PRAISE FOR **ADVENTURES OF V**

I0681738

With a few brush strokes, Reid creates a whole world. It's like magic –
the reader is sucked into that world, instantaneously. V swirls us into an
extravaganza, a detailed, delightful, dystopic, alien, familiar future – primal,
ferocious, and gratifying.
– Susan S. Senstad, author of *Milk and Venom* and *Music for the Third Ear*

Vivacious, vampish, victorious, voluptuous, vibrant, villainous … An
eternal 19-year-old, gorgeous vampire, monster-vixen named "V" – a pagan
Goddess, reborn as a super-heroine beauty who lives off the blood of the
bad, to rescue the souls of the good. Irresistible hijinks!
– Ed Cowen, producer, impresario

A wild ride into adventure, fantasy, and chills, V gifted me with glimpses of
arcane current and historical knowledge. Not for years have novels been as
much fun and enlightening.
– Chuck Shamata, actor

Utterly engrossing, rich, dark, and deep, Gilbert Reid creates worlds within
worlds of vivid, bold adventure.
– Bernice Landry, artist

Gilbert Reid's prose is so sensuous and evocative! When he takes you down
unfamiliar paths, and into situations that excite suspension of disbelief, you
follow him because the energy of V' s personality is so witty and alluring,
she charms you into the universe the author has created. Vivid, complex,
wildly imaginative.
– Diana Leblanc, actor, director

PRAISE FOR OTHER BOOKS BY GILBERT REID

PRAISE FOR *SON OF TWO FATHERS*

This epic, suspenseful love story set in the 1500s in Venice is filled with the dangerously wicked intrigue and counter-intrigue, with delicious atmosphere, texture, and, most importantly, historical context ... It is a rich tapestry of history, intrigue, and, of course, love.
– Lynne Deragon, actor

Deep knowledge of Italian history and culture, told with ribald humor, scandalous intrigue, and page-turning drama.
– Sandra Martin, author of *A Good Death*

Son of Two Fathers offers readers thrilling moments laden with suspense, scalding tension, and unpredicted twists and turns of plot – thoughtful explorations of subjects as diverse as visual art, theater art, philosophy, political history, and Jewish history. Readers interested in history will enjoy this book. Readers interested in Jewish history will delight in it.
– Mordechai Ben-Dat, *The Canadian Jewish News*

A dazzling kaleidoscope of vivid characters and settings, a perfect summer companion for anyone with a taste for adventure and romance.
– David Calderisi, director, actor

PRAISE FOR OTHER BOOKS BY GILBERT REID

PRAISE FOR *LAVA AND OTHER STORIES*

Very powerful, poetic and nasty and tough.
– Anna Porter, novelist, author, journalist

The writing is terrific. The characters are glamorous, decayed, old, young, loved, unloved. Reid inhabits each one. His raw, elegant prose, his vivid and sensuous images leave one breathless, with recognition and terror.
– Diana Leblanc, actor, director

The women, how they speak, what they confide, and omit, what they expose about each other! It's as if only sexuality happened that summer.
– Susan S. Senstad, author of *Milk and Venom* and *Music for the Third Ear*

PRAISE FOR SO *THIS IS LOVE: LOLLIPOP AND OTHER STORIES*

Reid's stories are in the great traditions of Alice Munro or Mavis Gallant.
– Margaret Macmillan, historian, author

Powerfully rendered and suspenseful.
– Joyce Carol Oates, writer, critic, teacher

An unerring and compelling examination of aggression and compassion.
– *The Vancouver Sun*

One of the 100 best books of the year.
– *The Globe & Mail*

VAMPIRE VS VATICAN

ADVENTURES OF V: VOLUME 1
"The Goddess is back. Her hour has come."
– Jules Cashford

VAMPIRE VS
VATICAN

by
GILBERT REID

TWIN RIVERS
PRODUCTIONS

This is a work of fiction. Names, characters, places, institutions, and incidents either are products of the author's imagination or are used fictitiously. Any resemblance to actual persons, living or dead, events, or locales, is entirely coincidental.

Copyright © 2020 by Gilbert Reid

All rights reserved. No part of this book may be reproduced in any form or by any electronic or mechanical means, including information storage and retrieval systems, without permission in writing from the publisher, except by reviewers, who may quote brief passages in a review.

Issued in print and electronic formats
ISBN 978-0-9953108-6-5: *Vampire vs Vatican:* Paperback
ISBN 978-1-9994790-1-5: *Vampire vs Vatican:* EPUB
ISBN 978-0-9953108-7-2: *Vampire vs Vatican:* Kindle
ISBN 978-1-7773141-0-1: *Vampire vs Vatican:* Amazon paperback

Cover and text design by Counterpunch Inc. / Linda Gustafson
Illustrations by Niki9door

Published by
Twin Rivers Productions
20 Bloor Street East
PO Box 75070
Toronto, Ontario, M4W 3T3

To receive a free book or novella, sign up at:
https://gilbertreid.com

Dedicated to my sister, Heather Reid

"The Goddess must die!" The chant was ear-splitting. Spread-eagled, manacled on the black granite altar, the young woman stared at the thick smoke that billowed against the chapel ceiling. Under the soaring fiery torches, her naked body, slathered in oil and sweat, glittered – pure gold. "The Goddess must die!" screamed the half-naked worshippers, "The Goddess must die!"

Echoing the thunderous invocation, the priest lifted the knife, intoning, "The Goddess must die!"

And, so, at the stroke of midnight, the dark, gleaming sacred blade plunged down.

CONTENTS

CAST OF CHARACTERS

*An asterisk denotes a real historical or mythological-religious figure.

Abdul – officer of the Presidential Guard, North African Republic

Agathon – V's husband, or Tanis's husband, when she lives in Cumae

Amin – officer of the Presidential Guard, North African Republic

Asherah – deaf-mute servant of Marcus and V

Asherah* – Phoenician goddess, often called the Queen of Heaven

Avatar – V's Avatar, her soul, mischievous perfect replica of herself

Amilcare – Chief Servant in the villa of Marcus

Baal* – Phoenician thunder and warrior god, god of life and fertility

Brother Basilisk – monk in the Satanic Order of the Apocalypse

Brother Filippo – member of the Satanic Order of the Apocalypse

Brother Filippo IV – member of the Satanic Order of the Apocalypse

Brother Mot – the greatest of Cardinal Ambrosiano's monkish slaves

Cardinal Ambrosiano – Leader of the Satanic Order of the Apocalypse

Corrado Ferrari – the absentee owner of Villa Mazana Nera

Count Marbuse – member of the Satanic Order of the Apocalypse

Crystal – a giant disco-ball-like alien artifact, Destroyer of Worlds

Elena Satti – copilot of a Dassault Falcon business jet

Fabio – young Roman gang member and killer

Father Alvarez – member of the Satanic Order of the Apocalypse

Father Delgado – member of the Satanic Order of the Apocalypse

Father Diego – member of the Satanic Order of the Apocalypse

Father Andrea – assistant to Cardinal Ambrosiano

Father Luciani – Italian Jesuit, an expert on the Gnostic heresy

Father Michael Patrick O'Bryan – Irish Jesuit, an expert on demons

Father Ottavio – director of the Satanic Order of the Apocalypse

Fiorenza Giordano – one of V's pseudonyms

Franco Leone – young Mafia hitman for U Pizzu

Paolo La Maestra – young Mafia hitman for U Pizzu

Gaetano Larione – Sicilian Mafia boss, U Pizzu's buddy

Gaius – Phoenician officer, a close friend of Marcus

Hugh Tillotson – forty-three-year-old English solicitor and serial killer

Irene Barzov – 18, a Russian dancer

Jack Larssen – pilot of a Dassault Falcon business jet

James Taylor Nimitz – Commander of the aircraft carrier USS Abraham;

Jeff Tyndall – Scarlett Andersson's boyfriend

Jian Chan – Handsome, brilliant, young Chinese-American

John – British-Italian Special Forces; helps V with logistics

Julia – Italian criminologist; helps V pick her targets

Kate Dawkins Thornhill – Daughter of Nobel Laureate Roger Thornhill

Lalla – servant to young Tanis in Ancient Phoenicia

Laura Thornhill – Roger Thornhill's wife, killed in Jerusalem

Marcello Mastroianni* – Italian actor, the epitome of the "Latin Lover"

Marcus – Phoenician warrior, merchant, conqueror of Tanis's city

Marina Elia – Italian millionaire, active in fashion and design

Mario DeLuca – Roger Thornhill's driver and friend

Martine – naked young French woman in the Roman Forum

Megan O'Connell – Scarlett Andersson's best friend

Michele Sindona* – Italian banker poisoned in 1986

Mohammed Ibn Khaldun – Commander of Presidential Guard

Paolo – night porter at Scarlett's hotel in Rome

Pascale Leone – nine-year-old boy murdered by Brother Filippo

Pope Benedict XVI* – Pope from 2005 until 2013

Pope Francis II – newly elected Pope

Roberto Calvi* – Italian Banker, hung in London in 1982

Roger Thornhill – Nobel Laureate, physicist, a dandy

Salvo Aiello – private security guard

Santino – Sicilian Mafia, U Pizzu's hitman and sidekick

Scarlett Andersson – 22-year-old American student

Signora Bianchi – Father Michael Patrick O'Bryan's landlady

Sister Kundrie – servant of the Satanic Order of the Apocalypse

Sister Ursula – long-time private secretary to Pope Francis II

Tanis – original name of superheroine shape-changer V

Tatania – young Russian-Canadian, her kids Chloë and Zoe

Tiberius* – Roman general and then emperor

Timothy Abraham – Executive Officer US Abraham Lincoln

Torelli – Italian doctor and explorer

Toto Riina* – Sicilian Mafia boss, head of the Corleone Mafia

U Pizzu – Sicilian Mafia boss

V – Reptilian vampire shape-changing superheroine vigilante

PROLOGUE – BIRTH

GREATER PHOENICIA – NORTH AFRICA – 589 BCE

Hazy golden light filtered down from above.

"Look at yourself!"

"No! Damn you!"

"Look! I command you! Look!"

"No! No! No! No!!" The girl turned her back. "Let all the devils take you! I will not look!"

"You must!" He pulled her to him. "See what you have become!"

Finally, Tanis – barely nineteen and the greatest beauty of the city – shrugged. She gave up. She glanced into the mirror.

"Oh!!" She recoiled.

Glaring back, out of the rippling silver surface, was a demon. Its golden eyes, the eyes of a serpent, struck, like a sword, deep into her soul.

"What have you done?" Her tears welled up, her voice broke, her hand, now a claw, went to her throat. She screamed, "That monster cannot be me!"

The demon's shriek echoed under the lofty vaulted ceilings of the vast room, with its tall windows, swirling frescoes of cavorting gods and goddesses, and smoky, gently fluttering torches.

Straddling the foot of a three-hundred-foot cliff of black granite, the villa's colonnades and gardened terraces towered above the Mediterranean.

Far below, in the harbor, galleys and merchantmen were just setting sail for distant ports. Over the sea, reflected in suave, rippling waves of gold, dawn broke, in all its fiery brilliance, above the eastern horizon.

It was that magic instant – the birth of a new day. The reborn Sun God, surging up from his watery nocturnal grave, shone on the towering columns of the Temple of Baal and Asherah that soared above the quayside. The God's rays sparkled on the spars and cables of swiftly moving galleys; his glow tinged, with a warm golden caress, the sails of round-bottomed, heavily laden merchantmen, just now billowing full-out, catching the morning breeze. The Sun God glimmered on tiers of lacquered oars, rhythmically rising and falling, on the straining arms of oarsmen, and on stacks of sweet-smelling cedar from the Land of Canaan, and bulging bags of spices and dyes from the Orient. His beneficent embrace lit up heaps of ivory from the Nile and folds of woven cloth – wool from Israel, silk from Syria, and linen from Egypt.

In the cool rooms of the villa, the blessings of the Sun God, and the sounds – the clanking of chains, the shouts of stevedores, the rhythmic cries of galley slaves – wafted in, muted echoes, from a distant, more luminous, world.

And, so too, did the sublime chant of an early-morning priestess – her transcendent, gently rising song came, it seemed, from another universe. Offered to the gods and goddesses, it coiled upwards, ever higher, exquisite and fragile, like a spiral of sweet, sacred incense. Wistful and divine, her voice took flight, soaring all alone into the pure, pale, empty sky. A bell sounded. Three times it sounded; then it was silent.

"Look! I tell you, look!"

"I cannot look at that monster! No! I cannot! I will not!" But, then, despite herself, Tanis clenched her claw-like fists, and glanced – once again – at her reflection in the mirror, as the man commanded.

The demon's heavy-lidded golden eyes sparkled with mischief. Its scales, stippled with points of gold, radiated a shimmering green and turquoise light. Seeming to grin, the demon displayed its long, thin forked tongue, its sharp, bright fangs.

"Is that me?" Tanis choked on her sobs. "Is that what I have become?"

"That is you, Tanis. That is what you have become."

At the edge of the demon's eye, Tanis saw one silver tear. Catching the light, it trickled down the scales of the brightly patterned cheek. With the back of her claw, she swiped at it.

"I am hungry," she hissed, "I must feed."

"I know," the man said, "Let us begin."

That is the way she remembered it, that defining moment, sometimes, in future centuries, if she thought of it at all.

Then, 2,571 years later …

PART ONE – IN THE GARDEN

CHAPTER 1

An hour before dusk, a sultry, stormy afternoon in early July 1982 – on an isolated country road in Umbria, a dusty black 1978 Mercedes with Vatican license plates, suddenly and without signaling, swerved off the road, and disappeared into a narrow entranceway hidden by overgrown shrubbery.

Rapidly accelerating, the Mercedes sped under an ancient, weather-worn marble arch inscribed with the faded words *Villa Monteleone,* and raced up a long gravel laneway lined on both sides with tall dark cypresses.

Sitting in the back of the car were two priests, both dressed in black with impeccable jackets, neatly pressed trousers, gleaming clerical collars, and highly polished shoes. The driver was a layman employed by the Vatican, and he wore the standard uniform of his kind – a dark blue suit, a white shirt, black shoes, and a sober tie.

At the end of the lane and framed by tall, shadowy cypresses, stood an ancient chapel. Its high-pitched roof, pale unadorned walls, and high oval windows were in the pure Romanesque style.

The chapel was known by the name of Our Lady of Sorrows. It, and the small, walled, garden graveyard attached to it, was all that remained of a seventeenth-century aristocratic villa, a late Palladian caprice, Villa Monteleone that had been blasted into oblivion in the Second World War, thirty-eight years before, when twenty-five Germans and thirty Canadians fought to the death over a hilltop and a few acres of stony vineyard.

The Mercedes pulled up next to the chapel. The driver backed the car into a blind spot, hidden between rows of shrubs and towering cypresses. The car must not be seen from the road. He turned the key and killed the engine.

Suddenly, there was silence.

The two priests got out of the car and stood for a moment on the gravel. The older priest, who was in his forties perhaps, was a cardinal – Cardinal

Antonio Xavier Paulus Ambrosiano; but he was not wearing the scarlet. An exceptionally handsome man, Ambrosiano radiated a sense of power that cast a dark shadow on the brilliant Umbrian afternoon. His skin shone – a waxen, translucent hue. His eyes, narrowed against the lowering sun, and yellowed as with jaundice, were slyly inquisitorial, giving him an appearance of infinite cunning, but suggesting, too, a secret, tragic melancholy. He looked up – dark clouds were rising in the west. Soon, it would rain.

"He is already here?"

"Yes, Your Eminence." Father Andrea, the younger priest, nodded. "He is waiting in the cemetery."

"Let us inspect the chapel first."

The interior of the ancient chapel was unadorned and empty. It smelled of damp and of flaking frescoes and stucco. The pale-yellow walls captured the reflected daylight in a soft caress, as if time had been suspended, trapped in this warm, sacred space. There was just the ghost of incense and floor polish. The wooden seats had been removed. The highly polished tile floor was naked blood red.

"This is ideal." Cardinal Ambrosiano smiled. In the cool emptiness, his voice echoed, strangely hollow. "It is isolated. Its austerity and simplicity are appropriate. Our Lord Satan will be pleased. There is sufficient parking, hidden from the road. The black granite altar of sacrifice should go there." He pointed, and then looked down. The points of his shoes, he noted with distaste, were tainted with a thin veil of white dust. "On this red tile floor, the blood of the goddess, when she is slain by the purifying sword, will wash off easily, and leave no trace."

"Yes, Your Eminence."

Cardinal Ambrosiano glanced at the afternoon light that filtered through the oval windows high above. Pale, milky, and warm, the light projected upon the yellow stucco walls a shifting, peaceful pattern of radiance and shadow. It was a beautiful place, a reposeful place, an ideal place for satanic sacrifice, an appropriate setting in which to call upon Satan, the Evil Force, the true Governor of the Universe. "Well, let us go and talk to Brother Filippo. If he does not agree to our proposal, then, perhaps ..."

"Yes, Eminence?"

"He should be sent somewhere – far away," the Cardinal fixed Father Andrea with his steady, pitiless gaze, "far away, forever, never to return."

"Of course, Eminence."

"But Filippo is so useful." The Cardinal's eyes narrowed and sparkled. His lips curled in what appeared to be a smile. "I would hate to lose him."

"Of course, Eminence!" Father Andrea swallowed; his Adam's apple bobbled nervously up and down. It made him self-conscious, the way his larynx had, of visibly swallowing. He recoiled. The body, which was frail mortal flesh, was corrupt in all its fallen wickedness, and had, alas, a mind of its own. This was far from satanic purity.

"Let us talk to him." Cardinal Ambrosiano gazed at Father Andreas. "Satan's will be done."

"Satan's will be done." Father Andrea inclined his head.

A few minutes earlier, on a main highway not far from the picturesque Umbrian hilltop town of Perugia – world-renowned for its university and fine chocolates – two Carabinieri had flagged down a customized black Harley Davidson FXB.

The motorcyclist signaled, pulled over onto the gravel shoulder, stopped, got off the Harley, and stretched. With her arms reaching straight up, her body arched, turning sideways, her wrists entwined above her head, she looked, in silhouette, like a slender ballerina, a sketch from a Degas pastel.

She relaxed, flipped up the dark-tinted visor that protected her from the lowering sun, took off the helmet, shook out her short, jet-black hair, smoothed it down, and stood easy, waiting for one of the officers to approach.

"Routine check, Signora." The officer saluted. He ran his eyes up and down the skintight black leather biker's outfit that sculpted the woman's body in ripples of light and shadow. In fact, her startling appearance was the reason they had stopped her. Both officers were bored. Stuck for hours in a sweltering afternoon on the dusty back roads of rural Umbria, they had decided to improvise an interlude – a little entertainment – to break up the tedium. The woman on the Harley was a gift from heaven.

"Of course, officer," she smiled.

Caught in her dark, hypnotic gaze, the policeman drew in his stomach, tightened his muscles, and cleared his throat. He inclined his head and glanced at her documents.

"Just a moment, please, Signora." He saluted a second time, walked back to his bike, and radioed in the information.

It took less than a minute for the answers to come back. The ownership of the bike was in order; her identification also; and attached to her documents, the officer noticed, was a business card indicating that the woman was a lawyer, specializing in the privatization of state assets and in international trade agreements, with offices in Rome, Milan, Paris, and New York. This meant, he presumed, that she had money, connections – and power. And it meant, too, that she was, discreetly, making him aware of the fact.

He walked slowly back toward the young woman. She stood waiting, relaxed and smiling, one gloved hand resting lightly on the saddle of the bike.

"Thank you, Signora." He handed back the documents and saluted. He held her gaze for a moment and noted – almost with a tremor of fear – that he had never seen a smile and a face so perfect. She seemed – and this was a strange thought – too perfect to be human.

Her skin was a flawless white, as if carved in marble, her smile was frank and open, her full lips a bright, seemingly natural red. Her eyebrows were jet-black, the eyes themselves dark, and her glance was hypnotic. In fact, she had the darkest pupils and irises he had ever seen; there seemed to be no distinction between the two. The pools of black light sucked him into a maelstrom. He blinked – and shook himself free.

"Thank you, Signora," he repeated. Again, he saluted, thinking she should be a model or a goddess, not a lawyer! Or – strange thought – was she a demon? From a sermon heard in childhood, he had always remembered one lesson: The fallen angels were the brightest, the most beautiful, the most tempting, and the most dangerous.

"You are welcome, officer." Her smile was even wider. "Have a pleasant evening."

"Thank you again, Signora. You, too, have a pleasant evening." He adjusted his belt and again tightened his stomach muscles. Making a conscious effort, he managed to hold her gaze.

She nodded, smiled again, and turned away. She slipped the helmet back on and locked the visor in place. Carefully she straddled the bike, kicked it into gear, and took off gently, with no showy spurt of gravel.

The sun caught the bike and glittered on the black metal frame, on a sleek, sculpted, silken leather thigh, on the black helmet. Then she was gone.

"Whew!" he exclaimed, the afterimage lingering.

"The stuff of dreams," said his colleague. "That bike made hardly any noise. Did you notice? It was like it was gliding."

"Yes. Now that you mention it ..."

In the distance, there was thunder, a slowly rising, angry rumble.

They both turned.

To the east, over the shadowy blue crags of the Apennines, a distant forked flash of lightning lit up the darkening sky. It was blindingly bright.

A few minutes later, the young woman left the *strada statale* and turned into a narrow dirt back road. After two miles she stopped, got off the bike, opened a metal gate, rode through, and stopped again.

She stepped off the bike, closed the farmer's gate, carefully clicking the latch down. She glanced at the sky, noticing the darkening clouds. Behind the visor, she narrowed her eyes. Soon it would rain. Soon it would be night.

She settled herself on the bike and rode silently for about seventy yards along the farmer's dusty, rutted service road. Then she glided to a stop just beside the high brick wall that hid the graveyard of the ancient chapel known as Our Lady of Sorrows.

Parking the bike behind a thick, dusty clump of flowering oleander, she unbuckled and pulled off her boots, unzipped the sleek, skintight biker's outfit, slipped out of it, and stepped daintily out of her panties.

Naked, she stretched in the sunlight – a voluptuous, rare pleasure. Then she draped all her clothes, carefully folded, over the bike.

The sun – now almost hidden by a towering steel-gray thunderhead – was low in the western sky. A small lizard, a colorful three-inch-long sliver of green, yellow, and turquoise, was lying on a pile of flat white stones, catching the last rays of heat.

The young woman bent over it. "Hello, Little Brother! Or is it Little Sister?" She reached out. The lizard looked up and leaped onto her hand. She ran her fingers lightly along its back, and then set it down. "Enjoy!" she whispered.

"Now, we'll give them the full Monty, shall we?" She took a deep breath, paused, and closed her eyes. In an instant, her body dissolved into a whirring blur of light.

The creature that emerged from the shimmering column of air – and that glittered, turquoise, scarlet, and gold, shining brightly in the lowering sun – was a thing of beauty perhaps. But it was not human.

The small lizard blinked up, admiringly, at its new-found friend.

The thing she had become sniffed the air. Yes, they were still there, behind the wall, in the graveyard. She could smell them.

There was a low growl in her throat as she pawed the ground and pressed her claws against the ancient brick wall, preparing to leap.

Inside the graveyard, Father Andrea, head bowed, stood a few discrete steps behind Cardinal Ambrosiano. The Cardinal was in an amiable but scolding mood. "Now Brother Filippo, this will not do! You really must control yourself!"

Brother Filippo was twenty-eight years old, and a member in good standing of Cardinal Ambrosiano's Satanic Order of the Apocalypse. But dear handsome Brother Filippo, in addition to his sacred satanic duties, had a deplorable vice, a habit of raping and torturing little boys – and, from time to time, killing them. As the leader of the Satanic Order of the Apocalypse, this concerned Cardinal Ambrosiano greatly.

One eight-year-old boy, forcibly sodomized by Brother Filippo only two weeks before, had survived the experience. Being a spoiled, precocious brat, the child had the temerity to complain to his father.

The child's father also happened – and this was truly regrettable – to be an eminent lay member of the Satanic Order of the Apocalypse. He was Adolf Tremonti, the Turin-based arms dealer and industrialist, a world leader in the manufacture of espresso machines, machine-guns, assault rifles, handguns, and motorbikes. Tremonti was not amused.

In the divine and satanic dispensation that rules the affairs of men and women, the children of the rich and powerful are not meant to be raped – or murdered.

Brother Filippo bowed his head. Fear and trembling washed over his soul. Were all his pleasures to come to an end? No, it could not be! He had been at his obsessive little hobby for almost twelve years. More than once he had been reprimanded, but nothing had ever come of it.

Cardinal Ambrosiano sighed. It was all very unfortunate. Several boys had disappeared. Either they had threatened to cause trouble or Brother Filippo's natural sadism and exuberant lust had gotten the better of him. And so, they died. Bondage, beating, and forcible penetration of a child will occasionally, if not carefully orchestrated, end in death, alas. The dead boys – luckily mostly creatures of no consequence – had been buried in various odd fields outside Rome, or had ended up in the Roman sewers, to be torn apart by rats. In particular, the ancient Cloaca Maxima, the Great Sewer, that once drained the Roman Forum, and still emptied into the Tiber, was, the Cardinal had been informed, one of Brother Filippo's favorites.

Brother Filippo's mind was stocked with delicious, titillating memories. One of the best featured Pasquale Leone, a charming nine-year-old imp from Naples; he was one of Brother Filippo's finest acquisitions. Pasquale was buried – one of Filippo's naughty little jokes – under the flagstones of the terrace of a celebrated beach-side restaurant in the resort town of Fregene – Old Nino the Fisherman's Place – frequented by film stars and princes of the Church.

Pasquale had been such an exquisite little monkey! It was if he had stepped straight out of one of those heavily shadowed, dramatically lit, teasingly louche, religious paintings by Caravaggio. Pasquale's soft dark skin, bright eyes, and his curly jet-black hair, always spilling over his forehead, were mouthwatering – purely delicious. His innocent laughter was enough to drive even a jaded connoisseur absolutely crazy! And when he was excited or happy, Pasquale stuttered, the poor vulnerable little dear! Yes, Pasquale had been a delicacy! A true discovery!

It was delicious, too, Brother Filippo mused, to think that, even now, five years later, starlets in bikinis – or topless – gossiping and sipping from a glass of wine, walked barefoot over the unmarked grave; or that a cardinal or bishop might discuss sin or charity or the financial affairs of the Vatican and its Bank – The Institute for Religious Works – a few feet above the bones and rotting flesh of pretty, young – forever young – Pasquale Leone, whose charming laughter and unending screams still echoed, deliciously, in Brother Filippo's mind.

But …

Cardinal Ambrosiano was staring at him – with those eyes the Cardinal had – like the deadly glance of the basilisk or the Medusa that could in an instant shrivel you into a statue of stone.

Brother Filippo bowed his head and clasped his hands together, in what he reckoned was a perfect imitation of submission and chastened humility.

The Cardinal sighed. This was annoying; it was a distraction from weighty matters of satanic grandeur. Such trivial misadventures were easy to cover up – and thus without significance – if the boys – and, rarely in the case of priests, the girls – were poor, or child prostitutes, or gypsies, or came from an orphanage, or were in a Catholic school for the poor. But they were definitely not easy to cover up if the child's parents were rich, powerful, or famous.

"No, it will never, never do," Cardinal Ambrosiano repeated. His yellow eyes bore down on Brother Filippo, and a thin smile – even more threatening than a frown – hovered on his lips.

Trembling, Brother Filippo cast his eyes down and stared at his clasped hands, while adjusting his stance to an even more carefully studied imitation of shame and contrition. He knew he could be very convincing. Barely suppressing his sobs, he stuttered, "I will control myself, Your Eminence, I will. I promise!"

The Cardinal's smile broadened. "We shall see."

In Cardinal Ambrosiano's view, such tastes were unchangeable and incurable. The best that could be done with Brother Filippo would be to transfer him to some small mountain village or to a parish overseas – in some powerless, poverty-stricken, war-torn country. There, under the cover of the surrounding chaos, he could rape – and, if he really had to, murder – the children of poor people.

But, no, the Cardinal had no intention of sending Brother Filippo away. Brother Filippo had useful talents – useful, above all, in Rome. Poor Brother Filippo! A little compassion was in order! Two decades ago, he too was an innocent – a filthy, ragged, orphaned street urchin. His mother was a prostitute, an addict, who died of an overdose when she was twenty-two. And Filippo himself, as a child, had almost certainly been abused, tortured, and raped by his mother's clients and other vagabonds in the shantytown just outside Rome where the boy managed to scrape out an existence.

And so, as a matter of survival, the child – who was unbearably cute and devilishly precocious – delivered drugs for the local gangs and made it his business to know all of Rome's secrets; and the Eternal City seethed with seamy secrets, which, as the Cardinal well knew, was part of its charm.

Filippo was invaluable. He knew who lingered, hopeful or desperate for sex, in the pastoral sodomite garden of Monte Caprino – the Hill of the Little Goat – under Michelangelo's palaces on the Capitoline Hill; he knew who hunted for thrilling nocturnal carnal encounters in the wooded, sprawling ruins of the ancient Baths of Caracalla; he knew who made assignations – with men or with women – during dinners at such ecclesiastically favored restaurants as The Living Fountain, or near Emperor Hadrian's Tomb, known in recent centuries as Castel Saint Angelo; and he knew who was in the habit of picking up transvestite or transsexual prostitutes on Lungotevere, the pleasant, plane tree-shaded avenue that ran along the Tiber Embankment in the center of Rome.

Brother Filippo knew which priests frequented transvestite balls – sometimes dressed as nuns or divas and dancing the can-can; he knew who, among the princes of the Church, could be found in exclusive, secret sex clubs catering for a wide range of specialized tastes; and he knew who among the powerful had an appetite for young boys; or, more rarely, for prepubescent girls; or, even – though this was a true rarity among the clergy – a forbidden penchant for single or married women.

Brother Filippo knew it all. For Cardinal Ambrosiano, this made Brother Filippo a font of invaluable knowledge – even a godsend, one might say, a gift from Satan. Brother Filippo was essential, too, for other dirty little jobs, for arranging *disappearances*, for obtaining prostitutes and catamites for visiting dignitaries, and for the occasional exercise in blackmail.

Above all, with his street smarts, sharp eye, and humble, winning manner, Brother Filippo, who was handsome in the decadent and dark gigolo style of Caravaggio, had a special talent – procuring sacrificial fodder for the Satanic Order of the Apocalypse.

Sacrificial fodder ...

The sacrificial fodder consisted of young women, incarnations of the ancient Goddess, of the Female Principle, the womanly presence in history and in divinity and in the human spirit. Femininity was insidious. It had to be exorcised – driven out – repeatedly and at all costs – as all the patriarchs of all the faiths had always known. To play the role of the Goddess, the young women had to be beautiful, authentic embodiments of fecundity and fertility, of rebirth and of burgeoning life, young women who, in their vitality, represented the best of the Female Principle – a principle naturally anathema to the Prince of Darkness and all his thundering patriarchs. The exorcism had to be repeated, over, and over, and over again. The struggle was unending.

The sacrificial women were almost always foreigners, most often tourists, and during the Order's secret ceremony, a black Mass of great antiquity, the sacrifice would be offered up to the sacred sword on a jet-black granite altar that had been in use for centuries. Her blood would be collected, and her heart would be cut out. The worshippers would drink and bathe in her blood and eat of her flesh. This ritual of cleansing – ridding the world of the power of femininity – was the centerpiece of the Satanic Order of the Apocalypse.

In brief, for the Cardinal, it would be extremely inconvenient to lose Brother Filippo.

Besides, pity was so amusing! It would be entertaining to spare the man. The Cardinal took an unctuous pleasure in exercising pity. Pity, in the Cardinal's eyes, was a form of power. "Pity," as the Cardinal had once remarked to Father Andrea, "is cruelty held in reserve." Pity was the mark and stamp of power; it was an IOU – the promise of cruelty to come.

After all, the Cardinal mused, the Church itself was built on such power – the power to exercise pity, to forgive sins and purchase pardon, the power to condemn to eternal damnation – to condemn sinners to writhe forever in boiling pits of sulfurous pitch – and the power to elevate the faithful to eternal bliss – basking forever in the Light of God's Love, singing praise forever in little pink clouds, and unending, untroubled, mindless ecstasy. It was a powerful mixture – pure terror, and absolute exaltation.

The Cardinal breathed in such power like a life-giving elixir.

The Cardinal's smile – and he now smiled broadly – was considered by many terrified priests and nuns more frightening than his frown.

"Well," he said, "We shall give you another chance, Brother Filippo, but I am serious: Any boy you covet must be vetted by Father Andrea. We must be absolutely sure the boy is – how shall I put it? – Eligible, yes, *eligible*. Can you control yourself to that extent?"

Brother Filippo bobbed his head up and down. "Oh, yes, Eminence, certainly Eminence, yes, Eminence, I will check with Father Andrea!"

Father Andrea nodded, swallowed, and stroked the stubborn dark stubble on his chin. He smiled a thin-lipped smile. Yes, he would indeed ensure that Brother Filippo "importuned" only those children who were not important. But, if something did perchance go awry, if an *inappropriate* child were somehow chosen and abused, Father Andrea was confident that, with his skills as an accomplished negotiator and diplomat, he could arrange a satisfactory cover-up.

"So that's settled," said the Cardinal, his benign smile broadening even further.

"Yes, Eminence," Father Andrea murmured; he bowed his head, clasped his hands demurely in front of him, and began, "This will be … perhaps … a new beginning, a purification of desire, and a truly lofty and worthy transition to those transcendent satanic spiritual values which are eternal and unchanging and not relative or ephemeral like the wicked degrading and hedonistic secular fads so appropriately denounced by His Holiness Pope Benedict XVI and which ..."

He paused. Something caught his eye, a flutter of movement. He glanced up. "My God!"

Something extraordinary was crouched on top of the garden wall. Father Andrea blinked. Time stopped. In an instant everything became preternaturally still. He was overwhelmed by a mystical clarity of vision. The wall shone with numinous intensity: the old reddish bricks were unevenly spaced, faded and weathered and sagging in places, with between them thin lines of ancient mortar, white and crumbling, flaking away. The wall was about ten feet tall and here and there overgrown with lush dark ivy whose waxy leaves and tendrils straggled right down to the ground, and it was topped, all along its length, with pointed, knife-sharp shards of green-and-red bottle glass. Every detail was translucent, weirdly clear, as if the instant had been translated into absolute stillness, into pure perception, into an intimation of Plato's eternal, timeless, and unchanging forms. The wall was supposed to guarantee the privacy, the intimacy, of the little garden cemetery. But, now, crouched on top of the wall ... Father Andrea was about to say something, when ...

Cardinal Ambrosiano turned and glanced up. He saw, perched on the wall, what looked like a gargoyle. *How strange!*

It was life-size, and female, voluptuous and exquisitely detailed. It glowed, metallic green and turquoise, shining forth in the dull golden light of the dying day, light that was now tinged with an ominous leaden tincture. In the heavy stillness foreshadowing the oncoming storm, the atmosphere had acquired an eerie clarity that illuminated every lineament, every exquisite detail of the gargoyle whose scales glittered with flakes of gold. It was utterly beautiful. What was it doing here? How had he not noticed ...? But then it moved. It was not a statue, not a gargoyle.

"By all the saints!"

The skin was reptilian, but the face was human, handsome, with an intense, alien beauty. The creature glanced calmly back and forth and seemed to be smiling. Cardinal Ambrosiano focused and suddenly he noticed – the glistening fangs, the clenched razor-sharp claws, and the acute intelligence in the big, bright, golden serpent's eyes. A demon, it was a demon!

"Gentlemen," the beautiful demon said – and it spoke in a soft, alluring voice, with a slight lisp – "Gentlemen, I have come for Brother Filippo. I would like, if you don't mind, a word with him."

Without uttering another syllable, the creature leapt from the wall, flew high in the air, almost straight up, and came straight down, landing on Brother Filippo. It sank its fangs into his neck, and shook him wildly, like a dog would shake a limp, bloodied rabbit.

Brother Filippo did not even cry out; the attack was so fast and so deadly.

He just fell to the ground.

As the demon crouched over the fallen body, it made a loud slurping, gurgling sound – like someone sucking a thick, lumpy milkshake through a clogged, narrow straw.

Father Andrea fainted, falling straight down into the rose bushes.

"My God," breathed the Cardinal. For all his dedication to Satan and human sacrifice, he realized – what horror! what shame! – that he was not prepared for this. He stood there, paralyzed, watching the creature empty Brother Filippo of his blood. "Satan protect me!"

The sucking sound was unbearable.

Father Andrea came to, looked up, and shielded his eyes.

In less than a minute, the demon had completed its feast. It let the body go. The shriveled and empty husk of Brother Filippo fell away. The demon looked up. Blood dripped from its fangs; its breasts were sculpted in a crimson sheen, with bright, gooey splotches of thick, scarlet gore. Its reptilian eyes – glowing like embers – stared straight into the Cardinal's eyes.

The paralysis ended. Cardinal Ambrosiano ran. His car and driver were waiting outside the garden cemetery; if only he could get to them, he might escape alive.

His heart pounding, the gravel crunching under his highly polished thick-soled black shoes, the Cardinal ran. The creamy white walls of the chapel beckoned; they were a refuge, a glimpse of paradise, of life, of freedom. The tall, dark, pointed cypresses offered sweet, sleepy, earthly oblivion; but, overhead, the immense electric stillness of the afternoon was sinister, unreal, pregnant with cosmic violence, violence that was about to explode through the thin membrane of what passed for reality, violence that was about to burst into this universe, into this world, into this garden, from … If only, if only …!

The exit was within reach!

The demon leapt in front of him. Suddenly, there it was, between him and the sagging, rusted metal gate – such a small, insignificant, physical object, that twisted rusty gate – the narrow road to salvation.

The creature stood there, hands on its hips, the reptilian statue of a young woman, chin and breasts brightly splashed with Brother Filippo's blood. The turquoise and green scales, the flecks of gold, glowed in the late afternoon light. Thunder rolled over the fields. The light trembled. Time stood still.

The Cardinal didn't dare move; he waited, his heart pounding. He must remember his dignity. If he were to die now, he must do it in style; he would accept whatever fate Satan had in store for him. For, undoubtedly, this creature was a demon, an emissary of Satan.

Or was it?

Would an emissary of Satan kill Brother Filippo?

The Cardinal swallowed.

The creature stepped forward.

Hypnotized by the diabolic stare, the Cardinal retreated.

He backed toward the cemetery wall, until he felt his shoulders press against the sun-warmed bricks. The soft brick dust flaked against his jacket. He could go no farther. The demon stopped. It stared at him. Its long thin forked tongue flashed out, thoughtfully licking traces of blood from its lips and fangs. The Cardinal cleared his throat. "What did you do to Brother Filippo?"

"I fed. I fed on him."

"Fed?"

"Yes."

"He's dead?"

"Yes. He's dead."

"Dead? Truly dead?" The Cardinal had read deeply in satanic lore and demonology; he had seen vampire movies. Would Filippo rise from the dead? And if he did …?

"Yes, truly dead. He will not rise again. If he has a soul, which I most sincerely doubt, it might possibly be on its way to Heaven or, if there's justice in this universe, it will, I suppose, be bustling along its crooked, misshapen path to Hell. Brother Filippo's stay on this Earth, in this life, is over. You have been aware for years of what he is and what he has done, Cardinal Ambrosiano. And yet you have done nothing. I have solved your problem for you. He can do no more harm."

The demon stepped forward. The Cardinal was pinned to the wall. The sun-warmed bricks pressed against his back, pressed against the palms of his hands. If only he could dissolve his way through the wall! He closed his eyes: In the name of Satan, he told himself, remain calm!

He opened his eyes. She – he now, suddenly, thought of "it" as "she" – was very close, almost touching him.

"*In the name of Satan, remain calm*," the demon repeated. "That's an interesting exhortation for a Cardinal to make."

My God, she could read his thoughts!

He realized too, with a shock, that she was at least six inches shorter than he. This was no consolation: a cobra, poised to strike, may be small, but …

The Cardinal was sweating heavily. He yearned to finger his stiff damp clerical collar, but dared not. The demon gazed at him – her expression serious.

He looked straight into the alien demonic eyes – serpent eyes. They were large, yellow and gold, with a horizontal elliptical black slit, enigmatic – he could read nothing in such eyes.

Soul! She had no soul!

"What are you?" the Cardinal breathed.

"Ah," she bared her fangs in a smile, "my dear Cardinal, not even I know that!"

Cardinal Ambrosiano swallowed. He was about to die. He could not move. To meet the Devil or the Devil's agent, directly, was awe-inspiring. But his intent had always been that he alone would be the orchestrator of his submission to Satan. He did not want some she-devil, some fallen angel, some *girl* demon, however beautiful, to usurp that role: He would *not* allow a creature such as this presumptuous *female* to send him howling bloodless and unmanned into dark eternity; he would not accept an undignified summary execution and sentence, without so much as a "by your leave, Your Eminence." No, he would not die, not now, not this way!

As he stood there, paralyzed, images raced through his mind. Physically, she was strikingly beautiful, a Renaissance or Gothic work of art. She was the Serpent and Lucifer, all in one, or the Serpent and Eve merged, earthy and female, bejeweled and resplendent, here in this earthly garden. She was the embodiment of Original Sin, a demon, transfigured into the image of a beauteous woman reptile. She was the Eternal Feminine, the Goddess, the Eternal Enemy of the patriarchal Satanic Order of the Apocalypse. Yes, perhaps she was the reincarnation, in demon form, of one of the ancient, glittering, magnificent pagan goddesses, who, by the power of that usurper Yahweh – that impostor, God – had been driven from the realm of divinity, and transformed into demons, fallen from grace, and destined to howl in sulfurous darkness for all eternity.

Yes, perhaps she was a goddess, who had come back from the dead, come forth from Hell, or from ancient times.

A rival!

In truth, she *was* beautiful. Even demonic, she was clearly a seductress, unearthly, literally not of this Earth. The fallen angels burn the brightest. Perhaps she was one of those, a bright angel, cast out from Heaven! Her physical strength was clearly extraordinary. The thought occurred to him. Was she really a she, or was she a masculine demon in disguise? The androgyny of angels and demons was well known. To die at the hands of such a demon, or under her fangs, would not perhaps be such an undignified consummation, to be –

"My dear Cardinal, I shall not, for the moment, inconvenience you or your Satanic Order of the Apocalypse further. You are an important man. I know you have much to do. You may wish, though, to dispose of the body – we wouldn't want any embarrassing questions asked, now, would we?"

She leapt to the top of the wall, turned, glanced at him, grinned, winked, and disappeared.

Thunder rolled.

The air darkened, shading into a deep leaden color, an immense purple bruise. A scorching wind rose, suddenly rustled the dark green ivy that clung to the cemetery wall. It stirred the dusty rose bushes and blistered the Cardinal's cheeks. But in the torrid heaviness, chilly winter reigned in the Cardinal's soul.

His lips trembled. Sweat snaked down his spine. He pulled at the stiff clerical collar, now soaked, hot and sticky. He yearned to tear it off. He swallowed. He would tear off all his clothes. He would go wild, naked, gnashing his teeth, howling to the moon, a beast of the fields, bereft of human speech, bereft of reason, utterly alone, an outcast from humanity. He would creep naked on all fours; he would growl and snarl and crouch in the slime; he would crawl and slither on his belly; he would become the hissing serpent; he would eat the lowly dust and gravel and grass, the weeds and the thorns. He would become the beast. He shuddered. What had she done to him?

He was terrified. But suddenly he felt something else – an intimation of something sublime, of a great force leaking into the world from behind the veil of appearances, an inkling of an immense and mysterious power beyond human imagining – of something invading the world and struggling to be born.

She was not of this world, he thought, the she-demon was not of this world.

She was something … divine … perversely divine.

She was a revelation. She was a goddess. She was the enemy.

But he wondered if he might strive, if he might attain her degree of strength, of evil – and, when the moment came, smite her, destroy her.

Yes!

The thunder spoke.

True satanic transcendence would demand more sacrifice.

The Goddess must die! She must die, over and over. Satan must be appeased. The Cardinal himself must feed his own satanic strength. This dangerous and seductive female demon – this goddess from ancient times – was a challenger; she must be destroyed, driven back whence she came. He would need a new Filippo – and new sacrifices to feed Satan's insatiable appetite.

Thunder rolled. Lightning flashed.

In a few moments, it would be night.

The Cardinal looked up, and felt, on his forehead, the first, soothing drops of gentle rain.

PART TWO – INNOCENCE

CHAPTER 2 – A GIRL IN SCARLET

Sizzling hot – August 15, 2027, Saint Peter's Square, Rome.

"JITTERS RATTLE SCIENTISTS! TREMORS JIGGLE GLOBE!" The electronic news tickers above the news kiosks streamed bright scarlet headlines: "Never seen anything like it," says Professor Blaise Bradley of the World Seismological Institute.

RUSSIAN BALLERINA VANISHES. Irene Barzov, 18, last seen three days ago in Piazza del Campidoglio, not heard of since. "She's ultra-disciplined. She would never just disappear. I am terrified," says choreographer Sergei Ivanov.

VATICAN COUP: Pope Francis II plans Surprise Vatican Bank overhaul. "The Pope must be careful. He is making some very dangerous enemies," says one Vatican insider.

"Okay, bitch! Strut your stuff!" Brother Filippo – Filippo the Fourth – wiped his forehead and fingered the hot drops of sweat gathering in the hairs of his chest, and trickling under the gold medallion, and his unbuttoned, neatly-pressed, white shirt.

Hidden in the shadows of the giant pillars of Bernini's lofty Colonnade that encircled Saint Peter's Square, Filippo stared into the viewfinder, focusing on the woman. What a find! He licked his lips.

Ten minutes ago, he spotted her. She was standing in the middle of the square, vulnerable, all alone, next to the Egyptian obelisk. He took a series of shots, plus a quick video. It was not enough. She had to be right – she had to be the *one*. The Cardinal insisted on the very best.

She was taking photographs – and with what looked like an antique Leica, a collector's item. The girl must be fucking rich! She crouched down – a fluid, graceful motion, sensuous, quick, feline. Filippo squinted. She must be a dancer, like that Barzov, the damned long-legged Russian.

"Turn, bitch! Turn, whore! I need to see your face!"

She had impossibly long legs, legs tanned gold, and the heels of her pumps were as high as stilettos. What a fucking show-off! A fucking exhibitionist! Maybe she worked in a nightclub, maybe she was a stripper, maybe … Her scarlet dress was skintight, brazen – shameless. And in Saint Peter's Square! All on display! *A body to die for*, people would say. *Yes, a body to die for.*

"Come on, turn, you bitch! I need that full frontal, damn you!"

She certainly *looked* ideal, undefended, all by her little old self, out in the middle of the vast empty square. Flaunting! And in the heart of Christendom! Shameless! Her fate would be more than justified!

"Turn, damn you!"

Her blond hair was tied up in a ponytail, away from the long, graceful neck. Finally, she stood up, swinging around in his direction, just for a second, smiling. It was a brilliant smile, a generous smile. She must be having a cheery thought. Filippo zoomed in – a close-up – three close-ups! Perfect! Yes, she was ideal, photogenic, with a beautiful smile – painfully beautiful!

"Got you!" he whispered.

Filippo could see her already – this blond goddess – the way she would soon be – drugged into slobbering servitude – splayed out, naked, groomed to perfection, coated in gleaming satanic oil, under the giant burning torches, manacled, spread-eagled, on the black granite altar; then there would be the plunge of the sacred knife, the geyser of blood, the ultimate sacrifice. The Goddess would die, once again! As she had, so many times before, over and over and over!

"Got you!"

The Cardinal would be delighted.

"Oh, not again!" Scarlett Andersson frowned. "Damnation!" The infernal scarlet dress was too tight, too short, and too bright. It literally glowed! And right now, the rascal had ridden up too damned high – again!

She tugged at the hem. "Scarlett, you are an idiot!"

She swung around and focused on an elderly Roman Catholic priest she had noticed just a few seconds ago, on the far side of Saint Peter's Square, just next to the Basilica.

The cobblestones shimmered under the pitiless sun, creating tricky glaring reflections that made getting the right shot a real challenge. Aside from herself, the old priest seemed to be the only other living person in the simmering vastness of Saint Peter's Square.

Defying the tight dress, she crouched low, hoping for a perfect image of the old priest. She held her breath. Maybe – and this was an exciting idea – he had just been to see the new Pope, Francis II.

Whirr ... click!

Whirr ... click!

Excellent! Behind the priest, Bernini's giant Tuscan columns soared upwards, supporting the vast entablature that enclosed the huge, key-shaped Saint Peter's Square in a maternal embrace. The shot was an implicit allegory – the tiny priest, the ephemeral fragility of flesh, set against the impersonal, massive, vertical permanence of stone.

Whirr ... click!

Whirr ... click!

The place might be a cliche, but it was irresistibly spectacular. She glanced around. It was all a superb stage set. Religion, after all, was show business – appearances *were* essential – and Gian Lorenzo Bernini, who designed and built Saint Peter's Square, was clearly a virtuoso showman, a magician, a seventeen-century Barnum and Bailey with a big budget and working in stone! Like Leonardo Da Vinci, Bernini must have delighted in putting on a flashy display.

The old priest lurched painfully forward. He had a terrible limp. How could he walk at all? In a rumpled sort of way, he looked very distinguished – dressed in sober clerical black; his shock of white hair neatly combed. Oh, that limp! She bit her lip and winced. The poor fellow! His trousers were creased and baggy, his shoes visibly dusty and heavily scuffed.

Wiping the sweat from her forehead, she glanced at her wristwatch: almost one hundred degrees Fahrenheit, thirty-eight degrees Celsius. Whew! The bone-dry air shimmered, dead still, not the whiff of a breeze.

She and the priest really did seem to be the only people in the whole huge, eerily empty place. Paolo, the night porter in her hotel, had told her that in mid-August Rome was a ghost town. She tugged at the upward creeping dress. Skintight and glowing scarlet! She certainly was, as her grandmother Charlotte would say, "quite a sight."

Since the day of the accident, on New Year's Eve fourteen years ago, when Scarlett was eight, Charlotte had stood in for both parents

Strapped in the back of the Mercedes, Scarlett was playing with her teddy bear Oscar. Daddy had just told a joke. Mommy and Daddy were laughing. Mommy reached out her arm to touch Daddy's hair and … They'd been to a neighborhood party. There was a brilliant white glare. Daddy shouted. Mommy cried out, "Oh, No, Scarlett!" A bright, dazzling, screeching, crashing, shattering – then, nothing.

Scarlett didn't remember much – a jumble of images and sounds. Her mother and father, they told her, had been killed instantly. It was, they said, a head-on collision. An out-of-control SUV, a drunk driver was fighting with his wife. Blinded by rain and headlights, he lost control and crossed into the wrong lane.

So …

Mom and Dad existed in isolated images, faded mental snapshots, like in an old photo album. There were lots of real pictures, of course, and family videos. But, as living people, James and Rosaline were gone, they were fragments of strangers, glimpsed, and lost.

Yes, standing there, alone, in Saint Peter's Square, Scarlett was, "quite a sight." The skintight dress had been a caprice, designed on purpose – it might as well have been – to get her into trouble.

That morning, fresh from the shower, and staring at herself in the mirror, she had spent some time calculating – silly girl – how she might catch the attention of a certain masculine person who happened to be staying in the same hotel. She'd glimpsed the guy briefly, only once, and she didn't even know his name. Damn! How stupid could a girl be!

Gazing into the mirror, she examined her naked self, frowned, bit her lip, turned this way and that, and twirled around in a light dance step. Not bad, really not bad. So – what to wear? Shorts and a blouse were too pedestrian, too touristy. After testing the effect in the mirror, she tossed her black jeans and black T-shirt onto the bed. It was too hot for jeans, too hot for black, and they made her look too sporty, too intellectual, too aggressive, almost military. Finally, in a moment of jet-lag tom-foolery, she plucked her disco-dancing, nights-out-only, knock-'em-dead Scarlett Special from its hanger. She licked her lips. It was bright scarlet – a shameless, skintight, spaghetti-strap, short, elasticized cotton whim – not yet worn, not even once. Hmm! Why not? She shimmied and tugged, working her way into it. It clung like it had been painted on. She stared at herself, twisted her face into a goofy cross-eyed clown mask.

"Okay, Scarlett Andersson, strut your stuff!"

She tied her blond hair up in a bouncy, cool ponytail, away from her neck. She slipped into high-heeled pumps, with no stockings – her legs were tanned, and, anyway, it was too damned hot for stockings.

Giving herself a critical once-over – her extremely judgmental, bitchy, schoolmarm gaze – she stared into the full-length mirror that graced her tiny hotel room. *Who was this floozy?*

She tried a sultry sideways Marilyn Monroe pout. Hmm … Did she approve of this shameless female? Hmm … There was clearly some deplorable ulterior motive behind the hussy's exhibitionism. She almost ripped the scarlet dress off and went for the black jeans and black T-shirt.

But, no …

The hell with it!

She'd been dawdling, indecisive, long enough; and …

Nothing ventured, nothing gained!

The scarlet dress was, and she knew it, a form of revenge – an assertion of her womanhood, her desirability, and her – goddamn right! – her sex appeal. So – Yes, Scarlett, go for it!

Because …

… because, four days ago, early in the morning, at Logan Airport, her Boston-Charleston flight had been cancelled. Mechanical difficulties, they said. No more flights that day.

Damn!

Fuming, Scarlett took the shuttle back from the airport, caught a taxi, let herself into the brownstone, climbed the stairs, and entered the second-floor apartment she shared with her longtime best friend, Megan O'Connell. "Hey, anybody home?"

Nobody answered.

She put her suitcase down in the hall, yawned, stretched, and opened the door to her own room – *to her own room!*

It took her a split second to understand.

What was she seeing?

Her bed was not empty!

Jeff Tyndall, her boyfriend, and her best buddy since kindergarten, Megan O'Connell, were in *her* bed!

Her bed! *Scarlett's bed!*

Together!

Jeff's pale skinny intellectual's ass, with the fuzzy sparse hair and those two dark moles, was sticking up in the air, bobbing and bouncing up and down, as he pumped away; Megan's long, perfect, tanned, toned cheerleader's legs were cantilevered up, wrapped around him, ankles locked together. Megan was screaming, "Fuck me, oh, fuck me, oh Jeff, fuck me!"

No wonder they didn't hear her!

Scarlett stood there, eyes wide, her mouth hanging open.

She blushed.

"Sorry," she stammered, "I should have knocked." She turned crimson. What a fucking stupid thing to say!

Megan screamed.

Jeff shouted, "What the hell?"

The grotesque image – the two naked traitors caught in mid-copulation, in flagrante delicto – etched itself into Scarlett's mind. It would remain there, she figured, to the end of her days.

"Sorry!" She repeated and backed out of the room. She shut the door carefully, quietly. She leaned against the corridor wall, gasping for breath.

Her world spun, topsy-turvy, upside down. Her man and her best friend were fucking their brains out, in *her* bed. Right under *her* bookshelf with *her* War and Peace and Moby Dick and The Great Gatsby and Advanced Molecular Biology and Crime and Punishment, and Stephen King's The Stand, and Karl Popper on the Scientific Method, and …

It was her sacred place; it was where she slept, where she dreamed. It was her refuge, where she curled up and hid from the world, where she recovered from the flu or a cold or a hangover. It was where she had made love – many times – *how many times?* – With Jeff!

The fact that the double betrayal was being consummated in *her* bed – *her* bed – on *her* sheets – not even changed, she noticed – made it so … so … obscene, yes, obscene!

I'm a fool!

I'm an utter total complete fool!

I am the most total idiotic complete fool who has ever existed on the planet Earth – ever! In the whole history of the human race – period!

Jeff and Megan must have done it before! How many times? And she knew nothing! Not the slightest inkling! How stupid! Of course, everybody else knew. All her friends – all *their* friends – knew! *What a fool she was! Really, wow – what an absolute fool!* Grrrh! She had had no clue! Now, she would be an exile from her own life! Wouldn't be able to show her face – all the titters and sly looks, all the false commiseration! "Oh, dear," they would say, "Oh, you poor idiot!" *Damnation!*

The betrayal was a double betrayal, certainly a long-term betrayal. All this time, they must have been laughing behind her back! Grrrh! She curled her fists. Her knuckles turned white.

She glanced around. What should she do? Should she faint dead away, play the fragile Southern belle? Scream bloody murder? Sit down and cry her eyes out? Or grab a kitchen knife and kill the two traitors in a frenzy of blood, and big splashes of gore?

Kill, kill, kill …

Yes, kill …

Her elegant black suitcase with the single bold scarlet stripe was standing there, in the hallway, a strange, unrecognizable object, an archeological relic from another world, from a dead universe: *life before, and life after.*

What to do?

She had her passport – always, for some reason, carried it with her. Then and there, she decided – and Cinnamon the cat, basking in the sun and blinking at her when she retreated in shock to the kitchen, totally agreed – that she would leave immediately.

A wise decision: Otherwise she would definitely kill the two of them. *Grrrh! Kill! Kill! Grrrh!* Blood all over the place! Gobs of gore splashed on the bookcase, speckled on the windows! And what did you do with the bodies? Chop them up? Dissolve them in acid? Flush the fragments down the toilet? She would need several big bottles of sulfuric acid and lots of old rags and mops to clean it all up. The plumbing would suffer. The hardware store would ask questions. Why so much sulfuric acid, Ms. Andersson? She would have to be very thorough. Forensic scientists can sniff out the details of a crime from a single molecule!

Lined up in a gleaming row, the kitchen knives hung neatly on their hooks above the cutting board. What a temptation! Let's see. What should she use? The serrated bread knife, or the long, sharp carving knife, or the fillet knife? Or – ah, yes, the big, bold, thick-handled butcher's hatchet!

That was the best!

Wild-eyed, spittle flying, screaming like a banshee, she would storm into the bedroom, foaming at the mouth, her hair a cloud of Medusa-like fury, her eyes glowing red with blood lust, the hatchet high over her head and, like Norman Bates in that old classic, Alfred Hitchcock's *Psycho*, she would bring the thick, razor-sharp blade plunging down … and down … and chop, chop, chop … over and over and over! Blood everywhere! Gore! Severed limbs! Eyeballs bouncing, careening up to the ceiling. Teeth shattered. Skulls laid bare. Scalps waving in the breeze. Ah, ah, ah! *Delicious!*

She would bathe in their blood!

She would feast on their bones!

Then, naked, covered from head to toe in a bright, glamorous sheen of scarlet and smeared with thick, scrumptious, dripping, drooling gobs of gore, she would tramp downstairs, slam open the front door, spread her arms, and reveal herself to the world – Behold! The betrayed scarlet woman … The assassin, the …

Well … no … maybe not.

She took a deep breath.

No, Scarlett, no.

They are not worth it!

She would hop on a plane, get on the next flight anywhere, wherever, whatever – the farther away the better. She knelt and scratched the cat behind the ears. "Bye, bye, Cinnamon!"

She went out into the hall and picked up the innocent suitcase.

As she headed down the stairs, she heard Jeff shout, "Scarlett, Scarlett! Please, Scarlett! Wait, Scarlett!"

What a jerk!

What a total jerk!

A hopeless jerk!

An irredeemable jerk!

That stupid, pale, hairy bottom of his – two bouncing buttocks! Why had she ever …? What did she ever see in …?

She slammed the front door. Suddenly, she was out on the sidewalk, trembling, psychologically stripped naked – every nerve-ending raw, bleeding – exposed, clutching the suitcase.

God! Where am I? What am I doing?

It was a crisp, absurdly beautiful, sensually caressing summer day. Totally unreal. How was it the whole world not withered and turned to ash!? The leaves glowed. The sun shone. The sky was cloudless, too perfect, too blue. Everything was too bright. The birds twittered in the trees. How dare they! In the gutter, water gurgled and sparkled, silver music. Mr. Murphy, the lawyer who lived two doors down, waved from across the street. "Hi, Scarlett!"

She grinned, somehow, and waved back. What a stupid, false expression she must have on her face. Her lips and cheeks were a plastered-on carnival mask, a goblin's grin. *My face rubber; my legs are rubber; my stomach is going to throw up.*

Two minutes later she was in a cab – seething!

At Logan International airport, the next available flight was British Airways, and it happened to be for Rome, Italy! One stop in London, and then Rome. So, Rome it would be. Scarlett, luckily for her, was a rich young woman, she was privileged, and she knew it. She flashed her Visa card. She phoned Charlotte.

"Well, Scarlett, that sounds delightful! Rome is so beautiful – and inspiring! It will be hot. Arm yourself with a parasol. A lady's complexion is part of her stock-in-trade. Don't do anything rash. Come back to me safe, Scarlett, darling! And, Scarlett – I hate to say it, but I was never very partial to Jeff. Brainy of course, gift of the gab and flashes of charm and all, but too skinny and pale and not a gentleman, not really."

"You were right, Charlotte, as usual!"

"But, Scarlett, don't give up on men – not entirely, not yet! There still are some good ones out there, you know."

No, Scarlett thought, I won't give up on men – not entirely, not yet, not forever. There might be a good one, out there, somewhere!

So that was how twenty-two-year-old Scarlett Andersson ended up in middle of Saint Peter's Square, displaying those long bare legs, and wearing that paint-on scarlet dress and those bright scarlet high-heeled pumps.

Exhibitionist, maybe. A mistake perhaps. Bad taste and provocative, in the present ecclesiastical context, almost certainly. But here she was, and what was done was done! And what would be, would be! *Che sarà, sarà!*

The old priest's limp looked excruciating. Scarlett refocused, widened the field, and clicked in a filter to dampen reflections, sharpen depth, and accentuate the contrast between the frail priest and Bernini's soaring columns of stone. The priest's battered black briefcase swung loosely by his side.
Whirr … click!

Whirr … click!

Scarlett wiped her forehead. Sweat dribbled into her eyes. She blinked it away. She should have worn a sweatband! She zoomed in on the priest's face – handsome and ravaged. Lots of character! He must keep his old things with him, a humble, modest man. Probably he lived in a rooming house, or perhaps a university residence, or an old rectory or whatever they called those things. Every week he would water the geraniums in his window; they would be the only things in his room to get a touch of sunlight, except perhaps a radiator and a patch of the highly polished wooden floor that smelled of wax; and he must have a buxom, middle-aged Italian landlady, probably a widow, who fusses over him and is secretly in love with him.

She knelt to catch the rippling sunlit geometric patterns of the cobblestones, and capture, in the background, more of the giant soaring pillars of Bernini's Colonnade.

Damn! The infernal dress! It had crawled up again! Diabolic! She might as well strip the thing off and go naked. The shameless man-trap outfit was not made for the quick paparazzi squat.

Damn!

The mischievous thing had already gotten her barred from Saint Peter's Basilica.

That stupid, sanctimonious gatekeeper had been such an ass! And it was absolutely hypocritical of the Church to forbid female arms and legs and bare shoulders, when they had a delicious, virtually naked Christ, in that luscious masterpiece, Michelangelo's *Pietà*, with the dead Christ lolling sensually, every muscle and curve of his flesh an intimate sculptural caress, slumped there, in his mother's lap, just inside the doors. *La Pietà* always reminded Scarlett of William Blake's poem.

What is it men in women do require?
The lineaments of gratified desire.
What is it women do in men require?
The lineaments of gratified desire.

Still …

Why the hell did she sculpt herself in this skintight neon-bright scarlet?!

Well … because of the Chinese guy …

At least, she *thought* of him as Chinese, but she really had no idea …

The Chinese guy – he looked like a Samurai warrior – maybe he was Japanese – happened two nights ago. It was just a glimpse. But it was enough. It sparked her interest – and, for some reason she had not fathomed, it sparked more than her interest.

Maybe it was exhaustion and excitement. Maybe it was the rebound effect.

Maybe it was desperation and depression – or jet lag. Who knew? Who cared? When the epiphany – instant lust at first glance – occurred, Scarlett had just arrived in Rome on her murder-avoiding escape to Italy.

It was night and sweltering hot. She was lying exhausted, totally burned out, on top of the big hard king-sized bed in her tiny room on the fourth floor of the ramshackle little hotel, the *Hotel del Teatro de' Fiori*, she'd managed to book into at the very last minute – a pure miracle. The hotel was perfect, located on a cobblestoned side street, only steps away from the picturesque old market square, Campo de' Fiori.

She had been telling herself that, despite Charlotte's sterling advice, she would swear off men forever – forever! *Yes, yes, yes, forever!*

No men, never again!

She'd get a dog.

She'd advertise for a sexy girlfriend.

Or maybe a cat.

Would she ever see Cinnamon again?

Who would get custody?

Having just had a shower, and groggy with jet lag, she drifted between wake and sleep, listening to people running up and down the narrow winding stairs, clattering footsteps, *thump, thump, thump*, and snippets of laughter and talk –snapshots of other people's lives – in Italian, English, German, French, and Japanese.

"They all have lovers, I'll bet! They haven't been betrayed by a #@%$ Jeff and a #@@ Megan! They are all having sweet romance with flowers and candles and chilled wine and oodles of endless, unbridled, luscious, loyal, loving, high-powered acrobatic sex! *Mamma mia!*"

She stared at the ceiling and blinked away what seemed dangerously like self-pitying tears. How disgusting! What a jerk she was! "Hey, Scarlett – you are a true idiot!" She laughed. "We are in Rome, Scarlett! Yippee! Let's forget about Jeff and Megan! Let's seize the day – or the night! You, Scarlett Andersson, really *are* in Rome!"

Her eyes closed. *To sleep, perchance to dream …*

Then …

Her eyes opened. *What was going on?* Something was not right. She blinked, suddenly wide awake. She turned on the bedside lamp. She sat up and listened. She stared at the slender little vase standing on a narrow wooden shelf opposite the foot of the bed. The vase was pale blue and red and white. It depicted a shepherdess holding a hooked staff, and a fluffy lamb and a cedar tree.

The bed jiggled. It bounced. The walls groaned. The ceiling creaked. What in the world? She must be dreaming! *No, this was real*: The room rose up, fell back. The little vase danced sideways along the shelf, and toppled off.

Earthquake!

Scarlett leapt from the bed and caught the shepherdess in mid-flight. *I'm not going to let you fall, honey – not if I can save you!* Just as she seized the shepherdess, something else caught her eye – right above her head: a thin black crack opened in the ceiling – *Gosh!*

The bedside lamp toppled to the floor. It went out. The room plunged into darkness. Dim yellowish light shone through the large, open window. Shouting and trampling echoed in the stairway. Car alarms blared. A siren went off. More sirens wailed. Scarlett's heart thumped.

An earthquake!

She laid the shepherdess down in the middle of the bed, pulled on shorts, a T-shirt, and sandals, snatched up her purse, passport, camera, and smartphone, and left the room, locking the door carefully behind her. The whole building was swaying.

Scarlett galloped down the steep, narrow stairs that wound down around an antique, open, metal-latticework elevator shaft. In front of her, two Japanese girls, dressed in frilly-doll cartoon outfits, sprinted and leapt down the steps, giggling hysterically. They made it to the lobby. The walls had stopped trembling.

"Yes, sir, it is an earthquake," the night porter, Paolo, was explaining, "A minor one, I believe." On the wall behind Paolo, a female anchor on a TV monitor was talking excitedly in Italian.

A young guy in dark blue jeans and a white T-shirt was leaning on the counter. His arms were smooth, with golden skin, and he had muscular, broad shoulders. "Do you know where the epicenter was?" the guy asked. He looked Chinese.

"Well, that's the strange thing, sir. There's not one epicenter. They've just reported quakes all over the world – California, Japan, Indonesia."

"That's weird." The guy in the white T-shirt turned and glanced at Scarlett.

Oh, he *is* Chinese, Scarlett thought, or maybe Korean. Or maybe Japanese. For some reason, she blushed – looked down, then up.

The Chinese guy smiled. He had a beautiful smile. "Earthquakes all over the place – at the same time," he said, still smiling, and turned back to Paolo. Then he glanced again at Scarlett, this time letting his gaze linger, widening his smile, taking her in.

She smiled back, wide-eyed. His eyes crinkled. Yes, he was drinking her in.

She took a deep breath. *So much for giving up men, you hussy!*

"Hi, I'm Scarlett," she was about to say, beginning to reach out her hand, when a person stepped between them, and then another person, and then there was a jostling crowd. Paolo beckoned. "Signorina Andersson, I have that brochure you asked for!" It was a locally produced brochure about the history of Campo de' Fiori and the surrounding area. Paolo explained some of the details. When Scarlett looked around, the Chinese guy was nowhere to be seen.

Her heart sank. In a flash, she had glimpsed a totally imaginary future – a virtual paradise – the inkling of an alternative life – the glimpse of a different self. It all evaporated. Poof! Gone! Just a glimpse! And she was in mourning – for a life that had never been, a love affair that was not even a dream, a Scarlett who never existed, a man she didn't know! Just imagined! And she knew nothing whatsoever about the guy! What an idiot she was!

Everyone milled around. Finally, Paolo told them they could go back to their rooms – the earthquake was minor, the authorities said; there was no need to be alarmed; the cracks in the ceilings meant nothing, happens all the time. Scarlett, bereft, returned to her room. Somehow, tossing and turning, dreaming of a ridiculous, impossible, imaginary life with a figment of her imagination, she fell asleep.

And that was why, two days later, not having seen her semi-imagined dream man, hoping he was still in the hotel, too shy to ask Paolo about the stranger, and in a mischievous devil-may-care, anti-Jeff, anti-Megan mood, Scarlett had shimmied and wiggled into her figure-revealing, man-trap dress. So now, exposed for all to see, she was the scarlet woman, a branded shameless hussy, the woman in the scarlet dress.

The Chinese guy would be nice to talk to, at the very least, at the very least … Those strong, chiseled features, those quick, intelligent eyes …

One result of this Scarlett caper was that she had been turned away at the entrance to Saint Peter's – and brusquely too.

"Your attire is immodest," the sallow, unshaven guardian announced, proclaiming it loudly, for all to hear, while he submitted her legs and figure to a leering – and prolonged – examination.

And so it was. Even with the long silk shawl she'd brought along just in case draped over her shoulders and down to her thighs, Scarlett was turned away at the temple door. She was unclean, unworthy. She wouldn't be allowed inside Saint Peter's to see Michelangelo's *Pietà*, nor Bernini's baldachin, nor the inside of the dome, nor the view from the roof.

After her encounter with that lascivious loud-mouthed lout, Scarlett felt she needed a hot soapy shower – to wipe the slimy residue of the man's eyes off her skin. The thought of it made her blood boil.

But, twenty minutes after she had been driven from the temple, Scarlett's spirits were fully revived. She was mercurial and she knew it. Bad moods rarely lasted more than a brief temper outburst; then – however furious the storm – she had to laugh at herself.

Right now, she was completely absorbed in watching the elderly priest limp his way across the square.

The poor man did look like he had the weight of the whole world on his shoulders. His face was care-worn, his jowls sagged, his eyes were downcast; his lips were moving; he was arguing with himself, or, maybe he was arguing with God.

The priest glanced up. He must have felt her eyes upon him. She flashed him a smile and a shy apologetic little wave. She was, after all, invading his privacy. He hesitated, nodded and waved back, a curt little gesture of the hand.

How lonely the poor man looked!

She imagined herself striding boldly over to him. "Here, Father, sit down, let's have a coffee, it's on me, it's on Scarlett, it's alright, it's not so bad! Life is not so tragic! Tell me your troubles – and they'll all go away!"

Absorbed in his own thoughts, the priest seemed for the moment to take no more notice of Scarlett, even though they were still, aside from a distant group of Japanese tourists, the only people in the vast square.

Maybe it was too hot for tourists. Paolo, the hotel porter, had told her that in August most true Romans abandoned the city for the mountains or the beach. "In August, the city is a ghost town."

"People are afraid, Signorina Scarlett." Paolo picked up a magazine. *Fifty-six Women Missing Over Ten Years: unexplained disappearances.* The cover featured images of women – all races, all young, all beautiful. "Why, just the other day, a Russian girl, a dancer, disappeared."

"Who is doing this?"

"Nobody knows, Signorina Andersson. There are rumors of a secret sect. Maybe it's slavery, or a prostitution racket, people smuggling of some kind. Be careful. Don't accept drinks from strangers. Sometimes they contain drugs. You fall asleep and – *poof* – you disappear! Stay where people can see you. Otherwise, Rome is a ghost town!" He spread his arms wide. "And it's all yours!"

Now, in sun-drenched Saint Peter's Square, virtually alone, Scarlett swung around, and got another shot of the priest, in profile this time. He was walking, his head bent, deep in thought. The huge Bernini columns rose behind him, a tiny human doll, dwarfed by giants.

With Scarlett framed in his telephoto lens, Brother Filippo took one last shot. She did move like a dancer. She was too good to be true.

Satan be praised! Soon, the sacred sword would flash down. Her blood – the blood of the Goddess – would gush up and spill over … Her heart, cut out, would be elevated! The satanic worshippers, in a bestial frenzy, would rush forward, eager to partake, to drink and feast, and to absorb the powers of the vanquished Goddess.

CHAPTER 3 – EXORCIST

"I am dead. If you are reading this note, Father O'Bryan, then know this – I am dead. And, the moment you read these words, you too, Father O'Bryan, will be in mortal danger."

Michael Patrick O'Bryan was a 56-year-old Irish Jesuit, author of many highly esteemed books and scholarly articles, and a world-renowned expert on ancient Semitic and related religions – the pre-Biblical polytheistic religions of the Jews, Phoenicians, Sumerians, and so on – as well as on witchcraft, exorcism, and demonology. He was particularly celebrated for his passionate, in-depth studies of demons and exorcism.

Three days earlier, an envelope had been left with Father O'Bryan's landlady, Signora Bianchi. The message came from a Father Luciani, a Jesuit priest whom Father O'Bryan had met casually, once or twice, at scholarly conferences on heresy and witchcraft. Just four days ago, poor Father Luciani had died of a stroke. Father O'Bryan had seen a small notice in the *L'Osservatore Romano*.

With Luciani's handwritten note was a key to a safe deposit box in Rome's Termini Station, and a warning. "Tell no one of this! And, when you go to Termini Station, be absolutely certain no one is following you."

"A young man delivered the envelope," Signora Bianchi told Father O'Bryan, but she didn't know who the young man was, had never seen him before. "He didn't give his name, and, Father, he did seem nervous and in a great hurry to get away."

Early the next morning, Father O'Bryan ordered a taxi, went to Santa Maria Maggiore, not far from Termini Station, walked through the Church, then out by a side entrance, and walked to the station, by an indirect route, glancing nervously around, thinking, rather wryly, that he was imagining himself inside an American spy thriller.

He opened the deposit box, took out a thick, brown, padded, legal-size envelope, stuffed it in his briefcase, shut the deposit box, leaving the key, and walked away as quickly as he could. At the side entrance of the station, he took another taxi, got out on Piazza di Spagna, just under the Spanish Steps, and, after walking nervously down a variety of side streets, he slipped into a fashionable café on Piazza del Popolo, and sat down at a corner table in a back room.

Eyeing the customers and waiters for possible assassins, Father O'Bryan glanced around. Satisfied that he was for the moment safe, he opened the envelope. What was all this about? What could possibly be so urgent and so dangerous? What could have come out of the dusty archives that would have so upset a modest unassuming scholar such as Father Luciani? For many years, Father Luciani had been involved in research on the Gnostics, an ancient heresy of Christianity. According to the Gnostics, the whole material universe, and all the bodies of the creatures in it, were the creation not of God, but of an Evil Spirit or Dark Force known as the Demiurge. The Demiurge was identified, in some eyes, with Satan. This creature was the true ruler and Creator of the physical universe. This was how the Gnostics explained the presence of evil in the world. It wasn't God's fault; it was the Demiurge that did it.

Inside the envelope, there was another note in Father Luciani's spindly handwriting: "Knowing I was interested in the Gnostics and other such Manichaean heresies that postulate a Principle of Good eternally at war with a Principle of Evil, and assuming that I had the ear of the Pope, a powerful layman – a Swiss banker – who had attended one of my lectures on "the Early Gnostics and the Myth of Helen of Troy as an Avatar of Female Incarnation" – delivered into my hands, under the strictest confidence and an assurance of his complete anonymity, some documents. They are terrifying. They demonstrate – I believe conclusively – that, nested in the very bosom of the Church, there is a satanic sect – *The Satanic Order of the Apocalypse* – which holds the most abominable beliefs, and practices the bloodiest, most repulsive rites, including, almost certainly, human sacrifice. This is a reversion to some of the earliest most detestable roots of religion. The order is led, it seems, by Cardinal Ambrosiano. You will find herein some of the material that has come into my possession. I have not yet had time to fully investigate, and, dear Father O'Bryan, I fear I am being watched and that my days are numbered. Yours in Christ, Luciani."

A waiter appeared. Father O'Bryan ordered an Americano – with a little pot of cold milk on the side – and a warmed-up chocolate croissant. The waiter bowed and left.

Father O'Bryan glanced around. A middle-aged woman in a tweed jacket was gossiping with another woman, and a man in a pinstripe suit was reading that pink-colored English financial paper, *The Financial Times*. Hmm. They didn't look like assassins. Father O'Bryan stroked his chin. He began to leaf through the material collected by Father Luciani.

The coffee grew cold. The chocolate croissant remained untouched. An hour later, when – looking rather concerned – the waiter asked him if everything was in order, Father O'Bryan looked up, startled, as if waking from a dream. "Yes, yes, everything is fine," he said. "Quite fine."

Father O'Bryan stuffed the envelope and its contents into his briefcase and paid the bill. When he came limping out of Canova's Café, into the Rome sunlight, the world had changed. The brightness, the crowds, the passing cars, the tourists, all seemed unreal, a phantasmagoric pantomime, behind which lay terror and gathering darkness. It was quite possible that Father Luciani had been murdered. Murder could easily be made to look like a stroke.

Father O'Bryan hailed a taxi and set off toward his office in the Vatican. There was nowhere else to go, not really, and, if the material in the envelope was authentic, there was nowhere to hide.

As soon as he got to the Vatican, Father O'Bryan locked himself in his office and wrote to the Pope. Then he sent it, a private handwritten letter, "For His Holiness's Eyes only!"

Father Luciani's file was still in Father O'Bryan's briefcase – complete with its drawings, diagrams, computer sticks and computer disks, all the information that Luciani had provided on *The Satanic Order of the Apocalypse*. Father O'Bryan wasn't going to let any of the material out of his sight.

Now, in the middle of Saint Peter's Square, Father O'Bryan stopped. He wiped his forehead. It was devilishly hot. Maybe it had not been such a good idea, sending that letter. He should have requested a private audience. If the Apocalypse story were true, sending the letter was dangerous – for the Pope. And indeed, for Father O'Bryan. He sighed. Ah, Michael Patrick O'Bryan, you certainly do have a gift for getting yourself in hot water!

Somebody was staring at him – he felt it, a tickling sensation. He glanced up. Ah! There was a remarkable looking girl – long, bare, tanned legs, and her dress was so red – well, scarlet – it glowed. A splash of color like that certainly did draw attention.

She was close to the Egyptian obelisk, crouching low, almost sitting on the cobblestones, a remarkable pose. Truly acrobatic! How did she not collapse onto her backside? What in the world was she doing? Ah, she was taking pictures. She swung around, aiming the camera, and Father O'Bryan realized that she was taking a picture of him.

He frowned. Hmm, well, Michael Patrick O'Bryan, you don't want this! You don't like this at all! Should he ask her to stop? He abhorred having his picture taken. Now, why was that? He rubbed his forehead. Was it vanity or atavistic superstition? Of course, some tribes believed that a photograph steals your soul. Idolatry. The image gives you control over the thing represented – like a voodoo priestess and pins and voodoo dolls. He blinked against the sweat; it was getting into his eyes. The graven image, idols, icons, totems, that sort of thing, objects that try to show the invisible, make the unseen visible, make the absent present. Spirits cannot be shown, or represented, nor God in certain religions. It's blasphemy to try. All representational images are sin, so some say, and lead to idolatry, to the worship of images. Even Islam. The Christian Puritans were iconoclasts too – smashing all the images. So many masterpieces lost! Old ideas, old taboos, old fears, linger, take on new disguises.

Father O'Bryan pulled a rumpled handkerchief from his trouser pocket. He wiped his forehead. Narrowing his eyes, he glanced a second time at the girl. She was certainly athletic – the way she moved. There was something Dionysian about her, a primitive elemental power. Of course, there is a sense of divinity in the female form – all the great artists – not only the men – and all the ancient religions thought so – the female is powerful and therefore dangerous. Sculpted, such a creature would be an idol of burnished gold, a goddess of war or of fertility, or, perhaps, of both. Ah, well, and then the Abrahamic religions and monotheism do rather neuter the female form. Fear, almost certainly, lust too, and awe. Certainly, that which you fear, even if it is what you desire, you must repress.

He glanced away, concentrated on the cobblestones.

But the image remained. He sighed. Such girls, to give them credit, are like the nymphs of old times. It was strange how the idea of the sacred had evolved. Eons ago, there was, it seems, the Mother Goddess who encompassed everything, the whole cosmos. Then came the pagan goddesses, incarnating war and fertility, destruction and construction, death and rebirth. There was Asherah, for example, goddess of the Canaanites and Phoenicians. Some old texts even claimed Asherah had been the wife of Yahweh, the wife of the God of Israel – the Wife of God Himself! Just think of it! Such an idea would certainly upset a great many theological apple-carts! God married – just think! Perhaps not such a bad idea, really …

He glanced up again.

She was looking around – her blond hair was pulled up into a perky pony-tail, long delicate neck. Fragility too – that is something sacred, something to be protected.

Yes, she was an incarnation, a goddess of light, all sunshine and energy.

A whiff of memory from a former life passed like a heady perfume through Father O'Bryan's mind. Ah, Michael Patrick O'Bryan, do not allow yourself to go there! He had to smile.

The exuberance of youth! Ah, women! So beautiful, so complex! Once, even after he was ordained, he almost succumbed. In Africa, a Frenchwoman, a doctor she was, and as secular as they come, a blonde too, with blue eyes, startlingly blue, not a believer, atheist or agnostic, almost certainly. He never asked; but a fine person still, an idealist, serving the poor, risking her life. Came to him one night, needed a shower. His bungalow had water, no one else did. She toweled herself in front of him, while talking about medical supplies, not modest, didn't even think about it, he thought she didn't … but maybe she did. Very polite, left laughing about something he said, afterwards all was normal, joking and friendly, just as before. He could be such a fool. Of course, she was offering herself – or tempting him. Teasing! Mischievous! He truly liked her. He sighed. There was much about his life he had never understood at all.

He glanced once more at the golden girl. She waved.

Well, he would give her a little wave then, no harm in it, just a short little wave, nothing personal, nothing compromising. Big smile she had, waving back, magnificent! And don't you know, the way she moved, the self-assurance! That girl must have charm in oodles, certainly gets her way, almost every time. But she wasn't spoiled. The wave and smile were too open, too frank.

Now she was crouching again – more photographs.

And of him! He sighed.

That scarlet dress! Ah, well, and it was tight! That was the truth! She moved easily, quickly, lithe like an animal, those long, tanned legs, good legs for running, showy, good genes, ideal mate, sprinter, easily escape from mastodons, tigers and wild baboons. Big prize for some caveman.

In Salem or Würtzburg in the old days they would have taken her for a witch and burned her at the stake or driven her naked out into the wilderness or stoned her to death in the town square. Or thrown her from a high window. It's the same old story! Women as scapegoats – to be sacrificed. That's what Jehu, son of Jehoshaphat, did to the Phoenician princess, Queen Jezebel – tossed her out the window. And so, the scriptures tell us, to defy the assassins and confront her own death, Queen Jezebel put on all her finery, makeup, and beautiful clothes. Had a sense of dignity, Jezebel, knew her role, stood up for what she believed in – the Phoenician gods Ba'al and Asherah. He'd always had a sneaking admiration for Jezebel! Mind you, it was theologically quite unacceptable, hush, hush. Top secret! Jehu ordered three eunuchs to throw Jezebel from a window. Then, dead, she was trampled by horses and eaten by dogs and her remains were left to rot in the sun. Not a pleasant ending for a princess. Not very gallant of Jehu. No gentleman, he. Terrorist, really. Jezebel's assassination was the death by proxy not only of her favorite, Ba'al, the Phoenician God, but of the goddesses, all of them – Asherah and all the others. The Patriarch triumphed. All the old pantheon, all the old gods and goddesses, marvelous and cruel poetic emanations of human energy and human dreaming, driven out of heaven and cast into Hell, transmogrified into demons, all their glory and beauty gone. So many human talents and instincts, demonized, cast overboard. One way of looking at it. Heterodox. Thought takes flight! Then you are back again, trapped in your flesh, a prisoner of your own body and your own beliefs. Jezebel certainly did have a bad press. Ah, well, the victors do get to write history.

The blonde was taking more shots, and again she gave him a timid wave. What was she saying? Ah, yes: *I'm invading your privacy, I'm sorry, I'm sorry!*

Something glittered, bright silver-white, in his eye, blinding for an instant in the sun. It was sparkling at her neck, between her breasts. Waving back, he blinked. It wasn't a cross. Not Catholic, then.

Like Kate Thornhill, poor dear beautiful Kate! Kate was not Catholic, not even a believer, Kate, his dear darling agnostic Kate, or atheist Kate, or skeptical Kate – he'd never pushed her on the point – she was like a daughter to him, Kate – dark, pale, tragic Kate.

He glanced at the blonde again, over his glasses, from under his tangled salt-and-pepper eyebrows. She was crouching now, taking yet another photograph. Such beautiful women were not safe, not here, not now, not in Rome. Young women were disappearing. Women were disappearing all the time.

There was a story in the papers about it. Russian girl who disappeared, musician or dancer, something artistic. He'd seen it in *Il Messaggero* or on the website. Photographs of the girl – beautiful, a tall blonde like this one. In the photograph, she was in a tutu, on tiptoes, pirouetting in *Swan Lake* or *Cinderella* or something like that. Exquisite, the human form! Maybe he should warn the girl photographer. No, that would be impertinent. Fussy old Irish priest with limp scolded me, she'd say ... And yet such beauty was dangerous these days, such generous, smiling openness.

He wiped his brow. The heaviness of the heat lay thick upon him; and the heaviness of the old, worn, over-full leather briefcase; heavy, too, the thick cloth of his black jacket, and his trousers, damp with sweat – a carapace, as if he were imprisoned in a shroud.

Beauty can so easily be destroyed.

Women, so often the chosen victims, and children.

He had seen so many. Dead bodies stacked up like firewood. Young women with bright smiles, joy and love in their faces, then, hours later, they were dead, rotting flesh. Buzzing flies. Blood in pools. Their children too. Breasts, arms, chopped off. Open wounds. Sores. No end to it. Machetes, assault rifles, machine-guns, napalm. No end to it. Laughing black faces, big smiles, and then they arrive, the masks of hatred. Helicopter gunships. Uniforms. All the best machines for killing, cutting-edge, lots of money involved. Diamonds, gold, copper, uranium, feed the slaughter. Yes, the children too they killed, women and children. This was a fallen world. Possessed by Evil, by Satan.

Those Gnostics Father Luciani studied, they had a point. How could God, the Creator of the world, omnipotent and omniscient, all-powerful and all-knowing, seeing the future and the past and all things, have created the world, knowing that, in this freshly created world, evil would flourish, such evil? How could He have overseen such evil, permitted such evil? And does such a fallen world – tainted by original sin – deserve to exist? *Original sin*, yes, that was the escape clause, that was what salvaged God's honor – Eve was guilty, and the serpent, not God! And all womankind suffered for it. Free will made love, and love of God, possible, and thus it made choice and sin possible too ... And a woman was the gateway to the abyss.

He wiped his brow. He had to wonder. Did this Satanic Order of the Apocalypse, if it existed, have a point? Was that strange, exalted, cruel Cardinal Ambrosiano a madman or a visionary? Was he possessed by a demon? Or was he merely evil?

Father O'Bryan turned and glanced up at the facade of Saint Peter's. Yes, there they were, the statues of the saints and apostles, and of Christ the Redeemer Himself, perched like bowling pins along the top of the giant facade that loomed above the piazza. It was all very splendid and grandiose, the Italian Renaissance at its most baroque and eloquent, and the Catholic Church, reaching out, with all its power and grandeur, speaking to the world of Salvation and Redemption.

He was almost out of the square now.

The old-fashioned newspapers pinned up outside the newspaper kiosks hung limp in the shimmering heat, *Le Monde*, *The International New York Times*, *die Neue Züricher Zeitung*, *die Welt*, *El País*, Chinese papers, Russian papers, Japanese, Korean ...

Father O'Bryan glanced at the bright banner headlines streaming in Italian across the top of one kiosk: RUSSIAN DANCER DISAPPEARS! *18-year-old Irene Barzov, of Saint Petersburg, Russia, was last seen ...* EARTH TREMBLES! *Seismologists puzzled. Tremors touch all continents. Is* WASHINGTON STATE'S MOUNT SAINT HELENS ABOUT TO EXPLODE?

Indeed, it was curious, simultaneous earth tremors everywhere! Strange indeed. But no casualties had been reported; so, if no one had been hurt, then, well, no real harm had been done. As for Irene Barzov, the young woman who had disappeared, well, that ...

He almost turned back, had a half-thought of going back to warn her – the golden-limbed blonde in scarlet.

He glanced at his watch. No, it was none of his business, really. He must hurry home, have a shower, take an afternoon nap, change into some new clothes – possibly polish his shoes and check that his trousers were properly pressed – perhaps Signora Bianchi, if she had time, would press them for him. Later, he would make his way to the Rome Institute of Cosmology to hear Roger Thornhill's talk on the frontiers of cosmological and astronomical research. Roger's marvelous daughter Kate was with him, so it would be a double pleasure.

There was one mystery in Father Luciani's Satanic Order of the Apocalypse material. It contained a list of scientists – mostly famous cosmologists and physicists – and Roger Thornhill's name was at the very top of that list. What could that mean? Could Roger be a secret member of the Satanic Order of the Apocalypse?

No, that was nonsense! Roger Thornhill was not even a believer. Roger was a pure scientist, and probably an atheist, certainly an agnostic. Roger, who was a Nobel Prize Laureate, would never be party to some silly Gnostic or apocalyptic plot. Perhaps the whole thing, the whole cache of documents, was somebody's cruel idea of a joke! Yes, it was quite possible the Satanic Order of the Apocalypse didn't exist at all. And yet, if it was a hoax, it was a very elaborate one. Ah, well, then, Michael Patrick O'Bryan, maybe you are getting yourself in a feverish tizzy about nothing at all ...

He crossed the line of white, inset into the black paving stones that, at the entry to Saint Peter's Square, marked the frontier between the sovereign Vatican City State and the Italian Republic.

Ah, my dear pagan girl, my dear blond nymph, in the scarlet dress, he thought, casting one quick glance backward, *Goodbye, Goodbye, Adieu, Adieu, Addio, Addio!*

As Father O'Bryan headed down via della Conciliazione, Scarlett turned her attention back to Saint Peter's Square, to the great Egyptian obelisk

The guidebook had informed her that the obelisk was four thousand years old; that it had been carved out of a single block of red granite; that it had been erected in the City of the Sun, on the edge of the Nile Delta in Egypt, and dedicated to the Sun God by Pharaoh Menacres in 1835 BCE. "Shaped like a sword – the word 'obelisk' meant sword – the Ancient Egyptians believed that the obelisk – a sword aimed at heaven – united the powers of the heavens and of the sun with the peoples of the Earth." What a poetic idea! Scarlett could see it – a flame from the tip of the obelisk flashing up to the sun itself.

The story was fascinating! So much history! Then, the Roman leader Octavius – soon to name himself Augustus, thus becoming the first Roman Emperor – after defeating the warships of Marc Anthony and the Egyptian Queen Cleopatra in 31 BCE at the naval battle of Actium, just off Greece, annexed Egypt the next year in 30 BCE, so the guidebook told her. It was said – but it was untrue – that Marc Antony and Cleopatra died, as passionate lovers should, in each other's arms. Very romantic! Scarlett sighed. The Romans, being practical people, wasted no time and looted the City of the Sun. Sixty-seven years later, in 37 CE, under the Emperor Caligula, the obelisk was shipped to Rome. Then, more than one thousand five hundred years after that, when Catholic Renaissance Rome was being rebuilt in all its baroque splendor, the obelisk was transported – in 1586 CE – to this very spot and placed, proudly upright, not an easy task in those days, in the center of Saint Peter's Square. It was quite a story!

Concentrating on the obelisk, Scarlett did not notice two tanned, muscular young men who had been tailing the old priest, and who now came out of the shadows of Bernini's columns and followed him down via della Conciliazione.

And she did not notice that someone was watching her; that, in fact, several people were watching her.

Scarlett and her bright, skintight dress were the starring attraction, that sunny sweltering summer's day, right at the center of Gian Lorenzo Bernini's grandiose Barnum & Bailey stage set.

"Francis, take your pills!"

"Yes, yes, Sister Ursula, I will, I will!"

"Well, I won't do another stitch of work, not until you've swallowed them all!"

"Yes, yes, of course!" Pope Francis II allowed himself a smile. Sister Ursula was sitting primly in front of her bank of computers. "I promise, Sister Ursula! Cross my heart and hope to die!"

The Pope walked over to the window, pushed aside a curtain, and took a deep breath. He hated the pills, but his heart was weak, so they told him, and he did often feel its weakness – palpitations, shortness of breath, and occasional numbness. So, with a resigned sigh, he put the pills into his mouth, turned to face Sister Ursula, and gulped down all three, with a drink of water. "See!"

"Very good, Francis. But I shouldn't have to keep after you!"

"I know, I know." The Pope gazed at her. Sister Ursula had been with him for many years. She was 65, a Swede of great beauty, great culture, and very strict principles. And, luckily for him, she was a formidable organizer. She had never doubted her vocation, not, it seemed, for an instant. But she was aware that he had often doubted his.

He gazed out the window at the blue sky, the immensity of it, burnished burning bright, a sky of pure metallic cerulean blue, glowing with the pitiless August heat.

He wiped his forehead. It was stifling – not even the hint of a breeze. Perhaps, as Sister Ursula had argued – and she really could be insistent – they should install air-conditioning or a fan. But, no, that would be a weakness, it would be an example of self-indulgence. He must set a standard of absolute simplicity.

Looking down, the Pope noticed – in the vast, empty square – a lone tourist, possibly American he guessed, from the way she moved, casual, yet with the quickness and grace of a tennis player. A splash of scarlet. A girl in a scarlet dress …

Yes, American probably, although, he mused, a Russian or Pole or Brazilian might dress like that. Daring for the middle of the day.

She was taking photographs. Following the direction of her aim, the Pope recognized Father Michael Patrick O'Bryan – one of his oldest, most trusted friends.

Seeing Father O'Bryan's limp, the Pope grimaced. It brought back painful memories. Father O'Bryan's infirmity was the result of months of torture – involving electric shocks, and drills and hammers – in a basement room in the Interior Ministry of a very corrupt African country that was, at that time, and still even now, torn by civil war. Before that, Father O'Bryan had been a great tennis player and always seemed much younger than he was.

And now Father O'Bryan believed he had discovered evidence – in a file of Father Luciani's – of a plot that threatened the very foundations of Catholicism.

Was this threat, this secret order, the Satanic Order of the Apocalypse, a figment of Father Luciani's imagination, or was it real? Father O'Bryan took it very seriously. Well, Michael did specialize in heresies, demons, and exorcisms, and …

The Pope wiped his forehead. The heat hung, glowing, in the air. It pressed on his skin, on his heart. The heat was real, not a fantastical satanic plot. The stone balustrade was real, not a phantom. He looked at his handkerchief – dark with sweat. The handkerchief too was real – and soaked with real human sweat. Not a figment of an over-active imagination.

If he had followed tradition, and Sister Ursula's urging, he would not be in Rome at all. He would be up in Castel Gandolfo, the Pope's summer residence, 30 kilometers north of the city, on the lip of an ancient volcano, and overlooking Lake Albano. There, on the mountainside, the air was cooler.

But, 78 years old and newly elected Pope, Francis II had insisted on staying in Rome. He was fragile. He didn't have much time left. There was much to be done. He had to act quickly. All was not well with Mother Church. New scandals were brewing. Sexual scandals, child abuse, and rape were rife. These scandals cast a shadow over the more than 400,000 honest and dedicated priests and nuns who sacrificed each day, each hour, for their vocation. It was a tragedy – mostly of course for the children and the victims, but not only for them.

Then there was the Vatican Bank – *L'Istituto per le Opere di Religione* – known by its initials, IOR. Its connections with the organized crime, and its money-laundering activity had never been completely cleaned up, despite the efforts of previous popes.

There were layers upon layers of deceit and corruption swirling around the Bank. More than anyone else, the Pope knew of the past scandals. He had prepared a confidential report on them for an earlier Pope – and had learned much about the deaths – clearly murders – of many people whose paths had crossed the Vatican Bank, including two of the Vatican's favorite Italian bankers – Roberto Calvi and Michele Sindona.

The Pope closed his eyes. Macabre images flooded his mind. Roberto Calvi, "God's Banker," as he was known, had been hanged by the neck by his killers. It was a ritual killing, an execution. Calvi had threatened to "spill the beans." He was a dour, clever man, sharp-featured and bald, with a moustache, and a fringe of wispy hair around the naked pale dome of his head. His body was found, swaying, wearing a long dark overcoat, its pockets weighed down with bricks, hanging by his neck under Black Friars Bridge, right next to the heart of the financial district of the City of London. The Capital of Finance and Black Friars! The symbolism – the message – could not have been clearer. Calvi had threatened to reveal secrets; and so, he had to die.

Then there was Michele Sindona, "The Shark," as he was called, another privileged partner of the Vatican Bank. Sindona was a handsome, dashing, charming, self-made man from near Messina, in Sicily, banker for the Sicilian Mafia, friend of the American Mafia, and partner of the Vatican. Shortly after he was convicted of contracting out a murder, Sindona died in prison, in Milan, poisoned – by cyanide in his morning espresso. How convenient! Sentenced to life, and apparently with nothing to lose, he too had threatened to reveal everything he knew. And so, he had to die.

Both should have known better.

Many other people connected with the Vatican Bank died – lawyers, detectives, journalists, policemen. Anyone who tried to get to the bottom of these murky Vatican affairs was in danger. Pope John Paul I, or Papa Luciani, as he was known, for instance. Luciani was an innocent, saintly man, who was possibly murdered, only 33 days after becoming Pope. He had declared that he intended to set up an investigation into the affairs of the Vatican Bank. That declaration, quite possibly, triggered his death warrant.

Father O'Bryan's letter suggested that Cardinal Ambrosiano's mysterious Satanic Order of the Apocalypse was connected to the Mafia, and to money laundering. Frankly, it sounded fanciful. Corruption was one thing, Mafia connections also. Murder and assassinations, too, were not unknown. But a *secret satanic sect* lurking in the very heart of the Vatican, in the very heart of Christendom, and whose aim was to bring about the Apocalypse? That was something else!

Father O'Bryan had limped his way out of the square, and was heading down via della Conciliazione.

The Pope put his hand on the window frame. A hot spasm rippled through his chest, but not enough to bother Sister Ursula about. He had his pride; he would not become a cranky old hypochondriac.

Grimacing against the pain, the Pope turned back to Sister Ursula and the work at hand. "Tonight, we will take them by surprise; it will be our little Blitzkrieg: We will announce that the Special Commission to Investigate the Vatican Bank has *already* been set up – and is fully staffed – it is a *fait accompli*. It is too late for anybody to do anything about it. So, now, you and I will prepare …"

As he turned away from the window, Francis didn't see the two young men hurrying to catch up with Father Michael Patrick O'Bryan.

Nor did he notice the rather flashy young man who slipped out of the shadows of Bernini's Colonnade and took one more photograph of the girl in scarlet.

Later, in very different circumstances, the Pope would remember what he had seen. And, yes, he would remember, vividly remember, the briefly glimpsed beautiful young woman – the girl in scarlet.

As Father O'Bryan entered the broad and empty via della Conciliazione, he felt a twinge of distaste. The avenue was Monumental Fascism. It symbolized one of the compromises the Church had made with the Devil, the Devil, in this case, being the Fascist dictator Benito Mussolini. The street had been built in the 1930s to celebrate the signing of a treaty between the Church and the Fascist Regime. The street was disquieting, desolate, and sterile, with its lineup of grandiose replica facades of Venetian palaces and soaring marble lampposts. It was a world of stone, he thought, as he wiped his forehead, a lifeless, life-denying, world of stone.

Behind Father O'Bryan, the two young men quickened their pace. Then they began to run.

As Scarlett turned her camera toward via della Conciliazione, she noticed two young men with backpacks. It looked like they were following the priest – and now they began to run.

Scarlett thought, but it was just half a thought, a semi-conscious inkling: *There was something not quite right about this picture, two young men hurrying, the old priest limping along in front of them.*

She was going to take another shot, but some pigeons flew up, whirling in a flutter of flashing white and black. Scarlett swung around, camera ready, to catch them in flight, soaring up beside the obelisk toward the hot empty blue sky.

Whirr, click, whirr, click – yes, great shot!

From behind one of the columns of Bernini's Colonnade, another camera clicked, taking one last photograph, one last image of Scarlett.

She was perfect! A dream!

The girl in the scarlet dress.

Brother Filippo glanced at his watch. He licked his lips. He could hardly wait. Cardinal Ambrosiano would be delighted.

CHAPTER 4 – CICADA'S SONG

The girl was still alive, barely.

It was a miracle, really.

The air stank of roasted flesh.

It was an isolated spot, a suitable spot, fifty miles east of Palermo, not far from the north coast of Sicily and its dazzling beaches.

U Pizzu took a deep breath. The blond girl – "collateral damage" in the sanitized lingo of the military – lay sprawled on her back on the other side of the burning Hummer. She was still breathing – but not for long.

One job was done – then there was that priest to be killed. What was his name? Oh, yes, O'Bryan, Father Michael Patrick O'Bryan, Irish, a Jesuit, a scholar, an expert on heresies and witchcraft, demons and possession and exorcisms, and other such nonsense. Apparently, he knew things he shouldn't know. He must be a nosy old coot!

U Pizzu glanced at his wristwatch. Well, that job too would soon be wrapped up. Right now, in fact, Father Michael Patrick O'Bryan would be taking his very last breath. Probably, he was dead already – God bless the man!

The black Hummer smoldered, flames crackled. The vehicle was slewed sideways, halfway into the ditch, the motor smashed, windows and doors shattered by the bazooka blast. Smoke drifted from charred, twisted metal. Seats sputtered with ribbons of fire. The interior was pasted with gore, dripping with bits of what had been, a few minutes ago, a human being.

U Pizzu – aka "The Cut" or "Mr. Percentage" – crossed himself. U Pizzu didn't believe in God, but he stuck to the old rituals and the ancient traditions. He took out a mauve handkerchief and wiped the sweat from his forehead. His white cream jacket and trousers were still impeccable, like his black shirt and white tie. It was late afternoon. The sun was low in the sky. A hot, glowing haze hung in the perfumed air, giving an extra edge to the drifting fragrance of burnt flesh and coppery tang of blood.

U Pizzu insisted on doing the important dirty work himself. It was a matter of craftsmanship and professional courtesy. He smiled – and it was a charming, open smile: *You gotta recognize a job well done! Gaetano Larione was history.*

Ah, poor, foolish Gaetano!

They were dining in a little roadside restaurant not far from Palermo when Gaetano told U Pizzu that he was going to end the money-laundering deal with Cardinal Ambrosiano. He even suggested that he and U Pizzu have the Cardinal assassinated, and he went on to say crazy things about the Cardinal being totally nuts. Cardinal Ambrosiano, Gaetano said, was planning to bring about the end of the world, like, the Apocalypse.

"The end of the world, eh?" U Pizzu toyed with his water glass. If any priest should be poisoned, it was the new Pope, this Francis II. Word was out the Pope planned to set up a Special Commission to "clean house" at the Vatican Bank – definitely a bad idea. Getting rid of this new Pope was something worth looking into. After all, John Paul I, Papa Luciani, way back in 1978, when he poked his nose into the Vatican Bank, he only lasted … what … a month … 33 days? Just over a month! Then – poof! Dead! And they couldn't bury the guy fast enough! As soon as he was dead, Luciani became a non-person, like he'd never been pope at all.

"If there's no world," Gaetano said, "there's no business."

"Yeah. Right. No world, no business." U Pizzu picked up a crusty piece of bread and stared at it. His old pal, Gaetano, had lost his marbles. Lack of marbles was bad for business. Gaetano, poor fellow, had become a threat to business-as-usual. Business-as-usual was true religion. So, alas, Gaetano had become a liability. And in U Pizzu's considered opinion, liabilities were to be gotten off the books lickety-split. So, regretfully, U Pizzu had informed Cardinal Ambrosiano's right-hand man, that spooky old geezer, Father Andrea, that Gaetano could no longer be trusted; that he'd made some incredible accusations; that …

A day later, word from the Cardinal had come down – eliminate the Larione clan.

"All of them?"

"All of them."

"The men, just the men?"

There was a hesitation on the other end of the line, then: "Yes, just the men."

U Pizzu sighed. For some reason, he was pleased they didn't have to kill the women and children. But the lesson was clear: Do not cross Mother Church!

Ah, poor old Gaetano! At their last meeting, just two weeks ago, Gaetano was, as always, bigger than life, bursting with energy. The two of them were sitting at a simple wooden table, under the awning, on the terrace of a restaurant near the beach in Cefalù. Gaetano had his sleeves rolled up and his shirt open, showing that silly big gold medallion he was so proud of; chest hair spilled out over his crisp, blue-striped cotton shirt. He was filling U Pizzu's glass, and saying, "That fucking Cardinal is a crazy son-of-a-bitch. He's got this idea he can destroy the Earth."

"Destroy the Earth? How?"

"We've got to stop him." Gaetano gave U Pizzu that warm, big-eyed, doe-like look – *we've known each other forever – brothers forever, right* – and fingered his sweaty chest medallion.

"How the hell is he going to destroy the Earth?" U Pizzu forked up a spool of spaghetti and one clam. "What's he got – an atomic bomb?"

"He's got something worse, much worse. This guy – an engineer from Bologna – told me. He said that the Cardinal has laid hands on something that can cause earthquakes."

"Really?" U Pizzu favored Gaetano with his most suave smile. U Pizzu didn't read much, but he knew science fiction when he heard it. "Cause earthquakes? I thought earthquakes were an act of God, like, you'd need a lot of energy for that, not even an atomic bomb can cause a quake, I mean, not a big one. Little ones, fine, even fracking will do that. But big ones?"

"Well, the Cardinal's got it, the energy, and he's gonna use it to blow up everything, sink the continents, empty the oceans, turn the temples upside down, make the fucking ethereal towers tumble into the fucking abyss, all kinds of biblical shit. The engineer guy said you tinker with that sort of gizmo, and you destroy everything, the whole Earth." Gaetano smiled at U Pizzu.

U Pizzu noticed, and not for the first time, that Gaetano had really sincere, charming eyes, wonderful warm brown irises, and big dark pupils, like you were looking straight into the man's soul. But U Pizzu had to wonder: Why would anybody want to destroy the Earth? I mean, Earth's our fucking home, right? "Sounds impressive!" U Pizzu grinned, "So what is this *gizmo*? What's it called?"

"It's a thing called the Crystal."

"The *Crystal!* My, my ..." U Pizzu risked a wistful smile. The Crystal sounded like something a fortune-teller would have in her tent in a circus. Once, near Piazza Navona in Rome, U Pizzu sat down with a fortune-teller; she had dark gypsy eyes, and a thin, handsome, deeply tanned face, lit up by the candle on the little wooden table she'd set up on the sidewalk; on the table was a little round piece of bubbly glass, which she called her "crystal ball," and, having gazed into it, and fingered the palm of his hand, she told him that women would always find him irresistible, and that next year would be particularly prosperous. Well, there was nothing wrong with that!

"If Ambrosiano dies, this thing doesn't happen." Gaetano speared a helpess, naked, unshelled clam.

"Thing?"

"The end of the world."

"Right – the end of the world." U Pizzu looked down, forked another coil of spaghetti, and impaled a luscious little white clam. "Well, we don't want the world to come to an end, do we?" He paused to savor the clam. "How you gonna kill Ambrosiano?"

"I'm thinking ..."

"You're thinking ..."

Gaetano Larione was a vain, overweight, jovial well-meaning son-of-a-bitch, who always made sure he had a good tan. He even sun-bathed in the nude, slathered in sun-tan oil, on the rooftop of his farmhouse, which was about twenty kilometers south of Corleone. This, even though Gaetano was one of his oldest friends, U Pizzu found disgusting and vaguely obscene. Gaetano was also a womanizer, a connoisseur of very young ladies: blonde, preferably; tanned, all over, preferably; smooth as silk, all over, preferably.

So, it was child's play to get Gaetano to a convenient out-of-the-way place for his execution. All U Pizzu needed was bait; and it hadn't taken his men long to come up with the sweetest kind of bait – a girl from Milazzo, an exquisite blonde, a student at the University of Messina, not connected to any Mafia clan, her family being honest folk, a small chain of eye-glass and contact lens and eye-modification shops – her father started from nothing and somehow stayed clean. Miracles do happen.

So, now, Gaetano was food for vultures.

Well, not really. What was left of Gaetano – a torso and bits and pieces – would be dissolved in acid, mixed in a barrel of concrete, left to dry, sealed, and dumped in the Tyrrhenian Sea where it was more than 2000 meters deep. The vultures wouldn't get a peek in.

The Hummer was still smoldering. A few bright crackles and sparks flashing here and there.

The sun was low. Etna, that glorious volcano, pride of Sicily, more than three kilometers high, hung there, a soft metal-dark shadow in the eastern sky. The light was golden. The cicadas, gone silent after the explosion, started up again, making a racket. Funny that such a rough sound could be so melodiously sensual! U Pizzu loved it! It was like the strumming of light on the sea, or the heat vibrating in the air, mirage upon mirage, something you could drown in – primal ecstasy, and pure delight, as good as sex; well …

U Pizzu had a weakness for the virginal, meaningless music of nature: The rasping of cicadas, the whirring of crickets, the whispering of wind in grass, the jazz-like splattering rhythm of breakers surging against a waterfront, the eerie hollow clatter of pebbles swept up and dropped in the surf, the harsh raw caw of seagulls, circling, skimming over the water.

Now, just before dusk, even with the trilling of the cicadas, which added to the intensity, the air was absolutely still, motionless, dead calm. It had an uncanny, transparent beauty. The beauty was so intense, it was almost painful – heavy with the pathos of the passing of time. U Pizzu glanced at Etna – he was proud of it, Europe's biggest volcano. And it was in Sicily! Majestic was the only word for it.

Hmm! There was something strange going on. A giant column of black smoke was rising from the volcano, climbing straight up, until, the ash particles getting too heavy for the thin upper atmosphere, the column flattened out and began moving southeast. Weird – nobody had talked about an eruption. Whatever was going on, it was impressive, even from halfway across the island. Could this column of ash have anything to do with the wave of earthquakes he'd read about? Two days ago, there'd been shaking and trembling everywhere – Japan, Turkey, Chile … U Pizzu stared at the rising pillar of ash, at how it caught the light. It looked like a cylinder of dark steel, a burnished sniper barrel – gunmetal gray. Ah, yes, it was truly beautiful.

He glanced at the dusty fronds of a nearby palm tree, seemingly so sleepy and peaceful. Ah, nature! U Pizzu breathed it in. People think the ground under their feet is solid. It isn't. It's at war. The Earth is a battlefield. Tectonic plates duke it out! Huge tensions, building up. Earthquakes and volcanoes! Everything we see is violence, struggle, conflict, all the time, everywhere. We are sitting on a live volcano, whether we know it or not! U Pizzu had read about it – geology was a fascinating subject, and volcanology and seismology;. He'd even read a few books on tectonics and volcanoes.

He sighed. People, so-called civilized people, didn't realize that civilization, well, so-called civilization, was a veneer, a masquerade, a perilous high-wire act, total artifice, a fairy tale. Underneath the good manners, human beings were cannibalistic savages. Strip off the Armani, take away the central heating and the plumbing, the corner café, the nail salon, and the pricey restaurant, and it is blood, fangs, claws, sweat, piss, and shit: jealous savages crouching among half-eaten bones.

U Pizzu adjusted his glasses. He wore special big dark Gucci Polaroids because they made him look like a film star and because they hid his eyes. His eyes were big and dark and sensitive, and, women told him, utterly beautiful. It was annoying. They made him look too handsome. His wife, Maria Grazia, said he looked like the famous Latin Lover in those old movies, Marcello Mastroianni.

Almost always, when he was finishing a job – killing somebody – U Pizzu would take the glasses off. The last thing the dying victim would see would be those big liquid romantic eyes, staring into his or her dying eyes, with compassion, with curiosity.

U Pizzu wondered what it was like, dying.

He stood up and walked around to the far side of the Hummer.

The bait, the young woman – a girl, really – was still alive. Amazing! Somehow, she'd survived the blast. She'd gotten out of the Hummer and tried to run. Tough little kid! She had a cell phone. He'd stopped her by shooting her in the back, off center, down by the hip, so she wouldn't die, not right away; he'd watched her fall. Then he'd walked up, turned her over, and shot her in the belly, again to the side; then he'd kicked the cell phone away and crushed it underfoot.

Now, he came back to watch. The kid was crawling on her belly, reaching out for the bloodied, smashed cell phone. She'd never make it. But she'd try, you had to give her that, a brave kid, and young, just 18 years old, a student in jurisprudence – top marks too! – making an extra buck, making ends meet. The girl had crawled quite a way already – leaving a streak of shit, bits of flesh, and blood. It didn't smell so good.

"Give it a rest, Signorina."

She was a pretty girl, more than pretty, the perfect blond trophy the

Larione boys loved to strut around – and thus the perfect bait. Only thing was, she hadn't known she was bait. She'd thought she was a favor – 3000 euros for a date.

"Just tell Gaetano you want to take him to this special little beach you discovered, real private – and you know how to get there, secret little side roads. It'll be a surprise!"

"What sort of surprise?" she'd asked.

"His birthday! But it's a secret, an absolute secret!"

She'd smiled – charming, really, and she liked surprises, or so she said.

You could see her thinking: If she had to fuck the guy, well … maybe she'd get extra money …

Maybe she'd get on a national TV show …

U Pizzu had hinted about links to the Prime Minister, links to show business, and the TV networks and game shows; and he'd sighed, romantically, "Favors draw favors, Signorina, favors draw favors."

In fact, when U Pizzu came to think of it, the cliché was true: There was a chain of favors going right from the ruined and smoking Hummer on this narrow little country road in Sicily to the Prime Minister's office in Palazzo Chigi and to certain ornately baroque rooms in the Vatican, to the Vatican Bank, and from there the chain extended to staid, ultra-respectable banking houses in Zurich and Lugarno; to banks in Frankfurt, in London, in New York and Hong Kong and Shanghai and Moscow and Seoul; and it spread to investments in real things – in restaurants, real estate, construction companies, casinos, pizza parlors, spas – in Canada, the US, Germany, Switzerland, France; and, last, but not least, the chain led to the office of Cardinal Antonio Xavier Paulus Ambrosiano, Prince of the Church, intimate of presidents and prime ministers, reputed mystic – and banker for the Mafia.

Everything's connected.

If he'd been able to trust the girl – well, she could have become part of that profitable chain. But she was too young, too innocent and naive, and, above all, she was *not one of us.*

The girl's perfect honey-like tan was like melted wax now, tinged with green. She turned, twisting around was hard, and looked up at him. Green eyes, the mouth set in a grimace, her teeth bared in a rictus, her silk shirt stained with blood and flecks of intestine.

Brave little bitch, she really was …

"*Per favore* … Please," she whispered. She really was a spunky kid. U Pizzu liked that … different circumstances and, well, he would have fucked her himself, showed her a good time.

U Pizzu pulled up his cream trousers, to protect the crease, and crouched down. The intense heat, rising from the cracked and grained asphalt, glowed on his face. The road stretched down and around the hillside. The cicadas were chanting even stronger now; the air was sweet.

U Pizzu caressed her hair, greasy with sweat and fear, plastered down, close to the skull; one of those perfect blond Sicilian girls from the time of the Normans and the Vikings – they were blond and blue-eyed or blond and green-eyed – genes from the forests and icy fiords of the far north – and yet as Sicilian as they come. "Can you hear the cicadas, Signorina? It's a love song. Beautiful, isn't it? Ah, life … life is so full, so full!"

She tried to speak, but only managed a gurgle in her throat. She reached out one slender hand, fine-boned, smooth skin, beautiful; she was gazing now, with just a sliver of hope, straight up at him.

"*Mi dispiace, Signorina.* I'm sorry, Miss." He pulled out the Walther P38, paused a second for effect, watched the newly startled terror, and shot her between the eyes.

Yes, it was a shame, truly a shame.

U Pizzu crouched there, suddenly regretting that he had forgotten to push the Polaroids up onto his forehead, so she'd see his soul peering into her soul the instant she died. He would have liked her eyes to be staring straight into his when she realized she was about to die, so their two souls would be locked in that moment of eternity, forever.

It would have been like love!

It would have been like fucking!

Caught in the instant, in eternity!

U Pizzu stroked his chin. In the old days the Mafia didn't shoot women, not usually anyway. But now other organizations, the Naples Camorra and the Calabrian 'Ndrangheta – not to mention the South Americans, the Russians, the Chinese, and the Arabs – were leaving Cosa Nostra, the old-fashioned, honorable Sicilian Mafia, in the dust. So, standards had slipped – it was regrettable.

He stood up, brushing down his trousers. "Okay, boys," he said into the short-range walkie-talkie, knowing the clean-up crew was just around the corner, parked next to a farmhouse whose peaked red tile roof he could just see over the fronds of a dusty palm tree and a straggle of bright red bougainvillea.

They'd be here in a minute and clean it up – spick and span. The road would be scrubbed down. Gaetano and the girl would never be found. The Hummer would be dismantled and scrapped. Any pieces that might identify the vehicle would be melted down and dropped in the deep blue sea.

U Pizzu stretched and yawned. The *lupara bianca*, they called it, the "white shotgun," or maybe, U Pizzu mused, "the ghostly sawed-off shotgun" would be a better way to put it. It was an appropriate metaphor for the death you never see and about which you know nothing. One day you disappear. You are never found, not a trace, not a whiff, not a hint – no body, no bones, no flesh, no blood, no clothes, no DNA, not a single tooth, not even a filling. Poof! You are gone, as if you had never been. It was so much more terrifying – for the dying and for the survivors – than knowing there's a cadaver you can mourn over and bury and visit.

It's like being killed twice – your soul is lost. People don't even dare speak your name.

If your loved ones mourn you, they mourn shamefully, curtains drawn, shutters closed, huddled in the silence of their own rooms. Your death is not a death; it's a curse. One that casts the shadow of fear over the family, over associates – forever. So, it would be with the girl – and with Gaetano, and with all the other Larione men – gone, just gone, forever.

The Larione Clan had made a fatal mistake – pitting its power against Cardinal Ambrosiano. Threatening to cancel the Ambrosiano connection was a death sentence.

Whatever had gotten into Gaetano, to make such wild accusations? A machine that could cause earthquakes! *The Crystal?* A machine that could bring about the end of the world?

In a week, there'd be no more Lariones alive, not to speak of.

U Pizzu flipped open his cell phone to tell Rome that "the problem had been solved."

"Yeah? Well, we still got that *other* problem," said the voice.

"Okay. Talk!" U Pizzu narrowed his eyes. Sometimes he found the indirection of Mafia Speak annoying. He understood the need for security and discretion, of course; but sometimes he wanted to scream: *Just say what the fuck you want to say for fuck's sake!*

"The priest. The fucking Jesuit …"

U Pizzu rolled his eyes. It never stopped. He was working with idiots. Nobody had any faith or trust any more. True craftsmanship was a thing of the past. "You told me about that problem already! I sent Franco and Paolo. They are looking after it. Or do I have to come up there myself?"

"Yes, boss, okay, they're looking after it."

"Fine. That means the priest is history already!" U Pizzu flipped the cell phone shut and walked down the road toward where his car was parked in a gravel side road. Problems, fucking problems! Some people, unwisely, couldn't resist dramatizing every little event – creating problems where there weren't any.

His mood darkened.

Killing Gaetano was like cutting out part of his own heart. He and Gaetano went back a long way. Their families – fathers, grandfathers, great-grandfathers – had survived the Mafia civil wars of the 1980s and early 1990s. Yes, somehow, they'd survived the bloodletting when Salvatore – Totò – Riina, the head of the Corleone clan, in a fit of crazy jealousy against the snobbish Palermo families that ran the million-dollar Europe-America heroin trade, had got it into his head to wipe out those Palermo-based families, the richest Mafia families in Sicily, and – clever underhanded bastard that he was – Totò had managed to do it; and, then, Gaetano's and U Pizzu's families had survived the crackdown of the 1990s, the crusading judges, the tough governments, the anti-Mafia laws … Gaetano and U Pizzu had grown up with all that history, all that tradition, behind them, and now there was only him, U Pizzu, the last of the grandees! Who could he talk to now? Who could he share his memories with? Gaetano was an asshole, but he was U Pizzu's asshole!

U Pizzu got to the side road – a sunken lane between two barren and scorched fields – where he had parked his car in the shadow of a eucalyptus tree. He stood there, breathing the air. The light was pure molten gold. Heat blazed off gravel and stones and piled-up earth and off the dried and yellowed grass and shrubs. The cicadas began their chant again, a vast rasping sound, vibrant, like the light, and as wide and deep as the landscape itself.

He opened the door and got into the car – his very own souped-up white Mini Cooper. Inside it was an oven. But he liked that. He opened all the windows and sat for a minute, just breathing it all in, the heat, the cicadas, the dust, and the golden afternoon light.

He turned the key, revved the engine, and spurted off down the dirt road before turning out onto the asphalt. It was a shame, a waste really, that girl. Lust rose in a tangle of images: legs, breasts, the girl's upturned face, her green eyes, her sweet soft lips, her bright, perfect, moist teeth. The lust subsided, dissolving into a warm pleasant feeling – a slight ache of nostalgia

He turned on the radio: the top of the pops, Italian style, and a couple of oldies, Neapolitan songs, in their American version, *"It's now or never …"*

And the Neapolitan version, *"O, sole mio …"*

Behind the Polaroids U Pizzu's eyes crinkled in a smile of anticipation. With luck, he could squeeze in a full hour of swimming. Swimming at sunset and even beyond, into the darkness, was one of his favorite things – then a chilled bottle of Regaleali and a plate of spaghetti with clams and he could just sit back, listen to the waves, and watch the darkness gather over the water – and maybe think about the 18-year-old, how sweet she would have been. What was the girl's name? No, it was better not to think about her. U Pizzu crossed himself.

The white Mini raced down the hillside, toward the glimmering coast, toward the golden beaches – and toward the sparkling, ever-changing, wine-dark sea.

CHAPTER 5 — BLOOD ON HER LIPS

WHAM! The first shot ricocheted three inches from Father O'Bryan's face; the second smashed into a loop of cable. Shards of stone splattered his jacket. Gunshots echoed, rippled down the sewer tunnel.

He flattened himself against the wall. *Who were these people?* It was chilly down here, but he was soaked in sweat. The beating of his heart, he was certain, could be heard for miles. When he'd pulled up the manhole grille and plunged into the sewer, he was sure he'd escaped. *Nobody knew these ancient tunnels like he did!*

Surely, the two killers wouldn't manage to follow him!

Surely, they wouldn't realize how he had disappeared!

But, by Jesus, Joseph, and Mary, they had realized; and, yes, they had followed him. There they were, behind him, lifting the grille, scrambling down the steel rungs.

Twenty feet below the sun-drenched sizzling cobblestones, in the ancient drainage tunnel, Father O'Bryan ran for his life. The shattered hip and limp were pure torture.

He was about to die.

Not yet, oh Lord, not yet!

Staggering around a bend, he careened against a stone wall, stumbled, caught himself – scraped his knuckles on the rough stone, righted himself, and splashed onwards, zigzagging, ankle-deep in runoff and rainwater. The blessed limp would be the death of him! But, no, he would fight! With God's help, he would survive!

The old sewage tunnel, its walls built of volcanic tuff, echoed with splashing footsteps. The tunnel was pitch-black, with dazzling circles of light every ten meters, filtering down from openings far above.

Soon the tunnel would branch into different tunnels, and then become a labyrinth. That was his only hope. If he could get far enough, then …

The spots of light, lighting him up from overhead, were the moments of maximum danger – and, at that very instant, Father O'Bryan reeled into a circle of hazy brilliance. The tunnel was drier at this point. Heart pounding as if it would burst, he weaved, twisted, stumbled, lurching to this side, then to that, desperate to dodge the bullets he knew must come.

A ripple of shots slammed into the tunnel wall. Bright flashing fragments of stone stung his face, smashed against his glasses, fracturing a lens, splattering his jacket.

Half-blinded, still lurching forward with his wild, ridiculous, limping gait, he glanced back. The two killers, thick silhouettes, legs pumping, caught in a spot of misty light, were closer. He gasped for breath. He was too old for this! He groaned. His heart thundered. For God's sake, he was a dusty old scholar, a pedant, not an Olympic runner!

Who the devil were these people? Why were they after him? Mafia? Cult members? Cardinal Ambrosiano's helpers?

And what, really, was the Satanic Order of the Apocalypse?

How stupid he had been! His letter to the Pope must have been intercepted. Who opened the Pope's mail? In whom did the Pope confide? It could not have been his secretary, or could it?

He held tight to his dusty old briefcase – it contained all the documents Father Luciani had left him.

A few minutes ago, life had been entirely normal. He was limping down via della Conciliazione, musing about the girl in scarlet when he'd suddenly stopped to look at a display in a bookshop window.

What caught his eye, among a mountain of guidebooks and devotional manuals, was a display featuring a new edition of the *Malleus Maleficarum*, the famous fifteenth-century treatise on witchcraft. It was a true classic, an exploration of how witches serve as Satan's handmaidens, how their carnal lust turns them into Satan's slaves, and how coupling with Satan is for a woman a most horrible sin, and how demonic possession and witchcraft are closely related! Ah, yes, demons and witches!

Glancing at the book, the image of the girl in scarlet again came vividly to mind. She was hardly a witch or a demon, though something had surely possessed her to wear such an outlandish dress.

He should have talked to her. And, in fact, just thinking of her gave him an idea. He would write an essay about the rise of feminism and the return of ancient goddesses – the return of the repressed Female Principle – the

Eternal Feminine – and he would link it with the cult of divas and actresses and pop stars – and relate this to the resurgence of pagan patterns in modern society, and to today's fashion for shameless, exhibitionist female attire, such as the girl in scarlet, and …

Suddenly, reflected in the window – superimposed on the image of a witch being burned at the stake – he saw something outlined in the glare of the midsummer sun. He blinked. The reflection was a dark cartoon silhouette: *a man drawing a gun.*

And … pointing it at him! Without looking around, Father O'Bryan ran. He sprinted, limping, as fast as he could. It was pure gut instinct, or perhaps the will of God that he was not to die, not now, not yet. As he ran, a shot whizzed past him, shattering a shop window. Yes, this was real.

He knew the Eternal City like the back of his hand; he turned down a side alley, slipped into an entryway, ducked into a side niche, lifted a manhole grille, and, pulling the grille shut behind him, he climbed down into an ancient Roman sewer where, years ago, earning money as a student, he had guided tourists. Here, he would be safe.

But, no, he wasn't! The two killers had followed.

Now, deep underground, he turned to look back. In that instant, a bullet ripped into his shoulder. A shot slammed into his chest. He doubled over, almost fell. He managed to straighten up. He gasped for breath, dizzy, disoriented.

Oh, Mother of God, I beseech thee!

Blood gurgled, coppery, bitter on the tongue; a wheezing sound, air being sucked in or out, bubbles of blood, sticky, hot. *The lungs are flooding. I'll choke on it. So, this is it!*

Suddenly he was calm. *Now, now, Michael Patrick O'Bryan, you must die like a man! Meet your end the way you should, even if unshriven.*

Then, a voice …

"This way, priest, this way!"

Oh, Mother of God! Father O'Bryan took a ragged, hissing breath. The bullets that hit him must have been ricochets; otherwise he wouldn't be alive. Blood, hot and sticky, seeped down inside his jacket. The wheezing bubbling clawed like fire at his chest.

"This way, priest, this way!"

What? He almost said it aloud. What was that voice? Where was it? Who was it? Dazed, feverish, he glanced around. On one side of the tunnel there was an alcove, a sort of shelter, with a grille up above. He stumbled – almost fell – into it. Sanctuary for a few seconds! He slid down, onto the cool wet pavement, his back against the wall. It was the end.

I'm dying, I'm dying.

Yellow rays of dirty dim light streamed down from the grille, projecting shadowy bars across Father O'Bryan's shattered, dying body. Part of his mind found it amusingly ironic. Bars like prison bars were closing upon him. The assassins would find him, and they would kill him; or he might already be dead.

Another shot scattered sparks on the stone.

"Priest!" The voice was a fiery hiss – impatient, furious. Father O'Brien looked up. At first, he didn't see anything. Then he glimpsed what looked like a black cloak, a monk, up above. Suddenly, the grille was lifted – a hand, a silhouette.

Another shot rang out. His heart skipped a beat.

"Priest!"

I'm delirious! He wiped his forehead; his hand, he noticed, was streaked with black in the yellow light – blood, blood turned black. *I'm going mad, I've been shot, I'm seeing things.*

"Priest!" the voice hissed – a mocking voice, playful and seductive: a child playing a game, hide-and-seek … *Yes, I'm losing my mind!*

"Priest! Up here! Hurry!"

Father O'Bryan groaned. A ladder, thick rusty iron rungs, dimly perceived, led upward, to the opening, faintly lit. He struggled to his feet, doubled over in agony, straightened up – another burning, searing pain. His fingers grasped the first rungs of the ladder, slippery, crumbling greasy rust. His undershirt, he realized, was soaked in blood. Warm sticky blood flooded his crotch, ran down his leg.

Climbing left him breathless. His lungs were on fire. Bubbles of gore burst from his lips.

He reached for the opening, a sort of manhole. But he couldn't make it. His strength failed. He hung there. "I can't!"

A hand came down. A slender, powerful arm. A hand with long sharp claw-like fingers grasped him by the arm, then under the armpit, and hoisted him up. It seemed to Father O'Bryan that he was, for an instant, flying – through the manhole and into a small space.

He landed on the floor and felt shock and pain and more hot blood soaking his jacket. He was breathless. His glasses were fogged, smudged, fractured, twisted sideways. He lay on the floor. He could not see the creature, whatever it was.

"I'm sorry," he began to say.

"Silence, priest!"

The shape was black – an ink blot hovering over him. He groped for his glasses. He must wipe them. He didn't have the strength. In that instant, his savior turned, and, in the yellowish light, through the smeared, fractured lenses, the face Father O'Bryan glimpsed, for an instant, was demonic – reptilian, green and turquoise scales, seductive, large eyes, a female!

The eyes were the eyes of a snake – sparkling, heavy-lidded, slits of green and gold. The mouth curved upwards. It looked like a smile. –And two long, gleaming fangs! My God! The tongue flickered. Forked!

A demon!

He *was* delirious! Or was he being carried off to Hell by the Devil or by one of his female consorts, a girl demon?

He opened his mouth …

"Shush!" A clawed finger raised to the demon's lips. "Shush!"

The demon's voice was caressing, suave, musical. She smiled.

The demon is delighted! She has captured my soul. I am surely not much of a prize! Was this a nightmare? Had he read too many dusty volumes about demons and witches? Had he performed too many exorcisms? Had she possessed him, already, without his being aware of it?

The demon turned away, leaned over the manhole, and she was gone, fluid as a shadow, plunging into the tunnel below.

Covering his mouth, trying to stifle the sound, Father O'Bryan coughed. Hot blood bubbled on his lips – bitter and metallic. He reached into his coat pocket, warm, and sticky, soaked in blood.

There were screams, a string of swear words in a Sicilian dialect, shots ricocheting off metal, more screams. It all came from far away, as if in a dream. There was a wet smacking sound, a sucking, and what sounded like the splash of a wave; then a breaking, a crunching of bones …

Slash, slash. Rip, rip, ripppppp! Shhhhuulluuuushhh …

These were not human sounds.

Father O'Bryan was not a coward, but he felt the chill of pure terror.

He groaned – then he must have passed out.

He woke up, blinking in pain.

"Shush!" The demon bent close over him; a suave leathery claw clamped down on his mouth.

Father O'Bryan fought back, tried to cry out.

"Shush, now, shush!" The smell of leather, the reptilian face close to his, a hint of perfume, then, something, a cloth, over his nose … chloroform, chloroform …

"Quiet! Quiet, priest, quiet!"

Father O'Bryan kicked, squirmed, tried to tear the claw away but, breathing in the bitter-sweet acid, he was too weak.

He flickered in and out of consciousness.

Darkness and oblivion

When he woke up – oh, the pain!

In a flash of light – which was perhaps just pain – he saw the face. The demon had changed. He was sure it was she. She was pretending to be human. Her face was only inches away.

He stared at creature's blood-red lips, and her eyes, which were dark, at the arched, coal-black eyebrows, the skin as white as alabaster, and a face of a purity and perfection that was too beautiful … too perfect … to … be … human … No, she could not be human.

"Do not move, priest!"

Red liquid dripped from the full, sensual lips, from the bright, perfect teeth – blood? Was it blood?

Her hand was under his jacket, reaching for his heart, digging into his chest, probing into his wounds, his blood gurgling up …

"*Oh, Mother of God*," he cried out; the words died in his throat, as did the prayer …

CHAPTER 6 – GOTH GIRL

"No worries, Professor." Mario DeLuca glanced at the digital clock on the Mercedes dashboard. "We're running right on time."

Ten minutes earlier, just after sunset, Mario had picked up Professor Roger Thornhill and his daughter Kate at the Rome Institute of Cosmology, situated on a street on the Esquiline Hill. A full-house crowd was pouring out of the building, a throng of VIPs, and VIP cars, and loads of security; but Mario had been able to park right across from the Institute in the special spot reserved for his Mercedes.

When he caught sight of Kate, Mario was leaning against the car, arms folded, patiently waiting. Kate was alone, apart from the crowd, and dressed all in black. She waved timidly.

Her father was surrounded. People were congratulating him and asking him questions. Looking both ways, Kate – a slender, shadowy figure, silhouetted in the glow of the street lamps and reflecting cobblestones – strode across the street, heading straight for Mario. Mario took a deep breath, straightened up, and smoothed down his tie.

"Mario, finally! Finally, we meet again!"

"Kate!" Mario rarely choked up, but this time he did. He'd known Kate since she was a little kid, only four years old. They'd never stopped corresponding. But the last time he had seen her was six years ago. Kate was a teenager and she was with her mother, Laura. Since then, there had been the tragedy – Laura was dead, assassinated, and …

Kate put her arms around him, hugged him, and kissed him on both cheeks. "*Come stai*, Mario? How are you?"

"*Piuttosto come stai, tu*?" Mario said. "How are you? That's more important!"

"*Sto bene, Mario, sto bene.* I'm okay, Mario, I'm okay." Kate leaned back, and stared at him; and, with the lamplight lighting up her pale skin and thick glasses, she feigned an appraising critical pout, head tilted to one side. Her face lit up. She grinned. "*Sempre lo stesso, Mario! Il più bello di tutti gli romani!*" You haven't changed, Mario – you're still the most handsome Roman of them all!"

"*Scherzi!* You're joking!" Mario laughed. "*Sono un vecchietto.* I'm a little old man! I'm 48!" He relaxed. Kate was still Kate. As a kid she'd been a hell-raiser, hilarious, always up to mischief!

"Dad is trapped by his fans." Kate put her arm under Mario's and turned to watch the crowd. More cars – Mercedes, Alfas, and BMWs – had drawn up to take delivery of the VIPs.

"He's an important man!" Mario felt a surge of pride – it was like they were family. Well, in a way they were. When she was fourteen, Kate had stayed a whole year with him and his wife and their kids. They'd gone on holidays – Venice, Sicily, snorkeling off the island of Vulcano, and then long weekends at the beach, in Fregene, where Mario had rented a cottage. Kate was like a sister to Francesca and Lorenzo and like a daughter to him and Elena.

"Yes, yes, you're right," said Kate, in a soft voice; with one finger she pushed her glasses up the bridge of her nose.

"He looks like a movie star," said Mario.

"Don't tell him that – people say he looks like –"

"… like Cary Grant," said Mario, "that old star from the –"

"Yes, but, like I said, Mario," Kate grinned, "don't tell him that."

Professor Roger Thornhill – Nobel Laureate and International Physics Wolf-Bergman Prize Winner – glanced across the street. Kate was leaning against Mario. Roger put his hand on Professor Giorgio Liberati's shoulder. "So, Giorgio, I'll see you later and we can pick up where we left off."

"Yes, Roger. See you later."

"That was a wonderful talk, Professor Thornhill," gushed a sleek, deeply tanned woman. She was the wife – Roger managed to remember – of the Italian Minister of Defense and, in her own right, rather well known. Yes, she was a Professor, at the University of Perugia, of something … Oh, yes, an expert on Dante, she and a colleague had translated the *Divine Comedy* into French, to very good reviews. "*Grazie, Signora.*" Roger inclined his head in a bow and gave her his special smile; then, touching her lightly on the arm, he moved on, and, catching the eyes of dozens of people, he managed, with a quick series of friendly, intimate glances, *just for you, just for you, and just for you,* to free himself, and cross the street, turning once to wave back at the crowd.

"Mario," he said, shaking Mario's hand. "Finally!"

"*Professore*," Mario said. "It's been a long time!"

"Too long, Mario, too long!"

That was ten minutes ago. Traffic had been backed up near the Institute and it had taken Mario almost the whole ten minutes to get down to via Fori Imperiali and now …

Now, a blinding glare surged up in the rearview mirror, as a car with headlights on high beam crowded in behind the Mercedes. Mario glanced into the rearview mirror. An Alfa, it looked like. The Alfa was too close, suspiciously close. But, as they approached the Colosseum, the Alfa fell back, the blinding glare faded. Other cars slid into the empty slot. Mario relaxed.

As the Mercedes raced past the Colosseum, Roger turned to stare at the towering arched walls. Unbidden, the images rose up – all the lions, Christians, and gladiators who had died in there, of all those blood-soaked stones, now trampled over by tourists and tour guides and archaeologists.

Blood-soaked stones … Images of Jerusalem …

Roger tugged at his shirt collar, and unbuttoned an extra button. As soon as he had gotten into the car, Kate had insisted on undoing and removing his tie. "Dad, it's too hot for a tie," she declared, tucking the tie into her purse.

"Really, Kate!"

"Yes, really! It's a very pretty tie; and you do like to be pretty. But you don't need a tie! You are perfectly handsome without it."

Roger frowned. He preferred to be formal and perfectly groomed; but if Kate insisted …

Suddenly, something struck him as strange. Father O'Bryan had not been at the lecture. Michael had assured Roger no force on earth would keep him away.

Kate said, "I wonder why Father O'Bryan wasn't there – it's not like him."

"No, it isn't."

Kate had tried Father O'Bryan's cell phone; nothing – not even his voice mail; when she sent a text message it bounced back. "Strange," Kate said. "Weird, really."

"I'm sure he'll get in touch." Roger smoothed down the lapel of his jacket. It was a fine white linen Hugo Boss jacket he had bought in Paris just last month and he rather liked it. It went very well with his tan.

"He's invited to the dinner, perhaps we'll see him there."

"Yes," Roger frowned. "I hope so. Still it is strange."

They sat back in silence, each mulling Father O'Bryan's non-appearance.

Roger glanced at his daughter. Kate was staring out the window, at the passing umbrella pines, at the few pedestrians, at the strolling, scantily clad prostitutes, some of them transvestites. The more outrageous or scanty the outfit, the more likely it was a transsexual or transvestite. It was dangerous, unpleasant work. Kate had once talked to a couple of the girls. But it was also for Kate part of the sprawling Felliniesque spectacle that was Rome, the Eternal City, steeped in wisdom and mysticism, sex and cynicism and scandal. As soon as she had tasted it, Kate had fallen in love with the whole unbridled, seething, amoral, circus-like feel of Rome. And now she felt her passion for the city roaring back, a taste of old times.

When she turned to look at her father, she was smiling.

Roger smiled back. He took a deep breath. It was the first time in a long time that he had seen Kate truly smile – a sardonic smirk, yes, a wistful pout, yes, but a real smile – no.

It was a miracle that she had agreed to come on the trip. Maybe she was finally returning to her sunny, outgoing, optimistic self. There was no kohl painted around her eyes, no thick, black lipstick, no dark, menacing airbrush tattoos ... For the moment, she seemed to have cast off the Goth-Punk affectation, the metal chains, the rings, the black makeup, and the false piercings. But maybe this return to the old luminous, mischievous Kate would be temporary. Maybe she would revert to darkness.

The old Kate vanished three years ago, the instant her mother and boyfriend were killed in a terrorist attack in Jerusalem. Kate was badly wounded. A razor-sharp, L-shaped piece of shrapnel had cut through her back and curled around her spine. It was a miracle she had not been paralyzed. Physically, she had recovered; but psychologically ...

At first, after the attack, Kate retreated into herself. Then, she suddenly adopted a Goth-Military-Punk style – heavy black boots, black T-shirts, black jeans, and a thick black leather belt. Without telling him, she took up martial arts, signed up at a rifle-range, and learned to shoot – a pistol, a rifle, and an assortment of automatic weapons – she knew how to operate half a dozen of them.

Roger went to the shooting range one day and watched her from afar. Dressed in black T-shirt, black jeans, and outfitted with military-style boots, Kate had the perfect shooter's stance; she was firing a Remington 700 target rifle. With a quick succession of shots, she scored bull's-eye after bull's-eye. Then she exchanged the Remington for a M16A2.

"Is she any good, that girl over there?" he'd asked an instructor who was standing watching, hands on hips.

The instructor, a beefy, muscular, ex-Marine, blond hair cropped short, grinned from behind his Polaroids. "That gal, sir, she is world class, a natural, could be a Special Forces sniper. I've never seen anything like it."

It was the same with her other new obsession, martial arts. "She's a tiger, that girl," the middle-aged Chinese trainer told him, "and, you know, she's strange – never talks to anybody, hardly at all. There is a lot of anger in there, all bottled up."

"Yes," Roger said, as he squinted toward the stranger his daughter had become. "I can see that."

Kate redefined herself, creating a severe, forbidding style. She pulled her beautiful glossy hair into a tight bun; she traded contact lenses for thick glasses with a heavy black frame. No makeup, except, when she went Goth-Punk, heavy eye shadow and black lipstick. Once, he'd asked her:

"Who do you hate, Kate – Palestinians?"

"No, I don't. I don't hate Palestinians. I don't hate Israelis. There are two Palestinians and three Israelis in my molecular orbital theory seminar. I like them all. We discuss everything, anything. They're just people. We're just people."

Roger wondered, "So …?"

"I just want to be ready …"

"Ready for what?"

"For anything."

That was that! His beautiful, sunny, mischievous darling had been transformed, into an ultra-serious schoolmarm packing a sidearm, a throwback to the pioneering 19th century. At other times, in her intensely dark mode, she was the reincarnation of a 1950s beatnik, or an angst-ridden Parisian existentialist. When the getup was extreme, she morphed into a fetishist version of sadomasochistic Goth-Punk. He didn't know what to think. But it did occur to him that her severity was a rebuke to him, to her dapper father who disguised his guilt and his grief – as he disguised everything – under an elegant and sunny optimism, an incurable stylish insouciance. Roger was exceptionally good-looking; and, as his wife Laura had often reminded him, he knew it. Unusually for a scientist, he was always elegantly dressed and took care to be perfectly groomed – *très soigné*, as the French would say – with the best shirts, and the best suits, and the best shoes. Roger, in short, was a dandy.

Once, when he and Kate were having breakfast in a café in Greenwich Village, Kate said, "That's a very nice shirt, Dad. What is it?"

"Ah, it's from Davies & Son, in London." He was taken aback; she had never commented on his clothes.

"Savile Row?"

"Ah, yes ..."

"It's very fine." Her dark eyes, heavily lined with kohl, bored into him.

"Ah, thank you." He held her gaze.

"You feel guilty underneath, don't you, Dad?"

"No, Kate, I ..."

"Don't deny it."

He looked at her, looked down at his plate, then up again, "I sometimes, think, Kate ... Well, yes, I do feel guilty. If I had not accepted that invitation to Jerusalem, Laura and Peter would not have died. It was very flattering. Vanity is a horrible thing, Kate, and I ..."

She'd laid her hand on his wrist. "It was not your fault, Dad. Things happen, things just happen." She paused, got up from the table, leaned over, and kissed him on the forehead. "You are beautiful, Daddy. I love you. I love you just the way you are." She pulled back, gazed at him, and sat down, primly. Carefully, she lifted the coffee cup to her black painted lips. "I've become a dull geek."

"No, you haven't."

"Oh, yes, I have! I'm a colorless, tedious nerd!" The voice was tight, angry.

He tried on his best smile. "You could never be boring, Kate!"

But ... he was uneasy; there was truth in what she said. She overflowed with violence and anger. A light had gone out; Kate's soul had been extinguished – or it had been stolen – by a bomb and by bullets.

The Mercedes approached the Avenue of the Baths of Caracalla.

Something in Kate was broken. Roger had no idea how to fix it. She had seemed, up until today, uninterested in other people – no boyfriends, no girlfriends, or very few – and she had no social life that Roger had been able to discover. He would try a diversion.

"Kate, do you think they liked the …?"

"They loved your talk, Dad! Absolutely loved it!" Turning toward him, Kate arched one jet-black eyebrow, an ironic smile hovering on her lips: How was it that her father, her brilliant, elegant, handsome father, had these bouts of self-doubt, of anguish? "You were a hit, Dad, a definite hit … but I do have a question, Dad …"

"Yes."

"Are you really sure that gravity cannot be manipulated, that …"

Roger frowned. This was a direct challenge to the core of his theory, the work that earned him his Nobel Prize. "No, it can't, not on any large scale, Kate. Gravity is a quality of the space-time matrix itself, Kate, a fundamental structure of the universe, as Einstein pointed out, and I think we can exclude the idea that –"

"You're sure? I mean string theory might … if the vibrational wave-forms at a micro-level, at a sub-quantum level, even below the quantum level, if the wave-particle duality, as regards gravitons, were to be …"

Roger sighed in mock frustration. "I see, young lady, that you're throwing down the gauntlet! I sense a challenge from the most brilliant of the new generation of cosmologists."

"Maybe." Kate grinned. Then she looked down, as if she were a little girl caught doing something naughty. "I just think that there may be a slim chance that –"

"You are a truly wicked girl, Kate, defying your ancient father's Nobel pedigree!"

"I know – I'm bad." The grin faded, but only slightly, as if she had suddenly thought of something else. She looked away, in a sudden shift of mood, sat back, and crossed her bare legs. The lamplight rippled on her thighs, a caressing shapely sculptural sheen. Kate, her father once again realized, was a very beautiful young woman.

Still smiling, he sighed. Kate challenging him – even if she was wrong – was a good sign. Her curiosity was roused. Her intellectual ambitions were revving up. He wiggled his wrist watch – a Rolex Submariner – out from under his shirt-cuff and glanced at it.

It was 8:15 p.m.

"We're perfectly on time, Professor." Mario DeLuca glanced in the mirror and winked; it was as if he always knew exactly what Roger was thinking.

"Great, Mario, that's good!"

Mario's black Mercedes sped along the broad avenue toward the ruins of the ancient Baths of Caracalla.

"So, tonight we have the dinner, Kate, and then, tomorrow, what's the schedule?" Roger gazed at his daughter. "You are the organizer of this jaunt, I believe."

"I'm your unpaid social secretary, you mean. Well, tomorrow, Dad, you can sleep in late, or linger over coffee on Piazza Navona if you wish. Then, there is lunch with the US Ambassador at her residence at 12:30 precisely, with just a few guests, the Minister of Scientific Research, a few famous scientists, journalists from *La Repubblica*, *Il Corriere della Sera*, and *Sole 24 Ore*, the BBC's Rome correspondent, *The New York Times International Edition*, *The Guardian*, a couple of film stars, and the wife of the Prime Minister. Being late is not an option!"

"Oh, right, thanks! Are you coming?"

"Yes, of course. I wouldn't miss it!" Suddenly, she turned away and looked out the window. "May I ask you a something?"

"Of course."

"That question the Frenchman, the bald one, what is his name ...? You know, the fellow who –"

"Marcel Pochon. He works at INP, the National Institute of Physics in Paris and he's –"

"Yes, he's one of the top cosmologists of the younger generation, or so I've been told." Kate was still looking away, the light reflecting off the tightly coiled bun of her hair. "That question he asked about whether the wave of earthquakes the other day has anything to do with –"

"– anything to do with the disturbance in the gravitational field that the satellites seem to have picked up? Ah, gravity! I see you are being naughty again! Yes, Marcel is an interesting theorist ... very imaginative ... perhaps too imaginative in my opinion. No, I think it's just ... a measurement problem, an anomaly of –"

"Professor, Kate – we're just going past the Baths of Caracalla ... You can just catch a glimpse of the ruins through the trees."

"Thank you, Mario!" Kate twisted around, toward her father, and suddenly smiled. Startlingly, it was a glorious open smile, the old, unreserved smile. Again, with her face entirely without makeup, Roger caught a glimpse of Kate as she used to be – curious about everything, delighting in everything.

Half hidden behind the umbrella pines, the giant brick walls of the majestic ruins of the Baths of Caracalla loomed up in the dusk. "Mario knows that this is one of my favorite places in Rome! Mario, do you remember when I first saw *Aida* there? I was twelve years old!"

"I remember, Signorina Kate!"

"Mario and Elena and Mom took me. It was outside. It was night. There were real elephants on stage! And camels and what seemed like armies in sparkling uniforms marching up and down and back and forth! It was awesome! There were thousands of people in the audience, up in the metal and wooden bleachers, whole families with their kids and babies and grandmothers and everybody. People drinking cheap Chianti out of those funny old bottles and salami sandwiches and it all smelled of garlic. Shouting and applauding and booing. It was chaos, a huge nighttime outdoor picnic. I loved it! We made friends with a family that was sitting next to us and we shared their sandwiches and mother let me drink out of their Chianti bottle! It was my first taste of red wine!"

"She did? She never told me!"

"No, she wouldn't have. You're such a prude!" Kate gave her father a friendly little poke. Being back in Italy, for the first time since studying in Rome years ago, made her feel reborn. She was just a twelve-year-old kid, when she first saw the towering, shattered brick walls of the Caracalla Baths. It had been a shivery thrill, a fairy tale.

The baths were an enchanted castle. Walking between the soaring walls, all the history overwhelmed her, the centuries and centuries, the splendor of the Rome Empire, the invasions by Barbarians, the long night of the Middle Ages, when Imperial Rome became a mere village, when peasants camped and goats pastured among huge ruins, then the Renaissance, the rebirth of Italy.

Then they'd got to the bleachers, rows and rows of seats, up on metal platforms, and the thousands of people, and then the opera itself, down on stage, brightly lit up, and the music, rising higher and higher. It made her almost drunk. Swept away into another world, Kate hummed.

Celeste Aida, forma divina,
Mistico serto di luce e fior,
Del mio pensiero tu sei regina,
Tu di mia vita sei lo splendor.

The Mercedes sped through the old gate in Rome's Aurelian wall.

"How far is it, Mario?"

"Not far, Professor. Five minutes. Not even."

Kate pulled out the invitation. "This post-lecture dinner, in honor of the distinguished American physicist, Nobel Prize Laureate, Professor Roger Thornhill, is to be held in the exclusive La Dolce Vita III restaurant. La Dolce Vita III is located just off the ancient road, the renowned via Appia Antica, in a Roman ruin, with a terrace looking out toward an ancient aqueduct, and a sumptuous swimming pool for our honored guests!"

"Honored guests sounds good." Roger touched his shirt collar. He'd have to be sharp, and look his best. There would be a lot of VIPs at the dinner.

"This will be fun." Kate realized she was famished. She even imagined herself – *how daring of me, how out of character!* – plunging into the famed Roman pool, "all cobalt blue with wondrous underwater lights." On the website, it looked positively luscious – she'd packed her new bikini just in case.

She glanced back – suddenly aware of headlights coming up very fast behind them. "I'm looking forward to a spaghetti primavera and a big glass of cool white Frascati wine ..."

"Ah, *i vini dei castelli*," said Mario, with an operatic sigh, "the white wines of the Roman hills ... Castel Gondolfo ... Pope Francis himself, you know, drinks those wines!"

"Yes," said Roger, "and I'm looking forward to having a friendly fight with Professor Martin ... Stigliano ... He's ..."

Suddenly, the car, coming up fast, overtook the Mercedes, passed it on the left side, then crowded in – aiming to drive the Mercedes off the road.

Mario swung the wheel. "What the fuck!"

The Mercedes careened to the right, a high wall of thin flat ancient Roman bricks surged up, a glaring russet and white blur, brilliant in the headlights skimmed past the windows.

Mario swung the wheel again. The Mercedes skidded past the wall, and plunged sideways into the roadside ditch, wheels spinning, the bottom of the car scraping along the side of the ditch, racing, racing ...

Mario gunned the engine. The Mercedes rocketed out of the ditch, swerved back, skidding sideways onto the pavement. The other car, and, yes, it was an Alfa-Romeo, fell back, behind them. But again, it came up – and fast. Mario swerved back and forth, zigzagging, blocking the road, trying to keep the Alfa behind them.

"Who the hell are they?"

"No idea, Professor."

"What do they want?" Kate stared out the back window. The headlights of the Alfa glared, its high beams blinding bright. Roman walls flashed away, into a blur of darkness, and a glimpse of one of the men in the car, a face, a white oval, briefly lit up. Again, the Alfa was gaining quickly, racing up. "Watch out!" she shouted.

The Alfa smashed against the Mercedes, a crunching, banging sound. Mario lost control, swerved to the right. The Alfa raced into the gap.

"Bastards," whispered Mario. "Hold on!" he shouted. He lurched the wheel left, smashing the Mercedes against the Alfa.

The Alfa bounced away, glanced against a roadside pillar. Kate saw it flying up, somersault style, into the air, a flash of tumbling light. Then it was gone.

The Alfa pressed up behind them, headlights flooding the interior of the Mercedes. "Bastards," Kate growled, "Absolute bastards!"

"They must want you, Professor!" Mario punched in the police number programmed into his cell phone. The Professor was world-famous, a valuable commodity. "This must be a kidnapping. I should have insisted on a police escort, Professor!"

"That would have been silly, Mario. No one could –"

The Alfa crowded in. The glare was blinding.

Kate blinked. Were those shots? Yes! Damn! They were shooting at the tires, at the fuel tank.

"These people are not playing games, Professor." The radio sputtered into life. "Mayday, Mayday," Mario shouted into the mike. "We're on the via Appia, kidnap attempt. I repeat, via Appia, kidnap attempt! Thank you. Hold on! Roger that! Just a second …"

The radio sputtered – police voices, police traffic …

"Please repeat? Kilometer …?" A police voice, a woman's voice; and then static.

"Get down, Kate." Roger was leaning over to protect her.

"Kilometer … Appia? Is that right?" Static, a female voice, bureaucratic, calm, routine – all in a day's work.

"Yes, yes, Appia."

Kate crouched forward and sideways, the seat belt straining, her father's arm pressing down hard on her shoulder.

The Alfa roared up again.

"It has a souped-up engine," Mario shouted, "and it's armored, slung low like that." He bent over the steering wheel – damn! – doing 140 kilometers an hour on a narrow road with bumpy pavement and the Roman walls on both sides closing in, no room to maneuver. But after the next curve, he'd be in open country. He clenched his jaw. Maybe he could outrun them, get to the restaurant – there would be too many people there for them to …

More shots, this time an automatic, a ripple of shots.

The rear window exploded. Shards, diamonds of glass sprayed over them.

Mario accelerated – 150 kilometers an hour.

"Who the hell are these …?"

The Alfa fell back, then rushed up, reaching them just as they came out into the open country and entered a curve. It rammed the back of the Mercedes – a massive jolt.

Mario struggled. Damm it! Could he make the turn? The Mercedes careened up on one side, two wheels on the ground, two in the air. It slammed down. The Alfa had caught up and was passing them again.

"Damn!" Mario floored the accelerator.

Gunfire ripped through the driver's door and window. There was a blinding flash, an explosion of red and white and gray …

Mario's head was gone, splattered over the windshield, the dashboard, and the passenger seat.

"Oh, my God!" Kate saw it in slow motion, blood, bone, and brain … red raindrops smeared over her glasses.

"Stay down, Kate." Roger unbuckled, struggled up, and reached for the steering wheel. His fingers closed on it. Mario's body had toppled partly to one side but was held back by the seat belt.

The Mercedes skidded sideways and raced forward. It vaulted off the pavement, slammed into the ditch. The steering wheel, greasy with blood and gore, slipped out of Roger's hands.

WHAM!

The Mercedes bounced out of the ditch.

Roger was tossed up, smashed against the roof. He fell across the back of the front seat, limp, arms flailing. The Mercedes rocketed ahead, Mario's foot wedged down, heavy on the gas pedal. The car careened wildly. It was in a field, then in a vineyard, skidding sideways. Wham! With an explosive impact, it slammed into a slope, rose up, plunged over the other side, and rolled over. Mario's body – with its half-stump of a neck keeled over at a weird angle – bounced away. The engine jammed, screaming, as the car rolled over again, ending up tilted half on its side, smoldering against a stack of hay. Suddenly, it was still.

"Daddy? Daddy?"

"Oh, Jesus, where …? Kate, are you okay?"

"Yes, I think so." Everything was a blur. Her glasses were cracked, twisted sideways, smeared with blood.

The electrical system crackled, sizzled, threw off sparks – *flash, flash, flash!* Kate wrinkled her nose. Gas! The gas tank must be leaking gasoline! And the stench of burnt rubber. Death! Terrorists! This couldn't be happening – not again!

"Can you move?"

"Yes. Can you?"

"Let's get out of here!" Kate pushed her way through the smashed, twisted back door, crawling, wiggling, squeezing. She was breathless, coughing, sucking in the burnt, tangy air. Her skirt caught on a sharp spiral of metal. It ripped. She jerked at the bloody thing. Half the skirt tore away. *Damn!* But now she could move. *No broken bones, at least as far as she could tell.*

She was outside, on hands and knees. Blinking through her smeared, half-shattered glasses, she peered into the murky wreck.

"Come on, Daddy!" Reaching through the half-crushed door, she grabbed her father's arm, slippery with blood. It was a tight squeeze, helping him through the twisted door frame. "Come on!"

Roger slithered and crawled out. His jacket was gone, his shirt torn off, just rags left. His belt was unbuckled; his pants were shreds, half his face and most of his chest were covered in blood.

"Is that your blood?"

"Mario's, I think."

"The bastards!" Dazed, still on hands and knees, Kate glanced around: A blurry out-of-focus impression – dim lights, sizzling sparks. The Mercedes was dripping gasoline. In a few seconds, it would explode in a pillar of flame. Above them, stretched shadowy trees, vague slopes and threatening shapes. The people who did this would not be far away. "We have to get out of here!"

"Yes. Up there!" Roger pointed up toward the vineyards where there appeared to be a cluster of trees.

"They're coming!" Kate shouted.

Roger glanced at the highway.

The Alfa-Romeo had pulled off onto the shoulder, maybe 200 meters ahead of them. It had turned around and was facing them. In the Alfa's headlights, Roger saw the silhouettes of two men running toward them.

"Run!"

Roger and Kate scrambled on hands and knees, clambering up the slope, dry hot clumps of earth crumbling under them. They struggled to their feet and raced into the alleys between the vines. They made it to the trees.

It was already dark. The two killers had flashlights. The beams shone through the vines, projecting a crazy quilt of shadow and hazy brightness on the glowing mist of the hot evening.

"I hear music!"

"Lights!"

"It must be the restaurant."

"Thank God. Just keep going, Kate."

Behind them, a huge explosion echoed, a blaze of yellow and white light. Pieces of glass showered up. *The Mercedes*, Kate gulped, *and Mario …*

"Bastards, damn bastards," she whispered, "I hate them, I hate, hate, hate them!"

Scrambling, running full-out, tumbling down, crawling on all fours, stumbling up again, they dashed through a small field, came to a brick wall, and ran along it.

Shots pinged off the wall, flashes, hot puffs of brick dust.

"Here! This way, Daddy! There's an opening!"

Climbing over a sagging barbed-wire fence, Kate tore a swath out of what was left of her skirt.

Damn, I will kill those people! I will! I will! I will!

Blinking, realizing she was lathered in sweat, she pushed the wire down. Her father, out of breath, stumbled over it.

She turned, eyes wide. A string of colored lights hung on an overhead wire. Under the lights, a long trestle table was set out with food and cutlery and candles. People were milling around, glasses of wine in their hands.

In giant red letters, a banner proclaimed: "Welcome Professor Roger Thornhill." Standing right under the banner was Martin Stigliano, head of the University of Rome's Department of Physics – one of Kate's former teachers. Behind him was Henri Girard, a French mathematician, and Melanie Hoffman, one of the top astrophysicists of NASA, and there was Marcel Pochon, good old Marcel, that ornery brilliant bald Frenchman, swallowing a glass of red wine and …

Shots rang out, zinging past them. Kate felt the air buzz next to her cheek.

"They won't kill us if they want us alive!" her father gasped.

"Come on, Daddy!"

Martin Stigliano spotted Kate and Roger coming out of the darkness of the trees. He ran toward them. "What's happened? Roger? Kate? What's going on?"

"Some guys are trying to kidnap Daddy," Kate stuttered, breathless. At twenty-two, she was less winded than her father, even if he was in great shape. "They rammed our car and killed Mario, our driver."

"Mario …? Jesus Maria!"

Shots rang out. Martin's white shirt, just where it was open, a little below his collarbone, blossomed in blood. He was thrown backward, a look of astonishment in his eyes, his mouth still open on the "Jesus Maria …!"

"God!" Kate swung around.

The killers were climbing over the barbed wire.

Two motorbikes roared through the restaurant gates and skidded onto the terrace. In a spray of pebbles and dust, they slammed to a stop. One of the bikers fired a salvo over the heads of the party.

A broad-chested man with a giant handlebar moustache came out of the restaurant's side door onto the terrace; he had a white apron, a cloth over his arm, and a bottle in one hand. He must, Kate thought, be the owner of restaurant. "But, gentlemen, what are you doing?"

The second biker shot the restaurant owner in the face. The man's neck and jaw exploded in a splash of blood. He stood gurgling, jaw and nose gone, eyes bugging out, then fell slowly, grabbing the edge of a tablecloth, pulling it down with him – pulling, in slow motion, off the table, bottles of wine, candles, glasses, plates, knives, forks, spoons … Kate gaped. The shots and the clattering sounds were unreal, coming from another universe.

What in the world was happening?

What did this mean?

The crowd panicked. People ducked under tables. Some froze. Henri Girard was standing stock still, pale as a ghost. Slowly, he took a sip from his glass of Prosecco. The Jesuit head of the Vatican Observatory, Father José Fernandez, had stepped in front of a terrified waitress who was standing as if petrified, absolutely still, her eyes wide, blinking. Marcel Pochon glanced at Kate, nodded, and picked up a carving knife and hid it behind his back.

The two men coming out of the vineyards were out of breath. The tall one said, in English, "We just want Roger Thornhill and his daughter, Kate."

Roger and Kate were standing, breathless, by the main table.

"If you don't come peacefully, and right away, we will shoot the others. Fabio, show them!"

One of the bikers picked a person at random – Kate could see that, behind the dark Plexiglas mask that moved back and forth, he was trying to choose a good one: and he did: it was a twenty-three-year-old mathematician from the University of Oxford, Julie Tett – Kate's former roommate in Boston. He shot Julie in the thigh; she fell back with an amazed look, her face contorted in pain. Kate could see her clenching her jaw, in a superhuman effort not to scream.

I will kill these people. Kate clenched her fists. *I will kill these people! I will tear out their eyes!*

"Take me," Roger said, "but leave Kate alone."

"No," said the gunman. "We need both of you. Fabio, make the point."

Fabio shot another of the guests – 56-year-old James Canon, a mountaineer and geologist, between the eyes. Canon's face shattered; his body flew backward, hitting a side table, knocking over bottles of prosecco cooling in buckets of ice.

Kate's heart rose into her throat. If she didn't control herself, she was going to throw up. "Daddy, it's okay. Let's go. If they want us so badly, they need us. If they need us, they won't hurt us."

"Kate, I'm not so …"

"Listen to your daughter, Professor Thornhill. Fabio, see that woman over there …"

"Alright, alright," Roger shouted. "But if you harm Kate …"

"No harm will come to Kate, Professor. She is as precious to us as she is to you. Get on the back of those bikes. Any tricks and people die!"

Roger nodded. "Okay, no tricks."

"Kick off your shoes, Professor."

Roger looked down – his shirt and trousers had been reduced to skimpy, muddy, blood-stained rags. Somehow, too, his watch was gone. Frowning, he slipped out of his black Louis Vuitton strap shoes.

"Here, put this on!" One of the killers handed Roger a hood. Roger grimaced. The hood looked like leather. It had a thick metal and rubber collar. He slipped it over his head; the man closed the collar, tightened and locked it. Roger was hooded and blind.

Kate swallowed.

"Kick off your shoes!" Fabio grabbed her by the arm – a grip of steel. Kate kicked off her black patent leather, low-heeled shoes, suddenly feeling the pebbles and gravel hard and warm under her bare feet. She stared at the visor of the biker – She couldn't see his face. She whispered, *Fabio, you are dead, you are already dead.*

Fabio pulled a leather hood from his backpack, slipped it over Kate's head, zipped it shut, and locked the collar in place. The world went black. The shattered glasses pressed hard against her nose. She was going to choke! She was going to suffocate!

Grabbing her by the shoulder, Fabio guided her onto the bike.

She steeled herself. Her heart was beating too fast. *I'm not going to be able to breathe!* Panic rose. *Calm down, calm down …* She slowed herself down, she concentrated hard, she breathed. *Easy, easy now.*

"Lock your fingers around my waist and hold on," Fabio said. "Don't try to jump off or I *will* kill you."

She did as he ordered – tightening her fingers around his waist – tight muscular abs. She tensed. This killer was young, in good shape, probably handsome. She would kill him.

He gunned the bike. It roared off the pebbly terrace and onto the asphalt and down the road.

And so, the two bikes took off – in different directions.

The carnage in La Dolce Vita III was left behind.

Fingers locked around Fabio's waist, holding on tight, leaning tight against his sweaty back, Kate focused: *Where was he taking her?* They were on pavement, it was smooth asphalt; they bumped onto a different surface; the jolts were irregular. It must be the big lava or tuff paving stones of the ancient Appia Antica, the *real* old Roman road. After a few minutes, they were on pebbles and sand; sharp pebbles bounced around the bike and hit her legs. So – this was a dirt road, a laneway, or a country side road …

The bike skidded around a corner, slowed, and glided to a stop, the motor idling. Kate heard voices, indistinct and muffled by the hood.

The bike gunned forward. Almost losing her balance, she tightened her grip around Fabio's waist, leaning closer, her body hugging the sweaty muscular back of the assassin, the man she would kill. She would strangle him with her bare hands, she would gouge his eyes out, she would – A slamming sound, doors being shut, big wooden doors.

The bike skidded sideways and jerked to a stop. Fabio said, "Get off."

Someone grabbed her arm, pulled her off the bike. Wooden boards and straw crackled under her bare feet. Through the hood, she smelled straw and manure. It was a barn. What the hell were they doing in a barn?

How long had it been? Ten minutes? How far could you go in ten minutes? Five or six miles? She'd lost all sense of time.

She stood there, naked legs pressed together, as still as she could, smothered, blinded by the hood. She controlled her breathing.

"Don't misbehave, little girl!" Fabio grabbed her wrists, pulled them behind her. Hard metal against her wrists. The handcuffs clicked shut. Ouch! She winced. Somebody else held her shoulders. Fabio manacled her ankles. "Ouch," she muttered, a muffled groan, trapped inside the hood.

Fabio grabbed her, his hot, sweaty, musclar arms tight around legs and torso. He lifted her up, carried her. Pressing down her head, he pushed her into a box. No, it wasn't a box; it wasn't a coffin. It was the trunk of a car. She curled up. Fabio pulled her arms and legs together, bending her backward, into a U-shape. He clicked more metal around her wrists and ankles. He chained her wrists and ankles to each other – it was a short chain.

The bastard had hogtied her!

"Ahhhh … Ouch!" Her voice was a snort, strangled, stifled by the hood.

"Shut up," Fabio snarled. "It's better if you cooperate, Kate."

She said nothing.

"Yeah, shut the fuck up, you fucking bitch!" It was another voice, speaking English, a thicker accent than Fabio's.

Curled tightly on herself, Kate's spine was twisted. She felt like a pretzel, could hardly move a muscle. Hogtied, an animal. God, it hurt!

The trunk thudded shut.

Muffled voices – in Italian.

"Father Ottavio wants her."

"Wants her for what?" Fabio's voice. "She's just a hostage."

"The ceremony."

"The ceremony?" Fabio yelled. "The ceremony! Fuck, the man's crazy! That's against the plan. That was not the deal! That's not what we agreed to! She's leverage; she's a hostage; she's not a sacrifice …"

"The Russian girl, the blonde they were going to use, she killed herself."

"That's no reason …"

"The fucking bitch jumped out a window …"

"… no reason to use this kid as a sacrifice …"

"Fuck, yes. If the Cardinal says …"

The voices faded. Kate swallowed. They probably didn't know she understood Italian. What ceremony? What Russian girl? What sacrifice?

Sacrifice?

Me?

She forced her breathing to slow down She counted: *one, two, three; uno, due, tre; eins, zwei, drei; un, deux, trois …* She was helpless, hooded, chained, hogtied, and locked in a trunk but … goddamn it … she would fight! Somehow, she would get out of this!

But …

Sacrifice?

The car began to move.

CHAPTER 7 – SNATCH

The man seemed harmless …

The sun had gone down; the sky glowed a dark shade of red and yellow.

Yes, the man seemed harmless …

Scarlett closed her eyes. Hot water splashed everywhere, flowing over her head and shoulders – she would damned well soap and soak every inch of her body, a total cleansing. Easier said than done: The cubicle was tiny, barely enough space to swivel around – but it was better than nothing. Actually, it was divine!

She'd come to Rome to escape her fate as a betrayed woman – to avoid going stark-raving-foaming-at-the-mouth mad, and chopping Jeff and Megan into bloody itsy-bitsy tiny little pieces with a meat cleaver and finding herself demonized and in the electric chair. And she'd come for adventure. Well, she'd certainly had an adventure and then some – Whew!

It began, in the early afternoon, just after she left Saint Peter's Square.

At first, the man seemed harmless, just a guy who wanted to help a lost tourist, or maybe – and this was much more likely – a guy who wanted to pick her up, for a date, for casual sex, for …

But it turned ugly fast. He swore at her, called her a whore, and then he pulled out a hypodermic needle.

Jesus!

It must have been the devilish skintight scarlet dress that did it!

She'd left Saint Peter's Square and was walking down a side street, wandering, dawdling, just drifting along, the heat was so voluptuous, an all-over massage, a natural sauna. She wiggled her shoulders in pure pleasure and gazed lazily, eyes half closed, at the scene around her.

The buildings in this particular street had big tall windows, stone facades, sharp, rectangular edges, and massive intimidating proportions. Scarlett figured they had almost certainly been built in the 1920s and 1930s, designed in the classic Fascist Modernist style and calculated to glorify the Party and the Leader – Il Duce Benito Mussolini – and make the citizen – or today's tourist – feel tiny and insignificant.

Scarlett shivered. She definitely felt appropriately tiny and insignificant. In fact, the buildings gave her the willies, a spooky uneasy feeling. Right here, Rome was a lifeless city, a city of stone, not a tree or plant in sight, not on this street, and no cafés, and no people. It was as if the whole of the Eternal City was a dead monument, an architectural model, a lifeless exhibition, a nightmare landscape, designed to intimidate her alone.

She glanced around. Something about the empty street and the blind facades, the deep, sharp shadows, and cruel, sharp angles of stone seemed extra creepy. She couldn't put her finger on it; but she'd better double back. Skedaddle, Scarlett, skedaddle!

Which way to go? She stood there, indecisive. Indecision, she knew, was ill-advised. She'd read the guidebooks. Pickpockets – and purse snatchers on motorbikes – had a sixth sense for the confused tourist. They homed in like guided missiles on anybody who looked hesitant, even if just for a second.

And then – at that very moment – there he was: *the guy*. Where the dickens had he come from? He was a good-looking guy too, sharp-featured, tanned, with old-fashioned Latin good looks, thick, jet-black hair, greased and curly. In fact, he looked like the classic cliché gigolo. A cartoon!

"Looks like you might be lost, Signorina," he said, with a big smile. His English was good.

She smiled back. "Not really lost, thank you."

"Where are you headed?"

"Campo de' Fiori," she said, and was instantly annoyed with herself for answering. Something was not right. The guy's smile was too bright, his gaze too intense. He was trying to hypnotize her – like a snake transfixing, with the pure evil force of its gaze, its prey. Was he on drugs? And why the hell had he turned up right here, right now?

His smile became even more intense. But only his mouth was smiling. His eyes were edgy, tight, calculating. It wasn't drugs; it was something else.

"Campo de' Fiori? Right up that little side alley," he grinned, "between those two buildings. It's a shortcut, it takes you right out onto the Tiber, and from there …" He moved closer now, the eyes bright, staring straight, fixedly, at her eyes.

She took a deep breath. A decision loomed – fight or flight?

His shirt was open; his chest was tanned; a medallion sparkled amidst the curly hairs. His teeth were too even, too bright, looked like special dental work. His trousers were sharply pressed, his black shoes highly polished. She took a deep breath. There was something – ah, something almost clerical – some odor of the church – about him, as if he were a monk in civvies, or a …

Scarlett glanced at the narrow alley between two buildings. She didn't want to be impolite, but there was absolutely no way she would go into that narrow shadowy slot – a perfect trap. She had backed away from the man, and was standing between two parked cars, her purse and camera dangling from her shoulder. He came along the sidewalk, grinning, getting closer. She backed out onto the street, carefully checking – no cars, no motorbikes, and – damn it – no people!

"I think I'll just sort of wander," she said. "Just take my time, you know." She beamed at him, her best most naive, most genial, Southern belle smile. Sweat trickled down her back. Her smile felt like a mask; her face felt like rubber; everything was false; her face didn't belong to her. For some reason, animal instinct maybe, she was really, really scared. If she screamed, surely lots of people would hear, and come running. Scream, or not? She tightened her grip on the Leica strap and on her purse.

"Hey, that's a great idea! Wander! I know everything there is to know about Rome, Signorina. I will be an excellent guide! And, who knows, perhaps we will dine and share a bottle of wine tonight! I show you Rome by night, eh?"

He was closer now, coming out between the two parked cars.

Scarlett stood indecisive, undecided, calculating what her next move should be. One of his fists was clenched. She could see veins, white knuckles. Behind the ingratiating smile lurked fury and hate. He was getting ready to strike. Oh boy, oh boy! This is what she got for dressing as the Scarlet Woman!

"That sounds really nice," she said, backing away, "dinner and wine, but I have to meet my boyfriend, and –"

"You don't have a boyfriend." He was close now. His chin down, his face lowering. A twitch flickered at the corner of his mouth. *Hate*, yes, that's what it was, *hate* flared in his eyes.

"What?" Scarlett wanted to turn her back and walk away. But she didn't want him out of her sight, not for a second. "What do you mean I don't have a boyfriend?" Had this guy been spying on her? Did he know about Jeff and Megan? Was he somebody sent to get revenge … but revenge for what?

"You don't have a fucking boyfriend!" His eyes narrowed. The smile was tighter. He was older than she thought. The mouth twitched again; it was creepy. The perfect teeth were marred, she noticed, by tobacco stains, yellow, close to the roots. Utter hate blazed in his eyes.

"You don't know anything about me – and besides what I do or don't do is none of your business." She backed away.

"No fucking boyfriend would let his girl – not a girl like you – dress like a whore."

"Okay, that's enough. I …"

His grin widened; there was something sadistic about it, an anticipation of cruelty, of violence, physical assault, even mutilation. "Is that what you are? A whore? You look like one, an expensive whore, all tanned and glossy and blond. Dressed to kill – right?"

"Look, I think maybe you'd better … shut up … and …"

"I'll bet you're tanned all over." The hatred sparkled. "I can just see it, probably shaved too, or waxed, Brazilian or Hollywood, I bet. Totally naked. Little Miss Sunshine the Whore from the Old South! Smooth everywhere. You give me a hard-on, you know, just thinking, what it will be like …"

He slipped something out of his pocket. It looked like … it looked like a syringe …

"My name is Filippo, Filippo the Fourth. When you bow down, naked, before me, and worship me, you will call me Don Filippo."

"I'm not going to call you anything." Scarlett was scared. But now she was furious. Her muscles tensed, anger soared, adrenaline pumped. She'd always imagined that if she were ever cornered by a rapist, she would scratch his eyes out. Easier imagined than done.

And there was that deadly thing in his hand.

The syringe clicked. The point of the needle snapped out. It caught the light, a silver flash. In one quick leap, he rushed her. She ducked, stumbled back, and swung the Leica as hard as she could. It whammed into the side of his head.

He swore, stopped, and glared at her. His hand went up to his face; he stroked his cheek. His eyes were empty.

He stepped forward.

She jumped between two parked cars and sprinted. He came after her. She swung the Leica again. He grabbed for it; she jerked it free.

She was on the sidewalk, sprinting – even with these damned high heels she could run, and fast. He was right behind her. She swung around and swiveled between two parked cars. She hammered her fist on the hood of one of them. The alarm went off. Beep! Beep! Beep! Good! She hammered the other car. A second alarm went off. Good! She saw a motorbike coming down the street. *Oh, oh, not so good!*

Filippo grabbed her by the arm; she broke free.

"*Cazzo, Carlo, aiutame! Questa qui è una tigre!*" he shouted to the cyclist.

Scarlett caught the gist. These two guys were working together. She remembered what the night porter had told her about women disappearing. Filippo plunged forward, grabbing for her. She staggered back. He caught the strap of her dress and tore it off her shoulder, down to her waist. Scarlett whipped around and smashed the Leica down on his fist. He dropped the syringe, swore, and curled his fist as if he were going to punch her. The biker leapt off his bike. He was behind her.

She was trapped.

The biker grabbed her around the waist and lifted her up. His breath was hot, he smelled of garlic. His sweaty unshaven cheek pressed against her.

Scarlett kicked, trying to get purchase.

Filippo picked up the syringe. "You are a true bitch." He smiled. "You are a feisty bitch. That makes it better. Your sacrifice will be sublime. You are perfect! You don't know how perfect you are!"

He raised the needle.

"It will be a sacred moment."

"Fuck you!" She kicked, squirmed.

"You will become a goddess – a painted idol – all lacquered and preserved, set in plaster – a statue, a beautiful statue, forever."

"Get away from me!"

"You will be perfect – forever!"

Scarlett kicked. Her legs flailed. She twisted, squirmed, desperately trying to avoid the needle. The other guy held her tight, crushing her ribs; he was really strong. Damn it, damn it, damn it!

"Hey, hey!" There were shouts.

A man appeared in a window above. "What the hell are you doing?"

A woman charged out of a doorway. "What you are doing. Criminals! Help! Criminals!" The woman was heavy-set, middle-aged, a white and black apron around her waist. She came striding toward them, with red thick arms, her fists curled.

"Help, please help me!" Scarlett gasped; she kicked again.

Filippo turned to face the woman. "*Vada via, Signora, questo non è affare sua!* Go away, Signora, this is none of your business."

"But it is my business, you scum!" The woman kept coming.

"You'll just get hurt, Signora!" Filippo turned back to Scarlett and raised the needle, but at that moment Scarlett kicked against the side of a car and she and the biker who had his arms locked around her staggered and tumbled back onto the street, falling onto the cobblestones.

The biker let go. He was under her. Scarlett rolled away. She got to her knees, but now Filippo with the needle was standing right above her. She flipped over, rolled, and crawled. Her dress was torn away, she realized. She was half-naked. Filippo stepped forward, grinning. "You're the best!"

On hands and knees, staring up at him, Scarlett raised her arm to parry the plunging needle … There was a sound, not far away, of revving, roaring motorbikes – police … Holding the needle aloft, Filippo turned.

Oh, my God, police …

Sirens …

Police on motorbikes …

Sirens …

The next few minutes were a whirlwind. The woman in the apron grabbed at Filippo. The other guy got back on the bike.

Filippo slapped the woman hard.

"Scum!" The woman kicked him.

"Filippo!" The guy on the bike was revving the motor.

Filippo glared at Scarlett; then he jumped on the bike and they roared away.

Scarlett leapt up, grabbed the Leica, and took three quick shots of the bike as it sped into the distance.

"Signorina! Are you okay?" The woman was beside her.

"I'm fine, *sto bene, grazie, grazie Signora*." Scarlett knew a few words of Italian. "But I'm mad as hell! … *Sono furiosa!* Did he hurt you, Signora?"

"No, no, I am fine. You are a brave girl, Signorina!"

A heavy-set older man came huffing and puffing up the street. "You are a fighter, Signorina! I saw it all! From my window. I called the police. I came as fast as I could!"

The two police motorbikes had roared off after the bike, but it had disappeared around a corner, into a very narrow alleyway, and was gone.

Then there was a confused time – first with the woman and the other people who had come running into the street, everybody asking her if she was okay, and Scarlett all the time clutching at her ruined dress – one strap gone and a hunk torn and hanging away – and saying thank you to everybody; and then an hour with the police – at the police station – they offered her coffee, two chocolate croissants, and asked her lots of questions, and took her statement. She gave a detailed description of "Filippo" and of "Carlo" and she helped the police upload the photographs – the bike and its license plate – to their computers.

"You are a lucky young woman," said one of the cops.

"And brave – a fighter," said another.

Two officers, a woman and a man, accompanied her back to her hotel. "I like your dress," said the woman cop. The dress in question was in bad shape; Scarlett had to hold it up and drape her silk shawl over her shoulders, otherwise from the waist up she was naked.

"It's not my usual style," said Scarlett. "I was mad at somebody."

"I understand," said the woman cop, blinking at her and smiling.

The male cop saluted, looking at her carefully. "Enjoy your vacation, Signorina Scarlett, but do be careful."

"I will. Thank you!"

They told her that she should stay in Rome. She might be called as a witness; the incident might be connected to the disappearances of other young women, including the Russian girl who'd gone missing three days ago.

"Saint Peter's Square is a pick-up place," said the woman cop. "So many tourists go there, so it's one of the places the vultures congregate."

Scarlett switched the hot water to cold – all the way. Brrrh! Wow, what a shock! Now it was like ice. Brrrh! But, coming after the heat, almost 100 degrees by now, it was luxurious, like jumping into a delicious sea of ice cubes. She held on, gritting her teeth, turning, squirming, and letting the freezing water cascade over every inch of her body.

Finally, trembling in an ecstasy of torture, she turned the water off, and stood there, dripping water, a naked statue of goosebumps, shivering, clutching herself, feeling shocked, cleansed and – reborn.

She reached out of the shower, grabbed a towel, and stepped out of the cubicle and into the bedroom. She shook herself like a dog loping out of a river – drops of water spraying every which way – then she toweled herself down, slowly, luxuriously, and stretched and twirled around like a ballerina. Oh, so glorious!

The window was wide open. It gave onto rooftops and a dark blue evening sky, where she could even see – caught in the city's glow – some early stars. A delicate breeze, just a suggestion, wafted in.

Arms outstretched, she turned around, once, then twice, then three times, just to let the moving air play against her skin. How sumptuous this was!

Still wrapped in the towel, she sat down on the wooden chair – it was only a stool really – right next to the window. She would capture every tiny puff of air. Living without air-conditioning in a climate like this was an interesting experience, an experiment in direct, tactile, animal pleasure. Every minuscule shift in the air impinged. Outer and inner weather merged. Mood and atmosphere danced in synch, a stimulating kaleidoscope of sensation, like being caressed all over!

Time passed easily as she sat next to the window, wrapped in the towel, luxuriating in the soft, hot, night breeze. She stretched and yawned. A drink would be perfect, a cool glass of white wine, maybe up on the roof.

She let the towel fall away, stood up, pulled on shorts, a T-shirt, and sandals, left her room, and climbed the narrow winding stairs to the roof, carrying a wine glass and a bottle of cheap wine from Frascati that she'd stashed in the tiny fridge in the corner of her room.

When she got to the top of the stairs there was nobody up on the roof of the hotel except – *Whoopee, this was serendipity!* – the Chinese guy she'd seen the night of the earthquake. He was in shorts and a T-shirt; he was leaning on the balustrade and looking out at the buildings glowing in the twilight. He turned toward her and smiled, a smile of recognition; and, yes, he *was* a dish. He looked like one of those perfectly handsome medieval Middle Kingdom warriors who conquers dukedoms and sashays his way, fighting the whole time, into favor with the beautiful doe-eyed princess. Okay, she thought, branded scarlet hussy that I am, I am going to be boldly brazen.

"Hi," she said, holding up the bottle. "Would you like a glass of wine? It's the cheapest of cheap whites."

"Hi. Sure! Thanks! I'll get a glass."

While she waited for him to come back up to the roof, Scarlett looked down at the narrow street below – just about where Julius Caesar was assassinated, over two thousand years ago, or so Paolo the night porter had told her.

When the Chinese guy came back, Scarlett filled his glass.

"Thank you," he said. He looked her in the eyes. "Do you mind if I say something?"

"No, I don't, go ahead; say it, whatever it is." She gave him her best smile.

He looked down at his glass, and then he looked up, directly at her. "I was hoping you were still here – I mean, I'm embarrassed, we don't even know each other's names, but I was hoping to see you again." Now he was giving her the look, straight into her eyes.

Scarlett gazed at him, levelly, over her glass. Her blue eyes blinked twice. "Me too, I'm embarrassed to admit it. But I was hoping to see you again too." Thinking, *now* I've done it.

For some strange reason, Scarlett Andersson's heart skipped a beat. Suddenly, she was breathless.

PART THREE – DEMON

CHAPTER 8 – DEMON'S LAIR

I am Father Michael Patrick O'Bryan, of the Society of Jesus, and – though I do say so myself – I am a well-known expert in demons, possession, and exorcism, or so I am usually considered by my fellow experts. But, to tell the truth, I do doubt, right now, who and what I am. Or whether any of this is real at all.

I have decided to put everything down in writing, as it happened, the way it happened.

Yesterday I was a dead man. Today I am alive. Thank God! Or thank the Devil. Or thank a girl demon or she-devil or whatever she is. I do believe I am going insane. If I don't survive, and if people find these notes, maybe they or others will have an idea what happened – perhaps they will be able to judge whether I am in my right mind – or not.

My jailers – for that is certainly what they are – have kindly given me a spiral notebook with lined paper and a neat collection of Bic ballpoint pens in various colors, but no computer, no cellphone, and – obviously – no Internet connection.

Yesterday, two young men I had never seen before tried to kill me. They were professionals, I am quite certain of that. They chased me down into the sewers of Rome – I know the sewers well. I thought I could escape – but I couldn't. These men shot me – twice: once in the chest, and once in the shoulder.

I would have died except – well, now I do think that I am insane – I would have died except that a demon, a female demon, saved me.

Demons, as we know (as I believe I have mentioned, I have studied and written on the question of demons and demonic possession extensively), are, in most cases, like fallen angels. Demons tempt the sons of men; and they do the work of Satan. Most demons – as demonology and tradition tell us – work

indirectly – through a person or a thing; that is, they take possession of someone's mind and body; or, sometimes, they will inhabit an object – a cast-off
ragged doll, say, or a place, a coal cellar in an old house or a hayloft in an abandoned barn – and do their vicious and evil deeds in this manner, using their
victim – or the object or the place – as their instrument. This female demon
breaks the rules; she does not hide. She flaunts herself openly, and, dare I say,
shamelessly. In this, she is unlike most demons who, as I said, mask themselves
and become manifest only through possession of a person, a thing, or a place.

I am now the demon's prisoner. Again, even just writing these words
seems to me pure insanity. In any case, insane or not, I shall just write down,
as clearly as I can, what I have experienced. When I say "demon" I literally
mean that. Of course demonology, as any theologian worth his – or her – salt
can tell you, is a complex science, and heretical beliefs and teachings in this
field abound, so, in the interests of clarity, I shall try to give as exhaustive and
precise a description of this particular demon as I can. As I already mentioned, the demon is female. It seems too that she has several forms. Clearly,
she is a talented follower, acolyte, and instrument of Satan.

Last night, after I was shot, the demon appeared, saved me, and gave me
succor. I then passed out, I think from lack of blood. When I woke up, I was
in the arms, as it were, literally in the arms, of the demon. She was cooing
something to me about not talking, about not wasting my strength. "Hush,
hush," she said, or, rather, hissed. She speaks fine English and I believe Italian
and Latin as well, and most probably other languages. Her fangs and slender forked tongue give her, when she is in her most demonic form, truly a
creature from Hell, a slight soft lisp, which is, I must admit, rather disarming.
But, then, the wiles of the Devil, like those of women, are infinite, and this
is a female demon – beauteous in her own strange way – and hence doubly
dangerous!

That is the last thing I remember – her face, looking down upon me, cooing something soothing, trying to assuage my fears.

Then I slept. I died to the world, and sank into oblivion.

This morning I woke up in a strange bed in a bedroom that I had never seen
before. It was – it is – a pleasant room, simply furnished, and with clear white
stucco walls. White muslin curtains billowed into the room from wide-open
French doors. They carried with them a warm breeze and bright streaks of
sunlight that reflected in loops and waves on the ceiling, as if the light were
rippling off water, a swimming pool, or a lake, or the sea. The breeze carried

smells of sunbaked earth, flowers, and fields of hay. I thought I heard the surf and rollers of the sea and seagulls cawing; closer by, birds were twittering.

I wondered, at first, if the previous night had been a dream. Perhaps I was dead already and this pleasant room was an antechamber leading to Heaven or Hell. Then I heard a voice.

"Welcome back!"

I was confused; and, I think, only half awake.

"Welcome back, Father O'Bryan, welcome back – to life!"

A man was sitting beside the bed. He asked me how I was feeling.

"Dizzy," I said, looking around, "and confused. And – ouch – yes, not so good!"

"You'll feel better soon."

He was a thin, clean-shaven, deeply tanned man, wearing a black T-shirt, black jeans and black, military-style, thick-soled boots; he was reading *The New York Times International Edition*. He told me to call him Giovanni or John, depending on which I preferred.

I have seen quite a bit of John since. I thought at the time that he might be ex-British military, probably Special Forces, possibly the SAS, the UK's Special Air Service, a man who knows how to kill – and I was right, as I later learned. Yes, John is a man who does know how to kill.

He is lean, all muscle, clever, and hard as nails. He always carries a pistol in a black shoulder holster, and he has a rather upper-class English accent when he speaks English, and a clipped military manner. As I learned later, he speaks Italian fluently, with a slight Milanese accent, and French in the elegant orthodox Parisian manner. His thick black hair was combed straight back from his high forehead. He is handsome in a chiseled, austere sort of way, a strong jaw and long, bright teeth, and a steel-hard amused look in his eyes. He told me I was lucky to be alive. *Ah*, I thought, *so I am alive!*

"Where am I?"

"In Tuscany. V brought you here last night."

"V?"

"The woman who saved your life." John touched an intercom button. "Father O'Bryan is awake."

"Thanks, John. I'll be right there." It was the voice from the night before; the voice of the demon.

I felt a twinge of fear. Last night had been a nightmare. "Who – *what* – is she, this V?"

He smiled. "Impressive, isn't she? Let's say V is a person – a being – a creature – of many parts, and she has a long history. She'll explain. She told me she wants to be frank – totally open – with you. You will find it very interesting, I think. She rather fits into your field of study – demonology and exorcisms, ancient pagan goddesses, and suchlike."

Then he stood up. "Well, I'll leave you two to it. I've finished with the paper, Father, if you want it." And with that, he laid *The New York Times International Edition* on the bed, and next to it he put my glasses, polished and clean and totally intact, though I was quite sure they had been shattered the night before. He then walked out of the French doors into the bright sunlight, leaving me to face this V alone.

There was one ominous detail that struck me. When he left, John pulled the thick side curtains – I could see that they were lined with black rubber or some such thick material – tightly shut, so that every trace of sunlight was abolished, and the room was plunged into darkness.

It hurt to twist around. I realized that my chest and shoulder were wrapped in heavy bandages. But I did manage to reach out and turn on the bedside light. I did not want to be left alone in the dark, not again, with the reptilian creature I had seen the night before. I wanted to be able to confront her in the light. What, I wondered nervously, did "V" stand for? And precisely what sort of a demon was she?

Demons, as I may have explained, and as I wrote in my book *Demons: A Theological Taxonomy* (Cambridge University Press, 2024), come in many forms. Not everyone appreciates this. Some theologians, indeed, such as Professor Erik Hoffdung of Heidelberg, allow themselves to be led astray into the most fantastical doctrines. But that, I suppose, in my present dire circumstances, is neither here nor there. So, as I was saying, there are demons who inhabit the living and capture their bodies and souls. These must be cast out by exorcism, which is a delicate and complex – and frequently unpleasant and dangerous – procedure. Then there are demons who have never had a corporeal presence, an earthly body. These wander about in disembodied form and, as I believe I've already mentioned, they can settle in objects or in places.

In ancient times, the Greeks often thought of such demons – or wandering spirits – as potentially good. The Greek word *daemon* has many meanings: it can be merely a spirit, or a lower deity, or a departed soul. But under the rule of God, the one true God, the spiritual landscape has been simplified:

The true nature of demons – of *daemon* – has become clear; they are fallen creatures, like fallen angels, unclean spirits, and instruments of Satan, the opposite of true angels and of saints.

Questions thronged my mind. What sort of demon was this V? Why had she saved my life? Why had she brought me to Tuscany? Was my soul so valuable that she wanted or needed me? But for what purpose? Perhaps it was my knowledge of ancient spirits, of exorcism, that draws her to me. And why did the two men try to kill me? Was it because of that extraordinary plot that Father Luciani believed he had uncovered? Was it because of Cardinal Ambrosiano? Otherwise why would anyone want to kill me? I am just a dusty old scholar. I did testify at the International Court against the deposed dictator of Zimbabwe. Could it be that? But that was years ago!

I began to pray. The founder of our order, Saint Ignatius of Loyola, prized simplicity and courage. And so, I prayed as I had learned to pray, with the utmost simplicity.

Soul of Christ, sanctify me
Body of Christ, save me.
Blood of Christ, inebriate me.
Water from the side of Christ, wash me.
Passion of Christ, strengthen me
O Good Jesus, hear me
Within Thy wounds hide me.
Suffer me not to be separated from Thee.
From the wicked enemy defend me.
In the hour of my death call me.
And bid me come unto Thee,
That with all Thy saints,
I may praise Thee
Forever and ever.
Amen.

I had just breathed out the word "amen" when the demon came striding into the room.

"Well, priest," she said ...

CHAPTER 9 – MEN OF HONOR

From his window seat, U Pizzu gazed at the hazy, blue Tyrrhenian Sea, rippling silver in the afternoon sun.

The phone call had come in the middle of the night.

"We got a problem …"

"*Madonna Santa, che cazzo hanno fatto sta' volta?* Jesus Christ! What the fuck have they fucked up now?" U Pizzu swore quietly, under his breath. Maria Grazia didn't like it if he swore or blasphemed.

Even the people he thought he could depend on, he couldn't. If you wanted something done right, you had to do it yourself! That's why he'd done Gaetano himself. He owed Gaetano that. No fuss, no mess; get it right the first time. Gaetano was dead before he knew it.

The Palermo-Rome flight had boarded at 12:30, just when a normal man should be getting ready to enjoy lunch. U Pizzu and Maria Grazia had planned a picnic down at the beach – ah, it would have been excellent: hot sunburnt skin, grilled sole, salad, and chilled Regaleali.

Then that phone call at two o'clock in the morning!

U Pizzu closed his eyes and returned to the moment. His hand had just been running up Maria Grazia's spine, a long spine, beautifully articulated, then along her side and up under her breasts, curving the heaviness, sculpting the warm ripeness … She was a goddess! Even after all these years together, he worshipped her!

Then, right in *medias res*, the goddamn phone rings and …

"We got a problem …"

"A problem? Don't fucking tell me!" U Pizzu rolled his eyes. In the bedside light, he saw Maria Grazia grin. Despite not liking the swearing, she enjoyed seeing him lose his temper. She told him he was just too funny – charming and ridiculously cute – when he got mad. And she did like scolding him too; it was one of their little games.

U Pizzu made a face, sighed, and said into the phone, "Okay, what?"

Now, ten hours later, U Pizzu was nursing – slowly sipping, making it last – a bitter espresso from a paper cup. He and his sidekick and favorite hitman Santino Salvato were sitting well behind the wing of the Airbus A 319 on the Palermo-Rome flight. U Pizzu had insisted on the window seat with Santino stuck in the aisle seat, and a pile of newspapers – *Corriere della sera*, *Il Gazzetino*, *La Repubblica*, *Il Sole 24 Ore*, and an old iPad – in the seat between them. U Pizzu was staring hard at the Tyrrhenian Sea.

"Hey, Pizzu, what are you thinking?"

"I'm thinking of paradise. Now shut up!" U Pizzu liked silence; but Santino found it impossible to keep his trap shut.

Someday, he'd shut Santino up real good, but not yet. That mouth of Santino's could cause trouble. Yap, yap, yap! Some people have to share everything, even their tiniest most insignificant thoughts. They tweet and they text and they babble. *I'm sitting on the toilet right now. The first turd is real difficult. The second turd – ah, oh – comes easier. My cat is feeling moody today!* Like kids texting or on cellphones. Fuck! Can't keep quiet for the life of them. *Quiet* is a prerequisite of *business*. Quiet is essential – though, even if you keep quiet, even if you are the smartest devil alive, there's no way you leave *the business* except feet first, sad fact, but true …

Ah, yes, once you were in the Honored Society, Cosa Nostra, there was no way out. Men of honor – *uomini d'onore* – must make their choices and live with them. U Pizzu glanced out the window. Seeing the glittering sea made him feel young, took him back decades, to when he became a uomo d'onore, he and Gaetano Larione, at about the same time.

It wasn't easy. To become a uomo d'onore – a *man of honor* – you had to prove yourself.

Sipping the bitter airline espresso, gazing out the window toward the Aeolian Islands, dark volcanic hulks, glowing in the haze, U Pizzu could see it now – how he'd told his old childhood buddy, Gaetano, all about his initiation as a man of honor, the two of them reminiscing, drinking coffee, out on Gaetano's boat, just off the island of Salina, twin volcanoes sticking up out of the water, the water lapping around the boat, the sun breaking apart into little golden coins and reflecting in the oily swell, ah, the old days, the good days …

"Yeah, Gae', so, first off, I had to kill a kid we all knew, a pal of mine."

"Who'd you kill, Pizzu?"

"Nino Minucci."

"Yeah, I remember Nino – skinny guy, a smartass."

"Yeah, a smartass."

"It's a test, I was told. Well, I knew that." U Pizzu narrowed his eyes. "So, I shot Nino. He's standing on a street corner in Palermo. I ride up on my motorbike, that old white souped-up Vespa I had. 'Hey, Nino,' I say. He turns, big goofy smile on his face (we used to play pool), and I shoot him like that, right square in the smile, three rounds. His teeth fly apart, and his brains. He splatters all over the wall and the plate-glass windows of the Gucci and Prada shops behind him, and he falls flat down between two parked cars, an old Fiat 500 and a 2001 BMW. So that was done. Nice and clean. A month later, I'm picked up by Tonino Panucci. You remember Tonino. He owned a gas station in south Palermo, Uditore neighborhood, near the autostrada exit. People said he had money, owned apartment blocks, and he was a man of honor. 'Come on,' Tonino says. 'Hop in,' he says. So, I hop in. He's squinting in the sun, and he looks across at me – that squint, all wrinkles at the edge of those snot-green eyes, face like tanned leather, that narrow-eyed squint makes it look like he's thinking, calculating, plotting something deep; it scares the shit out of people. 'We're going for a little drive,' he says. 'Okay,' I say, 'it's a nice day for a drive.' So, we drive. He says nothing. I think: Now I'm either a dead man or a *man of honor*. Then, after maybe thirty minutes, he says, 'People got their eyes on you.' 'Yeah?' I say, and I'm thinking: Is this good news or bad news, people got their eyes on me? It was hot and I'm sweating – despite the air-conditioning. Twenty more minutes. We head up a little country road, then we turn into a real long, real narrow laneway, and it leads to an old abandoned farmhouse, looks like nobody's lived there for decades: dusty palm trees, pale ochre walls color of watery piss, peeling stucco and plaster, a few broken dusty windows – out of sight of everything and everybody. I'm not sure this is good news. I'm thinking: This is the sort of forgotten isolated old place you go into and you don't ever come out of. Then I see other cars are there. That makes me feel better – I'm young, I'm not important enough for a big meeting. If Tonino wanted me out of the way he'd just shoot me on the side of a road and drop me into some ravine. So, I'm sweating a little less. We get out of the car and Tonino hitches up his belt and pants right over his belly, just under the ribcage – and we go into the house, a messy sort of entryway, broken wooden coat rack, crockery on the floor, a faded tinted photograph – Mount Etna – hanging sideways on the wall – and then we go into this bigger room, which is real dark. All the curtains drawn, keeping out the sun. Men standing around. It's all in shadow, candles, images – religious sort of shit. One guy, Don Pasquale Tremino, pricks my finger, takes blood. I gotta smear the blood on this little piece of paper with a faded colored picture on it, woman with a halo and a face like an angel, the Virgin Mary. So I smear the picture with the blood and I swear I'm gonna be loyal, I'm not gonna rat on nobody, and then Don Pasquale holds the Virgin over a candle, and he burns the paper with the Virgin until it's ash, and that's the symbolic act, like they say – that's what's gonna happen to me, and we all know it, if I violate my oath: I'll be burned until there's nothing left, not even the ash. And they tell me I'm a *uomo d'onore*. A man of honor. So, we drink some wine and later we go and have some food – it's a big feast, lots of pasta, lamb, pork, chicken, even a big side of grilled beef. Fine with me, I thought: Now I'm a *man of honor*, a Mafioso, though we all know the word is taboo. There is no such thing as the *Mafia*. It's an invention of journalists and foreigners and Northern Italians and Communists and people who hate Sicilians, anti-Sicilian racists one and all."

Gazing down through the Airbus window at the rippling silver Mediterranean, U Pizzu closed his eyes and mused on how, looking back, his whole life now seemed like a dream. After the initiation, he killed more people, transported drugs, got his own "zone" established, set up a heroin laboratory or two with trained chemists, eliminated rival bosses, recruited a network of "mules" and smugglers, and made sure the chemists and the mules and smugglers behaved, and expanded his business. And so, he made his reputation. It was hard work. He had to know who to trust and who not to trust. He had to learn about shipping, and air freight, and trucking companies, and customs officials and which politicians and police to pay off, and ferry and airline schedules; he had to know who loads and unloads and inspects cargo, and how money is supposed to travel and be hidden, and which friends you need in which banks. Above all, banks – banks and computer and IT and AI experts were important – and soon he had his own powerful "family" – picking up where his old "family" had left off. And so now, in his modest way, he was a boss, almost the "boss of bosses," if the truth be told.

Yeah, that was the way it was; that was the way he told it, many years ago, to his closest pal, to dear old Gaetano Larione, God rest his soul. The two of them out on Gaetano's boat, on the sparkling, wine-dark sea.

Life happens too fast! You blink once, and it's over. You wonder if you are asleep or awake. He opened his eyes, squinted out the window – into the brilliance. It eats you up, life. Far below, the Mediterranean glittered, vast and beautiful, indifferent to human destiny. Ah, he loved the local branch of the Mediterranean – the Tyrrhenian and its islands! A few volcanic rocks, small islands, soared up from the sea. Each of them – Filicudi, Alicudi, Salina, Stromboli – had its own personality and was different from all the others, and U Pizzu knew them all like they were part of his own soul – which they were. Each island tugged at his heart, and each in its own way.

He closed his eyes. Memories are like barnacles on a boat: The older you get, the more they weigh you down. Older men get wiser, sometimes; but they get heavier and slower too. They forget how to be fast.

He loved all the islands. The island of Vulcano, closest to Sicily, was – potentially – the most violent island of them all, a sleeping time-bomb. Right now, it was slumbering and had been since its last eruption in 1890. He pictured it: The white smoke rising lazily from the fumaroles on the steep stony slope of the large crater. Vulcano was the entrance to the underworld, the Greeks and Romans used to say, the gateway to Hell, where the Roman blacksmith god, Vulcan, hung out. But for U Pizzu it was a piece of paradise.

He and Maria Grazia had made love on Vulcano, late one summer night, naked, out on the beach. She was shocked and afraid that somebody would come along and had prayed to the Virgin Mary and crossed herself, but soon she forgot the Virgin and got into the spirit of it. U Pizzu felt he had a special talent for pleasuring women, and they deserved all the pleasure they could get.

He thought of the blond girl – nothing left of her now, not even ashes. So spunky, so brave – so young, so beautiful. Truly, it was a shame.

Business, business, business! U Pizzu tried to keep it all straight in his mind – these days the business was complicated, and you couldn't put hardly any of it on paper or in a computer or in the cloud.

Used to be, in the simple old days, a fishing boat would head out, rendezvous with a tramp steamer from Turkey or Lebanon, pick up a couple of cases of raw heroin and bring it back into port or to some beach, guys in a little van would pick it up, take it to a lab in Palermo or Castellammare del Golfo – or out in a hidden basement on some farm somewhere – and refine the stuff. Then you sent the product onwards in ships or trucks packed with fruit or olive oil or wine – to the States or to Northern Europe – where it was distributed through pizzerias, fruit and vegetable markets, restaurants, manicurists, funeral parlors, building contractors, fitness clubs, local gangs, and street dealers. The money got deposited in a friendly bank or sent by courier ...

Now everything was more complicated.

You had to be even more sneaky and indirect.

A good memory helped. Like: Could he remember what was happening right now? He took another sip of the bitter coffee. Let's see, a whole caravan of mules was bringing drugs from Colombia up into the States. Private aircraft were flying cocaine from Central America into Florida and Louisiana. A string of trucks was coming out of Turkey and through the Balkans, bringing cocaine into Europe – Amsterdam, Hamburg, Frankfurt, Paris, and Glasgow.

At the end of the line, at the retail level, the income was old-fashioned cash, grubby, heavily fingered US dollars, euros, British pounds, or Russian rubles. You don't put cocaine or heroin on your Visa or your American Express card – unless it's part of your fitness club bill, or a fake restaurant or nail salon, or any number of weird false invoices. And you can't put hundreds of millions of euros under your mattress.

So, what do you do with it? If you walk up to somebody and say, "I want to buy that apartment building or that mall or that casino for two hundred and forty million dollars or euros," you can't hand over a barrel full of old notes with a few coins thrown in.

And you can't deposit the money in the bank – the fucking Financial Police want to know where the goddamned money came from – where are the invoices, the receipts, the bills of sale, who paid what to whom for what, how, where, when and by what means? Where do all these dirty wrinkled dollars and euros come from, eh?

The paper trail, the money trail – that is the problem! It's even more difficult than the drugs themselves! You need a lot of loyal – or terrified – skilled accountants and lawyers – and friendly bankers!

U Pizzu hated paper and paperwork. Making the drugs and selling them were the easy parts. Cleaning up the money so it smelled as sweet as roses, *that* was the key – and the hard part. Make the money antiseptic and anonymous and liquid and with a nice pedigree – so it can be invested anywhere – in casinos, restaurants, discos, retail fashion, real estate and construction, resorts and hotels – yeah, that was the tricky part.

So, the Vatican Bank – and its partner banks, like the old Banco Ambrosiano run by Roberto Calvi, God rest his troubled soul – was a wonderful help! A godsend!

What could be simpler! You ride a taxi from Italy into Saint Peter's Square, or just the edge of it, and there you are, in a foreign country – the Vatican – with a suitcase full of euros.

Even better – you get a helpful priest or friar to deposit the money for you, through some charity with "Saint" in its name, or a Church-run hospital, or a local bank.

Or you get a bank to transfer money, little bits each time, to a religious account and then to the Vatican Bank or to its corresponding banks, and from there the money magically disappears – with no annoying controls, the Vatican being a sovereign country, its own little jurisdiction – off to Switzerland, or Luxembourg, or the Cayman Islands, or Canada – and then, through empty "shell" holding companies, all that invisible money can be invested back into the real world, anywhere, in anything. All the little electronic bits and bytes become real stuff, real assets, with real incomes – casinos, apartment buildings, malls, beauty parlors, restaurants, cleaning companies, construction … you name it.

Dirty money made clean, courtesy of the Holy Spirit. Like confession and absolution – and you just have to pay a percentage!

The Larione brothers had refused to understand that simple fact: the Vatican connection was essential – and if you must deal with a few crazy prelates like Ambrosiano and Father Andrea and with some corrupt Roman politicians, well, what the fuck, it's worth it!

And if you had to assassinate a Pope, well, that too was worth it. After all, this new guy was changing the rules! Maybe Francis II wants to be a saint; well, we can turn him into a saint, even earlier than he figured!

Gaetano Larione thought that Ambrosiano was the problem; no – Ambrosiano was the solution!

The end of the world – what a fucking stupid idea! The world is as solid as the rocks under our feet.

Now all the Larione brothers were dead: Gaetano, Maurizio, Michael, and Peppino – all disappeared, blown up, shot, dismembered, and dissolved in acid, never to be seen again. The Larione women were all wearing black; the kids were orphans – they'd need a protector.

U Pizzu mused: it might be nice to console Concetta, Maurizio's young widow, she was a hot dish and U Pizzu had always thought that just maybe she had a sweet spot for him.

But this was just a daydream. U Pizzu knew that sleeping with anybody's wife, even a dead anybody, was suicidal; adultery was dangerous. It was distracting. It could get you killed. The occasional whore or casual school girl or Milanese university student – that was different. They were nobodies, unattached, and unprotected.

He looked out the window – more rippling silver on the sea, the Mediterranean. Fuck, how he loved it!

The Cardinal was a looney with crazy ideas? Who cared? The man was worth his weight in gold, literally, even if he did take a whacking big cut!

It was for the Cardinal that U Pizzu had sent two of his best men to Rome to "clean up a little problem." It was just some priest who'd stuck his nose where he shouldn't have. But the two guys sent to solve the problem, among the best foot soldiers U Pizzu had, one young, one seasoned, had disappeared – poof! – into thin air, leaving no sign. Mystery!

U Pizzu didn't like mysteries.

So, feeling put upon and royally pissed off, U Pizzu was on his way to solve the problem himself, with hangdog hitman Santino along for the ride. One thing about Santino: He knew how to shoot, use a knife, and he could garrote somebody lickety-split with razor wire without even a whisper of sound. He was a fat nervous sweaty stupid talkative bastard, but he was fast.

"You should use deodorant, Santino," U Pizzu said.

"What?"

"Even that snotty little stewardess turns up her nose when she goes by."

"Fuck you, I smell like a rose!"

"Even roses wither and rot, Santino."

"What the fuck does that mean?"

"Nothing, Santino, nothing; I'm just daydreaming, just kidding! I know not what I say! I'm in a foul and melancholy mood." U Pizzu smiled. Truth be told, he loved beating up on Santino; and he knew, too, that Santino, secretly, loved being beat up on.

They landed at 1:30 at Rome's Leonardo Da Vinci airport. A breeze wafted in from off the sea, brilliant seaside light flooded the sky from above and below, balmy, inebriating. Bright sandy beaches were not far away.

U Pizzu closed his eyes. Maybe he could go for a swim – maybe he could skip the meetings; maybe he could just go to the beach, at Fregene, ten minutes away. Classy, expensive, brainy dames, topless and glossy with suntan oil, slouched in deckchairs, fingering a glass of wine, and reading the chic highbrow papers, *La Stampa*, or *Corriere della sera*. Good view, good fish, sit back and sip a nice dry white French Muscadet. Better Fregene than Rome!

U Pizzu hated Rome – too many politicians, too many cops, too much pollution. But there was no choice; Rome it was. Quick in, quick out – solve the problem and get their asses back to Palermo!

A black Mercedes was waiting for them. It had Vatican license plates.

"Obliged," said U Pizzu, climbing in. "Santino, thank the good man!"

The driver was a huge monk. The cowl hid his face. He turned around. His face was chalk-white, and his features were baby features, all squished together down at the bottom of his face. But his voice was a deep, echoing voice, like a voice from the tomb.

Where the hell did the Church get these guys?

Maybe Gaetano had a point …

CHAPTER 10 – MAGIC

"Well, priest …" The demon strode into the room.

And so, God willing, I continue my account.

At first, she looked like a normal woman – a human. She was wearing tight black jeans, a black hip holster, with the requisite sidearm, a thin white T-shirt with "I love Seattle" written, using the little red heart icon, across the front, and open sandals. She had a light gold tan, no lipstick, very dark eyebrows, and raven-black hair cut short. She radiated health and power – and sensuality.

When she got closer, I noted, I must admit with revulsion, that she was perfect – the skin was flawless, the features absolutely symmetrical.

She is not human, I thought, definitely not human. She is too perfect.

"Well, priest, you are awake," she said, adding, with a thin smile, "By the way, people call me V."

"So John told me." Echoes of the demonic voice in the sewer came back to me, the voice that had hissed the word *priest*; and the fangs, the reptilian face, the golden, heavy-lidded serpent's eyes staring at me, the forked tongue, the blood, the chloroform – it all rushed back. Could she possibly be the same creature? She came close to the bed and stood looking down at me. Suddenly I was terrified. I reached for my cross.

"My cross?" I always had it with me, dangling around my neck.

"Your cross? Here it is." She reached into the pocket of her jeans, and held it out to me, dangling it from its chain, upside down, holding it, I thought, as if it were something unseemly, polluted, or even obscene. It is well known that demons flee in terror at the mere sight of the cross, and holy water will wither and burn them – shrink their manifestations to a pile of ash or drive them, howling and cursing, out of those whose bodies they have possessed.

Her hands, I could not help noticing, were long and slender and delicate

– again, flawless. As she held the cross upside down, flaunting her resplendent beauty, I had to remind myself that Satan seduces with inhuman beauty, with seeming perfection; that Satan uses desire – and terror – to ensnare even the purest of souls. Beauty is a trick. Evil has many disguises. The world is a seething cornucopia of hidden and secret demons. Behind every passion, every weakness, every sin, every act of evil, lurks a demon. Maya, the Veil of Being, or the Veil of Illusion, is paper thin, and behind this mundane veil a myriad of diabolic tempters are sent daily to entrap us; it is with delight that such demons spawn and proliferate.

For some reason I thought of the young woman I had seen: the blonde in the scarlet dress, the pagan goddess celebrating her youth and beauty in the sun.

Was that yesterday? Only yesterday? It seemed like eons had gone by.

I was no longer the man I had been – yesterday.

The demon smiled, a perfect smile, beautiful! But underneath every form of perfection, we know, we will find only death, and putrefaction, maggots, worms, and sulfurous coiled intestines – piss, shit, and sweat. I would not allow myself to be seduced by this creature, whatever wiles she might deploy. I clenched my fists and reminded myself of the reptilian claws I had seen – and that had seized me – only yesterday down in the sewer.

"Thank you," I said.

Yes, it was indeed my cross – the silver cross I have worn around my neck through decades of adventure; it had been with me in joy and in sorrow. But now it was twisted, scarred, and blackened.

"Did you …?" I began to ask; I meant to ask: Did you destroy it, profane it?

"No, that wasn't me," the demon said, sitting down on the chair next to the bed, and pulling it closer. "I didn't profane your cross," she added, as if reading my thoughts. "It deflected one of the bullets and, I hate to admit this, priest" – she favored me with a sly smile – "but your cross probably saved your life. Without it, I would have been too late – it would have been impossible to revive you. It's enough to make a girl superstitious!"

It was perhaps foolish of me, but I righted the cross and held it boldly out in front of me. I stared across it, straight at her. She gave me an even fuller smile – a joyous movie-star smile. It made her look like a teenager. In a flash I saw that, whatever else she was, she *was* very young – 19, 20, 21, not much older. "Why do you smile?"

She half closed her eyes and laughed, as if we were sharing a joke. "How very medieval of you, priest! It doesn't work, your cross. Garlic doesn't work either, nor the Eucharist, with the consecrated wine and bread, nor holy water, if you are inclined to try. Now, a stake through the heart might slow me down a bit, but I would almost certainly bounce back even from that."

Her flippancy was intolerable! An irreverent, irreligious, mocking demon – and *female* to boot – that was doubly sacrilegious and a triple insult. So, wincing from pain, I put the question: "Who are you? What are you?"

"What am I?" She leaned forward. "Even I don't know the answer to that, priest. The simplest description, though, and I know this sounds ridiculous, is that I am what people call a vampire."

"You are quite right. That *is* ridiculous!" I knew now that she was a charlatan, an evil charlatan – she was a joke, not a threat. "A vampire?" I laughed. "Is this a farce? Vampires don't exist. That's eastern folklore. The Church believes there is no such thing. And neither do I!"

"No such thing as me? Well, I know it's hard to believe. But, priest, I'm not joking. I do exist, that I know. 'Vampire' might not be the right word. I have other – how shall I put it? – characteristics. I'm a hybrid of human and something else – a mongrel, if you like. Truly, I don't know what I am. But I do feed on human blood. It's my nature; it's certainly part of what I am."

"Rubbish!" I threw up my hands, and winced from the pain that flashed through my chest and shoulder. I felt a mixture of repulsion and disbelief. That this unearthly beautiful creature was claiming to be a foul drinker of human blood, a cannibal, a desecrator of humanity and all that is holy – it put me into a rage.

"This is a travesty!" I gasped.

"Don't worry, priest. I may be a vampire, but you are not on the menu! Not today!" She again displayed her perfect, even teeth, the brightest I'd ever seen. "But I do drink coffee, red wine or whiskey – so I can keep you company if you will have a Bushmills a little later."

She had named my favorite whiskey.

"That horrendous thing I saw last night?"

"The *thing* with scales and claws … eyes like a snake …?"

"Yes. That thing."

"That *thing* was me."

"You!"

"Yes, me. I come in different forms, or flavors. That was my demonic version." She favored me with an innocent, beatific, movie-star grin: I realized that the demon was a tease.

I was enraged. "Am I going mad? Am I dreaming?"

"This is not a dream, priest," she said. "Sit up. I want to see your wounds."

"Why do you call me priest? You seem to spit out the word! Why not Father?"

"I'll address you as Father if it pleases you."

"It would."

"Even from a vampire? Even from a demon?"

"Yes."

"Here, then, Father, sit up." As she put her arm around me, I caught the scent of that sweet and spicy perfume I had noticed the night before. Her hands were gentle. She levered me into a sitting position. Pain shot through my chest and shoulder and I was terribly weak and vulnerable.

She drew back and gazed at me, eyes narrowing, suddenly serious, like a doctor considering her patient, or a mathematician contemplating a vexing problem on a dusty blackboard. "If I hesitate to call you Father it is because I am not – let us say – an admirer of your Church. And your Church is certainly not fond of me. And, though you are a fine and admirable and brave man, Father O'Bryan, you are not my father."

"I've seen you somewhere before," I said. I had the sneaking feeling that somewhere, in some other guise, I had seen this young woman.

"Oh, where?"

I concentrated. I closed my eyes. For some reason there flashed into my mind the image of a little old bent-over nun, a wizened, mousey semi-invisible, cowering timorous thing, a creature whom I had seen once or twice in the Vatican Library, who brought me files, and made sure I wore gloves when handling the materials, who ...

"No, it couldn't be," I said. "You couldn't be ..."

"Yes. Sister Agnes."

"Sister Agnes!"

"Yes."

"How?"

"Let's say I'm good at disguises, Father."

"But why?"

"I wanted to learn what I could about the Satanic Order of the Apocalypse."

"The Satanic Order of the Apocalypse?" I said. "What in the world is that?"

She stared at me. The tip of her tongue ran along her upper lip. She looked like she might roll her eyes in frustration. She sighed. "As you certainly know, it's a secret satanic sect. I have been following them for, well, for centuries. In recent decades I had lost track of them. Now they have once again become active. They are more dangerous than ever. In the Vatican Library – and in some private bank vaults – many secrets are hidden. I don't have access. But – without knowing it – you, Father, and Father Luciani were on their trail. It was when you were doing your research on the Gnostic Heresy – so I was there to watch you. To learn, if I could, what you might stumble upon – or were about to stumble upon. I think Father Luciani was even closer to the truth than you, but then, he is dead, almost certainly murdered, and you … are my only recourse."

"Me?"

"Yes, you, Father. With Father Luciani dead, that leaves you. What I believe you have discovered is of great interest to me. And it is extremely dangerous, for you, for your Church."

I dared not move. Was this diabolical creature – she virtually spat out the word "priest" – intending to destroy the Church? I could not breathe. Did she intend to use me to attack it? To attack Pope Francis? Was she Satan?

"No, I am not out to destroy your Church, Father. I rather like Pope Francis. And, I can't be sure, but I really don't believe I am Satan, however flattering and exciting such an incarnation might be!"

I was startled. This was the second time the demon had repeated back to me thoughts I had not uttered. "So, you read thoughts, then, do you?"

"Just a little bit, Father, just occasionally, I read thoughts, surface thoughts. Except when I am feeding; then I go deeper, much deeper."

"When you are feeding …?"

Her eyes dilated. I have never seen eyes that were so intense, that bored into my soul the way hers did – they were whirlpools of darkness, an abyss, a hypnotic swirl of demonic blackness, a maelstrom of nihilism.

Slowly emphasizing each word, she leaned forward. "I want you to tell me, Father, everything – I mean everything – you have discovered about Cardinal Ambrosiano and the Satanic Order of the Apocalypse."

I laughed. "Satanic Order of the Apocalypse? What an idea!" While I uttered these words, I tried to veil my thoughts with irrelevant musings and mental static – reciting an old song I remembered from my days at the Irish College. This strange young woman – or demon – really did seem to be able to read thoughts. How to defend myself against her? Desperately, I changed tunes. In my head, I sang …

It's a long way to Tipperary,
It's a long way to go …

She tilted her head and grinned. "Come now, Father, you are not that old!" And, double mockery, she began to sing it, that old First World War song. She had a fine voice, rich and nuanced, and she even managed to give it a quivering, quavering period feel, as if heard on an old gramophone.

"You are making a fool of me!"

"Gosh! Sorry!" She looked down – a little girl about to be scolded – and then blinked at me from under her eyelashes – yes, no doubt about it! She was a shameless, irrepressible flirt.

I clenched my jaw. I would not be an accomplice to a campaign to cast disgrace on the Catholic Church. The Church is humanity's only vehicle of salvation. The activities of Cardinal Ambrosiano and his so-called Order are just the sort of thing that casts the Church in a bad light. When scandals turn people away from the Church, they are turning people away from salvation and leading them straight toward eternal damnation. Just think about it! There have been so many attacks on the Church – on its sexual doctrines, on its supposed indifference to sexual crimes, on its agreements with Mussolini and his Fascist regime, on its supposed complicity with Hitler and the Nazis, on its alleged indifference during the Holocaust, on its alleged links to the Mafia and reputed laundering of Mafia money …

I will not, I thought, be an accomplice of this devilish woman – this demon – and her plots against the Church.

"I want you to trust me, Father." She looked down, then up, and, gazing into my eyes, fluttered her eyelashes.

"I know nothing about you," I scowled. "And why is it important that I trust you? What do you want?"

"I want to save the world."

I laughed. "Save the world! That is sacrilegious, woman! That is mad! What is threatening the world?"

"I know it sounds insane, but believe me, I'm not crazy."

"Well? So, what is going to destroy the world?"

"Perhaps I am, by negligence."

"You?"

"Yes. You know, Father O'Bryan, I must confess."

"Confess?" What mockery was this – from a demon! A demon – offering to confess? She was playing with me – a sort of wicked spiritual hide-and-seek! A parody of contrition!

"I truly am guilty, Father." She looked down, again like a child caught doing something naughty.

"Guilty? How or why would a demon like you feel guilt? What do you feel guilty for?"

"I could have stopped Cardinal Ambrosiano."

"Stopped him – how stopped him?"

She looked at me sadly, tilted her head to one side. "I could have killed him. I should have killed him when I had the chance."

"Killed him?"

"Yes, I had the opportunity; but … I didn't seize it."

"Why?"

"I think …" She paused. "I think because I was showing off – I was showing him how strong I was, and how magnanimous. I murdered one of his acolytes – in front of him. So, I frightened the Cardinal – and yet I spared him, and I spared his sidekick, Father Andreas, too. It was pure vanity. I really am a showoff, I'm afraid. Then, too, I'd already drunk my fill. I was no longer hungry. I fear I was rather selfish."

"I regret to say I cannot pardon you, demon, or grant you absolution, for *not* murdering the Cardinal – a grievous sin of omission, I suppose. But let us not wander; let us not get off the subject." I wondered whether this strange demon wanted me to offer her absolution and impose thirty Hail Marys, because she had *not* killed the man. She obviously had a topsy-turvy sense of ethics and morality and her grasp of theology was, alas, very shaky indeed. But, of course, she is a demon. "Back to the question at hand: what is going to destroy the world?"

Her intense dark eyes stared directly into my mine. "There is an object, a sort of machine, buried in the desert in North Africa. And there is a key that controls this machine and …"

"A machine … I see." I had read some science fiction while holed up for months at a time in small frontier missions in Africa and I was prepared to be amused. "Is this machine a spaceship from Mars, full of nasty little green men, Martian leprechauns, or is it an ancient talisman from the Egypt of the Pharaohs, a casket which, when opened, will release all the whirling demons of Hell and turn everybody to skeletal dust? And I thought we Irish had imagination!"

She licked her lips and bared her teeth as if she wanted to bite me. Her teeth did look sharp. I was, I believe, getting under her skin. This gave me a strange, perhaps sinful, surge of almost physical pleasure. The demon was annoyed! Dark fire flared in her pupils. She leaned closer and lowered her voice, making it soft, barely a whisper. "This object – let's call it the Crystal – it looks like a gigantic crystal or disco ball – is designed to do many things. Among other things, it can destroy the planet we live on."

"Destroy the Earth? Destroy God's Earth?" I chortled. This was utterly absurd, not to mention sacrilegious. But I did have a flash of doubt; some of the sketches in Father Luciani's file did look like a disco ball – a Crystal.

"Yes!"

"What fanciful tales you tell, woman!"

"You don't believe me." She flashed that sweet wicked smile that was both charming and flirtatious, sharp-toothed and carnivorous – *the better to eat you with*. The dark flames in her eyes gave me the impression she was piercing through the very fabric of time-and-space, that she was looking right through me and into … depths of nothingness.

I was determined to stare her down. "I very much fear, my dear demon, that you are insane – and a fraud, a beautiful fraud perhaps, but a fraud, nonetheless. I don't know by what magic you appeared to me last night, by what magic you seem to have saved me, but I want you to let me go, and I want you to give me my belongings. I am going to leave – and I am going to leave now!"

I began to get up. Ouch! I winced – searing bolts of lightning shot through my chest and shoulder, reminding me that I owed my life to this insane young person. It also reminded me that there were people who wanted to kill me. I was overwhelmed by a sensation of weakness.

"Father, relax for God's sake, and don't be a fool."

"I, a fool? You – woman! – are accusing me of being a fool?"

"Sorry, I apologize."

"You have a quick temper, my girl."

"Yes, I do." She gave me that sheepish, worshipful, little-girl grin, fluttering her black eyelashes, and bit her lip.

"Hmmm," I frowned. This creature, this demon, this female, needed a lesson in humility.

"Father," she was almost gritting her teeth. "Are you not supposed to be a man of faith?"

"Yes. Certainly!"

"Can you not make this leap of faith with me?"

"No, I cannot. There is faith, and then there is faith. Faith in God and in His Son Jesus Christ and in Salvation, on the one hand, and faith in you and your fantastical tales, on the other, are two absolutely different things. I do not know what or who you are. You've told me you are a vampire and many other absurd and mad things – but I have no reason to believe you and every reason to doubt you."

I stared at her as if I could force her to wince, to confess the ridiculous nature of what she was telling me. But she just sat there, smiling, quite calm, waiting for the storm to pass. I could not stare her down. This demon was patient – she played a long game.

I took a deep breath, thinking, well then, let us see this through. "So be it! If we are to play games, I want you to show me what you really are. I want you to reveal yourself. I want to see the demonic shape I saw last night. I want to look into those diabolic serpent eyes. I want proof that I am not stark raving mad and that you are not an impostor, merely an insane trickster!"

"An insane trickster? I sometimes wish that was all I were."

"I insist! I want to see the mask removed. I want the truth!"

"You want to see me as I am?" She stood up and spread her arms, a beautiful young woman. "This is what I am!"

"No, I want to see the *other* you."

"You insist?"

"Yes."

"Well, Father, you shall have your wish!" She turned her back, and then swiveled around – she was unchanged except for two fangs that protruded from her mouth, and there were now shadows under her eyes; her lips were blood red, and her skin chalk-white with veins of blue, her hair unruly, in knots. She came close to me and knelt. "Happy?"

I was shocked. How had she done this? Was she a magician, a conjurer? Was she truly possessed? And if she herself is a demon, as I at first supposed, what sort of demon is she? The learned Father Leo Allatius in his *De Grae-corum hodie quirundam opinationibus*, an exhaustive catalogue of popular beliefs in Greece in the 17th century, stated that, according to legend, vampires were the work of the Devil, instruments and handmaidens of Satan. Could she truly be one of those, not only a demon, but a vampire too? This might require an adjustment of our doctrine on demons! The change had been instantaneous. "The vampire," I asked. "That's the vampire?"

"Yes, this is the vampire." She knelt close and ran her hand over my face, over my forehead. Her touch was as frigid as ice. The chill invaded my bones. I recoiled, shivering. But her breath was still strangely perfumed, a heady and spicy suggestion of forests and gardens. "Standard issue vampire." Her fangs grinned. "Cool, isn't it?" She brushed her icy fingertips over my lips. I hardly dared breathe. What little breath I had appeared as mist – condensing in the sudden cold.

"And the demon?" I whispered, "The creature I saw last night?"

"Ah, the demon!" She stood up, still in vampire mode, and then, in a blur, her features returned to normal. She was once more the perfect, perfectly groomed young woman I had been talking to a moment before. I blinked: she had not even turned her back; the transformation had taken place in front of my eyes. What satanic trickery was this?

"The demon." She frowned. "Well, Father, the demon is rather a production. It's better if I undress." She lifted off her T-shirt (she was not wearing a bra) and unbuckled the leather belt and opened her jeans. "You may want to close your eyes, Father. Becoming the demon – she's rather muscular and voluptuous – literally explodes my clothes, even down to the merest stitch. So, like Eve, when I am a true demon, I do without raiment and go naked."

"I've seen naked women before." I decided to be stubborn. I was not going to take my eyes from her, not for one instant.

"Oh, you have, Father? And where, pray tell?" She stepped out of her jeans.

"In Africa. Dead women, dying women, tortured women."

"Of course. How stupid of me. I apologize, Father. You were in the Central African Republic, in the civil war, and in other war-torn places. You stood up against the rapists and murderers. You were tortured. That's where the limp comes from."

"Yes," I said. I must admit, that, as I watched her, I thought if I were a lust-driven man (and what man is not?), I might easily lust after this creature – all her lithe beauty and youth! She had now stepped out of her panties, and had placed everything, neatly folded, on a dresser.

She turned to face me – naked. "Presto," she said. "You see me as I am! And now!"

Her body ... was a blur.

"Abracadabra!" She bowed deep, as if delivering a rabbit from a magician's hat. "*Voilà!* You see me as I also am."

I gasped.

The Demon stood before me. Yes, she was certainly more muscular, more voluptuous, than her human self. Scales covered her whole body – translucent, patterned, green, turquoise, gold, scarlet, iridescent scales. The fangs were longer than the vampire's fangs. Her hair had turned to a rippling tight-fitting cap of turquoise and scarlet scales. The eyes were the eyes of a serpent; they glittered with a golden light, and they had dark lozenge-like pupils; they twinkled with a malevolent, or perhaps a mischievous, gleam.

I was awestruck. All that I had read of demons was now incarnate before me. She was the very image of a pagan idol; she was an ancient Babylonian totem; she was the voluptuous statue of a naked goddess coated in sparkling gems. She must most certainly be a fallen angel turned demonic, one of the beautiful angels cast down with Lucifer. The gaze of her eyes was hypnotic. She could surely, with those serpent's eyes, paralyze her victims before she ate them.

She flexed her claws, opening them, and gazed at the result, pointed fingers outspread, like a woman examining her nail polish. She came over, knelt next to the bed, and looked me straight in the eye. Her tongue was forked and this gave her a slight, hissing, rather charming, lisp. "Now that we have summoned the demon, let us practice some demonic magic, shall we, Father O'Bryan? Let us test our faith! Let us release the powers of Satan!"

Before I could recoil, she laid one claw on the wound in my chest and the other on my shattered shoulder.

I was paralyzed – fascinated, repelled, and terrified. I didn't dare move. I didn't know what thought or emotion was – or should be – uppermost in my mind. I prayed, silently, desperately.

My duty, I knew, my sacred duty, was to destroy – as soon as I could – this diabolical spawn of Satan. But I had to bury this thought lest she read it.

With her claws pressed on my chest and shoulder, she seemed to be concentrating – though it was hard to read any expression in those reptilian eyes.

Warmth flooded through my chest and my shoulder. She held her claws in place and her serpent eyes gazed into my eyes. We stared at each other from only a few inches away. Her presence, as I had noticed before, seemed to exude a sort of sweetness, not cloying, but strangely invigorating.

"I read your book *The Witchcraft Trials of the 17th Century* with great pleasure, Father," she said, fangs bared, forked tongue flickering, and lisping slightly, and still intent on what she was doing, like a surgeon making casual conversation while disemboweling a patient. "I could probably tell you some interesting things – perhaps even things you don't know – about those times. I was almost burned as a witch, once, in Germany. Protestants tried to burn me, not Catholics, so I won't hold that episode against you. We should compare notes sometime."

"You were almost burned as a witch – how? When?"

"There!" she said, ignoring my question, and lifting her claws from my chest and shoulder. "Now, where is the trouble with that limp?"

Before I realized what I was saying, I told her that it was in the right hip bone; they had used hammers and, briefly, a Black and Decker power drill, the torturers, and shattered the bones.

I was, as it were, paralyzed, and didn't try to stop her. She laid her claw on my right hip, caressing, downwards, then upwards, over my hip bone.

"I apologize for being so intimate, Father."

She withdrew her claw; she was still kneeling next to the bed.

"Now you have seen the demon, Father."

"Yes."

"Here, Father, touch – touch the scales!"

I hesitated but then I ran my fingers over her arm, her claw-like hand. The scales were warm and smooth like the scales of a snake that had been lying in the sun.

"I am warm-blooded." The serpent eyes blinked at me.

"Yes, I see, I mean, I feel."

"Satisfied?" She stood up.

"I have seen what I have seen," I sighed. I suddenly realized that I felt much stronger. Was this her demonic magic? Had I been cured by Satan's mistress?

"You can get out of bed now, Father. Your clothes have been cleaned and pressed – there was a lot of mud and blood down in that tunnel."

I swiveled around and sat on the edge of the bed. I didn't feel any pain at all.

"We can take those bandages off now."

She lifted off the pajama top I was wearing – whose pajamas were they? I wondered – and used her claws to rip away the bandages. "This may hurt a bit."

It was disconcerting to have a scaly and fanged she-demon act as nurse; but there she was.

She brought a bottle of alcohol from the bathroom and cleaned away the remains of the bandages and adhesive and traces of blood. She was totally focused on her work, a true professional.

"There!" She was still kneeling beside the bed. "Have a look!" She handed me a mirror.

I took the mirror and angled it to my chest and then to my shoulder. There was not a trace of a wound on my chest or on my shoulder. There was no sign I had been shot – no sign at all.

"Try to stand up."

I stood up and took a few steps – the limp seemed to be gone. I took a few more steps. There was no pain! There was no limp. I felt years younger.

The kneeling demon looked up at me. "Well?"

"The pain is gone. The wounds are gone. This is a miracle!"

"Or demonic magic."

"Or demonic magic." I was suddenly cast into a somber mood. Such creatures as she, with all their wiles and powers, must be destroyed, no matter how charming and generous they may appear.

She stood up, moved to the closet, opened its doors, and brought me my clothes, neatly folded on a hanger. "I'll turn my back and become human again, while you dress, Father."

She turned her back. I saw the blur of flesh being transformed. And she was once again human, a naked young woman, with her back turned to me.

I did not want to look any longer. After all, I may be a priest, but I am still a man. And a demon such as she could easily draw any man – even an old man who has vowed chastity – into sticky tangles of curiosity, tenderness, and carnal lust.

And, it was clear; even her kindness and compassion were clever traps designed to snare the soul. I concentrated on pulling on my trousers; then a thought occurred to me. "Last night, what did you do to the two killers?"

"Ah, the two killers." She pulled on her jeans, "Well, Father, I'm afraid I lost my temper." She turned to face me and slipped the T-shirt over her head. She wiggled her torso, smoothing the T-shirt down; it was tight-fitting, almost transparent. This demon is not modest.

"Lost your temper?"

"Yes. I … well … I tore them apart."

"Tore them apart?"

"Yes." She sighed. "It was messy." She stared down at her hands and twisted them together. "I ripped them into tiny pieces. I obliterated them. I lost control. I don't usually do that. But I was angry, furious really. And I was in a hurry – you were dying, you were losing a lot of blood. I had to get back to

you. So, I drank quickly, and ripped them into itsy-bitsy teeny-weeny shreds."
She looked up at me and blinked.

"You drank?"

"Yes." She buckled her belt, slid the holster onto the belt and clipped down
the flap. "When I drink my prey's blood, Father, I absorb – I don't know how
it works – their memories and thoughts."

"I see."

"I lock, for an instant, into the victim's central nervous system; it's like
accessing a mental data bank, I receive flashes of information, images, events;
it's all pretty chaotic; I piece it together afterwards. And, of course, drinking
gives me strength, makes me perhaps a bit too feisty. Then I had to make sure
they were truly dead and could not rise again."

"Not rise again?"

"I swore an oath never to create any other creatures like me."

"Ah, I see."

"For twenty-five centuries I have not wavered from that oath."

While I was absorbing the idea of *twenty-five centuries*, and thinking for
an instant of the women accused in the witch trials of the 17th century (could
she really have been one of those?), I asked "Who were they – the two men
who were shooting at me?"

"They were Mafia foot soldiers – *soldati* or *picciotti*, as they call them.
Neither one was a *made man* or a *man of honor*; but both of course wanted
to be. Humans – particularly young male humans – really do have a death
wish. I suppose evolution prized warriors and soldiers and hunters. One of
the young men was called Franco Leone. He was twenty-two. He was from
Corleone, in Sicily, part of the gang that once, long ago, was led by the famous
Salvatore Totò 'the Beast' Riina. As you will recall, in the 70s and 80s, Totò
wiped out most of the big Palermo-based Mafia families in a fight for control
of the international heroin trade."

"I remember," I said. "It was a slaughter."

"Franco was young, but a killer; a cool character, a good shot. He delivered drugs, at the retail level; and he was an enforcer. He'd killed about fifteen people, I think, tortured a few more, and threatened many people
– shop-keepers, merchants, and businessmen, in the local extortion rackets
in and around Palermo. His I.Q. was not very high." She looked down and
adjusted her belt and shifted the holster further out onto her hip. "The other
killer was Paolo La Maestra, nineteen, a farm boy. He was less experienced,

but more intelligent. He was new on the job. He'd killed too – a family of three – and was very proficient, a good shot, a natural killer. But at the last moment, when Paolo realized he was going to die, he was just a kid again – I saw lots of images of his mother – in his mind, he was crying out to her. He was really scared, poor kid. They both worked for a Mafia boss called U Pizzu. He's the one who sent them to kill you. But U Pizzu, I think, was doing it for someone else, as a favor. These are the snapshots I got when I drank their blood."

"Well, well ..." I didn't know what to say. What do you say to someone who has just told you she drinks people's blood, eavesdrops on their minds, and rips their bodies to itsy-bitsy teeny-weeny shreds?

She blinked at me, all innocence. "I know, Father. It's not pretty."

Not wishing to dwell any further on the blood and gore, and curious to know more about my presumed killers, I asked. "Who is this U Pizzu?"

She closed her eyes – for just an instant – as if contemplating an inner image. "U Pizzu is a handsome charming fellow, so I've heard. He looks like Marcello Mastroianni, the actor who in the 1960s and 70s was the very paragon of the great Latin lover. I've seen photographs of U Pizzu, but I've never met him. He's the head of one of the old Mafia clans from around Palermo – and I think he has a big say in Corleone too. He's close to the Vatican Bank and to Cardinal Ambrosiano."

"Yes, I know about the Vatican Bank," I conceded, grumpily.

"U Pizzu sent the two boys to kill you. And I'm certain – well, almost certain – that Cardinal Ambrosiano asked U Pizzu to do it. You are dangerous, Father, even if you don't know it. U Pizzu will want to finish the job his boys failed to do. He will consider it a personal insult – an act of disrespect – *uno sgarbo* – that his boys were – ah – mistreated so."

"This U Pizzu, will he try to kill you too?" I found it hard to believe that I was dangerous; I was just a harmless puttering old scholar. But if there really was a Satanic Order of the Apocalypse, if there really was a plot to blow up something, then I suppose – thanks to poor Father Luciani – I possibly did know too much. But I found it hard to credit that Cardinal Ambrosiano, however monstrous he might be, could be involved in anything like a satanic cult or terrorism.

"Yes. U Pizzu will try to kill me – or punish me. But I'll find him before he finds me." She paused. "Father, you have seen what I am. Will you now help me? I need to know! The stakes could not be higher."

"I want to know more. I want to know more about you – and about this so-called Crystal. If I do not fully understand you and your mission, my dear demon, I shall be hard pressed to trust you."

She rolled her eyes and sighed. "Oh, Michael Patrick O'Bryan, you are a most difficult man! How your mother, dear sainted woman, ever put up with you I shall for the life of me never understand!"

I almost smiled, but managed to retain a stern countenance. Her evocation of my mother – a dear, dear, and infinitely patient person with the most wonderful smile – brought back sweet and painful memories; I again saw myself as a child, eight years old, playing hopscotch with nine-year-old freckled redhead Maggie O'Bryan – a cousin I was at the time in love with. We were on the sidewalk in front of our home in Dublin, oh, so long ago! As this image flitted through my mind, I said nothing. I merely favored the demon with my most obstinate glare.

V allowed herself a resigned, world-weary sort of smile. "Well, then, if you insist, I shall tell you my story. You, Father O'Bryan, shall be my confessor."

"Well, I'm not sure I would go so far as –"

"You asked for it, Father." She held up her hand. "You, Father Michael Patrick O'Bryan, of the Society of Jesus, shall now be privileged to hear the unvarnished shocking true confessions of a girl demon."

"Oh, dear, I'm not sure that I really –"

"You shall learn to savor, in gory infinite detail, dear Father O'Bryan, all of the demon's sins. Her splendid orgies and crimes, her bizarre copulations and innumerable murders, all of this will be laid out before you in the most lurid, graphic, titillating splendor!" She smiled the sheepish little-girl smile, then, staring straight at me, she licked her lips with the point of her tongue, as if I had just whetted her appetite.

Oh, dear, I sighed. What had I unleashed?

PART FOUR – CONFESSIONAL

CHAPTER 11 – VANITY

On his knees, ankles shackled, wrists manacled behind his back, and wrists and ankles chained tightly together, Professor Roger Thornhill, dapper gentleman, cosmopolitan dandy, Nobel Laureate, former President of the National Academy of Sciences, stared at a giant curved razor-sharp Ottoman scimitar – it was something out of the Arabian Nights – that was hovering just above his head. Klieg lights on metal stands projected a garish glare that glinted on the edge of the scimitar's blade.

The beheading, Roger hoped, would be quick. Sweat trickled down his spine. Six feet away a camera on a tripod was happily recording every detail of his humiliation. Presumably, this was for all the world to see. Roger grimaced. Miserable social media show-offs, incurable attention-seekers, these terrorists! No selfie, no terror!

The last few hours were a chaotic blur. He glanced at the hovering blade. It would not be a glorious death. He had a headache. He was virtually naked, filthy, streaked with blood, oil, urine, and dust.

And, damn it, he ached all over – maybe from the beating he'd taken. He vaguely remembered fighting somebody or something – and boasting about it, which seemed terribly bad form. Not like him, not like him at all! Right now, whatever had happened, he had a horrible hangover, static in his head, a blur in his vision.

He had been drugged and beaten up, that much was clear. The drug, whatever it was, had catapulted him into drunken boastful madness. Slowly, he was getting sober, or so it seemed. He remembered, quite clearly, how just a few moments ago he had been forced down onto his knees. The end, it seemed, would come just as he was sobering up. Rather unfortunate!

The camera's red light blinked. It was busy filming or transmitting. Roger stared at the camera's eye. To be exposed to the world in this way was damned degrading. Damned ignorant obscurantist terrorists! No sense of dignity! No respect for science! He gritted his teeth. His eyes were probably bloodshot, not terribly photogenic. On his knees, clothes reduced to rags, barefoot, unwashed, unshaven, haggard, hair all mussed up, he would not present a prepossessing image to the world. He was clearly being made an example of: Famous American scientist on his knees, bathed in filth, about to be beheaded by heroic dedicated most holy Jihadists. Humiliations aren't humiliations if nobody knows about them. The whole thing was distasteful. Sweat was getting into his eyes. He tried to blink it away. What kind of terrorists were these people? They'd almost certainly be posing and taking selfies before long – with him shackled and on his knees.

Towering over Roger, gripping the glittering scimitar, was his executioner, a weird-looking creature, a monster-sized, seven-foot-tall chap, with chalk-white skin, and who was clothed in a black cloak and hood that looked like a monk's habit. Strange uniform and interesting genetics. Roger squinted up at the fellow. What the duce was he? And what was he thinking?

The creature licked its tiny cupid-bow lips, narrowed its minuscule eyes, and eyed Roger's neck. He was visibly eager to swing the sword down, and lop off Roger's head.

Lop off the head of a Nobel Laureate! Damnation! What presumption! Such effrontery made Roger's blood boil. These people obviously had no concept of the vastly important original ideas buzzing around in this particular, extremely valuable head, of the contributions it still could make to science, to technology, to humanity.

Behind the terrorist in the black robe, somebody else appeared, emerging from the shadows into the bright circle of light.

Roger stared. It couldn't be! But it did appear to be – it was Cardinal Antonio Xavier Paulus Ambrosiano, a Prince of the Church, rigged out in full ecclesiastical regalia.

"Cardinal Ambrosiano?"

"Yes, Professor, it is I." The prelate beamed down on him. The smile was the smile of a convivial jackal. The bright glowing cartoon grin looked like it was about to pop out of the Cardinal's mouth. Was the man wearing oversized dentures?

Why was the Cardinal here? What was this about? Or was it all just a bad dream? Had the Catholic Church become a terrorist organization? Whoever these people were, Roger had seen that they were capable of anything.

They were as mad as hatters and they were cold-blooded murderers. Best to humor them.

"Dare I ask what is going on, Cardinal?"

"There are more things in Heaven and Earth, Professor, than are dreamt of in your philosophy!"

"I'm sure there are." Roger licked at the crust of blood at the corner of his mouth. What did *Hamlet* or Horatio or cosmology or the philosophy of science have to do with anything?

"Your so-called science is a petty, ignorant, pitiful thing, Professor."

"Perhaps it is." Roger studied the old man. "But if my science, as you call it, is so pitiful, why did you bring me here? And why did you take Kate?"

Suddenly, uttering Kate's name, Roger saw it all – Kate had been kidnapped too! Images flashed. Men on motorbikes. The ambush. The car chase. The Mercedes. Mario! The murders at La Dolce Vita! Kate! It became crystal clear. A surge of anguish and fury rose. He swallowed. He must, above all, stay calm.

The Cardinal beamed. The enamel of his teeth caught the light. "I want you to fall on your knees and worship, Professor."

"I'm already on my knees, Cardinal." Roger was about to lose his temper. Murders! Kidnappings! What was this ridiculous, crazy, presumptuous old codger up to?

"Yes, yes, true, true. More important, Professor, I want to you to confess your innumerable mortal sins, your arrogance, your ignorance, your hubris!"

"And Kate – where is Kate?"

"Kate is well, and she is safe. Kate is my insurance policy. It means that you will obey me in all things! So, now, I wish you to worship and to confess!"

"Really? You really want me to worship – you?"

"I do, I do, and I do!" A gleeful sparkle flashed in the old man's bright cloudy eyes. Did he have cataracts?

"And …"

"And … if you don't, well, Professor, then Kate will certainly regret it – and hence you will regret it. You will, as in the Old Testament or as in a Greek tragedy, lament and cry out and gnash your teeth and tear out your hair, perhaps rip out your eyes. You will become a tragic figure – not a hero, though, merely a maimed fool, naked, or in motley, an outcast beggar, a buffoon, a jester without laughter!"

"I see," Roger said.

The Cardinal rubbed his chin, pursed his lips, and adopted a pose of pensive melancholy. "Nothing, they say, is worse than a dead child – or a mutilated child. Without a nose, say, without a tongue, or lips, or eyes, or arms, or perhaps legs –"

"Cardinal, if you lay a hand on …"

"And it's a marvel what acid can do. Kate is a beautiful young woman, and exceedingly talented and intelligent – so I have been told. We would not wish to mar her beauty or destroy her mind, would we?"

If Roger could have killed the Cardinal he would have, and with his bare hands, and all those bloody monks too. He managed to form his mouth into a bitter smile – then a contrite expression. "So you wish me to worship you?"

"I do. I most certainly do!"

"Well, then, here goes." Roger looked up at the old man, and said it as levelly as he could. "Oh, Great Cardinal Ambrosiano, I worship you!" The scimitar hovered uneasily. Ripples of iridescent light fluttered on its razor-sharp edge. The executioner's thumb twitched.

"Very, very good, Professor. And now I want you to confess your sins!"

"Of course, Cardinal! Just what particular sins shall I confess to today?"

"Just repeat after me! I confess my sins …" the Cardinal beamed down at his prisoner.

"I confess my sins …"

"Of pride, and arrogance, and hubris, and practicing false idolatrous science!"

"Of pride, and arrogance, and hubris, and practicing false idolatrous science!"

"More feeling, Professor! No irony!" The Cardinal roared. "Do not take this lightly! Do not mock me!" All the man's pretend amiability had vanished. "Confess your blasphemy, your pride. Confess your dedication to the idols of so-called science, your denial of the Dark Force, your denial of Satan and of Evil!"

Roger clenched his fists. If he could, he would spring up, punch the Cardinal square in the jaw, explode those silly oversized dentures out of the old man's mouth, wrest the scimitar from the ridiculous monk-terrorist, and decapitate all of them; but, with his wrists handcuffed behind his back, and with the handcuff linkeded by a tight chain to the manacles that held his ankles pressed together, he could do nothing. Sweat pearled down his forehead. And – what was this damned nonsensical rigmarole about a Satanic Dark Force?

He blinked. The scimitar hovered, trembling. If they chopped off his head, what would become of Kate?

He swallowed. "I confess to all of it – to everything I have ever done or believed, I confess!"

"You think I am taken in, Professor? No, I am not!" The Cardinal roared, "Oh, you arrogant human, you arrogant overweening faithless miserable excremental biped!" Foam spurted from the man's mouth. Bending close to Roger, spraying spittle, he whispered, softly, into Roger's ear. "You are not sincere, Professor. Your confession is a travesty."

"I'm sorry, I really didn't mean to ..."

Drool dribbled from the Cardinal's lips. "Do you remember when you humiliated me, you irreverent fool! Atheist fool! Agnostic know-nothing fool!"

"You mean when we were on that roundtable at the Pontifical Institute?"

"Yes! Yes! Yes!" The Cardinal straightened up. He thundered. "You said I understood nothing. You said Evil was a mere word, you said ..." The Cardinal ranted on, and on, and on.

Roger frowned. What could he have said that made the Cardinal so mad? His headache was fading; his mind was clearing. Oh, yes, it was about the nature of evil. He had said that while people did very bad things, evil things, for evil motives, and with evil intent, intending to harm other humans and other sentient creatures, he nonetheless did not believe in an Omnipresent Evil Spirit that lay behind all such actions.

In response, the Cardinal, who had perhaps drunk too much, had begun to rant about the Evil Force, and demons, and everlasting Satan, and suchlike nonsense, and had generally made a fool of himself. Roger, as he remembered it, had not been scornful at all; indeed, he had tried – and it was hard – to be gentle with the raving old duffer.

Was this mock trial – and summary execution – revenge for a debate that had taken place years ago? Was this about Satan? What a ridiculous idea!

Suddenly, he had flashes of what had transpired – the assault on Mario's Mercedes, Mario's head exploding, the murders in the restaurant. It was a rush of confused images. He and Kate had been kidnapped. He'd been blinded by a leather hood, and carried off on a motorcycle, and then he'd been transferred to a car, and taken to a small airport where an executive jet was waiting.

Somehow, at one point, he had managed to rip off the hood. He fought with the kidnappers when they tried to bundle him into the plane. He remembered pounding some guy's head into the tarmac.

He was shouting, and he certainly must have already been drunk or drugged. "I'm a very important person, I hope you realize that! And Kate is a very important person!" He was smashing the guy's head against the asphalt. Blood was spreading. The guy's eyes were wide open, terrified. Then two other guys – then three – were tearing at Roger. Somebody hit him on the head.

He fell but got up again, barefoot, punching, swinging out with both fists, insane with anger. He had to save Kate!

He smashed one of the men in the face, kicked another in the crotch. And he had – he heard somebody say later – broken two arms.

Finally, five men – including two of the weird monks – overpowered him. They must have drugged him. The flash of a needle, the pinprick of pain – then nothing, then … delirium.

Now he was on his knees, sobering up, and about to be beheaded in a mock trial straight out of *Alice in Wonderland*, presided over by a totally nutty Prince of the Church, who was clearly living in some wild fantasy world of his own.

"Cardinal, I have confessed to everything! What more do you want!"

"And Evil, the Dark Force, the Principle of Evil? Do you recognize Evil?"

"Cardinal, you have convinced me, Evil truly exists!"

"The Dark Force?"

"Absolutely. I believe with all my heart in the Dark Force."

"Repeat! 'I believe in and worship the true Dark Force that reigns over the Universe, and the true God which is Satan!'"

"I believe in and worship the true Dark Force that reigns over the Universe, and the true God which is Satan!"

The Cardinal grinned. "Lift him up! His conversion is complete. This has gone far enough!"

They removed the chain linking Roger's ankles to his wrists. He was hauled to his feet, ankles and wrists still manacled. Maybe he was not going to be killed, not right away at least. Now he could think about how to rescue Kate.

With the huge monk – and his Arabian Nights scimitar – still hovering, Roger glanced around. So, this was his prison. He had to observe carefully. There might, even now, be a way out of this.

More lights went on, big floodlights mounted on metal towers. In a flash, they illuminated a vast space. Roger took a deep breath. What was this place? It looked like an immense cavern, the size, Roger reckoned, of a football field – or maybe even bigger, much bigger. The walls soared up, almost out of sight, and were of stone, possibly granite; they were ultra-smooth, sparkling with mica. The cavern looked like it had been carved out of solid rock.

Roger glanced upwards. The roof was far above, lost in shadows, and appeared to be sharply vaulted, like the soaring, pointed ceiling of a gothic cathedral. Lining the walls were arches of stone that rose up and disappeared into darkness. Who had created this place – and why?

Then, when he glanced behind the Cardinal, he saw it. Dominating the whole cavern was something the likes of which Roger had never seen. It was a huge glass-like sphere, a giant disco ball, perhaps six stories high. Millions of facets sparkled, as if it were a colossal diamond. It seemed to be floating – yes, floating – in a dense framework of dark metal that soared up around it. Metal staircases, zigzagging upwards, festooned the lattice-like cradle. They looked like old-fashioned fire escapes on a tenement building. There were a few platforms, at various levels. One platform, a little less than halfway up the sphere, was larger than the others. It was, perhaps, some sort of control center. There seemed to be a sort of vertical instruments panel, possibly attached to the face of the sphere.

To the right of the glittering luminous sphere was a vast dark open space, set up slightly above the floor of the cavern, like a stage or platform. It plunged into the depths, seeming to go on forever, perhaps behind the sphere, extending back until one could see nothing, only darkness.

Construction scaffolding had been erected on the floor of the cavern, and, glancing back, Roger saw the elevator that – if he remembered correctly – it was all a bit fuzzy – had brought him down into the cave; it was an open, construction-type elevator and it was attached to what looked like a rock face, with a sort of stone ledge at the top. Next to the elevator, there was also what looked like a wall of sheer stainless steel built into the rock face – it appeared to be very advanced, ultra-modern, and there was a doorway at the bottom – maybe another elevator? But this one was built into the structure of the cavern and was probably part of the original design.

Floodlights on stands had been set up around the cavern, and old-fashioned gas-powered generators were chugging away. Cables snaked along the cavern floor and wound up the dark metal grid where the huge globe of crystal was floating. The whole thing looked like a film set.

Roger turned to the Cardinal and nodded toward the shimmering globe. "What in the world *is* that?"

"It is a thing of beauty. It is the Dark Force made manifest!" The Cardinal gazed up at the sparkling sphere. "It is Satan incarnate!"

Roger stared. The old man was insane. Father O'Bryan would say the man was possessed. Maybe the good Father was right. Maybe there were such things as demons. Roger was beginning to think that anything was possible. Physically, the Cardinal was merely a withered, yellowed, waxen, old human being with a wide bright smile that made him look like he was wearing ill-fitting, oversized, off-the-shelf dentures – the brightness of the man's grin emphasized his decrepitude.

Standing around them were five of the monstrous monks. They looked like twins, cut from the same cloth. Their baby-like features were crowded down into the bottom of their faces and they had large putty-like hands. They were tall – over six-foot-five, Roger calculated, except for one, the executioner, who loomed over the others. He was seven feet tall, at least.

"What are you doing here, Cardinal?"

The Cardinal smiled; his yellow eyes gleamed.

"What are you *really* doing here, Cardinal?"

The Cardinal covered his mouth, tittered, and looked down, suddenly bashful. "My nuptials are about to be celebrated!"

"Nuptials?"

"I am getting married."

"Well, I suppose congratulations are in order."

"Yes, I am the bride." The Cardinal grinned. His lips curled up in a diabolic, clownish smile, stretching his ancient, yellowed, parchment skin into a mask-like grimace, an icon of madness. Roger swallowed. The man must be at least 100 years old. And totally deranged. "And you, Professor, are my witness! My bridesmaid!"

"Bridesmaid. Well, that is truly an honor, Cardinal." Roger looked down at the singed, burnt, blood-splattered rags – tattered boxer shorts – that were all that remained of his elegant attire. "I'm not sure I'm dressed for such an occasion."

"Oh, worry not your pretty little head about that, Professor, you will do quite nicely, just as you are! You see, pilgrims and saints often go in rags. And this wedding will be a truly spiritual ceremony. Your penitential garb is perfectly appropriate. Vanity and outward trappings are but flimsy illusions. My bridegroom you see, and he is my love, is the Evil Force, Satan Himself, the Prince of Evil and Darkness."

"Satan? Well, quite an honor, I'm sure."

"Indeed, it is! During the ceremony I shall be swept up into my darling's arms. I shall transcend all things human, I shall merge with Satan himself, it will be pure ecstasy."

"Ecstasy, Cardinal? What sort of ecstasy?"

"Well, that is the beautiful thing, Professor. It will be the ecstasy of destruction – of utter final obliteration. And you are my witness, my most privileged companion."

"What is being destroyed, Cardinal, what is the sacrifice?"

"The world, my dear Professor Thornhill, this planet that we call Earth. That is the sacrifice! You will bear witness to the end of the world, Professor. You are one of the few who can truly understand what will happen and truly bear witness to it. That is why I need you!"

"So, your Eminence, if your wedding signifies the end of the world, how exactly will this occur?" Roger's voice tightened. Frightful thought: There might be something serious behind the old man's madness.

"You see the glorious crystalline orb suspended above us? – the *Crystal* as I call her – she is such a sweet, obedient thing."

"Yes, I see her."

"Well, she, and she is most definitely female, she is an obedient emissary of Satan, a dark angel sent to usher in the final hour. She will bring about the end of the world and unite me with Evil."

"How?"

"She will destroy the veil of mere appearance."

"I see, but how will she do that?"

"Earthquakes, dear Professor. She will bring about earthquakes and tidal waves and tsunamis and super-volcanoes and superstorms and all sorts of delightful satanic mayhem. All of this is foretold in the Book of Revelations! It will be the Apocalypse and Revelation that we have all so eagerly waited for."

Roger glanced at the giant gently shimmering sphere, and he murmured, half to himself. "But *how* could it do that?"

"The Crystal can bestow wonderful powers – I myself have felt some of her transformative influence."

"Wonderful powers?" Roger shifted uneasily. His wrists, tightly hand-cuffed behind his back, were chafing. He was losing circulation in his fingers. He closed and opened them. The ankle manacles clinked if he made the slightest move. The monk holding the scimitar turned his heavy head and stared. His eyes were hidden in folds of fat and shielded by the shadow of his hood. Roger blinked. No, he would not let these maniacs see he was terrified.

"Yes, she has granted me satanic powers – very invigorating for a man of my age!"

Roger kept his gaze steady. The Cardinal was as mad as a hatter: No machine could destroy the Earth, not unless the Crystal was an immense bomb, some sort of …

The Cardinal licked his lips. A fleck of white saliva stuck to his lower lip. "My flesh no longer defines what I am!"

"I see. That is truly wonderful, Cardinal!" Roger opened and closed his fingers; feeling was returning, a burning, throbbing sensation.

"Yes, it is, it truly is. I have become, Professor, well, I believe the term is a 'shape-changer.' And I can work miracles."

"I see." Roger nodded. Mumbo jumbo was for children. Shape-changers belonged in horror movies or fairy tales. As for miracles, well, they belonged in fairy tales too, or outdated religions and myths. "You mentioned earthquakes, Cardinal. Are you suggesting that this thing, the Crystal, caused the wave of earth tremors a few days ago?"

"It most certainly did."

"That is … incredible!" Roger frowned. Could it be possible? What sort of device could cause earthquakes at a distance? If such a thing *were* possible, then he'd have to revise the very foundations of his theories. That was horrendous. That Frenchman Marcel Pochon would uncork a bottle of champagne! What an awful thought!

The Cardinal gestured toward the chugging motors. "We tried a number of tests – little jolts of electricity from our generators here. And each time, with a time lag, there have been tremors somewhere in the world."

"Extra seismic activity all around the world?"

"Yes."

Roger swallowed. This was appalling. If true, it might mean that the Crystal had manipulated the gravitational field. Roger had won his Nobel Prize for demonstrating – he thought definitively – that the gravitational field could not be manipulated, not on a large scale, not without the presence of a corresponding mass; after all, gravity was an aspect of the basic space-time matrix, and … Roger scowled. He would have to prove that such manipulation was not the case; or else, he might have to change his mind. Kate had suggested that maybe, just maybe, there might be a flaw in Daddy's theory … *Oh, God – Kate!*

"My dear Professor, I want you to examine the power of the Dark Force, incarnated here in the Crystal. I want you to bear witness to the end of the world, the Revelation and the Apocalypse!"

"Of course." Roger nodded. His mind was racing. If any of this was true, he would be forced to rewrite his last book. He would have to publish a retraction in *Nature*. The Nobel Committee would be miffed. The Royal Society would raise an eyebrow. His next meetings at CERN would be awkward. And the Pentagon! Well, the Pentagon would be tempted, if such a thing were possible, to exploit this object, this *Crystal*; it would be a weapon of infinite power. Hmm. Maybe Kate had been right, perhaps gravity could be played with. No, it was impossible. It didn't agree with his theories or his observations. He didn't believe it! He refused to believe it!

Kate … He must save Kate …

Roger glanced at the Crystal. He was beginning to think clearly. Questions were coming thick and fast.

If it truly could manipulate or control gravity, then the immense sphere floating peacefully, almost dreamily, in its latticework cradle was possibly the most powerful weapon ever designed; and if it could distort space-time, reconfigure the gravitational field, and redesign or reform fundamental sub-atomic structures, then …

Then it might travel through space-time … Then it was quite possibly not only a *world-destroyer*; but much more …

Who had designed and built this thing?

And why was it here?

Who had placed it here?

At first glance, floating in its framework as it seemed to be, it appeared to be far beyond anything humanity could have conceived or built!

"Cardinal," he said, "I need my computer to do any work on this – and I need to know that Kate is safe."

"Kate is certainly safe, Professor. You will talk to her later."

"No. I will talk to her now."

"Now?"

"Yes, now." Roger looked the Cardinal straight in the eye, holding the man's weirdly inhuman gaze.

"It shall be done, Professor. I shall arrange it. As for your computer, it is right here. We took your laptop from your hotel in Rome. We've downloaded the contents of your office computer in Stanford and the contents of the other desktop and mainframe in Cambridge with all the relevant data and programs, including from all your Cloud files and sites."

Christ! Roger was about to swear but didn't. "Does the Pope know what you are doing?" Roger had met the new Pope – before he became Pope – and was impressed by the man. Father O'Bryan, Roger knew, was close to the Pope.

"The Pope?" Cardinal Ambrosiano snorted. "That superstitious old dolt! No, he has no idea! What we are doing is utterly beyond his comprehension! What we are doing is beyond the mind of Man!" Again, that ghastly cadaverous grin. The teeth shone, glistening yellow fangs. The Cardinal lifted his arms, embracing the whole cavern, the whole universe. "The Pope will soon be merely a memory, not even that. Death, death comes so easily –"

"What do you mean?"

The Cardinal's mind flitted off in another direction. "My wedding will be the apotheosis, the end of human history! The single greatest event of all time! Greater than Napoleon when he crowned himself Emperor in Notre-Dame, greater than the Resurrection of Christ!"

Roger held his breath.

"But now, Professor, it is time for you to get to work. Let me show you your office!"

Roger's "office" was a steel cage set next to one of the stone arches that soared up the walls of the cavern, and close to the vast upraised platform that looked like an empty stage to the right of the Crystal.

The cage-office was supplied with computers, including Roger's laptop, a desk and a cot. Next to the cage was a portable toilet of the type used on construction sites.

Roger's ankles were chained to the steel chair, and his wrists were loosely manacled, just allowing him enough freedom to work the keyboard.

He had no access to outgoing communications. The computers were not connected to the Internet and they were monitored by some of the Cardinal's monks – hidden somewhere. Any connection to the Internet had to be physically set up and go through one of those weird monks. The material and programs Roger might need had already been downloaded.

Roger swore inwardly. He would stay cool. He had to, if he was going to save Kate, wherever she was.

Roger had been studying the calculations and the correlations of the electric shocks and seismic activity for about a half an hour when the Cardinal handed him a cell phone.

"Here is your daughter, Professor."

"Kate?"

"Daddy!"

CHAPTER 12 – HOSTAGE

"Okay, *basta, basta*: that's enough." The priest lifted the phone from Kate's hand.

"Thank you." Kate said. Remain icily civil, she told herself, remain icily polite.

The call lasted forty-five seconds. Just time enough to tell her father she was okay.

"We'll serve you breakfast in a few minutes," said the priest.

"Breakfast" in the man's mouth sounded like a threat – as if he were announcing an execution. The priest and the two monks left the room. Kate was alone. In the last twelve hours, she had come a long way.

The ride in the car had been torture. After Fabio stuffed her into the trunk, hogtied, the trunk was slammed shut. That was when she'd overheard someone say she was going to be a "sacrifice."

Sacrifice? Me? They can't be serious …

How long she'd lain in that hot, sweaty, stinky trunk, she didn't know, blinded and half-suffocated by the leather hood, strangled by the tight collar, her smashed glasses squished across her nose. Curled on her side, chained and manacled, wrists and ankles pinned together, she'd wiggled and squirmed. It was impossible to get comfortable. Her spine felt like it was going to crack. She focused on breathing – *slow and steady* – and on figuring out where the car was going.

The car backed out of the barn, turned around on what sounded like gravel. It accelerated, bouncing along a rugged, potholed road. Objects – tools, she supposed – shifted and rattled in the trunk. One of them, probably a tire jack, prodded her in the belly. It was metal and big, greasy and sharp.

After one last jolt, the ride was smoother. They must be on a highway. The car accelerated. It seemed to be new, smooth pavement, silky new asphalt, she imagined. She concentrated. Think about anything but the pain. There wasn't much traffic – it must be a local highway, not a superhighway. Silky new asphalt under the moonlight, in the mist – she forced herself to visualize the scene, peaceful, bucolic. Then the spooky thought returned:

A sacrifice – me!

What kind of sacrifice?

The car went uphill, slowed, turned, and accelerated again, easing, probably, into heavy traffic, to judge by the honking.

Then the ride was mostly smooth, but with bumps every few seconds; and then it was stop-and-go. Kate heard diesel engines, air-brakes, horns, engines idling. Probably they were on the ring road around Rome. She remembered, years ago, noticing the rhythmic thump, thump, thump of the breaks in the pavement, particularly where the ring road was elevated.

The car again entered onto a smoother surface, and there was less traffic. Hardly any traffic at all. *So, Sherlock Holmes, we've left the ring road. Now where are we going?*

The drive went on, and on, and on …

She tried to concentrate …

But blind, bound, half-suffocated, she was getting dizzy and nauseous. It was harder and harder to breathe … Her nose was running, clogging up her nostrils. If she threw up, she would drown in snot and vomit. *Don't panic: Do not panic, Kate! Do not panic!*

Avoid thinking about the last time! Above all, avoid thinking about the last time! But she couldn't help it; she couldn't help but think of it. The last time …

Four years ago … in Jerusalem.

Four years ago …

"The old city covers about a third of a square mile. It is home to …" Kate's mother, Laura, was reading from the guidebook; then she broke off to say: "Hey, Kate, Peter, look at how beautiful the light is on the tower!" Laura pointed at the huge square tower built by King Herod two thousand years ago. "It's really spectacular!"

In the morning sun the tower glowed like gold.

"Awesome," said Peter Ryland, Kate's boyfriend – not quite fiancé, not yet, but probably soon.

"There's the Museum of the History of Jerusalem inside the tower. I'm not sure when it's open." Kate was peering into her own guidebook; she noticed that a shoelace was undone, one end trailing on the pavement. Damn! She really hated shoelaces!

She knelt to tie it.

"I don't know if we have time for the museum," Laura was saying. "Roger's meetings should be over by 12:30 and –"

WHAM! WHAM! WHAM!

The square exploded in machine-gun fire; bullets splattered and ricocheted. Three bullets tore into Peter; they must have killed him instantly, one ripped off half his face. He fell straight onto the paving stones, a few feet from Kate, half of his face stared at her out of its one blue eye.

Two bullets hit Kate's mother, one in the chest, one in the stomach.

She fell next to Kate, reaching out one arm to break her fall.

Kate was down on one knee, tightening the shoelace, only beginning to register what was happening. The noise was deafening; Peter's blood and that of a Japanese tourist sprayed all over her.

WHAM!

A bomb blast. Glass, rusty nails, ball bearings, shrapnel, bits of brick and stone flew everywhere. Kate, beginning to stand up, felt a thud as if she'd been punched in the back. Pain seared up her spine, under her shoulder blades – fragments of glass and metal spun by; one cut deep into her side. In fact, though she didn't know it, a ball-bearing and two rusty razor blades – used as shrapnel – had cut into her back, missing her spine by a hair, one U-shaped piece of metal wrapped itself around the vertebrae, almost cutting the spinal cord.

"Mother," Kate gasped. She realized, as she spoke, that she was falling. It happened in slow motion. She was sprawled on the ground, the cobblestones hot, hard, whamming against her cheek, her face turned toward her mother.

"Kate!" Her mother's blood was running between the cobblestones. Laura's mouth was half open – the small gap between her two front teeth suddenly seemed black and enormous; it drew Kate in, a vortex, a spiral.

Sirens and shots. Police running everywhere. Kate struggled to her knees and knelt next to her mother, and she glanced at Peter. Half his skull was gone.

"Kate …"

"Mummy, hold on!"

Bubbles of blood, lacy foam dribbled from her mother's mouth.

The light faded from Laura's eyes. Those eyes were crystal blue, oh so blue, and the way they looked at you – generous, infinitely giving, focused, all for you, just for you … Mother like a sister, like a best friend, like a sweet judge and counsellor … Now, she was dead.

And Peter …

Peter Ryland – so optimistic, so full of fun, so funny, so strong … an Olympic ranked swimmer …

His one eye stared at her, the rest of his face a mass of red and white, clotted flesh, blood, raw bone … teeth …

A crumpled silver tin can, Coca-Cola, bounced down next to his ruined skull, bounced again, and rolled away, over the cobblestones. The young Japanese tourist lay face up, eyes staring, half her torso gone.

A deafening roar, echoing.

Smoke, bodies, blood, everywhere – no help anywhere.

Kate stood, alone, in the middle of swirling smoke and screams, a roaring sound, in her ears, like a hurricane … Which way to turn? What to do?

She fell to her knees. Pain shot up her back, lightning bolts through her arms. Everything whirled into slow motion, unreal, a nightmare; everything went silent. No sound at all. Was she deaf?

Medics leaned over her mother; then they were kneeling over her. They lifted her up, laying her on a stretcher. "I don't want to be on a stretcher! I'm okay!" She could hear her voice, echoing, hollow, coming from far away. She tried to lift her arm. She couldn't. Her lips were numb, her tongue useless.

She was strapped down, hooked to a drip, in an ambulance. It crawled through traffic, siren wailing.

The medic sitting next to her had deep brown eyes; Hebrew letters on the armband. "You've lost a lot of blood. You just don't know it."

Kate bit her lip. She wanted to scream.

This can't be happening! I want my mother! I want the clock to turn back; I want to go back to breakfast this morning, I want to make everything different.

She was back at the breakfast table in the hotel, buttering her toast, smoothing orange marmalade on the crispy surface, she was saying … if only she had said, "Okay, let's skip the tour, let's just stay in the hotel," or "Let's follow Dad around on his appointments," or …

Kate faded into blackness, silky forgiving blackness.

Kate was the only one in that small square who survived. It echoed with gunfire and explosions for forty-two seconds. As they later explained, she survived because she noticed the untied shoelace. She was kneeling just below the line of fire when the machine-guns opened up.

If you survive, you feel guilty. It's a well-known fact. Some survivors commit suicide. Even many years, even decades, afterwards. The guilt never goes away, not really, not really away.

Later, in one of the hospitals, they were playing an old song, in some other room, and Kate caught some of the lyrics, something about picking yourself up and dusting yourself off.

Okay, she thought, okay – that was what she would do; death would have no dominion. Then she thought of her mother and Peter; and she lived it all over again, and again, and again.

If only we had stayed at the hotel, if only we'd ...

Curled up, manacled, hogtied, aching all over, locked in the stuffy, jam-packed car trunk, under the clammy suffocating leather hood, Kate began to cry.

Then, darkness ...

What? she woke up and shook herself.

How much time had passed? Two hours, maybe three, maybe four? She must have passed out, or gone to sleep ...

The car was going uphill, a steep climb. She slid toward the rear of the trunk. The greasy jack or whatever it was pressed against her again, a sharp edge digging into her shoulder.

The car stopped. She waited, controlling her breathing.

Someone opened the trunk.

"Lift this thing out!" It was a rough voice, speaking in Italian.

Fabio's voice, in Italian, protesting. "It's not a thing – it's a woman, for Christ's sake!"

The chain linking the ankle and wrist shackles was suddenly released. Giant pudgy fingers grabbed her and lifted her out of the trunk. She could straighten her back! She wanted to scream, the relief was so great.

Huge arms lowered her to the ground, her bare feet touched down on cool damp pebbles. Dew! It must be dew. So, it must still be night. It smelled – even through the hood – it smelled like trees, damp trees, at night. *Mountain country?* Her ankles and wrists were still shackled, pinioned, locked tight together. She barely managed – wavering slightly – not to fall. Under the hood her face was soaked – sweat, dribbling snot, saliva ...

"So, there she is – in good shape, as requested," Fabio said.

His voice was cut off by a shot.

"*Che cazzo …?* What the fuck …?" Another voice, also cut short. But not by a shot – a gurgling, a scuffle, then a sigh and a cough.

"Get rid of the bodies. And get rid of their car too."

Kate stood still, frozen, shocked, trembling, imprisoned in darkness. Were her kidnappers, Fabio and the other killer, dead? Is that what just happened? It must be! What the hell was going on?

"Take her inside!"

The big clumsy pudgy fingers fumbled with the ankle shackles and handcuffs. They were unlocked and pulled away. Kate sighed. Finally! She adjusted her stance, legs slightly apart, naked toes gripping the pebbled gravel. She wiggled her shoulders and rubbed her wrists.

She was going to kill Fabio herself. Now she suspected she might miss the guy – he seemed human, at least. She was not so sure about these new creatures, whatever they were.

Sacrifice, the word came back, *she was to be a sacrifice …*

Fabio had objected. Now, Fabio was dead.

Therefore …

The pudgy fingers closed on her arm. "Walk!" the voice spoke in English, with an accent, not Italian; maybe German. It was a deep voice, cavernous, and very, very creepy.

"Walk!" The creature prodded her. Kate took a step forward, then another – she walked.

She walked. The soles of her feet, her toes, guided her. The pebbles became flagstones, rough surfaces, a rustic style, uneven, coated with slippery cool dew. Maybe it was the dawn of a beautiful day.

"There's a step!"

Yes, she thought, the voice, speaking English, was German. She stepped up, calculating the probable height of the step. She must not fall, she must not stub her toes. Careful now, careful! So, this was what it was like to be blind. The air wafted, cool, almost chilly, against her skin.

After the flagstones, came stone steps, to be navigated carefully. Blind, she was at the mercy of whoever was guiding her. She bit her lip. Hold yourself erect, don't tremble, don't cower; hold onto your dignity.

Now, it was a ceramic tile floor, cool and smooth, dry and waxed. Going barefoot certainly helped her figure out where she was, or at least what she was walking on. The sounds changed. Even through the hood she sensed it.

They were more resonant, more contained. She was inside a building.

"Keep walking!" The hand squeezed her elbow, pushed her forward. The arm was in some sort of heavy rough textured, loose sleeve – a monk's habit? A hand pressed against the small of her back.

"Ahead! Straight!" The voice was rough, deep, but there was something childlike, infantile, about it.

Kate obeyed. They were walking down a long wide corridor – at least that was the sense she got through the quality of sound; and, even under the hood, she smelled floor wax and flowers.

Two giant hands seized her shoulders and swung her around, a quarter turn, and pushed her ahead; she sensed they were going through a narrow door; they were entering a room, a small room; the sounds were sharper, harder. The hands guided her to what seemed to be a straight-backed metal chair. She closed her fingers around curved, cool metal – the back of a chair. A metal garden chair?

"Sit!"

She felt her way, turned around, and sat. Cool, hard metal. Her legs and thighs damp, naked.

"Take off her hood." It was new voice, a normal voice, a man, speaking in cultivated Italian, not street argot, not dialect.

The thick fingers fumbled with the collar of her hood. A click. The collar opened, freeing her neck. The hood was unzipped and lifted off.

Kate blinked at the sudden light. She could breathe. Her face was dripping sweat. Suddenly, her skin felt icy. With the back of her hand, she wiped at her nose – sweat, snot, saliva. Yuk!

Everything was a sticky blur, her glasses were cracked and smeared with Mario's blood, but not completely shattered. She began to distinguish things; it wasn't perfect, but she could see.

The room was small, cell-like, with white chalk walls, thick bars on a window that was too high up to look through or even reach, a fold-out cot in one corner, a highly polished burnt sienna tile floor. Leaning over her was an enormous man in a monk's cowl and robe.

She looked up and almost started back. His baby-like features were all crowded down into the bottom of his face. His tiny mouth, with its wet pink lips twisting nervously, didn't seem to belong to his face; the lips looked like two worms – two wet, pink, fat, wiggling earthworms.

The giant moved aside and there, opposite Kate, sitting on another white metal chair, was a man dressed in black, very elegant, with a priest's dog collar, a neat salt-and-pepper beard.

"You're a priest?" Kate asked, in English.

"Yes. My name is Father Ottavio."

"What is going on? Why am I here? Where is my father?"

"Your father is on a special mission."

"Mission?"

"And you are here with us to make sure he carries it out."

Kate struggled to keep her voice level. She wanted to scream like a banshee, jump up, and rip the man's face off. She took a deep breath, and kept her voice calm and matter-of-fact. "Who are you? You kidnap us. You kill people. You killed our friends! And you're talking about a mission? And you say you are a priest!"

"You will talk to your father tomorrow."

"Tomorrow!"

"Yes, tomorrow."

"Tomorrow is too late. I want to talk to him now."

"Perhaps. We shall see." The priest stared at her.

"Perhaps is not good enough!"

"You are a willful creature, much too stubborn." The priest sighed. "We shall see. Right now, you will shower and get some sleep. And you will eat. You will need your strength. Then, perhaps you will speak to your father."

"Shower? Where do I shower?"

"There is a shower behind you. We will provide fresh clothes. You need fresh clothes."

Kate looked down. Her jacket was partly burnt, covered in blood – *from Mario?* And her shirt and skirt were torn to flimsy tatters. "I see what you mean."

The shower was in a small cubicle of varnished white ceramic tile. The floor, ceiling, walls – all were made of the same shiny, slippery material. There was a large towel rack with towels. The water was hot and abundant, and lots of perfumed soap, a large sponge, and a prickly scrub brush were laid out on a little metal shelf.

Kate showered, she untied her hair and shampooed. Her hair, she realized, was caked in blood, thick with gore.

She scrubbed and showered and scrubbed and showered. Then she tied her hair – still wet – up in the severe bun, as before; it was part of her identity, part of her armor. She placed her now-scrubbed glasses – even though they were badly cracked – carefully back on her nose. The glasses were part of her mask too; with her glasses on, she was not naked.

When she came out of the shower, wrapped in a large white towel, her clothes were gone. Lying folded on the cot was a flimsy white gown, one of those humiliating, skimpy, open-backed, hospital gowns that tie up, more or less, at the back, but really leave you almost as naked as Eve in Paradise.

She lifted it up. There was nothing else – no underwear – just the paper-thin hospital gown. The towel was better than that! What did these maniacs want from her father, what did they want with her?

Wrapped in the towel she went to the door, tried to open it.

It opened easily.

Two of the monks stood on the other side of the corridor, opposite the door. They looked like identical twins. Both were well over six feet tall, with the same baby-like features, wet pink lips, and eyes she could barely glimpse, buried in folds of fat. It was unnerving. Were they looking at her or not? Both appeared immensely strong, with pale bulging hands, enormously thick fingers with ghostly pale fingernails. They made no sign they had noticed her. She decided to stick to English; there was no need to reveal she understood Italian and German.

"Where are my clothes?"

There was no answer.

"Where are my clothes?"

No answer.

She glanced up and down the corridor. It was wide, with a high, airy, groin-vaulted white ceiling, white stucco walls and a floor of brightly polished burnt sienna tiles. Several pieces of massive antique mahogany furniture – high-quality antiques, it looked like – lined the walls, and from the ceiling hung huge chandelier-like lamps of wrought iron; the style was rustic and Hispanic-looking. Farther down, the corridor opened onto tropical shrubbery, palm fronds and ferns – probably an inner courtyard. All along the corridor were giant brightly decorated ceramic vases overflowing with brilliant red flowers … a fortune in flowers. Everything sparkled and was spotless. The place reeked of money.

Where in the world am I?

Should she make a run for it, a quick sprint down the corridor? No, it would serve no purpose. They would catch her and, even with her martial arts training, she wouldn't be a match for those monks. She would wait, and watch, and then, when the moment came, she'd make her move.

A nun appeared, wheeling a metal trolley with what looked like a meal on it. The nun was a giant too, and, like the monks, she had small squished-up baby features at the bottom of her face. Her eyes were visible, barely – and, as she approached, Kate saw that the nun's eyes were a lifeless, mottled, snot-green.

The nun rolled the trolley up to Kate. Then she went away and came back with a small metal table. She carried the table past Kate and put it in the room. Kate turned around to watch. The nun set the meal on the small metal table, pulled the metal chair up to the table, and took the lid off the meal.

Kate's mouth was watering.

She was starving. Hadn't even thought of food up to now!

The nun pulled up the other chair and sat down. She pointed at the meal. Kate wondered if the woman was mute.

Kate pointed to herself – *this is idiotic; but maybe I can start communicating* – shrugged, and mimed eating.

The nun nodded. *Yes, it's yours to eat.*

Leaving the door open, Kate went in and sat down.

She hesitated. Was the food poisoned or drugged? It looked delicious.

She breathed in the smells of fresh steaming hot veal, mashed potatoes, and broccoli. They must have a good chef, whoever ran the show – there was a lot of money involved, that was clear.

Why would they poison her or drug her? She was a hostage, or so it seemed, a hostage to guarantee that her father did whatever they wanted him to do – and what could that be? What if he couldn't do it because it was something horrible, something that would kill a great many people …? Well, she couldn't think about that, no, she couldn't think about that.

The meat had been pre-cut and all she had to eat with was a plastic spoon. No weapon to kill with or commit suicide with. Hmm!

She picked up the spoon and glanced up.

"*Guten Appetit!*" said the nun. The tiny mouth twitched, the little worm-like lips squirmed and danced, but the expression on the rest of her face remained unchanged, impassive. Her voice had the high-pitched sing-song quality of a four-year-old child.

Kate didn't flinch, didn't reveal she understood the German – she was fluent – and didn't reveal she was surprised by the voice. She held the nun's gaze – staring into the green expressionless eyes buried deep in those folds of white fat. Then she began to eat.

CHAPTER 13 – PICCIOTTI

"What the fuck do we do now?" Santino wiped his forehead. He and U Pizzu were staring at a manhole that led down into the moldy dank labyrinth of the sewers of Ancient Rome.

U Pizzu smoothed the lapel of his jacket. The meeting at the Vatican had been helpful. They had learned that the last signal from Franco's cell phone had come from right here, at the corner of via della Conciliazione and via Grazia. With a little encouragement from the Vatican, the cell phone company had been very obliging in tracing locations.

"This is the last fucking trace. That's all we know." U Pizzu bit his lip. Franco and Paolo were young, but they were good. They had never fucked up before. And now they go and disappear – poof!

Father Andrea had told U Pizzu that Franco and Paolo's target, a Father Michael Patrick O'Bryan, knew the tunnels and sewers of Rome by heart. "When he was studying for the priesthood, Father O'Bryan earned pocket money guiding tourists down into the sewers and catacombs. So ..." Father Andrea had shrugged and spread his arms in a gesture of resignation.

"So, if Father O'Bryan got into the sewers, how and where would he have gotten into them? Who can guide us to the right spot?" U Pizzu had asked.

"I have just the person," said Father Andrea.

"And who is that?"

"She's a historian of Roman architecture, of the city; author of a number of books on Rome. Nobody knows the city like she does," said Father Andrea. "But I warn you; she is not privy to any of our little secrets; and she is not even Catholic. I rather suspect she is atheist – or agnostic. One of the old secular, liberal Italian families, from the north originally. They rather dislike the Church, I'm afraid. She is useful, but not to be trusted."

Caterina De Sanctis, to all appearances an aristocratic Roman, though originally from Lombardy, might be an atheist, but if she was, she was a very attractive atheist, thought U Pizzu. Might even get him to convert to godless! She was probably in her forties, he figured, and she was a snob, that was clear, and an intellectual, with her crisp diction, choice vocabulary, impeccable syntax, tight pulled-back, ballerina-type, jet-black hair, arched black eyebrows, fine-boned features, dancer's body, and rich person's tan. Centuries of fucking breeding, and centuries of fucking money! But she knew her stuff. At almost precisely the spot where the cell phone signal had ceased, she explained, there was a secret entry to a little-known branch of the ancient sewer system.

"Very few people suspect it exists," she said, pushing open a door, leading them into a marble-paved corridor, and pointing to an ornate, grille-like, brass manhole cover that was located in an alcove just off the corridor. "This is the entry. Most people think it is just decorative; but it isn't."

U Pizzu pulled up his trousers, being careful with the crease, crouched, and lifted the manhole grille; it came up easily. Leaning forward, he peered into the hole. Metal rungs led downward – he could see damp stone walls, cool shadowy air; then it faded into darkness.

Caterina De Sanctis was standing next to him, with her high-heeled highly polished black leather shoes, her impeccable dark silk stockings. "Father Andrea told me the signal ceased about two hundred yards from here, in that direction. The main tunnel runs precisely that way. I would guess that your friend's phone was underground."

"Thanks," said U Pizzu.

"You're welcome," she said. "You have my number – my office is right over there, just off via della Conciliazione. If this doesn't work, call or text me. Father Andrea said to offer you every assistance possible. You have my mobile number too, so don't hesitate."

U Pizzu stood up, went to the doorway, and watched the woman walk down the street, an elegant dark silhouette in the blinding sunlight. There was something deeply satisfying, philosophically fulfilling, about the idea of fucking an upper-class woman like that, a classy, proud aristocratic Northern Italian woman, even if she had adopted Rome as her residence. Yes, atheist or not, it would be a pleasure, getting her naked, taking her by force if necessary, but then making her howl with pleasure, like a wild animal. Enslave her! Make her beg for more! Fantasy, of course, pure fantasy! But it would be symbolic revenge – redemption for centuries of getting fucked – over and over and over – by the likes of her – by barons, counts, princes, Sultans, Vikings, Arabs, Frenchmen, Germans, Fascists, Christian Democrats, Communists, and politicians – and popes. Everybody and his uncle had fucked Sicily, since the beginning of time! Caterina De Sanctis disappeared around a corner; she hadn't looked back.

"So, what do we do now?" Santino's forehead glowed with beads of sweat.

"We go down there." U Pizzu nodded at the manhole.

"We really gotta go down there? I don't like it. I get claustrophobic."

"Claustrophobic, huh? Well, Santino, the way you overcome your fears is you face up to them." U Pizzu removed his dark Polaroids and peered down into the cool dank darkness. "If you fall off a horse, you get back in the saddle. If you almost drown, you go back out for a swim. If you meet a moray eel in a cave underwater, you swim back into that fucking cave and tell the moray eel to go fuck itself. If you get burned, you stick your hand back in the fire. We definitely gotta go down into the sewer."

"Shit," said Santino.

U Pizzu and Santino climbed down the greasy iron rungs and found themselves in the giant ancient sewer twenty feet below street level.

U Pizzu shone the flashlight. "Whole fucking world down here!"

"Yeah, whole fucking world down here." Santino was staring at graffiti scrawled in scarlet and yellow on the walls. *Giulia loves Tommaso, Luciano is a fucking imbecile. Enrico must die!* There were spray-paint phalluses or stylized pricks too, big tall ones, man size, and a couple of efforts at what looked like scary oversized vaginas. Some of them had teeth, no, more like fangs, big ones.

"Fucking sewage …" U Pizzu grimaced. Underfoot a rivulet of water, running between the paving stones, gave off a strange sea-like smell, a smell of ozone and oysters, not unpleasant.

"Mostly just drain-off," said Santino, "not turds, shit like that."

"Yeah, yeah," said U Pizzu, frowning. Sometimes the boy did use his noggin, should have been a civil engineer, the Einstein of Sewage, the Edison of Turd Disposal, a Ph.D. in Shit.

U Pizzu shone the flashlight down the tunnel. The beam lit up walls, pipes, and cables, and then faded into smoky darkness. "Okay, so if this priest comes down here, he'd go that way. Right? Down where she said the last signal came from. She said this way. Right?"

"Right!" Santino shrugged; U Pizzu liked to do all the thinking.

"Okay, let's go."

They started walking down the tunnel, trying to avoid the runoff. U Pizzu was fucking well not going to get his Ferragamo loafers wet. It was spooky, but at least it was cooler than up there in the blazing midsummer sun. U Pizzu felt little ripples of chilly air play ticklish, prickly games on his skin.

After four minutes cautiously advancing along the tunnel – and about two hundred yards from the manhole – they found Franco and Paolo – or what was left of them – bits and pieces all over the place, even on the roof.

U Pizzu glanced at his cell phone. No signal. He figured they'd better take photographs – proof of what happened – and get the hell out of the place. It stank like a slaughterhouse.

"What do you think, eh?"

U Pizzu clutched a mauve handkerchief to his nose. "What I think is I'm gonna fucking throw up."

Santino bent down to study something that looked like a thick piece of cable, a giant sausage. It was a bloated intestine.

"There's an arm over here." U Pizzu crouched down and shone the flashlight. "It's Franco's left arm, I think. Yeah, there's the Rolex. It's still ticking."

"What the fuck did this?"

"I don't want to meet it, whatever it is." U Pizzu shone the light up and down the tunnel. There was nothing out there. The beams made a smoky whiteness and then were lost in darkness. Streams of water dripped from above. He shone the beam up and down the walls. More bits and pieces of the two killers were splattered, gobs, here and there. The ammunition belts lay on the floor of the tunnel, the guns too … There were splashes of blood on the roof.

Santino crouched and took pictures.

U Pizzu closed his eyes. How many people had he killed – one hundred, two hundred? You lose track after a time. He'd shot them, garroted them with piano wire, slit their throats with straight-razors, beat one to death with a baseball bat, hacked one kid's arm off – the kid was fourteen years old and still alive, son of a turncoat who'd squealed on the clan. U Pizzu had used a machete on the kid, three blows before he'd sliced right through – the fucking blade was dull – and then, after a little chitchat, he'd strangled the kid, slowly, blood spurting all over the place. Charming boy, too, pretty, almost too pretty. It was a fucking mess, but he'd enjoyed it: the shot of adrenaline you get from taking a life, from having somebody absolutely in your power.

He grilled most of the bodies on his special barbecue, down in an abandoned sulfur mine, and then dissolved what was left in vats of acid. Did it all himself too! Proud of the craftsmanship. So, nobody could say he was a fucking sissy. But this, this was not natural, no, this was not natural. He wiped the back of his hand across his forehead. "I've never seen anything like this. Looks like the bodies were exploded."

"Yeah." Santino crouched over Franco's arm. The Rolex was still ticking. "But it wasn't an explosion. No signs – no powder marks, no concussion marks." Santino eased the Rolex off the shattered wrist and wiped it on his pants.

"Yeah, and the way the pieces are scattered around – it couldn't be an explosion – otherwise, there'd be nothing at the center here." U Pizzu stood up. "Let's get the fuck out of here."

"Yeah." Santino slipped the Rolex into his pocket.

They walked back down the tunnel.

"It sure wasn't the priest," said U Pizzu.

"Maybe the thing got the priest too."

"The thing? You believe in monsters?"

"I don't believe in nothin'."

"Right!"

"Right!"

"But," U Pizzu stopped, took out a turquoise handkerchief, and blew his nose, "something was down here." He didn't want to think about it. The first thing he was going to do, up in the light of day, was get a hotel room and take a long hot shower, then a cold shower – with a nice cool glass of wine.

It was unsettling: two of their best young guys, Franco and Paolo, two guys who never fucked up. The job should have been a cinch, and yet … Maybe the priest consorted with demons. Somebody had said he was an exorcist and expert in witchcraft. Maybe the good Father had gone over to the dark side. You never knew with priests, a lot of them were weird, more than weird.

"I think, in fact, that I do want to meet whoever did this," said U Pizzu, wiping his forehead. "And I'm gonna do to them just what they did to Franco and Paolo."

CHAPTER 14 – DISCO BALL

It was cool in the vast cavern.

Damnation! Roger Thornhill – wearing only his shredded, blood-soiled, oil-stained boxer shorts – tapped his fingers – his fingernails were filthy, he noticed – on the desk. This was a disaster! He had analyzed the information the Cardinal had given him – records of the electric shocks applied to the Crystal, the intensity of each shock, the length of time each shock lasted. He had matched these elements to seismic records of the earthquakes of the last few days. The result was horrible: All his most brilliant theories might be wrong!

He hated to admit it. There was a clear, statistically strong relationship, with a time delay of up to four hours, sometimes shorter, sometimes longer, depending on the distance to the focal point of the earthquake, and depending on the amount of time the electric shock was applied. The electric shocks to the Crystal – tiny shocks really – were correlated with earth tremors and violent freaky weather patterns all over the planet.

This was humiliating. If the shocks to the Crystal did what they appeared to do, then his theory regarding the stability of the gravitational space-time matrix was wrong. Damnation! Moscow's Vladimir Salnikov would be dancing a jig! Maybe Marcel Pochon's question was a valid question, and Kate's intuition was right after all! This would require some deep, brave thinking! Damn it! And he could use a shower. He didn't mind being naked; but he hated being filthy.

If there was a machine that could change the nature of – or manipulate – gravitons, the fundamental particles that mediate or carry gravity, then it could twist space-time, and, if it could do that, it could also disintegrate any structure – like the planet Earth – that found itself in any targeted space-time nexus. Such a machine would be a destroyer of worlds.

So ...

What was the Crystal? Who put it here, and why? And if the Crystal were properly activated, not merely attacked with electric pinpricks, what could – or would – it do then?

"Well, Professor?" The Cardinal hovered over his shoulder.

Roger stared at the computer screen. "From a theoretical point of view, your Eminence, this is annoying."

"I thought you might feel that way."

"The electric shocks must cause the Crystal to act on the particles that carry the gravitational force, and twist or scatter them in some way. It distorts the gravitational field. The stronger the shock, the more extreme the effect. The Crystal acts on space-time, at a very basic level, giving it a torque, twisting it."

"You see, Professor, your theories were built on sand; you were arrogant! You were presumptuous."

"Yes, well, it seems you were right, Cardinal."

"Ah, my dear Professor, you are so modest, so coy, such a blushing wall-flower, you are truly a darling – worthy to be my bridesmaid!"

"I am truly honored." Roger glanced at the giant sphere, so beautiful, shimmering, floating in its matrix of metal. "If you really kick it into action, you may not be able to stop it."

"You mean, if I give it a high-level shock, a lengthy shock, it may not stop?"

"Yes. We don't know how powerful the effects would be or what would happen to any given geological or atmospheric structure."

"Ah, fascinating!" The Cardinal beamed and rocked back and forth on his heels. "You are suggesting that the Crystal might create storms as well – super-storms! How delicious!"

"I'm not sure I'd say *delicious*, Cardinal."

The Cardinal spun around in a – surprisingly graceful – pirouette and grinned. "Oh, but I would. Plagues shall descend from the skies! And hail-stones large as boulders! The waters well up as blood. Frogs and toads rain down from the clouds. Roiling putrescent blisters will boil up on the smooth-est of skin. Beauty is rendered hideous. And all manner of suffering shall spawn and pullulate!"

"Indeed."

"And you know what it says in Revelations?"

"I have a vague idea."

"Well, let me refresh your memory, Professor. 'Lo, there was a great earthquake; and the Sun became black as sackcloth of hair, and the Moon became as blood; and the stars of heaven fell unto the Earth … And the heavens departed; and every mountain and island were moved out of their places.' That, Professor, is what I foresee."

"It won't be very pleasant, I imagine, your Eminence, mountains and islands moving out of their places."

"Pleasantness is so small-minded, so petty, so milquetoast, so cowardly – a symptom of petty-bourgeois mediocrity, don't you think?"

"Perhaps." Roger narrowed his eyes. However difficult it was, he must remain courteous, even courtly. This crazy old buzzard was holding Kate prisoner somewhere. And he might also hold the fate of the world in his hands. "The Crystal may also be a sort of travel or transportation device. It may transcend – or bypass – the constraints of the space-time matrix. It may open a gateway to other worlds."

"Yes," the Cardinal covered his mouth, looked down, and tittered, like a bashful debutante about to make a confession. "I've been there."

"What?"

"The Crystal took me, briefly, from over there! That is the launch pad." The Cardinal pointed to the vast, elevated, stage-like space that began only a few feet away from Roger's cage. "I was transported, and it changed me – it gave me new powers – truly satanic powers! This wonderful machine, placed here by Satan himself, has made me into a shape-changer. It has unleashed my true satanic nature. I am multitudes, as I believe a great poet once said. I am not me; I am another! It has prepared me for my nuptial celebration when I will be united with Satan."

"I see." Roger suppressed a grimace.

"No, you do not see! Like others of your kind, you are blind; but that is of no consequence, Professor. What else have you discovered?"

"Well, if it twists the space-time matrix, then, as I suggested, it may travel through time as well – but this is, of course, pure speculation."

"Let's try a little experiment, shall we?"

"I wouldn't do that, Cardinal, it may …"

"But I will do it, Professor, I will do it!" The Cardinal turned to one of the monks. "Generator! Give our dear Crystal a little taste of power!"

The monk went over to the stairs that zigzagged up the latticework and climbed up the side of the Crystal. Then, standing on what seemed to be its control platform, about forty feet up the Crystal's face, he clamped one of the electric cables to the metal frame, so the end of the cable was pushed right against the Crystal.

"Don't do this." Roger winced, anticipating the Crystal's pain.

The generator roared. Sparks showered from the end of the cables that were touching the Crystal, cascading in a Niagara of light down the side of the great translucent globe.

"Now, Professor, we shall see some results."

"But we don't know what they will be."

"That is part of the fun, don't you think?"

"Fun?"

"You see, Professor, I have decided to see how far I can go." The Cardinal favored Roger with a jovial wink.

"How far is that?"

"As I told you, Professor, I am going to go to the end, to the absolute end – otherwise known as the Revelation and the Apocalypse."

"Yes, yes – the Revelation and the Apocalypse."

"Indeed, Professor. The end of time! That is where I am going to take you. This world is an illusion, a wispy insubstantial veil, shielding us from absolute truth – and from the delights of absolute evil, the direct presence of Satan. We shall rip the veil away and reveal the true Godhead – which is Satan."

"I see."

"Yes, Professor, now you finally begin to see!" The Cardinal rubbed his hands in childish glee.

A few seconds after the electric shock was applied, the Crystal began to hum; it rose slightly from the matrix of metal, and Roger saw that, yes, the matrix really *was* a cradle. The Crystal was not locked in. It could move – it could float. It was free. God only knew what it would do if it moved. It could disintegrate the world and leave nothing behind but molten rock and a far-flung asteroid belt.

This would mean the destruction of the Earth, and of humanity and all that it had ever done and ever stood for. It would be as if humans had never existed at all. Even in the cool air of the cavern and next to naked, Roger Thornhill was sweating. Fear? Yes, it must be fear.

CHAPTER 15 – CONFESSION

My Irish blood is stubborn.

We Irish resisted oppression and persecution for centuries; we have a solid backbone, and, truth be known, we love a good scrap; a barroom brawl is just the thing to invigorate the Gaelic spirit, stir the poet in one's soul, and make the blood race faster. If this female demon wanted a fight, I was ready for it!

She had asked for my help. But why should I help a handmaiden of Satan bring discredit upon the Church? Why should I help her destroy humanity's only hope of salvation? I crossed my arms and scowled.

"What I want to know," she said, staring at me with those incredible dark eyes, "is where they hold their ceremonies and who is who in the Order."

"I'm not sure I can help you."

"I'm sure you can, Father. You don't know what you know. There is an object I have to find – a sort of key …"

"The key! The key! What the devil is this key? And what sort of mumbo jumbo is this?"

"You see, Father, I have been very negligent. I lost the key – the key to the Crystal, and …"

"If I am to help you," I said, stalling for time, "I need to know more – of what you are, and who you are." I put away my scowl and favored her with my most genial, most dissembling, priestly smile. "You said you were going to confess. Well, now I am ready. I wish to hear your confession!"

We were sitting at a large table in what seemed to be a dining room. Here, too, thick curtains were drawn. There was not a trace of sunlight; and, though it was clearly a bright sunny day outside, only a table lamp lit up the room.

The demon had offered me a whiskey, my favorite, Bushmills. I must admit the tumbler cupped in my hands was warm and comforting.

I felt full of vigor, younger than I had felt in years. My shoes were polished, my trousers pressed, my jacket felt as if it had just come off the shelf. There were no bullet holes in the cloth, which I found quite mysterious. My wounds were gone. The limp was gone. The demon had definitely cured me – simply by the laying on of hands.

I had to keep reminding myself that I had been cured by the Devil. Indeed, perhaps she *was* the Devil himself.

As I have perhaps mentioned, Satan does incarnate from time to time in the form of a lesser demon, or even, occasionally, in the form of a human, and, thus disguised, he can wreak all order of mischief.

While sipping the demon's fine whiskey, I was struggling with feelings of horror and misgiving. I was in danger of ceding to her charms. With her seductive energy, her flagrant sexuality, she stood for everything I abhor, and yet, and yet …

I looked down at the whiskey, then up, straight at her. "For me, V, you are, I want to speak frankly – you are, quite sincerely, an abomination – something to be destroyed. But I confess I want to know about you – to really understand who and what you are."

"An abomination?" She raised an eyebrow.

"An abomination," I said. "You are a product of Satan, of Evil."

"Perhaps. I am certainly a murderer." She took a thoughtful sip. "But, aside from being an abomination, what am I, Father? It's a long story. One you'll have to take on faith. Shall I tell you?"

"Faith," I smiled perhaps with complacency, but I did smile. "Yes, let us try my faith!"

"Here goes, then! Father, you shall hear my full and true confessions." She narrowed her eyes and smiled at me as if tempting my disbelief. "First of all, I am, as I mentioned before, almost two thousand six hundred years old."

"Twenty-six hundred years old?!"

"Give or take a decade or two."

"Nonsense!"

She half closed her eyes, ignored my outburst and took a gentle sip of whiskey. She was an excessively precise and delicate creature, almost faery-like in her movements and gestures. Her eyes were far away. She was voyaging in the distant past.

"Twenty-six centuries ago …

And so it was that V began to tell me her story.

Twenty-six centuries ago ...

I remember my father and my mother and the city where I grew up. It was a port, on the Mediterranean, on the coast where Tunisia and Libya are now. This was almost six hundred years before Christ, in the time of the Phoenicians and the Greeks – they traded in copper, brass, tin, gold, iron, dyes, wine and olive oil.

At home we spoke a version of Aramaic – Phoenician. It was the language of Carthage, a Semitic language, and, incidentally, as I'm sure you know, Father, close to the language of Jesus of Nazareth and of sections of the Talmud. We also spoke Greek, which my father had learned and perfected in his travels. We Phoenicians were very close, ethnically, to the Jews of Israel, though we were a trading nation, on the coast, where Lebanon is now, and the Jews, mostly, lived inland, in the northern kingdom, Israel, and southern kingdom, Judah, and were farmers.

But we, in my city, lived in North Africa, in one of the cities of the Phoenician diaspora, far away from our Lebanese forefathers and original homeland. My father was rich, and wise, and a wonderful teller of tales, and my mother was beautiful and patient with her children – including me.

They called me their "gift from the gods." I didn't know what they meant, but I do know they spoiled me above all my brothers and sisters. It made me, I believe, somewhat headstrong and gave me a rather exalted idea of my own importance and talents.

And we had – or I had; she seemed to be there just for me – a black Nubian servant, Lalla. Her people lived in the valley of the Nile, south of Egypt, and she told me wondrous stories of the great river and of the mysterious and rich lands to the south; Lalla was slender, beautiful, and very intelligent; she loved jokes. She never left my side.

I was nineteen years old when war came. My father said the war was a foolishness – a result of the illusions of angry old men and of the braggadocio of stupid young men who wanted to challenge a nearby city's trading rights – and that we would lose the war they had brought upon us.

And so we did; we lost. Our armies were defeated. And, after a last battle on the plains just behind our city, enemy troops broke through the city gates. My father died, a messenger told us, in the fighting at the city wall. My two brothers and one sister, too, had been caught in the marketplace; one of the servants told me how they were cut down without mercy by our rampaging enemies. Our mother killed herself when she learned of their deaths. I had been ordered to stay home. So I was alone in our home, with the corpse of my mother, with some of the servants and with Lalla.

We could hear the fighting getting closer – shouts and screams. Then people were hammering on the large wooden gate and the servants were in a panic, on their knees, wailing, rending their clothes, tearing their hair.

Lalla alone was calm. She led me away from the servants' quarters and hurried me down into the crypt beneath our home. She said that if I were in danger, she had been told to perform a ceremony – a ritual – that would protect me from enemies, whoever they were. She had a mysterious-looking needle and a small vial of liquid and she pricked the needle into my arm and made me drink from another vial – a sweet-and-bitter liquid.

"Lalla ... I ... I feel strange ..." I fell into her arms.

I was numb, paralyzed – I was asleep, but not asleep.

"I love you, Lalla," I murmured; those were my last words; I could no longer speak.

Lalla lifted me in her arms and laid me on the stone catafalque that stood in the middle of the crypt; it was where my father told me his body was to be laid. He was sure, he said, that he would die before I did. And, alas, he was right, but not, I think, in the way he had hoped.

Lalla arranged my limbs, putting my legs straight together, my arms straight at my sides, creating a dignified, mortuary, mummy-like pose.

"For the enemy warriors, you will be dead," she whispered, caressing my forehead, and smoothing a few strands of hair. "And then, when they are gone, you will rise again – and begin a new life."

She leaned over the catafalque and kissed me on the lips.

Her kiss was warm and smooth and lusciously tempting, but, though I tried, I could not return it. Nor could I say a word. She gazed down at me and then she lifted a small semi-transparent vial to her lips and drank the contents; the torches flickered with a soft flapping sound. The silence bore in on me. Lalla's eyes rolled up, only the whites showing, and she slid down, slowly, her hand holding my hand. As she fell to the stone floor beside the catafalque, her hand, finally, slipped from mine. She was dead.

In the vaulted crypt, the torches were still burning, licking the walls, smoky, throwing ghostly shadows on the columns, on the vaulted ceiling, on the urns and frescoes.

I was dead, or so it seemed. My eyes were closed, yet I could see and hear everything. I was outside my body, invisible, standing next to my corpse, but I was inside my body, simmering and alert, under my closed eyelids.

No, I thought. I cannot be truly dead. I clearly heard the shouting from above and from outside – the screams, and the blood-curdling cries. I smelled the smoke, the seared flesh, the burst intestines, and – above all – the blood. Blood was being spilt – I felt it; I yearned for it, my tongue thirsted for it. Clearly, as if I could see it, I heard the looting – vases being smashed, tables overturned, jars thrown against walls, chairs torn apart and piled up for firewood, curtains and tapestries being torn down and ripped to shreds. There were heavy footsteps overhead, a man shouting orders, other men shouting back, a woman screaming – or perhaps it was an animal, I don't know. When pain and fear are too great, we all sound the same – a squeal and shriek and then we are extinguished. The invaders were raping, maiming, and killing the servants. When she chose death, Lalla had chosen wisely. My hearing and sense of smell had become more powerful. Was this an illusion? My eyes were closed and still I could not move.

Then the door to the crypt opened.

I could not see it, but I heard the door swing back.

Two soldiers came down the steps into the crypt. At first I – that is, my disembodied, invisible self, the self that, suddenly, was standing next to the catafalque – saw their strong, naked, muscular legs, tanned, smelling of sun and salt and sweat and battle. They were from the enemy army – two of them – an older man, and a younger – both handsome.

My heart, a young woman's heart – but now a demon's heart, I suppose – thirsted for them. Blood, I realized – it was blood I thirsted for. It was a yearning like hunger, like overwhelming sexual desire, like unleashed lust. I was aroused. And, in that moment, I realized I could move my body. I was exploding with sparkling energy. The lust was fiery, awe-inspiring. Somehow I managed not to move. The moment was dangerous. It was better to be dead.

The younger man stood staring at me.

The older man favored me with a long, penetrating gaze, then came over, and touched my left hand, caressing my palm. He ran his fingers along the inside of my arm, where the skin is most delicate. Then, he frowned and muttered something to himself. "Well, well ..."

He knelt where Lalla had fallen and whispered what sounded like a prayer, but it was in a language I had never heard. He put his hand on her forehead and closed her eyes.

The young man was still staring at my body as it lay, inert, on the catafalque. "She's the most beautiful thing I have ever seen."

"She's dead, Gaius, she's dead."

"I must have her, Marcus. I must have her."

"It's unmanly to possess the dead. Besides, it's unhealthy."

"She's freshly dead, Marcus. She's fresh."

"She's not fresh, Gaius; when you are dead, you are dead. It only takes an instant. She's dead. She's brutish like death, all blood and slippery guts inside, slimy filth under the beauty. You make love to that and all you'll meet is pus. Blood and shiny entrails will slip and splash out at you like vicious hungry serpents and slap you in the face. Maggots and worms will spill out of her mouth and eyes and infect you."

"I don't believe it."

"Look, let me show you what she is made of!" Marcus lifted his broad sword and made ready to strike. I tensed, preparing to spring up and attack him – a rush of inner power told me I could do such a thing.

"No, don't, Marcus, you are right: I'll not touch her."

Marcus sheathed his sword slowly, as if with regret. "That's good, Gaius. Let me tell you, sex is one brief spark of pleasure followed by one long lamentation of regret. And as for her, she is not life; she is death."

"Still, she is beautiful!" Gaius ran his fingers up along the inside of my leg. The tips of his fingers were rough and warm and caused a tingling, rippling feeling in my belly and my heart.

"By all the gods, I conjure you, man, leave her alone." Marcus raised his voice, tightened his tone. "The dead are demons! Be done with her! Let's go. There is little time. The city is burning. The troops are out of control, rioting, raping, pillaging. Discipline is breaking down. Our men are fighting each other. There is a massacre brewing up above our heads. We must go."

Then Marcus turned and stared straight at the ghostly incorporeal me, where, standing beside my flesh-and-blood body, and invisible, or so I thought, I was watching and listening. "As for you, demon," he stared directly into my eyes and held up his sword, "I bless you with my bloodied sword – long life in death, long death in life." He turned his back and was gone up the stairs, his boots and armor clanking, his strong legs last to disappear.

Gaius, the younger warrior – not so young, perhaps; I would say about thirty-five – stood looking down at my body, his eyes blazing with desire. But he, too, turned abruptly away and was gone, up the stairs.

I lay still and puzzled over what I had seen. Why did the warrior Marcus pay such attention to Lalla? Of course, she was beautiful, and she was dead, and he was paying his respects; but there was something else. It was as if he knew her. And the language he whispered over her body, what language was it? And why did he use it? It was a language I felt I knew and yet did not know.

I lay there thinking. I was hungry. No, I was starving. No, I was ravenous. Saliva gushed into my mouth, overflowed. I bared my teeth and licked my lips.

What *was* this hunger? *Blood!* I yearned for *blood!* How horrible! What was happening to me?

Time passed. I don't know how much time – but the rising lust for blood was irresistible. I clenched my fists. I trembled with desire, with hunger.

I sat up and slipped off the catafalque. Adjusting my robe, I stepped carefully over Lalla's body. I knelt next to her: her face was serene and as if carved in black stone. It shone. She was so beautiful. My heart yearned for her laughter, for her touch, for her wisdom. I kissed her on the lips. I stood up and tore my robe in ceremonial woe, as I had seen others do, ripping it to shreds. I was shocked by my strength – my robe was instantly reduced to slivers and rags.

"By all the gods, Lalla – by Ba'al, by Astarte, by Anath, and by Asherah, if there are such things as gods, I wish you now to be and forever more in Paradise."

I added my caveat about the gods possibly not existing because my father was a skeptic and, age nineteen, I followed him – perhaps rashly – in his disbelief. But, like him, and following his example and that of my mother, I had always scrupulously observed the outer forms of our religion as a sign of respect to the living and the dead, and to our city, and to Lalla whom I had truly loved – Lalla, who, when she spoke of the gods, did so with humor as if they were particularly pesky neighbors who provided fodder for gossip – larger than life and very entertaining with all their cosmic love affairs and fights and oversized vices and virtues, but familiars just the same and not so different, in their virtues, vices, and passions, from mortals such as we. What Lalla really believed, I shall never know. But I do know she loved me, and I loved her – and always shall.

I left the cool of the crypt and went up the steps. On the last step, and before pushing open the door, I hesitated. Above, what horrors would I see? Finally, I opened the heavy crypt door – when I brushed it aside, it seemed as light as a feather – and I stepped into the ruins of our home – everything that could have been smashed was smashed. Everyone was dead. There were bodies everywhere. People I knew. People who had raised me. But, unlike Lalla, they seemed, somehow, in the short time that had passed, to have become strangers, strangers seen from a great distance. Blood was everywhere and was drying. I sniffed at it. My nostrils quivered. My stomach growled. I got down on all fours and crawled among the bodies. I would to lick and lap the delicious blood up! Saliva dripped from my lips. The tip of my tongue touched the first viscous drying pool of curdled blood. Ouch! I started back in disgust, in horror. This would not do! Dead blood was an obscenity! I needed fresh living blood. It was an unearthly, overpowering yearning – like the desire to possess and be possessed – and I was only beginning to feel it; I was an amateur, a neophyte.

I stood up, walked to the entrance, and pushed aside the shattered timber gate of our villa and stepped outside.

Even I, even the monster I had become, was shocked.

The city was a mass of flame. Bodies everywhere. No one was alive. The air glowed red with heat, and the smoke and haze were heavy with the stench of burning wood, charred flesh, blood, spices, and dung. Everything I had known had been destroyed.

I glimpsed a few enemy soldiers in the distance, but none close by.

I followed the wall around our villa until I came out onto the little square behind our home where there was a fountain Lalla and I used to come to for extra buckets of water. Lalla would splash me and I would run and scream and pretend to be frightened. Images of Lalla flashed before me. Her laughter echoed in the little square as if she were still alive.

Near the fountain I saw the younger warrior, the one called Gaius. He was seated on a low stone step with his back against a wall, his armor shattered and peeled away. His stomach had been ripped open. Blood and guts – that he was trying to hold in – spilled through his fingers.

He stared at me. His eyes – which were very blue – were glazed over with pain.

"Gaius."

"You," he said.

"I must feed." I knelt in front of him and put my hands on his shoulders.

"Feed?" he said, and put his hand, covered in blood, on my hand.

"Yes. I need blood, your blood." I felt a strange sensation as pointed fangs suddenly protruded from my mouth. They tingled. How horrible! How exciting, how divine!

"No," he said, "you can't." Blood dribbled from the corner of his mouth.

"I must. I must feed."

"What is your name?" He stared at me and reached out to touch my mouth, caressing my lips and stroking my fangs with the tips of his fingers.

"Tanis," I said. "Tanis is my name."

"I knew you would come," he said. More blood ran, just a small trickle, from the corner of his mouth. "Well, then, if you must drink, then you must hurry," he said. "I don't have much longer."

"Thank you, Gaius, thank you!" I brushed my mouth against his lips, then I plunged my fangs into his neck, his thick, muscular, brave warrior's neck.

He shuddered, but did not resist.

He locked one of his hands into mine, the fingers squeezing mine – it was like a caress. "Oh, my love," he breathed. "My true and eternal love."

As I drained him of life, his blood and strength flooded into me. I shuddered. Never had I felt so intensely alive. He, too, shuddered, a few spasms. Then, he was still. His fingers opened. His hand, which had been holding mine, fell away.

I drank until there was not a drop left, until I knew, instinctively, that he was truly dead.

"You are dead, my darling, truly dead," I whispered. "You will not rise again."

A kaleidoscope of images flooded my mind – I plunged into the pageant of Gaius's life. I *saw* it – his loving parents, his rigorous schooling, his training in wrestling, his sword fights, his first experience of sex – he was in his teens, she was an older prostitute, and he was very clumsy, and she had to show him what to do – and his friendship with the man called Marcus whom he loved. In that instant, I *was* Gaius and *he* was me.

Trembling in ecstasy, in a sort of total abandonment, and voluptuous identification with Gaius, I came back to consciousness of myself. Blood dripped from my chin and ran between my breasts. The few rags that were left of my robe were soaked, heavy, transparent with blood. I was fulfilled. Gaius would have died in any case; but that did not concern me. He had become my lover, we had been united, his soul had been swept up in mine, I possessed him, he possessed me, but not in the way he had intended.

I was still crouched over the body, my fingers on the leather shoulder pad of his tunic, softly stroking it, as if it were part of him, when I heard a familiar voice.

"So we meet again."

I looked up. It was Marcus, the older warrior. He was only a few feet away and he had unsheathed his broadsword. He had an amphora in one hand; he put it down, tensed his body, every muscle, and was readying himself, I could see, for the kill. I did not yet know my strength and I was afraid.

I was already coming back to my human form, the fangs withdrawing. I was almost naked, of course, with just the rags of my torn gown, and dripping with blood. What a sight, I thought, what a sight I must be!

Marcus gazed at me. A scar ran across one of his cheeks, the stubble gleamed silver and gold. His blond hair was curly and cut short. He smiled. I stared at him. His was the smile of a warrior who is about to kill.

I willed myself to gather together all my strength. I would be the killer, I would not give him time to strike. But I felt drowsy, perhaps I had drunk too fast, perhaps I was not ready, perhaps … Yes, this man, Marcus, was going to kill me.

He raised his sword …

And …

"May I top up your glass, Father?"

"What, yes, yes, of course." I handed her my glass. I had been lost, I must admit, in her story. Who would come out on top, I wondered – the warrior Marcus, or the demon-vampire V? But, then, V must have come out on top. Otherwise, she would not be here to tell me her fantastical story. The newly created demon-vampire must have overcome the veteran pagan warrior, Marcus. "So, my dear demon, just how, exactly, did this play out? You must have killed the man, because …"

CHAPTER 16 – BACCANALE

Scarlett yawned. Sunlight, reflecting off the buildings opposite, streamed in through the wide-open window, lighting up the white muslin curtain that lazily drifted into the room, carrying a fresh warm breeze and the smell of roasted coffee. She had just opened her eyes and was lying on her back, on top of the sheets. She blinked at the ceiling. It must be late. Maybe it was ten o'clock, even eleven.

She reached out. Her hand met his shoulder, oh so smooth, and then his back, oh so muscular! She slid her hand down his back, slowly, slowly, inch by delicious inch. He groaned. He had a marvelous back – she decided that she loved his back, that she loved his broad shoulders, that she loved the way his back tapered from the wide shoulders down to the tight, muscular waist. She loved his golden skin … What a night!

"Coffee?" His hand reached out, took her hand. He rolled over; she turned onto her side. They were face-to-face, inches apart.

"Yes, coffee." She breathed the word, a sensuous sigh. "Coffee!"

"On the Campo, on a café terrace." The sunlight shone off his eyes.

"Excellent idea." With the tips of her fingers, she caressed his forehead. "With butter croissants – and maybe butter, real butter, and jam."

"We will have to get up, then." His hand ran down her side, over the smooth, beautifully toned slope of her hip, and along her thigh, the long, tanned, shapely leg.

"Yes, just a minute or two more – here." She sighed, and kissed him, lightly, on the lips; she lingered, her lips caressing his, delicately moving back and forth. Staring into his eyes, she stroked the nape of his neck, the curve of his shoulder. She could caress him forever; she could eat him up. Yes, indeed, she was voracious, bathed in sensation, hungry for more; truly, she had become shameless, even more than before. It must be the Roman air.

His name was Jian – Jian Chan. He was three years older than she. The moment they met, in the twilight, on the hotel roof, they began to talk, and for hours they didn't stop talking. Of one accord they decided they would walk most of the night, explore the city, and then, later, maybe sleep … Well, *sleep* was the word they used.

Wired up from her fight with Filippo, from her narrow escape, and from her exciting interviews with the police, Scarlett was ultra-alert, ultra-sensitive. It was like she was a survivor, living on borrowed time. And, then, the tension was general. There was a tingling, post-earthquake electricity sparkling in the air. Nobody, it seemed, had gone to bed. The streets thronged with tourists, Romans, pilgrims, everybody. The cafés and restaurants and terraces were crowded with chattering, laughing, arguing people. The laughter was nervous, high-strung. Hysteria hovered in the wings. The heat weighed down, oppressive, sultry, humid, charged with explosive energy. The heat was as intense as the heat of midday, and this, in a city largely without air-conditioning, made it hard to sleep.

"This is really weird weather." It was the first thing Jian said when they left the hotel, and glanced up at the glowing night sky.

"Yes, it is. I wonder –"

"If it has anything to do with the earthquakes?"

"Yes." Scarlett took his hand.

At first, they roamed the small streets and alleyways near the hotel. Then, they headed across the cobblestoned market square, Campo de' Fiori, and entered Piazza Farnese, and admired the facade of Palazzo Farnese, designed, in part, as Scarlett pointed out, by Michelangelo. Through windows high up they could see brightly lit frescoes on ceilings inside the Palazzo. It was the French Embassy, all lit up. Maybe they were giving a party or reception. They wondered. Who might be at that party? They created ridiculous, imaginary scenarios of impossibly glamorous soirées, with brilliantly costumed guests from all centuries and nations. What would Albert Einstein say to Julius Caesar? They wandered down a series of crooked little streets, some of them mere alleyways, and then doubled back, and found themselves in the vast oblong space of Piazza Navona, once, in ancient and medieval times, a scene of races and athletic contests and mock naval battles.

One of the first things Scarlett noticed was that she and Jian began and ended each other's sentences. She knew what he was going to say; and he knew what she was going to say. Another thing she noticed was that they could, just by a glance, just by a smile, communicate a whole world of ideas to each other, or so it seemed. Jian glanced at a very angry old lady scolding a mischievous child, and then, with a smile, he glanced at Scarlett, and it was clear – they both saw exactly the same thing at the same time: The comedy of the old lady's expression of exasperation, the sneaky stubborn look on the child's face, and how underneath the surface drama the old lady and the child both knew they were playing a game, and that, even in the jousting and scowling, they were expressing their deep love for each other.

Scarlett, instinctively trusting Jian, opened up completely. She told him about Jeff and Megan – turning it into a comedy routine in which she was the naive fall guy, the ingénue caught in somebody else's scenario, goofing it up, looking at herself – and the situation – from outside. After all, the whole thing truly was a farce! It had happened centuries ago. She only vaguely remembered who Jeff and Megan were.

She told him about her grandmother Charlotte, a true lady, who was a doctor, kept a stable of horses, and was always full of charm and wisdom; she told him about her ambitions, about her hopes for a medical career, about her interest in neurology; about her love of Leo Tolstoy and Jane Austen – Charlotte was a very cultured person and had given Scarlett a taste for books. She told him about her interest in the history of science and technology; she told him about the scarlet dress – again the story turned into a comic routine – and how it got her into trouble. She told him of her fight with Filippo and Carlo – and how, after it was over, and when she was safe, she realized that, perversely, a part of her had enjoyed it; it was exciting, a real challenge, adrenaline pumping like crazy.

"You know, I didn't even think to shout for help."

"Really?"

"I was so busy fighting, and I was so mad and so scared, but ..."

"But ...?"

"I did think to bang my fists on the cars, and –"

"And the alarms went off!"

"Exactly! People came running."

"You are a true warrior!" He laughed and put his arm around her. They headed down a little side street, a shady, twisting alleyway.

She told him about the people who helped her – the tough lady who'd taken on Filippo and the stout man who'd come running, huffing and puffing, and who'd called the police. She told him about the police and how they had been so friendly, so generous. "Actually, I was terrified. At one point, I was certain I was going to die." She told him about the other young women who had disappeared, and how the police had shown her photographs of them. "I think something really bad is going on. Just the other day a Russian girl – a ballerina – disappeared too. And a famous scientist and his daughter have been kidnapped."

"Yes." Jian suddenly turned serious. "Roger Thornhill – I read some of his articles. He's brilliant. He makes science truly exciting, and he makes really complicated things seem so simple – which, of course, they aren't."

"Yes. They aren't simple. You have to be extra brilliant to make them seem simple." Scarlett put her hand on his chest – she liked touching him; it seemed natural and irresistible. She moved her hand – the tips of her fingers – up and down his chest – pectorals, abs … *Oh, boy!*

"I want to see that guilty scarlet dress." Jian narrowed his eyes, giving her a sly look, "the one that got you into so much trouble."

"Well, dear sir, you will be pleased to learn that I fixed it up when I got home and sewed the strap back on. So, maybe later, if you are very, very good, I can demonstrate how it works and put on a little show." She blinked her eyes at him and bit and wet her lips. *Oh, Scarlett! You shameless hussy, you!*

He pulled her to him and kissed her. It was the first time he had kissed her, and it seemed the most natural thing in the world. She returned the kiss and kept it going. She had a delicious sensation – she was melting into him and he was melting into her.

As they walked hand in hand through Piazza Navona and stopped for ice cream at one of the cafés, Jian told her about his ambitions and his past. His family was from Beijing; his father and mother had made a great deal of money in real estate and then in high-tech and in Chinese social media. He had studied at Stanford and at Cambridge in England, and he loved – it turned out – Russian literature, and American and English literature. So, strangely, they ended up talking about Tolstoy and Dostoevsky and Jane Austen and Dickens, and Carl Hiaasen and Stephen King, and various TV series, and movies, and art, and the history of science – it turned out too that he knew a great deal about Galileo and Isaac Newton and how the scientific revolution began. He was into the theories of artificial intelligence in a big way – and his ambition was to create a cutting-edge company that would explore the outer reaches of what artificial intelligence might do, and how intelligent biological and non-biological systems might be integrated. Scarlett was interested in neurology and how the mind worked. The overlap of their interests, in human intelligence and artificial intelligence, seemed just about perfect.

"Are we geeks or elitists? It's all pretty highbrow." Scarlett took a sumptuous lick and then a bite of her double scoop vanilla ice cream cone.

"Nothing wrong with that," he said. He had a splash of chocolate on his chin; she yearned to lick it off; she reached out with a serviette and captured it.

He smiled. "It's good to be curious – to ask questions."

"Still, are we insufferable snobs?"

"No, we're just interested in things. And we are lucky enough to be able to follow up on our curiosity." He put his finger under her chin. "I want to know how things work."

"Me too. But … you know, it's really creepy."

"What's creepy?"

"How well I feel I know you. I mean, I feel like I've known you forever."

"Me too. When I first saw you, I thought – I know her, I recognize her, it's as if I've been waiting for her my whole life. I knew you existed somewhere in the world. I just had to find you. And now I have."

"Yes, me too. That's exactly what I thought and what I felt. This is nuts! We are totally crazy." Scarlett touched his cheek. She closed her eyes, and let the tips of her fingers linger, touching his cheeks, his lips, his nose, his eyelids, his forehead. "Do you mind?"

"Are you kidding?" He leaned over and kissed her; they both tasted of chocolate and vanilla ice cream.

She opened her eyes. He was smiling at her – it was the sort of smile that speaks volumes: love, possession, desire, partnership, and understanding.

Scarlett turned to watch a group of people strolling by. The piazza was a perfect pedestrian parade ground; it was oblong like a small-scale race course, and once, she remembered, in Ancient Rome, it had been a stadium used for foot races and gladiator fights. "They even used to stage mock naval battles here; in the Middle Ages or in the Renaissance they'd fill the piazza with water and launch ships." Scarlett took a big lick out of her vanilla ice cream. It was melting fast. Whew! It was so hot – maybe 100 degrees Fahrenheit. If not that hot, it was close to it.

Water gushed from the Fountain of the Four Rivers. Swirling rocks rose up from the basin where kids were splashing in the water and being mildly scolded by a policewoman who was telling them to get out of the fountain.

Perched on the cragged swirl of rocks were four majestic river gods, representing the Nile, the Danube, the Ganges, and the Rio de la Plata.

"You're dripping ice cream."

"It's sticky."

"You have a moustache!"

"You have a moustache too!"

They left the café and began to walk, just strolling. They were tempted at each point to stop and make love, standing up, right there and then.

"I have a shivery feeling all over."

"Me too."

"Hmm." She kissed him, violently this time, a long, hungry kiss, and she pressed against him.

"I like the tension," he said, as she drew back. "I like the suspense."

"Yes. I like it too." She took his hand.

They walked around a corner, into a darker street. Wrought iron street lamps stuck out from the sides of buildings.

"Romantic, isn't it?"

"Like the Middle Ages."

"Yes."

"This is very, very tempting." He pressed her against a wall; they were in a narrow little side alley, empty, hardly anyone about. He seized her by the waist, his body close, hard, against hers.

"Yes, it is." She nibbled at his lips. She gazed into his eyes. The nibble turned into a kiss, the kiss became a deep kiss, a deeper kiss.

"*Ah, l'amore, l'amore!* Oh, love, love!" An old woman was leaning out a window, just above them, on the opposite side of the alley. "*Giovinezza!* Youth!" She blew them a kiss, waved, and closed her shutters.

"Guess we'd better …"

"Yes, maybe we'd better …"

They disengaged slowly and, hand in hand, walked on, and found themselves at the Pantheon, the "Temple of All the Gods." It was open and so they entered.

Scarlett looked up. There was a big round hole – the oculus – in the roof and through it moonlight streamed down. The building had stood for two thousand years. She took Jian's hand and they walked around the vast round cool space. There were tombs along the walls and the footsteps and voices echoed in a hushed reverential tone.

Jian put his arm around her shoulders. She was tempted to kiss him, but they were in a church. She'd got in enough trouble with religion today! He gazed at her, an amused look in his eyes. He knew exactly what she was thinking.

She put her hand to the side of his face. "You are the most beautiful thing I have ever seen!"

He laughed and looked down. "Ditto," he said. "You, my darling, are beyond beautiful. It is more than beauty ... I don't know how to say it, what it is."

They walked out of the Pantheon, and stopped to eat a quick salad and sandwich in a small hole-in-the wall restaurant. They had a glass of chilled white wine. The table was on the sidewalk. They were virtually sitting in the street, people brushing past them.

She held her hand against the side of his face. Then she kissed him. The kiss was returned. "I love you," he said.

"I love you," she echoed.

They headed back to the hotel. It was 11 p.m.

"So, this, sir, is the dress – the scarlet scandal." She held it out, stretched, so he could fully appreciate its daring. "Filippo tore off one of the straps, but I fixed it up – I always have my handy little sewing kit with me."

"It looks perfect." He was perched on the edge of the bed.

"Dancing. We could go dancing."

"My thought exactly." He glanced at his watch. "Even though it is past midnight!"

"So, shall I try it on?"

"Yes, that would be very fine. I'll close my eyes."

"Oh, sir, you are a true gentleman."

She stripped to panties – string panties.

She pulled on the dress, shimmied into it, adjusted it, smoothed it, and slipped into her high-heeled pumps. "You can open your eyes now, dear sir."

"Wow!"

"You like?"

"I like. I like very much."

He stood up. She slid into his arms. "So – we go dancing?"

"Yes."

They'd seen, on their way back to the hotel, a group of people dancing in a small square near Campo de' Fiori. So, they joined the crowd. It was a lamp-lit, carnival atmosphere. Couples twirled around the piazza.

"So, my friend, let us dance." Scarlett put her hand in the small of his back and pulled him to her, and they swung around, light-footed, in a waltz. He held her tight. Others joined them. Then they were dancing a tango.

"You know how to dance!"

"Some men do." He tossed her back, fiercely pulled her toward him, and kissed her on the lips as their bodies slid sideways side-by-side, skin to skin, they swung around, wildly.

People clapped. Three couples were now dancing, interacting as if they had known each other all their lives.

Scarlett felt it tingle in every fiber of her being. The earthquake scare had created a fierce, uninhibited community feeling, like an all-night celebration in some small village, a pagan carnival. The lamplight shone on the cobble-stones and on the fountains; the hazy air bathed everything in an aura of mystery and romance.

The music, coming from an iPad and speakers, seemed to come out of the walls and the ground itself.

People leaned out of windows clapping in rhythm.

Jian's arms were around her, his hands seized her waist, lifting her into the air, and she flew, literally flew, around, and around, and around.

Finally, exhausted, they sat down on the edge of the fountain. Kids were splashing in the water. Two guys were splashing their girls. The girls started splashing the guys. It ended up with everybody splashing everybody. Within seconds, they were all soaked, including Scarlett and Jian.

"Oh! Now look!" Scarlett stared down at her dress, now see-through, sort of, transparent, more or less, well, more, really, than less ...

"I'm looking," Jian said. "I can't stop!"

Scarlett gazed at him. "Neither can I." Jian's wet T-shirt and shorts outlined every muscle, sculpted his chest in the lamplight. His pectorals stood out. The slope of his tummy was tight. Ah, Scarlett thought – splendid abs, splendid pectorals, marvelous biceps, and wonderful ...

She licked her lips.

He was staring at her, his eyes shining.

"Your T-shirt is soaked," Scarlett said, "and transparent."

"So is your dress." He swallowed. "Really, really soaked."

"Yes, this dress is a curse. It will get me burned at the stake." Scarlett put her hand on his chest. 'I'm going to become a sculptor.'

"Oh?" He raised an eyebrow.

"I will mold you, every tiny bit of you, and recreate your body. I will take the clay and I will touch and explore and trace and mold and sculpt every inch of you." Her hands moved over his chest, up over his shoulders; her fingers caressed his biceps, slid down his tummy.

He shivered and half closed his eyes. His hands were on her waist, then on her backside. She leaned back, to gaze at him.

He was holding her, staring at her. She felt his gaze eat up every inch of her. He slid his hands up her sides, sculpting her. She felt she was naked, the semitransparent, drenched dress ceased to exist.

"Hmm," said Scarlett.

"Huh, huh," said Jian.

She moved her fingers over the curve of his shoulder. "Warrior muscles," she whispered. "I'm wicked."

"Not wicked, just observant." He grinned and kissed her on the forehead.

"Oh, and the man is vain too! It adds to his charm." She kissed him on the lips, tentatively, and then made the kiss linger, exploring, as they breathed each other in.

Hand in hand, they made their way back to the hotel and raced up the stairs to her room. And then, in the shadowy room, lit only from the street, there was a prolonged and playful striptease on the part of both parties.

"Okay, now, sir."

"Yes, madam, now."

"Now."

"Yes, now."

And so it was that they made love, for the first time, and so it was that, a number of hours later, after an exhausting night, love, over and over, and finally sleeping, then waking to make love again, they woke up, finally, to the sun streaming through the window and decided that they would go to Campo de' Fiori and have coffee and a breakfast snack. "Yes, butter croissants, with real butter – and maybe even jam or marmalade!"

Scarlett slipped out of bed, into the golden, cascading morning light.

Jian stared at her, watching her every move. He got out of bed slowly and gazed at her as if he wanted to take possession of all of her, right away, and forever. He took her in his arms and pressed her to him. She put her arms around him and held on desperately as if she would never let go. She took a deep, deep breath. It was indescribably exciting, having him in her arms, feeling his naked body pressed against hers.

"We could stay like this forever."

"Yes, we could."

"But, maybe ..." He kissed her.

"Maybe we should ..." She breathed.

"Get dressed!"

"Yes!"

"Croissants!"

"Cornetti!"

"Coffee and jam!"

"Yes!"

The sun shone. The air was balmy. The sky was blue. It was a sparkling brand-new day, and Scarlett Andersson and Jian Chan were in love.

CHAPTER 17 – AVATAR

The demon filled my glass and filled her own. Then she sat down opposite me. I expected her to pick up her story where she had left off. The enemy warrior Marcus was about to kill her. Or she was about to kill Marcus. I was eager, I must admit, to know how she disposed of this warrior, this Marcus. Did she tear off his head? Did she rip out his heart? Did she drink him dry?

She just stared into space and said nothing. I didn't want to hurry her, so I took a modest sip of the fine whiskey and savored the rich burning texture of the divine elixir. But, finally, I could wait no longer.

I coughed, cleared my throat. "You were saying? This Marcus raised his sword, and …? What happened then?"

"Yes." She took a sip of whiskey. Her eyes had a faraway look. She was gazing into some distant invisible landscape. I suspect she was reliving those bloody, suspenseful moments from long ago.

"So – he raised his sword, and he was going to kill you?"

No answer.

I sighed. Oh, well! I shrugged and took another sip of whiskey. My demon was lost in her memories. Even demons, I suppose, have yearnings, and regrets, and magic moments from their past lives. Almost like having a soul, I imagine, although, as a demon, all would be tinged with the melancholy and pain of her fallen state.

Finally, she roused herself, blinked at me, and once again began to tell her tale. "Yes, the warrior called Marcus raised his sword and …"

Marcus raised his sword.

I was crouched at his feet, half-naked, dripping blood, covered in gore, seemingly a young woman, seemingly vulnerable. All my muscles tensed. Fierce energy roared in my veins. I took a deep breath. I would spring up, leap on this Marcus, claw off his face, rip off his head. By fate, he and I were destined to fight, and we would fight to the finish. This handsome, powerful man was an enemy warrior. His soldiers had destroyed everything I loved and everything I had known; they had killed my family and every friend I had ever had. They had laid waste to the city I worshipped. And I had just drunk all the blood from, and murdered his close friend Gaius – leaving only a soulless empty husk.

I knew I had superhuman strength. I could do anything. Yet, I somehow knew too that this man Marcus was dangerous, infinitely strong, that he – perhaps – could defeat me, and kill me.

"Well, well!" Marcus gazed at me. Then, just when I was about to leap to the attack, he grunted, put his sword back in its sheath, and crouched down to face me.

I was wound up like a spring. Energy sparkled from my pores. His face was within inches of mine. I could smell his tanned skin, the meals he had eaten, the oil he put on his hair, the leather and metal of his tunic and armor, and the intense, intimate, peppery smell of a man.

"Your first kill, I think," he said, his eyes crinkling, his teeth shining.

I stared at him and nodded. I was still kneeling, we were face-to-face.

"You did Gaius a favor. He was going to die, but more slowly, more painfully. I had gone to get an amphora to give him water, but it would have done no good. I was going to kill him myself. But now, it is done. He wanted to consummate with you and now you have consummated – in your own way – with him." He scratched his chin and stared into my eyes. "So, now, you are what you are! You do realize you are no longer human, do you not? Where are you going to go? You can't stay here! This place is doomed."

I stood up.

Still crouching, he looked me up and down. "You'll need clothes."

I was shivering, but from strength, glowing with power, the blood drying on my shoulders and breasts.

"I'm Marcus," he said. He stood up and, in a gesture I had never seen before, he took my hand and shook it up and down. So, I shook his hand back. He grinned at me. He had strong even teeth. "You could use a bath." He nodded at the fountain.

"Yes." I let the remains of my robe fall away. I walked to the fountain, I stepped under the cascade, and I bathed.

A young man – Severus's son, who had had a lisp and who might perhaps, my father had told me, have become my future husband since his parents were very rich – was lying dead on the stone steps of the fountain. He and I had often laughed together as if we were two girls. He loved to tell tales from the market and the harbor. He was an incorrigible gossip. He would giggle at his own jokes and put his hand over his mouth shyly and look down as if he were a young virgin. And he knew many sailors. He had not yet grown a beard, not even a shadow on his upper lip.

Now, he just lay there, a dead thing. One of his sandals was half off, the sole of his foot was streaked with dirt, and his ankle was twisted at a strange angle. His head had been split open like a melon – it was white and gray and red inside. His expression looked like he'd been taken by surprise, eyes wide open, screaming, mouth agape – a silent black hole, no teeth showing.

When we were children, he and I played on the steps of the fountain, or in my family's courtyard. I adored him. In my head, I heard his voice calling, "Tanis! Tanis! Tanis!" But now I looked upon his body from far away. He was a stranger. I had known him in another life, which was no longer my life. I was a stranger, too, to myself, I realized, now that I was dead.

The boy's tunic and trousers were not bloodied. Marcus knelt and carefully pulled them off.

I dressed myself in the dead boy's clothes as Marcus watched.

"Come, young fellow," he said.

"Why are you doing this?"

"I'm a warrior," he smiled, "but I'm a priest too – a priest of the Sun God."

"The sun?"

"Yes, your enemy, the sun; the sun that will consume you and burn you and turn you into a pillar of flame and a pile of wispy gray ash." He clapped a hand on my shoulder. "Don't worry. The sun will not be up for three or four hours yet. We'll get you safely to the shade."

I bowed my head. I knew I was no longer human. I was now a dangerous monster. But I didn't understand how this man knew these things and why he was not afraid of me or why he seemed to be helping me – perhaps it was a trap.

We headed toward the city gates. The temple of Ba'al and Astarte had not been damaged. A priest was sitting mournfully on the steps, the columns of the temple soaring up behind him. He looked up and watched us approach, but did not say anything. He was unbloodied, and alone.

As we passed, a young priestess came out of the temple. She was beautiful, tall and slender and dry-eyed, and arrayed in all her gold and purple finery; she stared at us with her kohl-lined eyes, but said not a word. She calmly descended the steps, put her hand on the priest's shoulder, crouched beside him, and wiped away his tears.

Perhaps, I thought, even the looters feared the gods. The paving stones in front of the temple were black with blood, the smells were all-powerful, my nostrils quivered.

I had never smelled so many things, or so intensely – cedar and pine burning, wet and dry ash, scalded and burning flesh, wool and cotton smoldering, spices, horse dung burning, stone and metal heated by fire. The air glowed with flames and heat and smells. The smells touched and caressed and tickled every inch of my skin. I licked my lips. My mind throbbed, my curiosity was alight, my saliva burned with lust. I could feel with the point of my tongue the eager tingling sharpness of my teeth.

We walked through the northern gate. Smoke hung in the air.

The giant wooden doors had been smashed inwards; great beams and planks hung from their pinions.

"I am leaving the army behind." Marcus turned to me. "Riotous fools. His own men stabbed Gaius, you know. He was foolish, brave, and young in spirit – and of course a bit perverse. He liked forbidden pleasures. Well, all that is over now! How old are you?"

"I was – I am – in my nineteenth year," I said, thinking it was very strange to think of myself in the past tense.

"Yes, of course. That is right. Then you will be nineteen, or thereabouts, for all eternity. Though what eternity is, I don't know, nor what destiny or the stars have in store for us." He looked up. Stars, stars everywhere.

We were soon out beyond the city gate. The sky was clear, the air fresh and the smells were brilliant and sharp, smells of the country. Temples to the gods and goddesses lined the road, among the umbrella pines and the cypresses that stood guard, with some large impressive tombs of the very rich families.

"Gaius tried to separate two drunken idiots fighting over a purse – a month or two's worth of gold. He lost his life for a handful of gold and two drunken fools. By the gods, I sometimes wonder …!"

"I don't know what I am," I said. With the new intensity of sensation, I felt a new intensity of fear: What had I become? I wanted to growl and scream. I wanted to tear off my clothes. I wanted to crawl naked on all fours. I yearned to sink my fangs into Marcus's flesh and drink his blood, I wanted to hold his face between my hands, and kiss him, I wanted to drink him in, I yearned to consume him as a flame would consume a cord of wood, I thirsted for him to take me, twist me, fulfill me, destroy me, break me, possess me, I wanted to curl up and sleep. I wanted to love … I wanted to run my hands through his hair, I wanted to feel his body, warm and living and male, against mine.

"Ah, our horses are still here. You can ride?"

"Yes, my Lord." I bowed.

"Ah – '*Yes, my Lord*' – ah, it … it … I'm sorry … *she* … she has a sense of humor!"

I had to smile. "Why are you doing this?"

"Ah, that, my young lad, is for you to find out!"

At first, the horse balked at taking me. But then Marcus calmed it with soothing words, and soon I was astride holding the reins, riding as I had seen men ride, and the horse quickly recognized I was its master – I don't know how I willed that feeling into the horse's brain, but I did – and soon the horse and I were one.

"Good, good," said Marcus. "Excellent."

We rode for three or four hours, inland, away from the city and the coastal plain. We came to a ridge of mountains, a sort of escarpment rising to our right. The moon shone on ridges and layers of rock.

The eastern horizon began to glow – the rosy and lemon glow that precedes dawn.

"The sun," I said.

"Yes, the sun." Marcus turned to me. "Don't worry. There it is, in fact. Our timing is perfect." As we rode closer, in under the shadow of the escarpment, Marcus pointed. "This is it, if memory serves." He jumped down from his horse and I followed. We led our horses closer to the cliff. "There," he said.

It was the dark gaping mouth of a cave.

Marcus struck a flint and made a torch from some kindling. "You may not need this, but just in case."

He went a little way into the cave with me, then asked if I would be frightened continuing on my own.

"I am not frightened."

"Good, good. I didn't think you would be." He touched my cheek and looked into my eyes. Then he left me. I stood still, holding the torch, listening to his echoing footsteps as he made his way out of the cave, toward the light of the breaking day, and listening to water dripping and the other sounds coming from deep within the cave. At its mouth, I could see glimmerings of daylight and hear the sounds of dawn – birds, the stirrings of the wind, and the morning calls of animals.

Sleeping bats hung from the ceiling. They were kindred spirits, nocturnal drinkers of blood. Black, velvety, and thickly clustered, they hung together, in dark dusty bunches, like some satin-skinned luscious fruit just waiting to be plucked.

Their guano was thick on the ground. I stepped carefully, going deeper and deeper into the cave until there was no glimmer from the rising sun; and, when I found a clean spot far beyond the home of the bats, I extinguished the torch and lay down on the dusty floor and slept.

And so I slept through the whole day where the light of the sun could not reach me.

When I woke, I wondered where I was, who I was, what I was … Then I remembered.

Marcus was right – I didn't need the torch. I could see in the dark, not as clearly as in the light of day, but I could see. "Tanis, you are a creature of darkness," I muttered. "You are a monster of the underworld."

Marcus was squatting next to a campfire when I came out of the cave. I could see – and smell – that he had just eaten a small animal he must have hunted during the day. The last glimmers of the setting sun were visible in the west, reflected over the crest of the escarpment, a long ribbon of yellow and pink and a color that was almost green as if the sun had gone underwater.

He looked up. "Ah, my young friend!"

"You waited for me."

"Of course! I worship the day; you worship the night; we make a fine pair!"

I crouched by the fire, though I didn't need the warmth.

He glanced at me, one eyebrow raised, quizzical and amused. I could feel intelligence and courage radiate off him like heat. "Are you hungry yet?"

"No," I smiled. "You are in no danger."

"Good, good! I'd hate to be someone's dinner, even yours." He stirred the fire with a stick. It flared, lighting up his face. He was perhaps as old as my father; but I loved him, a new way of loving that I had not known before and that I did not fully understand.

He was thoughtful for a moment, staring into the flames. He looked up at me. "But we must go. It is a long ride. It will take us most of the night."

He doused the fire with sand and we set off.

My mount was by now accustomed to me. I think she understood that she and I were partners, not enemies.

I would soon need blood, much blood – human blood. But, in that instant, I felt strong, dangerously strong – as if any second I could burst out of my skin.

The moon came up – vast and yellow-orange on the horizon – then, as it rose in the sky, smaller and silver and bright, and finally high above, like a thin coin polished by many hands. Everything was coated in silver. I saw how white I had become – was it an illusion? I didn't know. I was as pale as a ghost.

We galloped and galloped.

We had just come out of a shallow valley where once there must have been a river – there were sandbanks with clusters of scrub, and small reefs and rippled ridges of pebbles that clattered under the horses' hooves – when I sensed something, something dangerous, heading our way. I galloped up to Marcus and put my hand on his arm.

We reined our horses in, to a halt.

Dust, silver in the moonlight, rose around us.

Silence.

We waited.

Silence.

Then I heard: horses coming toward us.

A minute passed. Now it was too late to escape.

"I hear them too," Marcus said, glancing at me.

Then they appeared. They were coated in silver moonlight: four men, riding strong horses. I instantly knew that they were bandits and dangerous – that they wished to kill us, certainly to kill Marcus, perhaps to take me prisoner, as a slave or to be raped.

"A very pretty young man you have there," one of them, I suppose the leader, said, as they reined up. His smile, large teeth, shone bright in the moonlight. "And gold, I suppose, in your packs."

"He's a pretty enough fellow," said Marcus, "but I'm afraid there's little gold, gentlemen."

"Let us see. Empty your packs."

"That, gentlemen, we will not do."

"You will not?"

"No, we will not."

They drew their swords.

Marcus turned his horse, dashed at one of them and with a single sweep of his sword cut off the man's arm. It happened so quickly the others had no time to react. But now they rushed him. I watched. I had no weapon. It turned out I didn't need one.

Marcus was surrounded; while he fought one rider, another closed in, raising his sword for the kill. I don't know how I did it, but I leapt. I flew. I literally flew from the back of my horse, my claws sprang out (I didn't know I had claws!), and instinctively plunging these brand-new claws into the attacker's face, I ripped half of it off.

He turned. His one remaining eye was wide in terror. He swung his sword. It gleamed in the moonlight. I swept his arm aside and, swinging around, I straddled his horse, clawed away his other eye, and plunged my fangs into his jugular. We fell together, in a tangle, into the dust. The horse reared up and backed away.

Blind and faceless, rolling in the dust, screaming, the villain grabbed for me, his bloody, skull-like mask turned up, bared teeth and gums, no eyes. I smashed him down, flipped him over, climbed onto him, and sank my fangs deep into his neck. I drank my fill – it was quick – draining him dry.

He was well and truly dead; he would not rise again.

I looked up. Marcus's first victim had bled to death – all that good blood wasted in the dust! The man was lying on his back, his ghostly pale face turned toward the moon, his one remaining arm stretched out as if in a salute.

Marcus had smitten another of the raiders with a clear cut to the heart – he too lay in the dust.

The last of the thieves tried to flee.

Marcus threw his sword. Glittering, it spun through the moonlight and slammed into the man, square in the middle of his back. He fell from his horse into the dust.

Marcus rode up to the body, dismounted, pulled his sword from the dead man's back, and then, wiping it on the skirt of his tunic and leading his horse by the reins, he walked slowly back to me. He nodded toward the man I had killed.

"Impressive," he said.

"I didn't know I could do that."

"Neither did I, know you could do that! Fly through the air!" He eyed me for a second, and broke into a boyish, mischievous grin. "You have untold and hidden talents, my lad! I wonder what else we shall discover."

I looked down at my blood-soaked arms, silver and black in the cool light of the moon. My fingers had extended into claws, but now the claws retracted, leaving just my normal hands with their carefully cut and manicured nails. "I don't know," I murmured.

I looked up. Marcus was still gazing at me, with that amused smile of his – as if, in a nice way, he understood much more about me than I did. He grinned. "Well, we must go!"

"Yes, we must go," I repeated, stupidly; I could feel myself blushing.

"Good horses," Marcus said, nodding at the bandits' horses, "but ours are better."

"Yes," I said.

"Go," he shouted. Their horses galloped off; we could hear them long after they disappeared.

Then we too galloped off into the night. The moon was setting. The sun would soon rise. Again, I had to find shelter.

After four days and nights we came, toward dawn, to the city where Marcus dwelt. It too was a port, far along the coast.

Marcus had a large villa on the edge of the city and overlooking the harbor. His home was like a fortress, with high walls, and it was built tall against a cliff. Parts of the building were built within the cliff itself, carved out of the rock face.

A servant opened the gates. He was a distinguished-looking, older man, and behind him stood two armed guards.

"Is this a slave, Marcus, or a prisoner?"

"No, this is not a slave," Marcus laughed and leapt down from his horse. "This is not a prisoner. This is a friend, an honored guest, and, by the way," he added, slapping the man on the shoulder, "in spite of the costume, this honored guest is a woman – the daughter of a great friend of mine. She will have the apartments next to mine. And no one shall enter her apartments or mine without first asking permission and having permission granted.

"Absolutely," said the old man. He took the reins of my horse. "Welcome."

"Thank you, sir," I said as I dismounted.

"You will find your accommodation comfortable, but if there is any problem, or anything you need, you merely have to ask."

"Thank you, sir."

"My name is Amilcare."

"My name is Tanis," I said.

"Then welcome, Tanis," said Amilcare, smiling at both of us.

"Yes, indeed," said Marcus, gazing at me, and putting his hand on my shoulder. "Tanis is a fine name; but when you are dressed as a lad, Tanis, let us call you, let me see – yes, let us call you Adonis."

I blushed.

"Then Adonis you shall also be," said Amilcare. "Welcome, Adonis, my Lord!"

"Thank you, Amilcare."

And so I was thus anointed – well, baptized or named – by Marcus, on the threshold of his home. I was to be both girl and boy, man and woman. I thrilled inwardly; it gave me a weird feeling – to be two persons in one.

Marcus soon settled me in. He provided me with a wardrobe – both masculine and feminine – and told me where I could usefully hunt when I needed to feed, which, it turned out, was roughly once every ten days. Various unsavory people camped outside the city walls. They were thieves and rapists and dangerous nomads, Marcus said, and it would be easier for me to move among them – and find my victims – than inside the city where, even in the prostitutes' quarter and down by the port, most people were known: a stranger, particularly a young lad of quite striking appearance such as I, would draw attention. But in the taverns and encampments, beyond the walls, all were strangers, no questions were asked, anything was possible.

So I would sneak out, every week, to prowl, to hunt, and, often, to feed.

Week by week, I grew stronger and more skilled at hunting.

Almost every day Marcus and I would have a long talk – at dusk if I was leaving to hunt, or at dawn or sometimes during the day.

The first few times I hunted, Marcus came with me, guided me, and indicated possible victims – or "candidates" as he called them. "Choose the most villainous, if you can, Tanis," he said. "Cleanse the world of evil."

"And if I find no villains?"

"There are always villains."

"But if there aren't?"

"Well, my lad, to live you must drink, must you not?" He laid his hand on my shoulder and smiled. "So, do what you must do."

My apartments were large and cool and far from the sunlight and they were built in under the cliff. Life was pleasant. I was treated like royalty or like a preferred and rather eccentric daughter. Marcus's servants had been with him for many years and it was clear they worshipped him. Strangely, for it was an almost unheard-of practice, most of them called him by his first name, and he did not mind if they disagreed with him; he would discuss things, as if with a friend, and mostly he was right – but not always. They were kind to me too. I was left alone in my apartments where I had oil lamps and games and manuscripts to amuse me. Of course, I slept during the day.

"You are a night owl, Adonis," said Amilcare, "a hunter."

"Yes, I am."

Amilcare liked to play board games, and he played Senet – something like chess is today – with me, particularly if Marcus was away and I was feeling bored.

"Check," he said.

"Checkmate," I said.

"Impossible!"

Sometimes I let him win; I had not realized I was so intelligent – but apparently I was. Perhaps it was compensation for no longer being human.

Usually, I dressed as a man, even while in my own quarters. But I also liked to help the women in the kitchen, and when I did that I dressed as a woman.

People addressed me as a man or as a woman, as Tanis, or as Adonis, depending upon how I was dressed. It was strange at first but rather pleasant really – I was two people, at least two people. The servants did not seem to find this strange at all. I am sure they had seen stranger things.

Marcus, I learned, was reputed to have great powers, and it was said, too, that he was capable of magic, great magic. He had a workshop and inner sanctum into which only Amilcare and one servant girl – a beautiful deaf-mute called Asherah – could penetrate.

Asherah had been named after the mother goddess, Asherah, consort of Anu the Sky God; according to some texts, the goddess Asherah was also the wife of the Israelite god Yahweh; she was often called the Queen of Heaven. In any case, Asherah, *my* Asherah, was soon assigned specially to me. She was gentle and kind and, as she spoke with her eyes and her hands, I soon realized that she was highly intelligent. We developed a system of hand signs and facial expressions. Not only was this useful but it was a game and we spent many hours inventing new ways to say things.

A serious, slightly haughty grimace meant *Marcus*.

A downward-looking scowl, eyes looking up, meant *Amilcare*.

With a quick curved cupping motion of her hands, Asherah would designate a pot, then with a quick shallow beckoning gesture with the curved fingers of her right hand, she would indicate "bring" or "fetch."
All was not perfect, of course.

One of the things that annoyed me most – in my new condition – was that I could not see myself in a mirror. Asherah would comb my hair and look at my face and signal to me that all was well, and she would help me bathe and, just occasionally, very rarely, to put on makeup, but, still, it was disconcerting not to see an image of myself in the brass or copper mirrors.

When Asherah first noticed that I was invisible in the mirror she offered me, she did not panic or shrink away in horror; she shrugged her shoulders and gave me a kiss on the cheek. I think Marcus had, somehow, prepared her. But not being able to see myself piqued my vanity; and it made me feel unreal. So, one day, I complained to Marcus.

"I cannot see myself in a mirror," I said, giving him my best pout.

"Others can see you – even if not in a mirror."

"I do not like being a ghost."

"Well," said Marcus, "we shall remedy that. We shall give you an image in the mirror. We shall make you real. We shall give you what the philosophers call a soul."

"A soul?"

"Yes, let us go and meet your soul."

"Marcus, you are making fun of me – you are teasing me."

"No, not at all."

"Yes, you are!"

"Tut, tut, no, I'm not!"

We went into his private apartment, where a bright fire was burning merrily. Marcus raised his hand. The wall dissolved and there appeared what he called the "reflecting pool." The reflecting pool was like a cool flat pond of silver water, but it was on the wall; it was vertical. I wanted to step through it, into the other room that it showed on the other side. "It's a mirror," he said, "A type of mirror." I had never seen anything so perfect. It did not seem real.

I realized that Marcus knew – and even possessed – many things for which there were no words in our languages, so he put old words together to make a big new word to describe those unique things.

Of course, in those days, as I have mentioned, we did have mirrors: small ovals of silver, bronze, or copper, highly polished, that allowed us to see ourselves, darkly, dimly. But we had nothing like this.

The mirror was, for me, horrifying. In the room in the mirror, Marcus was standing there, perfect in his tunic, sandals, with his broad leather belt, his finger hooked under the belt, his smile, his scar, his deeply tanned skin, and his sparkling blue eyes. Everything was perfect, it was another him. When he moved or blinked, the man in the room on the other side of the mirror did the same thing. But next to him, where I was standing, there was nothing – not even my cloak, not even my sandals. Just nothing.

"You see," I said, "I have no soul; I'm not there; I'm invisible. I even make the things I wear invisible!"

"Concentrate."

"Concentrate? What should I concentrate on?"

"Concentrate on the spot where you think you should be. Fill the space beside me with the sense of you!"

I thought I understood. I stared at the space in the mirror, at the deep illusory space behind and beyond the looking glass. As I stared, Marcus put his hand on the crown of my head. I could see his hand, his arm outstretched, his hand cupped over nothing. I closed my eyes, squeezed them, and forced myself to will myself into existence. The heat from his hand radiated down into my hair, my scalp, my whole body.

I opened my eyes. Underneath his hand, in the mirror, something like a cloud was forming, a mist. It swirled and swirled and then it made the outline of a person. It was magic, like a spell!

Suddenly, in a flash, a person crystallized out of the mist. A woman was standing there, staring straight at me. She had raven-black hair, dark eyes, dark arched eyebrows, prominent cheekbones. Her skin was pale gold, and she was wearing the simple sheath and sandals I was wearing. She was beautiful. I had never seen her before, not like this. I realized with a shock that she was me.

"Now, look." Marcus withdrew his hand from my head and I saw his hand leave the head of my double in the mirror.

"Now, watch carefully," he said, "for this is a very powerful mirror." Suddenly, the woman behind the glass smiled. This surprised me because I had not smiled – but, without thinking, I smiled back. Her lips, like mine, were crimson and her teeth were bright.

"Lick your lips," Marcus said, speaking to her, not to me.

She moved the point of her tongue along her lips. But I was not doing this. I looked at him. What was happening?

He said, very gently, "Be not afraid."

But whether he was saying this to the creature in the mirror or to me I did not know. I felt abandoned. I almost panicked.

My echo looked doubtful too. She took a step forward.

"Come," he said, "be not afraid, come meet your sister, your mistress."

He was gazing at her, not at me.

My double looked frightened and confused. I felt for her, whatever she was. She reached out and her image was troubled, as if a pebble had been thrown into a clear still pond. It rippled. She rippled. For an instant she wavered and floated, as if unreal; then, she stepped through the mirror, which now became clouded. A thick mist pressed against the glass and there was nothing left to be seen.

"Welcome," he said.

"I have come," she said.

"This is your sister, your mistress. You shall come when she bids you."

"Must I come for her?"

"Yes."

"Cannot I come for you?"

"No."

"Well, then, I shall come for her."

"Embrace," he said.

It gave me the shivers; I was afraid. Was I real or was I just pure empty invisible air?

She stepped forward. I reached out my arms, and so did she. I half expected my arms would meet nothing, just empty space, even though she was so vivid and radiated such energy and presence. But my arms met warm solid flesh, or at least such was the illusion, and I felt her arms wrap around me, her fingers pressing on the small of my back. I was flooded with warmth, with a sense of happiness, of peace.

"Now you kiss," he said, "gently, gently."

She smiled, leaned back, and said, almost gaily, as if it were a joke, "Must we really?"

"Yes," he said. "I see you have a personality."

She laughed; it was a full-throated happy laugh. "Whatever I am," she said, "she, my mistress, is also." She was looking straight into my eyes. She kissed me on the lips and I returned the kiss.

"Indeed," he said. "Repeat, I am you and you are me."

We repeated the line: "I am you and you are me."

"You will come when your mistress, Tanis, beckons."

"I will come when my mistress, Tanis, beckons." She looked cross. She folded her arms and lowered her chin in a charming pout. "Mistress Tanis, you are to have all the fun, I can see that. I am to be a mere assistant, a maidservant."

"Oh, your role will be exalted enough," Marcus said. "Let us sit down." And so we sat down on either side of the fire, exact twins. He told us that I – Tanis – was to live for thousands of years, that I was to guard and protect a certain secret, that I was above all to try to protect humanity – all the peoples of the Earth – and delay their final destruction.

"Final destruction – of all the people?" I could not conceive such a thing.

"Do you really mean that?" my twin said, looking at him.

"Yes, I do." He was quite serious.

I sat there wide-eyed, not really understanding any of this. But Marcus went on, and both of us sat there like good schoolgirls, rather stunned, I think, sagely not moving, not objecting.

He explained that my "soul" would help me in times of need; that when her services were not required, she could sleep in limbo or amuse herself as she wished in her own shadow world. But when I called her, she must come. And, then, too, whenever I looked in a mirror, she would be there.

"Well, I suppose, if I must, I must," she said.

"You are very high-spirited," I said. It was the first time I had addressed her directly, using my own words.

"I am part of you, darling, so you are just as high-spirited as I – more so, I believe, but you have had a series of, how shall I put it, shocks, emotional shocks, so you are hiding your strength. But when you need your strength, it will be there; and I will come when you need me. I will be by your side, even though I know I can be difficult at times – I can pout and stamp my foot and play practical jokes. Is that not so?" She turned to Marcus.

He laughed. It was a very frank laugh, unlike the constrained and digni-fied smile he usually displayed when he was amused or happy. The firelight shone on his short blond hair and on the golden stubble on his cheeks. It once again occurred to me that, in many ways, I was in love with him. And when I glanced at my double I could see, just for a second, the same emotion – rapt, almost worshipful attention – on *her* face. She flashed an enormous smile and said, laughing, "We must not be jealous. In fact, we can't be jealous because we are one and the same."

Marcus looked embarrassed. "Well, ladies, now that you have met, you will have centuries, millennia, to get to know each other."

He turned to her. "Now it is time to go."

"To go? But I've only just begun to play!" she pouted, casting him a fiery glance. "It's too early to go to bed!"

In her expression, I saw my own face and heard my own voice when I was a child, playing in the courtyard, and my mother or one of the servants or even, occasionally, my father, called out that it was beyond my bedtime.

"You must," Marcus said, quite firmly.

"Oh, well, if I must, I must." She smiled brightly. "But I shall be back," she said, turning to me. "Don't leave me alone too long. *You are me and I am you.*"

Marcus raised his hand, the palm flat toward her, closed his eyes, and she began to fade and fade until there was nothing left except something that looked like a wisp of smoke, and then that was gone too.

The fire crackled. Marcus and I were alone. He stood up, with his back to the fire. The cloudy mirror dissolved and became a wall of stucco and stone.

"So – I am going to live for thousands of years?" I looked up at him. All of this was too much to absorb – a mirror image of me, a magical twin, and eternal life – or almost. I was dizzy with strange intimations and thoughts. With the fire glowing gold behind him, Marcus looked like a statue, like a god, as if he had just descended from the heavens.

"Yes."

"I don't believe it."

"Do you believe what you have seen?"

I hesitated, frowned, clasped my hands and twisted them. "Yes."

"Well, then," he shrugged and smiled, his gaze holding mine. "What I have told you is true. You will almost certainly live for thousands of years."

"You are a god," I sighed. "You must be a god, to do such miraculous things, to make one live forever and to create life out of nothing."

"Not out of nothing."

"Then where did she come from?"

"From you; she came from you."

"Me?"

"From within you," he said. "To call her you must think or say the words

Avatar, my Avatar, and mentally focus on the bodily image of her – or of your-self. You can remember that?"

"I can remember that," I said, though I had no idea what the word "Avatar" meant.

Marcus put his hands on my shoulders: it was something he did, I noticed, when he wanted to tell me something important. "When you call her, it will require energy, it will consume energy, so only call her when you really need her, or when you are very safe and just want to talk to her and there is no danger. Understood?"

"Understood," I said. "She certainly is exhausting – and she has a mind of her own."

"Yes, she certainly has. That is because your mind is many minds, and she is part of you, a part you usually keep hidden. Indeed, each of us contains a myriad of minds – only most of us don't know it. In fact, most of us go to great lengths to deny it. But, with a little help, we can evoke and free all those hidden selves we carry swirling within us. It may be frightening, Tanis, but it is a source of great power."

I puzzled over this. I was bubbling with questions – about eternal life, about my Avatar, about each of us having many minds in one – but then Amilcare knocked and entered, saying that Marcus was needed for some urgent matter regarding the affairs of the city.

"Yes, Amilcare, I am coming!" Marcus turned to me. "You will not forget: 'Avatar: my Avatar!'"

"I will not forget." And I did something bold – I reached up and kissed him on the cheek.

Still feeling slightly unreal – having been faced with my high-spirited double, or Avatar – and very doubtful about the "thousands of years" I was supposedly destined to live, I returned to my apartments and to Asherah, and she and I whiled away the time inventing new hand-words for things and amusing hand-names for some of the funnier people we knew – the jovial overweight cook, one of the surly guards, the thin-as-a-rail Greek teacher who was a bit of a pedant, insisting that I memorize perfectly the inflections of the most unusual and difficult verbs, which I did, quickly and perfectly – to his considerable annoyance.

As for myself, each day brought a new discovery, since I was forced by my new condition, my new nature, to continually discover unsuspected aspects of myself and of this thing I had become.

Now that I had an Avatar, or soul, I could, even without calling her, see myself in mirrors; if I did not evoke her, she behaved just as a normal reflection would; and so, now that I could see myself, I felt I possessed that illusion, that ephemeral bit of self-reflection, that desperate yearning toward eternity and wholeness, and oneness, that people think of as a *soul*.

"Well, demon, this is a most incredible tale, this story of having your very own Avatar or soul. It borders on metaphysics and mysticism."

"I do apologize, Father O'Bryan. I am trespassing on your territory."

"No, no, not at all. Priests do not have a monopoly of … ah … mystical experiences. But I am curious. Tell me more. Did you ever meet your Avatar again? Did you have occasion to avail yourself of her services?"

"Oh, yes, Father, she is immensely useful, when I get in a real fix."

"A real fix?" I favored her with my most smug, my most unctuous, priestly smile. "Do tell, V. How is she useful?" In asking these questions I was, of course, curious about what she could tell me; but I was also playing for time, waiting for the right moment to strike down and vanquish this ingenious and inventive female demon. For die she must, of that I was sure.

"Well, Father," V licked her lips slyly, "once, I think it was in the 12th century – around 1190 CE – I was captured by some Crusaders who were on their way to the Holy Land to attack the Infidel, the Muslims who had conquered Jerusalem hundreds of years before, in 637 CE. As you know, Father, one man's Infidel is another man's Holy Warrior – hero or martyr or terrorist or whatever – depending on your point of view."

"Indeed." I was not quite happy to concede the point. "Go on."

"In any case, the Crusaders were raping and pillaging and killing people along the way; Jews in particular had been victims in some of the earliest Crusades."

"That is true, alas." I looked down into my glass and sloshed around the gold-amber liquid.

"In any case, I was captured by a sadistic but charming Crusader. This warrior had the bluest of eyes and curly blond hair and a complexion that seemed made of golden honey, rather like Richard Lionheart; and he was, like so many of them, and like Richard, a fanatic, an opportunist, and a cold-blooded killer.

"I had to get free of him quickly to save some children. Some of his fellow crusaders had decided to burn the children alive, and, well, my Avatar came in very handy, distracting the Crusader, who thought she was I.

"He bedded her in the straw in the stable where he kept me prisoner, and while he and she were thus occupied, I slipped out of the open gate and made my way to the village; I got there just in time to put out the fire that was about to consume thirty-two young souls – children and young teenagers – who had been locked in a barn, and destined for incineration, because their parents had not raised sufficient ransom.

"The Avatar conquered the blue-eyed Crusader, and tamed him for a whole day and night, openly consorting with him in the camp, though she did insult a lot of people she met on the way and made his life as difficult as she could. She is extremely opinionated – and outspoken. But I do love her dearly!"

"Well, well," I said. I was absorbing this, the Crusades, the Infidel, the Holy Land, the pogroms! Where had this demon not been?

"Well, enough of my Avatar, charming as she can be! Perhaps, someday, Father, you will meet her! And I suspect that you will prefer her to me, Father, and I warn you, I shall be jealous! I am horrible when I am jealous! I throw tantrums, I smash furniture, I scream, I ..."

"My God, Demon – calm down!"

"Of course, Father. Well, on with my story. If I am to have you on my side, it seems I must bare my innermost self, reveal myself to you in all my nakedness." She gazed at me and fluttered her eyelashes.

"Now, now, Demon!" I feared for a moment she was going to take off her clothes and start strutting around naked. I was not sure I could stand that!

She favored me with a warm smile. "Here, Father, you'll be wanting some comfort. Do have some more whiskey, dear Father O'Bryan!"

"Thank you!"

"It will steady your nerves!"

I gave her a look but did not deign to comment on her artful allusion to my moment of inner disarray and weakness. The image of this demon's nakedness, flitting through my brain, had deeply disturbed me, lighting up almost forgotten areas in my cerebellum where I had thought to have successfully extinguished, long ago, and for all time, the sparks, the flashy neon, the sinful gaudiness of fleshly lust; strangely, too, those images were overlaid with a brief, fresh flash – colored with a tincture of concern and regret – of the girl in the scarlet dress – such a sensuous and sensual and free-spirited-looking creature. It was clear that V had peeked into my mind and seen the reptilian masculine lustful monster crouching there. The Old Adam never truly dies, as long as there is breath in the body! And thus it is that the sacraments, and Saint

Francis Xavier, and other saints, and our blessed Lord Himself, and the dear, dear Virgin Mary, have put so many barriers, so many fences between us and our most inward, wayward, sinful thoughts and dangerously base proclivities.

Having blinked thoughtfully at me, and then topped up her own and my glass, V continued with her story.

"One day Asherah was with me in my quarters when something perfectly ghastly happened. It was the emergence of the 'me' you most fear, the 'me' that I was when I saved you down in the sewer. It was the first time I met the *demon*."

She paused, as if fearful of going on. I may be wrong, but it did seem to me that her eyes were wet. The glossy reflections of the lamplight shone on them, making her look blind. Was she mourning her lost innocence, her lost humanity, she who is now an alien, demonic creature?

The one table lamb lit us up, in obscurity and light, rather like one of those shadowy but richly lit paintings by Caravaggio. In this dimly lit room, sheltered from the sunlight, V's beauty was unearthly. In the lamplight, the half of her face that glowed was exquisitely sculpted and utterly hypnotic; the other half was lost in darkness.

This division – between light and shadow – was symbolic. I began to see that, raised, as she claimed she was, in the pagan cult of Ba'al and Asherah, in the ancient profusion of the sacred, and in the indiscriminate proliferation and promiscuity of gods and goddesses, and their constant mingling with humans and human destinies, she could easily believe she was a representative of those fallen divinities, once the brothers and sisters of God, and who had been cast down by Yahweh, and transformed into hideous demons, evil sulfurous warriors in the service of the Prince of Darkness.

That she had powers, and that she was a vampire – a foul drinker of blood – all of this was by now quite clear to me. And, in this, she was certainly at one with her brothers and sisters, the ancient gods and goddesses. Her thunder god, Ba'al, towering in the Phoenician pantheon, fed on human sacrifice – children falling from his arms into a blazing fire, burned alive to honor him and placate his rage and hunger. The screams must have been horrible. So, a demon she was, absolutely. Whatever else she might be, her powers and her beauty made her extremely dangerous.

She glanced at me, eyes wet, seemingly blinded by the lamplight, as if trying to read my thoughts.

"Do you wish to continue?"

She smiled. "Of course, Father. This is my confession."

"Do you expect absolution?"

"No, Father, of course not. However kind and generous you may be, absolution for me is, I'm afraid, impossible."

"I'm sorry, V."

"It is not your fault, Father." She smiled brightly and continued her tale.

I was in my apartments, walking back and forth, like a caged animal, as I sometimes did, if I could not sleep. Midday was midnight for me, the core of my sleeping time. It was cool in my shadowy apartment, but I could feel the vibrant heat of the sun, far away, outside the thick walls. An oil lamp flickered in the corner.

I yearned to rush out into the sunlight and run, and play, and talk to people, and laze and bathe in the rippling light. I wanted to worship the sun – just as I had when I was a child. I was tired of being a creature of the night.

I had asked for Asherah to come to me so that she and I could play a game of Senet. With Amilcar's help, I had taught her. She was a quick learner. And she did not seem to mind sitting with me, playing, in the shadows, far from the sun.

Beating her was hard. I had to concentrate, and I didn't always win – which made her happy and was good for me. Asherah's mind was swift and nimble and full of fun. And, since she could not talk, it lacked an outlet and overflowed with the need to play – just what I yearned for.

It was toward noon. I had called for her to come and duel with me in a fierce game of Senet when suddenly I felt very strange. Asherah came into the room. She took one look at me and put her hand to her mouth. Her eyes widened.

Something terrible was happening to me. My body was liquefying. My gown exploded, flew away in fragments, bits of cloth, some of them smoking and glowing. Some of them in burning brightly, flaring like little comets.

I screamed.

Asherah stood very still, her eyes growing wider, and her mouth open. Then, visibly making an effort, she came to me, and put her index finger to her mouth, indicating I should not make so much noise. She could not hear me, but she could see I was screaming.

My skin was on fire. I was as if insects were crawling all over me, a million tiny legs tramping around, dancing a devilish dance, every nerve end vibrating, enflamed …

I looked at my hands – and my arms – and I screamed as I had never screamed before.

Asherah grabbed my arms and gazed straight into my eyes.

Marcus came running into the room, his sword drawn.

"What is it?" He stopped and stared. I could see his eyes widen. Now he will kill me, now I am truly a monster. I was frozen in place, paralyzed by horror and revulsion, waiting for him to raise his sword.

Asherah turned to him, bowed and swung her arm out toward me, encompassing the new me, as if presenting me – an oddity and a freak– on a circus stage.

Marcus stood very still, apparently calm. He was clearly trying to control himself. Then, in a low, even voice, he said, "Well, well, Tanis, how do you feel?"

"What's happening to me?" I whimpered.

"Now, now …" He looked relieved. I don't know how I sensed this, but I immediately understood that my horror at my condition reassured him. I was still Tanis. I was still me. My mind had not turned monster. And for Marcus and Asherah, I wasn't a monster.

He motioned to Asherah to leave us – with a gesture that clearly meant she was not to inform anyone of what she had seen. She nodded and smiled her understanding – and, extraordinary thing, as she left the room she turned and blew me a kiss.

Marcus sheathed his sword, came up to me and put his hands on my shoulders. "This is natural; it is part of the process."

"This is horrible! This cannot be me!"

"It is you, Tanis. It is part of the process."

"Process?"

"Yes."

"Process? What process?" I was outraged at his calm – I wanted to hammer his chest with my fists – rather claws – but, as I wept, I realized I was comforted. His calm meant he accepted me.

So, instead of hammering his chest, I put my head against his shoulder and wept and at the same time I felt I possessed immense strength, immense energy, and boundless possibilities – that even though he was Marcus the Warrior, Marcus the Master, I could easily break him in two. But I was still a child – and I loved him.

He stroked my head. "Shush, shush," he repeated, in a rhythmic way, almost as if he were singing a lullaby.

"But what am I? What have I become?"

"You're a mystery, a beautiful mystery."

"Mystery! I am disgusting!"

"Just look at yourself! You are splendid!"

When I was calmer, I looked down at my body – at my arms, my breasts, my legs – all were more muscular, fuller, and stronger than before. My hands and feet had become claws, and my whole body was covered in scales, green, turquoise, gold, scarlet, shimmering serpent-like scales. I began to sob.

"Let's have a closer look at you."

He took me into his apartment, into the room with the vertical reflecting pool – the mirror – on the wall. "I believe this will be reversible."

"Reversible?"

"This is one of the forms you can take. If you concentrate, you can probably go back to what you were like before – to your human form."

"How do you know this?"

"I've lived for a long time. I know many things, though there are many things I do not know. In any case, you are beautiful now – and you were beautiful before – and you will be beautiful whatever form you take."

I sniffled again and rubbed my eyes with the back of my claws – careful not to claw myself. I shivered. "This is truly disgusting!"

Marcus unveiled the mirror. I gasped.

"Is that me? It cannot be!"

"It is."

"No, it is not me!"

"It is, Tanis, it is you!"

"This is what I have become?"

"Yes, Tanis, this is what you have become."

Staring back at me was a female demon, with large reptilian eyes and a body of shimmering scales. She was a voluptuous she-devil, too shapely to be real, a parody, a cartoon. She was like one of those impossibly muscular and statuesque female idols I had seen in the primitive temples in the slave quarter of the city, where strange rites from the farthest reaches of the Orient were carried out, with half-naked men and women convulsed in fiery dances under images of giant phalluses and monstrous hybrids of human and animal. I had become one of those primitive, frightening things!

"I'm a monster," I sniffled. My mouth was distorted into a reptilian grin by two long bright fangs. They were much more prominent than my normal vampire fangs. "I am truly a monster! Oh, the gods," I whimpered. I again began to sob. I watched with horror as the grotesque she-demon mimicked my sobbing. She was sobbing too! How horrible! We were one. "Oh, this is awful, this is terrible. I want to die."

"Now, now." Marcus put an arm around my shoulder. "Let us take a closer look."

We moved toward the mirror until I could gaze directly into my face, close-up, gleaming snout to gleaming snout: the serpent's eyes sparkled, gold, amber, silver, green and black. The nostrils quivered with emotion. The smile – and strangely it was a smile – was enigmatic, the fangs were a brilliant white. It was not me; it was a mask. A single tear wandered down one reptilian scaly cheek. I wiped it away with the back of my claw.

"You are beautiful." Marcus was smiling.

"Beautiful?" I exclaimed; and the demon in the mirror echoed, "Beautiful?" More tears ran down its cheeks. It hissed, "You call this beautiful?"

"Yes, you are beautiful – but I'm certain you can change back. Let us carry out a little experiment. Just think of the human you, the way you were just before this happened. Close your eyes and see – this is important, *see* – your human self."

The reptile eyes blinked and closed – I was plunged into darkness.

I concentrated. I pictured myself – my arms, my legs, and my face.

"Nothing's happening," I hissed.

"Keep going!"

I concentrated. I pictured myself, in my human form, running, riding on a horse; I pictured myself under the mountain stream, cool water pouring down over my shoulders, my back, my breasts and my stomach.

"Nothing's happening!"

"Keep trying!"

I pictured myself as a girl. I pictured myself as a woman. I pictured myself laughing with Lalla at the fountain, as we splashed each other with water. I pictured myself dressed as a young man, companion to Marcus. I pictured myself with my father and mother, in the courtyard, dining in the cool of the evening, gossiping, my father telling us stories of his voyages and of those Greek pioneers who lived, mining tin and gold and copper, on the windy islands, Lipari and Vulcano and Salina, north of Sicily, beyond Scylla and Charybdis, beyond the fiery mountain, Etna.

Suddenly, I felt a rippling all over my body, as if tens of thousands of ants were scurrying this way and that. Every inch of my flesh was aquiver. My sense of myself dissolved, went all blurry, shimmered and shivered, my skin withered; it burned as if in a flame, then it quieted. I felt as if I was me once again.

"Open your eyes."

I was visible, there, in the mirror, but it was the old me, the human me, or at least the human version of me. I no longer had any clothes – just a few fluttery specks of cloth that fell away from my nakedness like bright drifting motes in a beam of sunlight.

"Oh, thank the gods," I cried and threw myself into Marcus's arms.

"Now you are one in many and many in one." He stroked my hair.

"But what was that – that version of me?"

"Well, Tanis, that is a long story …" Marcus cleared his throat. He took on his serious expression, which he used when he was about to lecture me. This demonic form, he explained, was a version that came from deep inside me; that I should not be afraid of the transformation; that in my demonic form I would be even stronger than in my human and vampire forms; and that I should practice moving from one to the other. He told me that, at first, being the demon would consume a lot of energy, unless it was just in repose, and so, in general, I should transform myself into the demon only when I needed to fight a great and difficult battle or if I was going to sleep in a dangerous territory where I would have to be ready to fight the instant of wakening. With time, he said, the demon would become more natural. "The demon will become," Marcus smiled at me, "second nature."

When he said "demon" he said it with a smile. I still can see, years later, centuries later, that smile in my mind and wonder exactly what it meant.

"Second nature?" I hugged myself.

"Yes, Tanis." He took me in his arms, pressed me to him, his warm strong body comforting me. He kissed me on the forehead. I sighed. So many mixed feelings, all swirling together – love, hate, fear, horror, adoration! I looked up at him – my protector, my teacher, my mentor.

"Soon you will delight in this new you," said Marcus, his hands on my shoulders. "You must accept the new you, Tanis, and you must practice – back and forth, back and forth. It will become easy."

How he knew all this remained a mystery.

Over the next weeks, Marcus made me practice moving back and forth between my three versions – human, vampire, and demon. It went faster and faster, easier and easier, until it became automatic and I could switch in an instant, and at will.

Other than Marcus, Asherah was the only witness to my transformations. She would help me in my exercises, timing me by raising one finger, then another, then another, counting out silently how long it took me to whirl into the new version of me – and out again. At first, it took perhaps thirty seconds, and then it came down to five, and then to one. Eventually, it seemed almost instantaneous, a quarter of a second, or even less. Of course, I'm using our modern concepts of time rather than the more fluid and variable ways time was measured in those days.

Asherah even did, once, a sort of comic dance, which was an imitation of me morphing into the demonic. I laughed, then embraced her, and she kissed me on the lips. I kissed her back, and, right there and then, we invented a new hand-word, a sort of spiraling motion of the fingers, a swirling – and humorous – sculptural portrait, which meant: "Tanis transforming herself into demon and back."

I began to like being the she-demon. I was addicted. I wandered out into the desert alone; I practiced leaping over high walls, smashing stones in two. It was fun being so much more powerful than in my human form. What Marcus had said was true: So much frenetic and playful activity made me hungry. I fed more often.

In the weeks that followed, Marcus trained me, in my human form, in what are now called the martial arts – swordsmanship, throwing a lance or a spear, using a sling shot, killing or paralyzing a person by a single sideways chop of the hand. Asherah shared the exercises, and Marcus was equally careful in training her. Asherah would be my aid and consort, Marcus explained, when I needed one. As for me, I was to become, Marcus said, a warrior woman.

Marcus loved me whatever form I took. Asherah accepted me and loved to play and laugh with me whatever form I took. So, I learned to love and accept myself.

I began not only to like but to love my demonic form: it is wilder, freer, more natural, and more naked than my human self.

Sometimes I think I would prefer to live that way all the time, virtually invulnerable. But it would mean living in a cave, or forest, hidden from humans; and, at heart, I am a city girl. I really do like people – and I like meeting new people. Every single person has a lesson to teach. Every person is a whole universe.

And, of course, I need to feed. In the desert you do not find people, except perhaps nomads, or a solitary saint or two. But I do assure you, dear Father O'Bryan, I am not in the habit of feeding on saints, not when I can avoid it!"

The demon paused. She took a sip of whiskey and glanced sideways at me with that sheepish little-girl smile. She was being naughty – feeding meant killing people …

You are a strange girl, my demon, I thought. It is as if all of this is for you a game, and somehow not real, as if we humans were mere extras in a drama written by you and for you; we are shadowy creatures who live for an instant and who count for little – except as fodder and perhaps amusement.

"You were saying, V?"

"Yes, of course, of course." She stared at me, licked her lips, and once again continued her story.

Well, Father, one night I had a confrontation – well, a moment of revelation – with Marcus. The image of perfection he projected was shattered. Thinking back, I believe he did it deliberately.

We were alone in his quarters, though on this night the mirror was not there; it was only a blank stone wall. A small fire was burning in the fireplace, two logs, and bright embers. Marcus was sitting on one side of it in a chair of gold and silver and mahogany, with carved swirling images of Aphrodite rising from the sea at the end of the armrests. He had been drinking. There were beads of sweat on his upper lip, his eyes were brighter than usual, and there was the sweetness of wine on his breath. He told me to sit down. And, with a strange new type of fear rising in me, I did so, in a matching chair, on the other side of the fireplace. I was nervous. I clutched the armrests.

"Here, drink!" He offered me a glass.

I sipped the ruby red wine. "Thank you, Marcus." Drinking wine and not blood was a strange sensation, but not at all unpleasant.

"I want you to promise me one thing," he said.

"Yes."

"You will make no more of your kind."

"I don't want to make any more of my kind."

"Good! But swear that you won't!"

I raised my hand, my palm toward him, using a gesture he had taught me: "I swear!"

"Good!"

"But – if my kind is so dangerous – if I am so dangerous – why are you so good to me?"

"I loved one of your kind once."

"What happened to her?"

"I killed her." He looked at his hands.

I didn't know what to say. I wanted to touch him, to comfort him, but I didn't dare. If he killed her, why didn't he kill me? "How … how did you kill her?"

He looked up. His eyes, normally so clear, were bloodshot; he was crying, there were traces of tears on his tough, tanned cheeks.

"Why did you kill her?"

He didn't answer. He stood up, walked around the room, then came back and knelt in front of me.

Now I was really frightened. I clutched the armrests tighter, digging my fingernails into the wood.

As he knelt there, in front of me, tears streamed down his face. "I loved her, but such love is fatal. You know that, don't you? To consume such a love is fatal. I was crazy with love; it was a disease she and I shared; it was my passion; it was my world. Our love was an all-consuming fever. It had to be broken. I waited until she was weak. She had not fed for days. I kept her occupied, distracted. The weaker she became, the more passionate and inventive she became, languid and ultra-sensitive, playful and dreamy. We pushed our sensual games to the limit. I had never lived such ecstasy in my life – our bodies and minds were as one … But love with such as she must never be consummated – you know that!"

"Yes." Somehow, I knew that to consummate my love for anyone would mean their death. In my amorous passion, I would bite them, but not kill them; and, if I bit them, but did not kill them, they would become a blood-drinking beast – but, almost certainly, one without my self-control. I don't know how I knew this; but I did. If I loved someone, I would create a true monster, unchained, wild and deadly. It would be a plague. It would spread. It would mean the end of humankind.

Marcus stood up, drank deeply, refilled his glass, and stared down at me. His eyes were feverish. "I chained her to the bed. I pretended it was one of our erotic games. She trusted me. She put her destiny in my hands."

"Then …?"

"Then – I opened the curtains, unbolted the shutters, and let in the sun."

His face was like stone.

I held myself rigid, gripping the armrests. I trembled in horror and terror: I was the girl chained and bolted to that bed. I was the one staring up at my lover, at the man I worshipped, I was the one suddenly realizing he had betrayed me, that he was, in that instant, betraying me; that his love was false, that everything was a lie, that he had plotted my annihilation!

Marcus took a deep breath. "I shouted at her, asked her to forgive me. The rays of the sun, golden and warm, flooded the room. It was blinding. She was lit up as if by a giant fire. Waves of energy swept over her. Pure liquid gold coated her nakedness, shone in her hair, and filled her eyes. She twisted and turned. For a moment she was there, just as beautiful as ever, and relief flooded through me at the thought she was immune. *Why, why, why,* she cried, *I loved you, I love you, I love you ...*

"Then it began – first as a sizzling sound. Then cracks and veins appeared, her skin turned white, turned black, turned gray, turned to ash and fell away. Her eyes darkened to black, then white only, then one last long scream, *Why, why, why?*

"She was burning, as if on a funeral pyre, but alive, and slowly she died, slowly, each inch, each nerve ending, the skin and flesh frying, crackling, and peeling away. The screaming stopped. Only the skeleton remained. Then the bones snapped, one by one, and fell into dust. On the altar where we had shared so much passion, there was nothing but a handful of dust. I see it always. I cannot shut it out." He put his arm over his eyes, bowed his head, and was silent. He went down on his knees.

I said nothing. I felt as if I had been betrayed. *I was she; she was me.*

I got up, went to him, knelt next to him and held him in my arms.

And that, Father O'Bryan, is part of my story, part of what I am."

"Part of what you are, V ..." I stared at my glass. "Your roots go deep."

"Yes."

"It must be lonely." I hated to admit it, but I was moved by the demon's story, whether it was fanciful or not. It was a tale of impossible love and irreparable loss. But of course, all demons, exiled far from God, far from the light of redemption and hope, suffer irreparable loss; they are steeped in darkness and sin; and thus, imprisoned in nihilistic obscurity, incapable of love, they learn to simulate all human emotions, to feign empathy, just as clever psychopaths and serial killers do, while – silently – they are coldly plotting our destruction. "It must be lonely, V," I repeated.

"Lonely?" She smiled. "Remember – I am not human."

"But you feel human emotions."

She looked down and toyed with a steak knife that had been lying on the table, tracing one of the veins in the wood with the point of the knife, delicately, without scarring the wood.

She looked up. "I'm not sure I do feel *human* emotions, Father. Indeed, do you? Do you know what a *human* emotion is? I don't mean to be insulting or to question your sincerity. But are you sure what you call 'love' or 'jealousy' is what other people call 'love' or 'jealousy'? You humans are very proud of what you call your *feelings* – it is as if you and only you in the universe were capable of such things as *feelings*!"

I didn't say anything. I looked down at my hands; the ancestral, gnarled, heavy, weather-roughened hands of an Irish peasant. So now it is revealed, I thought, so now the abyss of hell will open and I will stare into it. This demon hates us. She despises us. I must not flinch. I wanted her to show all her hatred, all her hostility toward humankind. I wanted to feel justified in doing what I knew had to be done – I must kill her.

"You humans treat other creatures," she was staring at me, "as if they had no feelings, no thoughts, no suffering. You treat the whole world as if it had no existence, except its duty to serve you …"

"Ah," I said. "Man, the Lord of all Creation …"

"Yes, Man, the Lord of all Creation." She uttered the words with disdain. She looked at me again, as she toyed with the knife. It was a very fine steak knife, stainless steel, serrated and very sharp. But she handled it deftly, not scarring or marring the wood at all. Her eyes were so dark – so intense – but I could see nothing in them. Not even the reflection of the lamp.

She is, I thought, a soulless demon – to be cast out and destroyed. All her talk, all the pathos, all the humanity, is mere illusion. I was even beginning to like her! But she is like the pestilence. No, she *is* the pestilence. I have dealt with such creatures before. I know how to cast them out and cast them down. The Lord's will *must* be done.

She looked at me curiously, her head tilted to one side. "So, Father, you are going to destroy me, to cast me down … the Lord's will *must* be done."

"No, no … I …" I stuttered; I needed to buy time.

"The side of your mouth twitched, your forehead broke out in a sweat, you were reciting Biblical verse in your head, and you have the smell of hatred upon you." She bared her perfect teeth. I could not see into her soul at all – for, of course, the dear soul has no soul.

She leaned closer to me and whispered: "...*for, of course, the dear soul has no soul.*" She had it down even to the trace of an Irish lilt.

I stared at her. Satan could have no greater helper than she, charming, beautiful, a diviner of souls, reader of minds, and drinker of blood!

"Oh, Father O'Bryan, you are so honest, so sincere. You are a good man, Father, but you shouldn't believe in hobgoblins and fairies, and little green men from Mars. As for me, yes, I am a freak of nature, a mystery and a puzzle, certainly. But handmaiden of Satan – no, I don't think so! I am sure there is a rational explanation for what I am. I have tried to find out what transformed me. A vampire's bite? A magic potion? The needle Lalla pricked me with? The drink she gave me before she died? A virus? A curse? As for Satan, Father, I don't believe I am Satan, and I don't believe I work for Him. I've never met Him, or Her, or It."

She stood up and got the bottle of whiskey from the sideboard. "It's the only thing I drink, Father, other than wine, coffee, and human blood – my total diet!"

She poured me another glass and one for herself. "When I kill people, Father, I kill them; that's all I do; if there is a Heaven or Hell and if they have a soul, then they go their separate ways to Heaven or to Hell, though mostly to Hell, I suppose, given the way I choose my fodder. But I have nothing to do with that. I do not harvest or collect souls. Not everyone is interested in collecting souls. I am not a crusader. I am not you. I am not interested in souls." She raised her glass, hesitated a moment, as if in salutation, as if making a toast, and drank. "I leave the souls to the professionals!"

She sat down.

I knew what I had to do. I could not even think my intention – because, if I did, she would know. The curtains were right beside us. They were of course thick, impermeable to light, and closed tightly. I knew the sun was shining brilliantly, slightly to the west. If I ripped open the curtains, the sun would flood in, and she, like Marcus's bestial vampire lover, would die, consumed in a pyre of fire.

That was what I must do – and now!

I jumped up. Her demonic magic had been such that I was bursting with energy – not a trace of pain or stiffness from my wounds.

In an instant I was at the curtains. I seized them with both fists and tore them open.

The sun flooded in – brilliant and gold. It washed over her, covering the demon in a glittering sheen of light; it was blindingly bright, and sparkled on every inch of her – the wonderful, purifying power of the sun.

The demon would die!

I would watch her disintegrate, I would free the world of this curse. I would save my soul! The beautiful demon would die, disintegrate into dust, and be no more!

And, so, with bated breath, I watched …

CHAPTER 18 – NAKED

Wrapped in the big white towel, Kate sat on the white metal chair in the small white room, her hands clasped on the white metal table in front of her; she felt entirely normal and clear-headed; the lunch, it seemed, had not been drugged.

She had thought of all sorts of ways of escaping. Climb up the wall and crawl through the little window? The window was too high, barely large enough to crawl through; it was heavily barred; and she had no idea what was on the other side. Okay, so much for that! Sprint past the giant monks and make a galloping run for it? That was ridiculous! Where would she go? And, besides, the monks moved quickly when they wanted to; she'd seen them. Nope, that wouldn't work! Hit them over the head with the chair she was sitting on? Ha! Ha! Hide somewhere – say, in the shower cubicle – and ambush them? That was clearly silly! All the choices were dead ends! In the small room, with the heavily barred window high up and out of reach, there was nowhere to run and nowhere to hide. Damn it! It was impossible!

The nun entered the room, her expressionless baby-like face framed by the shadowy hood. She stared at Kate. "No towel," she said, and held out the skimpy thin little hospital gown.

"I prefer the towel." Kate clutched it closer.

"No towel."

Two of the monks entered the room. They stood and stared at her. Then they indicated – quite clearly, making tearing, ripping, wrestling gestures with their huge hands – that if she were foolish enough to resist, they would grab the towel from her. Or she could be wise and give it up voluntarily.

Kate stared back. She considered fighting, but then decided that discretion was, for the moment, the better part of valor.

"Okay." She stood up slowly, turned her back, opened the towel, and held it out behind her. The nun took it.

Kate looked over her shoulder. The two monks and the nun stared, expressionless, at her nakedness. The nun held out the hospital gown. Kate took it. Keeping her back turned to them, she put her arms into its sleeves. It was ultra-short, as thin as tissue paper, and semitransparent.

Damnation!

Worse – there was no way she could tie it shut. It had no twill tapes at the back – they'd been cut off. These people! *Double damnation!* She might as well be naked. She crossed her arms and held the flimsy tissue thing close and turned to face her tormentors. The situation looked more and more ominous. Was she just a hostage? Or was she in fact a *sacrifice*? And, if so, *a sacrifice to what?*

"Sit," said the nun.

"Sit," Kate growled, gritting her teeth. "Sit, Fido, sit!"

They didn't flinch. Kate twisted her lip. These creatures obviously had no sense of humor; they hadn't gotten the joke, or they didn't want to recognize it. Or they didn't catch the reference. Maybe they weren't even human! Kate fumed. The white metal chair was cold and hard under her naked backside. The gown fluttered and opened, slipping away from her shoulders; she pulled it back, crossed her arms, clutching the flimsy tissue close.

Then …

Nothing happened …

Kate sat erect, quite still, waiting, her heart beating hard, furious at herself for being so passive and helpless. The nun and the monks stood in front of her; they did not move, and they said nothing. Kate bit her lip. She must control her rage, her shame. This whole thing was intolerably humiliating. And she had to admit, if only even to herself, she was proud; she cherished a sense of her own dignity – and why not? She concentrated, listening for sounds that might give her a clue as to where she was – traffic, a train, church bells, construction work, animals … But she heard nothing useful, just a suggestion of air-conditioning running somewhere, just the breathing of the monks, and the occasional crisp rustling of the paper-thin hospital gown. Her own beating heart – that was the loudest sound.

Father Ottavio came into the room.

"What is this about?" Kate gave him her coolest, most level stare. "Why am I being stripped and humiliated like this?"

Without a word, he pulled the other metal chair over, sat down right in front of her, on the other side of the small metal table. He sat there and stared at her for a long time, inspecting her as if she were a piece of furniture.

Kate stared back: *I will kill you; I will damned well kill you.* Outwardly, she displayed the utmost calm. She studied the man, putting him under a mental microscope, as if he were an insect. She examined the coarse grain of his skin, the small scar by his left nostril, the gray and green striations of his irises, the neat cut of his salt-and-pepper beard, the white specks of dandruff in his hair and on the shoulders of his priest's black jacket, the blackheads on and around his nose, memorizing everything, trying to understand. *If I understand, I may find a chink of weakness.*

"Glasses," he said, holding out his hand.

"My glasses?"

"Yes, your glasses," his hand still extended, palm up.

"No."

Father Ottavio nodded to one of monks. The giant leaned over and with his huge pudgy hand grabbed the glasses, lifted them up, dropped them, then crushed them under his heel. The crunching sound was painful.

"What was that for? What are you doing?"

Father Ottavio didn't answer. Kate tried to focus. Without her glasses, Father Ottavio was a blur, a hostile blur; the monks and the nun too; they were looming blobs and smears of black and white, an abstract painting. Kate began to stand up, but one of the monks pushed and held her down, his huge fingers pressed on her shoulders. He was immensely powerful; his grip was painful.

"Hair down!" Father Ottavio nodded to the nun.

"What?"

Before Kate could react, the nun had cut the elastic and pulled at her hair, which fell free, down around her cheeks, "What the hell are you people doing? What is this about?"

"Good, very good!" Father Ottavio gazed at her, his face an oval smudge.

"What's very good?"

"Remove it," said Father Ottavio.

"What?" Kate's voice rose. The big monk lifted his hands off her shoulders and ripped the hospital gown from Kate's back before Kate had time to react. She tried to cover her breasts, but the monk grabbed her arms, twisted them, pinning them behind her back.

"You bastards," Kate whispered, "you absolute bastards!"

Father Ottavio said nothing. He just sat there, within a few inches of Kate, staring. The smudged oval that was his face looked her up and down; he was taking possession of her body, drawing up an inventory of her parts; Kate was about to spit in his face, but it would serve no purpose. These people killed without a second thought. Thrashing around and hitting out would be worse than useless. She said nothing.

"Stand up!"

"Goddamn you!"

The monk put his big pudgy hand under her arm.

"I can stand up by myself, thank you!" Kate shook him off and stood up.

"Turn around!"

"Okay. You're the boss."

Father Ottavio, still sitting, pushed the table to one side. He stared. Kate turned around again, then stopped. "Have you seen enough? May I sit down?"

"Arms above your head – straight up!"

"Okay."

"Turn around like that – arms up!"

"Okay."

"Tiptoes now and turn around."

"Tiptoes?" *Jesus Christ!* She did it, pirouetting, turning around and around and around … They were staring at her. Even without her glasses she could see that! The nun, the two monks, and Father Ottavio, all watching the naked stripper do her tiptoe pirouette. *Jesus Christ!* This was humiliating! She stopped turning. "Well, have you seen enough now? May I sit down?"

"Yes. Sit down."

"What was that about?"

"You'll do," he said.

"I'll do what?"

"She'll do." Father Ottavio stood up, "She's perfect. Prepare her." He leaned over and ran his fingers through her hair; he brushed her cheek with the tips of his fingers. The rough grain of his fingertips lingered, caustic, on her cheekbone. She felt the ridges of skin, as if he were leaving his fingerprint, his mark, on her cheek. He was branding her. He was branding the naked prisoner. She was tempted to jerk her head back, slap him, bite him, scratch his eyes out. She forced herself to stay absolutely still. She would not give him the satisfaction. She would not flinch. She would not react. His fingers lingered. She could hear his breathing. Then he was gone.

Naked, she was exposed, vulnerable, her identity soiled, despoiled. Part of her vital self had been stripped away.

She sat there, rigid, impotent, fuming. She was blushing, and she knew it; her eyes were wet, bright with anger, humiliation.

One of the monks was holding something. Kate blinked, trying to focus. What was it …? It was a needle, a hypodermic needle.

"What the hell …?" Kate tried to shield herself. The other monk seized her arms, and twisted them behind her back, pinning her, naked, against him, against the coarse, rough folds of his monk's habit.

"Goddamn it, you can't do this!"

The needle plunged into her neck.

The rest was darkness.

CHAPTER 19 – SUN GOD

And so, to kill the demon, I tore open the curtains.

Sunlight flooded in, golden, brilliant, hot sunlight!

Yes, I had my opportunity to kill the demon, and I seized it. It was my duty as a priest; it was my duty as a human. She was a demon-vampire; she would die as a vampire should die – as a demon should die – in flames, in the purifying destructive power of fire.

The beautiful demon had turned in her chair, and was watching me curiously – wondering what I was doing, leaping up like that. One eyebrow was arched, a half-smile on her lips. Then, as the curtains were torn aside, the sun came flooding in. She frowned, but she did not move.

I stood next to the curtains, stupidly, waiting for her to flee – or to burst into flames. The merciless purifying sun shone on her jet-black hair, on her flawless skin, on her bright lips. I expected her to scream, to writhe in pain, to shrivel into dust and ashes.

She sat there frozen like a statue, not attempting to escape.

Then she swiveled her chair around, so she was directly facing the sun – and me. For a moment she said nothing, then: "Father O'Bryan, are your fears and hatred so great? Is your desire to destroy me so great?"

I was aghast. There was no sign of disintegration, no sign of burning, and no sign – even – of suffering. She was stronger, more powerful than I feared, and, of course, that meant she was even more dangerous than I realized.

She stood up, fully illuminated in the glory of the sun. She was a proud creature, that was clear – her chin up, her eyes blazing. She did look like a goddess. She went to the sideboard and seized a large carving knife. She approached me. Was she going to murder me? "Here," she said, handing the knife to me. "If you wish to kill me, try this, Father. Plunge it into my heart."

I took the knife.

She was standing very close, three or four inches shorter than I, both of us caught in the blazing golden glory of the hot afternoon sun. She stared at me, her eyes dark and bright and damp, little golden tears caught in her jet-black eyelashes. I felt as if I were looking into the eyes of a lover or a child – someone I should protect, not destroy.

"Go on!"

A single tear had formed and was traveling down her cheek.

"Go on, Father! What are you waiting for?"

Her beauty was blindingly bright.

"Go ahead, Father! Do it!"

"I …"

"Go on, Father, kill me! You know it has to be done!"

My hand, grown sweaty, gripped the carving knife.

"I …"

"Well?" Her lips trembled. She was visibly struggling to hold in her anger, her dismay: I had betrayed her. I had listened to her stories, to her secrets. But I had remained unmoved. She had tried her charms, her wit, and her beauty. It had not worked. She had saved my life, she had cured my ills, but now I was about to destroy her. The single tear, glistening in the sun, had been joined by another. I tightened my grip on the knife.

Then … "No, child," I said, and I offered her the knife.

She hesitated, then took it. "Thank you, Father." She returned the knife to the sideboard. "I am sorry, Father. I have put you in an impossible position. I have forced you into what you see as an alliance with Satan."

"What about the sun?" Now I was worried – perhaps I had damaged her irreparably.

"Oh, the sun," she said, "Too much will harm me – that's why the curtains are all light-proof, though it's not really necessary. It's more for old time's sake. I am immune, pretty much totally immune."

"Immune?" I pulled the curtain shut, plunging us into shadow. We took our places once again, at the table, facing each other.

"Yes, immune."

"Tell me."

"Marcus, as I mentioned, told me that he worshipped the Sun God. I am sure he did not worship the sun, really; it was part joke, part metaphor. He had to speak in a way that I could understand. But he did know a great deal about the sun and about light – his science was immense – he made me immune to the sun."

"How?"

"Well, Father. It happened this way …"

"Tanis, I shall change the sun from an enemy into a friend." Marcus gazed at me, with one eyebrow arched, as if he were calculating my true worth.

"Really?"

"Yes, really." He grinned, giving me one of his most charming smiles, "Come!"

He led me to the innermost sanctum of his quarters, his private studio, or workshop, which was next to his sleeping chambers. He had many instruments and a sort of altar – or shrine – at one side of the room. There was a fountain, too, and a small pool; on one wall, there was a mirror, like the one in which my Avatar had appeared, and on another wall, there were some silver-colored metal things, tools or instruments. On the wall above the altar was a large image of the sun.

And so – the ceremony began.

"Stand here." Marcus looked me up and down, again as if he were considering selling me on the slave market down in the harbor. Then he smiled and told me to disrobe and to get down on my hands and knees, naked, and pray.

"Disrobe?"

"Yes."

"Everything?"

"Yes."

"Hmm." I gave him a look.

He grinned. I was to do as he said.

"Well, then …" I shrugged. I was not allergic to nakedness. And physical shame – or modesty – did not seem to be in my repertoire. I was dressed as a boy. I lifted off my tunic, stepped out of my sandals, took off my leggings and my undergarments, and folded everything on the raised edge of the pool.

"Kneel. Go down on all fours."

"If you insist, Master." I got down on all fours before the altar, my knees and the palms of my hands on the damp stone. For what should I pray? And to whom?

Marcus stood next to me and intoned a prayer to the sun in that mysterious language he had whispered to Lalla. It was musical and sweet and full of light.

Then, he rounded it off with some nursery rhymes and nonsense.

I looked up at him with a frown: Was he making fun of me?

He smiled and winked.

"On hands and knees, you look like a she-wolf." He was grinning.

I growled low in my throat, like a she-wolf. I bared my teeth and snarled.

"Exactly," he smiled. "That is excellent."

The image of the sun above the altar began to glow. It radiated warmth, a delicious, drunken sense of lightness and strength.

Marcus, turning serious, filled a bowl with a smoking white liquid. He ordered me to drink from the bowl, as I was, on all fours, to lap it up with my tongue, keeping my knees and the palms of my hands flat on the floor.

I growled and began to lap. This was rather exciting, being a she-wolf. The liquid tasted like gold, that's all I can say, though I've never tasted gold, or perhaps it tasted like thick sweet honey. I had a vague memory of what honey tasted like. It flooded me with warmth and strength such as I had never known.

"Do not move," Marcus said. He brought over a large vase that looked as if it were made of a shiny silver metal as smooth as a still watery surface at dawn.

I did not move. I was frightened now, but I trusted him absolutely. If he had told me to kill myself, I would have done it.

I remained on all fours on the cool damp stone of the workshop floor.

"Close your eyes and keep them closed. This is very important!"

I closed my eyes and I felt him pouring something over my body. It was cool and thick, and it smelled sweet. It smelled like paradise. It seemed to cling to my body, and it spread – crawling and wiggling everywhere, like something alive. Finally, it covered me entirely. I was conscious of every square inch of skin, of every subtle curve of my body, of every orifice and opening. I longed to shimmy and wiggle and shiver; but I didn't.

"Now you can stand, but keep your eyes tightly closed."

I rose to my knees, blindly, and stood upright. Marcus poured more of the liquid over me. It tickled. "This must cover you entirely, every inch of your skin and body – your eyelids, your sex, your scalp, the soles of your feet, the palms of your hands, everything."

The thick foaming liquid hissed and bubbled over my skin. Following his orders, I rubbed it onto my eyelids, and the soles of my feet, between my legs, between my toes, everywhere.

"Open your eyes," he said, at last.

In his hand, Marcus held a source of light – it seemed to be a small baton – and he was shining the light on me. It was blindingly bright – like a miniature sun – it glowed purple and hummed. He shone it up and down my body, radiating my body, I suppose we would say today, but with what form of energy I do not know. He was thorough, probing every nook and cranny. "Spread your legs, Tanis." I frowned. "Yes, sir!" I said and I did as I was told. When he came to my face, he said, "Now, close your eyes again and for the sake of the gods keep them shut."

Again, I did as I was told.

The warmth of the light – of the radiation – sank into my skin, into my flesh, into my bones. I became the light itself.

Finally, Marcus said, "You may open your eyes now."

He put the little baton away in a sort of drawer in the metal wall – a wall of steel, I think it was, now that I look back on those days, steel or a material like steel.

He raised his hand, palm toward the section of the altar's wall representing the sun. He said a single word in that mysterious language he shared with Lalla. The wall slid aside. Where the image of the sun had been, there was the sun itself, the brilliant rising sun.

We had been together all night. It had seemed no time at all!

The cocks crowed. The room was flooded with light.

My heart exalted. The sun! I adored the sun! And if Marcus wanted me to die now, I would gladly die; whatever purpose he had, I would serve that purpose.

I looked at my arms and legs. I was chalk-white. I looked like a statue of white marble, coated in the smooth liquid.

I glanced at the sun, rising from the glittering sea. I knew instinctively – or thought I knew – that the sun would set me alight. I would be consumed in a column of fire.

"Don't move!"

I stood quite still, naked, facing the rising sun.

The red and gold heat flooded over me.

Nothing happened. I merely felt great warmth, great happiness, great power, and profound love too, love for him …

"You may bathe in the pool," he said.

As I stepped into the pool, and under the cascade of water, the white liquid peeled away from my skin, like scales from a snake, or plaster from a wall. But my skin itself was chalk-white too, not the honey gold it had been. Startled, I scrubbed my skin with my fingers, trying to remove the white; but it would not go away. It was what I had become; I was a statue, flawless, but looking as cold as white marble. "You will regain color in time, even a tan," he said. "Do not worry."

"This is the way I will be?"

"Yes," he said. "Now you begin another stage of your new life."

When I came out of the pool, he was holding a fresh perfumed cloak for me. He put it over my shoulders. I pulled it around me.

"What I have done is not perfect, but it will give you a great deal of immunity, and the effect will increase over time. Still, in the beginning, it is best to avoid staying uncovered in the sun for hours on end. Just go out near dawn or at twilight. Later you will be able to go out at noon or any time of the day."

The wall of the altar slid shut. We were in shadow. I looked at my chalk-white hands. I did not like this new ghostly me.

"I am ugly," I pouted. "I am a piece of dead marble."

"No, you are beautiful."

"I look like the frigid people of the north. The ones with white skin from across the sea, the ones who paint their skins with blue mud, the ones who cannot read or write and who have blue eyes and golden hair and pasty white skin with freckles and who do not bathe and who eat people and fall down before strange ugly forest gods. I do not like this new me."

He laughed. "You are as beautiful as before, even more so perhaps, only different. This will fade and your skin will be like honey and gold once more. In fact, I rather believe that your skin will change shades and be pale or dark whenever you wish it to do so."

I took refuge in his arms, sheltering in his love. But, with my face pressed against his shoulder, I asked myself: Who am I? ? What am I? What will I become?

CHAPTER 20 – DELICATE BALANCE

"The sun, the sun, the sun!" Twirling around, tiptoe on the cobblestones, Scarlett lifted her arms straight up, ballerina-style, worshipping the streaming sunlight, the perfect blue sky. The air was balmy and still.

"The Sun!" Jian grinned. "Middle-aged star, approximately seventy-three percent hydrogen, twenty-three percent helium, with a scattering of oxygen, carbon, neon, and iron. Operates by nuclear fusion at the core, powered by gravity and pressure, fusion that converts hydrogen into helium."

"Spoilsport! Evil! Evil!" Scarlett stopped spinning and stuck out her tongue.

Jian laughed. "It takes a little over eight minutes for the light from the sun to reach the Earth. Little photons zipping at us at three hundred thousand kilometers per second!"

"You, Jian Chang, are absolutely evil. There is no poetry in you. Not an ounce, not a gram!" She moved into his arms, kissed him, and then swung him around so they were both facing the morning market in Campo de' Fiori.

"Food!" he sighed.

"Let's have an orange!" Scarlett had spotted some luscious-looking oranges piled up in a pyramid, just next to a profusion of flowers.

"Orange – citrus fruit of the …"

"Oh, shut up, you beautiful devil, you!" She closed his mouth with a kiss. He ran his hands over her, exploring every bit of her, down her back, to the very small of her back, and up, and over … Thin white T-shirt, skintight white shorts.

"We are being indecent," she whispered.

"This is Rome," he murmured into her ear. "Anything is possible."

"Well, then, if you say so, Signore."

"Let us eat, then, and drink caffeine."

"Yes!" Scarlett bent down and picked up an orange and asked how much it cost, and the lady told her.

Jian and Scarlett bought two ripe navel oranges, perfect juicy seedless messy food. They leaned against the lip of the fountain next to the market and ate the oranges, and then they carefully deposited the peels in a garbage receptacle and washed their hands under the little cast iron pump – Scarlett had discovered that the little nineteenth-century drinking fountain pumps were known known as *nasoni* – or "big noses." This one stood just in front of the brooding statue of Giordano Bruno – who, she informed Jian, had been burned alive for heresy on this very spot in 1600.

"Now the coffee."

"Over there?"

"Yes, over there."

They chose a little round table on the terrace of a café, and sat down, ordered coffee and croissants, and breathed it all in. The traditional morning market of Campo de' Fiori was in full swing. The sun shone straight down on the awnings of the market stalls. The vendors hawked fruit and vegetables, fish and meats. Huge bouquets of fresh flowers were piled high. Under the awnings, mountains of zucchini and lemons gleamed, and fresh strawberries, tomatoes, mushrooms, and fish – squid, octopus, anchovies, mullet, shrimp, cod, and mackerel. The vendors shouted, joked, and waved their arms, advertising their wares. The air was limpid, perfumed with all the rich, various smells of the market.

The capuccinos were delicious, and the croissants were fresh from the corner bakery. Scarlett plunged into her guidebook, and glanced up, pointing at a high, irregularly shaped building, on the far side of the Campo.

"That's where Pompey, the general, and Caesar's rival, built his theater, over there, I think, by that high building. It was completed in 55 BC. I think that building is above the ruins of the bleachers of his theater." Scarlett peered into her guidebook. "This place, the square, used to be a meadow, and that's how it got its name, the 'field of flowers,' though it says here the flower part may refer to the name of a woman, Flora, who was loved by Pompey and who lived near here. The square was only paved over in 1456."

"Very interesting. A love affair gave this place its name, two thousand years ago." Jian gave Scarlett the special look, eyes half-closed, lazy, intense. He reached out, his fingers caressing her hair, pure gold, sparkling in the sunlight.

"You are my golden girl," he said, "all sunlight."

"Oh, my dear gentleman, thank you! I can be stormy, too!" She put aside the guidebook and leaned close, putting her hand against his cheek. "I can be dangerous and capricious and intolerable and opinionated and just straight out crazy."

"I'm looking forward to that," he said. "Never a dull moment."

"Well, you have been warned. No guarantees here!"

"You smell like sunshine." He leaned close, nuzzled her hair, breathed it in.

"Lemon shampoo." Scarlett drew back and blinked at him. Wow, she just *loved* the way he looked at her! And she *adored* looking at him: His smile, the smooth muscles of his arms and chest, the way his eyes sparkled, dark and intelligent, the thick dark hair she was itching to touch, to caress, to mess up. She was deliciously insane – this was just too much!

"Tell me more, Princess," he grinned and lifted the coffee cup to his lips, still giving her the look, drinking her in.

And so, Scarlett, referring to the guidebook, took Jian through the history of Campo de' Fiori and the streets that ran off it, and of this part of the river Tiber, which was not so far away. "Many of these little streets are named for the old crafts and trades," she said. "There's the street of the tailors; and the street of comb-makers, or carders; there's the street of hat-makers, and the street of the cross-bow makers; and the street of the key-makers. And there's the Street of the Rope, just behind us here, since they used to hang people on the Campo – or burn them to death – like Giordano Bruno."

"Gosh!"

"I'm glad we live in the modern age."

"Me too."

"In the old times we would never have met."

"No," said Scarlett. "I'd be shoveling manure and milking cows and carrying buckets of milk – somewhere out in the far north of Sweden in the back-woods of nowhere."

"And I'd be slaving in a rice paddy south of the Yangzi River; or maybe scything wheat or casting a fishing net. And I'd …"

"… marry the girl next door."

"Exactly."

A noisy gaggle of kids, girls and boys, came along, shouting and laughing, and splashed themselves in the water from the stubby little cast iron drinking fountain – the *Nasone*. Then, absolutely soaked, they began bouncing a big red rubber ball, back and forth, just in front of Giordano Bruno, who stared gloomily down at them.

"A good way to keep cool."

"Yes. Maybe we should do it." Eyes narrowed, Scarlett gave him the look.

"Not very dignified."

"Well …"

"Hmm." Jian put his hand on her arm and stroked it.

Scarlett grinned and glanced down at her guidebook. "Giordano Bruno got into trouble because he had a lot of forbidden ideas – he thought that perhaps Christ was not divine, but just a great moral teacher; that Earth was not the center of the universe; and that, perhaps, the universe consisted not just of a set of spheres centered on the Earth, but that it might be infinite and unending in extent and contain an infinity of worlds."

"No wonder they burned him at the stake. It's very upsetting not to be the center of the universe." Jian glanced at his phone. "Talking of our little planet Earth, I really wonder about all these little tremors and earthquakes, all over the world, and all at more or less the same time."

"It is strange. I wonder if …" Scarlett bit her lip.

"… something deeper and more serious …"

"… is going on. Yes." Scarlett snapped the guidebook shut.

"When you look at the history of the world, I mean of Earth," Jian lifted the coffee cup to his lips, "it's sort of a miracle that it all worked out so we could sit here in the sun on an ancient and medieval piazza and drink Italian coffee and eat French croissants."

"Yes, it is."

"It's sort of a fragile miracle, a delicate balance that anybody is alive at all."

"Yes, definitely fragile, definitely delicate." Scarlett gazed at the market, the vegetables, the fruit, the fish, the flowers, the profusion of colors and sounds. It was so rich, this little planet humans called home, a cornucopia.

Jian leaned forward. "I think people – I mean, we, we humans – don't appreciate how fragile it all is. How precarious. The life around us. The animals, the plants, the weather, the atmosphere – and our own happiness."

"Yes." Scarlett blinked at him. How often had she had that very same thought, even using, in her head, almost the very same words!

"We get used to things. But everything is moving – even the continents are moving."

Scarlett touched his cheek with her fingers, tracing a line from his cheekbone to his chin. "That thought always makes me just a bit dizzy. I read the other day that North America and Europe are moving apart, about an inch a year. And I thought – oh, wow!"

"Yes, the two tectonic plates are separating, the break runs through Iceland. The ground is shifting under our feet."

"It does make me dizzy, darling. I mean, the whole essence of this is that we are living on a planet that is still fluid, still developing. It surely still has lots of tricks up its sleeve, lots of surprises."

"Yes."

They paid the bill, wandered through the market and then headed down a few of the little streets and alleyways, looking in shop windows, chatting with the shop owners.

Jian's hand rested on Scarlett's hip and her hand on his. They ambled easily, relaxed in each other's company, excited by each other's presence, exploring at random, just discovering things. Then, at the very same moment, staring into a bookshop window, they had the very same idea.

"A siesta?"

"A siesta!"

They headed back toward the hotel. The sun shone down out of a perfect blue sky; and the air was so dry and clear it seemed to bubble like champagne. On the hotel doorstep, they stopped and kissed. It was a long deep kiss, a caress, and it was, for both, a promise.

CHAPTER 21 – WORLD-DESTROYER

V paused, turning her glass in her hands. "So that, Father is how I became immune to the sun. Indeed, now, I rather worship the sun."

"Most instructive, Demon. He is a complicated man, your Marcus."

"Yes, Father, he was – he is."

"You worship him."

"I did. I do. I love him."

"Ah, my poor demon child, if only …" I made a helpless gesture with my hands.

"You are very kind, Father, very generous." She took a slow, thoughtful sip of whiskey. "But now, Father, I must tell you a more important part of the story – the part that will explain, I hope, a few mysteries regarding recent events – the earthquakes, mega-storms, and strange eruptions – and why I am so eager for you to help me. It is the reason I fear the world is in danger."

"So – you truly believe the world about to end? My dear child!"

"Yes, I believe there is a serious risk of the Apocalypse."

"Why?"

"Humans are not ready, Father, for some forms of knowledge, and power."

"But no humans have the power to destroy the Earth – civilization, yes, most of life, yes, but the planet Earth, no."

"One does – and he has it now, though I am certain he does not know, precisely, what power he has and what it means."

"Who is this person?"

"Cardinal Antonio Xavier Paulus Ambrosiano."

"Oh, this sounds fanciful, my dear child. Ambrosiano may be a villain, he may be a heretic, he may be plotting against the Pope, but how do you expect me to believe that Ambrosiano, a mere mortal, can destroy the Earth?"

My fair demon glanced at me, sighed and put her hand on my hand. "Oh, man of infinite doubt! How your God puts up with you, I do not know!"

"Ah, well," I spread my arms. "The Lord is infinitely forgiving!"

"He certainly must be!" She smiled – again it was the smile of a forgiving mother, a compassionate Madonna – and so my demon continued with her story.

Two nights after he made me immune to the sun, Marcus suggested, just after dusk, that we go up to the roof of the villa, above the terraces and hanging gardens. I followed him up the steep staircase, and we stepped onto the roof. He raised his hand in a gesture that imposed silence.

It was a perfect, clear cloudless night. A gentle breeze carried all the perfumes of the desert and coastal flowers and plants. The palm tree in the upper courtyard rustled gently, its fronds making sharp black shadows, like the blades of scimitars cutting the darkening blue of the sky. Up above us was a myriad of stars, but as yet there was no moon. The sea, beyond the port, was silken black, reflecting ripples of starlight.

"What do you see?"

I looked up. "Stars," I said. "I see stars, and I see a great swath of light, scattered in a huge line, like a royal road across the sky."

"A royal road across the sky," he said. "Yes, that's very good, a royal road across the sky." Then, he surprised me by saying, "Let us sleep here tonight. It is warm. I want to tell you a story."

"But it's night; I sleep in the day."

"You can sleep during the night, can you not?" he asked, half joking.

"Well, I'm sure I am able to sleep anytime I wish to," I said defiantly, protesting inwardly: I was not entirely a freak.

I was silent as he ordered the servants to bring up the mattresses and bedding.

We lay down. He said nothing. I listened to the rustling of the palm tree and stared at the stars.

The sky seemed deep. It was as if I were looking downwards, into the depths of the heavens. I might topple away at any moment and fall, head first, through the sky, ever downwards, into the dark ocean of the sky, toward the stars, forever.

"Those stars are very far away." Marcus paused as if he expected me to object; I said nothing; I waited.

"Some of those little lights are like our sun. They are great balls of fire that burn and give heat and make life possible."

"But they are so small."

"They only seem small because of the distance. They are like a roaring bonfire you see at the far edge of the plain twinkling like a tiny spark; or like a tall man seen from a mountain ridge, a full day's journey away – he is a mere speck; or a large torch on a ship at sea, hardly visible, far away in the night. The stars are farther away, infinitely farther."

Vertigo swirled within me. The heavens were vast, they spun, round and round. I clenched my fist, clinging to the mattress. Facing the sky, I was facing a vortex of infinity. I could fall into the stars forever.

"Some of the lights we see are worlds – whole worlds – like the land we are on now, with mountains and plains, and flatlands and oceans. And, farther still – in worlds we cannot even see, thousands of worlds – there are villas like this one, or cities."

"But they are just specks of light."

"So are we, here, just a speck of light, when seen from so far away. In fact, we are invisible to many worlds, and many worlds are invisible to us."

I sighed. I was dizzy, staring into a nameless abyss of stars. So much had happened to me in the last few months that I was willing to believe anything. Mostly, people in those days thought the sky was not so far up, gods could fly there, and eagles sometimes. When it was very blue and very clear, there were days you felt you could touch it.

Marcus fell silent.

The breeze caressed my skin and moved in my hair. Somehow, the soft touch of the breeze made me feel that I didn't care if I was a tiny speck on a tiny spark of light lost in the night. As the breeze touched my skin and stirred my hair, I felt part of the vastness, part of everything, at one with the palm tree, the air, and at one with the sea that I could smell and just barely hear, and at one, too, with the smallest twinkling distant tumbling star. As the night moved on, the sky turned in a great circle, carrying the stars with it. I watched one crisp, diamond-bright star, as it disappeared behind the sharp, dark fronds of the palm tree.

"It all moves," I said. "Everything moves."

Marcus said nothing; then …

"I am not from here," he said.

I waited.

He didn't say anything. I heard a boatman shouting and the oars of a galley splashing. I smelled the goat meat someone was roasting, probably in the servants' courtyard below us. A watchman rang his bell. The doves fluttered and settled in their cages. A dog barked. I could imagine and *see* the dog; I *felt* its breath; I *felt* the grain of its fur, I *felt* my hand caressing it, my nostrils sniffing it, as clearly as if I were crouching next to it and stroking its neck and back.

"I come from out there." Marcus cleared his throat. "Somewhere out there." His arm stretched up, pointing at the great road of mist, as thick as a scattering of milk splashed right across the sky. "Somewhere out there," he repeated.

I was silent. He was telling me he was a god. The heavens were the abode of the gods. I had not believed in the gods before now, but the gods, I knew, were capricious. They could love you, then turn against you and destroy you in an instant. They could crush the strongest warrior, break his limbs, blind him, tear him apart and confuse his mind so that he would become a wild beast, snarling, growling, and tearing out his own eyes, murdering all that he loved.

"So, you are a god," I said, with dread in my heart – for when the gods reveal themselves, the stories say, it means they intend to destroy you.

"No, no, I'm not a god."

"But …"

"I know, I know. It is difficult. Let us just say that I have come from a very distant place – and that I mean you no harm."

No harm … I was trembling. It was strange, I admit. I was what people would later call a vampire. I am immortal (more or less, and with luck). And I have powers that, as I was discovering, are superhuman. But I was still a frightened young woman, a child.

"No harm," he said. "Let us now sleep till the cock crows. Tomorrow I will take you on a voyage. Then perhaps you will understand."

The next day came and we made our preparations.

I was dressed, of course, in masculine attire. I was Adonis, a young gentleman, companion to Marcus.

Asherah and Amilcare came to the gate to say goodbye.

It was just before dusk when we left, riding on the horses we had used to travel from my dead and burning city. My mount nuzzled me as soon as she saw me – I had made at least one "conquest."

When we had left the city behind, Marcus said, "Show your face to the sun."

I turned my chalk-white face, my crimson lips, to the sun.

"It paints you red and gold."

"It is warm."

"You are immune now. But – remember – in the beginning, don't over-expose yourself. Too much sun and you die. And you must not die."

We rode in silence. "Why must I not die?"

"You must live because I have chosen you."

Again, we rode in silence. I let his words echo in my mind. He talked to me even when he said nothing.

"Why have you chosen me?"

He did not answer. For a long time, there was just the steady clip-clop of the horses' hooves on the dry earth. We rode out beyond the great estates where grain was harvested. Workers saluted us. They were returning from the fields. We waved and rode on, beyond the vineyards and the olive orchards. The light was dying. The sun was a vast ember, crumbling into dark chunks on the horizon.

Soon the sun was gone. Darkness cooled the air, the heat seeping out of the plants and the soil, dampness rising. My nostrils quivered. I could smell the plants and the sweat and the oil of the horses' coats, and I could hear and sense, vividly, the creatures of the night – scurrying, skimming, fluttering, and rustling. Even if immune to the sun, I was still a creature of the night, a hunter in the darkness. It was a melancholy thrilling thought.

"What have you chosen me for?"

"You are to be a guardian."

And that was it. He said no more.

We rode for several days and nights. During much of the day, when the sun was very high, I slept in caves in the mountains. Marcus knew the route well and always knew where to find me a refuge. It was as if he had prepared the way for me.

One whole day we spent crossing a desert – I kept my hood up, sheltering my face from the pitiless sun. Just after the sun set, we arrived at a tall escarpment that blocked the horizon. We dismounted and led our horses in single file into a narrow crevice that cut into the soaring wall of granite. By now it was dark. I glanced up and saw, between the towering cliffs, a slender slice of sky – and a sprinkling of bright stars.

"No one," Marcus said, "has been here since I left, or so it appears. It's far from all trading routes and outside in the desert nothing grows."

The crevice widened and became a deep, narrow, flat-bottomed canyon. We got back on the horses. Here the plants were luxurious with wide flat leaves and looked like nothing I had ever seen before.

We came to a huge arrowhead-shaped boulder that stood, very erect, near the foot of the canyon wall, next to some trees. It was like a giant finger pointing to the sky.

"Let us rest here."

We dismounted, tied the horses to the trunk of a tree. We lay down under the tree. Hours passed. The moon rose until it was almost straight above us. It painted everything silver, the soaring walls of the canyon, the leaves of the plants, the sand and gravel and rocks. I had not fed for three nights and three days, but I did not feel weak or hungry.

"I want to tell you a story."

"A story, yes," I said. "Tell me a story."

We sat up. He looked serious, even more so than usual.

"Many years ago, from an island that is far, far away, a great ship set off on a long voyage. The idea was to discover new lands, new islands, and look for new and unknown peoples. Also, to discover enemies or peoples that might one day become enemies, and prepare to destroy them if they ever got strong enough to become a danger. So, the great ship set off, traveling farther and farther. It went farther than any other ship had ever gone – it went, in fact, far beyond where it was supposed to go. The captain, I believe, was a bit of a rogue."

It was getting close to dawn. High above us, in the stretch of sky between the cliffs, the moon was gone, the stars were fading. Marcus followed my glance upward. I looked at him and he nodded.

"A great ship from the stars," I whispered.

"Yes." He seemed weary, even hurt.

I closed my eyes and tried to imagine what such a great ship would look like. Would there be galley slaves, rowing through the air? Would it be a trireme, with three levels of oars and oarsmen? Would it have huge billowing square or triangular sails and be driven by the wind? Would it be broad and round-bottomed like a merchantman or sleek and warlike like a galley? Would it pass between the clouds? Would it end up shipwrecked on reefs of cloud or marooned upon the moon or adrift, abandoned, among the twinkling brightness of the stars?

Marcus cleared his throat. "The great ship came to a sky-island, what we call a planet, it came to Earth, this place where we are now."

"Here?"

Yes, here. Here it left behind a sort of marker, a beacon."

"Here?"

"Yes, right here, below us. I will show it to you – it is like a castle, but under the ground – and I will explain."

Marcus got up and walked away – just a short distance from the tree under which we were resting. He stopped next to the giant arrow-shaped boulder that looked like a finger pointing to the sky. He struck a flint, lit a torch, held it high, and began to look for something on the face of the boulder. One of our horses neighed.

I followed Marcus, hanging back a little bit. The light from the torch's flame sparkled on the face of the granite boulder making it seem as if the stone were alive. It called to something in me, something fierce.

"Hold the torch," he said, handing it to me. "Hold it high!"

I did as he asked. His shadow danced and flickered on the face of the boulder.

"Good! Keep it steady!"

I concentrated on holding the torch. The tallow bubbled and the smoke curled up into the darkness.

The only sound was the bubbling, flickering flame. I felt I was looking at ghosts dancing on the rock. Little bits of mineral sparkled in my eyes like diamonds.

Then I saw it: the pattern of a hand, inlaid in the stone. It was brought into relief by the play of light and shadow.

Marcus laid his hand upon the hand.

A voice spoke. I couldn't see where it came from. It was a woman's voice and it spoke in the language Marcus spoke over Lalla's body. Now I understood – this was the language Marcus spoke; it was the language of the stars. The voice was graceful and musical and welcoming, soft and caressing as the night breeze from the sea.

Marcus answered in the same language.

I was overcome by a thrilling vertigo of fear. He had told me he was not a god, but I was not convinced; the stones spoke to him; he was surrounded by magic; perhaps I was part of it too.

I moved closer, so he would protect me.

The giant boulder began to move. It slid smoothly aside with hardly a sound – except for pebbles tumbling down and a hissing cascade of sand

– and behind it, fifteen footsteps inward over a floor of polished black stone, was a doorway, a shiny door made of metal. I had never seen anything like it. It shone like the blade of a burnished sword and it reminded me of the vertical reflecting pool – the mirror – Marcus had conjured out of the wall of stone and stucco in his inner sanctum.

"Come."

I followed him to the metal door.

I glanced back at the stone. It was almost as tall as the tower at the southern gate in my fallen city. "Will the great stone move again and crush us?"

Marcus looked over his shoulder and smiled. "No, the great stone will do what it is told to do, no less, no more."

"May I?" I asked, gesturing at the door with my outstretched fingers.

"Go ahead."

I ran my fingers over it. It was smoother than any metal or porcelain I had ever touched; it was like a hard, perfect skin, without pores or blemishes. I wondered if it might be a living thing, and I drew my hand back.

A beam of light, brilliant like the sun, narrow as a small twig but straight as an arrow, came out of a little hole in the door. It was rose-colored, or pink, like the sunrise.

Marcus put his eye to it. I wanted to cry out, *No, it might kill you or blind you!* The door spoke: it was the same voice, the woman's voice. First one word, which sounded like a word of welcome. Then two more words, which were perhaps a name. And the mirror-like door slid aside, disappearing into the canyon wall.

The opening was pitch black – blackness that was more than absence of light, it was blackness that was as thick as liquid.

"Are you afraid?" He was smiling.

"No," I lied.

"You are a terrible liar," he laughed and ran his fingers through my hair. Then he took my face between his hands. "But, you know, sometimes I'm afraid too. Sometimes it is wise to be afraid."

"Are the gods afraid?"

"The gods, my dear Tanis, the gods are always afraid." And he entered the black hole.

"Come." His voice echoed, as if from far away, as if – the thought flashed through my mind – his voice was coming from the stars.

I took a deep breath and stepped into the darkness. I shuffled slowly forward, feeling my way, afraid I might fall into a deep hole, the sort of trap I had seen hunters set for wild gazelle. The metal door slid shut behind me and we were in total blackness. Even the night had disappeared.

"Shut your eyes."

I did so and waited. In total darkness, what difference did it make, I wondered, eyes open or eyes shut? I heard a series of clicks; Marcus said something in his language that was like music. There was a hissing sound, like an angry snake. And then I could tell, even with my eyes shut, that wherever we were, it had been flooded with light.

"Now, slowly, very slowly, open your eyes. Slowly."

Blinking with fear, I eased my eyes open.

We were standing in a long, gently curving tunnel, with smooth walls and light coming from certain points in the walls, and, far down the tunnel, I caught a glimpse of a gleaming wall. It looked like the smooth metal of the magic door we had just passed through.

"Come. Follow me."

As we advanced, I saw that the tunnel continued past the gleaming wall and that the gleaming wall had a door. When we got near to the gleaming wall, the door spoke. It said the same three words I had heard at the metal entry that had slid aside.

"Even the stones and the metals greet you, Marcus," I said. "You definitely are a god."

"You are a very stubborn girl." He smiled. "No, I am not a god."

This new door opened. Inside was a small room or box. We entered. The woman's voice said something. The door slid shut. We were trapped inside the box.

"Don't be afraid." He put his hand on my shoulder. "The box is going to move."

"Nothing will surprise me now, Marcus," I said, puffing up my courage.

"Don't be too sure, Tanis," he said; and he whispered, half to himself, half to me, "There are always new things to fear."

He gave an order in the language of the stars. The box plunged downwards. My stomach leapt upwards. I slipped my hand into his and held on tight.

"A brave new world," he said.

I didn't say anything.

The box kept going down, a little light blinking inside it.

"Did the gods make this?"

"No."

"Did men make this?"

"Not exactly."

I took time to absorb this, afraid to ask the next question, but I did. "Are you a man?"

"What do you think?"

"You look like a man; you smell like a man; your eyes, sometimes, look at me the way a man's eyes would look … at a woman … but …"

He blushed; I could have sworn he blushed. But it was true: I had seen it in his eyes, that mixture of calculation and interest, of speculation and hunger, the gaze of a man who looks at a woman he thinks he might want to possess.

"But you are not a man – not human."

"No."

"What are you?" I was holding his hand tighter now.

"A stranger," he smiled. He took me by the shoulders and kissed me softly on the lips. No man had ever done that to me before. "Satisfied?"

"No," I said, leaning against him. "You come from the stars."

"Yes."

"But you are here."

"Yes." He was still holding me tight. "Shipwrecked. I'm a shipwrecked sailor, a stranger on strange shores, the only one left of my crew. So …" He spread his arms wide. "I've had to blend in."

The voice spoke: the strange language again. It startled me. I looked around.

"It's the box," he said. "The box – 'elevator' is its name – is speaking, telling us we are about to arrive."

"Is the box – are these things that speak – alive?"

"No." He stroked my hair. "Not really. It's a machine, a tool, like a hammer, or a cart, a piece of rope."

The elevator came to a slow stop. I felt dizzy. A new door on the opposite side of the box from the old door slid open and we were free.

We stepped out into a huge cavern. It was lit by strange torches high on the walls and that did not flicker or give off any smoke.

"Lights," he explained.

"Lights." It was a word; it didn't explain anything; but a word was better than nothing. "Lights …" I tasted the word, trying to make it mean something.

"Electricity," he said, creating, by adding little words together, a new compound word – "force-that-moves-and-changes." This new word meant even less. I shrugged. These mysteries were beyond me.

"It is like the flash of lightning you see in a thunderstorm," he said, "but it has been captured and made tame, so it can be of use."

"Oh," I said. I nearly added that if he had captured the lightning and the thunder then he most certainly must be a god, perhaps Ba'al himself, who specialized in thunderstorms and rain clouds; but I was sure he would laugh at me or scold me. So, I said nothing, though I was sure he was a god – there was no other explanation for the things he could do.

"Come on. Let's see what we have come to see."

We walked down a smooth ramp into the huge cavern. I had never seen such a vast space except outside in the open air. My eyes opened wide. On the other side of the cavern, opposite us, was a gigantic round jewel. It rose up much higher than the walls of a city. It seemed to float in its vast metal cage, and it glowed and flickered as if it were reflecting the torches – I mean, *the lights* – on the walls. It had many tiny facets that sparkled, like the jewel my mother wore on the little chain around her neck, a small but exquisite gem my father brought back from one of his voyages; this huge jewel was round, like the sun or the moon, and it was taller than even the Temple of Asherah and Ba'al. It was, I thought, as if the moon or sun had come to live here, in this cave. I spoke none of these thoughts; Marcus, I feared, would laugh at me.

"This," Marcus said, "is what I wanted to show you." He led me to a staircase that appeared to be made of wrought metal. The staircase zigzagged up the metal latticework beside the great jewel to where there were little platforms next to the curved surface of the jewel. We stood at the bottom of the staircase and Marcus looked up. "This sparkling globe is known as the World-Destroyer. Simply put, it can make the earth shake and move."

"An earthquake," I said.

I had been in an earthquake. For just an instant, the sick dizzy sensation it caused came rushing back. Everything rattled, water had sloshed out of the pool in our courtyard. After it was over, I had asked my father why everything moved like that. What had happened? Were the gods angry? My father said the priests said it was the gods, but he thought nobody knew; everything around us is mysterious, he said, including whether the gods exist or not.

Marcus looked at me, surprised I think by my use of *seismos*, the Greek word for earthquake.

"Earthquakes, yes," he said, "and volcanic eruptions."

"Where fire comes out of the earth."

"Yes, indeed. Where did you learn about such things?"

"My father traveled when he was young," I said. "He told me that sometimes he saw fire and smoke far up over the sea, as high, he said, as the clouds. On some days, he said, you could not see the top of the smoking mountain – because of the clouds."

"Ah," Marcus said, "your father must have sailed to Sicily, past Etna, perhaps up the Strait of Messina – past Silla and Charybdis – the land of whirlpools and of hot and smoky waters, to the islands of the winds, the Aeolian Islands, to Stromboli, which spits fire, and to the smoldering island of Vulcano, which some say is the entrance to the underworld."

"Some of those names," I nodded, "are familiar to me."

Marcus looked up at the great shining jewel. "The World-Destroyer is asleep now," he said, "and no human being on Earth knows how to wake it."

"Is it good that it sleeps?"

"Yes. Very good. I do not want it to wake up, for if it does, it will unleash the fires and forces from below that will destroy everything – all the houses, all the cities, the seas, the land, everything ..."

"Why do you not destroy the World-Destroyer?"

"I cannot."

"Why?"

"Oh, my young inquisitive drinker of blood, my young demon, you are so curious. I fear that one day humans – and you are still really one of them, you know – humans, curious and inquisitive and intelligent, like you, will find the Crystal."

"The Crystal?"

"Yes, that's its other name."

"Crystal," I repeated, savoring the word; it sounded beautiful, and not dangerous at all.

"Let me tell you a story." Marcus led me up the stairs that snaked up the side of the Crystal. Our steps rang and echoed, making a hollow, metallic sound. As we went up, the surface of the Crystal curved out toward us.

"May I touch it?"

"Yes."

The Crystal was utterly smooth and cool. It made my fingers tingle as if it were talking to me. It was a pleasant sensation. I withdrew my fingers. "It feels alive."

"Yes. In a way, it is. The Crystal does have a mind, a vast mind, and it does think, not exactly like you or I think, or like your soul, your charming and headstrong Avatar, thinks, but it does think deep vast thoughts in its own powerful way. It will obey when someone has discovered what it is and discovered the key that will wake it up."

We sat down on the stairs, Marcus two steps above me. I did worship him as if he were a god; and I think – no, I know – that I desired him as a woman may desire a man. He was staring down at me, again, the way a man stares at a woman.

But I also knew that such things as love were for me impossible, and that love between Marcus and me was doubly impossible, though I had only the vaguest inkling of why that might be.

Looking up at him, I blinked away rising tears. "You said you were going to tell me a story."

"Yes, yes." He shook himself. "Imagine there is a great and strong city. It is on an island and it commands that island. And it commands many other islands and its ships ply back and forth between the islands, carrying goods and people, just as the ships of, say, Carthage, ply back and forth, from North Africa, to Byblos and Tyre in the East ..."

"I understand."

"Now imagine this city is a jealous city. It does not want people to worship or obey any other city – now, or in the future ..."

"It wants to be powerful forever."

"Yes." He hesitated, looking at me as if I had said something incredibly wise. "It wants to be powerful forever. So, if its ships discover an island where there is a city that might become a threat, a rival, in the future ..."

"It destroys that city."

"No, no, not exactly." He tilted his head sideways, smiling his sad smile.

"Oh!" I tried to picture such a great city that could destroy any city it feared. I had read of such wars in the sacred books and heard of them in the poems the wandering bards recited at home when we gathered around the fire. The Greeks had many such tales of war and cities destroyed and long voyages by wandering warriors. And now, as my father had feared and foretold, such a war and such destruction had been visited upon us, upon my own city, and upon my own family. All those I had loved – all those I had thought I loved – were dead. "If they don't destroy the city, or the island, what do they do?"

"They set a Crystal on the rival island, the potentially dangerous island, a Crystal like this one. Then when the island-city has become powerful, they ask its rulers if they want to be friendly, to join their city in its friendship and alliances."

"And, if not …"

"If not, the Crystal becomes alive and the new dangerous city …" – he swept his hand as if he were brushing aside a fly or a particle of dust – "is destroyed. Nothing remains but a few pebbles and rocks floating …"

"Floating …? Floating where?" This was mysterious to me because rocks and stones did not float so far as I knew; they sank. The only stone that floated was the pumice I used to polish my nails.

"Well, V, he was obviously talking about space," I said, looking away from my talkative demon and glancing down into my glass of whiskey. I sloshed it around. "He was talking about space – and planets."

"Yes, Father," she said. "Marcus was describing the explosion of our planet, its disintegration, and the creation of a new asteroid belt in its place. And he said he would show me …"

"Show you?"

"He would show me how the world would end."

"He would show you the Apocalypse," I murmured.

"Yes, Father, the Apocalypse. And, let me tell you, it was spectacular …"

CHAPTER 22 – TENTACLES

"Am I alive or am I dead?"

She hiccupped.

"Is this real?"

She blinked. No, wherever she was, it couldn't be real. She was trapped. Covered in gluey sweat, lying sprawled, spread-eagled, naked, on a slab of black granite under a blinding, burning tropical sun. She twisted and turned, trying to wiggle out from under an octopus that had crawled on top of her, smothering her in a sticky multi-limbed slimy embrace. It was determined to couple with her; that was clear. She jerked her hips, first this way and then that. Nothing doing! She couldn't escape, couldn't move. Why?

Oh, yes! She couldn't move because her ankles, wrists, and neck were manacled to the granite. Damnation! Her body was coated in slime, burning with fever, glowing in sweat.

Out of the bright, perspiring, glowing sky, voices spoke.

"Is she ready?"

"Yes, whenever you wish, Father."

Who were these people? Where were those voices coming from?

They faded. Was it the octopus talking?

No, it couldn't be the octopus! An octopus can't talk. Or can it? The octopus was insistent, clearly intelligent, knew what it was doing. Its fat slimy tentacles snuggled up lovingly on all sides, exploring, and probing, slipping in everywhere, pushing themselves under her arms, between her legs, around her neck, tickling every opening, poking deep into every orifice. Two large gooey suckers attached themselves to her breasts, tried to suck.

"Get away, damn you!" She tried to shout. What came out was a whimpering, liquid, animal snort.

She tensed, heaving up her torso, trying to kick against the tentacles that had wrapped themselves around her ankles. Again, she tried to shout, "Get away!" The only result was …

Glumph!

No sound came, but a slurry, bubbly …

Glumph!

A fat tentacle slapped itself angrily over her mouth, spurted out a thick liquid, gluing her lips together, merging them – she could feel it happening – into a single monstrous lip, a pulsating, protruding, sensual, bulbous thing, a sort of blind, mouthless snout. She gurgled, growling deep in her throat. Glumph! Glumph! Voices, speaking in Italian, came out of the blazing cloudless blue heavens, vibrated out of the smooth black granite.

"Has Brother Basilisk readied the paints and lacquers?"

"Yes, Father."

"The material is quick-drying, is it not?"

"Yes, Father, all will be ready in time."

Two round octopus eyes on snake-like stalks stared at her. The eyes blinked, amorously. The octopus certainly was eager to mate. Or was it trying to eat her? Or both – Did it want to fuck, then eat, or do both at once? Eat and fuck? She growled, gurgled, deep in her throat. Her bulbous mouthless snout twitched.

Grrrh!

Grrrh!

She wiggled. Her hair – she could feel it – was glued flat to her skull; greasy tendrils twisted like ropes down her neck. Her shoulders and buttocks were pinned flat to the hot, hard granite, and her ankles and wrists tightly manacled. She wanted to bite the octopus, but she had no teeth, no mouth.

Grrrh!

Grrrh!

She wiggled. She squirmed. An angry tentacle slapped her across the nose. It smelled like an old-fashioned inkpot. She blinked, eyes sweaty, out of focus, half-blind. The angry tentacle coiled back, paused, and slapped her again, a resounding blow, and it glued itself to her face and wiggled and squirted black ink, jets of thick, gooey black ink, all over her, over her hair, over her face, everywhere. Other tentacles flailed about, spraying ink. The ink was viscous, like molasses. Squirts and fountains of thick black viscid ink splashed everywhere. The tentacles were like fire hoses, with nozzles, and along the sides were large and small suckers. The tentacle clinging to her face recoiled back, and aimed at her eyes.

She shut her eyes tight. The squirt – or blast – of gluey ink sealed her eyes shut. Damn! This was disgusting!

Grrrh!

Grrrh!

She no longer had a mouth, just a mouthless snout, and now she had no eyes, just a smeared, featureless mask. The inky glue filled her eye sockets.

Grrrh!

Grrrh!

Greasy tentacles wrapped themselves tightly around her body, slithering under her torso, snuggling up, closer and closer around her legs and arms. She wiggled and squirmed, but less and less.

Ugh! Levering up her torso, she tried to break free. A fat oily tentacle, studded with keen suckers, slipped between her legs and eagerly probed everywhere. A tentacle slapped itself over what had once been her mouth, and squirmed to open the swollen merged lips of her mouthless snout. She heaved and wiggled and squirmed. Suddenly, the tentacles flipped away. The creature let go of her. It was gone.

Whew!

She sighed. She must be dead.

It must be a nightmare.

Breathing in rapid gasps, she lay still. She opened her mouth, she opened her eyes. She had a mouth; she had eyes. She could see. But what she saw was a vague whiteness, a misty open space, a giant room.

A disk that looked like a desk lamp was floating above her, high in the featureless white sky. She drifted. Her body was transparent, unreal, a body sculpted of glass. Her mind took flight, slipped out of her body. She had no sensation of touching anything. She tried to sit up. She couldn't.

"Damn!"

She was pinned to a piece of paper. No, she was *inside* the piece of paper, she was part of the paper. It was thick drawing or sketching paper. Out of the corner of her eye, she saw big flat-headed drawing tacks holding the paper down; they were gigantic. A huge object approached her. It was the broad flat copper nib of an artist's pen. It had a big drop of ink on it.

"The drugs are ready?"

"Yes."

"Triple dose this time."

"Triple?"

"Yes, absolute irredeemable madness is what we want."

"Yes, Father."

She was part of a drawing! She was a prisoner in the paper! She had been reduced to a few strokes of ink. A few sketched lines. How humiliating! The artist hovered over her. He had a giant, puffy, alcoholic face, it filled the whole sky; it was the face of God. His skin had red splotches, and a pimple or two, and his nose was bulbous with a thick harvest of blackheads, and there were leaden circles under his eyes; his red-blond curly hair was dirty and greasy and just turning gray; his big droopy white-gray moustache was stained yellow with tobacco; his nostrils were enormous, both nostrils inhabited by jungles of untamed hair, enormous red and white and black hairs, going every which way, and even sticking out, like giant half-smoked filter cigarettes. Behind the round, metal-rimmed glasses, his eyes were green and bloodshot.

He touched the nib to the paper and made a series of quick, light, swirling movements. He was sketching her shoulders and now her breasts. She could feel her body taking shape, as a cartoon! *What a violation! She was a cartoon!* She wanted to scream. But he hadn't yet drawn her mouth or lips.

She was swimming in black ink.

The artist faded.

She opened her eyes. She was crawling on her hands and knees up a beach of fine white sand, crystalline, and pure as pure could be. She looked up and saw, above her, cliffs of dark granite that soared toward the sky. The sky was a deep unreal blue, almost cobalt. She stood up and looked down at herself. She was naked. Where had her clothes gone? She looked at herself again, she was striped, like a zebra, thick black and white horizontal stripes, from the tip of her toes all the way up! Her exclamation of surprise came out sounding like a pony's high-pitched whinny. Whatever was going on? She glanced up and down the beach and saw no one, no sign of human beings or civilization at all. No deckchairs, no beach umbrellas or parasols, no little bamboo-and-palm-frond bars serving cocktails, nothing. Just pure white sand, stretching off as far as the eye could see, with dunes of pure white leading up to the black granite cliffs.

She sat down and sifted the sand through her fingers. She tried to remember. There was something she had to remember but she couldn't remember what it might be.

"I'll be along in fifteen minutes."

"Yes, Father."

Voices, voices from nowhere! The water lapped gently on the shore, a line of pure white foam running along the pure white sand. The sun was high in the sky and it was much bigger and redder than the sun should be. She stood up and walked to the water's edge. Hmm! Nothing particularly strange about the water. The watery reflections of the sun were like little red waves. She crouched and splashed herself. She waded into the water up to her waist. She ducked under the water and swam for a bit. It was very pleasant, warm and soft. She splashed up out of the water. The zebra stripes had not gone away. They hadn't smudged either. It seemed they were permanent, part of her. Hmm. They were quite pretty. She tossed her head and whinnied.

She waded out of the water, crossed the beach, and climbed the dunes, heading toward the black granite cliffs that towered up like the wall of a forbidding fortress. Strange tropical fruit hung from a tree that looked, just a little bit, like a miniature palm tree. Where in the world was she? She plucked one of the large berries. It was as big as an apple. She sniffed it. She bit into it, wondering if she was poisoning herself. She walked up what looked like a path. It was narrow and perilous, and it wound up the cliff side. She continued to eat the fruit. The juices squirted out of her mouth and dribbled from her chin. It was delicious.

After some time climbing up the zigzag path she came to the top of the cliff. She was perhaps two hundred feet up. She looked out over the ocean. There was a triangular peak on the ocean's horizon, just a shadow floating above the sea. It looked like a volcanic island. Where was she? Grassland stretched behind her, with a few of the palm tree–like plants. She plucked another giant berry and stood there, munching on the fruit, letting the juice overflow from her mouth, dribble down her chin.

She must be dead. Or … Could she be dreaming? She walked along the edge of the cliff and came to a cairn, or what looked like a cairn, a stack of flat stones. She looked up, she didn't see any birds in the sky. The only sounds were the gentle rolling of the surf and the whispering of the wind in the grass.

She narrowed her eyes and again looked out to sea. The sun was lower in the sky; the sun did seem strangely large. And not quite the right color – redder than it should be. And then she noticed them – in the sky were two moons, pale red shadows, one a slender crescent and the other, toward the horizon, almost half full, both rather larger than the earth's moon. How could that be?

She heard a rustling sound behind her, and she turned. The creature was striped like a zebra, black and white. It had the form and size of a small horse or pony. It was gazing at her. It turned toward the wind, tossed its head, and whinnied. She whinnied back. The animal turned to her, came over, and nuzzled her. She stroked its sides, realizing that she and the zebra were striped exactly alike. Then it offered itself to her as her mount. She leapt onto its back, felt its warm strong flanks between her bare legs. They galloped off, and she felt the wind in her hair. She whinnied. Her friend whinnied back.

The world dissolved into a pack of clouds, scudding through the blue, cirrus, wispy curly little waves, in a pale blue sky. She found herself in the sky, amidst the clouds, and she was falling, falling, falling.

Then …

A giant pudgy hand was on her belly, its thick fingers kneading, massaging her belly. She wanted to turn over, to curl up on her side, but there was something stopping her – a tight feeling around her neck and ankles and wrists. Manacles! Oh, damn, the manacles! She was strapped down. She blinked. Her eyes filled with tears, she couldn't see anything, just a vague shadow at the edge of her field of vision. She tried to turn her head. She couldn't.

The pudgy hand stroked her sides, then cupped her left breast, pinching and massaging the nipple; then it was gone.

Half-conscious, she realized she was on a steel gurney, manacled down, drugged, dreaming, or maybe this was the dream. Maybe she was really a zebra or an octopus. She opened her eyes. Nothing but blankness. Or was it a ceiling? Maybe this was the dream!

Her head hurt.

Her lips were dry.

She wanted a drink of water. Please, oh pretty please!

Then, then …

She is lying on her back, spread-eagled, on a raft that is drifting, racing, down a river. The raft swirls through rapids, white water surges on all sides, and white flecks of foam splash over her. Pine trees and cedar trees reach toward the pale blue sky and race by in a blur. Drifting wisps of white cloud, slender filament-like trails of cirrus, smudge the pale delicate blue. The water roars, the roar gets louder. She is headed for rapids.

She tries to sit up. She can't. Why? She is tied to the raft, manacled down, spread-eagled, naked, chained in place.

How had this happened?

The breeze ripples over her skin, shapes her body in her mind. The rough-hewn, rough-grained planks are coarse and scratchy, pressed against her naked buttocks, back, and shoulders. She smells resin. The smell of sun-warmed cedar. Pine needles. It reminds her of retsina – the strong resinous Greek wine. She drank retsina one sunny day in Greece, on the terrace of a small restaurant in a port on an island somewhere. Lesbos?

When was that? Was it real? Who was she?

She is naked and tied down to the raft, yes. That's all she knows. But who is she? Who is this naked person tied down on the raft? Why is she tied down on the raft? She has no idea.

And who was the girl who one day long ago sat on a terrace next to the small fishing port, the light of the sea sparkling up, reflected on the striped blue-and-white awning, the girl who drank resinous wine and speared a tomato and slice of cucumber with her fork? And stared at a luscious large dark pitted olive – her next victim. That girl must be a dream. What was her name? Who was she?

The roar faded.

The river was gone.

The smell of cedar lingered, the taste of retsina.

She is on her knees, naked except for a loincloth, in some sort of ancient temple. Columns of stone soar up to a high roof of beams and rafters. The marble paving stones are warm under her knees. She looks up. A huge statue soars above her. Some pagan god. It has the face of a goat, the horns of a goat, the ears of a goat, the body of a man, with huge bulging muscles, a loincloth with an intricate design. Next to the god is the statue of a goddess – equally tall, extraordinarily, impossibly voluptuous, and naked except for a patterned loincloth like that of the male god. She shakes her head. What am I doing here? I must get away. A priest appears – in long golden robes. His head is shaved. His eyes are made up, kohl, startling, beautiful eyes. He holds up something in his hand. It is dripping blood, it is throbbing, beating, it is glossy red – it is a human heart.

"Now, arise," the priest says.

She stands up. She tries to remember who she is, what she is. She has no idea. She can't remember. Not an inkling. Her mind is a cloud, a drifting vaporous cloud. She is a vessel, an empty vessel.

She stands as erect as she can, a good little soldier, standing to attention. The priest approaches. He lays the heart in her open, waiting, cupped hands.

The heart is beating. It is her heart. The heart beats slowly. Blood squirts out and drips between her outstretched fingers.

"Now," says the priest, "now drink this, take this."

And he pours blood from a silver vessel over her shoulders. He smears blood on her face. She opens her mouth. The priest pours the blood into her mouth; it overflows. She swallows.

She is holding, dripping in her cupped hands, her own beating heart; and yet she is alive, somehow, she is alive. "For evermore," says the priest. "Alive for evermore."

Her vision is blurry.

She is lying on a sidewalk in some city that is perhaps Paris, bullets are flying around just above her, and people are dying. She knows people are dying. She can't do anything. She is paralyzed. She can just move her lips. She can just move her tongue. The city fades, and the gunshots, and the sirens, and the cries for help.

Sometime later someone gave her a drink of water, tipping a paper cup to her lips. It was a monstrous face, vaguely perceived, out of focus, like the back side of the moon, featureless except for craters. Then a tiny mouth appeared, and almost invisible eyes, peeking out, snot-green deadlights, from folds of white fat. The water dribbled from her mouth. She felt the water overflow. She swallowed. It was painful to swallow. The face was gone. The cool water ran down her cheeks and neck. She blinked. A bright light – was it the moon? And then the voices.

"She will be prepared. Give us a few minutes."

"She is, as I told you, exactly what we need."

"Yes, you were right. She is ideal."

"Satan's will be done!"

"Satan's will be done!"

Hands touched her breasts, moved over them, and cupped them. The hands ran down her leg, explored between her legs. She wanted to scream. But maybe all of this was just another dream. Her voice was not her own. She couldn't speak. Her tongue. She couldn't feel her tongue. No sound came. Had they cut out her tongue? Had they removed her vocal cords?

Who were they?

She had a flash image of someone's head exploding, shattered glass, gunfire, flames, and sparks. It was night. She was running through a field, the soft dry earth under her feet. A man beside her, running fast, helping her, taking her hand. Who was that man?

She must get out of this place, but she has no idea where she is or who she is or where she might go, if she did leave this place. Then, it all turns vaporous and misty. She ceases to exist.

She is nobody and she is nowhere and she will cease to be and nobody will ever find her or know she had ever existed.

CHAPTER 23 – THE END OF DAYS

"So, my dear Demon, that was the Apocalypse. Marcus was describing the Apocalypse, the breaking apart of the planet, to be caused by the Crystal."

"Yes, the Apocalypse." V nodded. Her eyes were far away. And so she returned to the past and to her tale of how she came to be the devilish creature she now is and how the planet is threatened by her so-called Crystal.

Marcus and I were sitting on the steps of the metal stairs leading up the side of the Crystal. Marcus stood up, took my hand, and led me down the stairs and out onto the floor of the cavern.

"Promise not to be afraid."

"I will not be afraid." But I moved closer to him, and he put his arm around me.

He spoke to the Crystal. It answered him, in the same suave female voice as before. The voice seemed to come from everywhere around us. My skin tingled. I was in the presence of divinity; I was experiencing the greatness of the gods. It seemed to me, too, that the voice asked a few questions and Marcus answered – they were talking to each other, Marcus and the Crystal.

"I have asked the Crystal to show us what happens when …"

"… when a dangerous sky-island is destroyed?"

"Yes. These sky-islands are round, like the moon, they are islands in the sky."

"And are we, here, on a round island in the sky?"

"Yes, like the others."

We were standing in front of a large open space to the right of the Crystal. The space was set up slightly, higher than the floor of the cavern, like a platform where religious ceremonies could be held. Behind the stage was only the vaulting darkness of the cavern.

Suddenly this vaulting darkness was filled with stars – as if we were look-ing at the night sky. And then, in the image was a large colored ball.

"That is one of the sky-islands."

The image of the large colored ball was replaced by images of towers, taller and grander than any I had ever seen. And there were strange creatures mov-ing on streets and carts without horses or oxen moving very fast and many other wonders.

"That is life on the sky-island."

"Those are cities?"

"Yes."

The towers began to crack, and waver, and fall; and the creatures were run-ning every which way. Huge clouds formed, monstrous waves tossed what looked like ships. Then we were again looking at the whole sky-island, like a ball in the sky. Slowly it cracked, pieces flew away, and it fell into millions and millions, an infinity, of pieces. And there was fire everywhere. It billowed into flame and then nothingness. Then it all faded.

"I am afraid." I sheltered in his arms.

"Yes, well, so am I, so am I." Marcus held me tight. "But wait … There are others."

He said a few words to the Crystal, and I saw another sky-island, and it too exploded.

Then another … a red-tinted sky-island, exploding …

Then another … a wonderfully beautiful turquoise sky-island, exploding …

Then another … a green and blue sky-island, with white ribbons running around it, exploding …

I cried, silently I cried, for each of the sky-islands I saw perish and all the creatures who perished in them – and I was standing beside the instrument of their destruction; the beautiful Crystal with the soft and alluring voice.

I had seen the Apocalypse.

I feared for myself and for all the creatures that live on our home, our only home – our own sky-island, the planet earth.

I did not want that Apocalypse to occur here.

"So, Father O'Bryan, now I have told you what the Crystal can do. What do you think?" I stared at him. I willed him to give me an answer.

Father O'Bryan gazed into his whiskey. His head nodded. He looked like he was dozing or deep in thought. Maybe he was just trying to see in his own mind the things I had described. Or I had just bored the poor man to death.

In spite of myself, I liked Father O'Bryan. He was of course stubborn as a mule – a good Irishman – and a good Jesuit – and he was destined, by his faith and his very humanity, to be my enemy. And he was right to consider himself my enemy. After all, I *am* a demon, a pagan from ancient times. I *am* a predator who preys on humans, and I *am* a mass murdering vampire. Whew! That's quite a list! I don't think I'd want to work with me!

For a few long seconds, the good Father said nothing at all. It was very stalwart of him. He knew how to hide his hand – he was playing for time; he did not want to be stampeded into working with a demon.

I could of course have bitten him, and sucked him dry, and extracted as much information as I could from his nervous system, harvesting synapses and neurons and coded electrical charges galore. But that would have meant killing him. And I really didn't want to do that. He was a good man; in fact, he was a very good man. Besides, he did not know what he knew – so, in gulping down his blood, and in murdering him, I might miss the – deeply buried, elaborately coded and unconscious – vital information that I needed to seize … And if the good Father were dead, that information would, quite possibly, be lost forever.

"So, Father O'Bryan," I said, "the Crystal is capable of blowing up the planet, and has now begun to act."

"What do you mean? Do you mean that …?" He looked up at me, as if waking from a daze.

"Yes, those earthquakes the other day; they are just the beginning."

"But those were just little tremors."

"Yes, but all over the planet – at virtually the same time."

"And you believe your Crystal did this?"

"I am certain of it. Cardinal Ambrosiano has discovered the Crystal – I don't know exactly how – and he has visited it, and I think he has some dim idea of what it might do – or be made to do – and I'm almost certain that Cardinal Ambrosiano has decided that we *all* should die – I mean the whole human race, and every other creature on the planet too."

"Oh, dear me!"

"Yes, Father – You can say that again: *Oh, dear me!* My guess is that his version of the Gnostic Manichaean heresy decrees that the physical world is fallen, or at least that it is a barrier to his idea of divinity – the Evil Force or Satan – and to his personal salvation – whatever that is – and that Earth must perish, and that, in that Apocalypse, some perverse form of Satanic Rapture would take place and those chosen, by Satan, will be swept up into the Arms of the Evil One. You know more about him than I, Father O'Bryan. And you certainly know that he is the leader of the Order of the Apocalypse, do you not?"

Without looking up from his whiskey, Father O'Bryan grunted – a non-committal grunt.

Boy! Was Father O'Bryan stubborn! I was getting fidgety! And the last thing you want to be around is a fidgety demon-vampire – or me in one of my moods! I stared at the man, willing him to tell me what he knew and answer a few vital questions: Who worked for Cardinal Ambrosiano? Who were his allies? What was his relationship with the Pope? And above all, where would the Cardinal hide something he considered valuable?

And this was the essential point: for, just a year ago, I had discovered, on my first visit in over two thousand years, that the door to the Crystal's cavern was open. In fact, it was jammed open. Someone had entered the cavern and seen the Crystal; and, even more important, a vital part of the Crystal was missing – the key to the Crystal.

Without the key, I couldn't control the Crystal or close the cavern door, and, worse, I would not able to stop or reverse whatever the Cardinal was doing. I needed the key to the Crystal.

"Well?" I was getting twitchy. I tapped my fingers on the table – a dangerous sign. I must control myself; otherwise fangs would spring out, and claws, and I ...

Father O'Bryan sat at the table, just opposite me, the whiskey glass between his hands, staring deep into the amber liquid.

He shook himself, stood up, and walked away from the table. "What you are telling me is really the most amazing story. I really don't know if I can believe any of it ..."

"But, Father, you must realize something very serious is going on. After all, people tried to kill you."

"Yes, they did ..." he muttered, absently. His expression was vague. Oh, yes! The memory of his near-death experience was fading. He had been cured of all the after-effects. His wounds were fast becoming not even memories. Pain is something humans are designed to forget. Otherwise, I doubt any woman would ever agree to give birth a second time. Trauma too is soon forgotten, if the pain is taken away. Humans are ephemeral creatures, living in the moment, forgetful of so much pain and so much joy. Sometimes I think they are not even real – these humans.

"And, Father, they tried to kill you because you know what they don't want you to know. They are afraid you might talk to the Pope."

"Yes, perhaps." He glanced at me with a strange, ill-disguised mixture of distaste and distrust and ... affection. He was beginning to like me, in spite of himself, and in spite of the fact that for him I am a demon, a daughter and handmaiden of Satan, and he hated himself because of this weakness. He grimaced, and then smiled. "And you saved my life, Demon. And I rather like you, though I know I shouldn't. So tell me more!"

I rolled my eyes. I really should eat the good Father up, munch, munch, munch, right now, suck him dry, right down to the marrow – slurp, slurp, yum, yum! *No, no, V. Don't do it! Resist the temptation! You really are too impulsive!*

I clenched my fist, carefully composed my expression, favored Father O'Bryan with my best smile. I fixed my most penetrating gaze on the man, hoping to will him into submission. He looked away quickly, clever fellow that he is! "Well, Father, this is the general picture, according to what Marcus told me. Marcus's Empire planted or built – I don't know which – these crystals wherever they saw a life form emerging that might be a threat to them. Then, ideally, they would monitor the rise of the technology and the civilization, and when the moment came, they would *negotiate* with the new civilization. If the negotiations did not prove fruitful, or if the new civilization proved too belligerent or too unstable, the Empire held the trump card. It could activate the crystal ... and ... goodbye sky-island, goodbye life, in our case, goodbye Earth. And the threat to Marcus and his Empire was gone."

"Well, what role do you play in all this?" Father O'Bryan glanced up. "What did Marcus want from you?"

"He wanted me, as he said, to be what he called a guardian. I was the only immortal on Earth, he said; he could not be the guardian, he was not immortal ..."

"Ah, your friend was not immortal ..." Father O'Bryan nodded.

"No, he wasn't. He told me that he would die ..."

"Really ...?"

"I will die," he said. We were standing on the floor of the cavern looking up at the Crystal when Marcus told me that he would die – and soon.

"Oh, no," I said, "you cannot die!"

"I can, I can. And I will."

"I will not let you to die!"

"Oh, Tanis, how sweet you are – and how good to me!"

He laughed, tousled my hair, then frowned, and motioned toward the Crystal. "You must learn how to control the Crystal, how to put it back to sleep if perchance humans discover it and wake it up."

I stared at him. Wake it up – what a horrifying idea!

"Here, let me explain." He took me up the staircase that led to a platform on the face of the Crystal. He showed me what he called, for my benefit, a "surface that gives orders and commands." In fact, it was a control panel, a smooth slab with little knobs or handles on it, and with a place that would fit a hand and an eye.

"Either from here," he said, "or if it had been installed, from a remote station in space, a sort of lookout platform in orbit beyond the moons of Jupiter, the Crystal can be awakened. Unfortunately, because of the accident, the remote station is not in place, so the Crystal can only be controlled from here."

"Moons of Jupiter," I said, sighing. I reckoned there was one moon and it was ours. There was so much I didn't know and didn't understand. My head was going to burst. Did Jupiter have moons? Jupiter was a little spot wandering in the sky.

"Here," said Marcus. "Do you see this piece of the Crystal?"

"Yes. It sticks out."

"Put your hand on it, turn it, and pull it out. Like this!"

I put my hand on the piece of crystal and turned it, as he indicated, once to the left, then to the right and then back, and I pulled it out and held it in my hand.

It was about three inches long, oblong, and transparent; it was octagonal, or eight-sided along its length, and it was inserted by one end into an eight-sided hole. It didn't look like a key, but that's what he said it was.

"This is the key to unlock the Crystal! It will allow you – and only you – to control the Crystal, to talk to it. It has to be inserted, and turned. Put it back in place."

I did, repeating the movements in reverse order. The key locked into place with a click. It stood out about an inch from the surface of the control panel.

"Now, put your hand on this space." The space was flat, but it had the rough imprint of a hand on it. The hand imprint had longer fingers than mine, and rather pointed fingers too; this was something I hardly noticed at the time but have thought about since.

I put my hand flat on the hand imprint.

"Good. Now put your eye to this hole."

I was afraid of being blinded, but I did as he told me. A bright light shone in my eye. It startled me at first, but then it felt warm, almost comforting.

"Now picture everything you have just done – picture it as if you were doing it, one step after the other, in sequence."

"Yes."

"I am going to put some ideas into your head."

"What – you think I don't have any ideas in my head?" I pretended to be insulted, but I quickly melted. "You may put all ideas you want into my head, Marcus. You may do with me what you will!"

I immediately sensed that my naive, unbounded, submissive love made him uneasy. "These ideas are instructions," he said, "instructions on how to talk to the Crystal."

He put his hand on the crown of my head. I don't know how, but he was implanting ideas – instructions – in my mind. He first projected colors, then a picture of the control panel, then all the actions I had to perform, as if my own body were performing them.

"Do you feel it? Do you see it?"

"Yes, Marcus."

"Does it hurt?"

"No, but it's a strange sensation. It is as if I am you, and you are me."

"Yes, in a way that is true."

Marcus was piloting my mind. Mentally, I went through the sequences of actions I had to perform to work with the Crystal, or to stop it, or control it.

Afterwards we climbed down the staircase, and walked across the cavern, away from the Crystal.

I looked back. The Crystal was huge; but it was familiar now, almost a friend. Its tremendous power gave me a thrill that was horrifying but also, I must admit, almost … almost orgasmic. It was as if I had been connected to the very powers that govern our universe.

The Crystal glowed gingerly and seemed to vibrate and palpitate. It looked like life not death; but it had a power not even the gods possessed.

We took the smooth elevator upwards and listened to the same suave voice.

At one point, going up in the box, Marcus said something in his own language to the suave voice, and the voice said, in my language.

"Hello, V!"

"V?"

"Crystal has given you a new name, V," said Marcus. "Henceforth you are V."

I glanced quizzically at Marcus and then I said, "Hello, Crystal."

"I am delighted to meet you, V." It again spoke in my language, with a most sweet accent, and with classical precision. My father and mother would have been delighted.

"I am equally pleased to have met you, Crystal." I was going to ask more but we arrived at the top.

"Goodbye, V. I hope we meet again."

"Goodbye, Crystal," I said, feeling I was leaving behind a new-found friend. The sweetness of her voice echoed in my mind and made me yearn for something I had lost, but I had no idea what it was.

"V?" I glanced at Marcus.

"V." He grinned and slapped me on my back as if at that moment I had again become a man, a fellow warrior with strong broad shoulders, not a fragile young woman disguised in a boy's clothing.

CHAPTER 24 – DEMON THIRST

Father O'Bryan is a difficult man. When I finished my tale, he glanced at me and said, "Very interesting."

Very interesting! We were contemplating the destruction of the planet and all he could say was *very interesting!* I wanted to scream!

But … *No, no, V,* I said to myself, *calm down! Don't let him get your goat!* Marcus did warn me. I am impetuous and too impatient.

"Very interesting, my dear Demon," said Father O'Bryan. He gazed at me through his glasses, a wonderfully complacent expression, looking very much the thoughtful old scholar that he is, a man used to shuffling papers and ideas in dusty libraries and silent study halls with polished mahogany tables and comfortable leather chairs and a glass of sherry and little desk lamps with narrow circles of light and pinched imaginations, squinting myopically at some infinitesimal detail of philology, a comma – or is it a period? – in some ancient dusty utterly irrelevant text, and bent over volumes of fine print telling infinite tales of much ado about nothing! Grrrh! I clenched my fists.

Father O'Bryan stood up and turned his back to me and topped up his Bushmills. "But how exactly does this Crystal work? How will it destroy our little sky-island, Earth?"

I composed myself. Patience, I told myself, patience, V, is a virtue. Perhaps I *will* become a saint. "Well, Father," I cleared my throat, "Marcus told me – but the terms he used were appropriate for a young woman twenty-six hundred years ago. He used metaphors and simple images to explain things. But let me summarize what I have understood over the years: I think – I'm not sure – but I think the Crystal distorts and then suspends the law of gravity; it distorts or twists space-time."

"You can't be serious?" Father O'Bryan came back to the table, topped up my glass and sat down opposite me.

"I am deadly serious, Father. It will start slowly, selectively, distorting or suspending the force of gravity in certain places. Gravity is the matrix of being, the latticework of existence. Since gravity holds everything in place, when it is suspended, or twisted, it unleashes immense pressures in the Earth, and earthquakes, tidal waves, and volcanic eruptions are the result."

Father O'Bryan frowned. "Can it be stopped once it starts?"

I hid my smile. Oh! My dear Father O'Bryan is beginning to believe! I have shaken him, perhaps, out of his dogmatic slumber! I gave him my best, most reassuring smile. "Yes, it can be stopped, and I know how – but to stop it I need the key."

"Ah, yes – the key! This mysterious key!"

"It's what allows me to control the Crystal and to talk to it. It is the key to saving the world. It is the *Clavis Mundi.*"

"Ah, the *Clavis Mundi*, the *Key to the World*. Marcus explained all this to you, then – did he?"

"Yes, as I told you, he explained it in terms I could understand." I curled my hand into a tight fist. Yes, I really should drink good Father O'Bryan dry, quite dry, down to the last drop; and in fact the whiskey would add a nice tang to his blood; I really should …

"And, then, afterwards, how did you become what you are? I mean to say, Demon, what happened next?"

"Oh, Father!" I literally rolled my eyes.

"Humor me, my dear, dear Demon!" He favored me with a benign, masterly, priestly grin.

Oh! All the Gods! I murmured: Father O'Bryan is a *sadist!* The man was enjoying himself – torturing a poor, innocent demon!

He smiled, an even more unctuous smile. I imagined he might rub his hands together in priestly delight. "It is part of my vocation, my dear Demon, to listen to stories, to listen to confessions. And as you so kindly put it, Demon, I am your confessor."

I gulped down some whiskey – in order to stave off my thirst for the good Father's blood – and, slurping back my saliva and blood-lust, I resigned myself to this torture and continued my story.

When we left the cavern, it was dusk. Outside, in the narrow canyon there was just a faint light high up, between the cliffs, in the jagged meandering strip of sky.

The horses were tethered where we had left them. My gentle mare seemed delighted to see me; she neighed, tossed her head, and nuzzled my neck and shoulders. I patted her, stroked her, and gazed into her big liquid eyes.

"Soon you must feed," Marcus said.

"Yes." I nodded. It had been days since I had fed. I was feeling a bit light-headed.

We walked, leading our horses through the canyon, under the narrow, luminous slice of sky, framed, up above, by walls of dark granite. Bats swooped in the twilight. The air was balmy, rich with smells. My senses were flooded with a symphony of perfumes, odors, traces and signatures of life.

Now, as a nocturnal predator, I knew how to interpret all these signs: Which animals had been where, which birds had taken flight, which insects had climbed over the rocks and then retreated when the sun went down, which flowers and blossoms had opened and closed, letting their perfumes loose on the air ...

"How were you shipwrecked?" I asked, still marveling that I was talking to a man – no, a god – no, a creature – from beyond the stars. I had no names for what he was or what he might be.

"A stupid accident."

"Accidents still happen in your world?"

"*Still?*" He turned to look at me. "Are you thinking I'm from the future?"

I frowned. *The future – from the future –* I was not sure what the expression meant – though I had of course thought about the next season and about the coming festivals and dancing in the summer, about growing up; about being mated with a man, about being a mother, and about growing old. My father had told me that everything teaches us that life is a cycle, turning around and around like a chariot wheel. The sun rises, crosses the sky, and sets and rises again; the moon moves through its phases, and then moves through them again, and again, and again; the waves wash again, and again, and again, against the shore; the tides rise, and then they retreat; the seasons come and go, and then return; the plants grow, are harvested, are planted, grow, are harvested; people and animals are born, make love, have children, grow old, die, are born, make love, grow old ... So, even naive as I was, I had certainly thought about this cycle, and perhaps about dying. Whether I'd thought about my own death, it's hard to say; but I had not thought about *the future*.

"My father says things move in circles and cycles, they go and they return, change is forever," I said. "But what is this '*future*' you speak of?"

"Ah, Tanis, I see that you are a philosopher. I am sure you asked your father such thorny questions."

"Yes, I did. And I asked my mother too. She knew many things. And if my father or mother didn't know, then my father would ask a merchant or friend of his or sometimes a scribe or a priest. But my father didn't have much faith in the priests. He said there are many things we do not know and there are probably some things we can never know; indeed, we do not know how ignorant we are. He said we should be very careful about claiming to know things."

"That is very wise."

"Big questions are good, my father said, but big answers are suspect. To justify the offerings given to them, the priests, he said, must seem wise and important; so they pretend to know all things and often, to hide their ignorance, they speak in riddles that must be interpreted, or they speak gibberish – but they do not know all things and to make such a claim to total knowledge of the gods and the world is, my father said, overweening folly."

"A wise man."

"Yes, he was," I said, wondering at how full and how empty my heart had become. I was a stranger to myself and to everything that, only a few months ago, I had been. I had not seen my father die, only heard how, fighting against desperate odds on the ramparts, he was slain, trying to save us, his children, his family, and his city. His last moments, I suddenly realized, must have been horrendous and tragic – he would have known that we were all doomed, and that everything he had lived for and that he loved was lost – and for nothing, in a stupid war he had bravely opposed.

Marcus and I walked on in silence. The horses too were quiet. The moon had come out, painting the top of the cliffs; and the air itself was like cool blue silver.

"I asked you …"

"Yes, the *future*. The future is many lifetimes away. It is straight like a line, not round like a circle. It stretches in front of us like a long road, going on forever. No one can see the end. And no one can see the beginning. We all travel that road. Things change. People learn to make new things. New tools, new crops, new animals, and new ways to do things, new ways to think, to believe. And they live on new worlds."

"And travel to the stars."

"And travel to the stars," he echoed, softly.

"And the accident – the shipwreck?"

"Ah, yes. It is a painful memory."

"You do not have to talk of it."

"No, it is simple enough. We had put the Crystal in place. This was perhaps two hundred of your years ago."

"You see, you *are* a god."

"I am an old man."

"For me you are young."

"Ah, you are good for me, V!" He laughed, taking delight it seemed in using my new name. "I had come back, alone, down here, to this sky-island, to finish my work with the Crystal. I was going to remove the key and seal the mechanism so that nobody on Earth could interfere with the Crystal. If the key is gone, the Crystal cannot be woken up by anyone here on Earth and can only be controlled from beyond this Earth Island."

"So, the Crystal is not finished."

"No, Tanis, she isn't. She can't be controlled from beyond Earth. And that's why the key is still here. That's why there's a danger. The Crystal *can* be controlled from here. That's why I need a guardian.

"Me."

"Yes, you."

"So, you were alone, and –"

"Yes, I was alone down here, and I was talking to the pilot on the ship about bringing me back up."

"Up to the sky?"

"Yes, up to the sky. My ship was circling Earth, floating above it, circling the Earth sky-island. Waiting for me to return. We were a long way from home, farther than any ship had ever gone. And we were a bit rogue …"

"Rogue?"

"We were doing what we shouldn't have done. Going where we shouldn't go. Going farther than we should have."

"You were pirates?"

"Well … let's say I was an independent explorer – going where nobody had gone before and where I wasn't supposed to go."

"You were the captain?"

"Yes, I was the captain, the leader."

"I knew it!"

He smiled and put his hand on my shoulder. "I heard shouting on the ship, and the pilot said, 'Captain, something is happening.' Then he said, 'Wait a minute,' and then there was static – just noise. A few seconds later I saw a great flash in the sky."

"Oh."

"There were no more messages. I waited. We were far from home and we had only one ship. And, since we had not received permission to go to this new world of sky-islands, we had not signaled where we were going. It was a secret."

"So, nobody knew where you were."

"Yes, Tanis. Nobody knew where we were. And, with the ship destroyed, so far beyond the reach of our usual voyages, there was no way for them to find us even if they did start looking. After a day or two of no news, I knew I was alone on Earth, on this sky-island, far from home, and that nobody would ever come for me. For years, I hoped they would, but no one did. So, I made my life here, I used my knowledge – and the tools and equipment I had with me – to voyage and explore, and to reinvent myself several times – and continue my scientific experiments – and, now, to become rich and powerful in the city and ..."

"... to become what you are, a warrior, a priest, a wise man."

We had reached the narrow crevice that was the entrance to the canyon. Walking single file, we led the horses through the passage.

I could see even better, I discovered, as the night darkened. It was not perfect vision, but I could see very well – the better for hunting, I suppose. Each day brought a change – and a new discovery.

"Your powers will increase with time," Marcus said, as if reading my thoughts, "and with practice. And, when you need them, you will discover powers you didn't know you had." His voice echoed between the narrow stone cliffs, like the voice of a prophet.

As we came out of the passage, the escarpment loomed up behind us, hundreds of meters high, silver in the moonlight. In front of us was the desert and, beyond it, grassland, and, far beyond that, to the north, the great wheat fields and vineyards of the estates outside the city. The smells were sparse. It was open space of scrub, sand, and sunburnt rock; the sky was immense, the air bone-dry and crystal clear, the myriad of stars hardly dimmed at all by the moon.

"Tomorrow, once the horses have fed, we will find fodder for you."

"*Fodder?* So – I am an animal like the others," I said, somewhat piqued.

He laughed. "And so am I! We are all animals!"

I swung up onto my mare, tight leggings and boots and a very short tunic making it much easier than the long and folded sheath that women in those days were usually forced to wear – though some did dress as men, and some, sometimes, went very scantily clothed indeed.

"So, let us go, Adonis," Marcus said. His smile was bright in the moonlight.

"Yes, let us go." I steadied myself in the saddle.

We rode off into the desert, toward new adventures and new dangers.

At the end of the following day, just after dusk, we happened upon an encampment of desert nomads. Marcus bought some food from them – many of the Berber tribes that voyage across the trans-Sahara trade routes were very welcoming to travelers – and we sat down among them. But, this time, around the campfire that burned brightly, in the shadowy faces, I sensed hostility and evil intent. It was soon clear that some of the men were ruffians – interlopers – outcasts even from their own people – and not members of this tribe whose hospitality they were abusing.

"And he does not eat, the handsome young gentleman?"

"No, he will eat later; he likes to watch."

"Likes to watch!" The men laughed; their teeth were big and bright in the light of the campfire.

One of them, dark, unshaven, and older, lusted after me as an older man can lust after a boy. I could feel his gaze intent upon me, his hot dark eyes.

"You have very pale skin," he said.

"Yes." I looked straight back at him.

"And bright lips."

"Yes. That too. What of it?"

"Oh, nothing," he said, and, looking down, toyed with his food.

The meal soon ended. The fires were doused. Most of the men wrapped themselves in blankets or returned to their tents – and their women.

I lingered, gazing into the remaining embers, poking at them with a stick.

Marcus glanced at me and then walked away to tend to our horses – leaving me to find my *fodder*, my "candidate" for that evening.

I would be my own bait, I decided.

I wandered off into the darkness; the lustful older man followed me. I thought, if he is gentle and kind, I will merely refuse his advances and send him back to the camp. And then I must look elsewhere for my meal. But if he tries to force me, I will satisfy my hunger.

I walked slowly, as if lost in thought, following a narrow path that led through some brush and scrub and sloped down toward a shallow ravine. I poked at the ground with the stick. The ravine was not deep but would shelter me – and my feeding – from the camp. I could see clearly in the dark. It was a strange sensation – to see where others were blind.

The moon broke clear of a bank of cloud and everything was, suddenly, doubly visible. Now my pursuer could see too.

He crept up behind me, in what he considered, I suppose, a cleverly stealthy manner, crouching low, moving silently, with careful, light footsteps, from bush to bush. He was not alone.

Two other men came behind him, whispering.

My senses had multiplied and were more than human – I heard, saw, and smelled things other people could not. Like a flame searing my mind, I felt the physical presence of the men, their cruel desire burning bright in the warm night, their lust to hurt, possess, maim, and kill. They were drunk with the power to hurt another human being – man or woman or child.

I came to a bar of sand, about two meters high; perhaps it was the bank or shallows of a river that had dried up in the dry season. I waited – yes, I was bait in a trap.

The man came up stealthily, or so he thought, and then, at the last moment, coming out from a bank of reeds, he rushed me, and put his knife to my throat.

"Please don't," I said. "I am yours."

He backed away slightly, releasing me, and gazed at me with a grin of pure lust. I sensed that he – that they – intended not only to rape and sodomize me, but also, after a session of torture, to kill me – and then of course to murder Marcus – and in as prolonged and painful a way as possible.

"Ah," I thought, "you make it easy, my friend!"

The moon slipped behind a dark reef of cloud. My assailant was caught in an instant of semi-blindness, of confusion.

"Now!" I leapt so high that I came down straight onto his back. I curled myself around him with the fluidity of a snake. I pinned his arms to his sides and plunged my fangs into his jugular.

He was so stunned he dropped his knife.

It fell straight into the sand, point first, and stood there, vertical, quivering. It will be useful, I thought. I will take it when I've finished.

He was too startled to cry out; and my fangs instantly paralyzed his vocal cords; he writhed and twisted, this way and that; his arms struggled, trying to unsaddle me. His voice gurgled. He pitched forward, straight down onto the sand.

It took only a few seconds. I drank, and drank, and, as I drank, the tapestry of his life was revealed to me, an endless sequence of adventure and crime, rape and violation. One flurry of images: It was night, he was pursuing a prostitute down a narrow alleyway, down stone steps where, under the lamplight, rivulets of waste and water ran. He caught her dress and tore it away from her. She was young, just a teenager really, a blonde – a northern slave girl from the icy seas beyond the mountains – and terrified. He grabbed at her ankle. She kicked herself free, scrambled to her feet, ran, screaming for someone to help her. No one did; the shutters were closed; fear and loathing lurked behind every window. He galloped after her, caught up to her as she turned a corner, smashed into her, slamming her with the bulk of his huge body. They rolled down into a wider street. He grabbed her hair, shouting, "Whore, whore, whore, you'll pay, you'll pay!" He seized her face, crushing her cheeks between his fingers, slashed at her with a knife, one quick razor-sharp stroke cutting her nose from her face. He stepped back, just for an instant, to contemplate his work – the gaping horror, skull-like, where her nose had been, her beauty forever gone, the wide staring eyes, the blood gushing, dripping like a droopy moustache and beard, black in the moonlight. Then he seized her and stabbed her deep in the heart and twisted the knife upwards. I felt in my gut the pain of her heart being sliced and cut out, I saw her killer through her horrified wide-open eyes; I saw how excited he was as he mutilated and murdered her, the blood pulsing, exalted, through his veins. I *felt* how excited he was. Cruelty! Ecstasy! I was the man; I was the girl. Then it went blank. She was gone. The scene was gone.

Emptiness.

He too was emptied. I had finished. I stood up. I checked. He was dead, truly dead. He would not rise again. I tossed the body to one side. The dogs, the wolves, the jackals would eat it.

Energy surged through me. I could do anything!

The others came up now, cautiously, hiding behind the reeds, giving their friend time to finish his work, expecting to find me helpless – but they too were to be caught and surprised. I could see and they couldn't. And I could move much more quickly than they ever could.

I killed them in the traditional human way – with a knife, the knife my meal had let fall. It was a fine-looking knife, twelve inches long, very sharp, and with a splendidly carved ivory handle, representing a phoenix rising from a sea of flame.

It took a few short seconds to kill the two rapists – slitting the throat of the first, cutting the heart out of the second. Marcus had taught me well. I sniffed and licked the villain's warm, bloody heart that I held in my hand, regretting that I could not eat it.

It was a good knife. I decided to keep it.

"You have fed?" Marcus was securing a pack to his horse. He tightened a belt and patted it down.

"Can you not see?"

Marcus peered into the dark. "Oh, yes, the blood!"

I glanced down at my bloodied clothes. "My table manners are atrocious."

"It was satisfying?"

"Very."

"Good."

"There were two others, his friends – they were going to rape me and kill me. They have killed before, particularly women, and raped and tortured. I killed them – all three."

"Excellent! You are a marvel, V, a font of good works," Marcus grinned. "We must leave before they notice that the swine are missing. In any case, your assailants were interlopers and bullies, parasites and extortionists, not at all popular with this tribe. They will not be missed. Indeed, you have done this little group a service. Tomorrow, when they break camp, they will do so without fear. By the way, I stole some clothes, a nice simple tunic, and some leggings, just your size. You can bathe and change later."

At first, we walked our horses in silence. Then we mounted and galloped away as quickly as we could. When we were at a safe distance from the encampment, we slowed and rode on through the beautiful night, rich with the smell of herbs and flowers. I drank it all in – never, when I was human, did I feel the full flavors of life as I did now.

We came to a stream that slowed down behind a dam of pebbles to make a wide shallow pool that rippled gently in the moonlight.

"You can bathe and change here if you wish."

We dismounted. I took off my bloodied clothes and waded into the water while Marcus sat on a pile of rocks and watched.

I plunged under the surface and, guided by the rippling shadowy moonlight, I skimmed along the bottom of the pool, just inches above the white sand and dark pebbles. I was gliding, flying in the water, naked, effortless, feeling as free and elegant as a slick, frolicking dolphin.

I splashed to the surface, dripping with moonlight, and climbed onto the rocks and sat next to Marcus. We didn't say anything. We let the night caress us.

In the silence, I felt we were one, Marcus and I.

Marcus put his hand on my hand and our fingers locked together.

Once or twice, Marcus squeezed my hand.

Finally, the beads of water evaporated – I was dry. Marcus stood up and held out the clothes, a tunic and tight-fitting leggings, with a finely wrought leather belt. I stood up and pulled them on. They were fresh. I had been created anew.

We mounted our horses and followed the stream in a leisurely fashion, making our way toward home. Hours passed. The moon crossed the sky and was lost behind a bank of clouds.

"Soon I will fall ill and die," Marcus said, out of the blue.

My heart, as if a thunderbolt had hit it, was stricken.

"No, it cannot be."

"Nothing can stop it."

"But you are young."

"No, I am old – for my race, I am old."

"But you are strong, full of fight. You are vigorous."

"Yes, so it appears. My people know how to keep the body lusty and young, for centuries, for thousands of years, but then the end comes suddenly." Marcus paused, frowned, and stroked his beard. "If I were among my own people, I could be *renewed*. For another hundred years or so, perhaps a thousand or two ... and then again ... and again ... but here ..." He waved toward the darkness around us.

I understood. We, on our sky-island, were primitive barbarians; we did not have the magic to save him.

"But I love you," I said. "I cannot – I will not – live without you!"

"You will, and you must," he said; his voice was hard. I hated him – how could he abandon me? How could he talk of his death with such calm? Then suddenly the hate dissolved, and I was consumed with a sense of love and of loss.

"Oh, Marcus!" Tears filled my eyes.

When we arrived home, Amilcare was at the gate with Asherah waiting. They always seemed to sense when Marcus was about to arrive.

Asherah favored me with a brilliant smile and kissed me on both cheeks. She ran a bath and had already prepared my bed just the way I liked it, the white linen sheets, with the top sheet drawn back at an angle, and had set out a game of Senet.

Even as she tended to me so joyously and even as I responded with affectionate delight, I felt an inner melancholy, even despair. I tried to hide it, but I knew Asherah sensed it.

We played Senet for several hours. It helped take my mind from what Marcus had told me, that soon I would be alone.

Finally, I was tired and wanted to sleep.

Asherah motioned: *Did I want her to stay with me as I slept?*

Yes, I nodded: *I did.* Her idea was that she was going to stand guard or sleep on the floor, but I told her that, if she agreed, she was to share the bed – it was certainly large enough. So, for the first time, we slept together. She fell asleep more quickly than I. I held her close and listened to her breathing, regular, and soft, and almost musical. It may seem strange that a creature such as I should say this, but I think there is nothing so sacred as sleeping with someone who trusts you absolutely, nothing so touching as listening to the even rhythm of their breathing, nothing so tender as watching in vigil over someone you protect, a woman, a child, or even a man. Such trust is like magic. It is like love. Often, it *is* love.

Soon afterwards, Marcus said I was to leave the city, I was to sail across the Mediterranean to the Greek city-state called Cumae, near what is now the city of Naples. I would begin my new life independent of him.

"What?" I shouted.

I did not want a life independent of him!

"What are you talking about?" I screamed. I stormed and cried and beat my fists on the walls. I tore my hair, I ripped my garments.

Marcus was not to be moved. He did not want me to see him grow old and frail and die. He wanted me to remember him as he was – not as he would soon be. "Besides, your duty is to survive," he said. "The future lies to the north, in Italy."

"The future!" I stamped my foot. "I do not want to even hear that word: *the future*! What a ridiculous idea – *the future!*"

Marcus laughed. "You know who you sound like?"

"No." I kicked the wall. "I do not know and I do not care what I sound like! Let all the devils take you!"

"Your Avatar, that opinionated, petulant –"

"Maybe I should summon her! Together we could give you a real thrashing and force you to change your mind!" What a tongue-lashing she would give him if I ordered it! In spite of myself, I smiled, then grinned, then began to laugh – though I was still angry!

Marcus wiped his eyes, laughing, while I simmered. Suddenly, I relented. "You are my master, Marcus." I wiped away my tears. "Decide my fate as you will!"

He took me to him and held me and comforted me, stroking my hair, whispering endearments and jokes into my ear. I would in future years thank him, he said, for sending me away. But in that, he was wrong. I could never thank him for leaving me. Love, of course, is selfish. It never wants to lose what it loves. I wanted him to live forever and to be mine – forever.

And so, Marcus sent me – dressed for the occasion as a woman – with a cargo of gold and ivory and valuable textiles, my "dowry" as it were – across the Mediterranean to Italy. I had my own personal guards – big muscular men who worked for Marcus and who would have laid down their life for him – and I am sure for me as well.

I did not want to dress as a woman. I did not want to *be* a woman. I disliked the long gowns I would be forced to wear. I loved the freedom of a simple tunic and leggings. I loved the boots men wore. And I loved having my knife by my side.

"You have no choice," Marcus said. And he explained: I would have a consort in Italy, a husband, a very wealthy and powerful man to whom Marcus had "promised" me. But Marcus told me that my future husband would not trouble me for the kind of love that usually marks intimacy between a man and a woman. "He likes women," Marcus said, "but his intimate tastes, his need for tenderness and sex and love, are directed toward men. He is very refined," Marcus added, "and he believes – rightly – that you are a sort of divine being, a creature with magical powers and special needs."

"Special needs," I muttered. "Eating people ..."

"You don't eat people; you drink them." Marcus was grinning. He liked it when I was testy.

"Well, that is entirely different," I pouted.

"Yes, it is!" Marcus said. "Blood is sacred; drinking blood is a sacrament."

"Humph." I crossed my arms and stared at the floor.

"Would you like Asherah to go with you?"

I looked up. "I would love it, Marcus – but you must ask her!"

"We will ask her together!"

Asherah did not hesitate. She clapped her hands and threw her arms around me. She immediately began to pack our things.

Just before dawn, Marcus took us to the port. We set sail within the hour.

Marcus stood on the quay and waved. He was still there when we went over the horizon and the city vanished; and then the cliffs too were gone; and then there was nothing but sea and sky and the ship itself and a few gulls flying behind us.

I had never been to sea before.

The crisp waves, the gulls following in our wake, the vast horizon, the brilliance of light, the salty tang in the air, the rows of oars rising and falling, gleaming in the sunlight, the sails, billowing and snapping in the wind – it all made me drunk with pure sensation.

Keeping out of the sun, I stayed below deck much of the time, reading some fragments of Greek poetry on a scroll Marcus had given me, but Asherah stayed up on deck, among the sailors, in the sunlight, letting the wind run through her hair, for almost the whole voyage. I had never seen her so happy.

We sailed across the Strait of Sicily, which separates the island of Sicily from North Africa, and then along the south and east coasts of Sicily, past Mount Etna, which, with its vast fields of lava, shone darkly in the sunlight. Then we sailed through the treacherous and narrowing Strait of Messina, which separates Sicily from the toe of the Italian boot, and where, at the northern end of the Strait, Scylla, a dangerous outcropping of rocks, and Charybdis, a treacherous whirlpool, lie in wait for unwary sailors. North of Sicily, we sailed past the Aeolian Islands, the Islands of the Winds, and up the Italian coast, till we arrived at our destination, not far from Mount Vesuvius, not far from the island of Capri.

As planned, we settled in the Greek city of Cumae – just northwest of where Naples now is. Adapting was easy because I already spoke fluent Greek. And so began my life alone, except for Asherah, my greatest friend.

Often, we went out at night together, when I went hunting. She would stand guard. She had learned martial arts from Marcus and from me, so she was a match for anyone we might meet.

My – our – patron, and my "husband," was Agathon. He was an immensely rich, extremely understanding fellow, fifty-three years old, who owned large estates and had extensive trading interests. He adored what Marcus called philosophic discussion. He was witty, and, amazingly for such a rich and powerful man, he was also a good listener. We dined often alone, unusual in that culture for man and wife, and talked and argued late into the night. He quickly learned to trust me. Indeed, increasingly, when Agathon traveled to his more distant estates or voyaged for business, he left the running of his establishments to me: I never betrayed his trust, and I quickly learned much about the business of buying and selling slaves, scheduling the arrival and departure of ships laden with goods, and making sure servants and slaves and freedmen on the estates managed things well: textiles, dyes, olives, grapes, wine, oil, metals, grains …

It was a busy life, and a full one.

Asherah went everywhere with me, beautiful, patient, wise …

The years passed.

I chose my fodder, when I could, from those who preyed on the weak – on women, children, the old – and on the poor. Agathon occasionally gave me valuable advice about those who could, usefully, be *vanished*, as he put it. Asherah hunted with me – as long as she could.

Asherah grew old – and I stayed young.

Of course, the day came when Agathon died. It was sudden – and during a feast to which he had invited some of his most brilliant young male companions – I was included and dressed in my young gentleman version, Adonis. All Agathon's intimates knew I often dressed as Adonis and they accepted me as one of them. Agathon was in splendid form, though perhaps he had drunk too much. He stood up to give a toast, finished his little speech, drank from the cup, and, while everyone was still laughing at his last joke, he turned to me, winked – and then fell straight to the ground, dead. That so much wit and graciousness could cease to be in an instant was a sobering thought. In our own quite separate and different ways Agathon and I had grown to love each other. I inherited his fortune through a trick – which he had exploited – in the law, though I shared it with some of his "favorites" – young men who seemed to have taken a liking to me, and I to them. And, having learned from Agathon, I continued to administer – and expand – the estates and his businesses.

And Asherah, too, eventually, died.

It was a warm, calm, perfect evening, with the stars in all their splendor. Asherah knew these were her last hours. She wanted to die under the stars – and so we arranged it. Reclining on a bed out on the terrace, with the soft breeze keeping us company, we talked and joked using our private sign language; and, after drinking one last glass of wine, she died in my arms.

Her last hand-sign to me was "love." She pointed at me and I returned the sign to her and kissed her. As she gazed at me, her hand stroking my cheek, the light faded from her eyes. I waited for a long instant, breathless with pain. Then I closed her eyes and kissed her lips.

I said to myself: "Now I know I am alone."

Oh, I am self-centered, I thought, even in the death of the one who – after Marcus – I most loved. I am a monster of egoism! But how to live without her amused and affectionate glance, the quizzical tilt of her head, her bright smile, and her silent laughter? How to live without her body beside me in the night? How to live without our games and caresses? How to live without her kisses? How to live without the joy of waking her or being woken by her?

After the funeral rites, the laying out of her body, the funeral procession, and the burial, the condolences and formalities, I wanted to be alone – to savor, masochistically, my solitude.

I slept in the stable that night – the warmth and the smell of the horses comforted me. I dreamed, and the dream was a vision of hell and of myself in my demon form, perhaps playing the role of Satan himself, with my serpent's eyes, gold with the dark impenetrable slit, staring back at me, accusing me. All around me rose sulfurous fumes, lava glowed and spurted from volcanoes. I clawed at my scales and as I stood outside myself, watching myself, I changed – becoming ever more demonic, with hooves, longer claws, horns, a forked tail, a vicious snout, and evil voracious fangs. I cried out, "No, No, this cannot be – this cannot be …"

I woke up, alone, lying on the straw, covered in sweat. The horses were neighing and pawing the ground, rearing up, kicking at their stable walls, terrified, their eyes rolling, their mouths foaming. It took me a long time to calm them down.

I breathed intense emptiness, knowing now I would forever be alone.

Later that day I morphed into my demonic self and wandered for three days and three nights, a naked beast, hiding in the forest. I climbed the side of the volcano Vesuvius. I breathed in the sulfur. I watched the clouds of rising hot steam. I crouched alone on the dark lava. I covered myself in ash. I cried out to the empty heavens. Truly, I was a demon. Truly, I had risen from Hell or Hades. Truly, I was the daughter of some unclean unsanctified cursed place. Truly, I did not deserve love. Solitude was to be my destiny. I waited for the sun to rise, then I hid myself from the light and cowered deep in the dark forest, weeping.

Finally, I came back to myself – stretched in the sunlight, yawned, cast off my self-pity and self-indulgent melancholy, and changed back into human form and returned to my home where the servants were calmly waiting for me – they were used to my strange habits.

And so my new life began – alone, far from everything I loved. Of course I never saw Marcus again.

And I was true to my word. I have never created another creature such as I."

As V told me this story, I could see that she was truly moved by her memories of Marcus and Asherah. Tears ran down her cheeks.

I coughed to break the spell. "So, you say Cardinal Ambrosiano is using the Crystal?"

V blinked at me. She blew her nose, daintily, with a handkerchief she pulled from the back pocket of her jeans. "Yes, he is certainly using it, though I am sure he doesn't understand what he is doing. It is my fault – my negligence. I know the Crystal has been activated. Nothing else would create this weird wave of earthquakes – and I have intercepted a few strange signals between Rome and North Africa that indicate that the Cardinal is with the Crystal now. Somehow, he is using it to cause earthquakes. And the earthquakes are just the beginning."

"Are you sure?"

"Yes. The Cardinal's secret Order aims at the end of the world – at the realization of the Apocalypse, as foreseen, they say, by John of Patmos. You know how it goes, Father. *And I beheld when he had opened the sixth seal, and, lo, there was a great earthquake; and the Sun became black as sackcloth of hair, and the moon became as blood; and the stars of heaven fell unto the earth, even as a fig tree casteth her untimely figs, when she is shaken of a mighty wind. And the heaven departed as a scroll when it is rolled together; and every mountain and island were moved out of their places.*"

"Indeed," I said, "you know the passage by heart, Demon. So it is foretold."

"The Satanic Order of the Apocalypse is an evil organization, Father. It is dedicated to human sacrifice, as I am sure you are aware."

CHAPTER 25 – ZEBRA GIRL

"Who am I? Where am I?"

Just now, she had emerged from the sea. She yawned. She was a zebra, striped like a zebra. She'd been coupling with an octopus. It wasn't very pleasant. The octopus had stared at her, slapped her once, amiably, on the shoulder. At one point, she felt the octopus would make an ideal companion. She and he should get married. Then it faded. Was the octopus real?

She tried to shake her head.

She couldn't; her neck was locked in a vice.

Her tongue, heavy and dry, lolled, useless, paralyzed, in her mouth. Her lips were dry. She was groggy. She had to pee. Bowels uneasy, intestines in a knot. She had to shit. She groaned. She tried to sit up. She couldn't. Her ankles and wrists and neck were pinioned down. What had happened to her? She twisted, she turned, she groaned, stretched out, manacled, spread-eagled, lying on something hard.

"Go to bathroom, have to," she whispered. "Pee, must pee …"

Her voice was hollow and hoarse and slurred. It was childish, too; it was not her voice. Her tongue flopped, useless, impossible to control. She dribbled. She licked at the saliva. Moisten my lips, she thought, vaguely, moisten my tongue.

"Go to bathroom, have to …"

No answer. Nothing, just silence; some machinery running somewhere; maybe a ventilation system, fans turning, blowing air, sucking in air. Difficult to think. Head full of clouds. Woolly, woolly, woolly! Vaguely, she recollected coupling with a large octopus, it was black and silver gray and slimy and it squirted ink all over her; then she was a zebra-girl crawling on a beach of pure white sand, and climbing a cliff and eating some sort of unearthly delightful banana.

That banana tasted delicious.

There were two moons in the sky.

"Go to bathroom. Have to pee!" She cleared her throat, clogged up with phlegm. Her voice was so weak!

"What?" A figure, a face, a huge white and black blur, loomed over her.

"Have to pee," she whispered.

"What?" The blur leaned close. The blur had a German accent. It must be that nun, that strange nun. The nun had no real face, just a little baby face, and she spoke like a child. German, yes, the nun spoke German. Kate remembered, she remembered who she was; well, she remembered a name; it was her name – Kate. *I am Kate, my name is Kate.* But where was she? And who was this nun, really?

"Pee! I have to pee!" Her voice was so weak she could hardly hear herself.

"*Einen Moment, bitte,*" said the little-girl voice. The breath smelled of something – cinnamon, probably cinnamon.

The face went away.

"I gotta pee!" She wiggled, trying to lever up her hips, but she was so tightly tied down, she could hardly raise them at all. She gave up. Maybe she would just pee here, now, soil her prison, soil whatever she was lying on – it was hard – a metal cot or gurney. A device to constrain a prisoner or an insane person. She would die in her own pee, soiled by her own shit, naked. Who cared! Nobody would know. Anger rose, subsided, dissipated, disappeared. Maybe she was crazy, maybe she was a crazy person. Maybe this was her reality – she was a crazy person in an asylum and that's where she'd been her whole life.

She had to sleep, she wanted to dream. The amorous octopus was better than this; and that beautiful otherworldly beach! She blinked. All she could see were vague shapes and lights. A ceiling, perhaps, it must be a ceiling.

The big pudding-like blur of a face returned.

Big fingers, arms enveloped in voluminous coarse-textured black, the nun's habit, fiddling with the collar around her neck. It opened. Kate tried to raise her head. It took too much effort. She lay back.

The hands opened the manacles – wrists and ankles. Kate lay there.

"*Aufstehen!* Up, get up," said the nun. "*Aufstehen!*"

"I can't."

"*Aufstehen!*" Two big pudgy hands and arms pulled her up, and swung her legs out into the void. Her feet touched down, the bare soles of her feet, touched the floor, recoiled from the cool tiles, then touched the floor again.

"*Sitzen!* Sit!"

Kate sat on the edge of the cot – it was a metal cot, made of steel, cold to the touch, and longer than a normal cot, and it had restraints with buckles and locks.

Yes, it designed was to keep crazy people pinned down, so they wouldn't hurt themselves or anybody else or escape and wander around in the streets and scare the good citizens going about their normal good citizen business. Was she a crazy person? *Am I a crazy person?* Her head spun. Round and round it went, round and round. Vertigo. Nausea. Vomit rising. She leaned forward, clutching the edge of the cot. She could hardly see anything – just a blur. Her own body was a blur; she looked down: Breasts, belly, thighs – blurs and smears of white. Naked. She was naked. She hugged herself. Sticky skin, gooey cooling sweat, shivering all over.

"*Aufstehen!* Stand up!"

She tried to stand. Vertigo. They must have put drops in her eyes, because she only saw the vaguest of shapes, much worse than when she just went without her glasses. Yes, they must have put in drops!

And drugs! She was drugged!

Of course!

How silly not to have realized!

A big arm under the voluminous coarse cloth of the nun's habit took her under the arm, pulled her to her feet.

What a humiliation, naked, soaked in sweat, needing to pee, eager to shit, unable to stand up. *Damnation!* The nun laid a huge hand on her shoulder.

"Bathroom! *Toilette!*"

Kate sagged. Her legs were rubber. Yes, they had drugged her, but what sort of drug was it?

"Walk!"

"Okay." Red and black splotches flashed, floating like motes of fire. She almost fell. She gagged, almost vomited. Held it in; the feeling faded. *Damnation! I must control myself.*

With the nun holding her up, she staggered along the corridor, around a corner – almost falling – and then to a door. The nun guided her through the door. Kate put her hand against the cool ceramic wall.

A sudden shock of icy cold, a chill. In an instant, it passed.

A toilet and, in another corner, a shower stall.

"Sit!" The nun stood over her.

Kate lowered herself onto the toilet seat, cold and hard. She pressed her legs together. The nun loomed. Kate peed. She shat. Okay, that was easy. At least she didn't have diarrhea, or constipation.

"Wipe!" The nun held out toilet paper.

Bending forward, Kate wiped herself. Four times, four strips of toilet paper. What a humiliation! A flush of shame. But the feeling drifted away.

Suddenly, she felt warm, drowsy, comfortable, horny, vaguely dreamy, floating; yes, horny – her Id was on the loose … Where was she? Who was she?

"Here," said the big blob in the dark robe. What was she? Who was she? Oh, yes, the nun. Why was she with a nun? Was she in a convent?

Who am I?

I have forgotten my name.

Is that possible?

Who am I?

The nun steered her across the room. Kate touched her breasts, her belly. Her body was slick with sweat, thick, slippery, and gooey. Had the octopus done that? Drugs can do that. Body trying to eliminate the poisons. Pores flushing the toxins out. Hmm! Had they poisoned her? Drugged her, yes, certainly, they must have done that. Think! Think!

She was in a shower cubicle, head down, leaning against the ceramic wall, staring at the patterned floor tiles. Was there some deep meaning in the pattern? She tried to focus.

The nun turned on the water. Kate's mouth hung open, her lips sagged, drooled. The water poured down. A warm deluge and then a hot deluge. She stood there, not moving. The nun began to scrub her.

I can do it, she wanted to say. No words came. She reached out to a small shelf. She took a bar of soap and a small rag-like sponge and she began to wash herself.

"Everywhere," said the nun.

Kate stared at the nun with dazed eyes. Why is this person my boss? Why is she my master?

She tried to say something. Out came an indistinguishable sound, something between a sigh and a croak.

She closed her eyes, turned her face up to the water, let it pour over her. She soaped herself all over, cleaned every inch, every orifice. The water poured down. Then it stopped.

The nun took an enormous white towel and rubbed Kate's back. Kate felt the water dribble way. Her hair was wet. It felt cool. The nun was strong, the strokes were vigorous. She was brushing down a horse, a pony.

They were outside the shower cubicle.

Kate stood, confused; which way was she supposed to go?

What was the next step?

Then …

It was toothpaste time, clearly. A sink and a mirror. Kate frowned, trying to see her face. Blurry image. White oval, black hair plastered down both sides, onto her neck, and over the forehead. A cartoon drawn in ink. She was a cartoon. *I am a cartoon!* She brushed her teeth. The foaming toothpaste overflowed. The nun cleaned it away with a towel.

"Rinse!"

Kate rinsed. She sloshed the water around in her mouth. She spat. She felt dizzy. Head lowered, about to gag, she put two hands on the sink. Hold on! Hold on! It passed. *Think, goddamn it, think!*

The nun took her by the hand. Kate allowed herself to be led.

"Lie down!" The nun pointed. The cot looked inviting. Kate slid onto the cot and lay down. Obedient little girl. The manacles and straps clicked into place – neck, wrists, ankles, and this time, her waist was buckled in too.

She lay there.

A few minutes later – or was it an eternity? It was difficult to tell. Somebody else was looking down at her. Another vague blob.

"Is she ready?" someone asked, in Italian.

"Yes, she is ready," said the nun.

"Time for the next injection, then."

"Yes, the injection."

"The paralysis must be total."

"Yes," said the nun in her wheezing, sing-song, little-girl voice, "the paralysis must be total."

When the needle plunged, Kate didn't even feel it.

CHAPTER 26 – TORMENT

I favored my demon with my most benign priestly stare. "So, you are saying the Cardinal is in North Africa – in the cavern you described?"

"Yes." Her gaze held mine.

"But if that's so, dear Demon, why don't you go there and stop him?"

"I need the key."

"You and Marcus left the key in the Crystal, did you not?"

"Yes. But it's not there." The corners of her mouth turned down, creating a delightfully comic expression of sadness, of contrition. My demon could, when she wished, play the melancholy clown. "My fault, I'm afraid," she said, with the pout of a guilty child.

"Ah, well, V, if the key is not there, where could it possibly have gone? You didn't misplace it, did you?"

"I do not know where it is. I have been sorely negligent, Father." Her eyelashes fluttered, truly meek now, blinking up at me, humbled, contrite. Oh, what an artist she is, a dissembler, a true actor!

"How so, my dear child?" I beamed at her. I felt quite comfortable in this role. She was a repentant sinner, and I was her benign confessor. It occurred to me that I would have to confess all these goings-on to *my* confessor – the thought gave me pause, but not much pause. I was not sure quite what sins I had already committed, if any, by listening to a demon's confession – though I was quite sure that if I allied myself with this demon in her strange enterprise, there would be sins to come, multiple sins, grievous sins, and soon!

"I failed to protect the Crystal and the key."

"But, my dear Demon, you could not be expected to stand guard over the cavern forever. How would you feed? And your mentor himself, Marcus, sent you far away, across the sea."

"Yes, that is true, Father. And for many centuries the Crystal and the key were safe. The climate changed in North Africa, the desert spread, and sand-storms buried the entrance to the Crystal for many centuries."

"Well, then." I spread my arms.

"But in the 1930s another vast storm swept away the sand. So, the cavern was uncovered. People could find it – and someone did find it."

"Really?"

"When I learned – only a year ago – that the storm had opened the canyon that leads to the Crystal's cavern, I immediately went to see for myself. The boulder that protected the entrance to the cavern was off to one side. The steel door was open. How this could have happened I did not understand – then I saw that there was a mark along the side of the cliff – a mark probably caused by a bolt of lightning, perhaps the lightning had been drawn by the metal in the cave, perhaps by the Crystal itself. The lightning had hit the boulder and the door. And it must have triggered the opening mechanism."

"An act of God."

"Yes, Father, an act of God." She smiled, and was, for an instant, once again her usual jaunty, high-spirited self.

"Go on."

"The tunnel was half buried in sand, but you could crawl down it to the end. The cavern was intact, just some shallow sand drifts here and there. But the Crystal was silent – a few lights flickered deep in its depths, but it was as if dead or sleeping a very deep sleep."

"I see."

"There were signs an expedition had entered the cavern – ropes and rope ladders, burnt torches, Italian newspapers from 1936, and a few tools. But that was it. I don't know who entered the cavern, nor exactly when. I climbed up to the control platform. The key was gone. The keyhole was empty. I looked everywhere. There was no sign of it. And, without the key, the Crystal did not talk to me, and I could not communicate with it."

"I see. So – the World-Destroyer is untended. And vulnerable."

"Yes, without the key, I cannot control it." She put her hand on my sleeve. "From hints I have heard, I am convinced Ambrosiano's Satanic Order of the Apocalypse knows where the key is. I need to find it. And, now, since the earthquakes have begun, I need to find it fast. Otherwise, accidentally or not, the Crystal could destroy the Earth."

"Why do you think they have it?"

"No one, I have learned, has recently visited the Crystal, or has entered the cave, except Cardinal Ambrosiano and his followers."

"I see."

"So, Father, you can see now why I need to learn everything about the Order of the Apocalypse."

"Well …" I glanced at her. I still don't know why I did it, but I decided to trust her and go along with the demon's game. "The problem is this: much of what I have found, I do not understand. It's all – most of it – in my briefcase."

"Shall we look?"

"You haven't done so already?" I had expected – now that I knew what she was and how badly she wanted the information – that she would have fully ransacked my briefcase by now.

V laughed. "I was sorely tempted, Father, but I decided I wanted you to be willing to help me – I would wait for your permission."

"Let us get my briefcase, then."

I went back to the bedroom where I had first woken up. There it was, sitting on a chair, innocently, next to the wall, my old battered, scuffed, black leather briefcase, with the loose handle that I had had repaired so many times by the shoe-maker just off Campo de' Fiori, whose shop, or so he says, is right next to where Julius Caesar was murdered by his friend Brutus and the other conspirators.

I picked up the briefcase and carried it back to the dining room where V was waiting.

I laid the briefcase down on the table, unbuckled the straps, and pulled out some of the material I had kept, plus my small, old-fashioned leather-bound spiral address book, another spiral notebook, and three old-fashioned computer discs.

Rather sheepishly I put some other items onto the table: a sandwich, gone bad, three rubber bands, four rumpled newspaper clippings from three months back, some unsharpened pencils, and packs of stick-it notes, a paperback guide to Pompeii, and an ancient muffin that was coated in what looked like greenish-blue moss.

"Ugh! That's disgusting!" V made a face. "Doesn't Signora Bianchi clean out your briefcase? I am going to have a talk with her; I will say I am your niece. She must look after you properly."

"I never let her near my briefcase. She wouldn't dare!"

I was about to give my young demon friend a lecture about privacy and independence, but I decided that I would not win that argument, so I changed the subject. I pulled out the thick envelope. "Father Luciani left me this."

I pushed the moldy sandwich and the mossy muffin aside. "I have not been able to open the files on the discs or on the memory sticks," I said. "They are old and most of them are in old codes and encrypted perhaps."

"Let's see," said V. She pulled a powerful-looking laptop out of the sideboard and set it on the dining room table.

"Some of these files," she said, inserting a disc, "I will send to John – right now. He can decode them and tell us what he finds. The others, I think I can decode myself; they look pretty simple." She stared at the screen. Files began to open, in windows, on the screen desktop.

First, there was the list of scientists, including my friend, Roger Thornhill, and other physicists. V ran her finger down it.

"Yes," she said, "the list includes physicists, geologists, seismologists, and climate scientists – so if the Cardinal drew it up, he has a rough idea of what the Crystal can do."

"So – what does the Cardinal want from these experts?"

"Who knows? Instructions on how to make the Crystal work? Witnesses to his triumph?" V flipped through a few pages. "I suspect he is insane."

"Insane?"

"Yes, a total loony. There's no telling what he might do – he's a trickster, a joker, and therefore unpredictable."

"I never liked him. But I thought it uncharitable on my part, and I suspected that part of me was perhaps jealous of his power."

"Sometimes our instincts are right, Father, and our principles, our scruples, lead us astray. A gut feeling is not something to be ignored."

"A moral philosopher, are we, V?" I raised an eyebrow.

She stuck out her tongue.

We went through the files that she could decrypt on the laptop. In separate files, there were notes on sacrifice; the rules for a black Mass; the idea that Satan really should be God and that God's creation – the world and humans in this instance – should be destroyed.

"Well, it looks like the Cardinal still wants to turn the Christian religion upside down," said V. "I was hoping he might have tired of that obsession, but obviously not."

"You told me you met him. You feel guilty you didn't kill him then?"

"It was, let's see," she closed her eyes. "It was the third of July 1982, toward dusk, a romantic setting in a little country graveyard. A protégé of the Cardinal, a Brother Filippo, was a handsome fellow – a sort of street villain from a painting by Caravaggio – and he was a pedophile who raped and tortured and murdered little boys. He also procured young women – mostly foreigners and tourists – for the Cardinal's black Mass ceremonies. After I dealt with Brother Filippo, the disappearances of young women ceased – for a time. I had a little talk with the Cardinal, but I should have killed him – and Father Andrea – right there and then. But I was enjoying myself too much. You see, Father O'Bryan, I am incurably frivolous. But enough of that," she said. "We must focus on the present."

"You said black Mass?"

"Yes." V was staring at the notes on the screen.

"Black Mass? You mean the Cardinal really has officiated at a black Mass?"

V glanced up. "He did. Many times. He does, almost certainly, still. Those young women who have been disappearing in Rome and Naples, I suspect that is his work. The Cardinal's version of the Holy Mass involves not bread and wine, but flesh and blood – and death. The Satanic Order of the Apocalypse has returned to an earlier, literal, form of sacrifice – human sacrifice."

"Oh, dear!" This, if true, was even worse than I suspected. I continued to rummage through the material. Tied together with an elastic were more handwritten notes, clearly made by Father Luciani.

V stared at them. The notes were in a scrawled and uneven cursive hand, a few lines, clearly scribbled quickly, in spotty blue ink, with a ballpoint pen.

"Are these notes written by Father Luciani?"

"Yes, almost certainly," I said.

"Poor Father Luciani." V ran her finger over Father Luciani's notes and, peering over her shoulder, I read them out loud: "Perversion of Gnostic doctrine, practice of black Mass, proof of kidnappings and killings, ritual killing of a goddess figure, links with Mafia ... Must report to the Pope ... I feel I am being watched ... Is there no place safe in this world, no wall without eyes, no alcove without ears ...? I can share this with no one, only with the Pope ... I am hiding this material now, here, where no one, I hope, will look. You, who read these notes, you will know what to do."

"Ah, ah," said V.

"I am a fool; I didn't really think it all through." I shuddered.

"You are not a fool, Father." V pushed another of the discs into the laptop.

A few seconds later, she murmured, "Yes, you are right, these are doubly encrypted. But I think I have a program that will open this one."

And she did.

"Well, well," V said, staring at the screen, "so it is true. Here is the proof. He's once again up to his old tricks! You don't have to look, if you don't want to, Father."

"I'll look." I got up and stood behind her.

On the screen was a photograph. It was pure pornography. A young woman, naked, manacled down, on an altar of black stone, possibly granite; large candles, held in elaborately wrought and monumental candleholders, were burning on either side of her; a man was standing over her, dressed in priest's garb, and holding a large knife high in the air.

Behind him, partly visible on the wall, was what looked like a cross, perhaps two meters high, but it was upside down, and it appeared to have been charred and twisted. The setting appeared to be a shadowy, dark place, possibly a cave or cavern.

"Oh," I said.

V clicked a button, and the slide show began.

It was a series of quick stills. The knife plunged down into the young woman's abdomen. Her blood splashed up over her. Her blood ran down onto the altar where runnels had been cut in the stone to catch and channel it.

The man dressed as a priest twisted the knife and cut out her heart. He lifted it up, displaying it, as if it were the Eucharist. He wiped the girl's blood on his face, very deliberately, on both cheeks, and on his forehead …

"Enough." I turned away.

"Do you know the priest?"

"No. I find it difficult to believe he is really a priest."

"Oh, he's a priest alright," V said. "His name is Father Ottavio. I saw him, once, at a cocktail party in Rome. We can check; but I'm certain it is him."

I swallowed. I had read learned papers on the Gnostic heresy, on the Cathars, and on Satanism by a Father Ottavio. "Could these images have been faked?"

"Yes, but they aren't. There's a video file, too. Let's see what it shows."

"Yes," I sighed. "Let us see."

V triggered the video file and we saw, suddenly, on the screen, Cardinal Ambrosiano. He was sitting behind a desk dressed in plain priest's garb, the collar, the black shirt and jacket, and his hair was carefully combed. He had once been, I had to admit, extremely handsome. But now he was a parody of the man I had known. His lips were thinner, his mouth turned inwards, and the corners turned down, as if in anger. His teeth, when he revealed them, were sharp, uneven, and pointed, like those of a rat. He clasped his hands in front of him on the desk, in that false-sincere way that salesmen, priests, and politicians adopt to demonstrate that everything is genial and cheerful and aboveboard. The Cardinal smiled; then he spoke:

"If you are watching this, then you will know that the end of time is near, that the countdown to the Apocalypse has begun.

"This is my confession, and confession, too, is merely an expression of vanity, or of despair, or of the loneliness of the self; there is no escape from the self, the source of all our anguish and all our joys.

"The self is a tissue of lies. But, no matter – all is vanity and so I shall express my vanity to the full! Our greatest fear, I think, is that we are invisible: no one truly knows we exist, we are entirely without significance, we live and die totally unknown to others, and unloved by them; we are prisoners in a cage that can never be opened.

"You know, if you look into your heart, that your true self is a knot of filthy little secrets, unknown to anyone but you. And thus, you have lived, trapped in your own iniquity, and thus you will die – utterly alone. This is the truth of all life – utter loneliness and perverse egoistic solitude. The rest is a mere charade.

"In confession, though, we are under the illusion that we truly reveal ourselves, and are known, and, being known and accepted, are saved. Since God knows us, we exist – and existence is love. Otherwise we are nothing – worse than nothing. Ah, yes, God – the solution to all problems!

"But God, my friends, is a fraud, an illusion; He is absent. He is not of this world, nor is He of any other world. The God we speak of is an invention of our despair, our fear, our vanity, our loneliness, of the desperate megalomania of a few who dared call themselves prophets, and of our yearning – of our need for love. He is the lie we all tell ourselves.

"As for me, I am fallen, and I exult in my fallen state.

"I will now confess how I found Glorious Satan – for Satan is Sin, Satan is Joy, Satan is the Dark Force, Satan is Freedom, and therefore He is our Friend – for only He can truly understand us, truly know us …

"Thus, to be truly ourselves, we must exult in sin!

"Only evil can understand evil. And so it is that, to go to the end of one's knowledge of oneself, one must go as far in the path of evil as is possible;

one must descend as deep as one can into cruelty, obscenity, perversion, blasphemy …

"This satanic epiphany happened one snowy night to a naive and idealistic young priest – who subsequently became the man I am now – Cardinal Antonio Xavier Paulus Ambrosiano.

"We are shallow-draft vessels, we humans. The slightest breeze will capsize us. And, accordingly, it was a minuscule and trivial event that overturned me, that sparked my epiphany – my conversion to the Truth of Satan and to the worship of Satan! I was at the time a hollow man. My understanding was narrow and merely human. My tiny insignificant epiphany was a beginning.

"The young priest I once was had passions – perversions. The young priest disapproved of his passions, his perversions. And, in his innocence, he prayed for enlightenment and purification. He wished to abolish his passions and transcend his perversions. He asked God to guide him. God told him that the World was a wicked place, that men and women were irredeemable sinners, that even the sacrifice of His son our Lord Jesus Christ had not been enough to cleanse sin from the world or to save the wicked. The fallen are forever fallen; there is no salvation.

"God whispered, 'I shall confide in you, oh lowly priest! The world was *not* created by me! It was – and *is* – the offspring of Satan.' The young priest recoiled in horror. This was the Gnostic and the Cathar heresy, for which almost a million Cathars had justly perished, under the sword, in the flames. Was God a heretic?

"The young priest felt the evil burning bright with an all-consuming flame within himself. If the world was created by Satan, then the world is evil, and we are evil. And then, evil is sacred!

"One bitter cold winter night the young priest closed his books, closed his eyes and sat very still, his forearms flat on the oak table in his small room. He felt the vast empty night pressing in around him. He was handsome and virile, this young priest, but his beauty and his virility were doomed to consume themselves in solitude and vanity. It was midwinter; and in the young priest's soul there was icy desolation. The night was dark; it was the holiday season; the young priest felt lost, distant from every other living being – not a touch, not a glance, not a word of comfort for him. Nor did he offer comfort to others. Love to him was unknown. His soul was an arid frozen desert. Nor could he worship or pray. God had retired from the world. God had drifted away and faded – leaving behind a chill white mist … nothing more.

"The young priest sat there, at his solitary simple wooden desk, the dark chill night closing in, close against the naked windowpanes. Ice clung to the thick lead bars between the small panes of colorless glass.

"The young priest, dressed in Jesuitical black, with his precise, impeccable white clerical collar, opened his eyes. He stood up. He put on his long overcoat and went out for a walk in the cold.

"The wind blew grains of icy hard snow off the roadside drifts. The road was empty, half buried in frozen snow that crunched underfoot. The night was bitter cold. It was a university town. Holiday lights shone in the trees, twined around lampposts, and shone too, like a welcome, on the porches and verandas of the big houses. Everyone had someone. He passed the windows of dormitories that glowed a warm, welcoming yellow. Behind the glass and the curtains there were, he was certain, scenes of voluptuous sinful abandon, orgies of copulation and fornication, bodies entangled in sweaty ecstasies of intimacy. His body was freezing. But his imagination was on fire.

"The young priest at that time was exceptionally handsome; and he knew it. It was a weapon, this beauty: he could convince or seduce anyone, or so he thought. But manipulating others did not liberate him from his solitude, his loneliness, his pain; his power was merely part of his prison.

"He walked for a long time that night. He stopped on a side street, a street of lonely houses with rubbish heaps covered in snow. This was a poor and neglected part of town. Suddenly, through a second-story window, he saw a woman who was wearing only a chemise. It was midnight. The wind had dropped. The snow was falling slowly, at a gentle angle; through the black air, thick, lazy, wet flakes drifted indifferently down.

"He moved to the left, to see the woman more clearly. Her bare arms shone like alabaster in the yellow light; her black hair was tied up in a glossy chignon.

"There was something slatternly, exposed and vulnerable, and infinitely appealing, about the woman – the casual abandon; one strap of the chemise down over her shoulder – it gave the young priest a rush of adrenaline, of dark seething lust. *Slut*, *whore*, *harlot*, he thought, with rising pleasure.

"She turned and glanced out the window; but she surely didn't see him. She was, he saw, young and more than pretty. He was truly excited now. In his fiery imaginings, he possessed the woman. She was tied down, bound hand-and-foot, splayed spread-eagled naked across a table; or standing erect, naked, with her arms pinioned behind her back, manacled to the stone wall of a dungeon, offered and helpless. He felt a burning desire to seize her, to subjugate her, to force her to her knees, to force her to worship him.

"As he was hypnotized by these reveries, he didn't notice how quickly time was passing. The snow fell, thicker and thicker. He was soaked and shivering. Ice formed in his hair. Finally, he turned away from the house, and walked down the hill, toward the university.

"He seethed with self-hatred. He was a pervert. He was lost in the eyes of God. He had fallen farther and faster than Lucifer.

"But he hated the woman much more than he hated himself. She was sin itself. She was Eve. She was Jezebel. She was temptation. She was weakness! Offering herself like that, shameless, lewd, with her bare arms, bare shoulders, breasts hardly hidden, then the strap of the bodice, hanging loose, an invitation to sin. She was the weakness, the inner weakness, threatening the mystically inclined, transcendent, soaring male ego: she was soft and all-enclosing; she was fertility; she was earth-like; she reeked of clay; she was lush, fecund, female, womb-like, amniotic; she was the origin of life, messy and mortal, soaked in blood and piss and shit, the whore, the earth, the soil, the Mother Goddess – she was *criminal!*

"He could not turn away from her. He could not escape. She was a physical presence in his gut, in his groin; she swirled around in a voluptuous vertigo-inducing dance; she was Jezebel and Salomé; clothed in painted splendor, she cast off her veils, she revealed all. She was alive within him, hollowing him out, invading, polluting, defiling – he must exorcise her, he must destroy this sacrilege! Burn her, scald her, cut her, destroy and obliterate her! Yes, exorcise her, cast her out, burn her alive!

"In a fever of rage and lust, he fled. He didn't stop walking until he was back in his room. The old, former Xavier, the naive young priest, felt that he should pray. But the *new* Xavier did not want to pray, to supplicate, to beg, to grovel before the idol, before the Empty One, the Void that called itself God!

"No!

"He stripped off the soaking clothes. He ripped off the collar. He poured himself a whiskey.

"*He would embrace Evil – not reject it!*

"He sat down and thought of the woman and of the unspeakable things he could do to her – binding, maiming, burying, and crushing. He looked down: he had an erection.

"How pleasing! How divine! Four hours ago, he would have chastised himself, prayed, imagined self-flagellation, forced himself to take a cold shower; but now, newly enlightened, newly liberated, he poured himself another whiskey.

"Since God was dead, *he* was God. Yes, he was God; he was without limit; he was eternal. Everything was permitted; nothing was impossible!

"'I am the phallic god,' he whispered. 'I am the fountainhead, the source. I am desire incarnate. I am unlimited untrammeled power.'

"He swallowed more whiskey.

"'I am the beginning and the end, the alpha and the omega.'

"Should he bring himself to orgasm? No, he would force himself to wait; he would store up the energy, the vital seminal fluid, the poisonous desire, and use it as energy! Sublimate! Sublimate!

"Later when he stood under the hot shower, he imagined the tortures, humiliations, degradations he would inflict on the whore; he would transform her into a female Saint Sebastian, naked, pierced, mutilated, and disfigured. Ah, yes, he had attained an insight into the true nature of desire and of evil.

"We are all, each one of us, in our innermost selves, diabolic; we are all servants of Satan. This was the new truth, the new theology!

"Since Satan, King of the World, had given the young priest this blindingly profound – and obvious – insight into evil, he decided he would exorcise evil by practicing evil; and he would find within the rotten shell of the existing Church a new pure core – the Cult of Truth, the Cult of Evil."

At this point, the Cardinal paused, beamed at the camera, and rubbed his hands. He licked his lips, the lascivious slurping lick of a wicked old man.

"He's nuts," V whispered. She clicked pause. "He's a prophet, maybe, a seer, maybe; but he's totally fucking nuts!"

I shot her a glance.

"Sorry, Father. I shouldn't use bad words!"

She clicked play.

A glimmer of drool remained on the Cardinal's chin and a slick of saliva on his sunken lips. He began, once more, to speak.

"Let me tell you, brother and sisters in crime, we *are* Satan. *We are Satan!* *We!* Why do we need fallen angels, when we have ourselves? Why do we need

Hell, when we can create all the wickedness and torture we desire here on Earth?

"Cruelty excites me, and why shouldn't it? I am human; therefore, I am a beast of prey, the deadliest and most cunning of them all, and thus I lust, I covet, I seize, I enslave, I rape, I mutilate, I torture, I kill! I murder and I take pleasure in murdering. And why shouldn't I?

"All our so-called virtues, our altruism, our kindness, our empathy, our so-called principles, are merely shallow masks for egotism and desire, for vanity and ambition, lust and power, and our appetite for slaughter. The religion of virtue is a religion of slaves, riddled with cringing hypocrisy, foul resentment, and craven weakness. But if I look into my heart, I find true divinity – the divinity of Satan and His – and my – dominion over the world

"And so, my dear invisible confessor, my dear audience, *mon semblable, mon frère*, this was the beginning – the modest beginning of my education. I plunged into the literature of evil. And that was how I discovered the Satanic Order of the Apocalypse. It had existed for many centuries – and it had, over millennia, transformed the Satanic Word into flesh and blood. The Order restored the original, dark, true meaning of religion – purification and rebirth through the spilling of the blood of innocence, the blood of the scapegoat, the blood of women, the blood of the Goddess. What is the religion of the patriarchs, after all, but an exorcism – ridding the world of the female principle, the eternal feminine, over and over. The so-called Holy Mass, and the Eucharist, with the wafers and the wine, is a mere parody, a pale adulterated mockery of the true meaning of sacrifice; and the true meaning of sacrifice is exorcism through blood and sacrifice, real blood and real sacrifice, the blood of the Goddess, the blood of woman, the blood of exorcism and casting out of the female archetype!

"And so, we have celebrated, for many decades now, the death of the Goddess, and the continual rebirth of Evil and of Satan's Reign on Earth. Now the time has come for the climax, time to bring the miserable charade of humanity and of so-called civilization to an end. Now the time has come to join with Satan in that nothingness that is absolute and true divinity! This world – this universe – is about to perish. So be it! Amen!"

The tape ended. The Cardinal, his hands clasped genially in front of him, grinned at the camera, a thick slick of saliva glowing at one corner of his sunken old man's mouth.

"Mad as a hatter," said V, "And yet ..."

"Yes," I sighed. And it seemed to me that it was quite possible that Ambrosiano had been driven mad, in a strange, perverse way, by his priestly ambition, by his desire for holiness, for perfection, for transcendence – all vanity and false ambition, in the end. If he couldn't be perfect in goodness, he would be perfect in evil. If he could not be godly; he would be satanic. Saints, I find, make the most dangerous sinners. Their very purity turns each virtue into vice. Desire for absolute purity leads to the guillotine, the gulag, concentration camps, terrorist bombs, and the killing fields. The quest for purity exults in uncovering scapegoats, in staging executions. Ambrosiano had tipped his saintly aspirations upside down, creating his own topsy-turvy world in which Love became Hate, Charity became Cruelty, and Life became Death. He wanted to be God. And so, he had to murder the divinity in every man and every woman. This was the antithesis of Christ ...

V, who was sifting through Father Luciani's notes, looked up. "There's a reference here to a drawing of something called 'the Torelli Jewel'!"

"The Torelli Jewel?"

"Yes. An interesting choice of words. The key to the Crystal could be described as a jewel. Let's look for the drawing."

"But where?"

"In your briefcase, Father. It is not yet empty. What else might your little cornucopia contain?"

"Well, let's see. You know I rather forget what's in there. I always am surprised by what I find when I delve deep enough."

"Well ..." V reached for it.

"Alright, alright, V, hold your horses!" I snatched my briefcase from her, turned it upside down, and emptied all the remaining contents: One navel orange, hardened to the consistency of granite; one banana (rather too ripe); an extra pair of reading spectacles of the cheap kind one can buy in a drugstore; three HB pencils; two ballpoint pens; a small octagonal yellow plastic pencil sharpener; and a slew of separate pieces of paper.

"Your briefcase is a whole universe, Father!"

"Well ..."

"I am most definitely going to have a talk with Signora Bianchi."

"I forbid you to say a –" I was stopped cold in mid-sentence ...

Everything trembled. The whiskey sloshed in the glass. One of the pens rolled along the table and fell off the edge. The navel orange turned around in a circle. The sliding doors rattled, the curtains in front of them swayed, swishing back and forth. What was happening? Then I realized – it was an earthquake …

"V …" John's voice was on the intercom.

"Yes, John, I know." V knelt and picked up the pen.

"It's beginning, V," John's voice paused. "And there are some things you and Father O'Bryan must see."

"We'll be there in a minute, John."

"Don't leave it too long, V!"

"Do you think that this is …?" I paused. Was this the beginning of the end?

"This is the Cardinal, this is the Crystal." V placed the pen back on the table. "Now, the Torelli Jewel."

"Oh, yes." I adjusted my glasses. "I do think I did see it. The drawing of the Torelli Jewel is in one of these notes, I do believe. Let me see." I began to sort out the little pieces of paper and stick-it notes that I'd accumulated to aid me in the act of composition of my great upcoming work on *Heresies and Demonic Possession*. They were all mixed in with the material from Father Luciani. Some of the stick-it notes had smiley faces, others had frowning faces, there were yellow ones, mauve ones, and pink ones. I used these little things whenever I wanted to organize a chapter, the different colors, I find, greatly facilitating clarity of thought. "Ah, here it is."

"Yes?" V perked up, a wolf scenting her prey.

"Let's see …" I stared at the drawing. It was of an oblong semi-transparent object, and along its length it had eight sides.

"That's it!" V stared at it. "That is the key!"

"And the note says, 'The Torelli Jewel is in the care of Father Matteo Ottavio.' Ah …"

V spread out a batch of photographs that were in the same bunch of papers as the stick-it notes and the drawing. "These are photographs of a Doctor Torelli. It seems he was an amateur explorer, poking around in North Africa in the 1930s. Here he is in a pith helmet. It's a nice photograph, rather faded though."

"Torelli …" I stared at the photograph. "So, he is perhaps the fellow who found the Crystal, in the 1930s."

"Yes, it must have been him … Hmm. Look at this." V held one of the photographs: Torelli standing with a camel, and behind him a silhouette that looked like a rock face. She pointed. "That's the escarpment, not far from the crevice and canyon that lead to the Crystal." She paused. "And Father Ottavio is almost certainly the same Father Ottavio as in the black Mass. He must have the Torelli Jewel."

"Let me see." I pawed my way through the masses of little notes, mine and Father Luciani's. "This last note is from – I'm sure it's from Father Luciani; I hadn't noticed it before. I just stuffed things into my briefcase. I was in a café, and I was in a hurry, you know; and I was afraid someone would see me … In any case, this note says …" I squinted at it. "… that Father Ottavio claims to have put the Torelli Jewel with custodians. It is in a safe place, the note says. The Torelli Jewel, it says, is a *fragment of the True Satanic Jewel and proof of the Cardinal's infinite satanic power, it* …"

"Who are the custodians?"

"It doesn't say."

"Where is this safe place?"

"It doesn't say."

"Damn!" She tapped her index finger on the table. "Damn!"

"But, my dear Demon, if we look for Ottavio, we shall find the custodians and then we shall find the Torelli Jewel. It is simple, is it not?"

The intercom spoke again. "V, I don't think we can wait any longer. You and Father O'Bryan must come and see this."

"Yes, John, we're coming!" V stood up. "Father, do you wish to come with me? Do you wish to see what we are up against?"

I hesitated for a second. Then I said, "Yes, I'm coming!" As the immortal Bard – even if he was English – put it, there is a tide in the affairs of men, which, if not taken at the flood …

"Good, then. Come, Father. Follow me."

I followed my very own demon along a corridor that was lined, on both sides, with bookshelves that were crammed to overflowing. Titles caught my eye – philosophers, theologians, and works of psychology, the classics of literature, history, and works of science, all in a variety of languages: English, Greek, Latin, French, German, Italian, Spanish, Russian, Hebrew, Chinese, Japanese, and Arabic.

"Your books?"

"I have lots of time to read, Father."

We came to a wall at the end of the corridor, it too covered with books.

V lifted out two recent English translations of *The Iliad* and *The Odyssey*, revealing a security panel; she punched in a combination and put her hand to a flat button. The wall slid open.

A stainless-steel staircase led downwards. It was amazing to walk down a staircase without having to compensate for my limp.

At the bottom of the staircase was an ultra-modern room – there were video screens, computer work stations, and what looked like controls for an elaborate communications and security system.

"This is Julia," said V, introducing me to a dark-haired, handsome, deeply tanned woman. She was dressed in a simple black skirt, a blouse, and a jacket. She looked like a Milanese lawyer or businesswoman, just back from a vacation. "Julia is a criminologist and a brilliant hacker too."

Julia smiled and shook my hand.

"John and Julia have been together ... how long?"

"Too long to mention," said Julia. "Almost 20 years now."

"Julia also helps me with my meals."

"You might say I'm V's dietician," said Julia. "John and I help V locate ... how should I say ..."

"... the *customers*," said V. "That's our usual euphemism; or as Marcus used to say, the *candidates*."

"People the world could quite well do without," said Julia.

As I listened to these two charming women, I realized how far I had traveled, in just a few hours! Oh, dear! Michael Patrick O'Bryan! I was conversing with an attractive, crisply professional lady who planned murders for her boss, a demon-vampire.

"So, now, listen to this." John was sitting at a console. He pushed a button. It was a TV-Internet news broadcast, in playback.

"In a spectacular and bloody kidnapping just outside Rome, one of the world's leading physicists, Doctor Roger Thornhill, and his daughter, Katherine, were bundled onto motorcycles and spirited away to an unknown destination.

"The kidnapping followed a car chase in which fifty-two-year-old Mario DeLuca, Thornhill's driver, was fatally wounded. Several leading scientists, who had gathered to honor Professor Thornhill, were murdered or wounded when armed gunmen opened fire on ..."

"My God! Roger and Kate are friends of mine, close friends."

"Thornhill was the first on the Cardinal's list, Father," said V. "He's one of the few scientists who might have an inkling of what the Crystal can do."

On the screen now was the title "Earthquake watch."

"Hello, I'm Cindy Tanaka, reporting from London. Experts declared today that the simultaneous seismic and volcanic activity around the world seems to have been the result of some sort of disturbance in Earth's gravitational field.

"Professor Raymond Blythe, one of the world's leading physicists, is here with me now. He has kindly agreed to help us understand what is happening in so many points around the globe." She indicated a world map with blinking red dots virtually everywhere.

"So, Professor Blythe, what *is* happening?"

The expert, a pale, gray-haired, gaunt gentleman in a tweed jacket, stroked his chin. "Well, Cindy, frankly, I don't think anybody has a clue. It's an absolute mystery. But one we are trying hard to solve. We are measuring all the variations that have been recorded in the gravitational field by satellites, by ground installations, and we are looking for a pattern."

"And is there one?"

"The disturbances have come in bursts, over the last month. The bursts have been getting stronger and closer together. But we do not know what is causing them."

"That sounds ominous – stronger and more frequent."

"It does sound ominous, but the phenomenon is probably natural, and it will probably pass. People must not panic. There are cycles in all processes, so …" The Professor suddenly looked uneasy, as if he had gone too far. "That's all I can say at this time."

"Well, thank you, Professor Blythe."

"Now, to other news …" The anchorwoman swung around and smiled her bright smile, which she kept tight to express, I assumed, the seriousness of the situation. "The US Department of Defense announced that US forces in the Mediterranean have been put on high alert. When asked if this had anything to do with the recent seismic activity, a Defense Department spokesperson refused to comment. The nuclear-powered aircraft carrier, the USS *Abraham Lincoln*, usually based in Naples, and currently on exercises in the Mediterranean, has been ordered to …"

Julia swung around in her swivel chair to face V. "If the US authorities have figured it out, then …"

"Then maybe they are planning an air strike or a commando raid." V tapped a pencil on the desk in front of her.

"An air strike would be faster, but the facility is buried deep in a cavern." John stood up and started to walk back and forth. "So, I think a targeted nuke, V, is the way they will go; that's a choice they could easily make …"

"Yes. You're right, John," said V. "But if that happens …"

"… then the Crystal would go into overdrive." Julia completed the sentence. John sat down looking grim.

"Yes," said V, giving the pencil one last tap, and setting it down. "Overdrive."

"Excuse me," I said. "What exactly do you mean by overdrive?"

"The Crystal is almost certainly immune to destruction by any weapon on Earth, including nuclear weapons," said V, staring at me but seeming to look right through me at something else, perhaps at an exploding planet. "But if you feed the Crystal lots of energy – certainly a thermonuclear blast would do that – then it will in all probability go ballistic and do to Earth what I saw its sister crystals do to other worlds. Marcus told me that any serious attack on the Crystal would cause it to destroy the host planet – and move elsewhere."

"I see." I sat down. *Was any of this real?*

"And look at this." John turned up the TV sound. "It was broadcast a few minutes ago."

The same anchor, Cindy Tanaka, was talking. "Pope Francis II today announced an official inquiry into the Vatican Bank. This surprise move by the Pope is expected to run into vigorous opposition from conservative Vatican circles and …"

John switched off the monitor. I sat there, aghast – Roger and Kate kidnapped! And more scandals involving the Vatican Bank! Such things threatened the very mission of the Church.

"So, V, what do we do? What's first?" John stood up and began to pace around.

"We find Father Ottavio and get the key," said V.

"Yes."

"And we warn the Pope." V glanced at me. "They are going to try to kill him – and soon."

"Kill the Pope!" I exclaimed. "Such a thing is impossible!"

"If the Pope touches the Vatican Bank," V said, "Cardinal Ambrosiano will almost certainly arrange for the Pope to be assassinated."

"Impossible, impossible," I muttered.

"If we try to warn the Pope now, we might just accelerate things." John was staring at V.

"Of course," she frowned. "He's under surveillance. If we send a message …"

"The killers would move – now."

"Yes."

"So, we wait."

"Yes."

Listening to this dialogue, I was appalled. It meant that by sending the letter about Father Luciani's suspicions to the Pope, I had endangered the Pope's life. What had I done?

Julia stared at her hands. "Father Ottavio, Father Ottavio …?"

"I think he was part of the ring that kidnapped girls." V half closed her eyes. "There was a monk who worked for them earlier, many years ago, a Brother Filippo. That Filippo worked for Ambrosiano too."

"Oh, yes, Brother Filippo was one of the recruiters for the Satanic Order of the Apocalypse." Julia was gazing at me. "He was also a child molester and a child murderer, 14 dead little boys, at least, and many others of course who had been raped. He was terminated on July 3, 1982, by you, V."

"Terminated," I muttered.

Fire in her eyes, V turned to me. "I already told you about him, Father. I killed him – okay? I drank his blood down to the very last drop – okay? I slurped it up. Yummy! Yummy! I enjoyed it. He was delicious. I had fun, yes, fun – okay?"

"Ottavio has a cell phone." John had turned his attention back to his computer. "I'll get a trace on his recent calls."

"There is something else," V said. "Yes, now I remember, Father Ottavio is a cousin of the industrialist Corrado Ferrari."

"Corrado Ferrari – why he's one of the richest men in Italy!" John looked up from his screen.

"About 17 years ago, Corrado bought Villa Mazana Nera," said Julia. "I did some research on Corrado just last year. Corrado is also related to Cardinal Ambrosiano."

"Really? Villa Mazana Nera." V leaned over and tapped the pencil on the paper. "That is interesting! Villa Mazana Nera was used by the Order in the seventeenth and eighteenth centuries."

"Yes, V," said Julia. "And didn't you have a run-in with a count who was the owner of Villa Mazana Nera in the early eighteenth century?"

"Yes, I did indeed. It was delectable. Yum! Yum! I must tell Father O'Bryan about it." She turned and flashed one of her carnivorous smiles.

"Well …" I shrugged. I wasn't sure I wanted to hear about this eighteenth century count, but I was – I must admit – curious.

John, who had been typing away furiously at his computer, said, "Okay, here are the results. The latest calls from Father Ottavio's cell phone are right about here on the map. Have a look, V."

"Well, well."

"Yes, that's the spot, isn't it?"

"Yes, that's Villa Mazana Nera," V said. "So, the Order has returned to its old eighteenth century lair. Let's pay Father Ottavio a visit, shall we?"

PART FIVE – FLESH

CHAPTER 27 – BODY ART

"Careful!! Do not bruise it!" The voice drifted out of a fog.

Kate was coming back to herself, bits and pieces.

Where am I?

Who am I?

This is a nightmare.

"Be careful! No bruises! No scratches!"

This must be a nightmare.

Who am I? Where am I? She tried to sit up; nothing happened. She tried to clench her fists; nothing happened. She tried to say "Shit!" Nothing! Her tongue lay useless, a heavy deadweight in her mouth.

Suddenly, she remembered – she was Kate, Kate Thornhill, daughter of Roger Thornhill. She had been kidnapped. She realized, too, that she was paralyzed – couldn't move a muscle, couldn't talk, could barely swallow. They must have given her a neuromuscular blocking drug – a strong one. Her eyes stared, unfocused, at the ceiling lights.

Focus! Focus! Focus!! She couldn't. Her eyes refused to obey. But her mind was waking up, sharpening.

Focus! Focus! Focus!

Above her, big blurry lights glared down – strange lights. What sort of lights? Ah, the lights of an operating table!

An operating table!

What?

Ice cold fear. Pure horror!

Someone was wrapping straps around her wrists, around her neck, at her ankles; they tightened the straps. The pressure of the straps was sharp against her wrists, against her throat. Horrible realization: She was strapped down, spread-eagled on an operating table.

What were they going to do to her?

Oh, God!

Her heart hammered, throbbed, faster and faster. Why the straps? They weren't needed. Whatever drug they had given her, it sure worked. Sweat was pearling on her tummy; she felt it. Helpless! Even unbound, she would be as immobile as a statue. Returning to full consciousness, she realized with greater and greater clarity, and in greater and greater detail, that she couldn't move a muscle – not a finger, not a toe, not an eyelid. It was a horror story, a classic: She was locked inside her flesh, buried alive.

What were these maniacs going to do?

The operating lights shone down, relentless, a brilliant blur – lights, instruments – like something in the office of an insane dentist or sadistic utterly mad plastic surgeon.

Amputation? Mutilation? Fear rose, pure panic. With all her might, she fought it down.

Suddenly, she discovered she could blink, but that was about it; she practiced – blink, blink, blink …

Okay, that was something; nothing else worked.

Yes, her tongue lay inert and heavy in her mouth; but she could swallow, and she could decide when to swallow. One step at a time, Kate, one step at a time.

Around her, voices:

"Careful, as I told you, the body must not be damaged."

"She will be perfect." The voice was a deep voice, basso profondo, a new voice, a voice from the depths of Hell.

A white blur appeared, above her, a face. It stared down, into her eyes. Kate tried not to blink; she stared, unblinking. The more helpless they thought she was, the better. The face hovered, close, framed by a black hood, the Angel of Death, sporting a black halo. It must be one of the monks – or maybe it was the nun? Cold hands prodded her sides, moved down the inside of her thighs, slid up over her belly, caressing, probing, exploring, moving to her pubis, violating.

I will kill these people – every single one!

Vengeance will be mine – for Mario, for Dad, for Martin, for …

"Now, for the pose – we were thinking, for the Russian girl, of *The Ecstasy of Saint Teresa*. She should have her head tilted back, limbs sprawled in a pose expressing, well, ecstasy, sexual and mystical ecstasy," said the basso profondo, "With one leg angled up perhaps."

"Excellent." Father Ottavio cleared his throat. "This creature is exquisite, even better for *The Ecstasy* than the Russian. She will make a splendid Saint Teresa, naked, of course. The mouth and eyes should be wide open – and the head tilted, too, quite far back. Use the photographs as a guide. And be creative!"

"Yes, Father."

"Satan's will be done!"

"Satan's will be done!"

Kate cringed. Strangely, she was embarrassed for the man. His voice expressed an obscene, lip-smacking relish, as if he were anticipating a sumptuous erotic feast; his sadism and fetishism were on full, uncensored, shameless display. "You may proceed: give her the full treatment – wash the body thoroughly, and of course, after the procedure, wash it again, very thoroughly. Use the laser too – no pubic hair must remain. Total depilation. And remember! Perfect condition – no bruises, no scratches. That is essential."

Kate blinked. She discovered that she could move the tip of her tongue across the roof of her mouth. Well, that was progress! She touched the tip of her tongue to the back of her teeth.

Her mouth was bone-dry. Swallowing was painful.

She was a mind entombed in a statue of stone, trapped, buried inside her body, her eyes staring, glazed; and almost – but not quite – blind, locked-in, a prisoner, like the locked-in syndrome. She tried to remember: Was it the Medusa that turned people to stone or the Basilisk? Or both?

She felt them free her from the straps and manacles, allowing the helpless-doll-body to flop around, surely the better to manipulate and move her, clean her and depilate her. Yuk!

Big black loops, like a black mamba or Burmese python, appeared just above her. It was a rubber hose! Whew! She blinked. The nozzle came into view and hovered, a few inches from her face, and then it rose up, maybe a foot, silver and round, with big black holes. Water spurted out, sprayed over her, warm silver droplets splashing into her eyes. Her eyes blinked shut. They were hosing her down!

"No pubic hair. Use wax. And the laser. Total, you understand."

"Yes, Father."

Kate's eyes blinked open: *I will kill these people, every single one, totally and forever!*

They began the treatment. She was blow dried, warm air rippled over her skin, through her hair and everywhere; and then they began with the laser and waxing.

She felt everything, each drop of water, each breeze from the blow-dryer, the tickling pulse of burning light, the wax being smoothed onto her skin with a spatula, then, more delicately, on the labia, probably, it seemed, with Q-tips; each time, she felt the hair ripped away; she felt everything, but she couldn't move a muscle. And then the laser – a burning sensation. And again, and again, and again. They were very thorough. Grrhh! Anger rose.

Eager hands moved everywhere, soaping, exploring, probing, rinsing. The greasy, slippery fingers tackled every inch, probed and penetrated, every orifice, every crevice and fold. Then they brushed her teeth, forcing her mouth open, forcing her lips back – an electric toothbrush, foam overflowing onto her cheeks and chin.

Then they were shampooing her, washing her hair.

She blinked. So, she was being prepared for sacrifice. But what sort of sacrifice? And what was all this talk about Saint Teresa? They were discussing a "pose," so they probably meant Bernini's sculpture of Saint Teresa. She knew it well. It was in her opinion a super sexy, but entirely proper sculpture. Saint Teresa was writhing in a swirl of robes, emblazoned in rays of light from overhead, her face tilted back, mouth half open, eyes closed, lying on her back, while a cute young male angel holding a heart-piercing spear hovered over her and fingered a fold of her robe while gazing amorously down on the saint's enraptured face.

Were they going to turn her into a statue like Saint Teresa? Like in some diabolic waxworks? Curled up on the old couch in the house outside Cambridge, eating popcorn, she'd watched lots of horror films. Being turned into a wax statue usually meant you died, burnt to death or roasted to death by the heat of the red-hot liquid wax, your skeletal and roasted remains entombed inside your own waxen image. Inwardly, she shivered.

What the hell did these crazies intend to do?

And her father? What were they doing to him?

She had to survive, for her father's sake.

311

CHAPTER 28 – BARE, FORKED ANIMAL

Filthy, sweaty, barefoot, and clothed in torn, ragged, soiled boxer shorts, Roger Thornhill gritted his teeth. He was a long way, now, from London's Savile Row or Milan's via Montenapoleone. He was a naked prisoner, slave to a madman.

But, however he looked and whatever he felt, it was trivial compared to the present danger. The Cardinal was like a spoiled two-year-old playing with a hydrogen bomb. It was now clear – damn it! The Crystal did act on the very structure of space-time, thus on gravity, probably through vibrations and waves, frequencies at a very basic level, below the quantum level, somehow acting on the gravitons, as Kate had suggested. It was beyond dangerous.

Twenty minutes ago, the Cardinal had ordered the Crystal be given an extra electric shock. For one minute, sparks flew. Then, after a delay of eleven minutes and ten seconds – Roger timed it carefully – the Crystal began to glow and hum. It was a static-filled glow, with flashes like lightning inside the Crystal's misty, stormy depths. Then it had quieted down, but still it hummed and glowed gently, like a benign, friendly, oversized Christmas ornament.

Now, twenty minutes after the electric shocks were applied, Roger felt a sudden chill. He looked up from the computer. A wall of mist surged from the stage to the right of the Crystal. The mist thickened into a fog, and the fog sent out long thick tentacles that probed everywhere. Soon everything around the Crystal was immersed in an impenetrable bank of fog.

"What is happening?" The Cardinal turned toward Roger.

"I don't know. You are poking at something none of us understands."

A crunching and groaning came from the mist.

"You are a scientist. You are supposed to know what is happening."

Roger shrugged. The man obviously knew nothing about science. The Crystal was beyond any previous experience. It didn't fit into existing theories;

there was no history of experimentation, no controlled tests, and no precise results upon which to base anything more than wild speculation. There was no way Roger, even putting on his Nobel Prize Genius Hat, could know, with any accuracy, what the Crystal was going to do.

A bellow echoed in the cavern. It sounded like a wounded elephant or perhaps some gigantic undersea creature.

"It's picking up sounds," Roger said. "But where the sounds are coming from, I have no idea." Roger sat back and waited. Could the Crystal pluck sounds from the depths of the oceans or from the Serengeti or from an outdoor market in Shanghai? Did it have sensors, perhaps scattered throughout the world? Could it send out feelers?

Another roar, a gigantic lion. Roger turned on the computer's recording device. Maybe the computer could identify the sounds. Roger frowned. Was the Crystal a transportation machine? Could it take you to another place? Maybe it could bring other places or objects and individuals here! The possibilities were infinite – and they were terrifying.

The four monks standing guard over the Cardinal raised their automatic weapons, clicking the safeties off.

The floor of the cavern trembled.

One of the monks stumbled, and, falling, he accidentally set off his automatic weapon. It made dull sparks in the mist. The sound – *rat, tat, tat, rat, tat, tat* – was muted, muffled, as if lost in an immense open space.

Something appeared in the fog: a shadow, the shape of a waving arm or a hose or …

"Look!" Roger stared.

"By Satan's lights!" The Cardinal took a step backward.

A huge tentacle, like that of a giant octopus, flew out of the fog and hovered over the fallen monk. The monk was crawling on his belly, desperate to get away, his habit flapping around him. It looked like he was trying to swim. He got to his knees, stood up, and ran. The tentacle shot out, snapped around the man, spun him in circles, wrapping him in a mass of coiled tentacle, lifted him up, and whipped him away into the fog. The monk screamed. Then there was silence, only a hissing sound. Then nothing.

"Satan be praised!"

Roger glanced at the Cardinal. The man was in a state of ecstasy, staring in adoration at the wall of fog.

"Satan?"

"The Absolute, Professor, Infinity. The Evil Force. Satan – whatever! Names for the Infinite are inadequate. The glory of Evil surpasses all human understanding! Language fails! Reason is baffled. Science is impotent!" The Cardinal turned toward Roger, his face shining.

Roger held his gaze.

The ground was still trembling, more gently now, a terrestrial lullaby, in gentle waves, the after-wash in the wake of a slow-moving, slowly disappearing, ship. The bars of Roger's cage creaked, groaned, and settled down.

Now, strangely, came the *sound* of waves, as if they were standing on the edge of an underground sea. The waves splashed and the wind roared; but nothing moved – the wall of fog had withdrawn to the deepest recess of the platform; it hung there, sending a few lazy tentacles of mist across the vast flat surface.

And still, the sound of waves crashing, wind roaring.

Roger expected a wall of water to come thundering in from somewhere and drown them all. Could the Crystal have opened a gate through time-and-space into an ocean? Were they perhaps two or three miles below the surface?

The ground stopped shaking. The fog cleared. The chill wore off. There was no sign of the monk who had been snatched away or of the giant tentacle.

As the last coils of mist faded, a body was revealed. It was lying on the platform. It looked like it had been freshly killed – there was a long, bright streak of blood. It was an animal of some sort.

"You will examine this," said the Cardinal.

"I'm not a biologist."

"You are a scientist."

"Well, Cardinal, if you insist."

One of the monks opened the cage door. Still shackled, Roger was led out of the cage. With two of the giant monks following him, their automatic weapons nudging his back, Roger shuffled and clanked his way across the stage toward the thing. It resembled an African warthog, but it had two sets of eyes. He knelt next to it, not easy, shackled as he was.

The creature almost certainly had never existed on Earth and it didn't exist now. Probably, it had never existed at all – anywhere. Roger could not understand why, in terms of optics and evolution, it should have two pairs of eyes, one above the other.

"The Crystal is traveling through time or it is accessing some other dimension, some alternative world." Roger touched the animal. The fur was still warm, the snout damp. He noticed, caught in its fur, a bit of black cloth, and strands of fabric – it looked like a fragment of the monk's habit. Could the Crystal have transformed the monk into ...? Or merged the monk with some other creature to create this weird amalgam? Or traded the monk for this animal, feeling, somehow, that it was a fair exchange? Was this a joke, a warning, or a demonstration? Or was it just a random event, created by the electric shocks acting on a complex system?

He stood up. "Or it may have effected a genetic transformation – reconfiguring the DNA and molecular structure – of some animal it caught, redesigning it on the fly. Or maybe this is a space-time travel mistake. Maybe, during transport disassembly and reassembly, the genetic codes got mixed up. I don't know." Roger stared at the deformed creature. He wasn't going to say it out loud, but he thought that – just maybe – the Crystal was playing games. The bits of cloth were, possibly, a hint, or a clue. Or maybe not. He looked up at the giant floating globe. I wonder, my dear Crystal. Do you have a sense of humor?

There was a brilliant flash, like lightning, and a roar; the mist began to return, thick coils of fog rose from the platform and the wall of the cave beyond.

Was this the Crystal's answer to his thought? Could the Crystal read minds? Shuffling, shackled, held by his two guards, Roger retreated from the giant stage. He didn't want to be caught in that fog.

"Well, what do you think, Professor?"

"The Crystal seems to be, among other things, a transformation machine, perhaps also a gateway ... But, listen, Cardinal. It's preparing something! I think it's going to perform more tricks for us!"

In fact, at that moment, from the Crystal – or from somewhere nearby – came more noises.

At first it was static and then it was ...

It was a medley of old radio and TV broadcasts. *I Love Lucy*, Ed Sullivan's *Toast of the Town* banter, Adolf Hitler ranting, and Winston Churchill orating, Russian broadcasts, Chinese broadcasts; there was the voice of a Cardinal announcing "*Habemus Papam* ..." Fragments from times gone by. "*Tales calculated to keep you in suspense*" ... *The Shadow Knows* ... *Deutschland über alles* ... *Johnny Dollar* ... The Beatles ... September 11, 2001. "*No, it can't be ... I believe ... No, the tower is no longer there. I don't know what to ...*"

Roger wanted to laugh; but he resisted the temptation.

"What is all this?" asked the Cardinal. "Why should the Crystal give us this? This is trivia, this is gross, this is ... Explain, Professor!"

"I have no idea. Your guess is as good as mine, Cardinal."

"If that is so, I can shoot you now and do away with your daughter too. I want your best thoughts, Professor. I want to enjoy this. The Crystal is an instrument of Satan, that I know, but I want details, details, details ..."

"Certainly, Cardinal! But I warn you, if anything happens to Kate, I will do my very best to kill you. Is that understood?"

"Perfectly, Professor Thornhill. You are a high-spirited fellow. I admire gumption and frankness in a man of science."

"Well, then, I think our friend here, the Crystal, may be giving us a play-back of things, things it recorded – maybe it is designed to pick up radio waves and television broadcasts. And it records what it hears, and we are getting a sampling."

"A sampling?" The Cardinal glanced up at the Crystal.

"Yes, the Crystal been listening to us, monitoring us – monitoring human-ity. And now it is reaching back into its archives and retrieving items, perhaps at random. Or, there is a more startling possibility. It may be traveling back in time – or glimpsing backward through windows in time – and picking up snippets of broadcasts in different time-and-space dimensions. That assumes, of course, that all time – all past time at least – still exists in some way."

"Of those two possibilities, what's your guess, Professor?"

Roger strained the chain and stroked his chin, by now covered in raspy stubble. "If you look upon the Crystal as a gigantic super-computer, or let's say an artificial mind, then it will have memories, a data bank. By giving it these random little shocks, you are prompting its memory, stimulating these playbacks. So, I think the Crystal is remembering things. We are poking into its neural networks. And we are also, almost certainly, giving it orders too, as you well know, but we are flying blind – we don't know what orders we are giving, or what effect they will have. The Crystal is not human. It is beyond our technology and our understanding."

"Wonderful!"

"Why wonderful, Cardinal?"

"We are playing Russian roulette with the world. Isn't this fun? Don't you find this exciting, Professor?"

"Well, yes – but, basically, no."

"No? I thought you scientists believe in blind chance. If pure chance – if the Darwinian struggle of claw and blood – created humans, isn't it appropriate to let pure chance determine its extinction? Why, then, does it matter whether we live or die? The only thing left is the thrill of destruction!"

"Your Eminence, Darwin did not postulate pure chance. He merely made a brilliant, very well informed, guess about a key mechanism which causes life forms – animals and plants and bacteria and viruses and so on – to change over time. That is quite different from pure chance. But, leaving Darwin aside, I believe we make our own choices – that we define and choose the good or the bad; that we choose the right or wrong way to act. Not believing in God does not mean one is necessarily a 'relativist' and that anything goes; or that one does not believe in free will; much that happens is indeterminate. Evil and good lie in us, not in our stars."

"Oh, bravo, Professor." The Cardinal clapped, lazily, limply.

Suddenly, the Crystal began to hum, again exuding wave upon wave of fog. Then there were waves of thunder from inside the fog.

"More amusement!" The Cardinal grinned.

The Crystal sent out a bolt of lightning that jolted across the giant platform, filling it with more streamers and filaments of fog. Within the thickening fog strange forms appeared, monstrous silhouettes – the universe, perhaps, was coming to pay a visit.

Roger felt that, all around him, the walls of reason were breaking down. There were no longer any limits to what could or might happen. Facts were no longer facts. Out of the mist, out of this cavern, what huge monsters might come slouching forth, what beasts and monstrosities, in the sleep of reason, what terrors might appear?

He closed his eyes. None of this could be real.

But it was.

And under his closed eyelids, he had a vision – Kate …

CHAPTER 29 – SUBLIME

"So, Demon, you believe we will find Father Ottavio in Villa Mazana Nera?"

"Yes, Father, his cell phone says so."

"What if he moves?"

"We move with him."

I glanced at my watch. It was ten minutes before two o'clock in the afternoon. No wonder I was hungry!

"Do you think the Order has any idea what the 'key' is?" I turned to V.

"They haven't used it yet. I hope they think it's just a souvenir of the Crystal. Just a trinket. If he knows what it is, the Cardinal will have it with him."

In this underground room with all its television monitors and computers, and the low hum of air-conditioners, everything was so massively built and so solid that I imagined it was also bombproof; a refuge as well as a communications center. It seemed impossible that such a place could be swept away in a volcanic or seismic cataclysm – but, on reflection, nothing is solid or invulnerable, not even Earth itself.

John had obtained the architectural drawings and schematics of Villa Mazana Nera from the Italian National Art and Archeological Archives, and V was using memories of her last visit – several centuries ago. Together they were building up a detailed plan of the villa and its defenses.

I listened with interest. As they described it, it seemed that Villa Mazana Nera possessed an underground chapel, with a labyrinth of tunnels and old volcanic hot springs and mud baths. Oh, yes, I thought. That would make the villa an ideal site for satanic rituals – linked to the sulfurous telluric forces of the underworld, an entry to the very gates of Hell, redolent of fire and brimstone. Volcanoes and other sulfurous openings often symbolized, in the Ancient World, the entry to Hades or Hell. The island of Vulcano off Sicily was often described as the home of Vulcan, the divine blacksmith and protector of blacksmiths, but it was also a gate to the Underworld; and on Mount Etna in Sicily and near Naples there are entries to the Underworld, as well as at sulfur-emitting spots in Greece and in Turkey. According to V, the villa had already been used for satanic purposes – for the celebration of the black Mass – in the seventeenth and eighteen centuries. It was apparently seen as an appropriate gateway to the Kingdom of Satan, the Kingdom of Death. While I indulged in these reflections, John was laying out the plans for our attack on Villa Mazana Nera. Security was tight, he explained, and the place was outfitted with quite sophisticated alarm systems. "It is best," John said, "that we wait until night."

"I prefer night!" V nodded.

Julia had noticed – from monitoring the telephone networks – that there had been a great deal of telephone traffic from the villa in the last few days. "Probably they are organizing something."

"So, when we pay a visit tonight …" John was looking at V.

"…we may break in on a black Mass."

"Oh, dear," I said.

"Would you like that, Father?" V raised an eyebrow.

I muttered that a black Mass would undoubtedly be interesting. In fact, in terms of scholarly interest, it would be right up my alley.

"These ceremonies can be spectacular," V added, "a return to some of the ancient primal roots of religion, human sacrifice; it would certainly give you interesting material for a new book."

"Perhaps." I pursed my lips. This demon of mine was indeed mischievous; she couldn't resist baiting me about religion, or about my scholarly obsession with publishing books and articles – publish or perish, as they say. But I was not going to rise to the bait, not this time.

In any case, she was quite right. Even the most sublime ceremonies of the most advanced and true religion have their roots deep in antiquity. Our knowledge of God is a long voyage and process of discovery. For eons humankind has groped toward a true relationship with divinity. Even in the most primitive forms of worship, even in the cruelest rituals, there are intimations of the truly sacred, vague inklings of the true God, rough sketches of what, ultimately, our relationship to God can and should be.

V half closed her eyes and fixed me with a sly, sleepy version of her intimidatingly dark gaze. Surely, she had eavesdropped on my inner reflections. She was enjoying herself; and perhaps, too, she was anticipating the hunt – and what she would do to, or with, Father Ottavio. She was truly a predator, a lion, or tiger, or panther. Still staring at me, her gaze locked on mine, she stretched, arms straight up over her head, arching her back in a most voluptuous way – with her T-shirt almost transparent, and her dark nipples clearly outlined.

"Wicked child," I muttered.

Her tongue just peeked, barely, between her lips, leaving a glowing slick of saliva, and she blinked; it was definitely a sensuous, come-hither, flirtatious blink.

This impertinent demon was sticking her tongue out at me! And flirting! Devilish imp! Again, the image of the beautiful blonde in the scarlet dress flashed into my mind – her huge smile, her friendly wave – different versions of the Eternal Feminine, I suppose – the ancient pagan goddesses, in T-shirts or red dresses, reappearing in modern guise. "Ah," I sighed.

"That girl of yours, your friend, the girl in the red dress," said V. "I think – I don't know why – but I am sure she is doing just fine. It was a close call, but she fought off the danger. Your fears have not come to pass."

I blushed.

Julia raised an eyebrow. "Girl in the red dress, Father? I won't ask! You have clearly lived an adventurous life, Father." She favored me with a beatific smile worthy of being immortalized by a Renaissance painter. This devilish demon's mischief was catching.

"As for the girl in red, Father O'Bryan is innocent of any untoward behavior. I vouch for him," said V. "They just caught a glimpse of each other in Saint Peter's Square, that's all. And Father O'Bryan was worried for her safety." My demon beamed at me – giving a Jesuit, a priest, and man of God, a character reference gave her, I do believe, great pleasure.

I was still trying to understand the implications of the position I was in. I – a member of the Order of Jesus – was becoming, slowly, by stages, the accomplice of a young woman vampire, who was also a reptilian demon and serial killer – and had been for centuries.

Of course, we Jesuits are trained to understand other cultures, to put ourselves, as it were, in the shoes of those we wish to convert, to understand, as people used to say, "Where they are coming from." But it is most definitely not true that to understand everything means that one must accept or approve anything. Exercising empathy and understanding must have limits and, in any case, it does not mean that one must abandon one's own values or one's own point of view. As for my present position, ethical and theological scruples swarmed into my mind. There was a distinct danger that I might lose my bearings and *go native*. If I was not very careful, I might jeopardize my immortal soul.

But, for the moment at least, V seemed, in some ways, to be on the side of the angels. If I allied myself with her, however evil she might be, would I be helping prevent a greater evil? What a pickle! Excuses and justifications for our actions can be extremely elaborate – and yet misleading. The ways of casuistry are infinite, and the pitfalls for one's conscience innumerable.

Finally, I must admit – and this, clearly, is a sinful admission – I was curious. I had studied the ways of Satan for decades. I had written learned volumes – one was almost 800 pages long – on demons and on possession by demons, and on exorcism, on witchcraft, black magic, on ancient Semitic religions, and the fallen angels; and now I was privileged to study, to get to know on intimate terms, a creature who, charming and beautiful as she might be, was undoubtedly a true and genuine demon, a spawn of Satan, a fallen angel, even, perhaps, a pagan deity – a goddess – exiled from her former divine status and cut off forever from the light of God. I was entering into a Faustian pact – I would help her, and I would possess all the knowledge and insight she could give me. It was a perilous journey! But then Dante, guided by Virgil, ventured into the heart of Hell itself, so perhaps I, a much humbler spiritual voyager, should screw up my courage and …

"It's almost two o'clock," John said. "I say we leave in the late afternoon."

"Yes," said V. "Julia, could you stay here and coordinate?"

"Yes, V. I'm always happy to miss the fun."

"Father – will you come with us, or do you want to stay here? You'll be safer here with Julia, I think."

"No." I put on my defiant face. "I must come with you. I must see for myself."

"Agreed then …" John smiled; he was, it seemed, pleased to see me along on this adventure.

"All the telephone activity probably means a black Mass," said V. "A Russian tourist, she is a dancer from Saint Petersburg, disappeared a few days ago. She is probably the sacrifice."

I thought of Kate, just kidnapped by gangsters. Could she be the sacrifice?

But, no, I thought, if they have the Russian girl, why would they need Kate? After all, Kate must have been kidnapped because of Roger. So, if we find Roger, we will find Kate, and we will save them both, God willing!

V stood up. "Come with me, Father. I'll give you a tour of my villa. You may find it interesting."

We left Julia and John and climbed up the burnished steel staircase.

V led me out through the sliding secret door, pushed the bookshelf with the English translations of *The Iliad* and *The Odyssey* back into place.

I noticed that there were various versions of *The Iliad* and *The Odyssey* – in Ancient Greek and various other languages, French, Russian, and German, Korean, and so on. The Devil, like God, must understand the tongues of men. V, I imagined, must herself be a bit of a Jesuit.

"Yes, Father, the Devil, my patron, and I speak some of the languages of men – and women." She poked me in the ribs and led me around a corner and down another corridor. "My sleeping quarters, as befits a vampire and demon, are down below, in the lower crypt, but I'll spare you that – for now!"

"Tell me, Demon, do you sleep in a coffin?"

"No, Father. Sorry to disappoint you. I afraid I'm unorthodox even in my sleeping habits."

"You are generally unorthodox, it seems to me."

"I shall take that as a compliment, dear friend."

I noted the "dear friend." Unaccountably, it gave me great pleasure; my face flushed. I felt honored by the demon, and I wondered greatly at myself.

We came out of the corridor – which was a tunnel through solid rock – into a spacious living room. It had an immense large-screen television and a splendid-looking stone fireplace with cut logs neatly stacked in a wrought iron firewood rack – black leather sofas and chairs, and raw stone walls of steel-gray. Overflowing bookshelves went along two walls, and the wall opposite us consisted of a floor-to-ceiling window of plate glass that looked out onto a large terrace and the pure bright blue sky. It was a midsummer's day! I had almost forgotten! These last few hours, except for the moment when I'd parted the curtains in the dining room, I'd felt as if I were deep in a twilight zone or trapped in the depths of eternal night. We went out through the sliding glass doors onto the terrace.

"This is magnificent." I was awestruck. We were on a cliff. In fact, we were inside the cliff. Much of the villa had been built into the side of the cliff, into the rock face. Behind us and above the plate glass, a wall of rock – red and gray – rose straight up. We were standing on a broad flagstone terrace that overlooked the sea. A huge expanse of water, sparkling in the noonday sun, stretched off to the horizon.

V gazed over the sea, and then turned to me. "The original villa, up above us at the top of the cliff, is ancient – bits go back to Roman times. In the

Middle Ages, it was a fortress against Arab sea-raiders, with a tower and look-out. I lived here in the seventeenth and eighteenth centuries.

"A Saracen Tower," I said, "against the Turks and North African raiders, who came ashore in search of booty and slaves. There is so much blood, so much history, along this coast."

"Yes, a Saracen Tower. The modern part of the villa is where we are now. I had it designed a few years ago. It is cut into the rock, below the old Roman fortress and below the sixteenth century villa."

I craned my neck. Above me I could see a few windows, or openings; they were set deep, so they fitted naturally into the towering cliff face, and were just barely visible; they looked as if they were fortified too; and undoubtedly the glass was bullet-proof.

"Yes, they are armored and, yes, the glass is bullet-proof." V was leaning with her back against the balustrade, arms folded, watching me; her smile was warm, like the sunshine of this splendid summer day.

"Most impressive." I felt I should say something; and it really was special, truly sublime. There was nothing between us and the sea and the sky; this was a place where one could commune with nature, and, perhaps, with infinity.

I put my hands on the stainless-steel balustrade. Far below, the sea rolled toward us, lines and lines of whitecaps marching onwards; a soft warm breeze caressed us; and up above was the untroubled brilliance of the burnished sky. I took a deep breath. Sea and sky unfurl and liberate the human imagination. I thought of a poem by Paul Valéry.

La mer, la mer, toujours recommencée
O récompense après une pensée
Qu'un long regard sur le calme des dieux!

Ah, if only one could find the words to express such feelings – to express, truly, what one feels! Like many of those who haunt musty archives in search of some ever-receding truth, I sometimes think that my dry and gnarled soul, the soul of a scholar-peasant-priest, dedicated to the pursuit of knowledge, has buried itself in dust; that my emotional joints have become arthritic; that my passions have atrophied. I wonder sometimes, too, if I have lost my way. To do unto others as you would have them do unto you, you must have the imagination to feel what others feel! What if I had, in my pursuit of know-ledge, killed my imagination, clipped the wings of my desire, and deadened my capacity to feel and to understand other people, all God's creatures? Imagination and compassion are related. Without the one, you cannot ...

V was staring at me; but she said nothing.

I bit my lip. In some ways, this female demon was like the eye of one's conscience, the eye – and this is most blasphemous, I know – of God. She sees into my thoughts and ferrets out, even without wishing to do so, my doubts.

"I don't think you are lost, Father." She flashed that same forgiving generous Madonna smile.

"You cannot truly be a demon," I said.

"Maybe time will tell, Father, what I truly am. You are very charitable, Father, and very understanding."

She led me along the stainless-steel balustrade, and ran her hand lightly along it, until we reached the end of the terrace-balcony where the balustrade curved back toward the rock face.

"Down below is my private paradise. See!" She pointed to an indentation in the cliff, far below. "It is a little cove, sheltered by two points of rock. There's a pebbled beach right behind that outcropping. That's where we go swimming – John, Julia, and I. It's a wondrous, secluded place. In fact, while you have lunch, I shall go for a swim."

"You won't eat with us, then," I said, forgetting for a moment that she was a drinker of human blood and that solid human food was not for the likes of her.

"No." She glanced at me from under her jet-black eyebrows and ran the tip of her tongue along her lips. There was something teasingly innocent and yet feral and ferocious – famished and carnivorous – about her expression. "But I will join you for coffee."

I thought, yet again: yes, we are her prey.

V bared her teeth in something that was not quite a smile. "Yes, you are right of course. We are predator and prey!" But immediately the expression was transformed into a human smile. "Now, Father, have a wonderful lunch – Julia is a marvelous cook and John is a very fine sous-chef. Go back through the tunnel, up three levels of the second steel staircase, and you'll be in the kitchen. I imagine lunch is already being prepared. I'll see you later!"

She walked over, put her hand to the side of my face, and kissed me on the cheek.

CHAPTER 30 – TROPHY

"Is she still paralyzed?" Father Ottavio gazed reverentially down upon the body. He laid his hand on the body's forehead, stroked its cheek.

"Yes, Father."

"Good. You can remove the straps and manacles, and position the limbs."

"Yes, Father."

Eager hands slid along Kate's legs and arms, over her belly, across her breasts. Fingers toyed with her hair, combing it, brushing it against her cheek. The hands levered her up and pushed some sort of frame under her back, propping her up.

They were toying, experimenting with the body, trying out various positions. Kate was a life-size rubber doll, a helpless plastic mannequin. Inwardly, silently, she observed, as if from an immense distance. They posed her lolling back, with her arms outstretched. Then, they placed her with her legs spread apart, lying flat on her back, staring straight up. Then, they positioned her with arms at her sides, and one knee crooked upwards, one leg straight out.

Gradually, they seemed to be getting it right. One knee up, one leg outstretched, and then one arm dangling down, and her head flung back, her mouth open, breathless with desire, with an inner clamp, pusing her palate up and her jaw down, to hold it that way. Posed thus, mouth wide open, she could hardly breathe. Her heart was pounding. Fear bubbled in pearls over her whole body. She imagined it. She *saw* it – her skin, covered with sweaty, sparkling drops of terror.

"Tilt the head farther back! That is better, more voluptuous."

"Yes, Father."

"Good. Now she is ready. Do it."

"Yes, Father."

They plugged her nostrils with little plastic tubes, they sealed her eyes shut with an elastic goo; they jammed a tube into her mouth, fitting it in between the clamp. They sprayed her with some sort of liquid. Oil? Grease? Her heart skipped a beat; her breathing faltered. She was going to gag. If she threw up, she'd choke on her vomit. They fitted a tight-fitting elastic cap over her hair. It snapped into place.

"Ready?"

"Yes, ready."

Warm, thick liquid, maybe hot clay, poured over her in a flood. What was this? What was it? She was being buried alive; she would drown; she would suffocate! If only she could break out of the paralysis! The voices, the voices were still there.

"Is she breathing?"

"Yes, still breathing."

The air hissed, sucked into the narrow tube in her mouth, and hissed and gurgled as it exhaled. She was breathing – barely. Her body was rigid, paralyzed, locked into the pose they had given her.

Time passed.

Her heart grew quieter.

The liquid hardened – It got hot. Her skin was on fire. It cooled – she was entombed. Her mind went quiet. A fierce mental clarity set in. She understood. They were making a cast. And, from the cast, they would make a sculpture, a sculpture of Saint Teresa. But why not just get a sculptor? In any case, Bernini had already done Saint Teresa, the best that could be done. Why create a copy? This was a sick travesty, a parody! She had to get out of here – but how?

Think, she told herself, *think!*

Ah, of course! The cast was a relic, a *trophy*! Once they had the statue they wouldn't need her – except for the sacrifice. The cast, the trophy, would remain – a memento mori, a reminder of the sacrifice, of death, of her death. So, that was it! She really was to be a sacrifice! And if she was the sacrifice, how would she die? By burning? By stabbing? Entombed alive? Crucified? Stoned to death? Torn apart by a mad mob? How many possibilities were there?

Her heart beat; her breath rasped, and gurgled; but he heard nothing else. She was alone, entombed, buried, forgotten. She dozed, she woke, she dozed. She heard nothing – no sounds, no voices, and no whispers. Where had the world gone? Was she dead? Was she already a ghost?

CHAPTER 31 – YOUTH

"Siestas are an excellent idea." Jian's hands were locked around Scarlett's waist, pressing in, setting fire to lots of tingling nerve endings, every inch of skin, every facet of sensuality.

"I'm not sure this counts as a siesta." Scarlett bent over him, her lips just touching, teasing his lips, her breasts brushing against his chest, back and forth, back and forth. Astraddle his midriff, she swayed, savoring each nuance of pressure, each point of contact. She leaned down, deeper, closer, and kissed him, a deep, hungry kiss.

He was thrusting up, deep inside her.

She bent back, riding him, tantalizing him, tightening, loosening, lifting herself up, and slowly, teasingly, lowering herself down. She shuddered and gasped, taking a deep breath, almost choking from anticipation. The tension was astronomical and mounting fast – Oh, oh, oh, oh!

Trembling, she bent forward, blinking, drinking him in. The reflected sunlight, wafting into the room and muted by the drifting white muslin curtains, turned him into a statue of gold; the light glittered on his skin, it glinted in his eyes; it shone off his hair.

"This is what siestas are for," he murmured, his breath close against her cheek, his lips moving along her cheek, to her mouth, to her lips – and then the kiss, the real kiss, the deep kiss. Oh, oh, oh!

"You think?" She swayed lower, her breasts feeling extra heavy, extra rich, brushing and pressing against his chest. Wow! Every part of her body was about to explode. "Oh," she whispered, "oh, oh, oh!"

"Yes," he whispered.

"Oh, do *that*, keep doing *that*!"

"This?"

"Oh, oh, oh – yes!" She shuddered, she trembled, she hovered on the edge, right there, suspended in time, hovering on the precipice, the absolute razor-thin edge, yes, of orgasm. His fingers were so deft, so delicate, so strong; and they knew exactly what to do and where and when to do it. And he was so deep inside her, so deep!

"Oh, oh, oh!" Scarlett breathed it out. This was ecstasy, absolute ecstasy, and it went on, and on, and on. Would it now come to an end? She resisted. She fought. She was determined to prolong the moment, to remain suspended in delight, in painful anticipation, forever and ever. Oh, don't let it stop! Don't ever let it stop!

Half an hour earlier, they had come back to rest, absolutely exhausted – they had been up most of the night, making love, again and again, and then they had gone out for their breakfast on the Campo; then they had wandered around the little streets, blinking at all the sights; and finally, ready to collapse into each other's arms, they had staggered back to the hotel, taken the keys off the little hooks, and stumbled up the stairs, already half-asleep, in a giggly drowsy daze, stopping a couple of times to kiss and grope.

They chose Scarlett's room, and, suddenly full of renewed, furious energy, they tore off each other's clothes, and somehow managed to squeeze, together, into her tiny shower cubicle. They showered slowly, pressed against each other, soaping each other, kissing, groping, touching, gazing, laughing.

Stepping out of the shower, and into the room, Jian grabbed a big fluffy hotel towel, and stared at Scarlett as she emerged from the sparkly downpour. She glistened with rivulets of steamy silver, her skin shone like gold, her blond hair was darkened, plastered against her cheeks, her eyes bright and dazed, wide open, blinking at him. He began to apply the big towel, slowly, touching each part, kissing her shoulders, the nape of her neck, her shoulder blades, the small of her back, her breasts, her tummy. He was thorough. He touched every nerve, every vital spot, every square inch.

"Ah, you," she whispered.

He knelt in front of her and kissed her, her tummy, her sex.

"Oh, oh, oh! Are we waking up, now?" She shuddered, clutching his hair.

He stood up, kissed her, and, teasingly, he entered her, slowly, delicately, tentatively, turning her to pure liquid, opening her to a ripple of delicious multiplying sensations such as she had never felt before.

"Oh, oh, oh," she sighed, her fingers in his hair. "Oh, oh, oh. Wicked man!"

"Yes." He gave her that smile. "We are waking up." He withdrew and knelt before her and teased her with his tongue. He brought her to the edge, again and again, to the edge, and back, again and again.

"Oh, cruel man – oh cruel!" She shivered.

He paused in his attack, and worked his way up her body, tummy, breasts, his lips and tongue and fingers everywhere, and then he kissed her full and hard and deep on the mouth, with sudden animal violence. She grabbed him by the hair and pulled him close to her.

"I'll take my revenge, I really will." She kissed him on the shoulder, on the chest. She worked her way down, and she kissed him and she caressed him everywhere. "Oh, oh, oh," she murmured, and she took him and made him ready once again, liquid and slick, and then, together, they tumbled onto the bed.

And so now, she was astride him, teasing him, mastering him, lowering her mouth and her breasts to him, rising, falling, riding him – her steed, her stallion, her lover. She half closed her eyes and groaned. Her imagination was running riot, thoughts, sensations galore. He was enormous within her, it seemed like he was swelling up and occupying every inch of her, that she was only an envelope, a thin membrane of pure sensation, struggling to contain him.

Outside the open window the air was golden with summer light.

Scarlett lowered herself, tightened her thighs, every muscle straining for control, for mastery – She was going to win this wrestling match, damn it! She leaned forward and kissed his chest, his shoulders, his forehead, his eyelids; she kissed him on the lips, and he returned her kiss, a ferocious kiss .... They ceased to be two people, they ceased to be Scarlett and Jian – they became one.

Oh, oh, oh, oh!

Oh, oh, oh, oh!

It went on and on – one long shuddering explosion, sweet, soft liquid explosion.

Oh, oh, oh, oh!

Oh, oh, oh, oh!

And then, finally ...

He moved gently within her; she moved gently, containing him, savoring him, holding him. It lasted for a long, long time, a long delicate sweet affectionate retreat and diminuendo.

"A truce?" she whispered.

"Yes, a truce," he said, grinning.

"Oh, boy!" She lay back and moved her hands in his hair, caressing, teasing, and staring at the golden light moving on the ceiling.

"Yes," he sighed; he was stroking her breasts; his hand moved on her belly, slowly, explored the liquid heart of her.

"Oh, boy!"

"Yes, oh, boy!"

"Is it just us, or does the whole world feel like this?"

"Since the beginning of time." He leaned over, kissed her on the mouth, brushed her lips with his, and looked into her eyes.

"Yes," Scarlett gazed at him, touched his hair. "Since the beginning of time. I guess people have been doing this – since the beginning of time."

They slept.

CHAPTER 32 – PRIESTLY PLEASURE

I am, and I am quite aware of this, a dusty old scholar; and I am also a man of God, but I am, as well, a man who loves this world. After all, is not "love" the central word in the vocabulary of our Savior, and are we not commanded to love God's creation? The kitchen in V's villa was splendidly equipped. My mouth was watering. I wondered if my newly awakened alertness to things material, to sensations, was due to the demon; I felt younger and more alive than I had in decades.

The sacrifices inherent in the priesthood do occasionally incline one to value the more innocent of the sensual pleasures. Gluttony of course is a sin, and a dangerous one, but a good appetite, a fine palate, sensitive to nuances of taste and texture, and a connoisseur's knowledge of fine vintage wines and subtle liquors, well, that is another thing entirely – that is a true appreciation of life, a true appreciation of God's gifts to humankind!

Julia had lined up on the cutting board a number of perfect garlic cloves and luscious bright ripe tomatoes that John had just brought in from the garden, and basil and Italian parsley. Splendid-looking slices of veal were simmering in the skillet. The smells were mouthwatering.

This performance, I was sure, would equal Signora Bianchi's cooking; and that was saying a great deal! Signora Bianchi's *spaghetti all' amatriciana* and her *spaghetti carbonara* are – I have no hesitation in saying this – masterpieces and excellent matches for the good rich full-bodied Barolo I often manage to bring home as a gift to Signora Bianchi and my fellow lodgers. When there is a chill in the air, and the winter tramontane, the dry bitter cold north wind, comes down through the mountains and whistles through the narrow, darkening Roman streets, bringing an arctic chill to the soul, making us shrink into ourselves, there is nothing more comforting than Signora Bianchi's command of the subtleties of pasta and minestrone and cheese and rich salad dishes.

V was quite right: Julia was clearly a talented cook.

A window was open; it gave onto the sea; and a warm sea breeze wafted into the kitchen. The bougainvillea just outside the window – a profusion of white and purple and cobalt-blue –were brilliant in the sunlight – everything added up to give one a sense of earthly life brought to a pitch of perfection – all the senses were gratified.

I had a surprisingly hearty appetite. Was this, I wondered, an effect of being shot, or of being cured, or of some other aspect of my demon's black magic? My saliva was bubbling over and eager, and my stomach had just made a few discreet rumbling noises.

John was chopping the garlic into thin slices and Julia was stirring the skillet. I had perched myself on a high wooden bar stool and I was sipping a glass of dry white wine and feeling idle and useless but extraordinarily mellow. "Do you mind if I ask you both something, Julia, John?"

"No, Father, go ahead."

"How did you come to work for V?"

Julia was just putting the pasta – long strips of fettuccini – into boiling water. "It's an interesting story, Father. Which one of us do you want to listen to first? V told us to tell you everything. She has decided that you are one of us."

One of us ... I gazed into my glass and wondered what had happened to that dusty, scholarly, old man, that timid priest, who – only yesterday – had limped his way across Saint Peter's Square. *One of us ...* What would Ignatius of Loyola make of me now?

"You go first, Julia," said John.

Julia stopped stirring to wipe her forehead. "I was brought up in Milan." She began stirring again and dropped a small handful of fresh herbs into the skillet. "We were a happy family. I had a twin sister, Alessandra, whom I loved. We were exactly alike, mentally, physically – two people, but, in some respects, one soul. We did everything together. When we were twelve, Alessandra was kidnapped, raped, tortured, and killed. Her body was found six weeks later, on the edge of a rice paddy, outside Milan, not far from Malpensa airport; the body had been left in the open, naked, not even buried. It had been eaten by rats, by dogs too perhaps. Only her scattered bones were left.

"The killer was caught; he was declared insane and put in an asylum. Two years later a psychologist, who was experimenting with some new methods of rehabilitation, declared that the man was cured. He was released.

"His name was Aldo lo Greco. Within two weeks, just outside Rome, near the old film studios of Cine Città, Aldo lo Greco killed again, a twelve-year-old girl, the daughter of a single-mother schoolteacher. In looks, features, and hair color, the girl was similar to Alessandra, and to me.

"So, in university, I studied psychology – to see how such a so-called science could be so wrong – and then I trained as a criminologist; when I did my Ph.D., I worked on serial killers. Finally, I wangled permission to see the killer of my sister. I had coffee with him in the prison." Julia's eyes were glossy with tears. She paused and then went back to stirring the pasta.

"Aldo lo Greco told me that I would have been perfect for him were I nine years younger. I asked him what he felt toward the girls he killed. He said that he loved and desired them and wanted to possess them totally; part of him, he said, wanted to *be* them, part of him *was* them. He hated and loved them at the same time. Those mixed passions and compulsions, he said, were the most powerful feelings in his life. They were a form of ecstasy, like the feeling a shaman must have when he is possessed by an animal's spirit or a ghost. Killing, he told me, was an exorcism, a sacred ritual, a casting out of his female demons. He said that he had tricked the psychologists into thinking he was cured. 'They are easy to trick,' he said.

"'Why are the psychologists easy to trick, Aldo?' I asked.

"'Because, Julia, they have theories, not feelings,' Aldo shrugged and smiled. He was a bald, thickset, short man. He hunched forward toward me, with his shirt sleeves rolled up, revealing his massive, hair-covered forearms; he was an animal, coiled and ready to strike. 'Besides, Julia, they are vain, the psychologists, most of them – vain about their intelligence, about their theories, about their insights. They are jealous too; they would like to be me; they would like to do what I do. Most psychologists are sick, Julia, that is why they have become psychologists; they are voyeurs; and most, mentally and morally, are very small people, timorous and limited, narrow-minded and short-sighted, bookish and unpractical; they do not have the courage of their sickness, of their madness, of their genius. They don't live their own lives; they live vicariously. They are afraid of themselves. For such beings, I make life worthwhile. They imagine what I am and what I do – they see it obsessively – and repeat the scenarios over and over in their little minds, and this obsession compensates for the emptiness of their own miserable insignificant little lives.'

"Two weeks later, while still in prison, Aldo killed a young nurse – she was twenty-two – it was a particularly bloody and gruesome murder; he held her hostage in the infirmary, and he dismembered her, amputating her arms and legs, doing some of this while she was still alive. And then, a month later, Aldo sent me a postcard. It pictured Saint Sebastian, naked except for the usual loincloth, and pierced with all those arrows, and on the back of the card, he had written, 'Dear Julia, this was proof, just for you, that for True Mystics, Death is the only cure, your very own, Aldo.' "

Julia took the skillet off the stove. John had been watching her carefully; now he finished tossing the salad. "Well, I think, Father," he said, "if you carry the bread and the wine out onto the terrace, under the white-and-blue awning, luncheon can be served."

This was a second terrace, just outside the kitchen; it was set into the cliff, and quite small and intimate. It overlooked the sea. The table was quickly set, simple, gracious, and exquisite. Julia and John were artists, and so, I suppose, was V, who had chosen the setting and whose design this villa was.

I sampled the pasta and said, "Absolutely delicious, Julia." This was, if anything, an understatement.

The sea breeze rippled the canvas awning that sheltered us from the sun. Invisible, far below, V was swimming, alone, my solitary demon, in the little cove, her *magic place*, as she called it. I could imagine her diving, surfacing, or suspended, just basking, in the clear translucent water. She was a voluptuous, sensuous, worldly creature – this demon of mine.

John refilled my glass.

"I knew then that I was the cause of the nurse's murder," Julia said, a forkful of pasta halfway to her lips. "Aldo killed her to prove something. If I had not insisted on interviewing him, if I had not piqued his vanity, that nurse would be alive today. I caused her murder – because of curiosity, because of academic vanity. And I had been vain in my own person too; I thought I could charm him; I thought I could reconcile myself to Alessandra's death by coming to terms with her killer, by understanding him. I thought I could prove to him that he had made a mistake killing her, and that even he would realize that. In a way, I thought I could charm him, seduce him; and cure him of his hatred. This is all very convoluted and foolish, Father, I'm afraid."

"Not at all," I said. "You were seeking redemption; it was a noble thing to try to do, even if he scorned you for it, and exploited you. He wanted to make you feel guilty. And he succeeded. It was part of his sadism."

"You are a good man, Father." Julia paused. "So I gave up serial killers, for a while, at least, and I became a policewoman in a special squad to track down sex traffickers and people smugglers.

"Trafficking in people – modern-day slavery – is, as you know, Father, a criminal business worth billions of dollars. My work involved information analysis – monitoring communications, investigating the gangs of enforcers who 'recruit' the victims, monitoring financial flows, and trying to model the contacts and family networks of smugglers, the logistics of shipping people across frontiers. But sometimes I went out on operations – in order to do my work, it was essential to see what was happening on the ground, in the front line.

"So, one night I did have a front-line experience. We had located a ship that was transporting young women to be used as prostitutes in Italy and Germany and probably the UK; it was a large ship – the *Maria Teresa* – with a cargo of timber from a Turkish port – and a shipment of almost 100 young women. It was night. As you know, Father, the traffickers are well armed, sophisticated, and ruthless. This was war. We were in a heavily armed police boat. We were closing in on the ship, which had stopped and was just drifting. We approached; we hailed it; we radioed it; but we got no answer; so we boarded the ship. At first, there was no sign of the crew.

"It was an ambush. Our own boat was blown up – I think by a short-range missile. Most of our team was killed on the traffickers' ship – cut down by machine-guns, grenades, booby traps.

"I was on the *Maria Teresa*, one of the ones who survived. Then I found myself in the water, I don't remember how. I must have jumped or been blown or shoved off the *Maria Teresa*. I was wounded and covered in oil and gasoline. One arm was limp. I couldn't move it. It was night; we were about fifty miles south of Sicily, and a storm suddenly blew up and was soon raging.

"I managed to climb onto one of our dinghy lifeboats. How it got into the water, and why it was still, miraculously, afloat, I don't know. Already one of our officers was in the lifeboat, but he was in no condition to talk. I knew him. He was a nice guy, a great guy really, Giorgio Marinelli.

"So, we were floating in the lifeboat, badly hurt: my arm was useless, and I'd been shot though my side, as I discovered from the blood. I was only half-conscious. Giorgio was lying beside me. He was dying. Oil was burning on the water, near the wreck of our patrol boat. Then I had a hallucination – a sort of reptile thing poked its head over the side of the dinghy, and I said, 'Oh, God, now I'm seeing demons. What the hell is that?'

"I tried to get my pistol out of the holster, but my shoulder had been dislocated; my arm was broken too, as I suddenly realized for the first time. So I tried to shift arms, using my left hand to get the pistol out and aim it – all the time I was covered in oil and grease, which could explode in flames at any moment if we were touched by a spark.

"In the light of the burning oil, the demon shimmied her way on her belly over the side of the dinghy. Kicking her legs to give herself momentum, she flopped down in front of me. I saw that she was indeed a female humanoid reptile. She looked glamorous – in a horrifying way. I saw that she was wearing a backpack. I wondered: 'Do demons from Hell, or monsters from the deep, carry packs on their backs?' It was a high-tech backpack; and she had a belt too, with a holster. 'Gosh,' I thought, 'the Devil has gone modern and military; or maybe there's an underwater civilization we've not been aware of!'

"I was sure I was delirious. There she was, the demon, on hands and knees, in front of me, looking up at me, with her golden eyes and her fangs.

"I finally got the pistol out of the holster, but I could hardly hold it, I was so weak. I struggled to aim.

"Still watching me, the demon sat up. She pulled up her legs, curled in her toe claws, and wrapped her arms around her shins; she just watched me. Her lips curled up, with those two fangs over her lower lip. 'Hi, Julia,' she said. 'Your name is Julia, isn't it?'

"I was so startled I almost dropped the pistol; the pistol, like me, was covered in oil and grease, so it was slippery to hold and I was trembling and shaking. I realized I might pull the trigger even without wanting to.

"'Yes, I'm Julia.'

"'I'm V, people call me V.'

"'People? People?' I said. 'What people? What are you?'

"'It's complicated,' she said, still smiling. 'Please don't shoot me.'

"I was fading fast. I blinked at her, thinking, I'll have to shoot her now; if I don't she will kill me.

"'I can help with your wounds,' she said, still sitting there, 'and I can help your friend too, if you'll let me.'

"The pistol fell from my hand and the demon was suddenly there, beside me; it was so quick I didn't even see her move. She had caught the pistol while it was falling, and put on the safety, which somehow I had managed to click off.

"I was losing consciousness and I slid sideways – paralyzed and half-conscious – and felt her smooth and slick reptilian body against mine. I felt her put her claws on me and I could feel one of her claws moving along my arm, and up my shoulder, and down my side, where I had been shot; and I felt a warmth flooding through me, and strength too. I began to struggle to sit up and get free, but she said, 'Just a second longer, Julia! Wait! Be patient!'

"I relaxed. If she wanted to kill me, she would have already done so. Then she released me. I felt better and sat up. 'What happened?'

"'You were hurt. I healed you.'

"'What are you?'

"'Let's help your friend first,' she said, over her shoulder. She had already turned to Giorgio and was crouched over his crumpled body. The flickering light from the burning oil reflected on the curve of her back, ripples of turquoise, blue, and gold; it was very sculptural, her spine, her shoulder blades, the nape of her neck. I was thinking: *what the hell is this creature?*

"I was checking my arm and my shoulder when the demon handed me my pistol. I put it in the holster, saying, a bit late I must admit, 'Yes, help him, if you can.'

"She put her claws, both this time, into the mess that was his belly, with guts bulging out, the muscles torn away. Dark blood, stained with shit, reflected the burning oil.

"Giorgio had no clothes left, just one sock. His body was covered in oil and grease and blood. As I watched, the demon seemed to mold his stomach; smoke or steam rose from it. She pawed away some of the flesh and guts. Underneath her claws his intestines, his organs, and his stomach were taking form, as they had been. Suddenly, it was over. Giorgio opened his eyes, blinked and said, 'What the hell are you and what are you doing?'

"I leaned toward him. 'She's a friend. She healed you, I don't know how she did it, but she healed you. And she healed me too.'

"He sat up. 'I'm Giorgio.' He reached out a hand. "Giorgio Marinelli."

"'Just a second, my claw is rather bloody.'

"'My blood?' Giorgio looked at the claw.

"'Yes.' The demon leaned over the side of the dinghy and washed her claws and then she held her right claw out and they shook hands – well, hand and claw. I thought either Giorgio is a very cool character or he's still in shock.

"So that's how I met V." Julia said, as she spooned out more fettuccini from the big pasta bowl onto my plate, with the luscious creamy sauce, the delicious steaming broccoli, peas, and bacon.

"Thank you," I said, as I reflected on what Julia had told me. V was clearly as much a healer as she was a killer. This confirmed my thought that she is indeed like those ancient female deities: Kali who destroys evil and brings life among the Hindus; Pele the fire goddess in Hawaii; Isis the protector of slaves and sinners among the Egyptians; and even V's very own Asherah, the Phoenician and Semitic goddess, wife and mother of gods, who is often linked, symbolically, to the Serpent, a symbol of death, rebirth, and healing, and to the Tree of Life. So many aspects of divinity and of the sacred – the cruelty and the drama and the fruitfulness – that are buried and lost in the past. Like those ancient goddesses, V brings destruction and rebirth. She is a goddess – or a priestess – of fertility and death.

The scorching breeze rippled the blue-and-white striped awning, stirred the purple and magenta bougainvillea, and rustled in the cedar and pine trees that clung to the cliffs on both sides of the villa. The stones glowed, white with heat, the cicadas sang their rasping, sawing chorus, and the sea, rows and rows of gentle whitecaps, marched incessantly toward the land.

As I swallowed another forkful of Julia's sumptuous fettuccini, I felt as if all the sensual wildness and all the sensuous pleasures of the Earth were aimed at me. They were pouring into my soul. I wondered if, in saving me, V had infected me with some kind of pagan exaltation in the glorious multifarious splendor of each instant of life. *Carpe diem* indeed! Seize the day! A thought flashed through my mind: Being alive is perhaps the most sacred thing there is!

Julia was pushing a small triangle of bread, mopping up the sauce on her plate, a charming Italian habit that goes, I believe, by the equally charming fairy tale-like expression, *fare la scarpetta*, or "to do the little shoe." One of the special pleasures of Italy – and of Italians – is, it has always seemed to me, the unpretentious and direct pleasure people – even extremely sophisticated and wealthy people – take in simple small things. It is the wisdom of an ancient civilization that still remembers its peasant and agricultural past – everything is rooted in the land, in the gestures and rituals and pleasures of each instant.

"So, Father, V got us ashore. She helped us save the women destined for slavery that the traffickers had managed to deliver to land in motorboats. V, Giorgio, and I ambushed the traffickers, freed the girls, and took the trafficking boss prisoner. When Giorgio went to get reinforcements, V said to me, 'If you want to watch, you are free to, Julia, but I am going to kill that man.'

"'Kill him?'

"'Yes. You see, I drink human blood; I am, in part at least, what is called a vampire. So if you want to truly know what I am, then watch me; and this will be our test – whether you can accept me or not.'

"I watched her kill the trafficker; and I did not judge.

"That same night V asked me if I would like to work with her. By this time I had lost faith in the justice system, which protects the powerful and the rich, but abandons the poor and defenseless.

"'I don't know,' I said.

"'Think about it,' she said.

"I went back to Milan; I worked on criminal cases for several years. I worked with one of the international courts. I dealt with murderers and rapists, serial killers and torturers, traffickers in human flesh and dictators who'd set up special squads to kill and torture people; I interviewed generals who'd murdered thousands of unarmed prisoners, officers who had presided over mass rapes and mutilations, hacking off arms and breasts and legs and hands. I saw many of these characters escape punishment. They had lots of money – stolen money almost always – and they had the best, most expensive lawyers; and they also escaped justice because some judges and juries were stupid, or corrupt, or ignorant, or biased, or racist, or misogynist; and because many of the guarantees a democratic legal system puts in place to protect the innocent end up protecting, even more, the powerful and the guilty – who then go on to kill or maim or enslave again and again and again. You know all of this as well as I do, Father. You have been there."

"Indeed, I have," I said, as gently as I could. Images of blood-soaked massacre and mutilation were always fresh in my mind. I think that they will not leave me until I die – and even then ...who knows? Perhaps I shall take such images with me to Heaven or to Hell, as part of my baggage.

"So, one day, sitting in my office in Milan, staring out at the gray-brown wintry smog, at the dark facades of the buildings, I shuffled some papers back and forth – it was a file – 832 pages – on a killer who had been released for good behavior, who had killed again, and who would probably get off, again, because of a favorable psychiatric evaluation. And of course, he would kill again. I hummed a song to myself, I think it was *La Marseillaise*, or maybe it was *The Internationale*. I was feeling feisty and revolutionary – I wanted to set up a guillotine – and I was disgusted. I yearned for a great purifying wind to come and sweep away all the corruption and evil and lies. I wanted a rebirth! I wanted a Revolution!

"I went back to my desk, got my cell phone out, dialed a number – it was a coded voice mail 'drop' in Luxembourg – and left a message: 'Hi, can we meet?'

"We met a few weeks later on the terrace of a café in the little Umbrian hill town of Spoleto; the café was on a steep cobblestoned street that ran between old white-gray walls of blocks of limestone hewn from the cliffs above the town. The terrace was in a courtyard. It was unseasonably warm and the walls were covered in ivy and bougainvillea. V was in human guise, just as she is now. I had only seen her demon version and I was quite startled. She looked like a model for Dior – or a beautiful investment banker, dressed in the classic Milanese businesswoman's uniform, Armani, high heels, black stockings, short pleated skirt, white silk shirt, black jacket. On the table was a bottle of Brunello di Montalcino. V glanced at me. I nodded. She poured me a glass. I clicked my glass against hers.

"'Now, Julia,' V said, 'this you must see,' and she pulled out of her briefcase a thick, ancient, leather-bound ledger; it was the record of her victims, or 'meals' as she calls them. The lists were written in pen, a fine, minuscule classic cursive script. We went through the lists; there were thousands of names.

"'It's not complete. Sometimes I forget to write things down. And in the beginning I didn't keep a ledger.'

"'I see.'

"'I apologize for that. I try not to kill innocents. I aim at making my feeding as socially useful as possible, and as positive as possible, ethically speaking.'

"'Ethical eating?'

"'Yes, you could put it that way.' V gave me that special look, from under the eyebrows. You know that way she has, Father, a rather shy manner, appealing and somehow sly, and seductively innocent. And then she said, 'But I need advice, Julia, I need help.'

"'Okay,' I said, 'but how do you know they are guilty?' I flipped about twenty densely packed pages back from the most recent entry. 'What about this one?' I pointed to a name at random; like all the other entries, it was written in the same elegant cursive script, undoubtedly with a steel nib dip pen, the date was 1837; the ink had faded to rich sepia brown.

"V closed her eyes, just for an instant. When her eyes opened, she was far away, in the past. 'It was April 4, 1837, in Paris, a rainy April evening, mist rising from the wet cobblestones. I waited outside the *Théâtre de la Gaîté* for my assignation, a fat, gray-haired fellow, a gentleman of independent means;

he had made his money in haberdashery; and, more importantly, he had been seen, three times, with young actresses and prostitutes who subsequently disappeared, or so I had been told. I lingered there and let him pick me up. He was polite, courtly even. He took me to a derelict building he said he owned. He led me down into the cellar to show me, as he put it, some interesting works of exotic art. There, in a sumptuous secret underground room, after a bit of dalliance, which turned increasingly demanding and violent, it became clear he intended to murder me – and use my lifeless body for his necrophilic pleasures – just as he had murdered and used the others. I turned the tables; I fed on him.'

"'He was guilty?'

"'Yes,' V blinked. "His actions alone indicated he was guilty. But then I had confirmation that I was right.'

"'Confirmation? How?'

"'When I feed, when I drink my victim's blood, I can read their thoughts, Julia. I access their feelings as they are dying. I think it must be a transfer of electrical energy, something like that – nothing magical.' V took a sip of wine and smiled at me, her sunny innocent Madonna smile. 'Yes, he was certainly guilty. Through his mind I *saw* him kill the other girls; I felt his randy feverish excitement and exultation in killing them; I became *him*; and I became *them*; and, through them, I felt their horror when they realized that they were trapped, that they had been seduced, fooled, betrayed; I felt their horror at their own stupidity, at their own *guilt* or *fault* for what was happening to them, which was of course not guilt or fault at all; and, dwelling in his mind, I experienced to the full his joy in destruction and cruelty and death; I experienced his relief and ecstasy the moment he exorcised his demons. I think that, for him, as for many serial killers, when they kill women, or children, or men, they are killing a part – an imaginary part – of themselves; they are killing the mother or the sister or boy within them. And I felt the girls' agony, at the moment of their death.'

"I stared at V, stunned.

"She lifted her glass, gazed at the dark red wine, leaned back and sighed. 'I'm a vampire. I am what I eat. And I suffer with those whom I see suffer. Sorry, that sounds pretentious. It's really just a form of temporary identification – empathy, loss of self, or invention of self. I don't know. I imagine it's something like acting.'

"'So,' I said, 'what do you want from me?'

"She refilled my glass. 'I want you to help me hunt. I want you to help me find the truly guilty, the truly dangerous, the truly deserving.'

"For a long time I didn't say anything. I looked at the ledger; the names were followed by the date and notes: 'serial killer,' 'torturer,' 'murdered his wife and three children,' 'tortured prisoners on the convict ship *Little Mermaid*, killing five of them,' 'raped orphaned children put in his care,' 'sadistically murdered her husband and her lover,' 'slaughtered members of the tribe of ...' I thought back to the dusty files piled up in my office, layer upon layer of cases where we knew who was guilty and we knew we did not have sufficient proof for a conviction. I thought of all the murderers, torturers, rapists, and child traffickers who had gone free.

"'I am yours,' I said."

"Thank you, Julia. That is a remarkable story." This was not quite what I was used to hearing in the confessional, but it was certainly instructive. I gazed at her for a moment. "And you, John?"

"Me, ah, me!" John displayed that warm, predatory smile of the true warrior – the bright, even teeth, and the perfectly tanned, toned skin. "Well, Father, my mother was Italian and my dad was a Brit, both were scientists. I was brought up in England, good schools, lots of rugby and games, with glorious summers in Italy. Against the wishes of both my parents, who were hoping I would be a physicist, I went to the Royal Military Academy, Sandhurst. I did fairly well, and was offered a position in Special Services."

"Yes, I imagined something like that, John," I said, helping myself to an extra slice of veal, and allowing Julia to top up my wine.

John's eyes crinkled in a brief, cruel flash of memory. "It was a botched undercover job that brought me to V. The actual epiphany – if I may call it that – occurred in Whitehall. I was sitting in the office of a civil servant, a top fellow in the Ministry of Defense, liaison chap interfacing with the Foreign Office. He was a slimy bastard, had his sticky hand in all sorts of dirty pots, and, as it turned out and became common knowledge soon afterwards, he was a spy for a group of Islamic terrorists we were trying to put out of action. He caused us – I mean the UK – some major embarrassments – and not a few dead bodies, civilian and military. In any case, this traitor chap – who was totally venal, sold his soul for money, not out of some perverted sense of idealism – was telling me that we were not going to be able to go in to save my men who had been captured by a Middle Eastern terrorist regime in a bungled operation, and that I was going to be set up to take the fall for the fiasco: it would be said that I had planned it badly, that I had abandoned my chaps, fled the scene, and so on. As it turned out, he was the one who told our enemies where we would be, when, and what we would be doing – it was a setup, and a trap. My chaps were the victims; I'd be the fall guy.

"I said, 'We have to go in to get my men.'

"He said, 'It would be politically unadvisable, John, politically unadvisable.'

"'*Politically unadvisable*, you fucking sod!' I almost jumped up and punched him.

"'John, I'm disappointed to see you adopt such an unhelpful attitude.'

"I muttered something impolite. I was still trying to figure out how to rescue my men. Their lives and my honor were at stake.

"'You're not seeing the big picture, John. You are thinking small, letting your emotions dictate your reactions.'

"'You're right. I am not seeing the big picture.'

"'Very sorry about that, John.'

"If I didn't like it, he explained, I was free to resign; in any case, they were going to *privately* pin the debacle on me. After a few years of torture, my men would be left to die in the Colonel-Dictator's dungeon. My punishment would be minimal, and I'd get a discreet recommendation, so I could join one of those private security firms that were taking over much of our defense and anti-terrorism work. 'You'll make a lot more money, John, even if your reputation will be a trifle sullied.'

"'Thank you,' I said. I got up and I slammed the door, went down into the street – it was winter and for once in London it was snowing; it was dusk, which filled the grayness of the street with a silver-pink fading light. Down at the end of the street I could see Big Ben through the misty snow, symbol of democracy and freedom and 'our finest hour' and all that; we shall fight on the beaches, and so on. I wanted to go and smash someone's face in.

"I thought: I will not leave my men in the hands of those terrorists. I shall sit down at a bar, have a drink, and think over my 'options.' I shall find a way to get them out of there.

"I pushed my way through the door of the local pub, my regular hangout when in London, went to the bar and ordered a double whiskey.

"That's when I spotted the lady – she seemed familiar and was staring at me, with a slight smile, as of recognition. She was very striking.

"'Hello,' I said. 'Do I know you?'

"'No, you don't, John. But I think one of your friends has told you about me.'

"Then it clicked. My friend, an old schoolmate who was in MI-6, had pointed her out once at a reception. He'd taken me aside and whispered, 'If we have a particularly sticky problem and we think that lady can help us with it, John, say a hush-hush assassination, or a cloak-and-dagger, undercover high-risk mission we have to be able to deny ever happened, we give the lady a ring, and if she's interested, she calls me back. I'm her contact man. She's the finest of private assassins, totally upfront, totally effective.'

"'So, John, what are you up to?' the lady asked.

"I honestly don't know why, but I told her everything, even though I had never met her before. If you'll excuse the comparison, Father, I think V is rather like a priest, she knows everything, and, like a priest in confession, she understands everything, and accepts you for what you are. I told her that my men had been betrayed, that I had been double-crossed and was, in effect, being blackmailed, that the government was not going to try to rescue my men or even recognize that they existed.

"'I think there may be a way to get your chaps out of there,' she said.

"'Really?'

"'John, I imagined you might come here. Our meeting like this is not a coincidence.'

"'Oh?'

"'Would you like to work with me – for me?'

"I hesitated. 'What would that mean, exactly?'

"Well, Father, the long and the short of it is, she explained what she was and what she did, and that some of her operations were complicated, some were under contract, as it were, but most were her own 'projects' and that she could use help with the intelligence and the logistics; she also said that she had a most charming criminologist who worked with her – a person I would share many interests with and very much like – and would I be interested? There was, of course, no obligation; I could back out after a trial period, if I wished."

At this point, Julia interrupted John and said, "I shall confide a secret, Father. I had caught a glimpse of John at a conference on terrorism. I managed to talk to him. I liked him. Actually, I had rather fallen in love with him – though he didn't know it. I confessed to V, and she said, 'Well, you two would make a formidable team. And we do need somebody to help with logistics and planning. Let's see if this John gentleman you've fallen for is interested.' "

"When I met Julia, I was instantly hooked," John continued. "And we did get my men out of the camp where they were being tortured. I am also pleased to say that the noxious bureaucrat, the spy who had caused the death of six of my chaps, well, he somehow fell off his yacht in Majorca, and his body, strangely, was never found. He made a very good meal, V told me; and he did reveal to her some useful secrets, which we passed on to MI-6 and some French pals over at the *La Direction Générale de la Sécurité Extérieure*, which we all call, as I'm sure you know, Father, the DGSE."

Just then, as our delightful luncheon was ending, with Julia serving an exquisite *crème brûlée*, V appeared in the frame of the door leading from the kitchen onto the terrace. She looked like Aphrodite risen from the sea.

"Welcome, Princess," said John. "We were just talking about you."

"Frightening the good Father out of his wits, I imagine. Murder and mayhem! He will abandon us and run for the hills."

"Not at all. Their tales were all extremely flattering," I said.

"You are too kind, Father." V was wearing a sleek one-piece black bathing suit and over her shoulders a white bathrobe that flowed open around her. She looked quite sporty and exotic, a fashion illustration from the 1930s. Her alabaster skin – with its tints of gold – shone with beads of water.

I wondered, for an instant, if she was jealous of our more varied diet.

"Well, Father, you have made a splendid recovery."

"I have you to thank for that, V."

"You are welcome, Father." She walked to the balustrade, leaned on it, and turned toward us. "It was a pleasure."

I noticed that, behind her, far out to sea, strange clouds were rising up, clouds that started out as wispy little white things, but almost instantly changed into towering thunderheads; I had never seen clouds form so quickly, not even in the tropics. Following my glance, V turned abruptly, saw the clouds, and said, "Time to go, my friends, time to go!"

We swallowed the last of the wine, picked up the plates and dishes and followed her inside.

"Is this the beginning?" I asked.

"Yes, it is," V said, over her shoulder. "It is the beginning of the end ..."

"Or the end of the beginning ..."

"Precisely, Father, precisely! Winston Churchill himself could not have said it better!" V turned toward me, and in that moment the light from the sea caught her alabaster skin, and her dark, dark eyes. Yes, I thought, yes – she is a goddess, a goddess, rising from the sea, and come back from ancient times, perhaps to save us, now in the present, and perhaps in the future too. Truly, a demon she cannot be, but a goddess, yes, she is, perhaps, a goddess.

PART SIX – PAIN

CHAPTER 33 – ICON

Standing in the inner courtyard of Villa Mazana Nera, Father Ottavio glanced at his watch. He looked up. The air was darkening. Evening was coming on. He could hardly contain his excitment, his lust, enlivened by the fecund earthy odors of the bougainvillea, the oleander, roses, and orchids. "Has the body been painted and lacquered? Will it be in position on time?"

"Yes, Father." The monk bowed his enormous head. The black cowl threw a sharp shadow over the vast, blank forehead. The creature's eyes were invisible, hidden in deep folds of fat. The voice reverberated against the courtyard colonnade. He held out an iPad. "Here, Father, you can see the images."

"Thank you, Brother Basilisk." Father Ottavio flipped through the photographs and the video, licking his lips, and murmuring little yelps of surprised delight. He turned to the monk. "I am pleased, Brother Basilisk. The Cardinal will be pleased. The pose is sublime. It truly captures Bernini's *Ecstasy*, without the robes of course, and with its eyes wide open, staring in terror; it is much more natural – the sublime nakedness of Eve in her fallen splendor, orgasm and horror, eroticism and shame, desire and death, all in one exquisite package."

"Thank you, Father."

"And no damage was done to the original?"

"None, Father, the original has not been marred or blemished in any way. The original is as it was."

"Good! You may go now."

The monk took the iPad, and lumbered off, his swishing habit darkening the air. He disappeared, a shadowy hulk, slipping away, under the arches of the colonnade.

Left alone in the courtyard, Father Ottavio reflected that the choice of sacrifice was satanic serendipity at its best, a gift of the Evil Spirit. The

Russian girl had of course been a lovely and graceful creature; but when one of the nuns turned her back, the girl had managed to jump out of a window, shatter her bones, and break her neck. And so, they had been left without a sacrifice. But then another promising candidate, a beautiful blonde in a scarlet dress, had turned up. She looked extremely lively and high-spirited, which was ideal. The livelier, the better, the more intelligent, the better, it gave the ceremony extra punch. The more exquisite and aware the sacrificed creature was, the more acute her suffering would be, and thus the greater the sacrifice. Filippo – Filippo the Fourth as he styled himself – had sent him, for approval, photographs of the girl in scarlet. Father Ottavio instantly texted his blessing. She would indeed be pleasing to Satan. Alas, the blonde demonstrated how lively she truly was; she fought like a tiger and managed to escape.

But Satan provides.

The creature upon whose image Father Ottavio had just now feasted his eyes was certainly as exquisite as the other two. And, adding to the pleasure and sacredness of the sacrifice was the delightful irony that her father was a world-renowned unbeliever, a rationalist. Why, the girl's middle name was Dawkins! Even better, this famous scientist had been promised, by the Cardinal himself, that his daughter was safe. *Betrayal*, ah, betrayal! Betrayal was a truly satanic virtue! Betrayal was transcendent: You knew things your victim did not know; you changed other people's lives while they had no idea their lives were being changed; in the art of betrayal, one was like a god, enjoying divine power. Exercising the divine irony of a puppet master who knows all things, you pulled their strings in ways that only you could see. And, truly, for the Satanic Order of the Apocalypse, and for Satan, all other people were puppets in the end – just puppets.

Father Ottavio glanced up. Just as he did so, the sun disappeared behind a high bank of cloud, bringing a touch of shadowy coolness to the courtyard. Ah, good, there would be a storm tonight. It would make the ceremony even more sublime.

He heard distant thunder. It was starting already.

He must ask Brother Basilisk to put the Mercedes in the garage; he had just had it waxed. It would be a shame if raindrops marred the immaculate finish.

Father Ottavio rubbed his hands. He would now examine the body and see it for himself. He could imagine the sublime moment when, totally at his mercy, she would lie, spread-eagled, naked and gleaming with satanic oil, her skin immaculate white, manacled to the black granite altar, fully conscious, acutely aware, and knowing she was about to be dismembered.

Sublime!

Yes, sublime!

The door of V's silver BMW shut with a satisfyingly solid chunk. It was just before dusk. We were on our way to Villa Mazana Nera.

John would be driving a specially adapted Toyota Land Cruiser with most of the equipment.

"We travel with two vehicles," V said, as she backed out of the garage, "Just in case one of us runs into trouble."

We swung around and drove down the long, cypress-lined lane that led from V's villa. John's Toyota Land Cruiser, already in front of us, pulled away and disappeared around a bend in the road.

Keeping a fair distance between the two vehicles was best, V explained, and, though we might be miles away from John, we were connected to him by instantaneous communications – by walkie-talkie-type sender-receivers independent of all other systems – and by GPS trackers, two on each vehicle, plus one on John's person and one, V pointed, in the lining of her jeans' pocket.

As we turned onto a country road, which opened onto a vast vista, I glanced toward the sea. More dark cumulonimbus clouds had formed, towering and threatening. They looked deadly, very much like the mushroom clouds of atomic explosions. They were piling up to the west. The brilliant afternoon sun was still above them, but probably not for long. The darkening walls of cloud lent an ominous dramatic air to the immense open sky and sea.

I still harbored doubts about the imminence of the Apocalypse. The ordinary and seemingly benign surfaces of life can lull us into an illusory sense of security. Here we were, driving in an ultra-modern car, a fine example of German engineering, in a green and beautiful landscape, through rolling fields, with, in the middle distance, upward sloping vineyards, and, in the far distance, the ragged bluish silhouettes of the shadowy Apennines, and, almost blending in with them, the rounded eroded shapes of ancient volcanoes. Here, in one of the most cultivated and civilized landscapes in the world, a cradle of some of humanity's greatest cultural accomplishments, I found it hard to believe that the Satanic Order of the Apocalypse really did

exist, or that anything could really have the power to bring the very mountains tumbling down. As for the idea of human sacrifice …

"A penny for your thoughts, Father," said V, glancing at me, and of course I
realized that she had been reading those thoughts.

"Well, ah, V …" I stumbled.

"Yes, I know, Father, you wanted to ask me why and how I first began to
follow the Satanic Order of the Apocalypse. Didn't you, Father?" Her irony
was often utterly transparent but playfully tactful. She knew I knew she knew
what I was thinking. To avoid embarrassing me, she attributed to me thoughts
she knew I did not have, at least not at that moment.

"Yes, ah, yes, V," I said, pretending to regain my composure. "Yes, yes, V,
that's exactly what I was thinking. I am very curious regarding just that particular point."

She stretched, holding the steering wheel with one hand, and reaching
up with the other, perhaps to relax the tension, in a fine fluid effortless feline
movement. I rather expected her to meow; but she said, "I may be a vampire and a demon, Father, but I am also a woman. I despise people who mis-
treat women – and children – or even men, for that matter – but especially
women and children. I first became aware of the Order because of a series of
strange cases in which women were disappearing – and the authorities, generally, were not particularly interested in solving the mystery – the women
were lower class women, or common prostitutes, so of no importance for the
authorities. The world has not changed. This was in Ancient Rome. At first,
I thought the disappearances must be the work of what we now would call a
serial killer. But I then discovered that these were ritual killings, and that the
rituals were not merely sexual – but involved black Masses. The killers were
a sect; they worshipped Satan and, in their diabolic version of the Eucharist,
real blood and real flesh, a living woman, took the place of bread and wine –
and the girl, often, was sacrificed on an altar. That was the Satanic Order. It
has existed for a long time."

"Why are women so often the victims?" I asked, though I had my own ideas
on this subject, having seen what happens in civil wars, and having also been
involved in judging several so-called honor killings.

"Oh, that, Father, is, as you know, a fraught and infinite subject. Why are
women so often victimized? You have written on it yourself; women are physically weaker; for men, they are an object of desire, and therefore of inner
psychological weakness and conflict. Desire is an unruly force; it disturbs the

peace of men's souls; it destroys detachment and self-mastery; it can turn the proudest man into a slave. It can easily take violent forms. Women possess mysterious powers – the power of procreation; they preside over birth and childhood; women are our portal and welcome into life, which is messy and chaotic and painful; and they govern us, as mothers and wet nurses and often as teachers, when we are still learning how to be human. Resentment can easily build up. Separation from our mother's body at birth is perhaps the first trauma we suffer. Such violence has a great deal to do with the need for power."

"All true."

"So, there can be a lot of anger."

"Yes."

"Even among women – just think of girls and their mothers!"

"Indeed."

"And you will I hope excuse me for saying this, Father, but God, the Jealous God of the Bible, Yahweh, decreed through his rather angry prophets that all the ancient goddesses were devils and demons. The monotheistic God is not very fond of women, at least so it seems to me. He drove all the females from the pantheon of the gods. No more divine women or goddesses! Banished! And Yahweh, rather unusual among gods, is a bachelor, though, as I am sure you know, there are texts that claim he was married to Asherah. And Yahweh, being unique and alone, has, apparently, no interest in sex! Except to demonize and repress it! God is a gatekeeper, protecting men's psyches – and women's too – from the upsetting, Dionysian, earthy, cyclical, blood-soaked, liquid, primordial force of womanhood. With the rise of this single monkish God, women's participation in divinity was denied. Women were cast out of the heavens – and, frequently, demonized, and blamed for all of humankind's woes, from Eve and Jezebel onwards."

I cleared my throat. "That God who is infinite is always represented as purely male does seem a paradox, I must admit." I sighed. "Pope John Paul I got into trouble because he suggested God is also our Mother."

V smiled. "Pope John Paul I – Papa Luciani – didn't last long."

"No, no, indeed, he didn't. Thirty-three days."

"And the Church, you will excuse me for saying so, Father, has done its best to write him out of history."

I merely coughed and watched the road and then I had to mutter, "That may be so, Demon. That may be so."

V swung us around a tricky corner; the road, perched on a cliff side, was literally carved out of the rock. Then, we saw, on the side of the road, where it opened onto a scruffy hillside meadow, a woman and a young boy herding a crowd of perhaps twenty goats. The woman and boy seemed to know V. They waved and smiled, and V and I waved back.

"Father, my Phoenician culture – the Culture of the Canaanites and of Carthage – was destroyed – by the Persians in Lebanon and then, later, by the Romans in North Africa. And our gods and goddesses were later transformed by the victors – and by our cousins the Jews and later by the Christians – into demons and devils – or, even worse, into mere fictions, mere creatures of the imagination. Yahweh commanded that his followers destroy the shrines of Asherah. Monotheists – unlike say the pagan Ancient Romans – do not have room for other people's gods. There is no pantheon, no gathering or community of gods. There is only one God. For the Hebrews, our god Ba'al became a synonym for Satan."

"Yes, but you Phoenicians practiced child sacrifice. You laid children in the arms of Ba'al, to be dropped into a raging inferno."

"That is true, Father. It was a cruel religion, just as life is cruel."

"You admit it then."

"Certainly. I saw it with my own eyes – children sacrificed. As a child, I even participated in several ceremonies. I was a sort of altar girl. But Yahweh's descendants are not entirely innocent either. Some of the Single God's acolytes take His hatred and mistrust of women to extremes. It goes deep – this male adoration and hatred of women – it takes forms that are sacred and profane, obscene and sublime, submissive and dominant, all mingled together in what often turns out to be a lethal cocktail of hatred and adoration, desire and repulsion. And then, too, men often have a hidden feminine side, which, often, they hate and wish to exorcise – to excise, to cut out of their flesh and out of their souls."

"Like Ambrosiano," I said, "and his hatred for the girl he glimpsed in the window. He knew nothing about her; but in his confession, it was as if she had become part of him; he wished to cut her out of his soul, out of his body. What he hated was his own desire, his own lust."

"You are right, Father, it was part of himself he hated, not her. The victim is the scapegoat. The victim – child, woman, or man – is a sort of *voodoo doll* in which, as it were, the pins of hatred and self-mutilation are stuck. Often hatred is, largely, self-hatred. Anti-Semitism and most forms of racism have similar roots."

V swung the wheel easily, with one finger, as we came into a sharp turn. "In any case, over the centuries I have had occasional duels with the Satanic Order of the Apocalypse. The Order began in pagan times, and its rituals evolved. Through the decades and the centuries, it appeared and disappeared. I would find it. Then I would lose trace of it. I would hunt down sect members; then the sect would disappear; and I would search out other food, other meals – ordinary killers, rapacious landlords, wicked pirates, slave traders, brigands and bandits. And I would move to other countries, other continents. But you may be interested to learn where I first ran into the Order in its modern form. It was in fact at Villa Mazana Nera. Do you want to hear the story, Father?"

"Yes, V, I do."

"Knowledge is power. The better to slay me, Father?"

"Perhaps, my dear Demon, perhaps."

"Well, then. In Florence, in the seventeenth century, the Order reemerged. Young women were disappearing. No one knew how or why. So, I set myself the task of solving the mystery. If there was a killer of young women, then he or, just possibly she, would be my next snack; if it was the Order, well, then I might be able to plan my meals for several months, since, potentially, there would be quite a few tasty and guilty parties. I shock you, Father?"

"No, not at all, V, not at all, I am getting used to this. I might even say it is uniquely edifying, learning about your eating habits." We were zipping around another hairpin turn. She shot me a look, with the sneaky little-girl grin, while swinging through the turn at top speed. She was, thank God, a skillful driver. And so, she began with her story.

"To track down my prey, I loitered in public places, disguised as a young man of the lower classes, a servant traveling with an aristocrat or rich merchant. I dropped in on inns, I gossiped with fruit vendors, butchers, and candle makers. I was curious, I said, about these young ladies who had disappeared.

"Ladies, you call them!" said one butcher, the bloodied corpses of slaughtered lambs hanging lined up on hooks behind him.

"What? Are they not ladies?"

"Whores for the most part," he said, and his fat wife nodded in agreement. "Whores," she shouted, "whores one and all! Whores from the tip of their painted heads to the points of their painted toes! If they die, it is only just." She spat on the floor, just at my feet.

Father O'Bryan, I am always amazed how we – I mean human women – are so ready to put each other down – to rejoice in the misfortune of another woman. Is it because we must sell our bodies that we feel obliged to sully the competition and exult in the downfall of the young and the beautiful? Is that why we are so eager to shame our fellow women? Is that the reason we rejoice in their death and misfortune? Is it because a dead woman – particularly a prostitute – is one less rival to worry about?"

"Ah, V," I said, making a helpless gesture. The ways of sin and cruelty are many, and most ingenious in all their related forms and motives, petty and grandiose. Monsters lurk in all of us, even in the ladies.

"I left the amiable butcher and his wife to stew in their self-righteousness, and sauntered out into the misty evening, and stood on the quay – a chilly fog was creeping up the River Arno, drifting under the stone arches of the bridges. As the chill entered my bones, I was struck by the melancholy of the empty, damp, darkening alleyways. I cocked my hat at a jaunty angle, clicked the heels of my boots on the cobblestones, and set off through the wet, icy air in search of a warm, comforting tavern.

And, that same night, in a tavern, after some discreet and oblique inquiries, I heard of a certain friar who, they said, was an excellent student of philosophy; he was also a bon vivant, they said, a man who knew a great deal about the shadowy side of the city, the cesspools of sex and frivolity and corruption. "Where there is sin and damnation," said one crotchety old man, who was all pointed chin and pointed nose, "I can tell you, young man, there the good Friar is sure to be."

I paid for the old man's glass of brandy, or burnt wine, as they called it in those days, and, departing with a low bow, I left him to enjoy his drink alone.

Finally, that night – after visiting several more taverns and brothels – I tracked down the fat Friar; and, indeed, it was true: He was a familiar of bawdy houses and taverns, of brawls and cock fights, of dog fights and bull baiting, of excesses of every kind, and he was also, it turned out, addicted to learned philosophical disquisition. He was reputed to be a man of infinite resource, able to arrange any sort of mischief in the lower depths of the city.

Clothed in my boy-servant attire, I slid onto a bench next to him in a dark backroom in the out-of-the-way tavern where I found him drinking alone. I offered him a tankard of the house's best red wine.

"Young man," he beamed at me, "you are a man of taste – a scholar and a gentleman."

"If 'tis you who says so, Friar, then surely I am."

The Friar gulped down a full tankard and then another. He discoursed, wiping his mouth with the back of his large pudgy hand, on the weather: Rain would rot the crops, there were too many clouds in the sky, surely a result of a wicked conjuncture of the planets, Venus doing nasty things with Mars, or some such ominous and wicked celestial copulation; he opined on the price of whores, soaring and unjustified by the declining quality of the merchandise; on the wife of our very own good innkeeper (opens her legs joyously and is worth a visit); he launched into a disquisition on the various proofs of the existence of God (he listed twenty-five at least); on the ideas of Plato – eternal, immutable, and sublime – and the poetics of Aristotle: We experience fear and terror vicariously, so said Aristotle, identifying with the actors on stage, and thus we free or purge ourselves of these emotions – fear and terror – in a manner similar, so elaborated the good Friar, to vomiting or pissing or shitting away the poisons that have accumulated in our bodies. That was the way the good Friar put it: A visit to the theater or to a recital of poetry being equivalent, in the Friar's opinion, to relieving oneself in the loo, outhouse, or water closet. It was all most instructive and delectable. I could have listened to him prattle all night; but I had business to conclude.

"And what of the missing women?" I asked, eager to prepare my menu for the coming week. My stomach was beginning to rumble.

"Tut, tut," he mumbled, "we must not speak of them."

"Oh," I said, letting the question hang for just a moment, "well ..."

"Into darkness they went ..." The loquacious Friar was suddenly somber. His thumb twitched; the corner of his mouth trembled. He reached for his tankard – then drew his hand away. "Sacrificed, sacrificed," he muttered, speaking really, I believe, to himself.

I remained silent, waiting.

"I am to blame ... I am truly to blame for the death of one of them." He wiped his forehead; it was by now gleaming with sweat and I could see that, in his tiny blue eyes, ripe overflowing tears were sparkling. He cleared his throat. "There was a priest – there *is* a priest – a man of great learning, you understand – a powerful figure in the Church, a man who can discourse delightfully on anything under the sun or moon, a man always dressed in black, a man who can charm the birds out of the trees. He, this man, he caught a glimpse of her ... alas ..."

"Of her?"

"Of Dimples ..."

"Ah, of Dimples ..." I buried my nose in my mug.

"So, this priest," the good Friar's mouth twitched, "this Prince of the Church, this Cardinal, inquired after my friend, Dimples, whom he had glimpsed, merely glimpsed; and I answered him, as I was duty-bound to do, saying who she was. I said she was a woman of the people, good-hearted, simple, full of goodwill, playful, innocent as a child, almost unfallen, such was her innocence ... And as I described her thus, the priest rubbed his chin, sighed, and said that, indeed being so innocent, she could use some instruction, but it must be discreet. No one must know."

The Friar stared into his tankard.

I waited.

Finally, still staring into the tankard, the Friar spoke, "I arranged the assignation. Several monks came to take her. I had never seen such creatures before. They were giants with faces like the backside of the moon, monstrous strange faces – all skin, all forehead, then, at the bottom, all squeezed up, little tiny wee features, the features of ancient wicked malevolent babies risen from the deepest depths of Hell. Dimples looked at me, surprised that such creatures should have come for her. It was horrible – her fear. She was sore afraid."

"So, what happened then?"

"It was near Villa Mazana Nera; it was there, near the count's estate ..."

"The count's?"

"The count's ... Count Marbuse. They do dark deeds ..." The good Friar laid his finger by his nose, suddenly become sly. His round blue eyes swiveled toward me. "Those that know, know. They know what they do there." He winked heavily; sweat beaded his brow. "Now, the powerful, they linger over the blood of the lamb, and they drink it."

"The blood ... of our Lord?"

"By God, the blood of the women – are you dense, man!"

"I ..."

"Dead women. Up on the altar they put them, and they enact the sacrifice; they drink of the blood and they eat of the flesh ..."

So! The Satanic Order of the Apocalypse had indeed returned. The missing women in Florence were not the victims of a single maniac but sacrificial fodder for the cannibalistic Order.

"So, Friar ..."

"Hair soft like down, sunshine-blond, blue eyes, innocent like nothing you have ever seen – Dimples! I never saw her again! She got into the Cardinal's coach and I never saw her again ... Never ..."

"The Cardinal ...?"

The Friar came back to himself. His round eyes came into focus. He wiped his mouth with the back of his hand. "You will be the death of me for telling you this, lad. I shall kill you myself. More blood on these hands will do no harm." He stared down at his large, pudgy, strong hands.

And then, out of the folds of his friar's habit he pulled a large knife. "Now, my lad, shall I carve you up, then? Shall I make you less pretty?"

"Careful, Friar, I am not what I seem."

"Oh, you're a spy then; are you going have me burned at the stake or broken on the rack?"

"No, no, I am not an inquisitor. I am not a spy! I am a more frightful thing, Friar." I tore off the moustache and beard. I lifted the hat and let my hair fall free. "No, Friar, I am worse than a spy; I am a woman."

For a long moment, the Friar said nothing; his eyes went rounder still, his small mouth twitched.

"Oh, the horror! That I have poured such wisdom and such secrets into the ears of one who cannot understand; into the ears of Eve who had commerce with the serpent and brought us all shame and death and toil and damnation."

"Do you truly believe, Friar, that I am incapable of understanding what you say?"

"Women do not have souls – or so it is said – and their minds are small, windy and vaporous – vacant noisy places, largely uninhabited, with many chattering voices, but all of little consequence."

I ignored this nonsense – though such views were at the time widely held – and I said, "I want to know about the Satanic Order of the Apocalypse. Those who took your friend –"

"Do not even speak the words, woman! Do not speak!" He looked around terrified, as if the walls would tumble down and punish him. "Go!" he whispered, "For the love of God, go!"

"Yes, I shall go," I said, getting up, pasting my moustache back on, tucking my hair under my broad-brimmed hat, pinning my beard to my chin, and feeling the humiliation of being a woman, a thing considered unclean, to be hidden away, to be cloaked in darkness, to be treated like a madman or a child or an animal. *Me - unable to understand Plato, the very idea!* I was tempted to run him through with my rapier, there and then. And, though I was not thirsty, I was sorely tempted to bite him deep on his plump neck and drink him dry.

"Go!" Tears streamed down his fat face. They were tears, I think, of fear.

"Well, I must go now, Friar, and thank you: I have learned much. Now, watch!" I showed him a trick that I rarely do. It is petty and demeaning, really, like performing in a circus.

I leapt up the wall, hung from a ceiling beam, and disappeared through the window. But I did leave sufficent coin for the drinks.

A few days later I found the Count the Friar had mentioned – Count Marbuse, who was then the owner and master of Villa Mazana Nera. I invited myself to one of his balls, a masked ball, a sort of carnival celebration, a genteel and aristocratic bacchanal. Manners in some ways were freer in those days, and one could, if one wished to risk one's life, enter a party to which one had not been invited.

So I slipped into the Count's masked ball in a feathered owl's mask of my own devising that left only my lips and eyes free, and wearing my best gown, a lavish but revealing dress of delicate black silk and see-through lace, which, I calculated, would tease the senses and imagination of the Count but entirely disguise who and what I was. It was a warm summer night. I danced as sinuously and seductively as I could, and Count Marbuse took note, and danced, as often as he could, with me, choosing me, as the evening went on, as his privileged partner, just as I had planned.

He, like all his guests, was masked.

"I am curious," whispered the Count, "as to what is behind your mask."

"Curiosity is a marvelous thing," I said, "but it only stimulates and intrigues so long as it remains unsatisfied. Slake your curiosity, my dear Count, and nothing may remain but ash."

"You are a philosopher, I see," he grinned, swinging me around in the gavotte.

"Oh, dear Count, I cannot claim so much."

The Count was a powerfully built handsome man with broad shoulders and strong arms.

"Let me show you something, my dear lady," he said when the gavotte ended. He led me off the dance floor and into a long corridor – or open colonnade – that looked out through rounded arches over the rolling moonlit countryside.

As we strolled, the moon shone brightly, gleaming on his white powdered wig; he smelled strongly of musk and, once we were alone, he leaned close to me, holding me tight, too tight, by the arm, and showed me his collection of lascivious engravings. Two exquisitely detailed engravings struck me in particular: in one of these, a young woman was, like the mythical beauty Andromeda, chained to a rock, or perhaps to the wall of a cavern; she was naked and about to be sacrificed, probably to a sea monster, for giant tentacles were hovering just at the edge of one side of the engraving; the other engraving showed a naked young woman kneeling, on all fours, head down, before an altar, while a severe-looking nun, standing behind her, raised a whip …

"Most interesting," I said. "'Tis done with delicate art."

"Indeed." His intense gaze lingered on me, just a bit too long, and his grip tightened, just a bit too much.

As the evening progressed, the Count entreated me to stay after the ball. He had a particularly delightful wine he wished me to try. He had hidden treasures he wished to reveal; architectural details I would find fascinating. In fact, he promised a cornucopia of exquisite pleasures. So, when the feasting was over, the last carriage had drawn away, and the last servant had wandered off to bed, I waited in the shadows for my assignation. I was trembling with eagerness. Hunting and feeding are for me like sex, dear Father O'Bryan, a strange cocktail of fear and desire. Every encounter entails risk. I was aquiver with tingling anticipation – but at the same time, I feared things could go horribly wrong.

And, then, I was not entirely sure the Count was my man, which added the spice of uncertainty to the challenge. Perhaps he would be a true gentleman, if a bit playfully sadistic and perverse, and in that case, I would acquire a new friend.

He came to me without his mask. He tore off his wig, revealing hair that was chestnut and thick and fell to his shoulders.

"Take off your mask." It was a command, and not spoken in the gallant and light tone he had used when we were amid the crowd. "Take off the mask, or I will rip it off – and your face with it!"

"Yes, my Lord," I said, curtsying. "As you wish." I lifted off the feathery owl's mask, laid it aside, and offered my face to his.

"So, my lady, you are as beautiful as I could have desired."

"Thank you, my Lord," I said, with a slight inclination of my head; I feigned not to notice the barbaric tone he had suddenly adopted.

"Unfortunately, my lady, you are also a spy!"

"A spy, my Lord, what do you mean, a spy?"

"A spy, simply, a spy," he snarled. "I have many enemies; they wish to discredit me, and to destroy me."

He pulled back, shot me a look of pure hatred, and unsheathed his sword. It was a short, sharp sword, not a gentleman's sabre, but a knife made for butchery, disfigurement, and murder.

"My Lord! Please, my Lord, I am no spy!!" Now I was afraid. If he was quick enough, he could do me real damage before I could disarm him.

He advanced and I backed away, along the corridor, feigning much more fear and confusion than I felt.

Just as I was steeling myself to make a stand, a few feet away from me, a door opened – well, it was a secret door. Part of the wall slid aside and out stepped two huge creatures in monks' robes, black robes with hoods, monstrous in looks and seeming exactly alike, like twins, just as my friend the philosophical friar had described. Both were armed with enormous spiked cudgels.

"Come, lady!" The Count seized me by the arm. "Let us visit the secret chambers. There we shall hear your confession."

The Count pushed me through the secret door and down some wide stone steps. I could have taken a stand and fought, of course, and torn him apart; but I allowed myself to be thrust before him. I wished to see his inner sanctum and fully explore the depths of his depravity. The walls dripped with liquid and shone with saltpeter; the air smelled of sulfur; the torches flickered orange and yellow; from the flames waxy smoke rose up, a dirty sinuous brown, and curled along the vaulted stone roof. Down and down we went. The Count's grip was like steel.

At the bottom of the stairs, we entered a large cavern, furnished and decorated like a Christian chapel except that, at the far end, above the flat stone altar, the enormous cross was burnt and scarred and charred and hung upside down.

Along the walls, in separate niches, were rough-hewn statues of naked women, twisting in contorted poses of desire, orgasm, or pain; it was hard to tell which.

A fire blazed in the center of the cavern. Various instruments – branding irons and other tools of torture – were glowing, white hot, in the fire.

Huge iron rings were attached to the walls, with chains hanging from them. And then I saw her.

Beside the altar a naked young woman was manacled to a thick column of stone. She was standing, but her neck, wrists, and ankles were enclosed in iron. Her head hung forward, and her hair, like a cascade of gold, hung free, and went almost to her waist; her pose was limp, held up by the iron manacles. I could not tell whether she was dead or alive. She was the mirror image of the Andromeda-like woman in the engraving the Count had shown me only an hour or two before.

The altar at the far end of the "chapel" was of black stone, black granite, it seemed; it glimmered darkly in the light of the torches, as if sprinkled with mica. Embedded in its polished and flat surface were more iron manacles. As the Count pushed me closer to what was clearly an altar of sacrifice, I noticed that runnels were cut into the stone and that they led to silver spouts, presumably to collect the blood of the victim so that the worshippers could drink it. I wondered how many young women and children had been sacrificed here.

Tunnels and smaller caverns led off from the sides of the chapel. A great pool of hot liquid clay steamed to one side, making the whole place clammy, like a steam bath, and giving it that thick clinging sulfurous volcanic smell I had noticed when we came down the stairs. The villa, I realized, must be built upon or close to an ancient volcano, and the clayey mud must be heated from a volcanic source.

"Who are you spying for, my lady?" The Count's grin, a tight, mask-like grin, was sepulchral, almost skull-like. The hedonistic and debonair Count had given away to another creature entirely.

"I spy for no one, my Lord."

He pulled me toward him, clutching my chin; our lips almost touched, our eyes blazed. In his, I saw no humanity, no empathy, and no compassion. His breath smelled of fermentation, of wine, a tang of bitterness.

"Really, really? How do you, dear lady, account for the fact that no one knows who you are? No one knows where you come from …"

"I am merely a simple woman. I …"

"You gave no name."

"No. I …"

"Do you work for the Inquisition? Did the Pope send you?"

"No, no, my Lord, no!"

"Are you in the pay of Venice? The patricians of the Most Serene Republic and even the Doge himself," he spat out the words, "would certainly like to destroy me. They are very envious, you know, of my extraordinary powers!"

"Your powers, my Lord?"

He let go of my chin and with a single quick swipe of his hand he tore my gown from my shoulders, ripping it down to my waist. Then he tossed me away, as if I were as light as a feather, and into the hands of one of the giant monks. The monk seized me, pinning my arms tight against my body. I knew I had to make my move soon; I just needed a second with my arms free …

"You know, my lady, half-naked you are even more beautiful than when fully dressed," the Count smiled and spoke once again with the tone of a gallant gentleman bantering in society. His smile, though, instantly turned to a grimace.

"Whenever I see anything as beautiful as you, I have a terrible urge, an overpowering desire, to destroy that beauty, to deform it, maim it, turn it into grotesque irredeemable ugliness." Curling his fist, he contemplated his fingernails. "I wonder, my lady, why that is?"

"I know not, my Lord," I gasped. The giant's grip tightened. I needed a moment of distraction. Then I felt, at my back, the giant's excitement: he was aroused, aroused by the image of cruelty, he was anticipating my disfigurement.

"Well," said the Count, "since the lady will not speak, let us have some sport!"

The giant groaned with pleasure. He shifted his grip, stepped back slightly. I leaned forward, ever so slightly, pressing myself against him and against his aroused member.

The Count tilted his head in a theatrical, contemplative, Hamlet-like gesture, one index finger to his chin. "So! Let us see! How shall we proceed? Branding first, and then cut out her tongue?" He pulled from its sheath his wicked short-bladed sword, and toyed with it, turning it this way and that, contemplating the possibilities. "Or burn out her eyes with the hot iron?" He smiled, the old charming smile. "There is so much … choice … Yes, yes, a spy without eyes … ha, ha … that's it." He lifted a red-hot iron from the fire and turned the point toward me. Already I felt the hot flush of glowing iron on my cheeks.

The manacled woman screamed, "Don't let him! Don't let him!"

The giant was surprised. He loosened his grip. I slammed myself back into him, smashing against his huge aroused, erect member. I am sure I didn't hurt him. But I did shock and surprise him. He let go of my arms.

I sprang away, leaping to the side of the chapel, and vaulting over the pool of steaming gray mud, a useful barrier between me and my assailants. I concentrated … I would change – and I would change NOW!

It was instantaneous: fangs, claws, scales, and reptilian, superhuman strength, and that strange sensation that comes when all the senses are multiplied in intensity, and thought and perception go so fast that time seems to slow down, and, even, in extreme cases, to stop altogether.

My fine silk and lace ball gown, which I had bought only two months before at Veronelli's in Milan and which had already been ripped and torn to the waist by the Count, now, alas, exploded. It made a loud bang and sent out a shower of sparks. Nothing was left but smoking fragments. Ribbons and tiny wispy glowing motes of cloth, mere embers, floated in a cloud around me. Damn! But then I remembered: I had the design; Eleanor, my talented seamstress, could make me another – and it would be much cheaper!

As I morphed, my back, for just an instant, was turned to the Count and his monks. I used the instant of repose to cogitate and plan. I decided I would kill the two monks first. Then I would deal with the Count.

I turned to face them. One of the monks was rushing toward me. He had not had time to register my transformation. I leapt into the air, flying toward him. He stopped, and looked up, gaping. He didn't believe what he was seeing. I plunged straight down onto him, knocking him backward. I sank the points of my claws deep into his eyes and popped them, exploding the eyeballs, like rotten grapes. *So much for losing eyes, my friend!* My claws, which were dripping blood and gore and torn eyeball, ripped across his face, tearing his nose and jaw away.

Swinging around, I took his great clammy bald head between my claws – his cowl had flopped back – and, digging the points of my claws deep into his flesh – he was beginning to emit a rising howl of bloody bubbling rage, pain, and fear – I twisted his neck and snapped it.

Crack – then silence …

In mid-howl, he stopped and collapsed in on himself, an oversized lifeless heap, shrouded in his monk's habit.

The Count, still holding the glowing pointed bar of iron, was unsheathing his sword. I could see, forming on his lips, the words, "She-devil."

I turned to the other monk who was also racing toward me, wielding an enormous, heavy, double-edged sword. The arc of its downward sweep, I saw, would cut right through my left shoulder.

I swiveled aside, leapt above the slashing arc of the sword, and dove down, seizing his arm and pressing it, so that the sword continued downwards faster, faster, and faster – with mighty force – and – SLASH – it cut off his right leg.

Only the stump remained – squirting blood.

He howled and toppled, slowly, as if he were a huge tree coming down in a forest. In that instant, the naked manacled girl screamed, "Look out!"

I swung around. The Count's branding iron was flying. Its glowing white-hot point was aimed at my heart. I ducked aside. As it sailed past – and I could feel the deadly heat – it touched a remnant of my dress – a fluttery bit of fine Spanish lace – that had unaccountably survived my transformation and was clinging to my shoulder. The lace burst into flame, a tiny yellow flare guttering on my scales, just above my collarbone. It tickled, pleasantly. The iron sailed on and toward the wounded monk who was writhing in a gushing fountain of blood on the floor, desperately holding his stump of a leg, and there it slammed its white-hot, stiletto-sharp point right in the middle of his strange baby-like face, right where, an instant before, his tiny, twisted nose had been. Now, his nose was no more. He let out a blood-curdling gurgling scream. The iron sizzled and the smell of burning flesh flooded my nostrils.

"What are you?" The Count was staring, wild-eyed; his sword was drawn, and he was coming in for the kill.

"You see, dear Count, as I told you, I am not a spy!"

"She-devil!"

"If you wish to call me that, Count, then that is what I am!"

"I shall kill you. I shall burn you alive!"

"We shall see." I was hungry now; in fact, I was famished; vigorous exercise will have this effect, and during the Count's ball I had done a great deal of quite fancy dancing; but, above all, I was furious – furious because I knew what this man did and what he had done. Also, I needed to understand – why and how he did it, and with whom. And if you truly want to understand a man, there is nothing better, for me, than drinking him dry.

He drew a short knife and threw it at the girl chained on the wall.

As the knife sped through the air, so did I – and just in time I knocked it aside. Still, it cut her shoulder, but not badly. He had aimed it at the center of her throat.

"That was not gallant, Count. You are not a gentleman!"

"She-devil! I cast the curse of Satan upon you!"

"Oh? The curse of Satan?" I raised my reptilian eyebrows. With those words, the Count had made it doubly clear that he was not a lone sadistic madman but a member in good standing of the Satanic Order of the Apocalypse, in league with the Cardinal the good Friar had mentioned, and who, apparently, was its leader.

"Come, Count! I am waiting!"

"Demon!" he screamed. "Demon! I will send you howling down to the lowest reaches of Hell. You will burn in eternal fire! You'll ..."

"Go on, Count! I'm listening."

He hesitated. His eyes flashed back and forth as if he were imagining a way to escape; once again it occurred to me that this was a very treacherous place, with secret devices and trapdoors and invisible entrances and exits placed everywhere.

Sure enough: The Count backed away from me, retreating toward a side wall. He reached behind him and pushed a small inset cog. A portion of the wall swung open. He sprang into the embrasure, clearly hoping to slam the secret door shut behind him.

But I was faster than he expected. In a flash, we were both in the hidden tunnel. The stone door thundered shut behind us. The Count sprinted away, his footsteps echoing in the narrow, arched passageway. Torches lined the tunnel, casting a gloomy yellow flickering light, and making a wavering slapping ghostly sound, as if they were in a breeze. And, in fact, there was a breeze, a hot sulfurous breeze.

A gateway to Hell, I thought, how fitting!

"My Lord, I am hungry," I shouted, racing after him, my voice reverberating against the narrow, sweaty, inward-sloping walls. I knew I must end the game quickly. I was weakening from hunger.

The Count raced around a sharp bend. And when I followed, he was ready for me.

He struck out – I was caught off balance, stumbled back, and fell.

As he plunged at me with his sword, I rolled aside and kicked out. The Count tumbled backward, but instantly sprang to his feet, turned tail, and galloped away. I leapt up and raced after him, almost catching, with my outstretched claws, the flapping tails of his gold-embroidered, pale mauve, silk jacket. He dodged and ducked and sprinted – he had strong legs, was a good runner, and a good fighter, supple, quick, and decisive.

We came to another cavern. There were more sulfurous fumes and pools of delicious gray bubbling mud. When the Count turned to fight, slashing at me with his sword, I swiveled aside, evading his first blow. I ducked under his second. I pranced – rather precious of me I must admit – around the third, a wild swinging sweep of his blade. I wanted to make him dance, to make him perform. But he was getting confused. It was no longer fun. His virtuosity was fading. So, losing patience, I struck: I smashed his sword from his hand and snapped his sword arm at the elbow.

He didn't howl – not at first.

He stood still, trapped, dazed, his eyes wide, his face drained of color; he was sweating heavily, and white as a ghost. His eyes darted this way and that. I leapt forward. He stumbled backward, and, grabbing for the torn ribbons of my splendid ball gown, he managed to seize my wrist.

He fell with a splash into the thick gray soup, dragging me with him. I had been too impetuous in my leap; my momentum carried me after him into the mud. I was not happy with this, plunging into the gooey slime, so I grabbed the arm that was pulling me, and I snapped it in two, again at the elbow.

I was on my hands and knees now, deep in the bubbly gray muck. It was warm and thick and sticky; in the right circumstances, and with the right partner, this would have been delicious slippery fun.

Lifting the Count up by the frilled collar of his fine silk jacket, I dragged him, kicking and screaming, out of the steamy clay. With both arms broken he was helpless, a dangling, hysterical puppet, a limp ragdoll. There was a small cascade of water at the far end of the cavern. I dragged him toward it.

"I do not understand, my Lord, why you do what you do!"

He was beyond giving answers. He just howled.

I pushed him under the pouring hot sulfurous water, letting it clean both of us.

The Count's eyes rolled in his head. Foam spurted from his lips. I wanted to ask him about the Satanic Order of the Apocalypse: I wanted to know how it had changed in during the centuries; I wanted to know who the other members were – what did they believe, what rituals did they perform, where and how did they recruit their victims?

But I was hungry, and he was delirious.

I propped him up under the warm cascading water.

He was saying crazy things. Words bubbled out of his foaming mouth. I was his mother, or so he thought. This often happens, I have found, to men – particularly to hulking bullies who have rarely met their match. When they are in a fever or facing certain death, they mewl and whimper and scream and return to the cradle or the swaddling bands or the maternal breast – or maybe, even, when truly desperate, they crawl back into the clammy darkness of the womb.

"I am not your mother, Count!"

The Count began to sing a ditty of some kind – a French ditty; it was a beautiful song by the poet Rutebeuf. I wondered at the complexity of the human soul. I plunged my fangs into the Count's neck and fed and fed and fed – he was very juicy – and the Rutebeuf poem echoed in my mind.

Que sont mes amis devenus
Que j'avais de si près tenus
Et tant aimés ?

What has become of all my friends, I held so close, and loved so strong?

Je crois qu'ils sont trop clairsemés
Le vent je crois, me les a pris,
L'amour est morte.

They were scattered like seeds, sown too sparsely; and the wind I think has carried them all away; love is dead …

Yes, indeed, I thought, love is dead. I drank and drank. I consumed the Count's blood till he was nothing but an empty husk; he was dead, truly dead; he would not rise again.

I washed myself in the fountain, then carried the lifeless dangling body down the tunnel, out the secret door, and into the main chapel. There I threw it into the fire so it would be consumed.

The two dead monks still lay there.

I went up to the young woman. She looked at me in horror. With my fangs, with my naked, scaly body, and with my claws extended, I was not, I think, a reassuring sight. She was a brave girl. She didn't scream. She simply stared at me. I concentrated my strength and ripped the manacles from the wall and snapped the manacles from her wrists and neck and ankles. She was trembling and her shoulder was bleeding from the grazing glancing blow of the Count's sword.

"I won't hurt you," I said.

"Who are you?" She gazed into my eyes. "What are you?"

"Let me help you."

She shrank back.

"Suit yourself, but I can cure that wound.

She stood defiant but then relented and let me approach her. I laid my claw on the shoulder wound: the energy flowed. Her ankles and wrists were chaffed – I knelt before her and breathed the raw redness away.

"Good as new, or almost," I said, standing up. "We must find clothes, but first I shall finish what I have begun …"

I closed my eyes and in a whir of movement I changed back into my human form – now naked as Eve of course.

The girl stared but said nothing.

Count Marbuse was burning brightly. His rib cage stood out, dark charred curved bones, and the flesh was peeling off his skull. The debonair smile was now truly grim, a lopsided sneer. The oily bitter smell of burning flesh was unpleasant.

I dragged the two monks to the deep bubbling pool of clay and shoved them in. They floated for a moment, then sank out of sight. A few gluey muddy bubbles rose to the surface and popped noisily. The monks were gone.

I went back to the Count and raked the coals. The flames shot up; it was enough. He was – aside from a few teeth – nothing but ash. The young woman watched my every move.

"Let us go," I said.

We went up the stairs into the villa and along a corridor that skirted a large interior courtyard. Luckily, we did not come upon any servants. Preparing for the costumed ball had demanded a great deal of work, I'm sure, and they had undoubtedly all been happy to go to bed. We found our way to the private suite and bedroom of the Count.

"We must dress as men." I opened the door of the great wardrobe. "We cannot travel naked, as we now are, nor as women – not women alone."

"Of course," she said.

"What are you?" I asked, staring at her. She was a beauty, fresh as a rose, and truly young, but as calm and resolute as a Stoic philosopher.

She was pulling on a pretty pair of two-colored hose, one leg black and one leg scarlet, and was eyeing a pair of breeches, which would go perfectly with the two-colored hose. "What am I?" she repeated, turning to me.

"Yes. What are you?"

"I was a nun," she said, as she slipped into a fine, powder-blue doublet. "Or rather, a novice. I didn't have the vocation – indeed I'd fallen in love with a neighbor, a childhood friend – but my family disapproved of him, and of his family, and would not allow the match; they forced me to become a nun. I fought against the discipline of the convent. I rebelled, and so, to punish me, the Mother Superior sold me to the Count."

"Ah, I see." I glanced at myself in the mirror. The feathered hat was pleasingly frivolous. I tilted it down at a rakish angle. "Perhaps the nuns have sold other young women to the Count and his confederates."

"Indeed, many young ladies have disappeared over the years, so the other girls told me. Yes, undoubtedly it is so." She flexed a leg and looked down at it. The soft leather boots she had chosen were quite fetching. She turned her ankle this way, then that way. The leggings, black and scarlet, were skintight and fit her perfectly. "Do you approve?" She cast me a fluttery sideways glance.

"I approve," I said, thinking, I more than approve. I tried to keep my expression appropriately stern and masterly; but I could not resist letting my gaze linger. I wanted to bed her. I wanted to befriend her. I wanted to tutor her. I wanted to make her my companion. Then, when she was ready, and if she so desired, I would find her a suitable mate – a man rich enough and intelligent enough to appreciate her and give her the life she deserved. I shook myself, looked away, smoothed down my own leggings, and pulled on the boots I had chosen, black boots, with rather fine heels.

"You look," she said, "almost human."

"You, my Lady," I smiled, "are too kind." I bowed low, like a young, over-zealous, foppish gallant.

In return, she sketched a low bow, even more elaborate, that of a true gallant, or accomplished fop, bending deep from the waist, swinging her arm in front of her, stretching one leg out, while the other remained behind.

"We make a fine pair."

"We do indeed," she said; she had the most wonderful smile. Inwardly, I sighed.

Attired as young gentlemen, we left the Count's private apartments – though I did filch a small vial of very expensive perfume on the way out – and we headed down to the stables where we found the Count's stable boys fast asleep. I laid my hands on their foreheads and breathed into their nostrils, thus making sure they would not awake until long after the sun had risen. I saddled two of the Count's horses.

"You can ride?"

"Of course," she said.

"And do you have somewhere to go? Will your lover take you in?"

"He will; he must."

"Farewell, then."

"Farewell," she said, mounting her horse, "and thank you!" With deep regret, I watched her ride away. That last glimpse of her – as she waved and blew me a kiss – has stayed with me, and kept me company, over the years.

Now alone, I rode with the wind in my hair. The moon sailed along next to me, gliding smoothly past the trees and the hills, racing behind woods, flooding valleys and ravines with gentle cool silver light. I rode swiftly. I felt like a god. The power of the universe pulsed in my veins. It was the feeling I always get when I have fed. My soul is swept up in drunken revelry. I am Dionysius, bubbling with energy, dancing with delight.

I kept to the shores of Tuscany on the Tyrrhenian Sea, to the empty beaches, with the moon riding in ripples of silver on the crests of the waves; I galloped over the low sand dunes and grassy hillocks; I rode among the silvery-gray shadows. The sea was low, the night warm and without wind. The waves gently lapped at the sand, up-and-down, up-and-down, a giant's peaceful breathing.

I was drunk with adoration for this world of ours!

Toward dawn I stopped at an inn I knew – and they immediately gave me a room. I slept much of the day before starting off again. After two days of travel, I came to my "lair" – which is the villa you know, Father. I have lost it several times over the centuries, but I reacquired it again, for I think the fifth time, many decades ago, after the Second World War.

In the seventeenth and eighteenth centuries, as now, it was surrounded by cedars, umbrella pines, and tall, dark, spear-like cypress trees. With the villa, which I had purchased two decades before these events, I had acquired two old retainers, a couple, Giuseppe and Marta, who were childless, and who were delighted that the new mistress desired to keep them on.

It was getting toward dawn when I rode into the courtyard.

Giuseppe had heard the hooves of my horse and he was there, holding a lantern. He and Marta were used to my nocturnal ramblings, my long absences, my masculine attire, my riding alone through the night. They knew me for what I was.

"Good evening, Countess."

"Good evening, Giuseppe, though it is, I fear, almost morning."

"Indeed, Countess, the cock just crowed."

While Giuseppe held the reins, I jumped down and a few moments later I was sitting in the great hall, my legs stretched out, staring into a roaring fire. Marta had set out my usual refreshment after a long absence or a nocturnal ramble – a single glass of dark red wine.

For a few decades I kept track of activities at Villa Mazana Nera. The Satanic Order of the Apocalypse continued to use the villa for its celebrations even without the Count and, on a few occasions, I interrupted its supply of young women by kidnapping the prey, returning the girl to her family or finding her a mate or a home, and hunting down and killing the master of revels or the procurer or procuress.

At one point, I also arranged for a secret "leak" so that the Pope – he was a good Pope, not an opportunist, self-serving, libidinous, profligate, nepotistic amoral, plotting, Machiavellian devil, as so many of them in that period were – could act against the Order. And act he did.

That drove them underground for a decade or two.

Then I lost track of the Satanic Order of the Apocalypse. I lived elsewhere – in France and England, in China and Vietnam and India, and, briefly, for a few decades, in the New World.

V ended her story, just as we arrived at the crest of a very high hill. Islands of light far below indicated villages on the great plain beneath us, and, further away, lit up by the moon, I could make out the glittering metal-dark sea; and piling up above the sea were tremendous black clouds.

We ascended toward another series of hills, shadowy forested silhouettes. The little twinkles of light in the distant mountains were, I suppose, mountaintop villages.

Small white striped pillars on the side of the road marked dangerous corners where the cliff fell straight away. V again glanced at me, her face pale, lit up by the reflection of the car's headlights.

"Soon, Father," she said. "Soon – it won't be long now."

CHAPTER 34 – SCULPTURE

The body glistened as if oiled – a true work of art.

"Sublime, beautiful!" Father Ottavio rubbed his hands. He clapped. He was sorely tempted to dance a jig.

The lacquer had dried perfectly. The finish was immaculate. The creature was exquisite, if perhaps a trifle over-bright and garish; but, then, the reduction of fluid, nuanced, living beauty to dead, brightly lit kitsch was essential to the irony, charm, and … the sublime perversity of the sacrifice! Father Ottavio bent to get a closer look. For the psychological – sadistic and satanic – effect to work, everything had to be precise, down to the last detail. The pose he had chosen, adjusted from Bernini's original for greater effect, was perfect.

The girl's eyes stared toward the ceiling; the pupils and irises were brilliantly delineated, sparkling with tiny shards and glints of gold; the mouth was half open, the expression startled, dreamily ecstatic. The sublime fallen creature was trapped in orgasm. She would remain so – for all time.

"Please adjust the spotlight to the left, Brother Basilisk? Let us throw the shoulders and breasts into sharper relief. A bit more shadow, and a delicate emphasis on the line of the shoulder bone!" Father Ottavio clasped his hands and rubbed them.

Brother Basilisk nudged the spotlight to the left.

"Yes, yes, that is perfect." Father Ottavio licked his lips. "She is ready, quite ready. You and Sister Kundrie have done splendid work!" He beamed at the monk. "And now you may go, Brother Basilisk. I wish to be alone."

"Yes, Father Ottavio." The monk shuffled off, a dark, massive, hunched figure, heading up the chapel staircase, leaving Father Ottavio to contemplate his exquisite parody of Bernini's Saint Teresa – the lips shone, a thick splash of glossy ecclesiastical crimson; circles of rouge, almost clownlike, brightened the cheeks, heightening the cheekbones; deep purple eye shadow gave the eyelids and eyes a mask-like, sensuous, parodic intensity. The eyebrows and eyelashes were sharp, jet-black strokes, standing out, stark, against the ceramic-like, chalk-white skin. Her hair was so luxuriant, so glossily black, and so perfectly real, that Father Ottavio wanted to reach out and caress and smell it; he resisted the temptation.

The right leg was bent, the left leg stretched out, and one arm reached up, as if she were trying to shield herself from too much ecstasy; the other arm, down by her side, had its fingers spread, as if she were steadying herself, trying to root herself on the earth, struggling to deny the overwhelming sexual and divine craving that was about to lift her up and carry her off into the empyrean – or cast her down to Hell. Truly, this young woman was one of their most sublime creations, perhaps the finest of all. The flicking light of the torches, alternating brightness and shadow, added an extra, vital expression to her garishly painted, half-open mouth and gleaming teeth; it looked as if she were breathing, or about to speak; it truly looked as if she were alive.

In fact, she seemed so alive that Father Ottavio felt he could – felt he must – talk to her directly, confide in her. "You see, my dear, with your help we shall rid ourselves of that foolish creature, the Pope! We shall initiate what will be, as it always should have been, the Kingdom of Satan on Earth; the unveiling of the revelation will be quite glorious, my dear, and you are part of the final ceremony! You should be honored!"

The girl did not answer – but, in her blind eyes, Father Ottavio was sure he had seen a flicker of understanding, awe – and worshipful submission.

Sublime! Utterly sublime!

Finally, turning away from the masterpiece, Father Ottavio climbed up the sloping stairs toward a large oak door. It automatically swung open as he approached; and it closed behind him.

He stepped into a spacious wide corridor, lined with huge Ming vases overflowing with freshly cut flowers. The terracotta tiles were dazzlingly polished, the mahogany chests that stood against the walls glowed with fresh wax, and the torches, in their black wrought iron holders, burned softly, without producing any trace of smoke.

Villa Mazana Nera was a stunning and worthy setting for satanic sacrifice! It was part of an ancient and glorious tradition! Father Ottavio glanced around with approval and, as he strode down the hall, he bathed in a voluptuous and overwhelming sensation of pleasure and luxury; and he carried with him, in his mind's eye, that delicate, fine-featured creature, that work of art, that parody of Bernini's *Ecstasy*, that image of the young woman known, once, as Katherine Dawkins Thornhill.

CHAPTER 35 – THE DEAD

"Professor! Professor!"

"What?"

"Wake up, Professor!"

Roger shuddered and woke up. The Cardinal was standing over him, just outside the bars of the cage. Roger shook his head, struggling to chase away the cobwebs; he had dozed off; he had been dreaming: he was with Kate's mother, with Laura; it was the first time they had made love.

Laura had just let the blue-and-white striped towel drop away. She was standing by the bed smiling at him. "Here I am," she said. "Here I am with one of the most intelligent men in the world!"

"What do you mean *one* – *one* – of the most intelligent?"

She jumped onto the bed, leaned close, and closed his mouth with a kiss – her eyes gazed into his, light and laughter sparkling. "Your vanity, Professor Thornhill, is without limit." She kissed him, a longer kiss this time, slower and deeper. Slowly, teasingly, she lowered her body onto his, her fingers caressing his hair, the tips of her nipples brushing against his chest, her legs wrapped around his legs.

"I love you." It was the first time she'd said it.

"I love you," he said. In truth, he'd loved her – desired her, needed her, obsessed about her – from the first moment he'd caught a glimpse of her. It was a crisp, bright, blue autumn afternoon, warm, and yet sharp, one of those autumn days New York does so well. He was on Fifth Avenue and about to miss his flight to Los Angeles. A meeting had run too long. He ran out onto the sidewalk, desperate to get a cab. And there – right in front of him – was a cab, just come to a stop. A woman was getting out. The first thing he saw were legs, long legs, dark stockings, a pleated skirt – stylish, elegant, just perfect.

Then, she emerged, stood up, held the cab door open for him, and smiled. "All yours, sir!" And, clutching her briefcase, she walked off.

His thought – and it was the first time he'd ever had such a thought in his life – his thought was: *I absolutely must not lose her.*

He'd wanted the cab for himself – the desperate race to catch his flight to Los Angeles! But, seeing another woman frantically signaling for a cab, Roger gallantly offered her his, bowing her in, holding the door, and all the while watching the woman he had just glimpsed walking into an office building. His whole life was walking away with her, into the revolving doors, disappearing, disappearing perhaps forever.

He ran.

At the end of their first date, she'd said, "You are very nice, Roger, and lots of fun, and you are the most handsome man I have ever met. But, Roger, you are too vain; it will never work."

He sent flowers. He left messages. He begged.

It took three months of constant bombardment.

"You're stalking me, Professor!" But she said it with a smile.

Finally, she relented. "You really are impossible!"

"I know."

"It's too flattering, all this attention."

"You deserve every bit of it."

"I'll bet it stops the instant you've got me hooked!"

It didn't. Roger remained infatuated – he was still infatuated the day she died. He was infatuated even now – four years after her death.

They were married in Boston. He was teaching at MIT. Her specialty was molecular biology, and it turned out she was more than brilliant. She easily found a job, as chief of research and development for an up-and-coming biotech firm. Then they moved to England, where he had a four-year contract at the University of Cambridge. She sacrificed her career for him. But her Boston-based biotech firm had a link with a firm in Cambridge, so she continued to work, as "Adjunct Chief of Research." And she loved it. She adored their little house outside Cambridge – a refurbished Tudor cottage with a thatched roof that had probably been there when Shakespeare was writing *Hamlet.* She'd been told she could never have children, but then …

Then they had Kate.

Kate … their miracle child.

"Professor! Wake up! Wake up! Welcome back, Professor!" The Cardinal motioned to one of the monks. "Open the cage. Let the Professor out! Let him breathe the air of freedom."

Still dazed, still half lost in the world of his dream-like memory, Roger stood up. Manacled hand-and-foot, with chains attaching the handcuffs to a collar around his neck, he shuffled out of the cage. His anger, darkened with melancholy and mourning, seethed.

"One of the more recondite pleasures of power, Professor Thornhill, as I'm sure you are aware, is to know things that other people don't know."

"No doubt," Roger said, reluctantly shaking himself free of Laura and of the dream of love, of her sparkling, teasing presence. "So, what do you know, Cardinal? What do you know that other people don't know?"

The Cardinal grinned and laid his hand on Roger's shoulder. "I know, dear Professor Thornhill, that in a few short hours the world will come to an end."

"Yes?" Roger glanced up at the Crystal, innumerable facets, glimmering, sparkling, reflecting, in a myriad of minuscule flashes, the floodlights the Cardinal's monks had set up. After the small electric shock, the Cardinal's generator had applied, there had been, after a delay of about two hours, seismic quivers and small earthquakes and minor volcanic eruptions and weird weather events all over the planet – nothing dangerous, but the electric shock had been tiny and brief. Now Roger was certain: The Crystal was capable of tearing Earth apart.

"My followers believe that I am about to usher in the Reign of Satan on Earth. They will be celebrating the event in a special ceremony in Italy tonight."

"A ceremony?"

"A sort of black Mass, I suppose you could call it, a bit of sacrifice, the usual mumbo jumbo and hocus pocus. Like most things, it's merely show business. And my followers are of course fools."

"I see." Roger was dying to scratch his back and hoist up his ragged boxer shorts; they had sagged dangerously low; an inch lower, and he'd be naked. He was filthy, covered in sweat and grime. He grimaced. He must smell like a skunk.

The Cardinal beamed at Roger. It was an exquisite pleasure to hold a man of such intelligence at his mercy, to see the elegant Nobel Laureate naked, grimy, and in chains, to know that this proud man's beloved and unique daughter *was* the sacrifice offered up to Satan. The Ancients had had a very good idea when they paraded their conquered foes in chains through the streets. The sacrifice of Kate – that, surely, was the most exquisite, ironic touch of all.

The Cardinal had already received the images. Katherine Dawkins Thornhill was a sublime Saint Teresa.

"But these petty details, and these little ceremonies, are of no consequence here!" He laid his hand on Roger's shoulder. "We shall shortly demonstrate more of the power of the Crystal, an appetizer, a warm-up, an aperitif!"

"Cardinal, if you destroy the world, you will be destroying yourself as well, you know."

"I have lived a long life, Professor Thornhill. I have grown weary of humans and of all their works. In any case, death does not apply to me. I am no longer human. The Crystal has granted me extraordinary powers, powers that came as a revelation. So, when the world ends, I shall transcend mere human existence, and I will survive. I am divine. I will be swept up in Satanic Rapture. And I shall live forever."

"A revelation?" Roger held the Cardinal's gaze.

"Yes, a revelation, Professor. Let me show you." The Cardinal withdrew his hand from Roger's shoulder and rolled up his sleeve. "You see my forearm and my hand, Professor?"

"Yes, Cardinal, I do."

"They are the forearm and hand of a very old man, Professor, skinny, wrinkled, pale, and mottled with age spots. Yes? Well, then, Professor, watch!"

Roger sighed. What crazy rabbit was the Cardinal going to pull out of his sleeve? There was a blur. The Cardinal's hand and forearm disappeared … or, rather, morphed.

Where the old man's hand and forearm had been, there was something else – a long, spindly, metallic-looking thing, articulated with complex joints. It looked like a metal arm, part of a robot, or part of a space arm. It looked like an insect leg. Yes, it was an insect's leg … No, it was a spider's leg, and much longer than the Cardinal's arm.

"What, precisely, is that, Cardinal?" Roger cleared his throat. This was more than a vaudeville trick. Did the Crystal really have the power to …?

"Why, Professor, I'm glad you asked!" the Cardinal tittered. "That is part of the other me!" The Cardinal glanced sideways at Roger and offered one of his ghastly lopsided grins. Roger wondered: Had the man suffered a stroke? That might explain the megalomania, the madness.

"The other you?"

"Oh, yes, Professor! I do love watching you confront this unprecedented fact – instant metamorphosis. Somehow you manage to maintain your sublime sangfroid, your calm scientific curiosity, your phlegmatic objectivity. Absolutely adorable!"

"Cardinal, you are too kind!" Roger's throat was parched. He needed a drink. A bottle of chilled Chablis, right now, would be very ... How long was it since he'd peed? His bowels rumbled. Diarrhea? Was he going to lose control? Would he shit himself? Had he eaten? He couldn't remember. Damn! He could use a shower, and some clothes!

"You see, Professor, this is one – merely one – of the other forms I have discovered I can become. I contain multitudes. I am not speaking metaphorically. And I am not what I seem. Now, in my present form, I am merely a humble larva, a chrysalis!" The Cardinal twirled around, sketching out a dance step. His ecclesiastical gown rippled. It floated up around him. The strange metallic appendage waved up and down, the pincer-like ending – something that looked like a robotic claw – opened and closed. "Soon I shall emerge, like a butterfly from its cocoon, and become truly, truly divine!"

"How nice for you."

"Tut, tut, Professor, such petty, effeminate, pinch-lipped, drawing-room irony is beneath you. You are trivializing the sacred works of Satan. I forgive you! The Crystal, you see, has the power to transform a living creature into ... into something else."

"It looks like a spider's leg."

"Brilliant, Professor! Full marks! Yes, it is: a spider's leg. Precisely." The Cardinal waggled the deadly-looking appendage, which looked like a weapon from some ancient or future war.

Roger blinked: If this were true, the Crystal could reconfigure matter and energy at the deepest level – and do it instantaneously – potentially turning anything, even living things, into anything else. It was unbelievable! Everything he thought he knew must be wrong!

"Perhaps the Crystal has a sense of humor," said the Cardinal good naturedly, wagging his spindly appendage under Roger's nose, "or perhaps a sense of metaphor. I have often been called 'the spider' in the past. The present Pope called me a spider once – which was an uncharitable outburst on his part – and untypical I must say – usually that milquetoast fool is absolutely mealy-mouthed and coweringly polite – but I will say this: for his lapse, for his disrespect, he will pay, and pay dearly!" The Cardinal's grin broadened;

Roger thought, for some reason, of the Lewis Carroll's Cheshire cat in *Alice in Wonderland* – an unreal grin, appearing out of nowhere and nothing, hovering in the air, belonging to nobody. The Cardinal was no longer human – if he ever had been.

"You can do this when you want, and reverse it when you want?" Roger paused. This would turn biology, molecular biology, quantum mechanics, and all the sciences upside down.

"Yes, I can reverse it, and I can do it whenever I want."

"And can you go the whole way?"

"Oh, yes, Professor! I can transform myself into a whole spider – he's quite large, or she, I'm not sure – perhaps I am female, I have discovered depths within myself I did not know I had! I have discovered, too, what my real mission on this Earth of ours is."

"And that is?"

"Well, as I told you, to destroy all life on this planet." The long spider leg quivered. It reached out and the pincers patted Roger on the shoulder. The cold metallic carapace felt eerily substantial, terrifyingly real, tickling his naked skin.

"And destroy the planet itself, I suppose," said Roger. The spidery Cardinal gave off a tropical sugary-sweet and rotten smell, like a dead dog, swirling with maggots, left too long in the tropical sun on the side of some godforsaken tropical war zone road. Roger sneezed.

"Yes, of course – the planet itself, that goes without saying." The spider arm waved in the air – dismissively. The gesture seemed to imply that Earth was a mere bagatelle, a mote of dust, to be brushed away, tossed into annihilation.

"Isn't that a touch excessive?"

"Tut, tut – no, not at all excessive! Satan has vouchsafed me a celestial vision, as I said, a revelation." The Cardinal half closed his eyes, dreamily, as if he were about to swoon. "I saw it all so clearly when I stood over there by the Crystal. Our planet was floating in space, with all its clouds, oceans, continents, and then Satan gave me his blessing, and the whole planet burst apart, flying outwards, until there was nothing but empty black space, a few rocks, tendrils and streams of molten rock, the innards of Earth, the magma turning into crystalline strands, frozen by the cold of space, and breaking apart into pieces. And then nothing. Humanity's adventure was over, as if it had never been."

"But this vision," said Roger, "maybe it was a warning, Cardinal; perhaps you misunderstood, perhaps –"

"Oh, *perhaps, perhaps ... maybe, maybe ...* You scientists are without faith – such great intellects and such small minds. You do not have that extra sense that grants true wisdom! Faith is like love, Professor: you must experience it to know it. For all your intelligence, Professor Thornhill, you are spiritually blind: you do not possess the divine antennae."

"No, I suppose I don't."

"But let us not waste more breath, Professor. Let us give the world a taste of what awaits it: terror and horror, cities and nations obliterated. Flesh turned to ash! Mountains of writhing bodies. You are my witness! That is the gift you give me, or rather it is *one* of the gifts you have given me." The Cardinal turned to the monks. "Start the engines. Give the Crystal a bigger nudge. Let us see some fireworks!"

Roger looked away. It would be useless to protest. He couldn't break the chains, or overcome the monks. He might as well ... But ... what did the Cardinal mean, "gifts" in the plural.

Then it occurred to him.

Kate?

Yes, Kate.

Surely, the man would not be so cynical, so evil – *but oh, yes, yes, indeed, he could, he would; it is precisely what he would do ...* Kate ... the ceremony ... the sacrifice ... How had he not understood earlier? Kate *was* the sacrifice. Kate was about to be murdered by this madman.

The Cardinal's reassurances were less than worthless. Why, the man even took a sadistic pride in betraying his own followers. They believed they were ushering in a new reign of evil on Earth, instead there would be no Earth – there would be no reign. They were going to die, all of them, murdered by the man they worshipped. Were there no limits to his cynicism, his capacity for betrayal?

Roger clenched his fists. He would wait. When the first opportunity came, the Cardinal would die – the Cardinal *must* die!

CHAPTER 36 – BASILISK

Wheeling the stainless-steel gurney out of the laboratory and down the corridor to the elevator, Brother Basilisk gripped the cool steel handlebar as if his life depended on it. He was fighting a desperate battle, struggling mano a mano against his most ferocious perverse desires. If he lost control, he would damage the sacrifice, perhaps fatally. The gurney didn't help. One of the wheels squeaked. The other wheel made a tantalizing smooth squishy rubbery sound – like that of a body slipping into skintight latex, of a body bound and manacled in thick black rubber, of a body tied down with straps, encased in steel, of a body, bound, manacled, and about to die. A phantasmagoria of sadistic, blood-soaked images flooded over him. Mutilation and amputation were among Brother Basilisk's favorite things – arms, legs, tongue, eyes … The temptation soared. The ideal victim was inches away, more beautiful than any before! She was lying, helpless and paralyzed, on the gurney. He had only to reach down …

He came to the elevator. He pushed the metal button on the flat metal panel. It made that reassuring *ding*. He sighed. More images of violence surged up. He clenched his enormous fists. He *must* resist! A small, round, blinking light told him that the elevator was obediently on its way up from the underground chapel. Inside the elevator, he and the sacrifice would be alone, far from prying eyes.

Brother Basilisk waited. He clutched his hands around the metal until his knuckles hurt. He must focus. Soon the faithful would arrive. They would disrobe, shedding their day-to-day profane selves; they would partake of the sacred drink and swallow the sacred biscuits; both contained a powerful cocktail of drugs that would create overwhelming hallucinations. Their human identities, and all decorum, would be cast off. Each one of them, man and woman, would become the true elemental, primal, satanic beast within.

All illusions, all personality, all humanity, would vanish. The veneer of civilization would vanish. Satan's Reign would blossom forth. The flock would become a herd of mad, naked, frothing-at-the-mouth fiends, wild-eyed, libidinous, blood-thirsty, easily disciplined, easily led. The beasts would wallow in filthy excess, demons rehearsing their roles in Hell, which, for the chosen few, would be Heaven. Then, most of them naked, reduced to slobbering obedience, hysterical with unreason, libidos unleashed and exalted into a frenzy, they would file into the chapel. And the ceremony would begin.

The elevator door hissed open. Brother Basilisk steeled himself. He wheeled the gurney into the elevator. The door slid shut. He was alone with the sacrifice. The elevator began its slow voyage down into the heart of the mountain, toward the chapel. His fingers curled and uncurled. He fought with himself. It was a titanic struggle. He swallowed – it would best if he spoke to the sacrifice. That might relieve the pressure.

"My dear, you must appreciate what a privilege it is!" He glanced down at the girl. His tongue passed over his lips. She was immaculate, unblemished, not a bruise, not a scratch. Her oiled skin sparkled, pure ivory-white, every curve polished to perfection, a statue carved out of the best Carrara marble. Her jet-black hair was perfectly combed, thick and luxurious, curling down to her cheekbones, and almost to her shoulders, framing the delicate, finely featured, oval face. She was as glossy and as finely finished as a Renaissance work of art.

Not a muscle moved. She was totally paralyzed. But – and this made it much more pleasurable – he knew that she was conscious, acutely aware of what was happening to her – and of what was about to happen. In fact, he had reduced the drug dosage, so she would be ultra-aware, lucid, knowing, feeling, what was being done to her.

"Soon, my dear, you will be united with the Dark Force, with Satan, with the Universe." Brother Basilisk ran his hand over the curve of her shoulder, down the length of her arm. He was sorely tempted to tear her arm off, but he didn't. The girl's face showed no expression. Her flesh was like warm, smooth marble, like satin or silk. Touching her aroused feelings for which there were no words. Brother Basilisk shuddered. The girl didn't blink.

Brother Basilisk straightened up. A little decorum! He must resist! This young woman was sacred, a gift from Satan. There had been no trouble with her, no trouble at all, unlike that Russian bitch who had broken loose when Sister Kundrie was not looking. That girl – an athletic long-legged blonde

– had climbed, naked except for the fluttering hospital gown, out onto a window ledge, just where the villa looked over a twenty-meter cliff. When they'd tried to trap her, and coax her back, she'd sworn at them in Russian. Then she had stuck out her tongue, and pronounced, "Fuck you!" very clearly, in perfect English – and jumped. She didn't even scream.

It was a great waste. She was a beauty, and high-spirited. Well, she had been. She was still alive – grotesquely mangled and with a broken back – when they retrieved her. But she wasn't alive for long. She was given to some of the boys to be disposed of. They were cruel, those young lads – they probably amused themselves, and at considerable length, before they allowed her to die. Brother Basilisk pictured the possibilities. He had to admit he was jealous.

The affair with the Russian had been an annoyance. There had been much trouble in procuring her. She had been suspicious of Filippo and had only been acquired by pure frontal assault – which was dangerous – and at night. Filippo had followed her for days to find the right moment. She was briefly alone, walking back to her hotel after attending a concert of Bach and Mozart on the Capitoline Hill. She stopped for an instant to admire the facade of a building – Palazzo Colonna in piazza Santi Apostoli – the street was deserted – and *snatch*, she'd been grabbed from behind, given an injection, and, collapsing and unconscious, she'd been bundled into a car. At that moment, tourists came out of a side street. It could easily have gone wrong.

Then there was the American – the Saint Peter's Square blonde in the tight bright scarlet dress, another perfect specimen, strutting her stuff – the whore! But she'd been lucky. She fought like a demon; people had rushed to help, then the police on motorcycles had arrived, and the whore had gotten away.

Satan works in mysterious ways. These failures had been satanic blessings in disguise. With the girl called Kate, they had reached a pinnacle of perfection. And they had taken extra precautions. She was clearly clever, tough as nails, and crafty; but there was not a single moment when she could have escaped. And she was intelligent enough to know it. There was nowhere to escape to. The window the Russian had crawled out of had been barred. And Father Ottavio was even more pleased with this one; he had told Brother Basilisk that Cardinal Ambrosiano was delighted. "This one," Father Ottavio had said, "is ideal!"

When Brother Basilisk leaned over her – saying, almost affectionately, "You really should appreciate what a great privilege it is" – and when his huge, strange, fat, babyish face was breathing heavily on her, within an inch of her eyes, Kate almost blinked, almost gagged.

But she managed to keep her stare unfocused and fixed. She must look totally paralyzed, utterly helpless, then maybe, just maybe, if they let their guard down, she could pull something off.

Bits and pieces of bodily control – fragments of her body – were coming back: eyelids, fingertips, hands, tongue. She had to keep her cool. She had to monitor and control the process. The last few hours had been absolutely crazy, and utterly terrifying. Being molded – buried – in plaster – that, maybe, had been the worst. She was sure she was going to lose it and scream – but of course – and luckily – her vocal cords were paralyzed. She couldn't have screamed, or even whimpered, if she'd wanted to.

Now, being wheeled along in the gurney, she experimented, trying to clench her fists. Would the monk notice? First, she clenched the right fist, and then the left; the fingers curled, she could feel them, her nails touched the palm of her hand; she pressed down. *Yes, she could do it! She could do it!* Both hands: she had command of both hands!

The elevator doors hissed open. The monk wheeled her out into what seemed to be a tunnel or corridor. Manacled down, Kate stared, fixedly, straight upward, utterly immobile. Her mind raced.

It was all vague, filtered through her extreme myopia, but the general picture was clear. The corridor had a vaulted ceiling carved out of pure rock; big torches, in black metal casings, gushed yellow columns of flame that snaked up the stone walls. Flames … Religious fanatics burned people at the stake, didn't they? What would it be like, being burned alive? Searing pain flushed through every nerve in her body. Oh, God, how horrible …

Years ago, still a naive teenager, she had stood in Campo de' Fiori in Rome, in the fruit and vegetable market, staring up at the statue of the philosopher Giordano Bruno. The Church burned him alive at the stake in 1600 for heresy. Picturing his fate, even then, she had been shaken by a shiver of fear. Then, there was Joan of Arc, burnt at the stake by the English in Rouen in …When was it? Yes, in 1431! Joan was nineteen years old; they burned her, still alive, an example to all. Thinking of it, Kate's leg twitched, a spasm of fear. Luckily, the monk seemed not to have noticed. Her body was coming alive! She clenched her fist, squeezing it. Whether these new powers would do her any good, she had no idea.

The monk's black cowl was at the edge of her field of vision, hovering above her. The vaulted ceiling rushed by, with its pointed and crossed ribs, like in a Gothic cathedral. It must have been a religious place once – but what kind of religion? The air was hotter, more humid. It smelled of sulfur.

"She is here, Father; the sacred whore – the reincarnation of the goddess – is ready for the supreme sacrifice."

"Excellent! The goddess must die." Father Ottavio's voice was grave, and yet eager, even exalted. "Let us begin,"

CHAPTER 37 – CHIMES OF MIDNIGHT

For the last half-hour, V had been silent. It had been a long drive. We entered the mountains again. I glanced at V. Her features were illuminated, pale and bluish, barely discernible, in the dashboard lights. Outside the car, it was dark. It began to rain, softly at first. Then, the storm came. In an instant, the downpour became a deluge, a body blow. The BMW shuddered. A virtual Niagara hammered the roof and hood. On both sides of the road, rocky cliffs flared up, lit by garish flashes of lightning.

The windshield wipers worked hard, *thump, thump,* pushing sheets of water away. It was clammy and stifling in the car. The windows fogged up. I couldn't see anything. The headlights struggled to pierce the walls of falling water.

"We are almost there, Father. You will see the villa soon, rain permitting; if the lightning flashes again, you will see it."

I waited for another flash and then I saw, through the veil of rain, the infamous Villa Mazana Nera, briefly silhouetted. It was far above us, on a mountain crest, with cypress trees crowded close. It looked ominous – a brooding castle, with towers and turrets and steep gables.

"It's less dire when the sun is out. Inside, the villa is elegant and even airy. It has a pleasant internal courtyard, open to the sky."

"When was it built?"

"It was originally a monastery, from perhaps the eleventh or twelfth centuries. Then it was transformed into a fortified villa; it overlooks a large swath of the countryside – the domain of Count Marbuse, back in the seventeenth and eighteenth centuries. Before the monastery, I think there might have been fortifications dating back to Roman, or Etruscan, or even to prehistoric, times."

"Do you think the underground chapel – where you killed the Count – is still there?"

"I imagine so, Father. They have probably modernized it, but it will be the same dank underground space, the entry to the underworld. And tonight – to judge by the traffic we've monitored – it will probably be filled with satanic worshippers."

"Ah ..." I tried to imagine it – the horrors of a black Mass.

Another five minutes passed. Then we turned up a small steep mountain road. It was unpaved and even narrower than the one we had been on. Gravel spurted under the BMW's wheels. After a minute or two, we came out into a small clearing, surrounded by thick bushes and shrubs. John was waiting for us, inside the Land Cruiser, all lights off except for what looked like one small reading lamp.

"Good." V turned off the ignition and doused the headlights. "Now, Father, we can begin – the time has come to confront the Devil. We shall fight him *mano a mano* – and to the death!"

I glanced at my demon. She was not smiling.

"Whatever will happen, will happen." The Cardinal spread his arms, like a bat about to take flight.

Roger ignored the Cardinal's words and concentrated on the sparks bouncing off the surface of the Crystal, as they hissed, sparkled, and cascaded to the ground. This was a recipe for catastrophe, but at the same time, there was something marvelous in the abyss that separated human technology, represented by the sputtering, coughing, smoke-spewing, primitive, obsolete gasoline-powered generators, and the giant Crystal that dwarfed them in size, beauty, and wonder.

The Crystal had turned his world upside down, imbuing him with a sudden new sense of humility. He had been so certain his theories were right; now, he was almost equally certain they were wrong.

The chugging generators with their cables and clamps, already antiques by human standards, looked ridiculously sinister, while the huge, otherworldly Crystal, stunning in its beauty and apparent simplicity, floated gently in its cradle, vibrating slightly in response to the minuscule electric shocks. It looked sublime.

Roger cleared his throat. "I imagine the Crystal might be a trifle annoyed with us."

"I don't care a fig what the Crystal thinks, Professor Thornhill. The Crystal is my servant. She is my slave. She works for the Dark Force! And therefore, she works for me. I am her master!"

The Cardinal waved his long spindly spider arm in the air. With its knobs and articulations and giant hairs sticking out like antennae, it looked like a bionic robotic limb from a malign future.

"I can see that, Your Eminence. But now, we must think of the effects of this little appetizer, these shocks you are applying to it."

The Cardinal smiled; he was becoming quite fond of this calm, fallible mortal, Professor Roger Thornhill, who now looked like a naked, filthy primitive, a Neanderthal, which was surely what, underneath the civilized facade, he was. Savile Row suits and fine colognes cannot mask the filthy beast within.

"Professor, you are blind. Like others, you grope in the darkness. But soon the blind shall see; the deaf shall hear. And in that instant, they will all be cast down into the eternal abyss. They will become nothing – which is what they always have been; from nothing they came, and to nothing they return."

"Well, this little foretaste will certainly give them an idea of what is coming, Cardinal. But if you want to save the bigger shock for later, you should let the Crystal relax now. And let's monitor the effects in one to three hours – that way you can orchestrate the crescendo of fear."

The Cardinal stared at Roger for a long moment. Then a dreadful smile spread over his face. "Yes, yes, yes, a wonderful idea! Turn it off!" The Cardinal shouted to the monks. "The phrase I might use is 'Orchestrate the crescendo of *terror!*' What do you think?"

"Yes. *Terror* is the right word, Cardinal. It's much better than fear."

The generators wheezed to a halt.

"Good!" Roger stared at the generators. By inventing this silly slogan, he had, perhaps, bought some time for humanity, for the world. Perhaps … And maybe there would be another way to interrupt the madness. The computers got their energy from the generators, and maybe, through the computers, he could turn off the generators, or at least some of them. Even without access to the Internet or direct access to the generators, he might be able to find some cross-circuit, some link, and somehow short-circuit the power, blow the fuses, do something to stop the generators.

"The towers and walls shall tumble, Professor, the trumpets shall sound." The Cardinal turned his ancient, withered face toward Roger. "The trumpets shall announce the Reign of Satan, Professor."

"Yes, the Reign of Satan, it will be very pleasant." Roger wondered if he could stir any remnant of empathy for human beings, any residual sanity in the old buzzard. "Your Eminence, as you know, the effects of the present dose of electric shocks may be felt anywhere, particularly where there are faults or volcanoes – in Hawaii, or in the Massif Central in France, or in Italy, or California, in Japan, in Yellowstone, under the oceans … The world's crust is riven with weak points …"

"Tut! Tut! Trivial details, my dear Professor. From our little cave here, we shall watch events unfold from a lofty cosmic and satanic level."

Roger glanced at the ceiling of the huge cavern. Might it collapse upon them as one effect of the Cardinal's tinkering with the Crystal? If it did, would this bring all the Cardinal's monstrous designs to an end? It was a fanciful thought, certainly, but Roger wished that, somehow, he could talk to the Crystal, perhaps persuade it to stop this nonsense.

The Cardinal beamed. His mouth was turned upward in a caricature of a grin. The man resembled an evil-looking clown Roger had seen many years ago in a country fair just outside Toulouse in France. The clown had scared the dickens out of Kate. Since that day she'd been terrified of clowns.

"*Orchestrate the crescendo of terror* – that is a wonderful phrase, Professor – thank you! I can see why they pay you the *big bucks*!" The Cardinal repeated the phrase with almost spinsterish relish.

Roger smiled. "Yes, the big bucks!" They seemed very small, now, all those big bucks, and fine cars, the beautiful clothes, the costly wines, and exquisite dining, the awards – the worshipful crowds – and the Nobel Prize. *Trivial indeed!*

Roger, chained to his seat, tapped his fingers nervously on the table top. If only he could talk to Kate about what he'd seen. If only he could sit with her, or go for a walk with her, and discuss all these untold and horrendous wonders.

There were things, too, he should have said long ago, but somehow had never said, at least not with the passion he felt, things he must say, when he got the chance; he had been a frivolous man, and a negligent father. But Kate must know how much, whatever his faults, he had always loved and needed her.

"Come on, Father! Let's get wet!" V opened the door.

We jumped out of the car and in an instant, we were soaked. As we ran toward the Land Cruiser, water splashed up around us, drenching my trouser legs. I muttered to myself, "'Tis an awful soaking you're getting, Michael Patrick O'Bryan, and, unless you watch out, you're going to catch your death of cold!" I could just hear Signora Bianchi: "Now, let me get that dried for you, Father, you can't go about soaking wet, Father! It is indecent to see a man of the cloth soaked to the skin!"

We climbed into John's Land Cruiser. The doors chunked shut. It was dry inside, but it was also like being trapped in a box, a metal coffin. The rain drummed on the roof. Even the solidly built vehicle seemed a puny refuge. But the dry warmth had already restored my spirits.

John swiveled a computer screen around, so we could see a satellite image of the villa from several hours ago, when the sky was cloudless, and it was still daylight.

"I've just now obtained some up-to-date schematics and additional aerial photographs. The villa has a new heliport." John used a pencil to point at the screen. "And there's a helicopter parked there – or was a few hours ago; it looks like a Sikorsky s-76."

"That could be useful," V said.

"So, to summarize: the plan is this. V, you go into the villa and neutralize the security system and the guards. Then you open the main gate so that Father O'Bryan and I can drive in with the Land Cruiser. After which you and I will eliminate whatever other security risks there are. Then we locate Father Ottavio and seize him. We use Father Ottavio to track down the so-called Torelli Jewel, the key to the Crystal – and you get from Ottavio whatever other useful information you can glean."

V nodded.

"And if a woman is being sacrificed?" I had to ask the question. Suddenly, I *saw* Kate being laid out on the black granite altar – the vision was instantaneous, vivid and physical, like a punch in the gut.

"If they are going to sacrifice a woman, we will save her, if we are in time." V was all business, her features deadpan.

John pointed to a new image: "This overhead schematic outlines the security systems installed five years ago, and modified two months ago."

"So," V stared at the screen. "What are we up against?"

"The outer wall, here at the perimeter, has been heightened. It's now about fifteen feet high. It has electrified razor-sharp barbed wire running along the top, several strands; above the barbed wire there are infra-red sensor rays that cover up to five feet above the wall, but not below the barbed wire."

V's eyes glowed. She wet her lips. "Plus, I suppose, below the wire, the usual jagged pieces of broken bottles, that sort of thing. Is there any space, here, between the wire and the shards?"

"Not much, V, about a foot, 16 inches in some places, the distance varies. The top of the wall is irregular. You might be able to slip under – just – at this point – here – but I'm not sure. In any case, you'll have to take off your backpack and haul it behind you."

"Okay, good."

I could see V's mind working. It was as if she had linked my mind to hers. And, in fact, she must have sensed this thought, for she glanced at me, winked, and gave me a warm smile that communicated many things: *Yes, I know, Father, we are linked together; and, yes, I know, Father, that you are worried about Kate Thornhill; and, yes, we will do our best; but, no, Father, I really don't think that you will lose your soul because of me; you are after all a good man and a man of God.* All this in a wink and a smile. It was uncanny. It was like having another soul. I wondered: am I learning, then, about love – about *agape* – about true friendship – and from a demon-vampire? Can this be, Michael Patrick O'Bryan? Or are friendship and love the same? How, if I am entranced and ensnared by this creature, do I stay true to myself, to my relationship with God?

Inwardly, I prayed for my salvation.

The image on the computer screen shifted again. It was now an overhead schematic of the villa with bright blinking dots at various positions.

John indicated one of the dots. "These dots are cameras; they are set at a variety of locations and cover almost all approaches to the villa; the cameras rotate; they do not cover everything all the time. For short intervals, five to ten seconds, there are blind spots. Here, you can see the arc of coverage for each camera." Each bright dot emitted a radiant arc, which swung back and forth.

"Okay." V nodded.

"You'll have to look for an opening. Vertical coverage by each camera is about ten yards near the perimeter wall; but parts of the wall are hidden from the camera by vegetation – here, here, and here."

"Right." V ran her tongue along her lips.

"There are pressure alarms on the lawn and in the shrubbery that will go off if something as heavy as a person steps on them, but not if something as light as a dog moves over them. However, we don't know where these pressure alarms are; they were installed by a different contractor."

"Okay," V poked John on the shoulder, "so you don't know everything, John! You are not God. I always wondered."

"Nobody's perfect, love." He paused. "Then there are two dogs, Dobermans I think, and three armed guards – plus one or two or more men in the control room on the second floor just to the right of the top of the main staircase – there. These guys watch the camera feeds in real-time."

"Right." V bit her lip.

"So first you will need to take control of the security control room. It is at the top of the main staircase in this wing." John pointed at the schematic. "Then Father O'Bryan and I will come in through the main gate, help you mop up, and grab Father Ottavio. Judging by his cell phone signal, he is still there."

"The challenge will be to neutralize the guards and staff before Father Ottavio is warned and has time to escape."

"In a nutshell, yes. Then you can drain his brain, and find out about the key."

"Okay, let's do it," V said.

And before I realized what she was doing she had slipped out of her jeans and T-shirt and underwear. "Sorry, Father, but you've seen me naked before."

"Indeed. So, I have!" Inwardly I said another prayer for the salvation of my soul. My curiosity, however, got the best of me, and so I watched as this remarkable creature slipped into an elastic, skintight, black, leather-latex synthetic catsuit. As she pulled it on, it snapped and hissed, almost as if it were alive. She tugged on high-tread, buckle-up, combat boots, slipped on a backpack and a sidearm, and grabbed a submachine-gun, which she hitched over her shoulder. Then she put what looked like a kit of needle guns on her belt and fitted what looked like a communications device into her ear. The total performance took less than a minute.

"This device, Father, will allow us to communicate." V tapped her ear. The outfit looked like she was naked, merely coated in matte-black paint. Here was an entirely new version of the demon – a high-tech, special-ops Amazon.

John began to apply camouflage makeup to her face, coating it in a pattern of thick, dull black alternating with matte, aquatic, lily-pad green; the whites of her eyes shone, startlingly bright against the black and green camouflage.

"Done?" she whispered.

"Done, love." John handed her the paintbrush.

"You know, John, I don't like the feel of this weather – there is too much electricity; something is happening, and it's happening too fast, a buildup of static energy."

She froze, a wary animal, listening. The rain pounded on the roof. She shook herself, rolled down the window. Even in the rain, the air outside pressed in, sultry, heavy, hot …

"Earthquake weather?" John asked.

"Yes. Even worse. It's something bad – and coming fast, faster than I thought." V began applying camouflage to John's face. "John probably won't need this, Father, if I do my job correctly, but if he has to rescue me in the villa's garden, the more invisible he is, the better."

At this point, I realized that John was in military gear too. He must have changed while waiting for us to arrive. His outfit was as skintight as V's, revealing a lean, hard warrior's body.

"Something *is* building up." V added a few finishing touches to the criss-cross pattern on John's cheeks. Then, leaning back, contemplating her work, she said, "You are a thing of beauty, John."

"Thank you, love!"

We climbed out of the Land Cruiser. Battered by the rain, we clambered up a narrow, slippery path, and came to a jagged outcropping of rock about twenty yards above our parking spot. John took out a pair of binoculars, and, cupping his hands to shelter them from the downpour, aimed them at the villa. From this position, we could see over the walls and inside the villa's compound.

"Here, Father, have a look."

I peered through the binoculars as rain streamed down my face and under my collar. I saw BMWs, Alfa Romeos, Land Rovers, and other luxury vehicles, all parked inside the compound.

"Usually the cult begins the ceremony, if they are following tradition, at 11:30 p. m." V glanced at her wrist watch. "And they make the human sacrifice at midnight, exactly."

"It's 11:30 now." John glanced at V.

"Okay. We go! And we go now!"

We ran toward the Land Cruiser.

CHAPTER 38 – MARCUS AURELIUS

"Weird clouds." Scarlett shivered.

"Yes, stormy – stormy weather." Jian stared at the swift-moving clouds that were piling up over Rome, and at the damp glowing air, reflecting the lights of the city and glowing on the burnt sienna rooftops, on the slender towers, and on the curved black cobblestones. There was something eerie about the intensity of the damp, glowing air, as if it were alive.

Scarlett shivered. "It's spooky."

Jian put his arm around her.

"So, this is the Capitol, the center of the Roman Empire." Scarlett looked around. "Il Campidoglio." She pronounced the word "Campidoglio" carefully, with the liquid "gli" sound, like "lee-ho." They were gazing up at the statue of Emperor-Philosopher Marcus Aurelius, astride his warrior steed, in the middle of the cobblestoned square, on top of the Capitoline Hill, surrounded on three sides by the arcades and facades of Renaissance palaces. On the fourth side was Michelangelo's broad gentle ramped staircase, the *Cordonata*, which led down to the center of Rome. The whole square had been designed by Michelangelo, and Scarlett thought it was a supreme balancing act, restful and intimate, serene, powerful and open – with a splendid vista over the city.

"He's one of my favorite characters," Scarlett said.

"Marcus Aurelius?"

"Yes."

"Emperor from 161 to 180 AD." Jian tightened his hold on Scarlett's shoulders, pulling her close.

"You, my dear Jian Chang, are an encyclopedia!" She pinched him.

"Ouch!"

"One of his sayings I really like," Scarlett said, "is '*It is not death you should fear; but you should fear never beginning to live.*'"

"Yes. People can die without ever having lived."

Scarlett leaned her head against his shoulder. "But not us."

"No, not us."

In a first-year philosophy course, Scarlett had read excerpts from the *Meditations* of Aurelius. She became interested in the man, gobbling up books about him, and imagining the philosopher Emperor out on the far northern frontiers of the Empire, bravely defending civilization from the barbarians, in distant forests, in snow blizzards, and in pouring rain.

"Look where you're standing," Jian said, pointing down.

Scarlett moved her foot.

Just at the point of her toe was a small round plaque. It said that they were standing at the exact geographic center of the Eternal City.

A church bell began to ring.

Scarlett glanced at her watch. "It's 11:30," she said. "Almost midnight!" She glanced at Jian and leaned up and kissed him. He put his arms around her and pressed his lips to hers.

"How strange it is," she said. "How weird."

"What?"

"That the two of us should have met like this – through pure chance. From the instant I saw you …"

"Yes. It was the same for me."

As they kissed, Marcus Aurelius suddenly moved. The pavement under their feet trembled. Sirens wailed.

Scarlett looked up; the night sky had turned deep orange; the air glowed, suspenseful, even heavier with electricity … Again, the earth trembled.

"Did we do that? Make the earth move?"

"I don't think so." Jian had to smile.

"It's another earthquake?"

"Yes, another earthquake."

CHAPTER 39 – SHE-DEVIL

"Fuck!" U Pizzu got off the bed and went to the window and looked out. "Fuck!"

It was 11:25 p.m. precisely.

It had been a long day.

He had booked into a hotel just off Piazza Navona, an elegant, small hotel, on a tiny tree-lined square, where prime ministers and presidents liked to stay. The hotel had comfortable suites hidden up under the steep tiled roof, and little balconies where you could sit and watch the night sky, if you were so inclined, and admire the chaos of old rooftops in this bohemian – but gentrified and expensive – part of Medieval and Renaissance Rome.

The lights of the city were reflected in mottled swiftly moving patterns in the sky, and to the west clouds were piling up in a weird unsettling way.

"Fuck!" The air tingled with menace. It was earthquake weather, no doubt about it, overcharged with static electricity, hairy hysterical weather, the kind of weather that drove birds, rattlesnakes and rabbits crazy. People too. Birds were swirling in the air, in disjointed formations, whipping back and forth, screeching like banshees. Fuck! They were having a collective nervous breakdown. Normally, the birds would settle down at dusk and snooze away the night perched peacefully in trees and nooks and rooftops. But, no, not tonight: here they were, almost midnight, swirling and screeching wild things – black omens of dire events to come.

U Pizzu closed the wooden shudders, shut the window and pulled the curtains closed, banishing the chaos of the night. The air-conditioning began to cool the room and dry the damp invading troubled air.

U Pizzu removed his shoes and socks. He pulled off all his clothes. He hung everything up neatly in the built-in closet, and he put his trusty Walther P.38 on the bedside table. He looked at the bed – queen-size – room for two people. He sighed. He saw the face of the dead girl from the Hummer staring up at him and he said, out loud, "*Mi dispiace, Signorina.* I'm sorry, kid, I'm sorry, I really am."

He rubbed his jaw. "I'm getting old. I'm getting sentimental."

He sighed. "Fuck it!"

He lay down on top of the sheets and stared at the ceiling. The life of crime was not what it was cracked up to be. It was not like the movies. It wasn't fucking glamorous! Most of the time, it was grimy and gritty and lonely – and boring! Death and fear and betrayal were everywhere. He reached over and turned off the light. The room now was velvety dark – just a little red light indicating the smoke detector.

He closed his eyes. What a weird meeting he and Santino had had at the Vatican! They had gone back to report to Father Andrea on what they had found in the sewer. The good Father was a weird duck. And he had a crazy theory about how Father O'Bryan had escaped U Pizzu's two hit men; about what had killed the two *picciotti*; about what had torn Paolo and Franco into little pieces of smoking meat and ribbons of uncoiled intestine.

"It was a demon," Father Andrea said, "a female demon; it was the she-devil."

"A *she-devil?*" U Pizzu glanced at Santino and winked. "*The* she-devil? Really? How interesting! Do you know her, Father Andrea? Do you know this demon, this girl *demon?*"

"Yes."

"You've met her?"

"Yes."

"Hmm. And what does she look like? I mean ..."

"Covered in scales, with fangs, yes, fangs, and claws, and snake eyes – and she was naked, she wore no clothes; she was turquoise, green and gold and ... beautiful in a way ... I thought at first that she was a work of art."

"Well ..." U Pizzu blinked. This took a bit of digesting, but it was in fact an interesting concept – a naked female demon covered in scales, hmm ...

"So, Father Andrea, let's be clear about this. This *demon* you're talking about is a *woman?*" U Pizzu was not superstitious and, though he crossed himself and followed the rituals, he thought that religion was bunk, silly fairy tales – smoke and mirrors and snake oil – for girls and gossipy old women and sissies and nervous Nellie fusspots; just another grandiose extortion racket. The priests were carnival shills and the believers were rubes and dupes. But after seeing the two bodies – or bits of bodies – in the sewer, he was ready to consider any explanation: demons; angels; witches; extraterrestrial aliens;

the Archangel Gabriel himself; crazy homicidal Nigerian cyber-bully dwarfs wearing black-and-red pom-poms; famished sewer-haunting urban legend albino crocodiles; anything.

U Pizzu narrowed his eyes and examined the priest. Father Andrea was in his late eighties at least, maybe even much older; he was gaunt, all bones, with waxen skin and milky eyes; but the good Father did know stuff, secret valuable Vatican stuff; he knew where the bodies were buried; he knew the money conduits and pipelines, the money storage tanks, the money valves, and the money control panels, and he knew who *owned* whom, who *owed* what to whom and *why*, that sort of stuff. Father Andrea was the indispensable right-hand man of Cardinal Ambrosiano, the crimson-robed, money-laundering machine.

"So, the demon is a *woman* ...?" U Pizzu let the question hang in the air. The good Father looked absent; he did not look in the best of health, even paler and more fragile than usual; maybe it was indigestion.

But Father Andrea wasn't absent. He was thinking – and for that he needed to quiet the tumult of his passions, and silence all the clamorous doubtful voices rising in dangerous revolt in his mind. For decades, he had worked for Cardinal Antonio Xavier Paulus Ambrosiano. In fact, he had dedicated his whole life to the man, more than to the Church, more than to Satan Himself.

"A woman ...?" U Pizzu said, trying to prompt the priest.

Father Andrea didn't answer. He slowly got up from his desk and turned his back on U Pizzu and Santino and stood for a long moment, hands clasped behind his back, looking out over the rooftops of Rome. As he stared out at the brilliant blue sky, Father Andrea had a bizarre, almost giddy sensation. He was suddenly certain he was about to be betrayed – betrayed by Cardinal Ambrosiano – but betrayed how? Did the Cardinal really intend to destroy the Earth? Was that possible? Was the Cardinal insane? But *how* would he destroy Earth? How?

"Yes," Father Andrea said, finally. He turned away from the window and focused his gaunt, hooded, watery gaze on U Pizzu. "The demon is a woman." He paused and swallowed, his Adam's apple bobbing up and down. "Many years ago, this she-devil killed a Brother Filippo, poor man, right in front of my eyes, drank him dry, all his blood – nothing left but a weightless, empty, rustling husk."

"Really?"

Father Andrea sighed. "She has interfered with the Satanic Order of the Apocalypse a number of times."

"The Satanic Order of the Apocalypse, eh?" U Pizzu frowned. "That's not nice of her, not nice at all! How dare she! Well, Father, where can we find this demon?" U Pizzu had a gnawing feeling he might already know something about this girl demon. What was it? He tried to remember. Life was full of incidents – murders, betrayals, disappearances, celebrations, fornications, births, deaths, birthdays, bank deposits and transfers, politicians to corrupt, bombs going off – so it was hard to pick out what precisely this intimation of a memory might be, and where it came from. And then, yes, in a flash, it occurred to him …

Yes, yes, yes …!

Something had happened, years ago … what? He'd have to figure it out because, yes, he wanted to meet this demon. It would be an interesting challenge, a unique experience: to look into the eyes of the Devil herself! What is death like? U Pizzu wanted to ask her. What is it like to be dead and to be a demon? How does it feel? He repeated, louder this time, "So, Father, where can we find her, this demon?"

"I … I don't know where to f … f … find her." Father Andrea was still standing but was even more pale than usual; and he had developed a stutter. U Pizzu waited. Santino, slumped down in his chair, said nothing.

Outside, far away, bells were chiming and, even farther away, music was playing, band music, very faint, a march of some kind, from another world, yes, a Sousa march, *Semper Fidelis*. Ah, yes, U Pizzu remembered. There was an American band in town, he'd read about it: The US Marine Corps.

Dum-dum, dump da dump, dum … The music invaded U Pizzu's head. Might have been nice to be a soldier. Of course, you get shot at … and then there's the discipline. Right! The discipline – no way he could have been a soldier.

"How many people have seen her?" U Pizzu was getting antsy. Outside, life was going on, life was draining away. The march, faint as it was, stirred the blood, brought rousing thoughts, aspirations, thoughts of sunshine and warm breezes and fluttering leaves and sweet lips. It was pure poetry.

Father Andrea closed his eyes and sat down heavily. The high-backed chair rolled toward the window. Startled, Father Andrea steadied it by blindly grabbing at the edge of his desk.

U Pizzu blinked and gazed at the priest. Things were maybe getting a bit too vivid for the good Father. You might be a priest and try to keep life – emotions, yearnings, sex, violence, truth, desire – far away from your innermost secret self, locked away in some safe deposit box deep in your mind, but then reality had a way of kicking in all the doors, slamming itself right into you – a punch in the gut, an ache in the soul.

Father Andrea swallowed. "I saw her – and Cardinal Ambrosiano saw her – he even talked to her. It was many years ago, when she killed Brother Filippo. It was when we were recruiting … ah, we recruit young w … w … women for our rituals."

"So I've heard."

"You've heard?" Father Andrea was suddenly alert. "What have you heard? From whom – and what?"

"From Larione, Gaetano Larione," U Pizzu said. "Gaetano was talking wild – something about sacrifices … I didn't pay attention." U Pizzu smiled. Of course, he had paid attention – to every word. "He's full of … he *was* full of, ah, shit, begging your pardon, Father Andrea. *Sacrifices* – really!"

"Religion always requires sacrifice." Father Andrea's face stiffened.

"Well, Larione ain't going to talk no more. Not about sacrifices. Not about nothing."

"Christ was sacrificed – blood and flesh." Father Andrea leaned back in his chair, his two hands flat on the desk. "And the sacrifice is repeated in the holy sacrament – literal transubstantiation, His real flesh and blood."

"Yeah," said U Pizzu, thinking, and so we are all cannibals, eating God's blood and flesh every Sunday or whatever. We should be crouching in a jungle beating the tom-toms with our fists, chewing on our neighbor's bones, not kneeling, hands clasped in submission, in a goddamn church. "Sure, but … Larione is not going to talk no more – ever. That's the important thing."

"Without sacrifice, there is no holiness, no satanic glory."

"Yeah, yeah, of course," U Pizzu said, thinking that maybe he didn't appreciate the subtleties of theology, but he sure as hell didn't understand what satanic glory had to do with Jesus. Maybe he should ask his wife. Maria Grazia read a lot of books, knew virtually everything, and taught history in a Palermo high school. Sometimes, late at night, when they both woke up and, suddenly, went at it, U Pizzu thought, with utter delight, he was fucking the sexiest librarian – and teacher – with the richest, best-stocked mind in the whole western world.

"All the evil in the universe has to find a home – a scapegoat." Father Andrea was staring at some spot in space about three feet to U Pizzu's left. "Total sacrifice means total redemption."

"Yeah, of course." U Pizzu frowned. He was wondering what in the world the old fart was talking about. These priests sometimes got caught up in high-falutin airy-fairy fishnets and spider webs of their own making. Too much thinking was dangerous – you let it take hold, like a fever, and you never knew where you were going to end up – totally crazy, mostly, and then dead.

"Sure, I mean, yeah, you're right, Father Andrea … that's what Gaetano did for us – he made the total sacrifice. Total sacrifice, total redemption. He won't talk no more." U Pizzu glanced at Santino; Santino rolled his eyes.

U Pizzu figured he'd try again. "Now look, Father, about this girl demon –"

"Oh, yes, yes. You must excuse me!" Father Andrea cleared his throat. "Where was I? Ah, yes, the Order recruits young women for its rituals, often young foreign women traveling alone, or walking the streets alone, at dusk. So many young women – and it's very irresponsible of them – traveling alone, walking alone." Father Andrea licked his lips. "They shouldn't walk alone. And certainly not dressed like whores. Such display and boldness are a pernicious result of the evil moral relativism of our modern godless secular age, as the late Sainted Pope Benedict XVI so often and so wisely pointed out. People no longer believe in Satan or Evil; they have no reference points, so they wander, blind to sublimity, without a moral compass, spiritually empty …"

Yeah, thought U Pizzu, like it's the girls' fucking fault they go for a walk – maybe wear some cute hot sexy outfit – tight shorts, tight dress, short skirt, whatever, gives everybody some innocent pleasure – and they get kidnapped and raped and killed by some assholes and this idiot blames the girls. What is the fucking world coming to? *Moral relativism of our fucking modern fucking secular age!* What is this fucking old dolt nattering about? So – people think for themselves, so they make their own fucking judgments; this is a crime? Isn't that what freedom is about? So, girls go for walks – so girls like to look good! They are a gift to the world! And they should be insulted, spit at, shot, kidnapped, and raped? U Pizzu's blood boiled. He looked around at Father Andrea's office, at the rows of books, at the Cross, at the image of the Holy Virgin.

What is truly infinite around here, U Pizzu fumed, was bullshit. Infinite bullshit! He thought of his own eldest daughter, Adrianna, pure as snow, a true beauty, sexy like her mother, super-intelligent, in her third year in business administration at the Bocconi University in Milan, already had a BA, will soon get her MBA, then get a postgraduate degree, maybe Oxford or Stanford, something like that, great sense of humor, top marks all the way, definitely her own boss; nothing is too good for that kid, and if anybody laid a finger on her, or on her two younger sisters, he'd …

He'd better change the subject. "So, this demon – you reckon she was the one tore my two guys into shreds, down in the tunnel?"

"Yes, it must have been her. You see, Father O'Bryan stumbled upon information about the Satanic Order of the Apocalypse, confidential information; and we know that the demon, from time to time, also takes an interest in the Order; so, putting two and two together … And talking of Father O'Bryan, what do we do about him? He's still a loose end. The Cardinal insists that he be dealt with."

"Maybe the demon killed him," said U Pizzu. "Or maybe she feels – how can I put this –a sort of tenderness for the *good guys*, eh, Father. And maybe, misguided as she is, being a demon and all, she probably lacks that moral compass you and dear old Pope Benedict were talking about, her values may be lost in relativity and all, and so, confused morally speaking as this demon undoubtedly is, she may feel that this Father O'Bryan is one of the good guys, it's a deplorable mistake, I know. So maybe she didn't eat him; maybe she's kept him for herself – like a pet or a consigliere or something. Maybe if we find Father O'Bryan, we find her; and maybe if we find her, we find Father O'Bryan. Let me think about it."

"Have you checked O'Bryan's rooming house?"

"Yeah, we searched the rooms."

Santino cleared his throat. "Landlady said he didn't come home last night, she's real worried; nice lady, Signora Bianchi, offered us coffee and chocolate brownies." Santino had been sitting sagely silent. Miracle of miracles, thought U Pizzu, what the fuck had got into the boy?

Father Andrea took a deep breath, and then he exhaled. "I don't know where the she-devil is, but, given that she has probably taken Father O'Bryan, I suspect she might want the Torelli Jewel, and I do know where the Torelli Jewel is."

"The Torelli Jewel," said U Pizzu, wondering what the hell this Torelli Jewel was. "What is the Torelli Jewel? And where might it be, Father?"

"It's a sort of crystal jewel and it's in a small museum, in a small town, in the mountains, in the Abruzzo region." Father Andrea made a little steeple of his hands and stared at the points of his fingers. "You see, we think the she-devil has been snooping around the Vatican. We know she asked a journalist considered close to the Vatican about something she described as an oblong crystal, something about three inches long, eight-sided. That is a very good description of the Torelli Jewel. The journalist made inquiries for her. Nobody told him anything. Well, nobody knew anything. But his snooping was reported to me."

"Why would the demon want it?"

"I don't know."

"What is it precisely?"

"I don't know."

"I see," said U Pizzu.

"I suspect the she-demon thinks the Torelli Jewel rightly belongs to her. The journalist said she seemed agitated, even angry. But otherwise – I have no idea why she wants it."

"Ah," said U Pizzu, thinking, if the blood-drinking she-demon is interested in the Torelli Jewel, then so am I …

When U Pizzu and Santino exited Father Andrea's office, they left behind them a large briefcase with roughly seven hundred thousand euros to be "invested" through the Vatican Bank, or the Institute for the Works of Religion, as it is usually known. The receipt, a scrap of paper, was in U Pizzu's pants pocket. It was written in a scribbled code and disguised as part of a casual and indecipherable restaurant receipt from a Tunisian resort where U Pizzu had recently spent a holiday; and indeed, he and Maria Grazia had eaten in that very restaurant, on that very day.

Just outside Father Andrea's office, a black Mercedes driven by one of the strange monks was waiting. "No, thank you," said U Pizzu. He turned to Santino. "Let's just walk – I don't want the Cardinal's spies listening to us. I'm getting a bad feeling about this."

"You know what, Pizzu?"

"No, what?"

"I'm going to become a fucking Buddhist!"

"Yeah?" U Pizzu thought for a moment. "Me too. You know, the priests are worse than we are. They *think* they are good – or at least they *claim* to think they are good. We *know* we are bad. Whereas …"

"Yeah, whereas …" Santino kicked at an empty cola can. "People shouldn't leave shit around. I mean, right here, in Vatican City!" Santino stooped down, picked up the can and dropped it in a garbage receptacle.

Santino, the good citizen! U Pizzu glanced down via Conciliazione, imposing stone facades and monumental lampposts, all stone, all dead marble, overall a desolate funereal feeling, all heading toward the Tiber and the heart of Rome. "Makes me nervous, the whole thing."

"Yeah, me too, nervous. I have a real bad feeling," said Santino, wiping his hands.

"That why you didn't say anything, why you were so silent?"

"I was depressed, fucking depressed."

"You still believed in Santa Claus!"

"Yeah, yeah, I did. And the Holy Ghost."

"And now?" U Pizzu gave Santino a fatherly look.

"Don't ask."

They walked in silence down desolate via Conciliazione, past crouching Castel Saint Angelo, once the tomb of the Emperor Hadrian; then they crossed the pedestrian Bridge of Angels with its statues of Saint Paul and Saint Peter and with the ten angels holding the various instruments of Christ's passion.

"How the man suffered," said U Pizzu, looking up at one of the angels.

"Who?"

"Christ the Savior," said U Pizzu.

"Oh. Yeah. Him."

They left the bridge and headed up through a series of narrow tangled cobblestoned streets toward Piazza Navona. Then they had a stand-up espresso at the Tre Scalini bar on the edge of the piazza.

"Let's go and eat," said Santino. "My stomach is growling."

"Always hungry! Ah, youth! But you're right. It's time to eat." U Pizzu glanced at his watch.

"Let's go to where the priests are and watch and learn."

The restaurant, the Living Fountain, was frequented by the princes of the Church. It was in a big vaulted space, just next to Piazza Navona, and not far from the Italian Senate. You entered the restaurant by stepping downwards to a tiny magical Alice-in-Wonderland door and pushing your way through the door into a heavily ecclesiastical and sybaritic culinary atmosphere. The place featured, as waitresses, alluring girls in native costumes, mostly from what used to be called "The Third World."

U Pizzu glanced around. The place was a favorite rendezvous for high Vatican officials, cardinals, and bishops, visiting priest VIPs, and, even, sometimes, for various Popes who graced such spots with their holy presence. A few years ago, some cynical and irreverent French journalists – obviously suffering from the decadent moral relativism of the modern age – had claimed that the place used indentured – or slave – labor. The girls, they implied, were virtually slaves. The Church of course closed ranks with the Living Fountain, and any of the girls who might have complained were reportedly intimidated – or chose to disappear. No one knew of course whether any of this was true. U Pizzu found such gossip amusing – and instructive. Dirt is gold.

While Santino ogled the waitresses, U Pizzu nursed his drink and pondered a number of events that might have involved this she-demon character that so fascinated Father Andrea.

The first was a mysterious affair that U Pizzu had never quite figured out. Years ago, a fishing boat had pulled out from a small fishing village on the Adriatic coast in Apulia, and it came back – after a rendezvous with a Liberian freighter ten miles off the coast – carrying a cargo of twenty-five girls aged between seventeen and nineteen from Ukraine and Russia and Moldova. Usually, the girls would come in by land, on trucks; but there'd been a little trouble up in the Veneto and on the Austrian border, so U Pizzu's suppliers wanted to "experiment" with a new route. It was a small shipment, but still …

Each girl would be worth about ten thousand euros when the pimps bought them; so, the shipment of twenty-five girls was worth, gross, two hundred and fifty thousand euros – peanuts, really, but it was just an experiment with the new supply chain.

It was night, and the fishing boat had made it in past the coastguard. It stopped about a hundred yards out from the beach, while a couple of rowboats went out to fetch the girls. The night was dark, and a truck was waiting. The girls thought they were coming to be domestic servants or maybe even strippers. But in fact, they were imported for prostitution. Disciplining the girls wasn't a problem. Since they didn't have papers, legally they didn't exist; they didn't speak Italian; they had no friends or contacts, so there was no protection for them. So, usually, there weren't any complications. The pimps and traffickers could keep a girl in line. They could beat her up in a way that left no marks; or scar and disfigure her so she was ugly and worthless, a freak, kept around to clean the toilets or for sadists with special tastes in the grotesque, and such girls, with their faces slashed up, were a warning to the others; or the pimps could just kill her or, better, they could hook her on drugs, or threaten to kill her father, mother, and sisters, nieces and nephews in the old country where, of course, the pimps and traffickers had contacts or "correspondents" in or near the godforsaken pissant little village she came from. If her sister's daughter disappears, well, the girl would stay in line. And if the girl had a kid of her own, left, say, with her parents, well, even better. The kid could disappear, maybe killed, maybe recruited into the sex life, maybe kept alive, just barely, in slavery of one kind or another. So, discipline was rarely a problem. Besides, mostly, the cops were not interested in girls who were whores, particularly whores from foreign countries – or, if the cops did get interested, the pimps could buy protection from the guys on the vice squad, if there was a vice squad, or blackmail a cop who had dirty hands, or arrange for it to look like the cop had dirty – really dirty – hands, if he happened to be a squeaky clean, non-cooperative, high-principled cop; the ways of the Lord are infinite.

U Pizzu didn't like prostitution – it was messy and involved a lot of unreliable lowlifes and, frankly, he didn't like the idea of women being exploited in this way – but he had to keep his finger in the prostitution pie, otherwise his competitors' appetites would grow. In the organized crime business, where all the markets overlap and are connected, if you aren't present everywhere, you end up nowhere. Drugs, arms, prostitution, slave labor, extortion, industrial espionage, money laundering, corrupt subcontracting, corrupt waste disposal, knock-off fashions and forgeries of all kinds were all part of one interlinked system, so he'd figured he had to finance this girl-import operation, however unpleasant it might be. Naturally he had to pay a percentage to the local Mafia of Apulia, the *Sacra Corona Unita*, the masters of the heel of the Italian boot, since the transit went through their territory, but U Pizzu figured that, after expenses, he'd still clear at least one hundred and twenty-five thousand euros, net, and tax free of course – all for making a few phone calls.

The truck was to take the twenty-five girls by gravel side roads to an isolated farmhouse, inland about twenty miles, where they'd be auctioned off. Drinks and a buffet had been laid on for the buyers – guys from Milan and Rome and Amsterdam.

The shipment was well protected. There was the driver and one guy with an AK up front, and two guys in the back of the truck with the girls, the usual Mafia *picciotti*, foot soldiers, with AK-47s and brass knuckles, in case the girls got any ideas. One of the *picciotti* spoke Russian, just in case.

So far, so good …

But then, things went wrong. The truck stalled. It ran out of gas, though it had been topped up just hours before. So there they were, stopped, on a country road, with twenty-five girls who were beginning to get nervous and suspicious – maybe they were thinking that being transferred to a smelly fishing trawler, then rowed ashore in darkness, and then taken in the back of truck, guarded by guys with AKs, was not an auspicious start to their new life in a new country, maybe not the way to become a domestic servant, or even a nightclub stripper ...

The driver, a thirty-three-year-old Sicilian from Castellammare del Golfo, Giuseppe Santoro, a solid reliable guy, had just flipped open his cell phone to call the farmhouse. "I think somebody punched a hole in the fucking gas tank!" And that's when things got interesting. U Pizzu could picture the scene.

It's night, on an isolated one-lane dirt road out in the country. Crickets and cicadas are making the usual reassuring racket; there's a nice warm salty breeze wafting in from the Adriatic; you can smell the hay, the dust on the road.

The truck has sputtered to a stop.

"What the fuck?" The two *picciotti* lower the tailgate and jump out. They tell the girls to stay put. They don't want a gaggle of Ukrainian and Russian and Moldovan blondes wandering around in farmer's fields and getting lost.

One of the girls says, "I've got to take a pee – please!"

"Okay, take a pee there, where I can see you."

So, the girl climbs out of the truck and goes to the side of the road, gravel and sand and dust, hitches up her dress, rolls down her panties, crouches in the ditch.

You can hear the gush of the pee and maybe, too, the breeze in the trees. It's a nice peaceful warm night: paradise in southern Italy ... then ...

Ping! Ping!

Ping! Ping!

The two *picciotti* are down. It is perfectly professional – two shots each: forehead, chest; forehead, chest; two shots for each man – to make sure he is truly dead, like in the elite special force's manuals; and whoever did it uses a silencer. The two *picciotti* are killed by a whisper.

The peeing girl screams; and maybe some of the girls in the back of the truck scream too.

"What the hell was that?" Pasquale Clerico, the guy who's riding shotgun and sitting beside Giuseppe climbs out of the cab, gun drawn, to see what the fuck is going on. He's dead before his foot hits the ground, falling face down, neat little hole in his forehead, neat little hole in his chest. His AK-47 smashes into the dust beside him.

Good old Giuseppe Santoro – sitting frozen with fear behind the steering wheel – figures he's a dead man. U Pizzu imagines it. Fucking horrible! You can have loads of experience, be a cool guy, brave as Caesar, still it gets to you. Your number's up. You know it. Cold sweat breaks out. Your days are numbered – in terms of seconds, maybe two, three seconds.

Giuseppe takes a deep breath. "I'm coming out," he shouts. "Don't shoot!" He climbs down from the truck with his hands in the air. Then, he says later, what he sees makes him think he's landed in a fucking Hollywood movie. Standing only a few feet away, on the edge of the road, is a woman dressed all in black, like a latex catsuit, skintight, like Angelina what's-her-name superwoman in those old archeology action films, with black-and-green military-type camouflage on her face.

She's standing, legs braced apart, in the classic shooting position, sniper rifle hooked over her shoulder, knife holster at her ankle, small backpack for other stuff, little mike at her mouth – which means she's not alone – and a neat little machine pistol pointed right at Giuseppe's forehead, and she says, with a smile, in Italian, and as polite and gentle as can be, "Giuseppe, would you please do me the favor of lying down on the road, face down, hands behind your back. And throw your pistol away too, please, Giuseppe, the one tucked in the back of your belt, and the straight-razor in your pocket. And your cell phone! Thank you so much!"

Giuseppe does what he's told. U Pizzu understands. If he had tried anything, the lady would have dropped him dead in a nano-second. She knew his name; she knew what he was carrying. It was like she had X-ray eyes. She walks over, calm, relaxed, bends down, and handcuffs him, wrists behind his back, and attaches him, still lying belly down, by a chain to the bumper of the truck.

Then she tells the girls, in Russian and Italian and English, to stay put, not to run away. "Help is coming," she says. Above all, they are not to run away.

"Ciaò, Giuseppe," she says. In Italian, she has a Tuscan accent, with a touch of Venetian maybe, Giuseppe says afterwards, and she had a real nice voice, sexy really, seductive and sweet, made you want to date her, or something stupid like that.

And she walks off into the night.

Suddenly the girls are all talking at once, making a terrible racket. Giuseppe doesn't understand a word, and there he is, handcuffed, lying on his belly in the dust, still chained to the fucking truck, fucking undignified. He thinks he hears, in the distance, a motorbike gunning into action, revving up, and speeding away, maybe *two* motorbikes.

Yeah, she must have an accomplice – backup, standing by.

Fucking superwoman! Jesus!

Only minutes later the Carabinieri arrive, and with them a carload of people from that Rome charitable organization that looks after ex-prostitutes and a guy from a Milan outfit that protects illegal immigrants, and a journalist from the muck-raking Rome daily *Il Messaggero,* a reporter from RAI TV, complete with camera, and a girl journalist from the weekly, *L'Espresso.*

So, it was a well-planned, well-thought-out job, even down to the public relations. The lady was very confident in her timing, down to the minute, a real professional. Must have had inside information.

But she was totally human. Both Giuseppe and the girls agreed she was a woman in a catsuit and camouflage; no mention of fangs, claws, creepy scales, or snake eyes.

But somehow …

Somehow … somehow, somehow …

U Pizzu wondered. Could this woman and the demon be one and the same …?

"You know what, Santino?" asked U Pizzu, as he eyed a particularly fetching – actually, stunning – waitress – she looked Ethiopian or Eritrean or maybe Somali. She was wearing a multi-colored, clinging, half-pareo and snug halter-top and she was weaving her way among the tables. Now she stopped and leaned over a stout red-faced prelate in purple, whispering, and laughing – sharing a joke it seemed. They looked like old friends.

"No, what?" Santino was staring too.

"I think that girl demon, the she-devil Father Andrea was talking about, I think she might be a fucking feminist!"

Later in the evening Santino took a flight back to Palermo. U Pizzu decided he would stay in Rome – alone. He had an idea. If the Torelli Jewel was so important, where the Torelli Jewel was, there the she-demon was sure to be. Well, not really; it might not be so neat; but the Torelli Jewel might give him a clue to this girl demon, what she wanted, and where she was; and if U Pizzu had the Torelli Jewel, and he let it be known that he had it, then the she-devil would come to him.

U Pizzu lay very still on top of the queen-size bed, staring at the invisible ceiling, and at the little red light of the smoke detector.

He turned on the bedside light, sat up, got his computer out of its case, and waited while it kicked into action. Dear Girl Demon, he thought, I really do want to meet you; I think you and I will have much to talk about ... Now, where was that little mountain town where the Torelli Jewel was said to be ...?

As for Cardinal Ambrosiano, and his band of clowns, well, that was another story, because Santino and U Pizzu had learned something that had changed everything.

The computer signaled that it was ready to play. U Pizzu began to type – entering items into a search engine.

Then – a weird feeling ...

U Pizzu stopped typing and sat very still ...

The room was moving, no ... Yes, it was really shaking ...

An earthquake, a fucking earthquake ...

U Pizzu glanced at his watch: 11:30 p. m.

CHAPTER 40 – CLOWNS

"Kill! Kill! Kill!"

"Kill! Kill! Kill!"

Smoke curled under the arched ceiling of the tunnel and a clamor of voices echoed from somewhere ahead. The monk was wheeling Kate toward what she figured must be the place of her sacrifice.

"Kill! Kill! Kill!"

A chorus of hysterical chanting voices.

"Kill! Kill! Kill!"

Oily smoke billowed up, filling the air, stinging Kate's eyes, making her myopic vision even blurrier. Tears coursed down her cheeks. She could feel them. Tied down, flat on her back, with her neck and ankles and wrists shackled, her gaze fixed, blinking at the ceiling, she was utterly helpless – even though the paralysis was fading.

"Soon, Katherine Dawkins Thornhill, you will be united in flesh and spirit with Satan," the monk confided in a theatrical whisper. His voice was hoarse, deep, and hollow. It came from some distant cavernous inhuman place. "It is the apotheosis, the transmutation – you will become one of us, soulless, a sex slave, and faithful minion of Satan."

Minion of Satan! Kate almost blinked. *These people were beyond crazy!* The gurney rolled smoothly, wheels squeaking, the monk's cowl looming darkly. With her head locked in position by the metal collar, Kate couldn't see much. But she could hear. The screams grew louder.

"Kill! Kill! Kill!"

"Kill! Kill! Kill!"

The air was suffocating, oppressive with oily smoke and the overpowering smells of sweat and sulfur. Each breath was painful. The arches of the tunnel paraded past in a blur, vault after vault after vault. The rhythm was hypnotic, hallucinatory. She and the monk were nearing the place of sacrifice. But she would not accept this absurdity; she would fight; she would not accept death – she would not give up, not even at the last second.

She sniffed – something new, a new odor …

Was it greasepaint? Why did it smell of greasepaint? *Clowns!* It smelled like the makeup room in a circus! *Clowns!* Were these people clowns? That was a horrifying thought! *Clowns!*

Once, with her dad and mom, she'd been backstage in an old-fashioned circus – somewhere in France. She petted the horses and talked to the dancing bear and peered, up close, at one of the tigers. But there was an evil clown, with shiny metallic button eyes, a big frilly collar, and a gigantic toothy smile. She never forgot him. Clowns were scary!

The monk wheeled the gurney into a larger space. Kate blinked. The tears were drying. Her eyes were getting used to the smoke. Even without her glasses, she could see the high arched roof, like a church, or a chapel; huge metal torches burned, yellow flames towered against the stone walls; the stench of sulfur and sweat and greasepaint was cloying, sickening. She had been plunged into a Hell of overpowering odors.

Out of the corner of her eye, she caught a glimpse of a man-sized wooden cross, hanging high on a wall. It swung by, topsy-turvy. *Damn!* It was upside down and burnt and charred. Did that mean that this was a black Mass? Did they burn people alive in a black Mass?

This was a stupid nightmare! It could not be happening, not now, not in this day and age, and it couldn't be happening to her! She was just a Ph.D. student. She had a paper due in two weeks, she had some neat ideas, and she was going to deliver it to her favorite seminar! Were these crazy people going to crucify her and burn her alive on that old upside-down wooden cross? My God, who were these idiots?

Two huge monks, both clad in black, suddenly appeared and unlocked the wrist and ankle manacles and opened the thick metal and rubber collar that held her neck.

In one single quick movement, one holding her ankles, the other her arms, they lifted her up. For an instant, she thought that this was the moment; she could test her strength and make a break for it.

But the monks were quick, and they had her firmly in their steel grasp. A breakaway was impossible. Maybe when they set her down, she could try to make a break for it. Her muscles tensed. She let her head loll back, looking helpless, a doll, a puppet whose strings had been cut. She caught an upside-down glimpse of the crowd – mostly older, but with some young people too. It was out of focus, but she could see them – the satanic worshippers. Almost all were naked. Their eyes shone, wild, rolling in their sockets. Most – faces and bodies – were painted in dazzling colors, blue, yellow, crimson, white, and …

So … it was greasepaint. They were clowns …

The monks set her down on a smooth cold surface of stone – granite, probably. She tensed her muscles, getting ready to spring up, but in the same instant cold metal clamps – *more manacles* – were pressed down over her ankles, wrists, and neck. Damn! It wouldn't have worked anyway. If she managed to spring up – and she didn't know if she had the strength – where would she run to?

Once again stretched out, spread-eagled, manacled, she couldn't move a muscle. She was on the altar of sacrifice! From now on there would be no reprieve, no salvation. This was where she would die.

Fuck!

She blinked. The monks stood back. The clowns were chanting, "Kill! Kill! Kill!" Off to one side, Brother Basilisk stood with his arms folded in front of him; the expression on his giant bland pudding face looked like satisfaction.

Kate tried to relax; she lay still. The metal shackles were not as tight as the ones on the gurney. *Maybe, just maybe …*

"Kill! Kill! Kill!"

"Kill! Kill! Kill!"

Kate's blood boiled. She was obviously not the first victim. These maniacs must have been sacrificing people for a long time, maybe decades, maybe more. But, now, she could do nothing. She lay quiet, manacled down – spread-eagled, naked, your classic virgin ready to be sacrificed – well, she was not really a virgin, far from it! Maybe she should tell them. "I am totally not a virgin!" Maybe that would disqualify her …

A smile flickered. She swallowed and ran the tip of her tongue along her lips, took deep breaths, readying herself for whatever would come to pass. If she had to die, she had to die. Her father would be devastated; he had already lost too much. If only she could talk to him, comfort him! Even if just for one last time.

Sheltering under a porch, thirty-two-year-old Salvo Aiello pulled a crumpled package of French cigarettes – *Gitanes Brunes* – out of his jacket side pocket. He stared at the white-and-blue package for a long unhappy moment. Then he pulled out a damp, wrinkled, unfiltered cigarette and, using a small blue plastic Bic lighter, he lit it – squinting against the flame, and cupping his hands to shelter the bright yellow guttering flame from the stormy damp air.

He inhaled – ah, what a relief – then exhaled, watching the smoke drift away, curling up into the wall of rain, thundering down, so close he could touch it. The humidity must be one hundred percent. His suit was wet, heavy, and clammy. A shower would be paradise, and a dry, cool, air-conditioned hotel room would be heaven.

Two feet away, beyond the overhang of the porch, the rain poured down; it was a dense silver curtain; the lawn smoked with mist that drifted in thick white tendrils just inches above the carefully cut grass, which in the security floodlights glowed bright lime green. The whole place was unreal.

Salvo would be damned glad to get home; for five days he'd barely had time to change his shirt. He worked in private security, for one of the best companies, and he'd been assigned for ten days to a documentary film crew shooting high up on the great Sicilian volcano Etna. The work was non-stop, fourteen, sixteen hours a day. Then, suddenly, at the end of the last day of shooting, he was told he had to get his ass to a place called Villa Mazana Nera; some secret organization was having some kind of conference, and needed extra security – three men, at least three men, outside the building. Salvo managed a quick shower in his Sicilian hotel, double tipped the kind Somali girl – cute and flirtatious too – who made him an extra thermos of coffee and a package of sandwiches, took the ferry across the Strait of Messina, then drove most of the day and part of a night, the last stretch taking him up intricate curving hairpin cliff-side roads. Finally, he got to Villa Mazana Nera. It was beautiful; but it was damned spooky, isolated up here in the mountains.

He stared at the rain. It was weird weather. He didn't like the feel of it. Strangely, the rain had brought no relief; the air was as heavy and as electric as before, clinging, humid and clammy.

He bit down on his lip and glanced at his watch.

What in hell were these people up to? They had arrived in their cars – lots of very expensive cars – and jeeps and SUVs – then they all disappeared into the villa.

He didn't like it.

He'd mentioned the weirdness to Tommaso Farro, his team leader, and Tommaso had just shrugged. "Salvo, let it rest; sometimes it's better not to ask questions. In any case, it's just a few hours, and we are getting paid triple."

"And the guys in the security control room?"

"They are not our guys – they're members of the organization, whatever it is; and they're priests, for fuck sake! They work with whatever outfit this is, so we just don't bother them, and they won't fuck with us."

"Priests?" said Salvo.

"Priests. And, like you, Salvo, I have absolutely no idea what this is about."

Salvo got the point: if the money was good, and it was *very* good, and if priests were involved, well, then, yes, it was better not to ask questions. "Okay, you're right, Tommaso, we just do our jobs."

"Exactly, Salvo," said Tommaso, patting him on the shoulder. "We just do our jobs and we get the fuck out of here."

Father Francesco Delgado stared at the security screens. "Father Alvarez, how many cars did you count?"

"Thirty-five – and one woman turned up on foot; she said she left her car down the hill, at the second lookout." Father Alvarez zoomed up on an image that had just been archived: a woman at the gate, good-looking, forties or fifties, maybe.

"And her name is?" Father Delgado was always very precise, military, really, a true soldier doing the work of Satan, *Opus Diaboli*.

"Let's see – Elia, Marina Elia." Father Alvarez scanned the document that the woman had presented to the guard at the gate. "The name may be Jewish – 'Eliyahu,' as you know, means Jehovah is God, or her family may originally be from the town of Elia, in Calabria, or both. And, of course, there is Saint Elia. Probably converted Jews, from way back – Middle Ages or the 1490s, something like that. She probably doesn't even know herself."

"What have you got on her?"

"It's her first time here; she's a designer, clothes, textiles, she has her own company, with factories in Prato and in the Veneto. She's rich; she's divorced; she has an apartment in Milan, a house in Porto San Stefano, a *pied-à-terre* in Paris, near the Luxembourg Gardens. She was referred by one Laura Conti."

"Good, good, excellent: open a file on this Elia. Father Ottavio wants everybody tabbed, as you know, and then he will ask for contributions. This Marina had better be ready to open her pocketbook!" Father Delgado leaned back and smiled.

"Oh, she'll be ready," said Father Diego, who had been watching the five monitors that covered the outdoor cameras that swung back and forth, covering all approaches to the villa. "They get hooked on this stuff, and if not, the photographs, the files ... all those things they don't want people to see."

"Yes, of course. Satan be praised!" Father Alvarez clicked on the keyboard, opening a file – *Marina Elia* ..." He glanced at the control room clock: it was 11:35 p.m.

V and John now presented two perfect painted savage faces, two pairs of bright eyes staring out of black-and-green jungle masks.

The rain had not let up and it seemed even more humid than before.

"See you in ten minutes!" V opened the door of the Land Cruiser and slipped out. She closed the door and disappeared – a glittering black silhouette – gone, in an instant, into the fog and streaming rain.

"God be with you, child," I whispered.

"Amen, Father, Amen!" John laid a hand on my shoulder and smiled a diabolical smile from his painted jungle face. "V, do you read me?" he spoke into the microphone attached to his ear.

"Yes, John, I read you."

V sprinted through the pouring rain, down the hillside, and through the woods, and came to the road that ran beside the Villa Mazana Nera's high stone wall. She glanced around. According to John's schematics, there were no cameras covering the outside of the villa's wall or the road except at the main gate. She hoped the schematics were right. She skirted the wall, running alongside it, as close to it as she could.

It was 11:38.

She came to the spot she had identified as the most vulnerable point of the wall – the easiest point to leap over it. She wiggled out of her backpack and dropped it next to her, keeping it attached by a thin cord that was hooked to her belt. She paused for a second, then vaulted up the fifteen-foot-high, smooth-faced wall, grabbing the rough-edged top, and clinging to it with the tips of her fingers.

In one smooth movement, she flipped herself carefully – precisely – onto the top of the three-foot-thick wall and slipped sideways under the electrified barbed wire, crouching low, on all fours, knees and belly and breasts just a feather's breadth above the razor-sharp glass shards that stuck up at all angles, and with her shoulder blades and buttocks less than two inches under the high-voltage wire.

Carefully she hauled the backpack up after her, unhooked it from the cord, and slipped it under the barbed wire. The deluge was non-stop. Rain poured down over her, splashed up around her, and streamed over everything. Silver-dark drops of rain were strung out, running along the barbed wire, like smoky silver pearls on a razor-sharp necklace. It was pretty, if only she had had time to admire it!

Thick curls of mist rose from the wall and from the trees, wrapping themselves around her like eager, probing tentacles. She growled. Her eyes glowed with disquiet and nervous energy. There was something unsettling in the air – some extraordinary energy, ready to explode. Was the great seismic event – the catastrophe – coming sooner than she expected? Had the Cardinal gone further and faster with the Crystal than she had thought? That would be bad news, very bad news indeed. She hooked the backpack, gently, to two cords and with flexible hooks; she lowered it, so that it hung halfway down on the inside of the wall.

Into the mike, she whispered, "One!"

"Roger – Alpha," said John.

"What is that, John?"

"V and I have a code for each stage of any operation when we are working together. It's like timed acrobatics. We have two or three fallback routines at each stage. V learned from the best."

The rain and darkness pressed against the Land Cruiser. I closed my eyes and imagined how, over the centuries, V must have learned from the Phoenicians, from Marcus – and from gladiators, and Roman Centurions, from Greeks and Crusaders, Arabs and medieval knights, Japanese samurai and Caribbean pirates, twentieth century intelligence agents and Special Forces – yes, our demon would have had lots of time to perfect her skills.

V rolled off the top of the wall, flipped over in midair, and landed, softly, on her hands and knees, between the wall and a bed of thick sheltering evergreen shrubbery.

There had been no alarm, not at least as far as she had heard or noticed. She released the backpack from the flexi-hooks, and caught it before it landed.

"Two," she whispered, as she slipped the backpack onto her shoulders.

"Roger – Beta," John answered, his voice comforting and intimate in her ear.

Crouched on all fours, not moving a muscle, V listened. The dogs! Yes, the dogs were on their way. They were coming. So, the dogs had heard her! But probably nobody else, not yet. Still on all fours, she crawled deeper into the shrubbery, and right to the edge, where, still hidden in the leaves, she peered across the lawn.

Two Dobermans. As they came trotting toward her, V backed deeper into the shrubbery. They ran quickly and silently; they were deadly, panting and eager, superbly trained; they came to the edge of the shrubbery. Then they stopped, sniffing, listening.

V growled, a warning growl. Still on all fours, she waited a moment and gave another warning growl, low in her throat: it was dog talk she had learned long ago. Once, she had lived alone, at the beginning of the nineteenth century, for several months with a pack of wild dogs, in the mountains of Sardinia when she was on the run from a particularly vicious "demon hunter." The dogs had adopted her; she became the head of the pack, though she had to kill one dog – the former alpha male – to become boss dog. And so, she was boss dog until she left to join Napoleon's army – as a drummer boy and spy for the Duke of Wellington. Well, that was long ago! She was pleased she could still growl up a storm.

The two Dobermans hesitated. They whimpered quizzically, front paws rising and falling nervously. V slipped her dart gun out of its holster.

Eavesdropping, V merged with their minds. They were asking themselves: Is this creature friend or foe? It was a female, that they knew; but was it a female to mate with or to kill? Or both? They were close now, peering between the leaves, but still they hesitated, wondering, attracted and yet fearful. Then they slipped into the shrubbery. Now their bodies would not be visible from the lawn, and V had a clear shot.

Two quick darts from the silent gun – pop, pop. The dogs were unconscious before they hit the ground.

"Three," V whispered. "Bow-wow."

"Roger! Gamma. Dogs down!"

V crept past the two animals, stretched out on their sides, rain pattering on them through the leaves, their drenched coats reflecting glossy glimmers from the security lights. They would have a horrible headache when they woke up.

Now V had to get to another part of the lawn – where the security camera coverage was intermittent. Streaming with rain, covered in mud, watching for wire traps and pressure alarms, V slithered flat on her belly through the drenched oozy wilderness of plants, ferns, oleander, and bougainvillea. The mist snaked around everything. The ground was a slushy morass of slimy clayey mud; the plants were thick, bright spinach green, and tentacular, an aggressive tropical jungle. She came to the edge of the shrubbery. Warily, she got up on hands and knees, keeping her weight balanced, distributing it among the points of her toes, knees, palms of hands – and keeping it as close to that of a Doberman as possible. She didn't want to set off any pressure alarms.

In front of her stretched a broad, immaculate, floodlit lawn; this zone was covered by a rotating camera and watched over by a security guard.

The lawn was totally exposed. Anybody or anything crossing it would be spotted immediately. The security camera, according to John's schematics, should be positioned up at the corner of the covered terrace just across from her; it would be moving back and forth. And, in fact, V spotted the camera's little red light, doing just that.

Standing in the covered porch, sheltered from the rain, the security guard was smoking a cigarette. Another man, dressed in a dark suit and white shirt but no tie – possibly the butler, to judge by his demeanor and clothes – came out of the villa, spoke to the guard, then went back inside. He didn't seem to push any codes or buttons – which meant, almost certainly, that the door alarms were off. That made sense if lots of people were in the villa, coming and going.

V observed the security guard's every gesture. He was a strongly built, sallow, thickset man with a big block of a head and thick black hair combed straight back from his high forehead. He squinted out into the thick steamy rain, took a puff, removed the cigarette, and looked at it, then put it back in his mouth. He repeated the gesture: a deep, satisfied inhale, a relaxed exhale; then he looked at the cigarette with something like loathing. V could see all the anguish in the gesture. The poor guy had been trying to quit smoking, but he'd fallen back into the habit and was disgusted with himself.

At one end of the porch, there was an ash receptacle set back against the wall. If the guard was the scrupulous, careful type he seemed to be, he would stub the cigarette out in the receptacle. That meant he'd turn away, if just for an instant. If that happened when the camera was turned away too, V would have her brief window of opportunity.

V waited.

After about a minute and a half, the guard turned toward the ash receptacle and – perfect timing – the camera was panning away from V.

V leapt. In a single bound she was across the lawn and landed, gently, almost silently, on the flagstones. When the guard turned, she was already on top of him. When he asked, "Hey, who are you?" his eyes wide in surprise, the needle was already plunging into his neck.

Still staring at V, Salvo Aiello made a gurgling sound deep in his throat; he swayed, his eyes clouded and turned upwards, leaving only the whites, and he collapsed, folding up like a puppet whose strings had been cut. The half-smoked *Gitane Brune* fell with him, still glowing, still smoldering.

V caught him in mid-fall. Salvo was a heavy man. His blue suit smelled of dark tobacco, of dry-cleaning, and, more faintly, of mothballs and sweat. So – he was a bachelor who lived out of his suitcase; he'd been working long hours, and not getting much sleep. She caught a whiff of sulfur, a particular bouquet. Yes, and he'd been working close to a volcano – probably, to judge by the smell, Etna.

"Sorry, my friend." She lowered him gently to the ground. His expression was locked in a friendly rictus, though his eyes, now, were closed.

V slipped the automatic out of Salvo's shoulder holster. A classic Beretta M9, well oiled. She balanced it in the palm of her hand – *neat!* She shoved it into her backpack. He also had a miniaturized walkie-talkie, with the little speaker and microphone wrapped around his ear. She took it, muted it, and hung it at her belt. She used self-tightening plastic cuffs to hand- and ankle-cuff Salvo, then a plastic loop to link the cuffs; he was hogtied. He'd probably want a cigarette when he woke up. In anticipation, V could feel his yearning for dark French tobacco – the hunger of it; rather like her addiction to blood. Poor guy! She picked up the smoldering cigarette and dropped it into the ash receptacle.

"Four," she whispered.

"Roger that!" John's cheery voice gave V a warm feeling. "Edward for Epsilon – outside guard eliminated."

V ran along the terrace and pushed open the French doors. Having watched the servant – or butler – come out and go back in, V assumed the alarm was off – and it seemed she was right: no sirens wailed, no lights flashed. The main staircase was there, right where it should be, across a large corridor, leading to the second floor and to the security center.

"Five," she whispered

"Roger – five – Zeta – you're in."

V glanced around. This part of the villa appeared empty. Polished tile floors, gleaming stucco walls. It certainly had changed since the seventeenth century. There was modern lighting everywhere, but most of it was dimmed, making the whole place seem half-asleep, an enchanted castle, drowsing under the rain and mist, waiting for someone to wake it up.

The monster-sized Ming vases lining the corridor overflowed with enormous bouquets of freshly cut flowers. The air was heavy – almost cloying – with their perfume. Villa Mazana Nera was a sparkling showplace; Corrado Ferrari had not spared any expense. Everything reeked money. It was all splendidly restored, authentic; but it was so sparkling that it looked like it had been built yesterday. Wrought iron chandeliers hung from the ceilings; the tables and sideboards and ornamental storage trunks were of oak and mahogany, and in the Hispanic style, all antiques, but gleaming with fresh wax. The tile and ceramic floors sparkled, and everywhere was the overwhelming smell of flowers, of wood and floor polish, and an indefinable odor of spices.

There was no one in sight; but the staircase did have a camera facing downwards.

V raced up the steps. She couldn't give the guards monitoring the cameras any time to react. If she were lucky, they wouldn't, in this instant, be focused on the monitor covering the stairs.

Father Alvarez was saying he thought something was wrong with the dogs and with the security guard who was covering sector 3. "I don't know, but I think something is –"

"What's his name?"

"Salvo, Salvo Aiello. He's supposed to push the silent all-clear button every ten minutes and he missed. It was ten seconds ago, and so far, he's been very precise, right down to the second."

At that moment, the door to the control room flew open, and a woman – well, a creature entered, an apparition, a warrior, a –

Only Father Alvarez saw her. Father Diego and Father Delgado were staring at the screens and had their backs turned to the door. Father Alvarez had the impression that, suddenly, everything was happening in slow motion, but also extraordinarily fast. His mouth opened to shout a warning. But no sound came. The woman, who was wearing some sort of black skintight special-ops outfit and camouflage makeup, had a weapon in her gloved hand. She had already fired three shots – *ping, ping, ping …*

Ping, ping, ping …

The woman was smiling, straight at Father Alvarez.

Father Alvarez's mouth was still open, still trying to utter a warning. He felt a stinging sensation and fell off his chair. As he fell, he noticed that Father Diego and Father Delgado were collapsing, slumping over the monitors and keyboards; Father Alvarez thought, how strange, how efficient, how wonderful this woman warrior was! They hadn't had time to utter a word.

Father Alvarez fell to the floor. His face landed next to the legs of the stool Father Delgado was slumped on. Father Alvarez's eyes, wide open and glassy, stared, sideways, at the woman's black military-type boots. They had thick tread soles and were splashed with mud, as were her legs.

Father Delgado toppled in slow motion sideways off his chair. Father Diego fell from his, too, seeming to drift toward the floor, his arm swinging slowly down, his fingers clasped. To Father Alvarez, it seemed like a ballet in slow motion. Then they were lying sideways, sprawled on top of each other, Father Delgado and Father Diego, on the floor facing Father Alvarez, their faces frozen in surprise, mouths open. Father Diego's tongue was hanging out. For an instant, Father Alvarez wondered – *do I look like that?*

The warrior woman leaned down. Her face was a face from the wilds of a jungle. She smiled – her bright perfect teeth framed by matte-black lips. "This won't hurt a bit." In her hand was a needle – it plunged downward.

Father Alvarez then felt nothing and saw nothing; the world folded into blackness; as he faded, he felt for some reason not afraid at all, but happy.

Is this what death is like?

"Six," V whispered into the mike.

"Roger," said John. "Eta – Hotel – You've got the control room."

"I'm opening the gate. You can drive in."

V pushed the button and watched as, a few seconds later, the Land Cruiser entered. She took a bundle of keys from Father Alvarez's belt, dragged the bodies of the priests to the side, took out plastic handcuffs and chains, and hand- and ankle-cuffed all three. They should remain unconscious for at least thirty or forty minutes. She checked everything, and left the control room, closing and locking the door.

V glanced at her wristwatch: 11:48.

Twelve minutes to midnight.

She ran from room to room, checking for "hostiles." It would probably take John about five minutes to "neutralize" the two other guards – one in the parking lot, one in the back garden – knock them out and truss them up under a palm tree or some shrubbery.

There was not, so far as V knew, any outside service attached to the alarm system; the Satanic Order needed this to be a secretive place; an outside alarm system would bring the police or the Carabinieri. The Carabinieri tended to ask awkward questions and stick their noses into everything. The Satanic Order of the Apocalypse would want Villa Mazana Nera to remain an isolated little universe.

V raced around the ground floor of the villa. It looked too pristine; she wondered if Corrado Ferrari ever used the place. There seemed to be nobody at home; all the servants were gone, dismissed, probably for the night.

Except for one …

V found the servant she'd seen earlier on the outside terrace. He was in the kitchen, his black jacket slung over the back of a chair. He was a distinguished-looking man with gray hair, and he was sitting in his white shirtsleeves at a big wooden table and eating a chocolate éclair.

"Hello," said V.

"Who are you?" Asking the question was not easy, as his mouth was full of chocolate. V was jealous. Chocolate was one of the things she'd *really* like to eat. The smell of it made her mouth water – which was not a good thing. Her hunger might get the better of her. She didn't have time, now, to leap on some poor innocent bystander – like a butler – and drink him dry – however much she might be tempted; and then, too, she always tried to choose her meals by sticking to her ethical principle – eat only bad apples.

"I am the Devil," she said, wagging the Beretta M9 in the butler's direction.

"Well, then, you've come to the right place." He had a distinctly British accent. He took another bite of the chocolate éclair. "Would you like one?" He motioned with his chin to the open box of éclairs.

"No, thank you."

"They are very good."

"And who or what are you?"

"I'm Signor Ferrari's butler."

"I see. Where is Father Ottavio? And what is going on in the chapel?"

"Ah, you must be that demon they've been worrying about – the she-devil."

"That sounds like me." She glanced at her watch. 11:54. "I don't have much time."

Suddenly John and Father O'Bryan appeared at the kitchen door. "Done," John said. "The two outside guards are resting under some trees."

The butler wiped his mouth, glanced at John and said, "Father Ottavio is down in the chapel – they are celebrating a black Mass, I believe."

"How many are there?"

"About thirty or forty, and Ottavio has three of those strange monks with him. They have a young woman," the butler got up and pulled on his jacket. "I'm not supposed to know this, but they have a young woman – they brought her here yesterday – and I think ..."

"Yes, we know. Take us to the chapel. Quickly!"

"Of course." He settled his jacket carefully on his shoulders and led the way out of the kitchen and along one of the principal corridors. "When they are preparing their little parties, the servants are given time off and the so-called monks come in to run the place. I really don't know what they are or whether they are totally human."

"And you stay behind."

"I don't like to, but Signor Ferrari wants me to watch over the ... furniture. I usually stay in my own rooms. Signor Ferrari doesn't want the villa damaged. He only comes here once or twice a year."

"Ah."

"He isn't very fond of his relative, that Cardinal Ambrosiano – nor of his cousin, Father Ottavio. I imagine blackmail of some kind is involved; otherwise, I doubt that Signor Ferrari, who's a decent chap, would tolerate this or would let these maniacs near the place. But, you know, everyone has a secret, everyone can be blackmailed. So, I think that Signor Ferrari is turning a blind eye to what goes on. He doesn't know; and he doesn't want to know. Here we are. This door leads to the stairs that lead, I believe, to the chapel. Most of the revelers – or worshippers – leave their clothes in this vestibule here."

V glanced at the large carved oaken door and at the alcove leading to it. Clothes were hung on hangers, shoes lined up – yes, about thirty or forty people; expensive clothes, luxurious shoes, rich people.

She turned to the butler. "Would you mind awfully if we handcuff you and knock you out?"

"Not at all; though I'd rather like to enjoy the fun if you are going to break this gang up. I was sitting there contemplating quitting. By the way, I'm quite handy with my fists."

John and V looked at each other and at Father O'Bryan.

"Well, if you wish," V nodded. "But I warn you, there will be blood – and I am, in fact, a blood-drinking demon – the rumors are true."

"Thank you. I'll be delighted to join you whatever you are."

"Speaking of which," John said, "I think, perhaps, V, that your demon version might be appropriate attire for such a sacred occasion. What do you think, Father O'Bryan?"

"They worship the devil," Father O'Bryan grinned at V. "Let's give them the devil!"

"The devil?" The butler raised an eyebrow.

V favored Father O'Bryan with a scowl. "Right!" she said. "You may close your eyes if you wish," she said to the butler.

He shook his head and kept his eyes wide open.

V slipped out of her boots, unbuckled her holster and backpack, unzipped the catsuit, and handed everything to John, who slipped it all away into his backpack. The whole action took about forty seconds. V stood there, naked.

"I say!" said the butler.

V's body rippled into a blur – and there she was: the demon.

"This is most interesting," said the butler. "My name is Henry, by the way."

"Henry, delighted," V said, thinking that his aplomb was such he should be called Jeeves.

John drew his Beretta M9.

"Okay," V said. "Let's go!" She pushed open the door.

Broad, high, vaulted, stairs, with walls of white stucco, a Hispanic look, and deep alcoves on both sides, led gently downwards. V could smell the sulfur from the underground springs. It took her back three centuries. There was chanting, but it was faint: there must be another door at the bottom: "Kill! Kill! Kill!"

"Oh, Jesus, Joseph, and Mary," Father O'Bryan was staring at the first alcove. Lit by flickering candles, there stood a naked young woman, crucified on a cross, her eyes turned upwards, in imitation of Christ.

"It's a painted statue," V said. "Here, touch it."

"I have never been down here. This must be the gallery of their victims," said the butler. "I recognize that girl. They brought her here two years ago."

Father O'Bryan put his hand against the statue's cheek.

"It must be from a cast," V said. "They did that when Count Marbuse owned the villa – they made casts of their victims, trophies."

"What a dreadful idea!" Father O'Bryan quickly withdrew his hand.

As they hurried down the gently sloping tiled pathway, they passed other statues, each posed in its own alcove, all of them naked, brightly lit and hyper-real; they seemed alive, more than alive.

The poses were copies of Renaissance religious paintings or other works of art. V was sure the statues had been cast live: how terrifying, having molding plaster poured all over you!

When they got to the last alcove, Father O'Bryan stopped; he turned deadly pale and almost fainted. "My God!"

"Bernini's *The Ecstasy of Saint Teresa*, but in garish Technicolor! She's beautiful, this girl!" V said, realizing that she was being outrageously insensitive.

"No, that's not what I mean." Father O'Bryan's face was as white as chalk. "That's Kate, that's Roger Thornhill's daughter!"

John and V looked at each other. "We go in – now!"

The door was of wood reinforced by iron.

Behind the massive door the chanting began again, louder and much more intense:

"Kill! Kill! Kill! Kill!"

"Kill! Kill! Kill! Kill!"

CHAPTER 41 – BLACK MASS

Marina Elia was forty-six years old, with curly red hair, green eyes, a peaches-and-cream complexion, full lips, and a sprinkling of freckles across the bridge of her nose that gave her a girlish, impertinent look.

Marina was from Milan, and CEO of her own business in the fashion industry, as well as having interests in textiles and several wineries.

She had been on holiday in Tuscany when her friend Laura Conti mentioned Father Ottavio's Order of the Apocalypse. Marina was an agnostic – well, really an atheist – and, like quite a few Italians, secretly *extremely* hostile to organized religion, and certainly more than suspicious of cults. But she was incurably curious.

"I'd like to come along and see what these things are like," she'd said to Laura over cocktails in a café overlooking the old harbor in the ultra-chic seaside town of Porto San Stefano. Since her divorce, holidays had turned out to be utterly boring; most of the men she met were duds or married or gay; she had, essentially, stopped looking, but, perhaps, not stopped hoping.

"Well, I can't go to this thing, whatever it is," said Laura. "I'll tell them you're coming. Here's my entrance pass. A Father Ottavio gave it to my business partner, who passed it on to me. I've never attended one of their parties – or ceremonies, or whatever they are. Be careful – I've heard these people are nuts. There's a rumor they practice human sacrifice."

"You're kidding!"

"No, I'm not. I've heard strange rumors. Be careful!"

For Marina a risk was a temptation. Danger was irresistible. She had been a daredevil since she was a teenager – and spice had been singularly lacking in her life since her husband had left her for an eighteen-year-old chorus girl three years ago. "Chorus girl" had been Marina's polite way of putting it, though the girl herself, when Marina happened upon her in the ladies' room of a fashionable restaurant in Florence, was quite charming, and even apologetic; they had exchanged opinions on a particular shade and brand of lipstick. She could be my daughter, Marina thought; and she realized that she liked the girl, she actually liked her! She found she had no rancor toward the young woman – and they remained in touch – but she did have quite a bit of rancor, which she tried to repress, against her ex-husband. Resentment, in Marina's book, was an unhealthy emotion; and the best revenge, she reminded herself, was to be happy and to live well.

Marina was in the third row of the satanic congregation; and she was horrified. At first, she had thought the girl on the altar was an actress they'd hired for theatrical effect, and that these people were playing at Satanism.

But now, suddenly, she was certain that the priest at the altar really did intend to plunge the knife into the girl's body.

This was not an avant-garde play; this was murder.

"Kill! Kill! Kill! Kill!"

"Kill! Kill! Kill! Kill!"

To Marina's right was a German banker. She had met him once in Frankfurt. Luckily, he hadn't recognized her. He was about sixty years old, seriously overweight, and naked except for a black leather jockstrap almost entirely hidden by his sagging paunch. He was covered in oil, sweating heavily, bug-eyed, drugged out of his mind, and, like all the others, he was chanting, "Kill! Kill! Kill! Kill!"

Before they entered the chapel, everybody had been served what to Marina looked like a lethal cocktail of hallucinatory and psychosis-inducing drugs; most of the "worshippers" were naked, having removed all, or nearly all, of their clothing; most had smeared their faces and bodies in hideous psychedelic colors.

Marina grimaced. Among other things, the whole ceremony was in dreadful taste.

She had pretended to take the drug but had dumped the contents of the paper cup into one of the giant Ming vases overflowing with flowers that lined the ground floor passageway. As for clothes, Marina had taken off her jacket and her skirt but had kept on a chemise and panties and her shoes. She'd even managed to sneak in her purse – strictly against the rules, they had told her – which contained her keys, a Swiss Army knife, cash, credit cards, and a cell phone. Luckily, in the crush to enter the chapel, nobody had noticed.

Now, cold-sober and terrified, she realized she had descended into a sort of raucous sulfurous parody of Satan's Hell. She was surrounded by people who had been magically transformed from their normal, banal, boring, elegant selves into primitive homicidal maniacs. They were screaming like banshees – a hysterical lynch mob hollering for somebody's head.

"Kill! Kill! Kill!"

"Kill! Kill! Kill!"

Marina's muscles were tensing. She was just trying to decide how she might stop the murder – by screaming, or by pushing her way through to the front, grabbing the priest's sword and tearing it away from him – when she heard some sort of ruckus behind her and turned to see what it was …

Father Ottavio lifted and tipped the chalice and let the golden oil spill over the supine body that was to be sacrificed to the Everlasting Glory of Satan.

The girl's eyes were wide open, staring straight upwards. Father Ottavio was delighted. She was fully conscious, her mind was clear, and she was aware of every little detail of what was about to happen to her. It made her suffering, her sacrifice, so much more intense.

The oil made that special little bit of aesthetic difference too. It spilled over her breasts, her legs, her arms, her hands. Now she would gleam like gold. In her moment of death and transcendence, the dying goddess would shine forth in all her splendor and glory.

The oil *did* make a difference. Kate could now move her hand, and even her arm. She compressed her palm into the smallest space possible, wiggled her right hand gently, relaxed the muscles – *relax, relax, relax* – and pulled it, now that it was well oiled, slowly, out of the manacle – *Yes!*

One arm was free.

Now – what to do next?

Her heart was beating like crazy, a hammering, thundering, pulse.

Adrenaline, yes, adrenaline.

A drumbeat in her ears, nerves tingling, sparkling alive.

The four huge wrought iron candleholders on the altar towered above her, sputtering, their giant yellow flames flaring upward, projecting circles of smoky light onto the vaulted ceiling. Red wax melted and ran down the wrought iron, overflowing the bases; hot wax splattered and dripped onto the toes of Kate's right foot and onto her shoulder – she could feel it; she wiggled her toes – which was definite progress – but couldn't move her feet. The manacles were too tight.

Her body was coming alive – but it was too late.

Standing above her, Father Ottavio intoned some rubbish in Latin. Some of it she could understand: Soon oil would mingle with blood and soon living flesh would become sacrificial flesh. Soon Satan would be appeased. Soon his thirst, his hunger, would be sated, his satanic desires fulfilled. Soon Satan would have a new member of his harem, an exquisite angel transformed into a sublime minion of Satan, a satanic whore and concubine, a brand-new, truly seductive demon of evil.

Father Ottavio glanced down. The sacrificial sword, its blade gleaming, lay on the black granite slab next to the paralyzed girl. The runnels cut in the granite stood ready to drain the fresh sacrificial blood to the dishes and vases so that the worshippers – the damned – could drink thereof and exalt in the sensuality and glory of the sacrifice, drinking of the sacred blood, eating of the sacred flesh, in Satanic Communion with the Evil Force.

Father Ottavio's heart rose in pure elation. He cherished this moment of dark epiphany and negative grace, just before the plunge of the blade. This was a moment of glorious anticipation, of ecstasy, of identification with the Godhead of Evil, with Satan Himself.

"All will kneel before the sacrifice!" Father Ottavio looked out over the feverish bright-eyed gleaming painted faces – slaves, all slaves.

All the slaves knelt – before Satan, before the sacrifice, and before him, before Father Ottavio, Permanent Secretary of the Order of the Apocalypse!

"Oh, Divine Satan, we cry out to you," he intoned, "Creator of this World and all that is in it! Font of all wisdom! Savior of mankind! Guarantor of our rebirth in Evil! Hear us in our hour of exaltation! Hear your sons and daughters, we call unto you."

He lifted the full goblet of wine to his lips. He gazed out over the smoky incense-filled room. It was sublime; it was poetic! The torches illuminated the skulls along the wall, *memento mori*, the trophies of past sacrifices.

Each skull with its fleshless cheekbone, and ghostly, empty eye sockets, and unchanging grin was perched in a shallow niche; each glimmered with its own individual satanic light, and each one had a name: Marie-José, Angela, Mary-Lou, Katya, Veronica …

Most of the congregation were kneeling now, groveling in an ecstasy of abasement and abandon, saliva drooling from their open mouths. Here and there a few were still standing; but all their eyes were fixed upon him and on the pure oil-covered, ivory-white body manacled on the altar.

Father Ottavio drank the wine slowly, savoring it.

Unlike the others, he was soberly dressed, in priestly garb, as befit the solemnity of the occasion.

The countdown to the final revelation had begun. Only he and the Cardinal knew this; only he and the Cardinal knew that humanity was about to be reduced to dust and ashes, to deserved slavery. The nations of Earth would bow down before the Weapon of the Apocalypse – and the Reign of Satan and of Satan's minions on Earth would begin. The Satanic Order of the Apocalypse would have accomplished its mission!

He cried out, "Satan's will be done!"

He finished the wine. He set the goblet down.

At the far end of the chapel – near the entrance – the charcoal fire burned brightly, and the seven-foot stainless steel spit over the grill turned slowly, glowing, ready for the body that soon would be offered onto it, skewered onto the sharp-ended rotating steel rod. The meat would be delicious. A morsel for all the worshippers, for all the damned! And the fire, fueled by extra fuel from two jerrycans, then afterwards the acid, would peel away what remained – leaving the skull to add to the collection: a *memento mori* of the highest quality: *Katherine Dawkins Thornhill* – thus the plaque would read.

"Through the body of woman, we came into the world," Father Ottavio thundered. "Through the body of woman, we engender the world. Through the body of woman, we redeem the world. So, it has been, so it is, so it shall be, forever more."

He looked down.

The girl's lips were moving. She was struggling to say something. Father Ottavio leaned close – what mystical insight might she offer him on the verge of death?

"Asshole … Asshole!" she whispered.

"What, my child?"

"K … kitsch!"

"What, my child?"

"You are an asshole! This is a … a … all … k … k … kitsch," she stuttered, saliva on her bright lips. "You are a c … c … clown," she whispered, the words barely making it past her lips.

Father Ottavio was outraged. Without even looking for it, he reached for the sword.

His hand met nothing.

His face was still close to hers when a burning pain slashed and seared across his chest and arm.

He started back, hand to his chest, and saw that his arm and chest were covered in blood.

With her one free hand, Kate had raised the sword, the sword of wrath, and had stabbed out with all her might, slashing through the man's ecclesiastical garb, into muscle and bone. She had tried for his neck but couldn't reach so far.

Tears filled Father Ottavio's eyes: *It hurt! God! Did it hurt!*

The girl was still pinned down; only one arm was free. How had she done that? She should be helpless, at his mercy.

Her hand still held the sword.

Staring at him, she shouted, louder, distinctly now, "You … creep! You absolute asshole! You … murderer!"

"Sacrilege!" Father Ottavio screamed. He clenched his fists: he would grab the sword and finish with this insolent bitch for once and for all!

He could see her muscles tense as she tightened her grip on the sword. Her eyes flashed.

"Kill! Kill! Kill! Kill!"

"Kill! Kill! Kill! Kill!"

Father Ottavio hesitated. If he reached for it, she would slash out again.

He stepped back and was about to risk it all and lunge for the sword. At that moment, the torches flickered and wavered in a sudden gust of air.

Father Ottavio looked up.

Someone had entered the chapel. This was absolutely forbidden! Who could it be? This had never happened before. There were vague figures at the back of the room, silhouettes in the smoky atmosphere.

As his vision cleared, he saw a man with camouflage makeup in a shooting stance and, just behind the marksman, a strange demonic figure. It must be the she-devil he had heard of! The she-demon! And with her were two other men – one of them a priest!

A shot rang out.

Father Ottavio spun backward, a searing pain in his shoulder.

The believers stared, feeling that this, perhaps, was part of the spectacle.

"Kill! Kill! Kill! Kill!"

"Kill! Kill! Kill! Kill!"

At the entrance to the chapel, the two monks guarding the burning grill turned to face the door that had suddenly whammed open. The larger of the two monks, Brother Basilisk, seized a glowing branding iron from the grill, raised it, and ran at the demon and her three companions.

The demon turned, a Beretta M9 in one claw, smiled, said "Sorry!" and shot Brother Basilisk between the eyes at point-blank range. The six-foot-five giant tumbled backward, his monk's robe flailing upward. He careened, smashing into the grill, sending live flaming coals and embers showering outwards. Red-hot coals spilled onto the sandaled feet of the other monk. His robe flared up, flames licking at his face. The monk screamed and jumped back, smashing into two large jerrycans of fuel, which tipped over. With a second bullet, the she-demon put him out of his misery.

Fuel – gasoline – bubbled out of the cans and spread toward the kneeling and wailing believers. Among them were some of the richest and most powerful people in Europe, people who had discovered the ecstatic amoral beauty of their unleashed Dionysian selves in the Cult of Satan.

Father Ottavio, shot in the shoulder and reeling back, saw and understood all of this in a flash: the overturned grill, the gasoline flooding over the floor; the embers that had spilled out of the grill ... When the embers and the gasoline met, the chapel would explode; this was truly the death dance, which preceded the end of time. These writhing bodies were heralds of Armageddon!

Suddenly, the she-demon, her fangs gleaming, her eyes glowing, as beautiful and seductive as Satan, was upon him: she had leapt from the back of the chapel to the altar in what seemed like one fantastic stride.

Wounded by the slash from Kate's sword and by John's bullet, Father Ottavio cowered, trembling in pain, under the burnt inverted cross, his mind a swirling kaleidoscope of images. The pain in his shoulder and chest roared like fire; his left arm dangled free, useless.

He fell to his knees. "Oh, Satan! Oh, Satan!"

He closed his eyes. Perhaps a death-blow would be delivered.

But, no, he half opened his eyes. The demon had not killed him. The demon had turned aside. She was leaning over the naked young woman spread-eagled on the altar; she was leaning over the sacrifice.

Jesus Christ, thought Kate, what next?

Leaning over her was a creature out of a nightmare – a reptile with a woman's face. A scaly demon!

It leaned closer; its bright red forked tongue flickered.

This is too much! Was this a real demon or an actress?

Kate clenched her fist around the sword handle, getting ready to kill the demon, slash out with the blade – cut off its head.

Kate was furious. This must be the creature these idiots worshipped!

Kill it and kill it now!

The kneeling believers stumbled to their feet. The drugs they had drunk had left them wildly libidinous, all their humanity lost, drowning in psychotic hallucinations. They groped each other, kissing, caressing, slobbering, and, here and there, squirming on the ground, attempting feverishly to copulate. Under their bodies the gasoline was spreading.

Marina Elia had seen the demon's arrival, seen the brazier explode, and seen how it had sent out embers and burning coals; she smelled the gasoline and realized what was going to happen. They were all going to die. She really should never have come to this infernal event! Oh well, as her mother had often warned her, curiosity did kill the cat!

She grabbed a garish-colored silk shirt somebody had draped over a chair. She could at least throw this over the poor naked girl; it would be better than nothing.

She fought her way out of the crowd of slobbering shouting worshippers, climbing over a skinny ancient couple – all sagging flesh and mottled skin and fragile bones – who were humping frantically on the ground; she pushed aside the dazed and the crazed, and she jostled and elbowed her way to the altar.

Father Ottavio recovered his nerve. The demon was distracted, leaning over the sacrifice. What was the demon going to do – eat the girl? Yes, undoubtedly the demon was jealous and considered that the sacrifice rightly belonged to her. But then a man – Father Michael Patrick O'Bryan – surged up. His death had been decreed. But here he was, alive. What was Father O'Bryan doing with the demon?!

Suddenly, Father Ottavio knew he had to escape. The demon was not what she seemed – she was clearly not of Satan's Brood. But if not, then why had she come here? What was she going to do with the sacrifice? And what would she do with him? *Would she eat him?*

He levered himself up, staggered to his feet, and glanced around at the seething mass of worshippers. Limping badly, doubled over and swaying from side to side, he stumbled out of the nave and staggered into a side gallery; there, he opened an invisible door that was disguised as a blank-faced alcove and plunged into a tunnel that was a secret escape route; it would take him out of the depths and to the surface. The worshippers – the damned – would die, the demon would die, the sacrificial young woman would die, Father O'Bryan would die – but, he, Father Ottavio, would live!

The demon stared down at Kate. In the torchlight the demon's scales rippled with color – turquoise, green, and gold, with streaks of scarlet. The demon was so close, Kate could see her clearly, in exquisite detail. The lips were full, the nostrils fine, and the patterned colors of the scales sublimely decorative. The creature was a bejeweled stature, an idol, pagan goddess, like those to whom, in the old days, tribes and empires sacrificed chickens and goats – and living children. Kate realized that, in a terrifying way, the demon was beautiful – beautiful as only the devil could be beautiful.

All around were screams of pain or joy, of ecstasy or lust – Kate couldn't tell which. This must all be hallucination and madness; she must already be dead. Maybe she had died in Jerusalem. Maybe all this, her whole life since, had been a dream, a dream of her dead or her dying.

Her fingers gripped the handle of the sacrificial sword, waiting for the right moment to plunge the knife straight into the demon's heart or swing wildly and cut off its head.

The demon's reptilian eyes glowed, golden sparks. "She's alive!" the demon shouted. "She's alive!"

"The demon talks!" thought Kate.

It leaned closer. "Kate, can you hear me? Kate?"

It knows my name! How can that be? Her fingers tightened. Goddamn! If I can, I will cut off its head. Kate's body arched up in pure rage and she struck out with all her might. The blade swung upwards in a deadly arc. But at that very moment Kate heard another voice. It was a familiar voice. It was Father O'Bryan's voice, saying, "Thank God!" And in the same instant she saw his face appear behind the demon.

"Oh, my God," thought Kate. "Maybe I've made a terrible mistake!"

Marina Elia reached the altar, just in time to see the girl swing the sword up at the she-devil – one swift sweep of the glittering blade.

Oh, my God, thought Marina, what is going to happen now? But a fraction of a second later she saw the demon catch and hold the girl's arm, gently remove the sword from the girl's hand, and place it back on the altar.

"Kate, I'm not the enemy," the demon said.

The priest who was standing beside the demon leaned forward. "Kate, she's right. She's not the enemy."

The demon released Kate's wrist. "I must go after Father Ottavio."

"Go. We'll free Kate," said the priest.

"Father Ottavio escaped down there. There is a tunnel. It will be the way out of here, for everyone." The demon nodded at the side gallery, then she glanced in the direction of the flames and spreading gasoline.

"I understand," said the priest. "We'll follow you."

"John?"

"I heard you, V. The tunnel! We'll follow you!"

Marina Elia stared; the she-demon and the priest and these other people were working together; and they seemed to be on the side of justice and reason; this was getting stranger and stranger.

Just as the demon seized her wrist and as Kate felt the sword removed from her hand, a woman appeared beside Father O'Bryan. "I'll help," she said.

Kate tried to mouth the words "Who are you?" but her voice was hoarse. It came out as a barely audible whisper.

"Don't worry, child," said the woman. "My name is Marina. We'll get you out of here – that is, if we don't all burn to death."

Marina glanced back at the seething mass in the chapel. When the gasoline and the hot coals met, it would be a holocaust.

She took out her Swiss Army knife.

V dashed down the tunnel in pursuit of Father Ottavio, thinking: She's a spunky girl, that Kate; she was going to try to kill me! We will be friends, I am certain of it.

V sniffed the sulfurous air, her nostrils damp and quivering. This was certainly close to one of Italy's ancient volcanoes – a magma chamber must be below and not too many miles down. A whole string of volcanoes, running along the fault line separating Europe and Africa, stretched from Tuscany to the African coast. She wondered how deep the underlying magma chamber was and how explosive it might be. If the gravitational field were disturbed …

A breeze wafted over her. It carried the clayey, fecund smell of wet earth, of primal mud and ooze. Water was sinking into the depths, then, heated by the magma or by strata of heated rock, it was forcing its way back up, creating hot water springs, and pools of sulfurous mud. V remembered some rather luxurious open-air mud baths she had enjoyed, in the company of a very handsome and sporty Roman centurion, and how under the moonlight they had …

Well, enough of that!

The tunnel split in two, both branches lit by burning wall torches and primitive electric lights strung along the center of the roof.

V glanced down one tunnel, then the other. Her nostrils quivered. She picked up the odor and scent of the man, Father Ottavio, his fear, his sweat, and – his blood. He was bleeding heavily.

Blood, his blood – fresh blood!

Her pulse quickened. That was the way! The branch that curved off to the right!

Her saliva rose. It flooded her mouth, coated her tongue. Her fangs dripped silver liquid; they tingled, eager, excited. Slurping back the electric yearning, she repressed the flash of hunger. She sniffed the air. She pawed the clayey ground. And she plunged after her prey.

The priest's running, staggering footsteps were ahead of her; she followed them.

Blood, his blood – fresh blood!

The tunnel opened into a cave. V found herself in a shadowy cavern, with alcoves and various tunnels leading out of it. Which way to go? Her forked tongue flicked, silver drops of excited hot saliva flew every which way in a misty spray. *Oh, she was so close now, so close to the kill!*

And there he was – in the shadows – heading into another tunnel, limping, lurching wildly from side to side, clutching his shoulder, and dripping blood – precious blood – from where John had shot him, and Kate had slashed him with the sword. Double yummy! Blood, blood, blood! V could taste it, his blood, intense and coppery, dark and delicious! She gulped back the warm viscous flood of saliva. *She was famished, she was famished!*

But no! She had to control herself. Ottavio was not just a quick snack! He had information she desperately needed! It was best to obtain it while he was still able to talk, but if not … she would drink it out of him. She was hungry, oh, so hungry! She sped after him. *I want to feed; but I must hold myself back for – just long enough.* She willed her fangs to stop tingling, she ordered her saliva glands to behave themselves, she commanded them to hold back on the squirting juice.

The second tunnel opened into another large cave. It had a low roof and a large central pool of smoky gray mud. Father Ottavio cradled his bloodied arm and lurched his way through the shadows and across the cave, skirting the smoldering gray volcanic slime.

V leapt, smashing into the man, sending him sprawling back toward the pool of bubbling clay. He stumbled, tottered, fell into the steamy gray liquid, creating a slow-motion splash, a miniature tsunami. He struggled to his feet, dripping mud and fighting against the muck. Weighed down and staggering shin-deep in gluey clay, he struggled to wade away from V.

Ashes to ashes, V thought, mud to mud …

Blood, his blood – fresh blood!

More saliva rose; she slurped it back, sloppily; it drooled from her chin; little bright red sparks of blood thirst burst like Roman candles in her eyes. She waded lustily, eagerly, into the steaming muck. In quick splashing strides, she plunged after the staggering, wounded priest. "Hey, you, hey, Father Ottavio!"

She grabbed him by his clerical collar, dragging him down – splash! She lifted him up, intending to haul him straight out of the viscous pool. But he stumbled back, a swirling dead weight of a man, his arms and legs flailing, and – damn him! He dragged her with him, and they both fell into the sulfurous goo.

"Yuk!"

She dug her claws deep into the priest's shoulder. She and her victim thrashed and splashed and stumbled in the mud. Enough! She sprang to her feet, picked the man up, and dragged him out of the pit.

"Father Ottavio," she hissed, fangs bared, "at last we truly meet! What a pleasure this is!"

"Take me," he shouted, as she dragged him away from the pool. "I am not worthy, Demon, but take me!"

"I will indeed take you, Father!" She hauled the shrunken trembling creature to his feet, "but first, Father, I must know this: Where is the Torelli Jewel?"

"I don't know what you are talking about."

"You lie, priest!"

"No! I know nothing!"

"I have other ways of finding out."

"I cannot tell you anything! I'm … I'm afraid."

"It is too late for fear."

"I cannot! I dare not!"

"I don't have time for your scruples or your fear, Father Ottavio!"

"Do what you have to do, Oh, Demon, Oh, Satan!"

"I shall, Father! I shall!" She plunged her fangs into the priest's neck, closed her fluttering, golden eyes, and drank and drank and drank.

Blood, his blood – fresh blood! V exulted as the crimson life force gushed into her, gurgling up, spreading out, ramifying in every artery and vein, incandescent with energy. Blood and gore overflowed, dripping from her jaws.

With the surging energy came all of Father Ottavio's knowledge – all his thoughts, fears, hopes, passions, and all his secrets, in a lightning flash reverberating through her mind …

CHAPTER 42 — CARPE DIEM

After the paving stones trembled under their feet, and Emperor Marcus Aurelius wobbled on his pedestal, Jian and Scarlett decided – in unison – that life was too short and fragile for dawdling; that the future was uncertain; indeed, that there might be no future at all; so, sex should be first on the immediate agenda. Seize the day was the motto – or, in this case, seize the night.

The only question was, "Your room or mine?" It turned out, as before, to be her room – the bed was bigger.

So, they were going to offer themselves another luxurious night, a full, long night of unbridled sensational sensuous pleasure.

Jian's stamina, it turned out, was astounding.

About three hours after the session began, Scarlett lay sprawled on her back on the king-size bed that filled most of her tiny hotel room. She was limp as a rag, but also, inwardly, full of beans and bubbling with plans for more mischief. With her right hand she stroked Jian's chest. Tonight, so far, had been damned amazing – totally amazing – for tenderness, goofiness, laughter, sensuality, and … pure, pure sex. Gosh and golly! She smiled. It was unbelievable, unbelievable!

"You are amazing," said Scarlett.

"You're the amazing one," he said.

"Oh, no," she whispered, nuzzling him. "I'm a slouch!"

"Not true," he bit her, gently, on the lip. "You are a goddess come back from ancient times."

Right next to the bed, the window was wide open. The night was sweltering, edgy, sensual. Outside, just a few feet away, long streaks of rain slanted down like ribbons of gold, lit by the streetlamps. The lamps in the room were off; reflected light from the street burnished their naked bodies with ripples of gold and rose. Jian lay next to her, blinking at the ceiling, his hand on her tummy, caressing the ripe smooth fertile downward slope between her hips.

"Oh," she groaned, "you have no pity."

"Can't resist," he whispered.

"Hmm."

Time passed. They lay peacefully, dazed, half-awake, half-dreaming, exchanging light, tentative, tender little caresses.

"Tingle, tingle." Scarlett opened her eyes.

"Tingle, tingle?"

"I feel like I'm tingling. Tingling all over. Like I'm electric." She rolled over to face him. She snuggled up closer, sliding her hand up and down his chest.

"I feel it too." He caressed the side of her face.

"The air is tingling."

"Yes." His eyes were half closed. "Maybe the whole world is tingling."

"Did we do this?" A mischievous sparkle glowed in her eyes. "Create the tingle?"

"I'm sure we did." He kissed her.

"Oh, boy!"

"Oh, boy!" He echoed her, a friendly echo, just whispered.

"Darling, darling, darling!" Scarlett rolled over, kneeled above him, kissed him, and then, in one fluid, dance-like movement, she stepped off the bed, crouched in front of the little fridge, and pulled out the bottle of white wine she had bought when they were returning to the hotel.

She crawled to the bed and, on all fours, holding up the bottle, looked up at him. "This should be perfectly cold by now."

"Does it tingle?" He gazed up at her, in the golden light, drinking her in.

"Definitely!"

"Well, goddess, let us drink!" he whispered, and reached out to touch her hair, and caress her cheek. "My golden goddess!"

A few seconds later, they were sitting facing each other, cross-legged on the floor on an extra-large red towel Scarlett had unfurled onto the rug. Jian had just lifted a glass to Scarlett's lips. She was sipping from it, a cool splash of wine dribbling down her chin and down to her breasts, and thinking: *Oh, how fabulously right this all is!*

And in that very instant it happened.

The little shepherd girl statue bounced along its ledge; the refrigerator swayed; the bedside lamp fell over; the bed creaked and groaned; car alarms wailed; the streetlamps blinked, once, twice, three times, and then went out, plunging the room into darkness.

An earthquake.

"Oh, God!" Scarlett whispered, wine spilling from her lips.

"It's happening again." Jian reached out to hold her.

"Clothes!"

"Right – clothes!"

"Where are they?"

"The bed – maybe under the bed!"

They crawled, on all fours. They groped, blindly.

"I don't see them."

"I don't see anything."

They collided – on all fours, body against body. "Oh, you!" "Oh, you!" They groped, they kissed, they grabbed each other, they kissed … Then they were sliding down on each other, down onto the towel. They turned over, their bodies pressed together. She kissed him, deeper, longer, stronger than she had ever kissed anybody in her life.

Then, in an instant, he was on top of her, suddenly, blindly. He slid into her, deeper, stronger, faster, easier than he had ever slid into anyone in his life, the rhythm rising, her legs wrapped around him. "Oh, oh, oh," she cried. "Oh, oh, oh," he cried; her hands grappled with him, caressing him, pulling him deeper into her. She kissed him.

"This is crazy!

"Yes, this is crazy!"

"We're crazy!"

"Yes, we're crazy!"

Sirens wailed.

She kissed him again. It was a deep, unending, eternal kiss; it sealed their union; they became one, one creature, one wave of sensation, one rhythm; he moved within her, quickly, brutally, slowly, gently, tenderly, Oh, oh, oh, oh …

Sirens wailed.

They came. "Oh, oh, oh, oh …"

"Oh, oh, oh …!"

"Yes, yes, yes …!"

Sirens wailed …

They lay in the darkness, blind, gasping for breath, laughing, out of control, laughing. Then, slowly, blindly, sliding up onto all fours, they kissed, and stroked and caressed each other, their hearts beating hard, as one. And then, with one voice, they said, laughing, "Where are they? Where *are* our clothes?"

The sirens wailed.

Cloaked in velvety darkness, covered in steamy heat, fumbling for her panties, Scarlett slid her body along Jian's. This was, she thought, as, deep in her throat, she purred, this was positively languorous – in the almost mystical sense of calm and peace and unity that sometimes comes post coitum – and very, very exciting, as if anticipating and warming up for the next round. She was still hungry for him, yearning for him.

She moved her hand blindly down between his legs. "Naughty, naughty boy!" she whispered. "Very naughty!" He kissed her. The kiss lingered, soft and liquid and sublime. Scarlett just hoped they wouldn't die. Tonight was the wrong time to die, definitely the wrong night to die!

CHAPTER 43 – CRESCENDO

"See those squiggly lines, Cardinal? Those are anomalies – minuscule seismic movements. Earth is trembling, deep down, in the weak points."

"Where, dear Professor?" The Cardinal put on his spectacles, leaned over, put one hand on Roger's naked shoulder, and peered at the screen. The Cardinal's hand trembled. And his chin was trembling too – perhaps from excitement. There was a slick of saliva at the corner of his mouth.

"These are just preliminary tremors; the full impact will come, I think, in a few minutes." Roger suddenly had an image of the planet Earth. It was an old baseball with frayed seams dividing its skin into sections; the sections were tectonic plates. Some of the plates were pushing their way under, or over, other neighboring plates. Some plates were moving away from each other, ripping open a gap. Some were sliding, more or less easily, past one another. At the seams between plates, or where the plates themselves were porous or thin – at "hot spots" like Yellowstone – the world might quite easily begin to come apart at the seams, with plates clashing and tearing at each other, and with huge pools of molten magma spurting up from below, ripping the skin into fragments. Roger saw the baseball exploding, in slow motion, ripping apart …

"Where, exactly, Professor, are these little preliminary tremors?"

"Where you might expect, actually." Roger pointed at the large map on one of the screens. "Near tectonic plate boundaries, or near hot spots – for example, along the ring of fire around the Pacific. There are tremors in Sicily, near Mount Etna, then near Naples, in the shadow of Vesuvius, in Yellowstone National Park, and along the San Andreas Fault, in the Cascade Mountain Range. There's a cluster here, near Japan, which looks like one of the worst. And a few in Turkey, near the southern coast, so far; there will probably be more. There are some minor shocks near Rome, possibly in the city itself."

"Good, good! That means our message – our love letter – is being received all over the world!" The Cardinal beamed at Roger. "We are ecumenical!" He rubbed his hands. "We will kill everybody everywhere! No distinction of race, religion, or nationality!"

Roger said nothing; he held the Cardinal's gaze.

"Well, Professor, this is just an experiment, you know! Tomorrow, we will try something serious."

"I am not sure that will be even necessary. The quakes are already amplifying." Roger turned his attention to the seismic monitors. Several the inky-black lines were beginning to oscillate more fiercely. Roger clenched his fist. Every tiny jiggle in every tiny line could destroy hundreds, or thousands, or even millions of lives.

A few lines began to oscillate madly …

"Damn it," Roger muttered.

"Don't worry, Professor." The Cardinal smiled a mischievous smile. "None of this is your doing. I hereby absolve you. You will die with a clean conscience. You are merely an observer. You have nothing to do with the end of the world." And he raised his hand in benediction. "*In nomine diaboli, spiritus maligni, et aeterni mali.*"

CHAPTER 44 – PURIFYING FIRE

Father O'Bryan struggled desperately to loosen one of the manacles that held Kate down. He'd never felt so clumsy. His fingers seemed enormous, and made of rubber.

"Kill! Kill! Kill!"

"Kill! Kill! Kill!"

The zombie-like worshippers advanced steadily, an empty-eyed, slobbering phalanx headed toward the altar.

"Kill! Kill! Kill!"

"Kill! Kill! Kill!"

"Stand back or I'll shoot!" John held the Beretta M9 steady, aimed at the biggest of the three men who were in the front line, shuffling slowly toward the altar. They were indeed like zombies. Their empty soulless eyes shone like polished coins. Their attention was centered on the altar, on the naked girl. They slobbered and growled. Their hands opened and closed, like claws. Their intention was clear, they were going to tear the girl apart – and eat her.

John handed his machete to Henry. "Use this if you have to."

"Absolutely, sir," said Henry. "With pleasure."

"Call me John."

"Kill! Kill! Kill!"

"Kill! Kill! Kill!"

John shot two of the men point-blank. They fell, but behind them more were advancing. "Stand back or I'll shoot!"

"Kill! Kill! Kill!"

"Kill! Kill! Kill!"

Henry slashed at two heavy-set naked men, forcing them back a step, but others pushed forward; one was a gaunt ash blonde, a woman who had probably been beautiful, or was still beautiful when she was human. They shuffled forward, drooling, their vacuous bright gazes focused on the gleaming ivory-white body of the sacrifice splayed out on the altar.

"This is terrible," said Henry, "humans who have lost their humanity."

"Yes, it is." John pulled the trigger, again and again, and four of the men – and one of the women – the gaunt ghostly blonde – went down.

"And I think, John, this hellhole is about to go up in flames."

"Yes, Henry, I believe you are right."

John calculated they had a minute, maybe two, maybe not. The gasoline was seeping very close to where the embers were scattered and glowing. The chapel was a ticking time-bomb. The fuse was short.

Marina Elia crawled under the block of black granite, lay on her back, and stared up. The manacles on top of the altar were too strong and too tightly locked to be pried loose; but they were screw-bolted into the stone from below – if she could loosen the bolts, then the manacles would free up, and Kate would be able to get her wrists and ankles free …

Maybe …

Marina had already freed Kate's neck, and she was now loosening an ankle bolt with the Swiss Army knife. It was imperfectly bolted; she chipped away at a bit of rust, and layers of old clogged blood, and unscrewed it quickly. *Good, good, thank God!* Luckily, the bolts were greased; there was not too much rust, just a thick buildup of gore and encrusted blood. You'd think they'd clean it! The altar must have been in constant use: dozens of young women manacled down, disemboweled, bleeding to death …

"Okay, that one's done," said Marina; she crawled out from under the altar and stood up.

Father O'Bryan mumbled and groaned as he struggled with the one wrist manacle that was jammed. He pulled, twisted, pulled, grunted, sweated, but to no avail.

"So, one wrist remains," said Marina. She frowned. If they didn't get the girl out of here soon, they would all die. She glanced at the bowl of oil. She picked it up: *Yes!* It was half full. "Here," she turned to Kate. "Try to wiggle your hand out." She poured the golden oil over Kate's one manacled wrist.

Poor delusional true believers! John shot two more of the zombies point-blank. More were coming – a solid wall of gaily painted, groaning, snarling, naked, oiled, empty-eyed flesh. Some groveled on the ground, crying out prayers to Satan, others copulated in a welter of greasepaint, oil, and sweat. The stench of gasoline was overpowering.

"It's going to explode." Henry took a swipe at a very portly gentleman, forcing him back, just a few feet, but the man, thrust forward by those pressing from behind, came at Henry again, growling and slobbering, so, with one downward sweep of the machete, Henry split the man's skull in two, muttering, "I'm awfully sorry, sir."

The man's large, red, sagging face, with its heavy, creased jowls, looked shocked; his blue eyes bulged. Blood streamed down his forehead and down both sides of his bulbous nose. He keeled over.

"Yes, Henry, any instant now, and this will be an inferno." John shot two gentlemen in the legs and stepped back. If they got involved in hand-to-hand combat with these people, it would be impossible to disengage. In John's experience, the insane – and the possessed – could be much stronger than even the best trained normal human being.

Kate pulled her feet from the loosened manacles. Only that one wrist was still caught. She looked up at the woman – her name was Marina – who was pouring oil on her hand. Kate wiggled her wrist, squeezed her hand, pulled and wiggled and pulled – and, *Eureka*, the hand slipped free!

She was free!

She tried to sit up, felt dizzy, and almost fell back.

Father O'Bryan and Marina helped her sit up. "Here, dear," said Marina. She held out a garish shirt. "It's all I could find." She helped Kate pull on the shirt.

"Versace?" said Kate.

"Yes. I believe so."

"I'm not sure I *like* Versace." Kate buttoned it up – only three buttons … Even the simplest act was an effort; her mind moved slowly, and her arms and legs seemed far away, but she could move.

She pushed herself off the altar and stood up.

"Good girl!" Marina beamed.

"Kate, we must …" Father O'Bryan took her by the arm. "We must …"

Whoosh! The leaking gasoline touched the embers. A flame leapt up. Then another, and then the fire whooshed up. A wall of flame raced toward the center of the chapel.

Whoosh!

The oil and paint on the greased bodies of the damned ignited. In an instant, each believer became a living torch, and the chapel was a writhing inferno of screams and bodies in torment.   The fire filled the chapel.

"Follow me!" John shouted. The only possible way out was, as V had indicated, through the tunnels.

"Can you walk, Kate?"

"I'm dizzy."

Marina and Father O'Bryan grabbed Kate and ran toward the side gallery. Right behind them came Henry and John. Into the tunnel they ran.

A wave of scalding heat rushed behind them, slammed into them.

They staggered and raced down the tunnel. Behind them, screams and shrieks from the dying were drowned in a roar of fire.

WHAM! WHAM! WHAM!

A huge billow of fire flooded in.

The fire must have reached the jerry cans.

"Don't look! Don't look back!"

They faced a fork in the tunnel. "Which way? That way!"

"Any way!"

They ran to the right. Kate stumbled, half carried, half pushed, by Marina and Father O'Bryan.

Just as they entered a wide, low cavern, there was an immense explosion in the tunnels behind them – a huge, echoing boom. A wall of heat smashed into them, propelling them, staggering and tumbling, all the way into the middle of the space.

WHAM! Another wall of heat!

Kate fell to her knees. The Versace shirt billowed up around her. Father O'Bryan, thrown against a wall, just managed to stay upright.

Kate got to her feet, smoothed the Versace down. "Let's get out of here," she shouted. Her mind was suddenly clear; she felt a surge of energy. A wall of flame was rushing down the tunnel.

John led. They plunged into a side tunnel. Behind them, they could still hear screams – was that an illusion? – and the roar of flames.

"V!" Father O'Bryan shouted. His voice echoed.

"V!"

"V!"

There was no answer.

"She must have found a way out."

"Who is that demon, that thing?" gasped Kate.

"A friend," said Father O'Bryan. "In spite of appearances, a friend."

Kate's blood was pumping, adrenaline surging. She didn't need help, she was running on her own.

Father O'Bryan was huffing and puffing. "I'm getting too old for this. You go on. I'll sit here and rest for a moment."

"Father, you can't stay here, the fire is getting closer. Here, I'll help you." John took Father O'Bryan by the arm.

"No, let me just rest here."

"You'll do no such thing, Father!" It was V, still in full reptilian demon mode, covered in mud, her chin and breasts dripping with fresh blood.

"Where did you come from?"

"I followed your voices. Let's go. I think I've found a way out."

V draped Father O'Bryan's arm over her shoulder and hoisted him up.

"Father Ottavio," John asked. "I suppose you …?"

"I fed. He is truly dead. He will not rise again. He was absolutely delicious, truly tasty, even if a trifle too muddy for my taste."

"Here, V. You lead the way. I'll look after Father O'Bryan." John slung his arm around Father O'Bryan.

V moved up ahead, looked over her shoulder, and shouted: "This way."

John urged Father O'Bryan forward. They raced and stumbled down the tunnel. It was hot as a furnace. Again, Kate wondered who on earth these people were.

"This is the way out." V pointed. "At least I think it is."

Kate sniffed the air. Her senses were extra alive. It smelled even more strongly of sulfur; the air was incandescent.

The electric lights flickered. The flaming torches, hit by a sudden rush of air, suddenly went out.

"Oh-oh," said Henry.

"I don't like this." John wiped his forehead.

"Keep moving," said V. "Something is going to happen."

"Oh, boy," said Kate. "You mean, *more* stuff is going to happen?"

They stumbled into a large cavern. A string of lightbulbs hanging on a wire clipped to the walls cast a ghostly sheen. Pressed against one side of the cavern, they skirted a sulfurous waterfall that cascaded into a wide pool of bubbling gray mud; tendrils and veils of steam spread like ghostly tentacles over the pool. Kate was wide-eyed. This was spectacular – and spooky.

The electric lights flickered.

V stopped. She held up a claw and sniffed the air. A breeze was coming from the tunnel to the left. Her nostrils twitched. It smelled like fresh cut grass, like a breeze from the sea; it smelled like wood smoke; it smelled like the outside, just a hint, but it was enough. "Come on! This is the way."

Then, just as she entered the new tunnel, V paused. A weird serpentine wave of energy was building up, tingling in every nerve ending, a hint of a rapidly accumulating electric charge, an inkling, an itchy premonition.

"Stop! Listen!"

They stopped; they listened.

In that instant V realized what it was she sensed. How could she have not recognized it before? Even before she attacked the villa, she had felt it – in the unnatural heaviness of the air, in the nervous sultry immobile heat, in the buildup of static energy that lay heavy on the land. It was the Crystal in action, as foreseen, as foretold. The timetable of destruction had accelerated. The end of the world was hurdling toward them like an out-of-control freight train. She slurped back her saliva. She suppressed her excitement. It was coming; it was going to happen; and part of it was going to happen now. "It's an earthquake!"

A deep rumbling, then a rippling roar. The cavern shook, swayed, jumped upwards; the ground heaved up; rocks fell, one wall collapsed inward – a thundering cascade of rock, rubble, and dust. John grabbed Father O'Bryan and pulled him out of the way of a careening block of stone.

Shielding Father O'Bryan, John was wacked on the shoulder by a fragment of the block. A bouncing rock whammed Marina on the temple, knocking her down. Sand and clay poured in everywhere. The earth trembled and shook. Henry bent over Marina, determined to protect her.

Torn away from Marina, Kate was sent spinning sideways; she fell on her backside, grabbed for the ground, and scrambled to steady herself, clawing at the dirt. John grabbed her and pulled her to her feet.

"Thanks," she breathed, holding tight to his gloved hand and looking up with startled eyes at his wildly painted camouflaged face and black skintight outfit; she'd hardly noticed it before. So many things had been happening.

Holding her breath, Kate held fast to John. The surge of energy came, wave after wave of it, splitting rocks, shattering the cavern walls, snapping the lighting cables, tearing them from their moorings. The lights flickered. The waterfall slowed and stopped; it went dry; then it bubbled up again and a huge wave of water flooded the cavern. The lights flickered again and went out. Total darkness. They were trapped – and with a rising flood of water! John's hold on Kate tightened.

"Don't move," V shouted.

As the flood swirled and gurgled up around her thighs, V grabbed a high-powered light from her backpack, clicked it on, and fastened it to her forehead. The raw white light lit up a jumble of rocks and cascading dust – and water boiling up all around them. "It's flooding the whole tunnel!"

"Is everybody okay?" Holding Kate close, John pulled an equally powerful lamp from his backpack; he fastened it to his forehead. The two lights lit up the scene in a garish ghostly white.

"I'm fine," said Father O'Bryan. "Shaken, but fine."

"I'm good," said Kate.

"I took a knock on the head," said Marina, white with mud and dust, "but I'm okay."

"Feeling splendid." Henry was next to Marina, and knee-deep in muddy foam. "Totally chipper."

"I'll see if the path is open." V waded deeper into the water – up to her waist. She faded, a luminous flickering sliver of turquoise and gold, and then she was gone. After a few seconds, she called out, "It's clear! Follow me!"

Kate glanced at John and raised an eyebrow. *Follow the demon!* It was like a game you could play in kindergarten, dragons and dungeons, or demons and caverns. She almost giggled. *I must be delirious. Follow the demon girl!*

John nodded, grinned, and winked. "Let's go."

With water bubbling up around them, with the headlamps bobbing up and down, with garish circles of light penetrating the smoky darkness, with dust raining down everywhere, they struggled onwards, mostly in single file. For the next thirty minutes, they navigated through the narrow ruins of the tunnel; they crawled through minuscule cracks; they slithered, belly-down in sloshing soupy mud, through shattered openings; they crouched and waddled, bent in half, under low, half-collapsed ceilings; they waded through a cauldron of thick clayey bubbling muck. Sometimes, rarely, they were able to walk upright, but even then, they had to grope through a tight, jagged, zigzag maze of fissures and crevices; they climbed, sloshed, and crawled over heaps of muddy rubble that reached almost to the ceiling; and even then, squeezed against the ceiling, they had to slip through on their bellies with only inches to spare.

Slithering through a narrow, swirling, bubbly morass of guck, Kate's mind was racing. She was stronger and stronger. The sooner they got out of this mess, the sooner she could find her father. She squeezed between two slippery boulders, and helped Marina slip sideways through the narrow opening. Thigh-high sulfurous mud swirled around them, warm as pea soup, thick as molasses. In the light of John's headlamp, Marina suddenly looked extra pale and ghostly. "Are you okay?" Kate took Marina's arm.

"I think I am." Marina gave Kate one of her best, warmest smiles.

Minutes later, in a narrow, half-flooded passage, Marina slid down, with one hand grasping a slippery clayey wall. She sat down in the muddy cascade of water.

"Marina needs help!" Kate shouted and knelt next to her.

John and Henry pulled Marina up and guided her through the last slimy space and up onto a bit of relatively dry ground, a sodden ledge of clay.

"V," said John, "this lady needs one of your talents."

Kate watched. What were they doing? The V creature, the demon reptile woman, brightly lit up in the spotlight of John's lamp, came wading back, climbed up onto the ledge of clay, and crouched down next to Marina.

"She's got a concussion." V knelt over Marina, put her palm on Marina's forehead, closed her eyes, and concentrated.

Kate stared. V was intensely lit up by the two lamps. It was like the demon was performing on a miniature movie set. Was this demon a witch, too? A faith healer? An angel? Or what? What was she doing – a "laying on of hands"? Ultraviolet light radiated from the demon's claws.

Marina opened her eyes. "I'm sorry. I must have fallen asleep."

"We're almost there," said V, lifting Marina to her feet. "My name is V, by the way."

"Thank you for saving us." Marina gave V her most dazzling smile.

"We're not out of this yet. But you're very welcome."

"You have a charming lisp."

"Fangs," said V. "And the forked tongue."

"Very elegant, the tongue, the patterns," said Marina. "I work in design."

"Thank you," said V.

Gosh! Kate stared at the woman and the demon. They were in danger of being buried alive and these two girls were talking demon design.

The demon turned to Kate – and winked.

Kate's eyes opened wider. Did the demon just read her thoughts?

It took them another twenty minutes to get to the entrance of the tunnel. The air was hot and heavy, but fresher than in the satanic chapel and deeper tunnels. Kate smelled plants, wood smoke, and fresh night air. They had almost reached the surface! She tightened her hold on Marina's hand.

Silhouetted against glimmers of the burning night sky that came through a tangle of vines, was a dark metal grille. It was a barred gate that blocked the way and it had not been destroyed by the quake. It had a heavy lock. V examined the lock and the gate. V glanced at Kate and then she seized the gate and ripped it off its hinges, swinging it around and leaning it against the wall of the tunnel. The way was clear, except for the jungle of vines and vegetation.

"I take back everything bad I've said about you," said Kate.

"You haven't said anything about me, Kate," said V. "Not yet."

"That's true," said Kate, with a grin. The lady demon was indeed an elegant and gallant demon – in fact, with the patterned scales, the fangs, the bright slender forked tongue, the glowing eyes, the whole ensemble was, as Marina said, very stylish. V could be turned into a wonderful line of accessories!

"I heard that," said V. "*Accessories*, eh?"

"You read thoughts?"

"Uh huh, sometimes."

"Accessories – not a bad idea," said Marina. "Definitely not a bad idea. Handbags, for instance."

"Women!" V probed forward with the flashlight. Beyond the grille, the exit tunnel was partly hidden by the vines and by a pile of flat stones. There was also an electric fence blocking the way, and two closed-circuit security cameras pointed at the exit, but V saw that the cameras were dead, their cables and power supplies almost certainly destroyed by the earthquake; and when she got to the electric fence, she discovered it was dead too, and torn open in places. She swept it aside and opened a breach big enough for all of them to pass through. And so, they all emerged, finally, into the free air, halfway up a steep mountainside that looked over the vast coastal plain that reached to the sea.

Kate took a deep, deep breath.

"Well, at least it's not raining." V gazed at the sky.

"Yes, the storm has passed." John wiped his forehead. He was still in full warrior makeup, his eyes shone, bright moonlit pools in the black-and-green patterned face. There was a rumbling sound. He turned.

"What is … that …?"

"Another earthquake or an aftershock!"

Rocks tumbled down the hillside and rolled past them. Pebbles skittered and bounced and disappeared downwards. Father O'Bryan felt his feet slip from under him. Trying to regain his balance, he spun his arms; it looked as if he were trying to take flight. But he managed to keep his footing and remain upright.

Henry stared at the countryside far below on the plain – there were fires everywhere. Kate steadied herself against Marina.

"I think this is the beginning of the final stage." V turned to Father O'Bryan.

"Ambrosiano's Apocalypse?" Father O'Bryan, still shaky from his near fall, and dusty, muddy, and disheveled, crossed himself.

"Yes." V slid out of her backpack. "Don't watch if you don't want to," she said to all of them, but particularly to Kate, who was staring at her.

"Don't watch what?" asked Kate.

There was a whirr and a blur that lit up the livid night air. The reptile woman disappeared, and the human version of V suddenly stood there, naked. "Don't watch that, was what I meant." V's human body shone, bright ivory, in the moonlight, but flecked with reflections of fire, splashed with mud and dust. Her face was still half painted in zebra-like camouflage and trickled with spatterings and flecks of blood. Kate stared; this was unbelievable – like magic! V unzipped her backpack and began to pull on her matte-black catsuit battle gear.

"Awesome," said Kate; she glanced at Father O'Bryan, who didn't seem surprised or shocked at all. "You knew about this? You've seen this?"

"Yes, Kate, I've seen a great many things in the last day or two."

"You said 'the beginning.' The beginning of what?" Marina blinked at the half-naked warrior woman.

"The beginning of the end!" shouted Father O'Bryan, spreading his arms, and, in an almost jovial oracular tone, he cried out: "the Apocalypse, Armageddon, the End of Days, and the Final Revelation!"

"He's giddy," said Marina. "The excitement has been too much for him."

"Yes, yes, you're right, Marina. I am indeed giddy. I've lost all sense of what is real and what isn't. I am a dusty old library mouse. I'm not used to such adventures."

"Look at that!" Henry pointed upwards. The moon was shrouded in a cloud of red dust. In the countryside below them, on the plain reaching to the sea, the fires continued to rage.

"Oh, boy!" Kate gazed around. It did look as if the world was coming to an end – the sky was red, the air was filled with dust, buildings and farms and villages were burning. It looked like they had landed smack in the middle of Dante's Inferno – or maybe something even worse.

Wham!

There was a huge explosion; they all turned …

CHAPTER 45 – INTERLUDE

Still tangled together, Scarlett and Jian groped in the darkness – searching for their clothes. The hotel room swayed. Drunken shadows from car headlights danced a tango on the walls. The room rose up in a giddy rolling motion, and then plunged down. They were in a small boat lifted – then dropped – by a giant ocean wave.

"Oh, boy – are we going to die?"

"No, because I love you," Jian's lips brushed hers, a light fast kiss.

"And I love you!"

"We are not allowed to die!"

"Right, dying is absolutely not on the menu!"

The floor swayed. A grinding, rising to a roar, overwhelmed everything. For a dizzy moment, the hotel room seemed to have turned upside down.

Then it settled.

Wham!

A huge crack of thunder echoed; and a sudden, instant deluge of rain roared outside the window – a Niagara.

Crawling under the bed, Scarlett found her panties and one of her socks.

"I've got a sock!" She backed out from under the bed and glanced at Jian. He was on hands and knees, his body ripping streams of reflected amber and gold.

"Do you really need socks?" He raised an eyebrow.

"You're right. I don't need the sock," Scarlett said. "I'm not going to wear the sock." Lying on her back, she levered herself up, and slipped into her panties. "I'm not going to wear the other sock either."

"That sounds about right." His grin was just visible, shining in the flickering reflections.

"Oh, my love!"

Shouts, screams, and trampling feet! People were stampeding down the narrow stairs just outside their door. Some were laughing; others were shouting. It was a babble of languages.

More sirens wailed.

Jian crouched lower, got down on his belly, and probed under the bed. "Got them!" He handed Scarlett her shorts and T-shirt.

Her purse and scarlet rubber flip-flops were sitting sagely next to the bathroom door. Scarlett crawled toward them. Jian pulled on his jeans and T-shirt. They checked for cell phones, keys, wallets, cameras and passports. Scarlett spotted the little shepherd girl; she was lying on the rug, unscathed. Scarlett picked her up and put her on the bed and tucked her safely between two pillows.

Wham! A giant flash of lightning lit Scarlett and Jian in a fiery red, coppery-gold glow; it was everywhere at once, shining out of the walls, radiating out of their bodies, glimmering in their eyes. The rain was coming down faster, heavier, a roaring Niagara. Screeching voices called out, for help, for friends, for each other; more sirens wailed, but all the sounds were drowned in the roar of the rain.

The door to the landing was jammed. "Uh, oh," said Scarlett.

Jian smashed into it with his shoulder; it sprang open.

On the landing, garish, white, battery-powered emergency lights glared down, giving panicky faces a ghastly hue. Like an Ensor painting, Scarlett thought, like rubber masks, not like people. She tugged on the door, managed to pull it shut, and locked it. Everybody coming down the stairs was talking, Italian, French, German, Mandarin, Japanese.

The building shook. The elevator cage swayed and creaked.

"Okay, down we go," said Jian, taking Scarlett's hand.

In the lobby, Paolo, the night porter, was organizing people and giving them instructions – bottles of water from the kitchen and chocolate bars and power bars from a dispenser. He glanced at Scarlett and Jian, said, "So you two found each other – I was sure you would!" Then he turned to the crowd. "Everybody, it's better to stay outside, in open spaces, as far away from buildings as you can."

A few seconds later, Scarlett and Jian found themselves out in the street, blinking up at the buildings. Nothing seemed to have collapsed. The sky still radiated that strange bright ominous coppery color. The rain slashed down, filling their eyes, hammering their faces. In a few seconds, they were near-blind – and soaked, T-shirts clinging, transparent as glass. In the distance, above the rooftops, bluish flashes leapt across the sky – followed by rippling waves of deep, rumbling thunder that shook the cobblestones and made Scarlett's teeth chatter.

"Oh, boy," Scarlett whispered into his ear. "This is exciting."

"More than exciting!" He kissed her and pressed her to him.

At that instant, the whole sky lit up. A huge arc of blue, a vast lightning bolt, jumped from one horizon to the other, flooding the whole atmosphere.

Fuck! U Pizzu was fucking well not going to budge, not a fucking inch. If the hotel fell down around his fucking ears, well, that was just too fucking bad. When the second shock came, he was lying naked on top of the covers on the queen-size bed, staring at the ceiling.

The lights went out. The air-conditioning fell silent. "Fuck!" U Pizzu got up, opened the window, pushed aside the creaky wooden shutters, and looked out. It was raining, a fucking deluge; the sky had turned from black to a deadly glowing coppery red. What the fuck could cause such a thing? It looked like the end of the fucking world! He'd better fucking well book a ticket on Noah's Ark. Poor old Gaetano, God rest his soul, the man had been a prophet!

U Pizzu pulled the shutters to, closed the window, drew the curtains shut, and went back to the bed and lay down. There are times when you want to shut the whole world out, curl up, and suck your thumb. It had been an instructive evening. After dining at the Living Fountain, U Pizzu and Santino had strolled down the sultry, crowded cobblestoned streets to a bar-restaurant situated in a small, intimate square a couple of blocks away.

They sat down at a table on the terrace. It was a great place to watch soccer stars, models, and starlets strut their stuff. The lamplight reflected on the green ivy that clung to the burnt sienna walls of the little Renaissance palazzo opposite. The cozy well-lit little piazza was like a film set.

"Look at that girl," said Santino. "All legs … and nothing else."

The model, who had just stepped out of a black SUV, displayed golden-tanned legs a mile long and a mini-dress that rose almost above her hips.

U Pizzu was toying with his espresso cup.

"Hey, Pizzu, you got to cheer up!"

U Pizzu was thinking just how easily Santino cheered up – one minute he's sunk in theological despair, no meaning to life, Santa Claus is dead, God has skipped town, Mother Church is truly the corrupt Whore of Babylon that heretical critics and Protestants always said she was; then the next minute he's ogling the merchandise, all alive, all sparkly, all bubbly! Oh, well, Santino was young; and then, too, he did have the attention span of a gnat.

At that point, as they sat in the café, and just after the waiter had delivered their coffees, U Pizzu's cell phone rang. He flipped it open and listened.

"They did what?" He frowned. Then he scowled. "No, no, no! That is absolutely against the …! Okay, okay, yeah, calm down. Yeah, you are right! That is so stupid! It means trouble, alright … Thanks."

He listened some more, then flipped the phone shut. He looked glummer than before.

"Who did what?"

"I don't know if I should tell you."

"Why, why not tell me?"

"Because, Santino, you are a sensitive soulful youthful impressionable son-of-a-bitch and it might upset you as much as it upset me. I don't want to ruin your evening."

"I am not – sensitive, I mean."

"Okay." U Pizzu lifted the espresso, took a careful sip. He was fucking well going to control himself; this was a personal insult, a grave personal insult, *uno sgarbo*! And in Sicily, for a man like U Pizzu, the maintenance of whose reputation was essential for business and even for physical survival, fear and respect being his first line of defense against enemies and assassins, and fear and respect being also his stock-in-trade, the basis of all extortion rackets, a *sgarbo*, an insult, was unforgiveable; it was a betrayal – and a deadly challenge, a risk to everything. He put the espresso cup down carefully. "You know that terrorist attack on via Aurelia last night?"

"Yeah, I saw that: the bastards shot up a high-class restaurant and kidnapped some fucking big-wheel American scientist and his daughter."

"Well, it wasn't a terrorist attack."

"It wasn't?"

"No." U Pizzu took a deep breath, and then he enunciated, very carefully, emphasizing each syllable. "It seems that on explicit orders from Cardinal Ambrosiano, the Garibaldi Street Gang – who are supposed to be our correspondents – our partners – here in Rome and keep us informed of what they're doing – did the job."

"What? That can't be – fuck!"

"It is – and it gets worse. As you know, they shot dead a couple of famous people, I'm saying like world-famous, like scientists with Nobel Prizes and bells and whistles and so on; and they wounded a bunch of other important people, including some famous foreigners; and they hurt some women. And they left a hell of a lot of witnesses."

"Jesus Maria!"

"Right," said U Pizzu, "*Jesus Maria!* And the worst thing is ..." U Pizzu paused. "The worst thing – and I don't fucking believe this – Cardinal Ambrosiano's guys, those crazy monks, and that madman Father Ottavio, killed the kidnappers. They murdered Fabio Ciotti and Gigi Viola – Pino Viola's son! They fucking murdered the guys who kidnapped the scientist's daughter and delivered her to that fucking villa Gaetano told me Cardinal Ambrosiano uses for his secret orgies."

"What? They killed the Garibaldi Street guys – Fabio and Gigi? Christ! I used to play poker regular with Gigi! Straight-faced Gigi, we called him!"

"Yeah, they killed them." U Pizzu gazed at a black model, a dish, in a short silver dress, who was laughing about something. Her hand was on her companion's shoulder. Some people were happy, innocent and happy! "Fabio's cellphone was open when he was killed. Old Francesco Ciotti, his father, heard the whole fucking thing – on speaker. Francesco's mad as hell and he's screaming murder!" U Pizzu emptied his espresso; he was very un-Sicilian, and he knew it, in the way he drank his espresso: real slow, a sip at a time, savoring it, like you savor life, letting it cool, taking his time, tasting things to the fullest. He half closed his eyes. He liked the way the black girl laughed. She was famous. He'd seen her in ads. She did charity work. Was super-nice to her staff, so the tabloids said. Yeah, she did look like a nice kid. "I don't fucking believe it!"

"This is fucking screwy! Why the fuck would they do it?"

"You know, I hate to say this, I really hate to say this – but Gaetano Larione was not nuts," U Pizzu said. He stared into the empty espresso cup. And he'd killed him, he'd killed his best buddy for telling the fucking truth, and for warning him, for being up front with him, up front as a best friend should be with his oldest buddy. "Right! I'm going to get that fucking Torelli Jewel or whatever the fuck it is! And I'm going to find that fucking demon and I'm going to ask her some hard questions! If anybody knows what the Cardinal is up to, it'll be this fucking girl demon."

"Yeah, but we don't know what the fucking Jewel is – or why it's fucking important."

"Look, nobody knows what it is or why it's important. Remember – Father Andrea said it's a piece of something called the Crystal, which is down in Africa somewhere. But Ambrosiano put the Torelli Jewel away for safekeeping; I think he didn't know what the fuck to do with it. But I do. I figure I can kill two birds with one stone. If I have the Torelli Jewel, the she-demon will come after me. See what I mean? And if I get her, I get revenge for our boys down in the tunnel – but also, with luck, I get information. Before I kill her, she'll tell me what I want to know. *Capisci?* You understand what I'm saying here? You gotta figure all the angles, Santino! You gotta triangulate! This stuff is strategy, it's fucking trigonometry!"

"So, when do we set off?"

"Santino, I got to do this one alone. This is on me. This is solo."

"Ah, Pizzu." Santino's eyes narrowed; his lips puckered up, he fingered a sugar package, turning it round and round; it looked like he was going to cry.

"Santino, you go to Palermo." U Pizzu took off his dark glasses, held them in front of his chest, stuck out his chin, and, narrowing his eyes, gave Santino the look. "You see the shop is okay. And, Santino, look after my family."

"Look after your family?" Santino wiped his eyes, just a little moist. He blinked and stared at U Pizzu; he worshipped the man: "*Look after your family?* I don't have a good feeling about this, Pizzu!"

"I think I'll have the lemon sorbet," said U Pizzu, settling his glasses back down on his nose. The black model walked past their table, glanced at them, and smiled. U Pizzu smiled back. The girl disappeared inside the café. U Pizzu sighed and fingered his lapel. He figured that, in many ways, the she-devil herself was the Jewel; she must be the key – the key to what was going on, the key to infinity and to death. She would know about the Crystal; and she would know what the fuck that old bird Ambrosiano was trying to do with all this nonsense, kidnapping famous scientists, killing the sons of his old friends, setting up black Masses, and babbling about the end of the world.

Now, three hours later, U Pizzu watched the ceiling lamp sway – back and forth – just like a rocking boat. He stroked his chin. In fact, everybody – the whole world – was sitting in a little boat, it was called Earth, and it was the only little boat they had; and, if Gaetano Larione was right, a big wave was coming, and their little boat, the wonderful green and blue planet Earth, our own little paradise, might just capsize or explode. Fuck it! Like Gaetano said, the end of the fucking world would be bad for business!

The swaying subsided and stopped. The quake was over.

U Pizzu swung his legs off the bed and sat up. It was time for action.

As he pulled on his trousers, he thought about how Santino had hugged him, arms wrapped tightly and desperately around him, holding on for dear life, and wouldn't fucking let go. It was clear Santino felt death was about to divide them. Finally, U Pizzu had to say, "Santino, your taxi is waiting. You're gonna miss your flight, Santino."

As the taxi drove away Santino had turned and looked back. U Pizzu could still see Santino's face, ghostly pale behind the glass, eyes wide open, already in mourning, with one hand pressed flat and white against the glass. "Goodbye, U Pizzu, goodbye!"

U Pizzu didn't want to – he felt it would look sentimental – but, just the same, he did it; at the last minute, he waved. The taxi turned a corner, and Santino was gone.

CHAPTER 46 – INFERNO

Holding the soaked, muddy Versace plastered against her body, Kate stared at the deadly, spectacular light show. The explosion echoed against the cliffs. Villa Mazana Nera was a towering column of fire, a huge twisting geyser of flame rising straight up – up, up, up – into the sky.

"Well, well." V was perched on a crag of rock, staring at the inferno. Yet again, part of her life was being peeled away. More of her memories were being consumed into ash – the dance with the Count, the underground chapel, the kitsch statues, the night she had saved the girl chained to the pillar of stone, that beautiful blonde, that gutsy tempting Andromeda …

"Most of the cars are on fire," John said. "There'll be no driving to Rome tonight."

"The guards," said V, "will be dead, or dying, and those priests I left tied up; they wouldn't have had a chance. Maybe the dogs are okay."

"The flames must have gone up the staircase to the fuel tanks," John said, "unless the earthquake created a short circuit somewhere."

Flames billowed out of windows and towers. More explosions echoed across the hillside. Cars and SUVs and jeeps were going up in great whooshes of red and yellow flame.

"Signor Ferrari will not be pleased," said Henry.

"No," said Marina, "he won't."

"Looks like I'm out of a job."

"I need someone, if you are interested."

"Indeed, I'm quite interested." Henry had already given Marina Elia a discreet once-over; he now took a closer look: all mussed up and covered in mud, dressed only in panties and a shirt, Marina had one arm around the girl, Kate. At first glance, he had sensed that Marina was a classy brave lady.

"Good," Marina said. "My Ferrari should be safe. It's down there on the side road, well away from the villa. I didn't trust those people."

"If you don't need us anymore," said Henry, glancing at V.

"No, thank you for everything," said V.

"Good luck to you both," said John. "And thanks."

"Then we shall just saunter down there and take our chances," said Marina. "Take care, my darling!" She hugged Kate and kissed her on the forehead. Then she shook hands, rather formally, with each of them. To V she said, "Whatever you are, you're an angel!"

"Thank you, Marina, you are too," said V.

"Well, goodbye, chaps, and good luck," said Henry.

"Goodbye, and God bless you!" Father O'Bryan made a vague sign of the cross, a gesture of adieu.

"And you, Father!" Marina blew him a kiss.

Marina and Henry began to make their way down the hillside. More enormous explosions shook the ground – it was the final death agony of Villa Mazana Nera, a secret gem, one of the most exquisite Renaissance villas in all of Italy, a masterpiece of sixteenth century architecture.

Father Alvarez smelled smoke – bitter, acrid, heavy smoke. His ears were filled with a roaring sound, an infernal roaring. He was swimming through molten lava. His flesh was peeling away. He stared at his hand. It was mere bone, chalk-white spindly, skeletal fingers and thumb. The bone-fingers and the bone-thumb fell off, leaving only smoking stumps, steaming in the heat. It must be a nightmare! Father Alvarez screamed. He heard himself scream. Yes, it must be a nightmare!

Suddenly, he was awake; his eyes stinging, glazed, sweat pouring from his forehead. The heat was overwhelming. There was smoke everywhere. Fire raced up one wall of the control room. He tried to move but couldn't. His hands and feet were bound. He was lying sideways on the floor, helpless.

Levering his back against the computer desk, he wiggled into a sitting position. Blazing smoke and flame were everywhere. Father Delgado and Father Diego were still out cold, hogtied, on the floor. He tried to kick them, hoping to wake them. Maybe there was a way out of this.

The smoke was thicker now, closing in. Father Alvarez choked. His throat, his nostrils, his lungs were burning. The pain was horrible, unbearable. There was a huge whoosh and a roar and what seemed like a wall of flame. Father

Alvarez didn't think much about anything anymore, though he did wonder, just for an instant, whether he was the one screaming. The scream stretched on, and on, and on ...

Perhaps screams echoed forever in the Kingdom of Satan.

Perhaps the last instant of consciousness is, in fact, eternity.

Perhaps the mind stops, and just goes around and around and around, in an endless eternal loop of suffering.

Those thoughts did cross his mind.

To burn in hellfire trapped in inferno, forever, and ever, and ever ...

Eternity!

No, no, no! It could not be!

"Our BMW, HIDDEN UP THE ROAD is probably okay. But with all the chaos, driving to Rome would take all night," V turned to John, "and we don't have all night."

"Yes," said John. "And I'm afraid our favorite Land Cruiser has gone up with the rest of the vehicles."

"Look at the traffic." Kate pointed.

"Yes, you're right." V glanced at Kate – except for the shirt, the girl was naked, and she was barefoot. V sat down, unbuckled her boots, pulled them off, and handed them to Kate.

"Why?"

"This ground is rough."

"Okay. Thanks." Kate shot V a shy grin, sat down on an outcropping, and pulled on and buckled up the boots.

"So, the roads are impossible." V stared at the plain below them. There were endless lines of lights, an exodus. Terrified of the next earthquake, millions of people were fleeing cities and towns and heading to open country, away from buildings. Every road up and down the peninsula would be snarled in a monstrous traffic jam.

"Well," John said, "the villa has a helipad. And last time we looked – a couple of hours ago – there was a helicopter. It is far away from the buildings. It may have survived. Shall we try that?"

"We don't have a choice." V glanced at John. "Yes, let's do it."

Kate looked down at herself. What a sight she must be, clothed in the Versace shirt, and nothing else; the shirt itself was muddy and soaked and almost see-through; and now, of course, she had handsome black thick-soled military boots. It was a great combo. She was tempted to laugh, but …

"What about my dad?"

"We'll find your dad," V said.

"Where?"

"In Africa, I think."

"Africa?"

"I'll explain later. Let's go."

"Okay! Right!" Kate figured the demon knew what she was doing. Questions would have to wait.

They started up the hillside toward the helipad.

V took a deep breath. The pebbles and sand and rock under her bare feet linked her directly to the Earth and the cosmos. She felt the last embers of solar energy radiating into the night air; and, ominously, she sensed the trembling of the vast tectonic forces wakened by the Crystal – the elemental forces just waiting to be released, including the huge chamber of magma that lay below them, roughly five miles down and off a few miles to the west, she guessed; it was stirring, beginning to press upwards. With the shifts in the gravitational field, there was movement everywhere. And so, linked to Earth's nervous system, united to the forces that had formed the planet, synchronized with the stars from which the atoms and molecules of her body and mind had been born, V felt, echoing in her bones and nerves, the immense energies that drove the whole vast mysterious endless universe. The message she was getting from all these sources was not good. Red lights were blinking everywhere. The end, for Earth, her home, was nigh.

"We don't have much time." She took the lead.

They climbed a steep and crumbly path toward the villa's helipad.

Father O'Bryan took Kate's arm. "I do believe, dear Kate –"

"Silence!" V dropped to her hands and knees and gestured: Crouch down, everybody!

John crawled forward.

V whispered, "Two o'clock: just ahead to the right."

John squinted, scanning the crumbled black rock that slanted upwards, matte-black and garish red in the dusty red light of the moon. Then, he saw it: Yes, on the crest of the hill, the moonlight reflected on a smooth strip of metal, the barrel of a machine-gun. John signaled to Kate and Father O'Bryan to lie flat.

John eased his pistol out of its holster and peered upward. He and V were below the shooter's line of sight; but the guard – if there was a guard – must have heard them coming up the path. Hopefully, the gunner didn't have grenades! V made a jagged motion with her hand and John noticed that, in front of the gunner's position, was a line of coiled barbed wire, low and close to the ground, almost invisible. How had he not seen that? He should have seen it! He must be getting old! V had the eyesight of a lynx.

A new giant blossom of billowing red light lit up the sky. John turned. The fire consuming Villa Mazana Nera towered even higher, lighting up the dust-filled heavens. The moon was blood red. Immense clouds of dust transited through the night, like vast dark sea squalls.

With a quick flip of her hand, V indicated to John that he should go to the right and she would go left; that they should close in on the machine-gun from both sides – and from behind. John nodded, twisted around and motioned to Father O'Bryan and Kate to stay put, and not talk.

Swiftly, John worked his way, crouching, along the edge of the hill. It was rough, friable, crunchy volcanic soil. He had to be extra careful not to make noise. He wondered how V would manage – barefoot.

Crawling on all fours, V slithered and zigzagged like a savvy dust-hugging serpent over the debris and ancient volcanic slag, her feet and hands fitting easily to the broken earth; her jet-black matte catsuit getup made her as dark as night and merged her with the volcanic rock; her eyes and the few bits of her face shone white where her camouflage makeup had been wiped away by her double morph and by the water and mud in the tunnel.

She circled around the slope until she came to what she reckoned would be one of the gunner's blind spots. Crawling on hands and knees, she kept as low as she could, so as not to be silhouetted against the glow from the fires up at the villa and down on the plain.

She leapt over the low tangle of barbed razor wire that ran near to the crest of the hill and found herself on a path that ran along the hillside parallel to the barbed wire, skirting just below the crest. She crawled quickly along it on the points of her fingers and toes.

She stopped. At the machine-gun post there was in fact a single guard. Despite the chaos, the explosions, and earthquakes, he hadn't abandoned his position. He must be one of those unimaginative or stubborn stalwarts who just follow orders no matter what happens. He seemed oblivious. So, he had not heard them coming up the path. He stood up and yawned, stretching his arms up into the air. V leapt, instantly morphing into vampire mode, her fangs and claws eager and extended.

He didn't have a chance. She seized his arms, pinning them behind his back, and plunged her fangs into his throat. Oh, that was so good! That was so luscious! She was still hungry, indeed famished, even after feeding on Father Ottavio; and she knew she would need extra energy for the battles to come. Blood bubbled and gurgled in her throat – a rush, an elixir of life, a tidal wave of energy.

"What the fuck?" a voice said.

V heard the click of a gun. She turned. Another guard was standing on the edge of the gun pit – he must have gone off to have a pee. He was looking down at her. How could she have been so careless? Caught feeding, she was dangerously vulnerable. How stupid she had been! The barrel swung toward her. "What the hell are you, bitch?"

"I …" she began, playing for time, realizing that the slightest move on her part and he would shoot her, between the eyes; that might be a bit too much, too fast …

"What, what the hell are you?" His finger tightened on the trigger.

"I'm, I'm … a …"

He pulled the trigger, she leapt aside, the bullet grazed past her shoulder. The man she had been feeding on was still alive. He began to stir. If he awoke, he would morph into a raging monster, and she would have two problems.

The guard pulled the trigger again. V leapt away just as the rock splintered under her feet. Now he had her centered. "I asked you a question," he said. "I am going to give you -"

A shot rang out. Wham! The guard's head exploded. His body toppled over, down into the gun pit.

John came out from behind the rocks.

"Are you okay?" He looked down at V, a wild, blood-soaked, disheveled, crouching, savage-looking vampire.

"Yes," she said. "I was distracted … I needed …"

"You needed to feed." John could have sworn he saw tears in her eyes. The moon – maybe the moon caused the illusion.

"The other one is still alive." John nodded toward the dark shadow that was now groaning, trying to get up.

"Yes. I must finish. Leave me!"

"No. There might be others."

"Turn your back."

John climbed down into the gun pit and crouched next to her; he looked into her eyes – yes, tears. "I've seen you feed before, V. It's not new."

"You're right. I'm being silly."

As V fed, John crouched beside her and scanned the hilltop, alert for any other guards, but nothing moved, nobody came. Probably there had been only those two men, left to guard the helicopter. V fed silently, though John did hear occasional sucking and gurgling. It seemed a long time; but it was all over in about forty seconds.

"I have to make sure he's truly dead," V said, biting her victim one last time. Crouching low next to the body, she used the man's uniform to wipe the blood from her face.

"Take your time." John scanned the rocks, the sky.

"Yes, he's truly dead," V stared at the body. "He will not rise again."

John took V, pulled her to him and hugged her.

She drew away, and sniffled. "Thank you, John."

"You are never alone, darling." He put his hand on her shoulder. "You must remember that."

Five minutes later they were at the helipad. An undamaged Sikorsky s-76 was tethered on the landing pad. Not far away, geysers of hot steam were spraying up in vast plumes. V frowned: heat from the magma chamber was leaking upwards into the water table and into the underground streams; time was running out. She glanced around. Would the whole area go volcanic? John glanced at her and nodded. He was thinking the same thing.

"This helicopter can easily take all four of us." John opened the door and motioned to them to climb in.

"Where are we going?" Kate's eyes were bright. "I want to know how we can rescue my –"

"We go to Rome," said V. "Then to Africa."

As she climbed into the Sikorsky, Kate pulled the tattered Versace closer. Everybody seemed to have forgotten that she was naked. Well, not entirely naked; she did have the shirt; and, if slimy gunk counted as clothes, she was modesty itself, covered head to toe in mud and dust and sweat and oil and blood. What she wouldn't give for a long hot shower! "What makes you think dad's in Africa?"

"Later, Kate, later."

Kate stared for a moment, tempted to protest; then she nodded: *Okay.*

As they buckled in, John ran his fingers over the controls.

He turned to V. "I'll fly over the mountains and then along the coast, then inland to Rome."

"Where do we land in Rome?" Kate tightened her seatbelt.

"The Vatican has a helipad," said V.

"The Vatican?" John raised an eyebrow; he revved the motor. The helicopter lifted off, tilted to the side, and began its journey.

"Why the Vatican?" Father O'Bryan had to shout to be heard.

"Tonight …" V hesitated. She was gazing out the window at the fires burning, at the lines of headlights blocking the coastal and cross-mountain superhighway. She shouted, over the sound of the motor, "Tonight is the night Cardinal Ambrosiano is going to murder the Pope."

"Oh!"

Nobody said anything.

"You are going to ask me," V shouted, her tongue probing at some blood at the side of her mouth, "how I know."

"Well, the question had occurred to me." Father O'Bryan stared at his demon friend. The light from a burning hillside town lit up V's face from below – turning it into a crimson mask, startling in its youth, its primitive wild beauty, one half painted in black and green stripes, one half blood-splashed ivory.

"When I drank Father Ottavio's blood," V shouted, "I drank his memories and his thoughts. The murder will be tonight; the Pope's murder is meant to signal the beginning of the end. Father Ottavio was exulting, but also in despair."

"In despair?"

"It suddenly occurred to him that Cardinal Ambrosiano is going to betray them all – that the end will really be *the end*; that the Cardinal doesn't intend to frighten the world, he doesn't intend to *rule* the world; he intends to destroy it. Father Ottavio didn't want to die."

"Oh, dear." Father O'Bryan frowned. Poor Father Ottavio, he had perished unshriven, without the sacraments, in a state of mortal sin, and drunk dry by a vampire, and, horror of horrors, that would mean that his eternal soul would –

"What does my dad have to do with all this?" Kate shouted.

"Your dad," V leaned close to Kate, "is one of the few people who can help the Cardinal understand what he is about to unleash – the Cardinal is vain;

he will want to know exactly how the end of the world is coming about. He thinks your father is one of the few minds in the world worthy of him – a worthy opponent and a worthy witness – that's my guess at any rate."

"Wow!" shouted Kate. "Dad's in on the end of the world?"

"Your father is alive," said V, putting her hand on Kate's shoulder. "I feel it; I know it; we just have to get there in time."

"To Africa?"

"Yes, to Africa."

John checked the coast. He could see the lights of another superhighway, and, farther away what looked like the lights of the Eternal City itself. There were no fires burning in or near Rome that he could see.

"It may be too late for the Pope," said V.

"The cell phones are down," John shouted. "Radio is all confused. Internet is not working. There is no way we can warn the Pope."

V smiled and put her hand on Father O'Bryan's shoulder. "Well, then, Father, we shall pay your good friend the Pope a surprise visit."

PART SEVEN – RESURRECTION

CHAPTER 47 – CRUCIFIXION

Eyes wide open, Father Andrea lay flat on his back in his office in Vatican City on top of his very large desk, his face turned upwards, both his eyes mindless, staring, without any expression at all, at the fine vaulted ceiling, at the allegorical figures – painted sometime in the seventeenth century – that swirled delightedly above him.

Four twelve-inch-long rusty nails had been hammered through the palms of Father Andrea's hands and the arches of his feet.

Father Andrea was still alive when the nails were driven in; and then one of the two monks who had come to kill him had leaned down close, as if he wanted to kiss Father Andrea on the lips, face-to-face; he had taken Father Andrea's head between his hands, waited for a long instant, hovering, and then, with one quick jerk to the right, and then to the left, he had broken Father Andrea's neck.

When the two monks appeared, unannounced, in his office, clearly emissaries of Cardinal Ambrosiano, Father Andrea realized he was doomed. His office must have been bugged. He had spoken to U Pizzu and Santino of things that must not be spoken of. He had spoken of the Satanic Order of the Apocalypse, of the black Mass, of human sacrifice, and of the she-demon. And so, he realized that, for this sin, for this betrayal, he was about to die.

In his last moments, Father Andrea was overcome by anger. Above all, he was angry with himself. How could he have been so stupid? How could he have been so blind? How could he not have seen what was as clear as day: Cardinal Ambrosiano was insane, truly insane. How could he have dedicated virtually his whole life – those long, arid, self-sacrificing decades of self-denial – to the caprices and cruelties of a madman? How could he not have realized that the Cardinal intended to betray and destroy everyone and everything; and that the Cardinal, true to his nihilistic and satanic beliefs, and true above all to his own supreme egotism, would delight, above all, in betraying those who had most faithfully served him?

In the rose-tinted twilight, the frescoes of the ceiling, lit by the curtains' shifting shadows, looked like they were alive. Mischievous cupids danced and flirted, lofty sweet-faced angels winked at each other, and solemn, sad-eyed, bearded saints took a bow. Lifted into the room by the gentle warm gusts, the white muslin curtains lightly touched and caressed Father Andrea's impaled, curled left hand. One length of curtain, caught on a bloodied nail, was trapped by the twisted head of the nail. Stuck there, it fluttered – and fluttered, and fluttered, in vain, struggling to be free.

Three little pills cupped in his hand – Pope Francis popped them into his mouth, picked up the glass of water, and washed the dreadful things down. Ugh! He really didn't like taking the pills; but he had to; he could sense the telltale fluttering of his weakened heart, suffering from the strain of what had been an exceptionally long day. It must be way past midnight. What time was it? Two o'clock, two-thirty, three-thirty?

The last tremors had subsided, and, aside from a few minor shocks, the Eternal City had been spared. The Vatican was untouched. The Pope knew something about the geology of the Eternal City. It sat on layers of sediment and lava that had been poured forth when a great rift between the African and European continental plates had opened and let immense fields of magma pour out. So, Rome was sitting on a deep pillow of porous lava – and ocean sediment – that helped cushion the shocks of underlying seismic events.

Francis II was originally from Venice, not Rome, and he retained a gentle Venetian singsong accent that had a touch of gallantry and courtliness about it; when excited, he sometimes found himself using dialect words and expressions he had picked up in the *calle*, the pedestrian walkways and alleyways of Venice.

But Francis had fully embraced his new home, the Eternal City. He loved Rome's complexity and over-ripe cynicism, its vast wealth of human experience, its talent for – well, in the end, he supposed – for compassion. The Romans, like the Venetians, had seen so much; they understood so much, and forgave so much – they were very human, almost too human, the Romans.

The Pope massaged his forehead. He closed his eyes. He was exhausted. He had moved his bedroom next to his office and taken to working excessively long hours. Today had been worse than most. In the morning, he had announced the Official Investigation into the Vatican Bank. Then, after the earthquakes began, he had made three broadcasts in Italian from Vatican radio. He had visited two hospitals as the first casualties – outside the city the damage had been much worse – were coming in; he had spoken with the President of Italy and the Prime Minister; he had assured himself that the Church was doing everything it could do to help people. He had worked with at least five committees to coordinate relief efforts, had made special broadcasts in English and French and Spanish, Polish and Filipino, to Catholics – and others – throughout the world. There had been earthquakes virtually everywhere, some of them quite severe. Finally, Sister Ursula had insisted he stop working, eat, and get some sleep.

Cardinal Ambrosiano had sent a messenger and had said it was urgent. But the Pope had demurred. He did not want to see the messenger. He was too busy to deal with the Cardinal and he needed time to think. He no longer trusted Ambrosiano. Father O'Bryan's letter had alarmed him. He had read it carefully, three times. Then he had burned it, lighting the match himself, gathered the ashes and flushed them down the toilet. Whether they were true or not, the accusations contained in the letter were explosive.

The Pope knelt by his bed and prayed. He had his very own very peculiar way of praying. He feared the worst – but what precise form the worst would take he didn't know. Cardinal Ambrosiano was clearly a dangerous man – the Pope was beginning to wonder how dangerous. Perhaps Father O'Bryan's warnings were justified.

Kneeling next to the bed, he felt a sudden draft, but when he looked around, he saw nothing, just the gentle breeze blowing the curtain of the large window inward. It was the night breeze, the *ponentino* celebrated by poets and lovers. How refreshing it was, here in Rome, especially on such a torrid muggy night. The gentle wind again touched his skin with its magic. Perhaps it would blow away the earthquake haze that had engulfed the city; the ash and dust and the reddish color from the fires throughout Italy suggested the dawning of the Inferno.

The Pope thought he detected a perfume, delicate and sweet and slightly spicy. He looked around. There was nothing, just the curtain, wafting softly into the room.

Then – WHAM! The door to his bedroom burst open.

The Pope was still on his knees. He turned toward the door. "What is it? Who are you?"

The visitor was dressed in a black cloak and hood, a friar's habit. He must be at least seven feet tall.

"My son, what is the meaning of this? Why have you come?"

The monk said nothing. There was something abnormal about him. He was huge and hulking, but his features were hidden by the black cowl.

The monk stepped into the light. The Pope saw the face: the eyes were tiny, and the features were all crowded together, twisted at the bottom of the face, eyes, mouth, and chin, wrenched sideways in what looked like an evil grimace, a snickering parody of evil intent.

The monk slammed the door behind him. They were locked in – alone.

"I have come." The monk's voice was deep, cavernous, a voice from the Underworld, from the Kingdom of the Dead. He enunciated with difficulty. Saliva shone on his thick lower lip. "I have come with a message from Cardinal Ambrosiano."

"Yes, my son."

In a single leap, the giant monk was across the room. He seized the Pope by one arm, lifted him up, and in an instant of blinding terror the Pope saw, in the giant's other fist, a needle, about to plunge down.

The Pope closed his eyes. So, it had come, death! And what a strange and useless death it would be! There was so much to be done, so much left unfinished, and –

"Stop right there," a voice commanded, a woman's voice.

The monk hesitated. The Pope opened his eyes, the needle was plunging down, and a shot rang out. The arm holding the needle flew backward, blossoming in blood. The needle spun away, clattered on the floor, skittering under a table.

The monk howled and staggered backward, dropping the Pope, who fell, sprawling stomach down on the floor.

The Pope shook himself and tried to get up. Still on his knees, he turned and saw a woman who was dressed in what seemed like skintight black leather or latex. Her legs were spread apart in the shooter's pose. She was barefoot and she was aiming a pistol at the monk.

"I do apologize, Your Holiness." The woman spoke Italian. Her voice was soft, cultivated and warm, with a touch of Milanese accent. "I do apologize for breaking in on you like this." She must have come from the window, from behind the curtain, but how …?

The monk stepped forward.

"You," the woman shouted, suddenly harsh. "One move and I blow your head off!"

The monk hesitated. He was holding his bloodied and shattered arm. His tiny eyes gleamed with hatred. Foam flecked his fluttering minuscule lips; drool dripped from his triple chins. "She-devil," he hissed. "I know you, she-devil!"

"Guns are rather clichéd." The woman took one step forward. "When I kill, Your Holiness, I usually use other, more primitive methods. I am not a good person, Your Holiness."

"She-devil," hissed the monk. He stepped forward.

"Oh, shut up! And stay back or I *will* kill you," V said. "Your Holiness: you'd better stay out of the line of fire. He may have other weapons, other tricks."

The Pope rose and came toward V, careful to keep to one side, out of the line of fire. "Who are you? What are you?"

"She-devil pretty well describes me, I'm afraid." V nodded, keeping all her attention focused on the monk, who was losing a lot of blood.

The Pope noticed as he came closer to V the perfume, that spicy, indefinable, attractive scent. Soothing warmth radiated from her. So that was what he had noticed when the breeze lifted the curtain. He saw that her outfit and face were streaked with mud and camouflage makeup and something else – was it blood?

There was a knock at the door. The Pope glanced at the woman. Was he, he wondered, being kidnapped, was he the prisoner of terrorists? The woman nodded.

"Come in!" the Pope said, in a voice so loud he surprised himself. The Pope frowned. "I didn't mean to shout."

The woman smiled. "A natural reaction, Your Holiness: I imagine you are rather wound up."

"I hate to admit it, but truth be told – I'm terrified."

The door burst open.

"They are all dead." It was Father Michael Patrick O'Bryan, and right behind him was a deeply tanned tall man the Pope didn't know, dressed in an outfit that echoed the woman's, with camouflage makeup on his face; he was holding a pistol, and had a light machine-gun over his shoulder. And following them came a young woman wearing boots. She was streaked with mud and wrapped in a garish muddy shirt but nothing else! A naked young woman! My God!

"Father O'Bryan!" The Pope exclaimed. "Who are all dead? What is happening?"

Father O'Bryan was ghostly pale and covered in mud.

"They are all dead. Your staff! The people who protected you – Sister Ursula, Brother Gabriel, Father Joseph, Sister Beatrice, the four Swiss guards."

"All dead … what …?" The Pope groped for a chair. "Sister Ursula …"

Still keeping her pistol pointed at the space between the monk's eyes, V pushed a chair toward the Pope.

As he sat down, he turned to Father O'Bryan. "Tell me, for God's sake, Michael, tell me! What is going on?"

Father O'Bryan glanced around. "This man – the monk – was sent by Cardinal Ambrosiano to kill you."

"But how would he dare? How dare he violate the …?"

"I'm afraid he's daring even more than that," said V.

"V … This is V …" said Father O'Bryan.

"V …" echoed the Pope, inclining his head with a touch of dazed irony.

"V discovered that Cardinal Ambrosiano intended to have you … ah … eliminated."

"Eliminated …" The Pope stared. "Eliminated!"

Suddenly, V sensed danger – and a dangerous odor. Her nostrils quivered. It was something familiar, something lethal – Semtex explosive, made in the Czech Republic – yes, that was what it was.

"John, frisk that fellow, would you please – be very careful. I think, I think …" V said, and she saw movement as the monk dropped his raised arm and reached under his tunic.

V shot him between the eyes.

He fell heavily, his fingers not yet under his cloak.

The Pope's eyes widened. "But …"

John approached the twitching body. Kneeling next to it, he carefully opened the giant monk's cloak. "There's a bomb, Semtex, I think," John said, calmly, with professional detachment. "Yes, Semtex. He was about to set it off …" John frowned. He was staring at a small box with red numbers racing down toward zero. "It also has a timer. We have thirty seconds," John said. "Out now! Everybody out now!"

"My God, I can't leave," said the Pope. "I can't abandon –"

"Yes, you can," said Father O'Bryan.

Pushing the Pope in front of them, they scrambled out of the papal bedroom. A man lay sprawled stomach down in the entry office. A nun lay spread-eagled face up just in front of the door. It was Sister Ursula, her brief-case in her hand. Her face had been ripped away; all that remained was a mask of pulp and blood. A priest lay nearby, his arm stretched out, reaching for an alarm button. Another priest lay face down farther on. Four dead Swiss guards lay near the staircase.

They ran, they ducked behind the outer doors, two rooms away from the Pope's bedroom.

V shouted, "Down! Your Holiness, down! Father O'Bryan, get over here, get behind me. Yes, you get behind me, too, Kate! Everybody down!"

"Cover your ears," Kate said, "and close your eyes."

"Yes, yes, of course," said the Pope. "Thank you, ah …"

"Kate, my name's Kate, Your Holiness."

WHAM!

The doors of the Pope's private quarters and office burst outwards. The explosion ripped through the papal apartments. The flash was seen in Saint Peter's Square, and beyond.

Reporters and news crews, standing by their TV vans and mobile studios, and habitually on guard on Saint Peter's Square, but particularly on this night full of earthquakes and bizarre events and ominous portents, looked up. The windows of the papal bedroom exploded outwards. Sparks, dust, bits of masonry and fragments of flesh rained down. Smoke drifted across the great square. The explosion echoed in Bernini's great colonnade.

A news flash went around the world. Pope Francis II had been assassinated by a bomb in a terrorist attack. "Perhaps the fanatical leader of …"

The Captain of the Pontifical Swiss Guard was furious with himself. How could this have happened? He insisted that the Pope had to be protected at all costs, so there were guards stationed everywhere now, on all sides.

"I really don't know who to trust," Father O'Bryan said.

The Pope – still in shock – was drinking a very short hot espresso, eating a chocolate croissant, and trying to control his emotions. "So, Father O'Bryan, you are telling me that much more is involved than merely a plot to kill me."

"Yes, much more. Now, Your Holiness, this will seem incredible, I know, but it seems that Cardinal Ambrosiano intends to destroy the planet. You were to die first. This was part of a little personal vendetta, a score to settle with you before the end came. He feared you, and what you intended to do

– particularly your investigation of the Vatican Bank. He wanted you to die alone, to know you were dying, and to be helpless to do anything to stop it."

"Ambrosiano wants to create a crescendo of terror," V said. "Now that this plot has been foiled, the Cardinal will probably accelerate his main plan."

"But if he thinks I am dead … No, I cannot let the faithful think I am dead."

"Yes," said V, "you're right, Your Holiness. You have a duty to hundreds of millions of the faithful. In any case, I'm sure the Cardinal already knows that we broke up his little black Mass and prevented the planned sacrifice." V glanced at Kate. "So, he'll already be on high alert."

The Pope considered his savior, this young woman who appeared so sure of herself, presumptuous even. "And, who, may I ask, are you, Mademoiselle V?"

"We will declare that you have survived the attempted assassination," said Father O'Bryan to the Pope. "We'll put out an announcement shortly. If you agree, of course."

"I agree."

"Good. I'll talk to those who remain – ah, alive – in the Secretariat."

"Mademoiselle V." The Pope was still staring at the young woman who, he now realized, was of extraordinary – almost unearthly – beauty; she was so unsettlingly beautiful that he found himself wondering whether she was fully human.

"She saved my life," said Father O'Bryan.

"Yes, Michael, she saved mine too; but who – or what – is she?"

"May I speak to you, Your Holiness?" V inclined her head toward the Pontiff. The Pope inclined his head in response. "Of course, my child." He stood up, and he and V moved away to a corner where they could talk without being overheard.

"What, I wonder, are they going to talk about?" asked Kate. She held the bloody Versace shirt close – she was getting used to being naked. Nobody seemed to have taken the slightest notice. "Is she going to say, 'Sorry, Your Holiness, but I'm a barefoot vampire in a muddy black catsuit; I run around and kill people and drink their blood. I've been doing it for centuries. Please, Holy Father, a few Hail-Mary's.'?"

Father O'Bryan smiled. Kate had clearly recovered enough from her ordeal to be her spunky impertinent old self.

"Oh, dear, dear Father O'Bryan, I love you so!" Kate blinked at him; her image of the good Father was a bit fuzzy, but, strangely, she noticed, her eyesight seemed to be getting better, in fact amazingly better – why, she wondered, why in the world would that be?

"But I don't believe in vampires," the Pope said.

"Well, neither would I, Your Holiness, except that I happen to be one – though I'm not, I believe, one of the living dead as vampires are supposed to be. I seem to be very much alive. In any case, right now, it doesn't really matter what I am – I live by drinking human blood. It is my nature and my fate."

Below them was Saint Peter's Square, usually almost empty at this hour, but now filling up with more television and radio crews.

"A vampire," the Pope muttered.

"Yes, in part at least, Your Holiness, a freak of nature, perhaps an abomination, as Father O'Bryan keeps telling me, in a very friendly way of course, and certainly a murderer."

The Pope looked out at the television crews setting up their equipment, the trailers with antenna disks at the edge of the square. "I am not sure why I am going to do this," he said, "but I am going to tell you something I have told no one. It is a measure of my trust that I know you will never share this knowledge with anyone. The strange thing is I don't know why I trust you."

V merely nodded. Swearing to keep the Pope's secret – whatever it was – would be redundant; it would be an insult to this frail – she sensed the weakness of his heart – and brave old man. And, sensing the flawed heart muscle, she allowed her hand to brush close to his chest, just for a second. Energy leapt, creating a small, almost invisible bridge of light. Well, that should fix that, for the time being at least! Sometimes she felt she really *should* believe in magic; but, strangely, she didn't.

"You do not believe in God," said the Pope, suddenly feeling a surge of warmth in his chest – a strange sensation of peace and strength.

"No, Your Holiness. Anything is possible, I imagine, but, in my fallible ignorance, finite and tiny as I am, not even a speck in this vast universe, no, I do not believe in God. I have no knowledge one way or the other of whether He or something like our idea of Him exists or not. So, no – I do not believe in God."

The Pope sighed. He put his hand on the window ledge and he looked out at the empty night air and the crowd gathering below. "Neither do I," he said; he glanced back at V, shyly, slyly, almost with suspicion: how would she react? Would she cry out against his hypocrisy?

A smile flickered at the edge of V's lips. "And yet you became Pope."

"Yes."

"I think it must be a great burden, being Pope."

"There are certainly worse burdens, much worse." The Pope hesitated. "For many years, I believed in God; it was the meaning of my life, it was the very substance of my thoughts, my yearnings, and my consciousness. When I prayed, I felt someone was there, someone was listening. He was there, answering me, like a friend, like a companion, always there. But … then …"

The Pope paused. V was gazing at him with eyes that seemed to the Pope to be infinitely deep, like a window on darkness, on utter nihilism, on cosmic emptiness, but also filled with light – and sympathy.

"I began to doubt," he said, looking away, toward the night sky. "I began to doubt when I saw children die in a senseless war. It was stupid of me, I know, and naive. Children have always died in senseless wars; men, women, children, the young, the old, the innocent, the less innocent, the guilty, all have died, all have suffered. But one death, one single death, affected me more than any other, I do not know why. One child died in my arms. She did not die a painless death. Nothing I could do, or the nurses could do, could ease her pain. We had no morphine, no drugs."

The Pope closed his eyes. He could see it as if he were still there, a young priest, fervent in his belief in the redemption of humankind by Christ, by the Church, by the saints, by the sacraments; he was sure in his own modest way, and merely by virtue of his priestly function, that he carried with him the gift of eternal salvation, eternal life.

The temperature must have been one hundred and ten degrees. Flies buzzed everywhere. The screens in the windows had been torn away, the doors ripped off their hinges. The mission buildings were empty shells. When he'd tried to stop the violence, the rebels had merely knocked him down and knocked him out. He was lucky they hadn't killed him or mutilated his body.

When he woke up the damage had been done. The small mission clinic had been levelled to the ground, set to the torch, by Marxist rebels – so-called Marxist rebels – he doubted if any of them had the vaguest idea who Marx was, or what his ideas were. Many of the African staff had been murdered. The women had been raped, mutilated – arms, breasts cut off, vaginas hacked out – before they were killed. The men, many of them, had been forced to castrate or disembowel themselves; and then they were shot or hacked to death. Many of the children had been taken away, the girls to be used as prostitutes and slaves, the boys to be drugged, addicted, and turned into child soldiers and child killers.

All this had happened – and still he kept his faith, still he worked to save those who could be saved. After the rebels moved on, the government troops came and did much the same thing with the buildings and people who remained – pillage, rape, mutilation, murder …

"There are so many horrors," said V.

"Yes, and I accepted them all. I didn't lose my faith. But, two years later, in yet another war, there was a little girl. She died of a fever, a little bug, a lack of hygiene; it was pure chance; it was bad luck. I brushed the flies from her lips. I dabbed cool water on her forehead. I looked into her eyes; I listened to her screams; I felt my own impotence. I felt love for the little girl. I was desperate to help her. But there was nothing to be done. I felt the impotence of God. Then I felt – it was like a sudden physical blow, like a blinding, burning, infinitely painful revelation – I felt the *irrelevance* of God. God had nothing to do with this tragedy. God had nothing to do with anything. Things just happen – that was that! People murdered other people. It was a fact. It had no metaphysical dimension at all – individual tragedies and mass tragedies have no relation to anything beyond themselves. I prayed for enlightenment, I prayed, and prayed, and prayed. No answer came. They heavens were empty, and so was my heart."

V nodded.

The Pope looked down at the people gathering in Saint Peter's Square – the media, the faithful, the curious. "I saw so clearly there was no benevolent deity, no God who was interested in human suffering or human destiny." The Pope wiped at his forehead. "The girl died. The light faded from her eyes. Her screams ceased. She was dead flesh, a dead animal. She, who had been so alive, so intelligent, so mischievous, was now no more alive than the pebbles on the edge of the road. There was no one to mourn her – no mother, no father, not even aunts, uncles, or cousins – all were dead. I went through the rituals at her death, and for her burial. Then I sat down in a corner …"

V nodded.

The Pope turned away from the window and gazed at V, but still it was as if he was not looking at her, not looking into her eyes, but instead looking through her, staring at some moment in the past, the distant past, at the life of another man, a man who no longer existed. "I sat down in a corner. I listened to the distant gunfire, to the screams, the explosions, and the faraway fluttering whirr of a military helicopter. This new war was moving on. It was now on the other side of the river – in another country. Already the violence seemed like a dream, vague and abstract; it was distant, like the ancient fading fresco in the little church outside the village in the Veneto where I was born, the bright colors dimmed with time, the violent gestures and deadly struggle brought to stillness, reconciled in death, everything formal and silent and hollow and strangely hieratical, frozen forever in a distant past." The Pope looked away for a moment and stared into empty space and then he turned directly to V. "The little girl's screams, her tears from a few minutes ago, were already fading memories. And I felt guilty, doubly guilty. I fell ill, with a fever."

V nodded – she knew how easy it was to forget suffering and death, to put them out of one's mind; forgetting *had* to be easy; otherwise how would anyone live? How would *she* live?

The Pope nodded. He understood – and he didn't know *how* he understood – what the strange young woman – *the vampire* – was thinking. "Yes," he sighed. "How *can* one live? How *could* one live? As I'm sure you know, the churches taught that such violence and such cruelty were an expression of human perversity, and human perversity was an expression of evil; and evil needed an explanation – for if God was good, if God was love, if God was all-powerful and all-knowing, and if God had created the universe and everything in it, then where did evil come from? How did evil and suffering creep into God's creation? Human evil, natural evil, was a mystery; and that mystery needed an explanation. So, the explanation, thought up by some ingenious poet, was, of course, the original sin of Eve listening to the serpent, eating the apple, handing it to Adam. The Expulsion from Paradise was the story that explained death, that explained knowledge, and consciousness and self-consciousness, that explained evil actions, murder, torture, cruelty, that explained shame and guilt, that explained viruses, mosquitoes, black mambas, plague, war ... and the death of a little girl."

The Pope took a deep breath. "I suddenly thought, in a flash of horrible insight: it was an absurd presumption, an obscene imposture – the whole idea. The myth of original sin was a mere excuse for our own impotence, our own evil. God was absent. God was gone. There was no God, at least not a God interested in humans, and there never had been. Nor had there ever been a fall from grace. There never had been any grace at all! There had never been a state of innocence. You will laugh at me – I was so naive. I believed in fairy tales!"

"Not at all, Your Holiness. We have all asked such questions, even if the terms we use are slightly different. And we all believe in something."

"You are right, Signorina. We are questioning creatures, we humans, but also presumptuous, I think, always wanting to be at the center of the universe. It was pure vanity to think that the universe was created with us in mind – vicarious vanity, empathetic and generous vanity perhaps, loving vanity sometimes, consoling vanity often, aspirational vanity, but vanity nonetheless – to believe that God is interested in the sufferings of a little child or in the destiny of a lonely sparrow that falls."

Outside the window, the breeze rose slightly. V's nostrils quivered. The Apocalypse was in the air.

"There was no Eden; there was never any perfection; and, since there had never been perfection, we were not created in God's image. But without original perfection, evil needed *no* explanation; *it just was – it just is*. There was no *Fall*; there is no *Resurrection*. Christ, the prophet, spoke, like all the prophets, in deep, enlightening images and parables. Even the *soul* is merely a metaphor, an image, for the sense of continuity of self that we feel and – another expression of vanity – another expression of our desire to be greater than we are, to be immortal. To be immortal like the gods we have created, often in our own image."

V nodded. The air outside the window glowed. The breeze rose again, wafted the curtains inwards. The menacing night was heavy with electricity.

"I no longer believed. If I had been brave enough, I would have resigned the priesthood, become a militant atheist or at least an angry skeptic. I was tempted; I was angry at what I saw as so much deception, so many lies. I could have become, probably would have become, one of those burnt-out ex-priests, men haunted by the emptiness left by their former faith, the void of sense and meaning, by bitterness for their loss, men nostalgic for salvation, for a mission and for meaning, men – and women – mourning the lover and the love they have abandoned, men – and women – who exist as shadows in the shadow of the Church. But then I thought, perhaps this is merely a temporary loss of faith."

"But it wasn't?"

"No. It wasn't. I lay ill in that cot in the mission hospital in Africa and as the days passed and the fever lessened, I listened to the sounds of battle fade and then to the ordinary sounds of life in the hospital and in the camp as people began to pick up their lives and begin again – the diesel motors, the generators going on and off, the singsong voices, even the laughter of children, as life returned, the cicadas and the birds and the animals – and I realized: The world is a wondrous place, life is a wondrous thing, consciousness is a gift; there may be no giver behind the gift, but just to be here, just to be alive, is an enormous privilege."

"Yes, it is." V gazed out at the brilliant hot dangerous night. That all this – the brilliant beautiful Earth – could perish, and in an instant – was a horrible thought. She shivered. Dust and smoke hung in the luminous air. The warm breeze caressed her skin, tingling with awareness. The whole miracle of the world, of the planet Earth, was in delicate balance, its very existence poised on the edge of the abyss. V cleared her throat. Her eyes, she realized, were wet. "To be alive is sublime."

"Yes, to be alive is sublime." The Pope turned toward her and noticed the dampness in her eyes. "Then I thought: The Church – the Catholic Church – is an immense force for good but also for evil in this world. If I want to serve the good, then perhaps I will better serve if I remain and work *within* the Church, if I disguise my lack of faith. And so, now, I am Pope. Of course, who am I to judge what is good, what is right? Perhaps I am the greatest hypocrite of all."

"I doubt it, Your Holiness."

"Yes, you are right, Signorina, you have an acute moral and psychological eye, I see. You are right. I flatter myself. We are vain even about our sins, our faults, are we not? We aspire to greatness, even in perversity, even in crime. Perhaps that is what drives Cardinal Ambrosiano – the desire for greatness and purity, even if it is greatness and purity in evil and cruelty."

"Yet your friend Father O'Bryan believes," V said, "and he worked in Africa too."

"Yes. It was in Africa that we came to know each other." The Pope glanced at Father O'Bryan, who was deep in conversation with one of the Pope's secretaries. "He is a brave man. He confronted death many times. He was tortured. He never gave in, he never gave up. They broke his body; but they did not break his spirit. Michael's faith was strengthened – he felt that, if there is no hope in this world, then there *must* be hope in the next; that only faith would give people the strength to endure and to do the right thing; that people need ideals and beliefs; they need a story – a magnificent, transcendent story – to make sense of their lives, they yearn for an opening onto the ideal, the sublime, and the Church is the custodian of that hope and the vehicle for meaning and salvation. Michael believes that man was made in God's image; that even if we were, in fact, never perfect, never innocent, we do have the ideals of perfection and of innocence and goodness within us, that those ideals and yearnings must reflect the presence and the word of God within us, but that we have fallen away from God and without Jesus and without His sacrifice and His message there would be – there will be – no redemption, either here on Earth, or in Heaven; for striving toward God is what makes us human."

"He considers you his best friend," said V. "He admires you greatly."

"Father O'Bryan would be a much better Pope than I," said the Pope, turning to V. "But, alas, Michael has never been interested in politics."

John was talking over the security situation with one of the Swiss Guard specialists, but he was also watching V and the Pope. It was quite amazing. They were talking as if they were old friends. He had noticed, too, the way she had just, casually, brushed her hand against the Pope's chest, and he knew what that meant.

And he could see from her gestures that V was now explaining the Crystal, and the Torelli Jewel, key to the Crystal, the *Clavis Mundi* as she had once called it, the *Key to the World*, and the urgency of stopping Cardinal Ambrosiano's plot. He wondered – Would the Pope understand, would he believe?

She is a most amazing creature, John thought.

"I realize, Your Holiness," V said, gazing straight into the Pope's eyes, "that you are making a great leap of faith – regarding the Crystal and Cardinal Ambrosiano."

"Faith is my business." The Pope smiled. "But, Signorina, what if you fail to stop the Cardinal?"

"Then, Your Holiness, nothing will matter – nothing, nothing at all."

"Go, then, Signorina, and do what you can do."

"Thank you, Your Holiness. I shall."

"I will not say 'God bless you, my child,' but you have my blessing, the blessing of a deeply imperfect and frail old man."

"Thank you, Your Holiness. Goodbye."

"Goodbye, my child. Goodbye, my friend."

"What in the world did you talk about, V?" asked Father O'Bryan.

"Faith."

"Ah!"

"I told the Pope about the Crystal."

"The Pope believed you?"

"Yes, strangely, he did. And I told him that this morning's news item – that the aircraft carrier *Abraham Lincoln* is moving east – is related to the earthquakes, that the Americans are almost certainly positioning the *Abraham Lincoln* for an attack on the Crystal. If they do decide to nuke the Crystal, then the Crystal will destroy the planet, instantly. If the danger of an attack presents itself, the Pope is going to try to convince them not to do it."

Father O'Bryan contemplated this possibility. "Ah – well, yes, the Pope is an old friend of the American President."

"If they try to nuke it, well, then," V grinned, "we are all angels – except for the devils, of course; and as far as devils and demons go, I have a head start."

"Ah, V, perhaps you are really an angel in disguise!"

"Oh, Father O'Bryan." V gave him her magic smile. "You are a most kind and generous person, and I do indeed love you!"

Father O'Bryan blinked at her; then he looked down – and blushed.

"In the meantime, Father, I must get the Torelli Jewel. It is the key to our salvation. It will allow me to speak to the Crystal. If I can talk to the Crystal, I will be able to ask her to stop and, if she can, reverse what Cardinal Ambrosiano has put in motion. When I drank Father Ottavio's blood, I learned where the Torelli Jewel is hidden – in a mountain town not far from Rome."

"Ah, so there is hope ..."

"Yes. While I get the key, John will arrange for a plane, a private jet, near Naples. It will take us to Africa. Will you come with us?"

"Of course, V. But Kate will insist on coming too. She's convinced we'll find her father there."

V glanced at the young woman, who was talking to a handsome young Swiss Guard, seemingly totally unself-conscious, holding the Versace shirt close with one hand, gesturing with the other. "She's brilliant at physics, right?"

"Yes, Kate is a sort of prodigy – a younger version of her father."

"And physically, she's ...?"

"... an adept of yoga, and an amateur acrobat," said Father O'Bryan, with almost paternal pride, "She's also a crack shot; after her mother was killed, Kate became obsessed with the martial and deadly arts."

"I see. Well, we'll let her come. The more the merrier. But ..."

"But what?"

V smiled and pointed: "Perhaps we should get her some clothes."

"My God, V, you're right! The poor child is naked!"

V laughed. "Yes, she is, Father. And, as you will have noticed, nobody here seems to have noticed – or cared. She's like Eve before the Apple, innocence itself. But, don't worry! I'm sure the nuns can find her a T-shirt and jeans. Later, John can fit her out in some of my war gear – Kate and I are about the same size. When I slipped into this armored catsuit, I saw a sparkle in her eye; I think she likes the girl warrior look. In any case, it'll be better for her to get into the fight than to brood."

"Absolutely right. Action is the best therapy."

V glanced at her watch. "Two hours to dawn, Father, and a brand-new day!"

CHAPTER 48 – A NEW DAWN

Shortly after sunrise, John and Kate and Father O'Bryan left for Naples in a specially modified, souped-up, Toyota Land Cruiser that John kept – with abundant backup supplies, and several of V's motorbikes – in a highly secure underground parking lot in Rome.

John was armed with a letter from the Pope – saying he and his group were on emergency work for the Holy See – and a letter from the Italian Ministry of the Interior and another from the High Command of the Carabinieri – saying that they were on an emergency high-priority mission for the Italian government. V, Julia, and John always kept, in Rome and elsewhere, supplies of documents, genuine and forged, and backup Internet links, and contacts with friendly officials ready to confirm whatever needed to be confirmed. The documents, hard copy and electronic, could be instantly updated, signed – with a forged or genuine signature – and used in emergencies.

The A-1 superhighway heading south toward Naples was crowded with military and police transport. The earthquake had set the whole security apparatus of Italy and of the NATO naval base in Naples on high alert. Smoke was rising from villages where fires had started during the earthquakes. Civilian cars and trucks had been pushed off to the side of the road; there had been looting, and a wave of murders, as people had commandeered other people's cars.

Kate stared at the screen of one of John's smartphones. The second wave of earth tremors had spread around the world, but had not yet caused huge damage; the news outlets were reporting that minor earthquakes had occurred all along the margins of the world's major tectonic plates.

"This doesn't look good. It means the stresses are everywhere," Kate said. She had managed a quick shower in the Vatican and from one of the nuns she had borrowed a pair of tight black jeans and a black T-shirt, rather chic, really, and a perfect fit. The nun was cute, Kate's age, very helpful, and not at all shy. She'd make an interesting friend, Kate thought. Maybe, after all this was over, the two of them could have lunch. As she stared at the smartphone, questions flooded in: Why were all these earthquakes happening at the same time? And why now? Was it a disturbance in the gravitational field? If V's so-called Crystal could distort gravity and manipulate space-time, then it could certainly cause earthquakes, volcanic eruptions, and super-storms. It might even make faster-than-light travel possible – maybe to other suns and other galaxies. Her father would be annoyed by all these unorthodox events and speculations, but he'd be inspired too. He would sink his teeth into the problems. She was dying to talk to him about it. Her secret dream – *one* of her secret dreams – was to work with her father. They would make a terrific team!

"Deep in thought, Kate?" John glanced at her.

"Yes, I am wondering ..."

"She's a deep one, my Kate." Father O'Bryan nodded.

"A nerd, Father O'Bryan," said Kate. "I'm a nerd."

"A glamorous nerd, an exceptionally beautiful nerd," said John, "but not just a plain, old, everyday, colorless, run-of-the-mill, off-the-shelf, insipid, uninspired, wallflower nerd, most certainly not."

"John, you are a truly gallant gentleman, and very talented polysyllabic flatterer!" Kate blew him a kiss and stretched, reaching her arms up above her head, and as she did so Father O'Bryan noticed that she had the same feline grace, the same dancer's fluid beauty of gesture and movement he had noticed so often in V.

With a red rotating light flashing on the Toyota's roof and with their special passes, they were able to drive, at top speed, along the shoulder of the highway, reserved for ambulances, police, and military vehicles. They even had, for much of the way, a Carabinieri motorcycle escort.

V was averaging ninety miles per hour on her sleek 185-horsepower titanium-frame Macchia Nera motorbike as she raced up to Santo Paolo in Monte Bianco, the little mountain town that was, in Father Ottavio's mind at least, home to the Torelli Jewel, though Father Ottavio had had no idea what the Torelli Jewel was; which probably meant that the Cardinal didn't either. But he did know it was valuable; and he almost certainly knew she was looking for it.

Racing along the highway was pure pleasure. The day was just beginning; but it was already hot; the sky was pure robin's egg blue; a white haze hung low over the hills and in the valleys. It looked like there were traces of snow, even in midsummer, on top of some of the higher mountains. The dust from the earth tremors and the smoke from the fires gave to the lower air a dreamy ethereal haze.

V went over in her mind how things had gone so badly wrong.

Was it her fault? She would indeed be furious with herself if humanity's long struggle, and that of all the other life forms on the planet, were to come to an end, and the beautiful planet cease to exist because she, V, idiot that she was, had failed to protect the Crystal and the key. Damn it! She reviewed everything she had learned over the last two years – and the last two days.

For centuries she had not had to worry about the Crystal. And it had never occurred to her, over those many years, to worry about the key. She growled. *How* could she have been so stupid?

Marcus had told her that the key was safest with the Crystal, and that it should stay with the Crystal. Then, two thousand years ago a series of sandstorms out of the Sahara had buried the canyon, the cave, and the Crystal; the problem seemed to have been solved, perhaps forever. For centuries the Crystal remained invisible, hidden under hundreds of feet of sand; no one, it seemed, would ever be able to find or tamper with the Crystal. V felt safe. The Crystal and the key were sealed away, far from, and inaccessible to, any inquisitive bipeds. And then, too, V herself was far away, exploring countries and continents, and fighting to survive, hunting down her food – her victims. As far as the Crystal went, she relaxed.

Indeed, she had remained serene and untroubled until a year ago. Then, for the first time, she became aware that a new storm, in the 1930s, had swept away the great dunes of sand and uncovered the narrow canyon that led to the home of the Crystal. Father Luciani's discoveries, and Father O'Bryan's files had revealed much of the story – and uncovered the name Giuseppe Torelli, medical doctor, and explorer and adventurer, who had discovered the Crystal and the Torelli Jewel.

The final pieces of the puzzle regarding the missing key were revealed when V drank Father Ottavio's blood. Father Ottavio knew part of the story. It had been told to him by Father Andrea, in an unusual moment of confidence

– Father Andrea, apparently, was strict and austere and self-sacrificing in his personal life, and he was not used to drinking wine, except for discreet sips during the Holy Mass. And so it was that a bottle of Barolo at the restaurant the Living Fountain had loosened his tongue. Father Andrea had become expansive. This was unusual for him – and Father Ottavio had learned about a mysterious small object, the Torelli Jewel, that was in the possession of Cardinal Ambrosiano's family and that, through sheer chance, Cardinal Ambrosiano had inherited.

The story was this. In 1936 Doctor Torelli had discovered the ravine that led to the Crystal's home, and he stumbled upon the entry to the cavern, where the stone had moved aside, and the steel door was wide open, apparently because a lightning strike had triggered the mechanism that opened the entry to the cavern. And so Torelli had entered the cavern itself and had found the Crystal.

Torelli was a devout Catholic and, by pure chance, was related to the family of the child who would later become Cardinal Ambrosiano. Torelli's cousin, Ambrosiano's grandfather, was a member of the Satanic Order of the Apocalypse, though Torelli did not know this, and almost certainly had no idea that such an order existed.

It was clear from Torelli's notes – and from Father Andrea's account – that Torelli had decided that the Crystal's existence was too amazing – and too unsettling – to be made known to the general public – or to anyone.

It indicated a civilization that was infinitely superior to the most technically advanced of human civilizations of the mid-twentieth century. Such a revelation would be a blow to the Catholic faith, and to humanity's faith in itself. And, in the mid-1930s, the world was in a deep economic depression, with fanaticism and evil rising on all sides. Torelli, who was an idealist, feared that knowledge of the Crystal would add to the crisis. He also feared that the technology embedded in the Crystal might be used by humans, particularly by Fascists and Nazis, to evil and terrible effect.

While he didn't know who made the Crystal and what it was for, Torelli did discover that a small oblong segment of the Crystal could be detached from the Crystal.

He managed to pluck it out of the Crystal. And he took it with him – almost certainly as proof of what he had found. Even this little object was clearly not made by any human civilization: its crystalline structure and molecular makeup were unique. At least, that's what Torelli thought. And, apparently, he was right. Before he left, Torelli made detailed drawings of the Crystal and its latticework metal cradle and took a few photographs.

From 1939, the Second World War – with fighting in North Africa – and the eventual defeat of the Axis powers, including Italy – made any further exploration of the ravine and the cavern impracticable.

After the war, Torelli moved on to an entirely different career. He specialized in plastic surgery and moved to California, where he treated aging film stars, and never mentioned, so far as anyone knew, the Crystal or the jewel. He died, a bachelor without a family of his own, ninety-six years old, in 2006 in San Diego. In his will, Torelli left what came to be called the Torelli Jewel – and a sealed envelope with a memo describing the Crystal and directions as to how it could be found – to his distant relative, Cardinal Ambrosiano. It was clear, from what V had gleaned, that Doctor Torelli knew nothing of the Satanic Order of the Apocalypse, and that he believed Ambrosiano would be a trusted and safe custodian for such dangerous knowledge – but by this time Ambrosiano had already been, for decades, the leader of the secret Order.

And this too V had learned from Father Ottavio: that the key, the Torelli Jewel, had been put on deposit by Torelli in a municipal museum in the small mountain town where the Torelli family had its summer home. There the Torelli Jewel remained, as a dusty curiosity, all these decades, through Depression, the fall of Fascism, war and peace, the liberation, the post-war boom, all the Italian crises, and the independence of the countries of North Africa.

Then when the museum was closed – two years ago – for restoration work, the key had been transferred to the mayor's office for safekeeping.

Now, according to Father Andrea's account to Father Ottavio, and following Father Ottavio's own knowledge, which blossomed instantly in V's mind when she gulped down his blood, the rest of the story went like this:

Cardinal Ambrosiano was at first skeptical and not very interested in this tale about his ancient relative. He had never known Torelli – a distant half-mythical rather eccentric old man who lived in faraway California – and he didn't have any faith at all in the doctor's drawings or his account of the Crystal. It was all just too fantastical. But finally, piqued by curiosity, and convinced this was perhaps a "sign" from Satan, Ambrosiano got around to secretly visiting the site of the Crystal early in 2023. He was awestruck by what he found and decided that the extraordinary object, the Crystal, must be a gift from Satan. In his excitement at finding the Crystal, Ambrosiano almost forgot about the small oblong detachable piece of the Crystal stored in the Torelli Collection. In any case, he certainly didn't realize its significance.

So, the "Torelli Jewel" was left in the Torelli Collection in the small local museum, sitting in a dusty case with a handwritten note explaining that it was an object that Doctor Torelli had found – or possibly purchased – during his adventures in Africa.

But once he had seen the Crystal itself, Ambrosiano did want to know what it did and how to make it work. He asked a leading civil and electronics engineer, Pino Moretti, who was a solid family man and a conservative Catholic – and who apparently had no knowledge of the Satanic Order of the Apocalypse – to go with him, on a secret mission, to see the Crystal. Moretti was fascinated and suggested the Crystal might respond to electric shock – frequencies and vibrations and electromagnetic energy. Then, to keep the secret of the Crystal intact, Cardinal Ambrosiano arranged to have Pino Moretti murdered – dropped out of the airplane that was taking him back to Italy. So far as the world knew, engineer Pino Moretti had simply disappeared – into nothingness. It was rumored that he was secretly gay, had acquired a boyfriend, and was now living, incognito, in Patagonia. The rumor was spread by Cardinal Ambrosiano's right-hand man – one Father Andrea …

As she raced toward the small town of Santo Paolo, V reflected that Professor Roger Thornhill was almost certainly the Cardinal's new in-house expert and victim, the new Pino Moretti. How long would the Cardinal feel he needed the Professor? V crouched lower over the motorbike and accelerated. Would the Cardinal keep Thornhill to the end? Or would he toss him away – murder him – when he felt the Professor was no longer useful? And just when would the Professor cease to be useful?

At an Esso station just outside Santo Paolo, V stopped and got off the motorbike. She patted the cowling. "Thanks, darling," she whispered, feeling the warm metal under her hand. V had a weakness for elegant, fast, powerful machines.

She used the Esso washroom to change from her synthetic leather-latex biker catsuit to more suitable attire for a meeting with the mayor of Santo Paolo.

When she emerged from the washroom, V was impeccably civilian, dressed in a sober but chic Armani suit, black patent leather high heels, sheer dark stockings, short pleated skirt, perfect little jacket, large sunglasses.

Except for the backpack, she looked every inch the successful Milanese – and international – lawyer that she was supposed to be, Fiorenza Giordano, the CEO of Laura Giordano International & Associates, a firm founded, so went the tale, by her grandmother Laura Giordano, who was, of course, V herself, in an earlier incarnation.

In her backpack she had her full military kit. In her purse, she had her Beretta M9.

She hitched up her skirt, rode the bike slowly into town and parked it in an open parking lot near the mayor's office. She asked a young man who was loitering nearby if he would watch her bike and gave him a very substantial tip; she promised him much, much more, later, when she returned. He saluted and said he would defend the bike with his life. Reading his mind, V knew he meant what he said.

Taking her backpack and briefcase with her, V walked along a narrow, steep, cobblestoned street toward city hall. The town was charming, with all the simple houses hewed out of pale mountain stone.

The mayor had been forewarned of her visit by a phone call from the office of the Pope and by a call from the Ministry of the Interior – John and Julia had pulled out all the stops.

City Hall was a neo-classical building of white stone in the main square; broad steps led up to the main doors, which were framed by giant Corinthian columns, over which, on the fronton, were written the proud letters, *Palazzo del Governo*.

The mayor's deputy, a tall, striking-looking woman wearing a black jacket and short skirt – with marvelous cheekbones, big friendly eyes, and wonderfully long legs, all which V took in with an appreciative smile – came to meet her at the entrance. "Delighted to meet you," she said. "My name is Jeannie. And that is a wonderful jacket!"

"Thank you, Jeannie. I'm Fiorenza, Fiorenza Giordano. Jeannie's an unusual name for an Italian."

"I was born in the States – Chicago – and my family came back when I was fifteen, so I have a foot in both worlds, a bit schizophrenic really."

"I can sympathize," said V. "I always feel I am living in several places at once."

High heels clicking, the two women walked along the marble-floored corridors. V noticed that weddings were being celebrated. One round-eyed, red-faced bridegroom had a crooked, goofy, embarrassed grin. Either he was scared out of his wits, or he couldn't believe his luck; V couldn't decide. His blue trousers were too short, his yellow-and-red plaid socks didn't match, and his shoes were scuffed. The bride smiled at V and looked down, blushing. She was olive-skinned, slender, and very pretty; and she was perhaps twenty years younger than her husband-to-be. V wondered at it. The bride was clutching an oversized lavish wedding bouquet. Red roses, hyacinths, and lilies spilled over in profusion.

Babies were being visited by doctors and registered at a health office. One baby waved a pudgy hand at V, gurgled, blowing a few bubbles, and gave her a bright-eyed smile. The mother – who looked about eighteen years old – said, "He likes you!"

"I like him too!" V gave the baby and mother her biggest movie-star smile. The whole place was impressive. All sorts of civic activities were concentrated in this one building – it was a microcosm of the life of the town, a true community. "It's a real circus," said V. "All of life is here."

"Yes," said Jeannie. "Generally, this is a very happy town."

"You must like it."

"I do. I love it."

The mayor was waiting for them, alone, in a rather large conference hall. "I'll leave you two here," said Jeannie. "I have to see about the firemen's yearly fund-raising dinner. And one of the local schools is putting on a pantomime. The children are very excited."

"Thank you, Jeannie," said V.

"Delighted to meet you, Ms. Giordano," the mayor said. "My office is being redecorated, so if you don't mind, we'll conduct our business here." The mayor was a tanned, handsome, impeccably groomed man in his forties, distinguished streaks of gray in his hair, and dressed in the sort of expensive perfectly tailored suit that Italian politicians of all parties seemed to favor.

"Delighted to meet you too, Mr. Mayor." V dropped her backpack beside the chair, sat down, and put her slender briefcase sideways on her lap.

Still smiling, the mayor lowered himself into his chair. "You have come for that interesting artifact that was deposited in the museum by Doctor Torelli back in 1936."

"Yes, exactly." V smiled and patted her briefcase as a good lawyer might do.

"That's very interesting …" said the mayor. He was gazing at V, appreciating her extraordinary looks. V could see the question in his eyes: *Was this woman real?*

"Yes," said V, "I have a letter here from the Holy See and one from the

Ministry of the Interior. And you did get our message about the danger of earthquakes and about how vital it is that I –"

"Yes, yes, yes," said the mayor, shaking himself, waking up from his fascination with V's cheekbones, skin, and lips. "Thank you for the warnings, this is earthquake country; the museum is undergoing restoration, so the Torelli Jewel has been put, temporarily, in a safety deposit box in the Catholic Bank of Upper Abruzzo; but, well, there is something strange … some mix-up, I suppose, because a gentleman was here just fifteen minutes ago, with a letter from Father Andrea in Cardinal Ambrosiano's office, and he said that you were delayed, so he was going to pick up the artifact for you …"

"Oh?" V said, raising an eyebrow, keeping her cool – but furious at being outmaneuvered. "What did the gentleman look like?"

"Very handsome, in fact, he looked rather like –"

"Marcello Mastroianni?"

"Precisely." The mayor smiled. "He is an extraordinarily handsome and charming chap, and when I told him about your note, he said he was a very good friend of yours. I gave him the key to the safe deposit box and one of my staff took him to the bank and –"

"Get down, Mr. Mayor," V shouted. She grabbed her backpack and briefcase, leapt over the table, shoved the mayor to the floor, and pushed him under the heavy conference table. She crouched down, next to the mayor.

"What in the world are you doing, Ms. Giordano?"

"Stay still, please."

"I really don't know what this is –?"

WHAM!

The first shock hit. The floor rose up, twisting, groaning, crunching; V stiffened. This was a real earthquake – not just a tremor, not just a warning shot, but the beginning of the final bombardment. A chandelier fell, smashing into the chair where the mayor had been sitting three seconds before.

"Ms. Giordano, how did you know –?"

"Shush, keep down, Mr. Mayor!"

WHAM!

The room cracked, twisted, seemed to be ripped in two. V sensed the catastrophe happening, all around her: A huge gap opened and snaked across the floor. A Renaissance painting of the Virgin Mary fell from the wall with a crash. A photograph of the President of the Republic flew spinning across the room like a frisbee. An architect's table bounced into the air and landed upside down. Plate glass windows burst outwards with an explosive roar. Marble tiles shattered. The conference table under which they were crouched flipped over, and a portion of the wall crashed down on V and the mayor.

WHAM!

The floor buckled. The marble floor burst upwards, splitting into huge fragments. V was crouched down in a compact ball next to the mayor, but the upward thrust of this new impact sent her catapulting, tumbling over herself, a double somersault, to the middle of the room. The mayor disappeared under an avalanche of rubble.

WHAM!

Beams crashed down, the reinforced concrete frame split; iron bars sprang out, snapping in two, whipping and swirling like wild serpents. Metal exploded – tangled lengths and coils of rusty inch-thick, snake-like cable, whiplashing, snapping, cracking. Dust swirled in the mangled thunderous air.

It calmed – for a moment, it calmed.

V was sitting – feeling dazed and a bit silly – on her backside. She got to her feet. At that moment, next to her, part of the ceiling came crashing down; a wave of chalky dust engulfed her, catching her in a tornado of powdery stucco; she covered her face, shielding her eyes, mouth and nose.

The roaring settled.

V was still in her Armani suit, which was reduced to ribbons; and she was now chalk-white, a plaster statue. She sneezed and stepped out of the swirling column of dust and climbed over heaps of rubble to where the mayor had disappeared. She pushed some of the stone and stucco and one large wooden beam aside and dug down, trying to reach the mayor. Vaguely, through the ringing in her ears, and from far away, she heard screams – other people were trapped, or hurt, or dying.

A ghost came out of the clouds of dust, a long-legged ghost, jacket gone, blouse torn, and covered in white – Jeannie.

"The mayor," she said. "Where is the mayor?"

Ah, thought V, *she's in love with him! Poor girl!*

"Oh, my God," said Jeannie.

"Over here. He was hit by a falling wall." V was clawing at the debris. "He's buried. Let's get him out!"

"Yes, yes – oh, please, please ..."

Daylight floated in through clouds of dust, through cracks in the half-fallen walls. Jeannie climbed over crags of broken stone to reach V.

The mayor was trapped under a huge ribbed beam of gray steel. V hesitated. The beam was too heavy for her and Jeannie, and it was too heavy for V in human form; she had to make a choice: *Damn!*

"Mr. Mayor, can you hear us?"

"Yes, yes, I can hear you, but I'm trapped; go and help the others, there must be many people who need –"

"We'll get you out, Mr. Mayor." V turned to Jeannie. "Jeannie, I am not what I seem, I'm going to change into a stronger version of me." She was already stripping off her clothes and putting them on a table that had, miraculously, remained standing.

"Another form? A stronger version?" Jeannie stared. *Was this woman mad?*

"Another form, like a demon, but a friendly demon." V was naked, dusty, but naked. "It's rather hard to explain." She morphed in a blur and stood there – reptilian, glittering, but still streaked with dust.

"Jesus!"

"Takes some getting used to, but I'm much stronger this way. Here, help me! You pull the mayor out from under this beam while I hold it up." V levered the giant double-ribbed steel beam up. Jeannie, still staring at V, pulled the mayor out from under it.

"Thank you, thank you, Jeannie," the mayor said, crawling out of the stucco and brushing at his suit. He looked up. His eyes opened wide, blinking against the falling dust. "What is *that*, Jeannie, what is *that*?" Staring down at him was a reptilian fanged demon.

"That's Ms. Giordano," said Jeannie, kneeling over the mayor, who was struggling to sit up.

"Ms. Giordano, but –"

"It's a long story, Mr. Mayor," V said, as she gently lowered the steel beam back down. "I'm stronger this way. But I can't show myself to too many people, so I'm going to change back to human form. Can you stand up, Mr. Mayor?"

"Yes, yes, I think I can." Keeping his eyes, hypnotized, on V, he stood, and brushed at his jacket.

V dissolved in a blur of light and reappeared in human form, but naked. "Sorry," she said, and quickly slipped back into what remained of her clothes, still plastered in dust.

"I'm astounded," said the mayor. "But I won't ask any questions. Thank you for saving me, Ms. Giordano, you and Jeannie."

"Let's see who else we can save," said V, picking up her backpack – strangely intact, as was her briefcase – and buckling it to her shoulders. "It would be best for all concerned if you didn't mention my little metamorphosis – people would think you are insane – that would be bad politics – and it would also be extremely inconvenient and dangerous for me."

"Silence is golden," said the Mayor.

"My lips are sealed," said Jeannie.

They made their way through the rubble to the exit sign – *Uscita* – which hung, blinking, half out of its frame, over the door; electric sparks cascaded down, bright yellow streaks, looking incongruous, flashes of lightning, in the dust-filled air. They climbed through the crooked doorframe, and, pushing aside the shattered door that hung from one hinge, they came out into the corridor. It was an obstacle course, twisted steel rods, shattered desks, fallen beams and smashed chandeliers. The walls had caved; in some places the ceiling had collapsed.

White dust cascaded from the cracked ceiling; everything was covered by a veil of falling white. The beautiful young bride and the goofy-looking groom lay dead under a thick veil of stucco, looking like ashen bodies from Pompeii, sculpted and frozen in death, and thickly encrusted with gray. V stared at them: Dead for seconds or dead for centuries, what difference did it make? The young woman, eyes wide open and staring at the ceiling, still clutched in one hand the bouquet – the flowers now chalk-white. She had been cut in half at the waist – by a snake of steel. The groom lay face down; one trouser leg was curled up or torn off; his shoes were gone; one of his plaid socks had a large hole at the heel. The building shook. An aftershock or just the settling of smashed foundations?

A baby was crying somewhere, howling.

They climbed over the rubble carefully, not wanting to endanger anybody who might be buried underneath. Bodies were sprawled everywhere – a woman lying halfway out of a doorway, a man in a fine business suit face down, his back torn open, merely a bloody hole – his head crushed, around it a halo of dark dust-soaked blood.

A child lay sprawled in the middle of the corridor with a woman, it must be her mother; pools of blood, darkened by dust, surrounded them.

There was another baby – the baby that had smiled at V – lying on the floor next to its mother. V crouched over it. The baby was alive, bubbles on its lips. V picked it up. Its chubby fingers grasped at the lapels of her jacket and held on. V gently detached his fingers and handed him to Jeannie.

V and the mayor levered a section of wall off the young mother, who was still alive – just barely – but very badly hurt, a huge gash in her abdomen and her intestines showing.

"We're going to help you," said V. "You'll be okay."

"Yes, yes, we'll help you," said the mayor, glancing at V: *How* could they help her? It was clear she was dying.

"I'm going to try something," said V, turning to the mayor. She knelt next to the young woman, pulled away the remains of her torn and bloodied blouse, and, concentrating hard, laid her hands on the wound. A purplish light radiated from V's fingers. The mayor and Jeannie looked at each other. Jeannie put her finger to her lips: *Not a word!* The mayor, his face a mask of pantomime white, nodded. As they watched, the wound closed, visibly healing. Then the wound was gone, as if it had never been. The young woman's eyes opened. "What happened?"

"There was an earthquake. Here, see if you can stand up." V and the mayor helped her to her feet. She looked down at herself. "I thought I was hurt, I was …" Her dress was torn, her blouse was gone, she was covered in gore, but underneath the blood and gore she was whole, unblemished.

Jeannie and the mayor looked at each other, and Jeannie handed the baby – who was reaching out – back to its mother. "Here, here you are – you are lucky, both of you made it."

"Yes, thank you, we were lucky," said the young mother, looking bewildered. And to V, "Thank you, thank you for everything," she said. "He liked you from the first."

They finally made it out of the building onto the piazza. The giant marble fronton proudly proclaiming *Palazzo del Governo* was now half-shattered and crooked, hanging awry.

The mayor stared at V with wide eyes. Here, in the light of day, she appeared to be entirely normal, merely a slender, pale woman, extraordinarily good-looking, in the torn rags of an elegant suit, covered in blood and dust, toting a backpack and clutching a briefcase; she seemed, like everyone else in the piazza, to be a bloodied ghost, an ordinary mortal who had risen from the dead.

Rescue workers were climbing toward them.

"Miss, miss, do you need help?" One tried to take V's arm.

"No, no, I'm fine."

"Thank you for everything." V shook the mayor's and Jeannie's hands. "And good luck." She kissed the young mother on the forehead, and offered the baby her finger, which it eagerly took; and then she left, as quickly as she could, pushing past the people who were gathering in the center of the town square, getting as far away from the unsteady and crumbling buildings as possible.

"I should really mind my own business," V muttered, both pleased and displeased with herself for saving lives and revealing her demonic self – a dangerous form of exposure she rarely indulged in.

Now she had to find U Pizzu – she was sure it was U Pizzu – she'd never met the man, but she was quite aware of his reputation. Damn it, the Mafioso probably had the Torelli Jewel. And he'd gone after the Torelli Jewel because he was going after her – that was clear. He would have no idea what the Jewel was. But he was ahead of her and he could already have gone to the bank and taken the Jewel. Or maybe he got caught in the earthquake. She looked down at herself – miserable rags! She couldn't go anywhere dressed like this! *Damn!*

She turned into a narrow street that, luckily, seemed totally untouched by the earthquake. She saw a cellar window in what looked like a derelict building. That was just the thing! She really did need a change of clothes! She knelt and crawled through the window, and, in the dark, dank cellar, she stripped off the ragged remains of the Armani suit.

"Well, goodbye to all that."

She looked around. The place was an authentic old-fashioned cellar, with cobwebs and heavy ceiling beams and dark dank corners, and some complicated sort of furnace or water heater in dark metal that looked like it had been patched up and repaired over the decades and turned into an extravagant surreal version of a Rube Goldberg Machine with an unbelievable number of pipes, levers, wires, and struts. She unzipped the backpack and peeked into it. "So, let's see, what …?"

At this point, she was rudely interrupted by a shadow. She turned. The shadow had surged up at the cellar window; it was a bulky thing in a dark cloak. The bulky thing climbed through the window and straightened up, in so far as it could. Damnation! It was one of those cursed monks!

The monk must have been six foot five at least, maybe six foot eight! V focused her night vision, compensating for the dimness of the cellar. The tiny twisted features crowded at the bottom of the large blank face were partly hidden by the black cowl. V took a deep breath. This was an unpleasant surprise. Those monks Count Marbuse used to keep as servants or slaves still existed – even now, three centuries later! They must be a special breed – servants or slaves, bred in secret over the centuries by the Order, an antique and diabolic form of genetic engineering.

"Demon," the monk growled, "She-demon, your hour has come."

"Oh," said V. She was feeling rather underdressed, naked as she was, except for dust, dirt, plaster, and a few fragments of the Armani that still stuck to her skin, but not in the right places. "I imagine you've been following me. How nice! I'm fine, thank you. And, how are you?"

"She-demon, thou shalt not escape!"

"And what about thou, my dear monk, shalt thou escape or shalt thou die, here and now, this very instant, and be cast down to Hell and everlasting torment, hopelessly distant from the love and light of Divinity?" As she spoke she was thinking: Let's see, I've already fed abundantly, I drank Father Ottavio dry, I drained every drop out of the poor machine-gun sentry; but it would perhaps be useful, given the present impending situation, which will undoubtedly demand considerable stamina, to store up on more vitamins, proteins, corpuscles, and amino acids, since the next forty-eight hours do promise to be hectic and grueling. This super-size monk was perhaps a godsend.

"So, monk, what do you say?"

He snarled.

"Come on, now, I'm sure you can say more than that!"

"She-demon," the monk hissed. "She-demon!" He leapt across the dark musty cellar, literally flying, skimming just under the roof beams, the sagging cobwebs, the dusty water pipes.

Well, well, thought V, this might be a challenge. In such a confined space one's room to maneuver was sorely limited. She slowed perceptual time down to a gluey molasses dribble. The seconds stretched out. The Doppler effect kicked into action. The sounds decelerated and deepened. The visible spectrum shifted toward infrared. She watched the monk fly through the dusky air, his habit flowing out behind him, rippling and snapping slowly, like a witch's somber ball gown caught in the wake and after-turbulence of a supersonic broomstick. His black cowl slipped slowly off his huge pale naked skull. With his monstrous arms and pudgy hands stretched out before him, he looked like a grotesque version of Superman.

Frowning pensively, V thought, the poor chap is going to try to break my neck – how very inconsiderate of him.

She slowed time down still further. For an instant, it stood still. She stepped lightly aside, using an old ballerina or was it bullfighting two-step she had once learned – was it from Ernest Hemingway or Margot Fonteyn? She couldn't remember – just a twirl of the ankles and hips, and – *voilà!*

So ...

She was not where the monk expected her to be.

The moment the flying monk passed her, within a whisker of her elegantly turned, chalk-white, mud-splattered, naked shoulder, she whipped around, leapt onto his back, crouched low, ripped away the crumpled cowl with her claws – thinking, it's rather fine material, this cowl; they treat themselves terribly well, these slaves of the Satanic Order – and plunged her wonderfully pointed fangs – which, like her claws, spouted bravely, conveniently, and precisely on cue – down through the monk's neck fat, down through the neck muscles, into the deeply buried, richly coursing jugular.

Splat!

The monk slammed head first into the far wall of the cellar, just next to the overelaborate water heater. He fell with a monstrous thump onto the stone-and-concrete floor. V rode him easily, clinging gracefully, staying with him, curling up upon him, amorously, and drinking, and drinking, locked delightedly into his whole cardiovascular system, every drop and capillary of it. Lying on the floor, he thrashed and thrashed. And then, in one mighty spasm, he tried to throw her off. But it was all in vain. His strength ebbed. He twitched and writhed, lying there, curled up, on his side, a giant ghost-white, black-robed fetus. V sucked him dry, down to the very last drop.

She stood up, wiped her mouth, and, then, just to be sure he was no longer dangerous, she ripped his head off, and placed it carefully, lovingly, upright on the floor, like a bald, chalk-white, Halloween pumpkin.

His eyes had rolled up; between the folds of fat, only the whites showed. White on white, thought V, very old avant-garde. To be hung on the best walls in the best museums. Dear, dear, she really was becoming too cynical for words!

In many ways, the poor creature was just a child.

She crouched over the headless body. This little dance had been extraordinarily messy. Blood dripped from her lips. And her face – she could see it in her mind's eye, as if in a mirror – was a bright-eyed, garish, sanguinary mask. Yum! Yum! It pleasantly echoed ancient blood sacrifice and delicious blood feasts. Her loins thrilled with the primitiveness of it all! She was wet with nihilistic excitement and ancestral lust. She slurped back a flood of saliva. Her dust-powdered, chalk-white collarbone and breasts shone with sparkling gaudy bubbles and splashes of festive scarlet.

Hmm!

She stood up.

The meal had been informative. She had learned much. She looked around. There was no water, no way to wash. She went to the water heater, knocked on the tank. It was rusty – and empty, dry as the mouth of a drunkard lost ten days in a desert.

She shrugged. She would just have to change as she was, coated in a lurid sheen of monk's blood and gobs of gore. How indecorous! She frowned. She licked her lips. Slipping into her warrior's garb would be warm and sticky, like applying a glaze of thick warm grease under the skintight catsuit – but, what the heck, it would be a sensuous experience, and she was glowing, now, with extra energy, bubbling with ideas – effervescent!

Too much blood in too short a time was dangerous! Of this she was quite aware. Right now she could sit down and write a thousand-page novel in about two seconds flat, or run a hundred-mile marathon before even leaving the starting gate, or maybe lift two five-hundred-pound dumbbells two hundred times in the blink of an eye, or jump over the moon, or recite *Hamlet* from beginning to end in less than ten seconds, playing all the roles herself, or ...

Dust drifted down from the ceiling in heavy veils – more miniature aftershocks. V put her hand to her nose; she wanted to sneeze. She resisted the temptation. She wiggled her nose and sniffled. Even sniffling offered a sensuous delight. Everything was just too delicious! Light filtered dimly through the single cellar window.

From her backpack, she pulled out her martial kit, and changed into her military gear; the skintight armored matte-black catsuit, the knife sheath, the pistol holster, and the grenade belt. Slipping into the elastic catsuit was a squishy and slippery business, but not at all unpleasant. The latex-like material squeaked and protested. It was like a deliciously smooth and viscous mud bath in one of those ancient spas in the Tuscan hills she'd so often visited in Caesar's time. For a moment, she shivered, shimmying in pleasure – What memories!

She zipped the suit shut and clicked the armored collar into place. Sitting down on a plaster and dust-covered wooden bench, she pulled on her military boots, buckled them up, and then stuffed the tattered remains of her Armani elegance into the backpack. Agnes, her longtime seamstress in Milan, would make her a replica Armani or personalized knock-off. She stretched, in pure voluptuous pleasure. "*You are getting giddy,*" she told herself. Watch out! If you overfeed, V, you can really screw things up! She frowned. One danger of overfeeding was a sensation of light-headed invulnerability, and that led directly to hubris, or overweening pride, and hubris led directly to stupid, frivolous mistakes, and mistakes led straight to catastrophe. *So, calm down, girl!*

She stood up, put her briefcase into the backpack, slipped the backpack over her shoulders, settled it snuggly, and locked it in place.

She glanced back at the dead monk whose head was sitting expressionless and sagely separate from its shattered empty body. The bloated body lay sprawled out, bloodless and much deflated, next to the Rube Goldberg water heater.

"Adieu, sweet monk, adieu!"

Boots and legs first, she slithered out of the basement window, stood up, and glanced up and down the narrow little street – nobody, no monks, no crying babies, no falling buildings, and no people buried under rubble.

She sprinted down the street, and skidded to a stop in a small, open square, her boots striking sparks on the cobblestones.

She looked around – dust was still rising from the earthquake. All the plants in a little vegetable garden on one side of the square were covered in a patina of white.

A barefoot young woman in white shorts and a black T-shirt, her hair tied up in a dark chignon, was kneeling next to a row of tomatoes, inspecting the damage; chunks of stucco and roof tiles had fallen into the garden, decapitating some of the tomatoes. The young woman glanced up at V – her pale face shocked and her eyes widening. She quickly looked away.

V frowned. She hated it when she had that effect on people!

Oh, well, it's to be expected! My face and hair are covered in blood, blood is still dripping, I'm sure, from my lips, and I'm wearing a skintight excessively revealing, fetishist's delight, black catsuit, and carrying an extraordinary assortment of deadly weapons, and …

She glanced up at the sky – a few wispy, ragged, high-altitude cirrus clouds. Otherwise, it was a splendid day, the sky a pale, soft, inviting blue.

She set off, jauntily – feeling much too peppy – and followed a cobblestone side street that wound down toward the Catholic Bank of Upper Abruzzo, where the Torelli Jewel should be tucked away in a safe deposit box, and where U Pizzu had been headed, probably, when the earthquake struck. Handsome devil, U Pizzu, she'd studied photographs of the Mafia boss carefully. Know your enemy. Would the bank still be standing? And if it had collapsed, had it buried U Pizzu and the key – the Torelli Jewel – under a pile of rubble? If his reputation was anything to go by, U Pizzu had probably made it out of the wreckage, and he probably already had the Jewel.

V climbed up some stone steps.

She hummed a jaunty little tune.

Oodles of fresh blood make you feel like dancing!

Still, she wondered about U Pizzu ...

"Fuck!" U Pizzu brushed the dust from his jacket. He had just left the bank when the first shock hit, and was heading down a narrow side street, with four-story houses of ancient white stone, on both sides, one of the worst possible places to be in an earthquake.

When the earthquake hit, U Pizzu looked up, saw the towering stone walls sway, back and forth, back and forth. A flower pot fell on the cobblestones two feet in front of him. It splattered earth and geraniums all over the place, even, annoyingly, onto the toes of his freshly polished shoes; a few windows exploded outwards, shards of glass showered down; a woman began to scream; fire alarms and car alarms went off, making a horrible racket. But the walls in the little street did not come tumbling down.

"What a day!" U Pizzu pulled a neatly folded mauve handkerchief from his vest pocket and wiped his forehead; he shook his foot to get rid of the twisted red geranium – he never did like the bitter smell of those things – and to shoo away the chunks of impertinent dirt from the shattered flowerpot.

It had been hot and dusty before; and now it was even more so. Dirt drifted down from the buildings. The ground was steaming, puffing up smoke. U Pizzu again wiped his forehead. Now would be a good time to be lying on a fold-out deckchair on the beach, with a bottle of white wine. Or snorkeling! If you are going to face the end of the world, that would be the way to do it, on the beach, with a plate of *spaghetti alle vongole* – ah, yes! Of course, at the seaside one faced the danger of tsunamis. Maybe a nice azure swimming pool inland, far from earthquake zones. Hmm! Then again, maybe no place was safe!

U Pizzu folded the handkerchief, returned it to his breast pocket, and patted it down; he looked back toward the bank. All he could see was a cloud of rising dust. Could the building have fallen down? The dust settled. U Pizzu squinted through the veil of white and saw that the bank was no longer there. Just a big hole, and the pale blue sky, where a few minutes ago there had been a bank. "Fuck!"

He headed back to see if he could help but when he got to the square, he saw that medics and crowds were already beginning to arrive, so he figured he could relax. The experts didn't always appreciate amateurs. He looked around. Much of the town was in ruins.

U Pizzu turned and walked back the way he had come. He didn't know what the "Torelli Jewel" was – though he knew the she-devil wanted it. He was frustrated by the whole thing; a riddle wrapped in a mystery wrapped in an enigma, as that great British Prime Minister Winston Churchill had once said. And mysteries were fucking *unhealthy*; mysteries got you killed. Cardinal Ambrosiano was a mystery and he was an evil joker; he was like a spider, at the center of many webs. How many people are caught in those webs? Was he, U Pizzu, one of them? Who had been using whom and for what purpose? Maybe laundering money through the Vatican Bank had not been such a hot idea. Lots of important people who had any dealings with that bank had ended up dead – shot, garroted, hung by the neck, poisoned. U Pizzu wiped his forehead. And then, returning to the present, there was the Torelli Jewel. What the fuck was it? Another mystery? Why did the she-devil want it? He didn't like going on a treasure hunt when he didn't know what the fucking treasure was.

And – what was worse – in the safe deposit box in the bank, there had been no Torelli Jewel. Instead he had found a note. A little joke on the part of the Cardinal!

A note … He'd been lucky it wasn't a bomb! Open up the safe deposit box and – boom – you are reduced to ash! U Pizzu had no idea what the note meant. He frowned. What did he do now? Minutes earlier, the town had been a shitty little provincial town, lost in the mountains – definitely not Palermo! Definitely not Corleone! Definitely not Cefalù! Not a palm tree in sight! And now it was a pile of smoking rubble. He should never have come here; and he didn't have a clue where to go next. He'd seen no sign of the she-devil, but he had to figure out how to get in touch with her.

He walked around a corner into a small side street, or what was left of it, and came face-to-face with …

"Shit!"

"*Ciaò*," V said.

She was standing in the middle of the street, just in front of a pile of big square stones that had fallen when a building had collapsed; her legs were spread apart, in cowboy-style shooting stance, but she had no pistol in her hand. Still ...

High Noon, thought U Pizzu.

Duel in the Sun, thought U Pizzu.

Annie Oakley, thought U Pizzu.

"Signorina," he said rather formally, nodding in salutation. "Miss." He didn't approve of the way young people used "*Ciaò*," coming, going, or just passing by, with a casual wave from the other side of the street: "*Ciaò!*" It showed a lack of respect, a lack of dignity. "Or is it Signora?" But she didn't look to him like the marrying kind. Do gun-toting demons hook up? No, she looked like a bachelor-girl, a single-girl, special-ops warrior, the most dangerous kind, with her sleek high-tech catsuit, high-tech weapons, and face streaked with dust and mud and blood; yes, definitely, blood.

She was smiling.

"Signorina will do." She took a step forward.

"Stop right there, Signorina!" U Pizzu pulled out his P.38.

"Certainly, sir, as you wish." She stopped and stood quite still, legs together now, as if standing at attention. Looked like she was having fun. U Pizzu had never seen her before; but from all the descriptions, he was sure this was the killer who had "liberated" the shipment of girls in Apulia. And maybe, too, this was the demon that had drunk the Cardinal's pimp and procurer, Brother Filippo, dry.

"But I might ask the same, that you stop right there, Signore U Pizzu."

"Only my dearest friends are allowed to call me that."

"Maybe we can be friends."

"I doubt it." U Pizzu frowned. Was this dame nuts?

"You are here for the Torelli Jewel." She tilted her head; the smile made her look very young.

"I don't know what you are talking about."

"Up till now, you have been acting as Ambrosiano's errand-boy. He was using you."

"So ..." U Pizzu shrugged.

"And he's going to double-cross you."

"Oh? Just how is he going do that?" U Pizzu held the P.38 steady and slipped his dark Polaroids up onto his forehead. He wanted this mysterious demon – if that's what she was – to be looking straight into his soul when he plugged her between the eyes; and, besides, he was intrigued. Who or what exactly was she? And what did she know about the Torelli Jewel?

"So, it's true, then," she said.

"So, what's true, then?" he asked, mimicking her.

"That you look like Marcello Mastroianni."

"Fuck! Do I have to hear this all my life?"

"It could be worse. I mean, he was the great Latin lover, right?"

"Great Latin lover! He was an actor, for fuck's sake! You want the great Latin lover, you gotta speak to the right people!"

"Like you, for instance."

"Right! Like me, for instance!" U Pizzu couldn't believe himself – yakking about the great Latin lover while there was real business to be done. She was hot-looking, though, maybe twenty-two to twenty-four, a bit splashed-up right now, maybe; but this added to the attraction. His own person he liked to keep impeccable; but mussed up in a beautiful woman, done the right way, that was exciting.

"What's that stuff all over your face?"

"What? This?" She felt her face. "Oh, that's blood. It's caked in dust, though."

"Blood." This was more like it, thought U Pizzu; now we can talk professional, man-to-man. "Whose blood?"

"Somebody I pulled out from under the rubble."

"Ah," said U Pizzu.

"Then I had to kill one of those monks. There was lots of splash and squirt when I tore his head off. Most of the blood is his."

"You tore his head off?"

"Yes, it was messy."

"I see." U Pizzu didn't like those monks either, but …

"The monk was here to stop me from getting the Torelli Jewel. And if you got it, he was going to kill you and take it – or kill you even if you didn't have it."

"Kill me?"

"Yes."

"They wouldn't dare."

"Yes, they would."

"How do you know this?"

"The monk: I found out from him."

"He confessed?"

"Yes, in a way he did, as he was dying. I can read the thoughts of those I kill."

"Oh, come on!"

The woman's eyes flashed – and, just for an instant, U Pizzu caught a glimpse into the deepest pit of Hell and the highest reaches of Heaven. He smiled. He'd always wanted to look death in the face, and here she was, Signorina Death in person! And if she really could read the souls of the dying, well! "Okay, let's say I believe you."

She stepped closer.

"Hold on! Hold it! Stay right there!"

"I want to propose a truce," she said.

"A truce?"

"You know some things; I know some things. We could work together."

"Maybe." U Pizzu held the pistol steady, aimed at her heart. "But I want to ask you one thing, ah, Signorina."

"Yes?"

"Was it you, way back, years ago, in Apulia, I had a shipment of girls –"

"The fifth of July 2003, at about 11:16 p.m.?"

"Ah, could have been, yeah, sounds right; anyway, a shipment gets interrupted and I lose three picciotti and maybe two hundred and fifty thousand euros of good young flesh."

"Yes, that was me."

"Fuck!" U Pizzu scratched his head. "How old were you then, two-and-a-half?"

"I was the age I am now."

U Pizzu stared at her; this was no ordinary killer. "And was it you did my two boys?"

"In the sewer tunnel, the other day?"

"Yeah."

"Yes."

"Jesus!"

"I apologize. It was messy. I used excessive force. I shouldn't have."

"Excessive force?!"

"I do apologize."

"Apologize?!"

"Yes."

"You pulverized those guys!"

"Franco and Paolo, yes, I'm sorry."

"You know their fucking names?"

"Yes."

U Pizzu thought for an instant: the past was past; the dead were dead. "Well, people die," he said. "People die all the time."

"Yes."

"It's business. That's the way it is."

"Yes."

"Okay, maybe that's water under the bridge."

"Good. Thank you!"

"You are fucking polite for a killer."

"Thank you, Marcello."

"Stop that!" U Pizzu had to grin.

"Well, is it a deal?" V took one step closer.

"Look, I …" U Pizzu steadied his aim.

"I'm a killer; so are you, Marcello, we are made for each other." She gave him a big wide smile.

"I'm not sure I …" U Pizzu felt obliged to smile back.

"And – if the world comes to an end, it will be bad for business – right?"

"You read minds too?"

"Yes, Marcello, I do." She gave him that smile – that flirting, deferential, entrancing female glance, face tilted down, eyes looking up, pushing all those old buttons, showing she was truly the worshipful female, gazing in adoration up at the masterful virile male, though he knew that worshipful was the very last thing this creature was; but – he sighed – sometimes a man has to risk everything.

"Okay," he said, giving her his best grin, "so if we're going to sign a truce, what do we do now?" He put his P.38 away, tucking it into the small of his back and thinking, I'm an utter fool; if I die now, it's because she's a sexy dame; all men are idiots when it comes to sexy dames, and I'm the biggest idiot of all – a true sucker!

"We find the Torelli Jewel. And you know where it might be."

"Yeah, maybe I do, I'm not sure." U Pizzu straightened his tie. He felt he should look as elegant as he could for Lady Death. "There was a clue. But I don't want to go chasing after something I don't know nothing about."

"The Torelli Jewel is a piece of crystal, about three inches long, eight sides along its length, and it has a mandala pattern inlaid at each end. It looks somewhat like a phallus. It's a key, actually. It is the key to the machine that is creating these earthquakes."

"So, the earthquakes aren't natural?"

"Not these ones."

"*Mizzica!* If that's true …"

"It is true. And, yes, what you've already begun to suspect is also true: Cardinal Ambrosiano does want to destroy the world, the whole planet, using that machine."

"That's what Gaetano Larione said."

"Well, he was right."

"Poor sod. My best buddy. I killed him … for telling the truth."

"I can use the Torelli Jewel – the key – to stop the machine and stop the earthquakes."

"Where is this machine?"

"Africa. Now, Marcello, where's the key?"

"Okay. I'm trusting you on this – and I don't entirely know why. The Torelli Jewel was not in the safe deposit box. And the piece of paper that *was* in the box says that the Jewel is under the third paving stone south from the sundial-stone, the sundial figure carved in the paving stones on the main platform of some place called Villa Jovis."

"Villa Jovis?"

"Yeah. The note says, 'It's the site of our greatest ecstasies and most delicious crimes,' and 'the height from which falling is so easy!' I don't know what the fuck that means or where the fuck Villa Jovis is!"

"Capri," said V. "It's on the island of Capri."

"Capri?"

"Yes. Villa Jovis – the Villa of the god Jupiter – was the favorite residence of the Emperor Tiberius for about sixteen years. It's a ruin now, in a park, on a very high cliff overlooking the sea. It's one of the most beautiful places on the planet. Ambrosiano has a villa on Capri. I've heard he held orgies at Villa Jovis when the tourists weren't there, after hours, maybe even a black Mass or two, so it's a joke on Ambrosiano's part. He may have thrown his sacrificial victims over the cliff. He would consider that amusing, I think."

"Yeah, he would. The Cardinal is a clown, a joker." U Pizzu patted his forehead with the mauve handkerchief, then folded it and put it back in his breast pocket.

"In some ways, he is."

"Clowns are fucking dangerous unpredictable bastards. You know, I go to a circus, it gives me the willies, just looking at those guys, they romp around, all giggly, with all that makeup, you can't see what the bastards are thinking. They're fucking ambiguous! And ambiguous I definitely don't like! Ambiguous is dangerous! They're all perverts! And they're spooky."

"Well, this particular clown certainly is."

"So, we go to Capri!"

"Yes."

"We get a vacation," said U Pizzu, grinning. V gave him a look. "Okay, okay," he said. "A *working* vacation."

"I have a bike," V said. "At least I think I have a bike."

"A bike?" said U Pizzu. "Like two wheels and a handlebar?"

"It's pretty fast, Marcello. You'll like it."

CHAPTER 49 – ISLE OF CAPRI

The island of Capri is a sharp-peaked mountaintop that rises like a giant arrowhead out of the glittering Mediterranean, just off the steep mountainous cliffs of the Sorrento peninsula and Amalfi Coast. The island is a broken-off piece of the Apennine mountain chain that is the backbone of Italy: Capri is a stacked-up, folded-over, fractured platform, layers of limestone and sandstone, blocks of material once deposited on the seafloor of an ancient sea from eons ago – the Tethys Ocean.

The cliffs of Capri plunge straight into the sea. It has only a small port and a few pebbled beaches and grottos hidden here and there. With its high cliffs, Capri is almost invulnerable to attack. It once provided a comfortable refuge for Roman emperors, such as Augustus and Tiberius; and it has, for millennia, also been – and still is even now – a playground for the ultra-rich. With its lemon groves, olives and vineyards, its warm sunny microclimate, refreshing sea breezes and spectacular views, as far back as human memory goes, Capri has been considered a paradise on Earth.

As the hydrofoil raced over the crisp blue waves, V stood at the railing next to her new comrade in arms U Pizzu; but her thoughts were lost in the distant past, almost two thousand years ago.

She had gone to Capri to meet with Emperor Tiberius. He had been a brilliant general, fighting for years against the German barbarian tribes and consolidating the Empire's northern frontiers. But he was a gloomy man and a reluctant politician. He never wanted to be emperor. And he had never recovered from being forced, by his patron, the first emperor, Augustus, to divorce Vipsania Agrippina, his pregnant and beautiful wife, whom he never ceased to love, and to marry Augustus's daughter, Julia. Becoming emperor for Tiberius was a poisoned chalice.

Eventually, to escape the corruption and dangers of Rome, Tiberius

retreated to Capri, and lived in a magnificent palace on its northeastern mountain peak, a palace that towered directly over the sea. This was Villa Jovis.

V visited the emperor there. She had been sent by a Roman senator who
wanted a favor and who had great faith in V's charm and persuasive powers.

Tiberius was gloomy and depressed – V could see that quite clearly – but
he was very gracious to V. He took her on a tour, showing her the splendors
of the villa, its baths, its water reservoirs, its magnificent reception rooms –
and its view from the loggia – from which, it was later rumored by Christian
propagandists, Tiberius threw to their deaths women or young boys of whom
he was tired or with whom he was displeased. Tiberius told V how he missed
and loved his first wife; once, he said, he had caught a glimpse of her in the
Forum and followed her, but in vain; she refused to speak to him, turned
her back, and disappeared in the crowd; he confessed to V how he hated
and despised his second wife, Julia, known as Julia the Lascivious, Julia the
Promiscuous, Julia who shunned and mocked him, Julia the Unfaithful, Julia
who organized private orgies and who haunted the Roman Forum in the heat
of summer nights in search of casual sex.

"So, my dear, you see, my gloom and cynicism are perhaps justified," he
said, gazing straight at V.

"But perhaps, my Emperor, this bitterness eats at you, and not at your
enemies."

"Perhaps … perhaps." He nodded to a servant that their glasses should be
refilled. Then he sat for a long time without saying a word – the sun was
setting and the vast panorama of the wine-dark sea, stretching toward the
horizon, turned from crisp blue to smoky turquoise; the milk-pale sky shimmered, crisscrossed by long feathery trails of rose; a few faint stars twinkled
in the fading glow. Finally, Tiberius smiled, rather shyly, V thought, and
turned to her. "Tell your senator his request is granted. And tell him that he
owes this favor to the beauty and intelligence of his messenger."

V left for the mainland that night – in a swift galley, the oars making a
rhythmic splash, the stars by now precise, bright, and multitudinous in the
slate-black sky, the dark waves crisp, and a brisk but warm breeze sweeping down from the north through the Apennine Mountains, a harbinger and
foretaste of winter, with its cold winds, icy black nights, and flakes of snow
and sleet. V stood on the deck, conversing with the captain and letting the
warm air caress her. She was not fond of winter and dreaded its coming. Back
in Rome, the Senator was delighted – and V was richly rewarded.

U Pizzu, who had been leaning into the wind, turned to V. She'd told him a little about her life as a vampire and U Pizzu felt it was pretty romantic to be heading off to the beautiful isle of Capri with a gorgeous vampire – Lady Death herself – and he began to sing the *Isle of Capri*.

"Oh, Marcello," V sighed and flapped her eyelashes, "so you do a wonderful imitation of good old Frankie Sinatra too!"

"Good old Frankie, yes," U Pizzu said. U Pizzu was proud of his singing, a talent honed in the church choir back in Corleone. "I see you're a girl who appreciates art!"

In Capri's port, V reserved a water taxi for their return trip, "just in case," she said, and paid the skipper a very hefty advance. "You'll be here when we need you?"

"I'll be here," he said.

"No matter what?"

"No matter what, I'll be here."

From the port V and U Pizzu took the funicular up to the village square – the Piazzetta. This little spot of ground, with its crowded cafés and shops, was said by some snobs of V's acquaintance, Neapolitans mostly, to be the most fashionable square in the world. V had her doubts. U Pizzu glanced around. It would be a fine thing to sit down at a café and have a cappuccino with his glamorous sexy new friend – get to know her, show her off, impress the waiters and the millionaires – but they were on business, after all. They left the elite village behind and walked through the fields and lemon groves up the steep hill to Villa Jovis, of whose splendor only a few ruined brick walls and several empty platforms remained. The ruins were perched on the very edge of the cliff. At the entrance to the Villa Jovis Park a little sign on a chain across the path said, "Closed for Repairs."

"Saves us the entrance fee," said V, as she stepped over the chain.

"This guy Tiberius had a great view," said U Pizzu when they got to the main platform, one of the floors of the ancient villa. He looked around. "Boy, oh, boy!"

"Yes, not many people come here – strangely. It's a place I absolutely love!" V half closed her eyes against the billowing brightness, sky and sea united in one vast luminous panorama.

The platform opened onto the sea and the distant cliffs of the Sorrento peninsula. "We're sitting on top of the world." U Pizzu beamed at V. "We should have brought a picnic." He looked around. They had the whole place to themselves – perfect!

Bougainvillea and oleander grew in the walls, and vines, and the ancient bricks seemed dusty and drowsy, asleep and dreaming, in the warm sunlight and gentle breeze. V looked around. "So, what are we looking for?"

They paced the floor, and found the ancient sundial, carved into the stone. "So, it is three stones to the left, which would be right here," said U Pizzu, pointing at a paving stone.

V knelt down and slid her fingers into the narrow crack and lifted the paving stone up and slid it aside: it was so simple – it was suspiciously simple.

"*Et voilà,*" said U Pizzu, crouching down carefully, keeping the crease of his trousers just so, sharp as a straight-razor.

"Yes." V glanced up at him.

Packed inside a small rectangular hollow was the glittering octagonal crystal tube, the Torelli Jewel – the key to the World. They stared at it. The key was wrapped in wires, different colored wires.

"It's a bomb, a booby trap," said U Pizzu.

"Let's see if we can …" V was feeling feisty; the beauty of the place was inebriating; the imperial memories it evoked made her feel all-powerful; and the handsome, dangerous Mr. U Pizzu was a charming stimulating companion, sexy and funny. Just the kind of bad boy she liked! And, of course, she had drunk too much blood – Paolo and Franco, Marcello's two virile young *picciotti* whom she'd eaten down in the sewer; savory Father Ottavio; the poor innocent machine-gunner; and the super-sized yummy monk in the cellar. She felt like a god. She could do anything! Part of her mind was desperately whispering "hubris" – "*Watch out, V, you are drunk on blood!*" She spurned the little voice. She was having too much fun – *and* she was showing off – for Marcello!

"I don't know if we can." U Pizzu chewed his lip. He could be bold, he could be excessively, even foolishly, brave, but, generally, he figured caution was the better part of valor – bombs he didn't like; he had seen what they could do.

"I'll do it." V decided to be stubborn; braggadocio is not a male prerogative. *Hubris, V, hubris,* whispered the tiny voice from deep down in her mind, *Hubris! Watch out! Watch out!* V pushed it away.

"I don't know …" U Pizzu felt unmanned – letting a dame do the dangerous work. "I'm good at setting bombs off, but I'm not very good at …"

"Don't worry. You stand back. If something happens …"

"You're sure now?" said U Pizzu.

"I'm sure." V licked her lips; this would be *fun*!

"I don't think you should."

"I can do this!" V looked up at him, sharply.

"Okay, okay, but I got a feeling …" U Pizzu backed away to what he felt was a safe distance; he was just getting used to this dame. If she blew herself up he would be very, very pissed off. Besides, if she blew herself up, she'd blow up the key too, and she was the only person who knew how to stop the Crystal, so if she was gone and the key was gone, the Cardinal could blow up the whole planet. And that, as good old Gaetano had pointed out, would be very bad for business, not to mention there'd be no more romping on the beach with Maria Grazia, and eldest daughter Adrianna wouldn't get to graduate, and his second daughter, Rosa, headed for the Sorbonne, wouldn't get that studio in Paris she wanted, and his third daughter, Paola, true scholarship material, wouldn't get to Oxford, and nobody, but fucking nobody, would live happily ever after.

U Pizzu took out his mauve handkerchief and wiped his brow. Right now, he was dying to jump into a shower, first cold, then hot, then cold; and then he would change his clothes – choosing something nice and snappy for Lady Death. He looked around – the sky was vast, and open, and blue, the sea sparkled, the distant cliffs of the Amalfi Coast seemed to float, purple shadows, drowsing in the brilliance of the afternoon sun, and the air overflowed with perfumes of countless plants and flowers. That Tiberius sure had an eye for real estate. Life was good! U Pizzu took a deep breath. Yes, that old emperor friend of V's had had a fine idea – get away from it all! And he'd chosen an ideal spot. Just standing here, you felt free, infinitely free. U Pizzu glanced at V. The lady was concentrating, crouched over the bomb – U Pizzu hoped she knew what she was doing.

The whole world was bathed in a sudden immense silence.

Kneeling over the trigger mechanism and the explosives, V concentrated. The wires were wrapped around the Torelli Jewel and the Jewel was held in place by steel clamps. Undoing the steel clamps would trigger the bomb, but maybe if someone were watching, they could trigger the bomb by tugging on a wire, or by remote control. V glanced around. Would the explosion destroy the key? She looked back at the key and frowned. Her nostrils quivered. Then, suddenly, her mind slammed into red alert. Then full alarm. Panic!

Something was wrong. There was an odor, an *extra* odor of – explosive. She'd made a mistake, a stupid mistake! There was a tiny extra trigger, she just now spotted it. It had been tripped when she lifted up the paving stone. So the stone itself had a delayed reaction connection. There was, almost certainly, another bomb – that was what her nostrils had picked up – a second bomb, but on a timer … And that second bomb, on the timer, was nested below the first bomb and hidden by the key and by the first bomb.

Yes, the Cardinal was a trickster, definitely a joker.

WHAM!

WHAM!

A blinding flash! It tossed V twenty feet in the air, smashed her down, bounced her, and careened her against a low ruined brick wall. What was left of V was crumpled up, smashed to pieces, a shattered, limp, bloody ragdoll of a thing, hardly human.

U Pizzu was somersaulted backward and landed on his backside. "Fuck!" He wondered whether his back was broken. A storm of pebbles and sand rained down. He put his arms up to protect his head. When the rain of stones stopped, he peeked out from between his fingers. He couldn't see V or anything – just a veil of dust and smoke. Then he saw her. She was a crumpled mass, lying like a broken doll.

U Pizzu got up, brushed himself off – he was covered in dust, *damn it!* He approached cautiously.

"V? Hey, Signorina? Signorina!" The explosion was ricocheting in his ears. His voice sounded like a warbling echo from some underwater musical. Sounds rang like church bells.

V was on her hands and knees. At least she was still alive. But when she turned her head toward him, he recoiled in horror. Her face was a mask of blood and gore, bone and teeth. It was no longer a face: it had no eyes, no nose; and one half of her teeth and gums and jawbone were showing where her mouth had been blown away.

"She looks like a fucking anatomical drawing, no, not even," U Pizzu muttered. How disgusting that such beauty could be ruined in a split second. But part of him was excited. Should he kill her now? She couldn't do anything; she was going to die anyway. He really should put her out of her misery.

"V?" He knelt next to her and drew the P.38. It would be an act of mercy, definitely. He always insisted on looking into the eyes of the person he was about to kill – but here there was just a bloody mess; there were no eyes to look into. That fact alone was disgusting.

For reasons he didn't entirely understand, U Pizzu felt heartsick. A deep burning rage filled his chest. He'd fallen for a fucking vampire superwoman and now these fucking bastards had killed her! He would strangle Ambrosiano! He would crush his fucking bones. He would rip the fucker apart! He would grind the man into tiny pieces!

The bloody mass that had been V's face turned toward him. She struggled to sit up. The remains of the tongue – a tangle of red meat – moved in the mangled half of her mouth. It was grotesque; but she managed to whisper, slurring the words, the syllables bubbling up through a sea of molasses, "Monks coming! Watch out!"

"Right." U Pizzu looked around. "Yeah, okay, right!"

He stood up and strode to where the Villa Jovis terrace ended in a balcony-like overhang. From here, he could see down into the trees and overlook the stairs that led up to the villa. Fuck! Coming up the steep stone steps were three of the oversized, baby-faced monks, those fucking diabolical creations of what must be the Order's breeding experiments.

"Right, don't worry! I'll look after them," U Pizzu said. "And you, V, what about you?"

"Don't worry about me," the bloodied mass slurred.

"Okay, I'll be right back." U Pizzu walked over to the broken body, leaned down and squeezed her arm. "Don't worry, V, I'll be back!"

The answer was a gurgle of blood and spittle.

U Pizzu ran to the top of the staircase. The monks were at the final landing. He drew his pistol. He would pick them off on the stairs, where there was nowhere for them to hide. He glanced back at V. He was getting soft. He didn't want her to die. It was like she was his own daughter. She was so fucking young. The monks had seen him. They stopped. Their blank faces looked upwards. U Pizzu saw no emotion in their expressions, none at all.

He picked off one monk – right in the forehead – single shot. Skill tells! He got the second just below the neck, at the level of the collarbone – not so good; the fucker probably wouldn't die immediately. The third monk took flight, literally flew up the stairs, his monk's habit wafting out behind him – the fucker was flying through the air!

This was not good! Not good at all!

U Pizzu fired three shots. The monk was a blur; his billowing habit hid his body. He swooped down, like a huge bird of prey, and hit U Pizzu with a smashing blow – then bounced up again.

U Pizzu staggered against one of the villa's brick walls. This fucker was a rubber ball! U Pizzu fired two more shots. Both missed. It was like the monk was flying at the speed of light. Now the fucker came straight down. He landed on top of U Pizzu, smashing him into the ground.

They rolled along the foot of the wall. U Pizzu kicked himself free, tried to get up, tried to get the switchblade out of his pocket. The monk grabbed him by the arm and lifted him into the air – it was effortless, as if U Pizzu were as light as a feather. U Pizzu got the switchblade out, snapped it open; but one of the monk's huge hands closed on his wrist, twisted, and plunged the knife sideways into U Pizzu's shoulder – ripping the blade sideways.

U Pizzu wanted to scream, but there was no fucking way he was going to scream for this weirdo monster. No way would he give the guy the satisfaction! Where did these fucking brutes get their strength?

The monk wrenched U Pizzu's left wrist straight back; the knife dropped; U Pizzu felt his wrist breaking, *crack, crack* – the bones snapping, shattering, into pieces, the useless fingers spread in agony. The monk bent them back – one by one – until they snapped, broken, one after the other.

Jesus, U Pizzu thought, without me, V is going to be helpless. This fucker will eat her alive!

The monk lifted U Pizzu up and dangled him out at arm's length. U Pizzu kicked, tried to get at the guy's gut; he waved his arms, trying to get the fingers of his good hand where he could scratch the guy's eyes out. His reach was not long enough. The monk was enormous! The monk's face was expressionless. It was as if U Pizzu didn't exist.

This was not the right way to die! Fuck! U Pizzu was furious with himself for the thought. Dying – out of the question! He was not going to fucking die. He clenched his jaw. Cancel that thought about dying right now! I'm not gonna fucking die! And I'm not gonna let this monster get his hands on V.

He kicked. His toe caught the monk in the side, a glancing blow. The monk slapped at him casually as if he were swatting a fly.

Carrying U Pizzu out at arm's length, the monk strode to the edge of the cliff. The sea roared on a jagged tangle of sharp rocks three hundred yards below. U Pizzu glanced down. Fuck! Nobody would survive that, nobody – not even U Pizzu!

The monk's muscles were tensing. "The fucker's gonna throw me now!" U Pizzu closed his eyes. Death, finally, death …

Suddenly, the monk roared, and spun around, carrying U Pizzu with him. U Pizzu opened his eyes and dared to look down. Surprise – he was above solid ground. Whew!

He looked up. There, clinging to the monk's back, was this – this thing – it looked like a demon. It *was* a demon, a girl demon – it must be the she-devil Father Andrea had talked about, it was just as he'd described her!

She was grappled onto the monk's back like a giant leech.

The monk dropped U Pizzu. U Pizzu fell on his back, rolled over, and crawled away as fast as he could, using his elbows and holding his broken hand up off the ground.

He looked around for the P.38. There it was – lying in the dust at the foot of the brick wall. U Pizzu crawled for it. The monk was screaming, an ululating wail, high-pitched and childish. It was fucking spooky.

"Serves the fucker right!" U Pizzu reached the pistol. His right hand was useless; waves of pain shot up the arm. So much goddamn fucking pain! He grasped the P.38 with his left hand – for once he wished he was a leftie – lifted it and tried to aim.

The monk was spinning around, trying to beat off the she-devil. She was still crouched, clinging tight, on top of his back. U Pizzu grimaced. If only he could get a clear shot!

U Pizzu focused, the P.38 trembled and shook – impossible! The monk was spinning toward the edge of the cliff, going around and around. The demon had its fangs sunk deep into the monk's neck! It was drinking the monk's fucking blood! Well, goddamn! U Pizzu would just let her drink her fill. He sat back on his heels. The full waves of agony from the knife wound in his shoulder and from his broken shattered hand invaded his mind. Then, through the veil of pain, he realized what the monk was trying to do. The fucker was trying to reach the edge of the cliff and jump over; he wanted to take the she-devil with him, kill her, even if he had to die himself. No way would U Pizzu let this happen. He would save the she-devil. My enemy's enemy is my friend. Using his left hand, U Pizzu took aim. The P.38 trembled, difficult to keep it straight …

He fought against the waves of pain, against the weakness. The barrel wavered. Fuck it! The barrel just wouldn't hold still.

The monk staggered, turning in circles, staggering, whirling. He made it to the brick safety wall, he reached out to climb over the iron railing; but then he faltered, turned heavily in a circle, once, twice, a third time, and then he stood absolutely still, and crumpled up, falling in a heap, with the demon still crouched on top of him, her arms and legs wrapped around him, her fangs plunged into his neck.

U Pizzu finally held the P.38 steady. That was good. It was good. But it looked like she didn't need his shot!

He watched, fascinated, as she drank and drank and drank. What would she do when she finished? She looked up, as if sensing his thought. The reptile eyes sparkled – took him in. She looked away and drank some more from the monk, deep slurps, more slurps, blood splashing. Then she let go, sat up, stared down at the body, bit it again and shook it like a dog would shake a dead rabbit, then she dropped it. The monk crumpled up, a deflated balloon, an empty husk. The demon crouched over the body for a moment; then she stood up.

U Pizzu's finger tightened on the trigger. The she-devil wiped her mouth. What was she, the sister of V? Her demonic twin?

"Are you okay?" she asked.

U Pizzu almost pulled the trigger he was so startled by the demon speaking directly to him. He didn't think of her as a person, but as a thing, an animal – you don't strike up a conversation with a boa constrictor!

"I'm okay," he said. "The bastard broke my wrist and fingers and stabbed me in the fucking shoulder, but otherwise –"

The she-devil bounded over to him. Again, the movement was so sudden, so swift, that U Pizzu almost pulled the trigger.

"Do you mind aiming that thing somewhere else?" she asked through her fangs, her forked tongue flickering, her reptilian lips curled up in what U Pizzu figured was a smile. "It might go off."

"Yeah, yeah, okay, I'm sorry."

"Let me have a look." The she-devil knelt next to him. "Now don't shoot me," she said, noticing U Pizzu's nervousness. "I think I can help."

She laid her claws on his shoulder.

"You should help V. She needs help more than me."

"V's okay. Don't worry about V."

She moved her claws lightly back and forth over his shoulder. What the fuck was she doing? U Pizzu felt warmth spread through his shoulder, the pain eased, then went away. "Where's V? She's in real bad shape. You need to help V."

"So you don't know – do you?" the demon asked. She paused and looked straight at him, with her gleaming gold serpent eyes, like a friendly, sexy, flirtatious girl-dragon out of some old-time fairy-tale cartoon.

"Don't know what?" It was weird speaking to a reptilian demon, even if she was a fucking knockout – I'm fucking falling for a snake! Jesus Maria, this is sick!

"Silly of me," said the demon. "I didn't tell you. I'm sorry."

"You talk in riddles too, I guess, like the Sphinx."

"Yes, sorry – you see, I *am* V."

"You're V? No way!"

"I'm a version of V. I'll revert to the V you know in a minute."

"But V was all smashed up, she was blind, she was …"

"Yes. That's why it took her – I mean, *me* – so long to come and help you fight the monks. I had to repair the damage. Let's see your hand." She cupped U Pizzu's hand between her two claws.

"There!" She stood up. "Let's see."

U Pizzu got to his feet. He flexed his hand. It was as good as new. He slid it under his jacket and shirt – no shoulder wound, not that he could feel, skin as good as new! Maybe not even a scar!

"A miracle!" he said, swallowing. Now he owed this reptile demon-broad, he owed her big time. "Thanks!"

"I've got to get my dress, my backup dress," said the demon, "and clean off this blood."

"That's not your blood," he said. "Not V's."

"No, it's mostly the monk's. There's a garden hose around here somewhere."

"Yeah," U Pizzu pointed. "Over there."

The reptile-girl headed for the garden hose. "We have to see if the key is somewhere around here; and if we can find it; or if it was destroyed."

"If it was destroyed, I guess we're fucked."

"Precisely. Look, I'm going to revert. You can turn your back if you wish."

"You're going to *revert*? Go back to being V? You mind if I watch?"

"No. Go ahead."

"But I'm worried – V was pretty badly … well, she was really fucked! I mean, how can you fix all that? She had no eyes, for fuck's sake!"

"You can watch and check, tell me if I got anything wrong during the restoration work." The demon, fangs and eyes glowing, grinned at him.

"Okay. I wouldn't miss this for the world!" U Pizzu grinned back. This fucking demon was a flirt; she was a goddamn flirt!

"Right, then. Here we go!"

U Pizzu watched. The she-demon became a blur, a mini-nanosecond tornado. Around her the air vibrated, shimmered, and turned a glassy green. Then she was in focus again. The human V stood there, rubbing her eyes; her back was turned to him; she was naked.

"*Cazzo,*" said U Pizzu. He was afraid that when she turned around he'd see that ruined face and be sick to his stomach. He was getting soft; it was a bad sign.

V turned to face him.

"*Cazzo!*"

"That bad, huh?"

"No, perfect! You're perfect! How do you do that?"

"Good. I'm delighted you like it."

U Pizzu came closer. "More than perfect!" And, yeah, she was naked. U Pizzu desperately tried to focus on her face. Not even a hair seemed out of place! "Just the blood," he said. "You're still covered in blood."

"Yes, the garden hose," she said, giving him – goddamn it – that flirtatious smile – face down, looking up through her eyelashes – the worshipful female animal, gazing up at her master. Flattering, but U Pizzu was fully aware that V surely *had* no master.

"Right, the garden hose," he said.

U Pizzu went over, leaned down to the little old rusty wheel-like handle at the end of the water pipe, and turned it. V was holding the end of the hose and the water splashed straight onto her face. "Brrrhhh! It's cold!" she spluttered.

U Pizzu tried to look away but couldn't. Golden beads of water sparkled on her skin, the late afternoon sunlight glistened off the curves of her body; she shimmied in a sensual, shivering, curvaceous dance, laughing all the while. He couldn't keep his eyes off her. She didn't seem to mind. He cleared his throat and forced himself to walk over to the stairs leading up from the park to see if anyone was coming: even if the site and park were closed and the place was pretty isolated, somebody must surely have heard the bomb explode and the gunshots – and he and V had three dead bodies to explain.

V finished soaking herself. "Did I get it all?"

U Pizzu came over to inspect. "Turn around."

V spun around, in a sort of dance step.

U Pizzu swallowed. "Yeah. You got it all."

"Thanks, my dear. You're an absolute darling. My jeans and T-shirt are goners, I'm afraid." V knelt by her backpack, pulled out a short elastic rose-colored cotton dress, rose-and-white string panties, with a floral design, and high-heeled scarlet sandals.

U Pizzu sighed. Some old writer, a German guy probably, had said that, once you'd seen Naples – it was so stunningly beautiful – then you could give yourself permission to die: "*Vedere Napoli e poi muori.*" U Pizzu watched V; he drank her in. Now he could die. Now he had seen everything. Now he could allow himself to die. V finished dressing. U Pizzu applauded. "It's like a miracle!"

She turned to him. "Now, Marcello, don't get all religious on me." Her smile was fully human, teasing. "Let's see if the key survived."

The Torelli Jewel was sitting all by itself in plain sight on top of a low brick wall – totally unharmed. V plucked it from the wall, turned it around in her hand, and showed it to U Pizzu.

"Looks just like a big stretched-out diamond."

"Yes. But with this simple little thing, Marcello, we may just save the world! All this!" V opened her arms wide.

"Yes." He gazed around – at the dazzling sunlight, at the boundless open sea, and at the bright overflowing cornucopia of flowers. He breathed it all in. Yes, this was life; this was the world! This was the planet Earth! This was home! But then he frowned. "V, we got a problem."

"The monks." V nodded and slipped the key into her backpack.

"Yeah, the monks – and the cops. We got three dead monks lying around and the cops are on their way – I'm sure of it – up from the village – they would have heard the shots. This island's got lots of cops. A load of VIPs live here, they need high-class protection. Usually it's elite cops too."

"Over the cliff."

"Right."

Luckily not much blood – nothing very noticeable – had been spilt on the staircase. The few traces that remained, V seemed to vacuum them away with a sweep of her hand.

"How you do that?"

"Magic, Marcello, magic!" She glanced up at him, offering him that intense worshipful gaze, from under those fluttering eyelashes.

"You are a fucking number! You know that?"

They dragged the two monks up the stairs, lifted them, and tossed them over the cliff. U Pizzu had the feeling that V was doing all the work and could easily have dragged and tossed the bodies over the cliff herself. Then, they picked up the monk that V had drunk dry. He was the lightest of all three. And over he went – head first.

It was interesting to watch. The bodies bounced down the huge white gleaming limestone cliff, arms and legs flailing, black habits billowing. They bounced and bounced and bounced, then landed, with a tiny distant splash, in the surf far below. As the bodies plummeted down, dense flocks of birds flew out from the cliff and swirled around, furious, cawing, screaming, circling, a black swarm, like locusts. Almost instantly, the bodies of the monks were invisible, lost in the turbulence of waves and foam. The birds settled back into their niches. The cawing ceased. The fuss was over.

V stared down the vertiginous cliff. The air was bright with the sharp tang of the sea, the warm scent of sunburnt brick and stone. She turned to U Pizzu. "This is exactly where Tiberius was said to have tossed women – and young boys – when he had finished with them or when they somehow displeased him. Personally, I think the stories are Christian propaganda. I found Tiberius to be a perfect gentleman and he could have been a very capable emperor – but he was frightened for his life, and toward the end he became disillusioned and cynical – and he lost touch with what was going on in Rome."

"Really, so it's true," said U Pizzu. "You really – I mean, really – knew Tiberius? I mean, like, wasn't he dead thousands of years ago?"

"Yes. He died in 37 CE. He didn't have the patience to be an emperor and … Oh, oh, those elite cops you mentioned are coming. I can feel their presence!"

"*Cazzo!*"

"Here," said V. She slipped one spaghetti strap off her shoulder, baring a breast.

"Hey!" said U Pizzu, his eyes widening: for some strange reason V half-dressed was even sexier – if that was possible – than V not dressed at all.

"Make love to me, Marcello! Come on! Quick!"

"Hey, don't you eat people you fuck? Didn't you tell me that when we were on the hydrofoil? Isn't that part of the gig?"

"Yes, sometimes. Kiss me, Marcello! Put your hand here! Pull down my dress! Pull up my hem right up my thigh!"

"Okay, ah, let's see."

"And keep your left side away from them!"

"What's wrong with my left side?"

"Blood on jacket," V whispered, fiddling with his lapel. "Now, kiss me, Marcello, kiss me!"

U Pizzu was glad he'd seen her rinse her mouth. He didn't relish the thought of drinking – or licking – monk blood.

He took a deep breath and puckered up and kissed her.

She responded. Her lips explored his, delicately. It began as a little waltz of hesitation, of advance and retreat, first the warmth of contact, then a timid withdrawal, then she advanced again, the tip of her tongue playing with his lips, just teasing, almost merging, and then withdrawing. U Pizzu sighed. Now this was something, really something!

"Ahhhh, Marcello!" She gazed into his eyes, sighing with a throaty voice. U Pizzu knew she was imitating somebody, ah, yeah, the Swedish actress, Anita Ekberg, in that old Fellini film, *La Dolce Vita*, the scene where the unbelievably stacked Swedish beauty wades into the Trevi Fountain, water gurgling down over the statues; she's in her long dark evening gown, and …

"Ahhhh, Marcello!" V's lips now met his with fire; it was as if her lips were supercharged with hot red pepper. She slid the tip of her tongue along his upper lip; he could feel himself getting excited. Then, delicately, hesitantly, as if asking for an invitation, she entered his mouth, exploring his tongue, his teeth; she raised one leg against his, as if closing him in a vice. It was as if …

Ouch!

She had moved a hand down and seized his erection; she teased it, delicately, with a small pinch – a joke – another little pinch and artful twist – another joke! *Cazzo!*

V was having fun. This was a dance; her every move told him that she wanted him to have fun too. They were acting out their desires – their lust – together. He could feel the almost surgical precision of her fingers as they touched him – and twisted, and teased …

"Hey! Hey!" Two police officers had arrived.

V disengaged herself slowly, blinked at the two officers – a woman and a man – and clumsily, hurriedly pulled at the strap of her flimsy little skintight rose dress. "Oh, I'm so sorry," she said, in a little-girl, bubble-brain, breathless, high-pitched voice. "It's all my fault!"

"The site is closed this afternoon, you know, repairs are scheduled; you really shouldn't be here," said the woman.

Yes, V was thinking, U Pizzu was right: Capri had a lot of rich residents

– prime kidnap material, so the cops were elite cops – good-looking, not to spoil the atmosphere; and they were probably incorruptible.

"Did you hear an explosion, any shots … see anybody with a gun … see anything suspicious or unusual?" asked the man.

"An explosion? A gun!?" V rounded her eyes and mouth in what she took to be the classic Marilyn Monroe style. "A gun!? Oh, golly!" Then she hesitated. Maybe she was overdoing it. The two cops were too bright to be taken in by clowning. *Tone it down, V!*

U Pizzu was busying making a show of getting his shirt and pants in order, while keeping the bloody shoulder of his jacket out of view. The P.38 was lodged safely at the back of his belt. He wouldn't open his mouth. Some people, locals and even Neapolitans (and these two were worse, he could tell, they were northerners), tended to get a bit suspicious and inquisitive when they heard the Palermo or Corleone accent.

V's eyes were round in feigned shock. "Gosh! I think we did hear some sort of big bang – and maybe a couple of gunshots, didn't we Marcello? I mean, I thought they were maybe firecrackers … somewhere over there … you know, far away … but we were … distracted … We apologize for being here. We didn't notice it was closed. Time is so precious and it's so romantic …"

"Don't worry about it," the male cop said.

"The exit's down that way," the woman cop said, motioning with her head. "Take your time. It's a beautiful day."

"Thank you!"

"Thank you very much." U Pizzu said in English, sounding flustered and managing a good approximation of a Bronx American accent.

The two cops saluted and sauntered down the steps and the path, then were out of sight, though V could hear their voices, the guy saying, "… caught with his pants down …" a quiet ripple of laughter, and the woman, laughing, "You're just jealous!"

Then there was nothing – just the twittering of the birds, the breeze in the cypresses and cedars, the sunburnt walls of Tiberius's villa, and the distant roar of the surf.

"Whew!" V breathed out a sweet sigh of relief.

"Yeah! You know, if you were acting, that was pretty good acting."

"Well, you're pretty good yourself, Marcello." She sighed his name languidly, drawing it out in a low, silken, old-fashioned, femme-fatale movie-tone groan. "But we had to make it convincing, you know! I thought your American accent was awfully good."

"From singing Frankie," U Pizzu said, beaming, "and watching TV!"

When they got to the little port of Capri, excited crowds were gathering to take the ferry or hydrofoil back to the mainland. Their water taxi was waiting.

"Signori, am I glad to see you two!" The water taxi driver grinned at them, the sun making crinkles around his eyes. "I almost didn't wait. People are nervous. There's talk of something going on with Vesuvius."

"Yes, thank you for waiting." V climbed on board and reached her hand up to help U Pizzu step down into the boat.

"Well, let's go!" The driver revved the engine. "If you look over there, you'll see what I mean."

V and U Pizzu glanced toward the mainland. Vesuvius was hidden by the hills and cliffs of the Sorrento peninsula, but V could see thick clouds piling up above the volcano; the air pressure was changing; electricity was building. Her skin prickled.

"Is that …?" U Pizzu raised an eyebrow.

"Yes," V said. "It's beginning – *again*." She narrowed her eyes against the light and glanced around. An eerie quiet had descended over the vast city of Naples, a stillness that spread out across the broad sparkling Bay of Naples itself.

"You were, ah, feisty, back there," said U Pizzu.

"Ah, well, Marcello." She leaned close and straightened and stroked his tie. "Death is so invigorating, don't you think?"

"I never met anyone, up till now, who really understood that."

V kissed him, pressed her body against his, thinking that it was so sweet, the two predators, he and she, Marcello and V, their bodies entangled, their souls for a moment mingling, almost as one.

With her head pressed against U Pizzu's chest, and listening to his heartbeat, V stared at the glittering expanse of water. Time was suspended, sizzling with suppressed tension, in a waiting mode. The afternoon sun shone brightly, sparkling on the crisp waves; ships and hydrofoils plied peacefully back and forth; but everything, people, machinery, birds, the sea itself, seemed muted, as if immobile, energy building up, as if waiting for something to happen, something grandiose and terrible. It was uncanny. V shuddered.

"We'd better hurry," she said.

"When you said it's beginning *again*?" U Pizzu stared at the gathering clouds. "What do you mean by that?"

"Another wave of whatever the Crystal is going to do." V kissed U Pizzu on the lips, gazed through his Polaroids into his eyes, and laid her hand against the side of his face. Then she turned away and stared at the approaching shoreline. The water taxi was speeding toward Naples, toward the private jet that would get them to Africa.

"I don't want to die," U Pizzu muttered. "Not now, not now that I've met Signorina Death herself."

V glanced at him; she took his arm in hers. "Seize the day, Marcello."

"For tomorrow, we die." U Pizzu half closed his eyes.

"You don't have to come with me, Marcello, you really don't."

"You kidding me? Of course, I'm coming!"

"You have to think of Maria Grazia, of Adrianna, Paola and Rosa."

"I already made arrangements, I …"

"Santino?"

"Yes."

"Well, then, Marcello …." V lightly caressed his lips with hers. "It is so wonderful to meet someone who is …" She paused; the darkness in her eyes sparkled, seemed to consume him.

U Pizzu waited.

"… someone who is like me," she whispered. She gave him her special, secretive, shy, little-girl smile, and looked away.

Vesuvius was in eruption. Roger stared at the computer screens and news feeds. A great column of ash towered over the volcano.

He turned to the Cardinal. "A state of emergency has been declared in Naples and around Naples. People are scrambling to get away. It will be a catastrophe."

"Yes, I know. When you kick an anthill, the ants all begin to scurry in great confusion."

"I suppose they do." Roger glanced back at the monitors. One showed a street full of cars, piled up, an impossible traffic jam, trying to flee. A boy was carrying a baby, running along a sidewalk, glancing back at something that terrified him. It looked like a wall of black fog, sweeping down the street.

Then, there was a long shot, an image of Vesuvius, flames and smoke flaring up from its flattened volcanic peak, a stream of red-hot lava coming down one side. This, Roger thought, was just the beginning.

"Many people will die." Roger was even filthier than before, and now clothed only in a skimpy rag loincloth – his boxer shorts having fallen into total ruin. He was chained to the steel seat and steel desk, all welded together; his hands were manacled together in a praying position and chained to the steel collar he was wearing; now, he could not even reach the computer keyboard. Helplessly, he watched as planet Earth unraveled.

"Soon it will be time to give the ants a *real* lesson, Professor!"

Roger closed his eyes. He didn't want to think about it.

By the time V and U Pizzu came ashore close to Naples' Capodichino airport, the sun was veiled in darkness. The water taxi sped off and V and U Pizzu leapt onto V's Macchia Nera, which was loyally waiting in an abandoned engine repair shed where V had hidden it.

"Damn it, where is V?" John stood in the cockpit of the Falcon 3000 executive jet and peered out into the darkening day.

"We can't wait much longer." Jack Larssen, the Falcon's pilot, stared out the cockpit window at the blackening air, the falling ash.

"Any more ash and the engines will get clogged." Elena Satti, the copilot, was monitoring radio frequencies. "And we'll explode like a Roman candle or just crash into the sea. At this rate, we might not be able to take off."

"I know, I know." John stared into the deepening gloom. "She'll be here. She's never failed yet."

Ash began to rain down on the runway. Smears like raindrops splashed against the Falcon's windows.

Visible on the plane's television monitors, Vesuvius was in full eruption. Panic was everywhere. Roads were clogged. Reports said a cloud of hot volcanic ash was flooding down the slopes of the mountain, down through the vineyards and farms, spilling over fences and woods, engulfing whole villages. The lighter ash, carried by a rising wind, covered the whole sky, and was drifting over Naples itself, and toward the airport.

Kate stared out the window. The dusk was full of flashing lights and a column of flame had risen, towering, over Vesuvius. Flashes of lightning lit up the sky. Flaming rocks, like little meteorites, were raining down a bit farther inland, maybe a mile or two from the runway.

V's motorbike, with "Marcello" riding pillion, skirted a link fence, zipped through a half-opened gate, leaving two guards shouting at them, leapt across a ditch, and then sped across the tarmac toward the Falcon.

John was getting a radio feed – a report from the Campi Flegrei area, just west of Naples. Hidden under the Campi Flegrei was a sleeping super-volcano, a vast chamber of magma that had last exploded, so the experts said, almost forty thousand years ago. He turned to Larssen and Satti. "They say the ground is moving at Campi Flegrei. If that blows, life in Europe might just be finished – for a couple of thousand years."

"Right," Larssen murmured, almost absentmindedly. He was staring at the radar screen, which showed a wall of hot ash sweeping toward the airport. "That wall is moving fast."

"Too fast." Satti glanced at the instrument panel. "If we're going to take off, we have to take off now. And I mean *now!*"

V skidded the bike to a stop and kicked the stand into place. She glanced inland. Vesuvius was glowing like a strawberry-colored electric ice cream cone. Below it was something that looked like a tidal wave, a tsunami of ash; it was spreading across the plain toward them: it was a pyroclastic flow. Pompeii all over again.

"Gonna leave it behind?" U Pizzu eyed the bike.

"Yes, Marcello."

"Shame, real fucking shame." U Pizzu looked up. Giant black flakes were beginning to flutter down over the runway. "Fuck – my suit!"

"No time, let's go." V was halfway up the Falcon's fold-out stairs.

U Pizzu leapt up the stairs, only two steps behind her. To judge by the ash, it looked like they were about to become the next Pompeii. He didn't intend to end up as a fucking plaster statue in a dusty glass case in some fucking museum for fucking future tourists in loud shirts to gawk at.

They were inside the plane; the door-stairway swung up, clicked shut. U Pizzu glanced through a porthole. The flakes were getting thicker – what the fuck would those things do to the jet's engines?

Father O'Bryan was safely buckled in, beside Kate. The good Father was impressed. This was a marvelously appointed aircraft, with wide comfortable seats, spacious armrests, and multiple little screens in front of him with a variety of video-audio information flows. Kate had been silent for the last few minutes, staring at the screens and occasionally looking out the window. Father O'Bryan gazed at one particular screen. Even when it was in its most destructive mood, God's world was so utterly beautiful. On the screen, the distant view of the tsunami of ash looked, in the dimming light, like a water-color or delicate oil painting, or perhaps a pencil drawing; it was ash-gray and metallic gray, and you could even see the billowing brushstrokes. The camera text said it was a slow-motion replay of what was happening – real-time, delayed by a second or two.

"Pyroclastic flow," Kate said, in a whisper; she was extra pale.

"What?"

"That's technical talk – Greek, actually, or, if you like, Geek Talk – for a cloud of ash and rock and gas, spit out by the volcano, probably super-heated; it's dense and heavy and so usually stays close to the ground, and usually moves fast."

"How hot?" Father O'Bryan was watching one screen that showed a distant view of a village being overwhelmed by the wave of ash.

"Up to one thousand degrees Celsius. That's about one fifth the temperature on the surface of the sun." Kate stared at the same screen. This was death coming, in its purest most absolute form – death, inescapable death.

The image shifted to a view of a traffic jam on a narrow road. The cars were so piled up they looked foreshortened; people were getting out of the vehicles and running, and scrambling; one man, in ragged blue jeans and a bright Hawaiian shirt that was flapping wildly, was carrying a little girl; then, suddenly, the cars behind them flipped over, people were blown into the air, as if a giant invisible finger had flicked them; the houses at the side of the road exploded, walls, roofs, careening up into the air, shredding into swirling fragments; the man and the little girl disintegrated into a blur; then the dark wave of ash overtook everything; the camera went dead. Kate blinked and swallowed. Tears were rising.

"I see – only one thousand degrees! And it goes fast, you said. How fast?" Father O'Bryan tried to fight back the utter horror.

"Maximum about six hundred to seven hundred kilometers an hour. That's about 10 kilometers a minute, or six miles a minute, ten seconds to cover a mile, to give you an idea," Kate said evenly, in her most level, matter-of-fact, scientific voice; she knew that she and the good Father might die in a few minutes, maybe less. "It pushes air in front of it too …"

"I see, and this creates turbulence …?" Father O'Bryan shifted in his seat, felt for the safety buckle, and tightened it.

"Yes. The wall of turbulence or a shock wave will probably hit us before the ash does."

"How will we take off?"

"We have to."

"You have faith, Kate."

"Yes, in spite of all this, I have faith, Father, I do have faith!"

V was in the cockpit in a flash, U Pizzu right behind. Just as U Pizzu entered the aircraft, the door had already swung shut and the Falcon was moving.

"Go, go, go!" V shouted.

"We're going as fast as we can." Jack Larssen glanced up. "Hello V, welcome aboard." He raised an eyebrow at V's skimpy skintight elastic cotton dress, and the scarlet high heels.

The engines roared, the plane accelerated.

"Thank you, Jack." V gave him a smirk.

"This is Elena Satti, our copilot."

"Elena," V said, "I'm V. This is Marcello."

"I'm John." John held out his hand to U Pizzu, and grinned. So V had made another conquest; she and U Pizzu would make a good pair, in some ways at least. V was certainly dressed to the nines; and U Pizzu was elegance itself.

"Pleasure." U Pizzu shook John's hand, sizing him up: this was definitely not a guy to mess with, but friendly, not jealous, V's working partner.

"Better buckle up tight," Jack Larssen announced over the speaker system. "Do it quick! Now! We're going to get slammed. And I mean – slammed!"

John stayed up front, buckled into a special observer's seat. V and U Pizzu headed back to the passenger cabin, and buckled themselves in, opposite Father O'Bryan and Kate.

The pyroclastic flow was only a few hundred yards away as the plane raced down the runway. The takeoff lights shone into thin waves of ash sweeping in front of the cockpit.

The plane lifted off – veered toward the open sea.

"I'm not sure we're going to make it." Jack Larssen gritted his teeth. He was pushing the aircraft beyond its limits; trying to outrun and get above the shock waves and the tsunami of ash and hot gas that was thundering over the ground and headed straight toward them.

Behind them, the wall of ash slammed into the hangars. Even before it hit, the hangars flipped over, the control tower exploded, planes were tossed like toys, disintegrating into millions of flashing fragments.

Larssen veered straight out to sea, ascending as fast as the plane could.

"Everybody's dead back there," muttered Elena Satti.

"Yes." Larssen was pushing the Falcon toward its top speed, almost five hundred miles an hour.

The engines screamed.

"Landing gear up."

"Roger, landing gear up." Larssen flipped a few switches.

Splatters of ash blackened the cockpit windows, but the plane swept out from under the edge of the ash cloud, the ping, ping of ash and dust echoing on the fuselage. Then ceasing. Now, suddenly, the plane was above the flood of ash.

"I think we made it. For the moment, we've made it." Larssen allowed himself a sigh of relief.

The Falcon headed south over the Tyrrhenian Sea, which, beyond the clouds, was still sparkling bright, seemingly normal and untroubled – the sun was low in the western sky. Surprisingly, it was still day.

The screens showed the pyroclasticwall of ash flooding down streets in Naples, buildings exploding, a huge traffic jam on the ring road, vineyards flooded with ash, a red snake of lava flowing down one side of Vesuvius.

"Pompeii in 79 CE," Kate said, in a whisper.

There was a huge lurch, as a wall of air slammed into the Falcon. Shuddering, the plane rose up, then spun around, the engines wailing and throbbing; the plane shot up, fell straight down, then, finally, it raced ahead.

"Yes, we're outracing it. If nothing else happens, we may just make it." Jack said to Elena.

"Yes, cross my heart and touch wood etc. etc.!" Elena blinked at the instruments. She wiggled her shoulders. She realized she was so tense every muscle in her body ached. She wiped her eyes. They were glistening, wet.

They were over the sea. It was calmer – and a few minutes later, suddenly, it was night. In the windows, stars shone.

Below them, the volcanic island of Stromboli was in eruption, but that was normal, it was always in eruption, a red glow in the midst of the sea. Then Etna, also in eruption, a larger red glow and a column of smoke and ash drifting over the Sicilian city of Catania.

Father O'Bryan glanced at Kate. She nodded and turned off the info screens. Suddenly, it was peaceful. They were in a small, self-contained world, flying three miles above the Mediterranean.

"And who is your new friend, V?" asked Father O'Bryan, nodding at the dashing, elegant, tanned man wearing dark Polaroid glasses.

"Oh, yes, sorry! Father O'Bryan, I want you and Kate to meet my new friend, Marcello."

"She means U Pizzu," U Pizzu said. "Marcello's her little joke. Sorry about trying to get you snuffed the other day, Father. Nothing personal. Glad it didn't work, actually."

Kate frowned. What was this about? Was V pals with somebody who'd tried to murder Father O'Bryan?

Father O'Bryan stared at U Pizzu, then cleared his throat, and shifted uneasily in his seat. "No problem, don't mention it. It happens every day, I'm sure. I'm pleased to meet you." He glanced at V. She shot him a wide smile, all sunny innocence, as if she had absolutely no idea that he might be the slightest bit flustered by meeting the infamous killer and Mafia boss who had put out a contract on his life – and who now seemed to be V's new best bosom buddy. V and this U Pizzu seemed to be – ah – very intimate. Father O'Bryan was shocked to recognize in himself a twinge – just a twinge – of jealousy.

Father O'Bryan sighed. He now found himself in league with a friendly she-devil or demon, and vampire, who just happened to have saved his and Kate's lives and that of the Pope – and these were not minor merits – and who had just brought on board their plane – and their expedition – one of Italy's most successful Mafia bosses and killers, the famous U Pizzu, "The Cut," known by other nicknames too – the Knife, Black Beauty, the Butcher, and now, it seemed, "Marcello." Father O'Bryan glanced down at his lap. Perhaps he should write a book of theological and ethical reflections about these adventures, if he or anyone survived to write anything about anything. Let's see, *Dialogues with the Devil, The Demon Wears Armani* … hmm … Certainly,

V's present skintight rose-colored outfit was not Armani. It was very fetching, far *too* fetching in fact! Had she put it on for U Pizzu?

V glanced at him and grinned.

Father O'Bryan blushed. *Oh, Jesus, Joseph, and Mary!* V had been reading his thoughts again; she had been tracking his vain little musings on the title of his future best-seller and his rather judgmental and catty observations about her scandalous dress, mixed with a tiny tincture of lust, and his timorous allusions to his own jealousy. He blushed again and looked down at his lap.

"I think *Adventures with a Naughty Demon* might be a good title, Father." She gave him a lazy wink. Then, suddenly turning serious, she added, "Excuse me for a moment, please – Father, Marcello, Kate!" And she got up and went forward into the cockpit. The battle for Earth was about to begin.

PART EIGHT – SEA & SAND

CHAPTER 50 – THE MIDDLE SEA

Jack Larssen was one of John's old pals, an English SAS paratrooper who'd retrained as a pilot. Elena Satti was also ex-military, American, an ex-USA special-ops scout and sniper; she was a thin, muscular, dark-skinned Italian blonde from Arizona; her family originally came from Sicily, so there was undoubtedly a mixture of Norman, Greek, German, and Arab blood – maybe even Phoenician – in her veins, all of which background John had briefed V on; a neat mixed heritage, V thought, if they went back far enough, Elena and she would probably discover they were distant cousins.

"So, let's tune in to the news, shall we?" said John. "See what the Crystal is up to." The headlines came up on his iPad: earth tremors were reported from just about everywhere; there had been an explosion – or eruption – in Yellowstone National Park; but reports so far were sketchy. Naples and the surrounding region of Campania had been declared an emergency zone. There were earthquakes in Japan and Indonesia, as well as a new volcanic eruption on Java. "Looks like it has started." John glanced at V.

"Right. No time to waste. I'm going to change." V left the cockpit and went back through the passenger cabin and entered the washroom. She stepped out of her high heels, slipped out of her cotton dress and panties, and took a quick shower. She dried under the full body blow-dryer and changed into her backup special-ops catsuit. It zipped – invisibly – up the back, had invisible armor, and was made of skintight black synthetic material that looked like a mix of fine-grained leather and pure latex. She clicked the armored collar shut, pulled on the warrior boots, buckled them, and returned to the cabin.

When V appeared, Kate gave the warrior outfit a careful up-and-down once-over. Wow! The skintight suit displayed V's body to perfection; it radiated a sense of power and of female warrior-girl virility. Kate licked her lips and bit and twisted them. What would it be like to wear something like that? Pretty exciting! But would she dare?

"What if you want to do Demon?" U Pizzu favored V with an appreciative, lingering, almost proprietary gaze. "I mean, change into your other self? How do you get out of that thing?"

"I unzip and pop out; or I burst out, depending."

U Pizzu sighed: *This woman is a goddess!*

As she stood in the aisle, next to Kate and Father O'Bryan, V buckled her holster to her belt, adjusted her ankle knife, her machete, and her stop-watch. She knelt to check the backpack and zip it shut, then looked up at Kate. "Father O'Bryan tells me you've trained with guns. What weapons are you comfortable with?"

"Various pistols," said Kate, "machete, and submachine-guns, Heckler & Koch MP5, for example. Also, a baseball bat … I can wield a mean hatpin too!"

John, who had come back into the cabin, handed Kate a Beretta M9. "You know how to use this?"

"Sure … But I'm short-sighted, and I don't have my glasses. I mean, my sight does seem to be getting better, but …"

"Short-sighted? Don't worry about that." V put her hand on Kate's forehead. "I have a little magic trick you might like."

Kate blinked and stared. What was the woman doing? Suddenly she could see every detail of V's face, the curls and individual strands of V's hair; she could see the stitching in the armored collar of V's outfit, the ultra-fine grain of V's black synthetic armored skin; and, over V's shoulder, she could see, as sharp as if under a microscope, John's smile, his lips, the grain of his skin, the way the five o'clock shadow merged with his tan, and the striations in the pupils and irises of his eyes. Her vision was suddenly more than 20/20; she could change focus, far and close, instantaneously, without even trying; everything was sharp, etched, colors were vivid; shapes and depth were ultra-clear. "Wow! What did you do? How did you do it?"

"It's one of the perks of being a demon. Father O'Bryan can provide a testimonial to the health benefits demons can provide."

"Indeed." Father O'Bryan turned a delicate shade of crimson, looking both honored and just a tiny bit put upon, as if an intimate secret had been revealed.

"Well, whatever you did, thanks," Kate said; and, at that, V flashed an extra-special warm smile that sent a strange, unfamiliar, shiver down Kate's back – a weird but totally pleasant, even luscious feeling.

"John," V glanced at him, "have we got an extra armored suit?"

"We have several, V, as usual – backups."

"Perhaps Kate would like one."

"And look like super comic Superwoman? Wow! It would be ultra-cool," said Kate, "I used to read these comic books when I was a kid, and I had a whole collection. I still have the whole collection, stored away."

"The outfit is just like V's and it's ultra-fashionable." John lifted a kit out of one of the boxes he'd stowed on board. "Here, Kate. It's body armor. It adds strength too, amplifies the effect of your movements, like having an extra set of muscles. V will brief you on the special features and the weaponry."

Kate fingered the material. "This is really, really interesting. You're sure?" She glanced at V and John.

"Absolutely!" V and John said in unison.

"If you don't like it, Kate, you can always just take it off and return to civvies," said John, "but it will be helpful for you to be well-equipped where we are going. We don't know what we are going to find there."

"Hmm. Okay."

And Kate went back to the washroom to change.

"What will dad think of this outfit?" Kate handled the material. She stroked it; it was ultra-smooth, slinky and satin-like. This was amazing equipment; it was more sophisticated than anything she had ever seen. She took a deep breath. Yes, things were going to turn out okay; they were going to find her dad, and save him, and she would be there for him; she'd become the invincible, invulnerable warrior woman she had dreamed of becoming.

She lifted off her T-shirt, wiggled out of her boots and jeans and folded them carefully. She bit her lip and then finally dared look in the mirror. She hadn't really seen herself since … since before Villa Mazana. At first, seeing the image in the mirror, she could hardly think. For the first time in years, she saw herself clearly – without glasses. Was the woman in the mirror really her? She grinned, frowned, made a goofy face, stuck out her tongue, crossed her eyes, lifted her hair up, let it tumble down, and then pinned it back up. Without those thick glasses, she was an entirely different person. She had forgotten who she really was. She looked down at herself. A naked body – raw material, the naked human body, a blank canvas. Now, for one more transformation!

"Okay, here goes!" She took a deep breath, and slid her legs into the bodysuit. It uncoiled by itself, and, as it quickly slithered up her body, enclosing her torso, it hissed like a snake, automatically adhering, molding her body, and, in a few seconds, becoming a tight, caressing second skin, a skin vibrating with a lusciously sensual – and thrillingly illicit – strength. This was clearly no ordinary material; it was something really, really advanced. It seemed alive. Who could have made such a thing? What was the science behind it?

She ran her fingers down her thighs, closed her eyes. Strange sensation! Like she was naked, directly touching her skin, as if her skin and body had merged into the catsuit. Reaching behind her back, she zipped the suit shut – again, it seemed to close by itself, with another quick rippling hiss.

She turned to the mirror and swung the side mirror out to check her back. The seam and zipper were invisible. Amazing!

She clicked the high armored collar into place, then sat down and pulled on the boots and then the gloves. There!

She glanced into the full-length mirror. She turned around, considering various angles. This outfit was a fetishist's dream! If she turned up at the shooting range in this, dear old Colonel Keenan would have a total heart attack! That, or he'd fall on his knees! Probably both!

The battle gear fit her perfectly. She tied her hair up in a knot. She frowned. Maybe that evil late unlamented creep, Father Ottavio, had had at least one good idea. She should try letting her hair down. And so, she did.

Again, she stared at the mirror. "Who are you? Who the heck are you, anyway, Katherine Dawkins Thornhill?"

Kate came out from the washroom and walked down the aisle.

U Pizzu took off his Polaroids and allowed himself a sustained appreciative gaze. He nodded his approval.

"My dear Kate!" Father O'Bryan blushed. He didn't know what to say or where to look. He wondered what Roger would think of this transformation of his scholarly, perfectionist, shy daughter.

"So, Father, you like?" Kate gave him a sultry, pouty look, head down, her tongue running along her upper lip, jet-black hair tumbling around her cheeks, and one gloved hand posed jauntily on her hip.

"Ah, ah, well, Kate …" Father O'Bryan tried to hold her gaze. What had gotten into the girl? She was flirting! She was teasing him! Wicked girl! He wouldn't let himself be flustered! He would have to brazen it out. Perhaps he should talk to V about her influence on young people! He cleared his throat. "Ah, well, Kate, it is very … attractive … I must say."

"Oh, you are so sweet and so infinitely understanding. Dear Father O'Bryan, I love you so and I always have!" She knelt next to him, took his face between her gloved hands, and kissed him on the forehead. She really did adore it when the good Father blushed.

"Kate, Kate …" Father O'Bryan turned as red as a beet. Not in decades had anyone touched him in such an intimate, innocent, and loving way, and now, in the space of a few hours, V had kissed him on the cheek; and Kate had kissed him on the forehead. *Oh, women! Oh, demons!*

"Here, Kate," said V, patting the seat next to her. "Sit next to me. I'll explain the suit's features."

Kate sat down. "I always wanted to be Superwoman – or Catwoman – protecting the weak, avenging crimes and misdemeanors. Jumping over buildings must be really cool."

"This outfit was made just for you," said V, gazing into Kate's eyes and brushing her fingers lightly against the girl's cheek. "Now, let me explain how it makes you safer." And she explained the suit's hidden devices – its ultra-sensitive nervous system, its chest armor, its special joint-armor, its electric insulation, its automatic temperature adjustment that would compensate if Kate found herself in a very cold or very hot atmosphere, and the way the collar protected the neck.

Three hundred miles west of the speeding Falcon, the 100,000-ton, 1,092-foot-long aircraft carrier USS *Abraham Lincoln* swung around into a light breeze coming from the east. Its captain, James Taylor Nimitz, was staring at a "TOP SECRET" coded message that had arrived directly from the Situation Room in the White House.

Aside from himself, only his chief officer and his intelligence officer were authorized to look at such messages.

"So, what do you think?" Nimitz glanced at his Air Intelligence Officer, Diane Macpherson.

"It's pretty clear, sir, we are to attack a terrorist weapons base that is one hundred miles inland from the North African coast – but before we attack the US Government is giving the country in question an opportunity to explain itself, and if the White House feels it has not explained itself sufficiently, then we will almost certainly receive an order to nuke the site."

"Precisely. *Nuke* – it's such a small word." Nimitz frowned, his fingers spread on the table, pressing down on the map surface. "*Nuke.* A one-syllable word."

"Sir, a lot of our guidance systems and GPS coordinates seem to be – well, not entirely reliable at this point," said the Executive Officer, Captain Timothy Abraham; Tim Abraham was a black man who was so handsome that he probably should have been a film star; but, since he was extremely capable, unflappable, and a logistics and organizational genius, Nimitz was happy to have him right where he was.

"The schematics of the target are extremely imprecise, sir," said the Air Intelligence Officer, Diane Macpherson, flipping the screen to the schematics. "These were acquired by satellite. The only thing they reveal is that, whatever this base or weapon is, it is deep underground, at least nine hundred, maybe even fifteen hundred feet, below the surface. And, whatever it is, it projects screens of interference. It doesn't want us to know what it is or what it is doing."

"That's pretty advanced technology, isn't it?" said the Captain. "I mean, blocking our surveillance, and – if this report is to be believed – twisting the gravitational space-time matrix, or weakening it."

Tim Abraham frowned. "Yes, it's beyond anything –"

"Beyond anything *we* know." Nimitz looked up from the schematics and glanced at his Air Intelligence Officer. "So, Diane, we don't really have an idea of what we are dropping these nukes on?"

"No, we don't, sir." Diane Macpherson pushed a strand of blond hair back from her forehead and glanced at Abraham; they both thought the upcoming mission could prove to be extraordinarily tricky – extremely dangerous, and not just for the ship. Dropping a nuke on some unknown but super-sophisticated weapons site, well, it raised a lot of questions, to say the least.

"Do we know what sort of counter-measures this, ah, target, might adopt if we do attack it?"

"No idea, sir." Macpherson looked him straight in the eye. "All we know is that the weapon seems – if the analysts and scientists at NASA and at the European Space Agency, and at the Russian, Chinese and Japanese agencies, I might add, are right – to be able to distort gravity and that it is the cause and origin of the recent wave of earthquakes."

"I wonder if this is really such a good idea."

"*Ours not to reason why*," said Diane Macpherson, "sir."

Abraham cleared his throat. "Hmm."

"But the charge of the Light Brigade didn't end so well, did it?" said Nimitz.

"No, sir."

"Absolutely not," said Tim Abraham.

"Well, let's hope this particular country can solve the puzzle – and give the White House answers – before we storm in, violate their sovereignty, and drop a couple of nukes on something way beyond our understanding and that may not be too pleased to be nuked. And if it's this sophisticated, it might know what we are intending to do before we do it."

"Yes."

"Yes, sir, indeed, sir." Tim Abraham picked up a small electronic organizer. "Shall we choose the pilots for this mission and give them a pre-briefing now, sir, or should we wait …?"

"No, let's choose our people now and brief them, and let's have a series of backup plans in case this thing reacts or blocks our initial attack."

"Yes, sir!" Both officers saluted and set to work.

Looking out the window at the dark sea far below, V put her hand against the cool glass. The news from everywhere was catastrophic: Almost a million were feared dead in Naples from the super-hot gas, rocks, and ash that had swept over the city; in Japan, there had been terrible destruction from a massive earthquake on the northern island. An initial burp from the Yellowstone caldera had caused at least three thousand deaths.

And yet, here, flying toward North Africa, everything seemed so normal, so peaceful. The moon, seemingly untroubled by all this terrestrial turmoil, was shining brightly, and the Mediterranean was its beautiful sublime self, a rippling sheet of metallic silver and black.

V loved the "Middle Sea." It was her spiritual home. She swam in it almost every day. She had crossed it so many times, for the first time in bright sunlight on a Phoenician galley when she and Asherah had left North Africa for Italy. Four hundred years later, V had crossed it – several times – during the one hundred and eighteen-year-long series of wars between Rome and Carthage, wars that had ended in the destruction of Carthage and her Phoenician homeland. All that V had originally held dear – her language, her nation, and even the myths and those gods and goddesses she didn't take so seriously – all of that had been destroyed, wiped from the annals of history by the Roman conquerors, and lost to the memory of man.

V's eyes were glossy with tears.

"You okay, Signorina?"

"Yes, Marcello, I'm fine – just memories, that's all." She squeezed U Pizzu's hand and leaned against him.

U Pizzu put his arm around V and adjusted his Polaroids. He sighed. "I know, I know! Memories! Signorina, I get an ache in my heart just thinking back on the first *spaghetti vongole* I ate, you know; I had just come back from snorkeling and it was a balmy evening out on the island of ..."

U Pizzu's voice was a soothing lullaby. V leaned closer against him, listened to the beating of his heart, and drifted back in time. After the fall of Carthage, in later centuries, V had often, as a citizen of the Roman Empire, been a passenger on Roman ships crossing the Mediterranean between Italy and Africa, or Italy and the Levant. She had watched the galley slaves, striving mightily, chained to the oars, muscular, virtually naked, and filthy, sweating under the pitiless sun, while she, now a privileged and wealthy Roman, walked up and down, sheathed in a gorgeous gown or, if she was traveling – which was more usual – in masculine guise, dressed in a rich young man's tunic, only a few feet away from the slaves. How easily, and depending on pure chance, a few yards could separate a life of enslaved misery from a life of freedom, wealth, luxury, and pleasure!

"... now, there's a little beach on Panarea; you'd like it, Signorina, it's isolated and you can take a little boat, a bottle of wine, and ..."

V snuggled closer, as U Pizzu tightened his arm around her. Once, in the Middle Ages, hundreds of years after the fall of Rome, she had been caught adrift in the Mediterranean, aboard a ship marooned in fog, with not a breath of wind, in an icy cold stillness, the water as immobile and flat as glass. For some reason, she never forgot that moment – the sensation of vast and utter stillness.

When the Arabs dominated the Mediterranean, and when they conquered Sicily, she had been there; and she had been there, too, when the Normans – blond, blue-eyed warriors from northern France and the fjords of Scandinavia – seized Sicily from the Arabs.

She had been with the crusaders – and often these were Normans too – when they sailed their fleets toward the Holy Land and Jerusalem – invading what had become Arab and Muslim lands in order to, as they declared, "take the Holy Land back for Christendom."

She had fought with pirates and privateers, and, in 1798, she had watched the fleets of Napoleon and Nelson duel it out – in a storm of smoke and fire and cannon-shot – at the Battle of the Nile.

She had gone ashore with Allied soldiers when they landed in North Africa in November 1942; and, in July 1943, she had followed them onto the beaches of Sicily, and then, in August, into mainland Italy.

Blood and treasure had been spilt on virtually every square inch of land and sea. And under the land and under the sea, things were equally violent, with clashing tectonic plates, underwater volcanoes, earthquakes and eruptions.

V wondered if it was the violence, or the beauty, or both, that drew her back, again and again, to this part of the planet.

"Oh, look, Marcello! Malta!" She sat up.

"Right, yes, Malta ..." U Pizzu straightened up, smoothed down his tie, and looked out the window.

Below them were the lights of Malta. Malta – one of the homes of the prehistoric Mother Goddess, her cult, and her temples; and it was also another battleground, fought over by Phoenicians, Romans, Greeks, Arabs, French, Germans, Italians, and British ...

And if all this history, all these memories, all these lives and humanity itself were to be swept away? Just because she had failed to be vigilant?

"Oh, Marcello," she sighed. She kissed U Pizzu on the cheek; and, concentrating, focusing closely, she carefully straightened his tie.

As the USS *Abraham Lincoln* streamed full speed toward its launch point, Captain Nimitz was again meeting with his executive and intelligence officers, Diane Macpherson and Tim Abraham.

"The GPS and all guidance systems are acting very strange. GPS essentially is offline, useless." Macpherson peered at an array of screens. "We may have to guide our bombers in manually, visually, and using our own radar."

"Can we trust the radar?" Nimitz frowned.

"So far, it seems, we can trust radar. There are some fluctuations in the readings, but generally ..."

"Fluctuations in the readings?"

"As if the speed of light were changing." Tim Abraham indicated an array of trembling graphs.

"What?"

"Electromagnetic waves of all kinds are acting strange – strange is the only word for it – across the spectrum."

"I see."

"Maybe GPS will come back online," Macpherson said, "but everything is weird right now."

"And the ultimatum expires in three hours." Nimitz gazed away and rubbed his chin.

"Yes, sir." Abraham nodded, the light from the multiple screens reflecting off his thoughtful, handsome face.

"At that point we will be given a 'go' from the President – or a 'no.'"

"Yes, sir."

"We have to do this right." Nimitz frowned; it was a stupid thing to say; of course, they had to do this right! Resorting to an empty cliché was a sign of tension, he figured, and of his ambivalence about the mission.

"We have to stop this damned thing, whatever it is." Macpherson glanced at some of the newsfeeds.

"Yes, no doubt about that, Lieutenant, no doubt about that." Nimitz stared at the news streams: lava flows and minor explosions in Yellowstone, obviously these were warning rumblings from the super-volcano that lay under Yellowstone National Park; Mount Helena had just exploded, which meant the Cascades might also erupt; and there had been a major earthquake along the San Andreas Fault in California. Disaster in Italy at Naples, where NATO was based. Several volcanic eruptions in Indonesia, Japan in difficulty …

"Let's talk again in fifteen minutes." Nimitz saluted the two officers.

He went out onto the deck, smelled the night air. Violence – violence everywhere! Around him, the Mediterranean stretched out under the moonlight, a calm, beautiful, warm sea, one of the cradles of human civilization; there were small twinkling lights in the far distance, probably fishing boats. A strand of cloud, luminous, delicate, feathery cirrus, passed in front of the moon. Ah, but Earth was a beautiful, fragile place! And it was the *only* place, our only home.

CHAPTER 51 – PLACE OF DESOLATION

A column of armored cars raced across the desert toward a cliff-like escarpment in the middle of nowhere – a site known, mysteriously, since ancient times as "The Place of Desolation."

Thirty-eight-year-old Colonel Mohammed Ibn Khaldun, Commander of the Republic's Presidential Guard, felt that the name itself was of ill-augur. Legend had it that anyone who approached the place either died or went mad. According to tribal legend, ghosts haunted the cliffs. One ravine in the cliff face was said to be particularly dangerous, and it had been scrupulously avoided by the nomads since time immemorial. Such were the superstitions and old-wives' tales handed down from generation to generation. One legend had it that a beautiful succubus – a female spirit or she-devil who often disguised herself as a young man – haunted the place, drank the blood of voyagers, sucked out their life force, and left nothing but an empty shriveled and withered husk, a mocking parody of the living person, behind.

Mohammed stared at the fragments of desert. Scrub and dunes of sand rushed forward, brightly lit in the headlights. He wondered what the mission was really about. They had been traveling at top speed for six hours. The tanker vehicles – with extra fuel – could barely keep up.

Why hadn't they just parachuted in a small group of crack troops? Personally, he would have been happy to lead such a group – clean, get in quickly, exploit the effect, perhaps, of surprise, and hopefully get out quickly. Maybe the President-Leader wanted to make this a real show of force. He'd have his reasons, undoubtedly; he always did – even if they usually remained mysterious to ordinary mortals.

The President-Leader had received a warning, direct from the American President, that there was a terrorist organization or machine or weapon, apparently buried deep underground, out in the desert; the American

President said that this machine, whatever it was, was causing the global wave of earth tremors; that this was a terrorist attack against all the nations of the Earth. The President-Leader, it was said, had declared that he knew nothing of such a machine. The American President, reportedly, had said, "I'm afraid that's not good enough, Mr. President!" The President-Leader responded politely, it was said, but he was furious – the honor of the nation – and his personal honor – had been impugned.

"It sounds like science fiction," said Lieutenant Abdul al-Rashid. "Nobody knows how to build a machine that could cause earthquakes all over the planet." Abdul had studied physics, had done graduate work in London, and was hoping to do his Ph.D. at Princeton or Oxford. "I just don't believe it!"

"Neither do I, but the Americans, I have been told, will attack the site with nuclear weapons if we do not solve this mystery."

"And have they given us a deadline?" asked Captain Amin ibn Abdul-Aziz.

"Probably sometime tomorrow morning," said Mohammed, suppressing his anger. The Americans were so impatient, and so bloody arrogant, always blundering into situations they didn't understand! "Let's go over the schematics again."

"A lot – too much – depends on us." Abdul shuddered at the idea of nukes; he had read whole books on what happened at Hiroshima and Nagasaki.

"It's supposed to be just a mining site, not a military base." Mohammed pointed out the features – a small landing strip, a cliff, and a narrow canyon or ravine – the ravine haunted by the mythical she-devil – that led to the mining site, which was, apparently, inside a deep cavern – all this was in a part of the desert where not even nomads ventured. The myths and fears had kept them away from the Place of Desolation. "We don't know anything about the cavern. We must act quickly and be prepared for anything. We'll deploy in a 'U' formation, surround the airfield, and then enter from the center and from both flanks. We don't know whether we will be meeting hostile forces or not, so we proceed carefully."

He passed the orders to all fifteen armored cars racing across the desert.

The Cardinal had been twirling around, for some time now lost perhaps in a world of his own imaginings, miming some dance step; his white ecclesiastical gown – which looked like an old-fashioned nightgown – floated out, and twirled and swirled with him; his bright scarlet ecclesiastical shoes, of which he seemed inordinately proud, stirred up eddies of dust on the cavern's floor.

The monks stood in a row, impassive, watching the performance. The Cardinal was remarkably light-footed; at least such was Roger's impression, though the old buzzard must be at least one hundred and twenty years old!

The Cardinal stopped his whirling-dervish performance, wiped his brow, came over to Roger's cage and peered through the bars. "Have you ever jumped over the moon, Professor?"

"I can't say that I have, Your Eminence."

"You should try it sometime."

"Well, certainly, first chance I get, Cardinal."

"It is so invigorating."

"I see, you're saying you really have jumped over the moon?"

"I most certainly have." The Cardinal's yellowish eyes took on a vague absent cast. He was far away, lost in memory. "I saw the dark side, the mysterious side that is always turned away from Earth. I saw the man in the moon, too, and very amiable he was. He was not made of cheese. He had horns and a tail. He spoke to me, most kindly."

"I see."

"This has been most pleasant, Professor. I do so enjoy our little chats. But now I have something urgent to attend to."

"Don't let me detain you, Your Eminence."

"Most kind, you are most kind." The Cardinal beamed at Roger. It was an endearing, affectionate smile, as if they were longtime bosom buddies. "I must take care of a little business up top, as they say. We are going to have some visitors shortly, and I want to show them what I can do. I shall give them a little demonstration of my powers."

"How we gonna land this thing in the desert?" U Pizzu had never been to a real desert; he wasn't sure he'd like the experience.

John pointed to a map. "They have their own landing strip. The Crystal is about one hundred miles in from the coast. Nobody lives nearby, and nobody goes there. Officially the site belongs to the Mediterranean Mining Corporation, but, behind that facade, and behind several holding companies in Switzerland, the site belongs to the Four Horsemen Mining and Security Corporation. It was acquired by them on a lease from the government two years ago."

"What sort of defenses do they have?" V scanned the map.

"Not much," John said. "It's supposed to be a civilian and private security installation – there are a couple of anti-aircraft guns. They have radar. They'll see us coming. If they don't want us to land, they can always block the runway. They might have ground-to-air missiles. Those are a dime a dozen." He unfolded a sketch. "Here's a rough map of the installation, made partly from what you've told me about the place, V."

They were entering North African airspace – and flying over the country that, after a series of revolutions and civil wars, now had a relatively benign dictatorial presidential regime. John and Larssen had arranged for clearance to enter the nation's air space.

Larssen spoke to the regional air controller.

"We may be met at the landing strip by some of the Republic's Presidential Guard. They are heading there overland. Apparently, they're only minutes away."

"Oh?"

"I don't like the idea of a Presidential Guard," said U Pizzu.

"What does this mean for us?" V glanced at John, while with one hand absent-mindedly stroking U Pizzu's tie.

"I trained some of their officers," said John. "I was at Military Academy Sandhurst with the head of the Presidential Guard. We used to play poker. I'm told he's leading the group himself. I consider him a friend and I think he feels the same way about me. He's why we have clearance to enter their airspace – and to land."

"So, we may be able to turn this to our advantage?" asked V. "They will be useful allies."

"Yes, probably. I'm sure they want the same thing as we do: to shut this thing down."

"I think we should tell your friend to be very careful about approaching the ravine and the Crystal."

"Right," said John, glancing at Larssen.

"Right," said Larssen, handing the microphone to John.

U Pizzu glanced at V: she was really in her element here. The girl was a fighter, a born warrior. At the same time, she was affectionate and even tender, and not afraid to show it. He felt proud to know her. For some reason, he wanted to tell Maria Grazia about this superwoman. Maria Grazia was, on the surface at least, very understanding about U Pizzu's amorous adventures. Above all, he wanted to tell his daughters, Adrianna and Rosa and Paola, about V. It would be an inspiring story for young women – a role model, that was what they said, wasn't it? Yes, V knew her own mind. She would be a great role model for the girls.

The elevator doors slid shut behind the Cardinal. The construction elevator cage, in its improvised steel tower, began its slow trembling journey upward. Cardinal Ambrosiano hummed to himself. Outwardly, he was just a frail old man, but in reality, he was much more, infinitely more.

The ants in the ants' nest had been stirred up. And the she-devil, the demon he had first met in the garden cemetery of Villa Monteleone – oh, so long ago – had returned – a worthy opponent! She had found the Torelli Jewel; and she had somehow evaded the little trap he had set for her at Villa Jovis. The Torelli Jewel must have great and magical powers if the demon pursued it so. She had murdered the three monks sent to kill her and that charming but foolish Mafioso, U Pizzu; and she had also saved the life of that doddering hypocritical naive old dupe the Pope! Truly, this she-devil was a mischief-maker of the worst sort! But she would get her comeuppance! Hers would be a most horrible fate, totally appropriate, one she truly deserved.

And, then, there were the Americans, threatening to drop an atomic bomb – always the Americans! In their naivety, they thought that their power, which was quickly fading in any case, could solve any problem; that they merely had to push a few buttons, drop a few bombs, and – presto! The problem would go away. But, by the time they sent their piddling little atomic bombs, it would be too late!

He licked his lips and probed his pointed ragged teeth with the tip of his tongue. They know not *who* I am! They know not *what* I am! They know not what I can do! Fools! Fools! Fools!

Ah, yes, and the President of this flea-bitten Republic had sent some of his toy soldiers to deal with him, ha! They had no idea what they are dealing with – but they would learn – ha, ha, when it is too late.

The elevator doors slid open. Wiping away a streak of drool from his chin, and glancing around with his hooded yellowing eyes, the Cardinal stepped out of the construction elevator onto the open platform that overlooked the cavern. He gazed at the winding tunnel that led out to the ravine, which then led to the airfield.

He knew from his informers that the approaching armored cars were equipped with electronic controls and electronic-controlled weaponry. The

North African Republic was rich from its vast oil exports and the President-Leader like to purchase, for his armed forces, all the latest gadgetry.

The Cardinal smiled. That the Republic's soldiers were equipped with the latest gadgetry was good – it was a weakness. The Crystal had transformed him, the Cardinal, into a most deadly weapon. He now transcended matter. He had become pure mind. He was mind! And mind was electricity. Therefore … Mind over Matter!

The Cardinal tittered.

Ah, how wonderful it was – to be like a god!

He really did like Professor Thornhill. The man was charming. When the Satanic Rapture swept them upwards, he would dearly like to keep the Professor with him. The Professor would make a good pet, obedient and slavish, to be led about on a leash, transmogrified perhaps into some horned and cloven and hairy hooved beast, with an ugly snout, a shrill inarticulate whinny for a voice, a long slippery bright red drooling tongue, and hooves for hands! How delicious! Since the man was highly intelligent, handsome, and vain, it would be delightful to transform him into an inarticulate, ugly, slobbering monster!

The Cardinal came to the end of the tunnel and emerged through the open steel door into the narrow crevice-like ravine. He stood for a moment gazing up at the sliver of sky, visible between the towering rock faces. It was night. Oh, delicious night! Soon the night would be eternal.

As he walked down the canyon the Cardinal cast off his ecclesiastical regalia. First went the biretta, then the bib, then the long white gown, then his shirt, and then his trousers, and undershirt and underpants, until everything was gone. What emerged was a skinny, wispy-haired, naked old man with shrunken shoulders, pipsqueak arms, withered skinny bow legs, walking slowly, bent forward, through the shadows of the narrow deep ravine.

Dust stirred at his feet; the air shimmered and twisted around him, as if distorted by a giant invisible lens. The old man was changing.

Knotty protuberances pushed out of his rib cage; his facial features – mouth, nose, eyes, cheeks – dissolved; his head lost its shape and grew larger, and larger; his neck, a scrawny pitiful human neck, shrank, and disappeared; his body split into two linked armored segments; the protuberances rapidly extended and became thin, metal-like limbs; his legs and arms morphed into spindly long bony appendages; and his eyes turned first to a mass of jelly and then spawned a myriad of little eyes, which multiplied and became multifaceted enormous spider eyes, eight of them, like a spider, but a hybrid design, containing many elements from many sources; he grew, he expanded, he swelled up, he got larger and larger and larger.

His body was fluid – it could twist and bend, expand and shrink! It was mind; it was pure energy, pure liquid energy. How wondrous the Dark Force was – its gifts, transmitted through the Crystal, were infinite; he could morph into anything, into anything at all.

The creature that had been Cardinal Ambrosiano leapt up onto the rock face and crawled sideways along the rocky wall for about fifty yards.

Here the creature – a giant spider – squeezed through the narrow mouth of the crevice and leapt from the granite wall to land on the hard-packed desert sand; its multiple beady eyes scanned the horizon, registering a wide frequency of wavelengths; it scurried toward the airstrip.

In the distance, the spider saw the headlights of the armored column, approaching fast, in U-formation, some to the south, some to the north, and a central group heading straight for the small airstrip.

The Spider-Cardinal mewled. Oh, how clever their commander thought he was! Oh, how foolish these mere mortals were! How ridiculous with their puny toys and infantile stratagems!

The Spider-Cardinal was a creature that had never existed on the planet Earth – nor perhaps on any other planet anywhere. Crouched in the darkness, it waited, and it watched through its gleaming many-beveled eyes. Its jaws drooled acid and venom.

Through this new body, the Spider-Cardinal felt a stream of power so great it was overwhelming. He squealed in delight at the solemnity.

I am a vessel, Oh, Dark Force, Oh Satan! I am your gateway, Oh Divine Darkness! I am your portal into this world.

I am the Spider-God!

The Spider-Cardinal – or Spider-God – watched as the two columns of armored cars, deployed in classic pincer formation, plus a central striking force, raced closer to the airfield.

The Spider's multilayered mandibles clattered and drooled, moving their many overlapping segments, ravenous for prey. Acid-slobber splashed onto the sand and hissed.

The armored cars, all three columns, entered the mine fields – special mines designed to be undetectable by electronic means.

The great beady eyes, all eight of them, and each of them about a foot across, blinked with pleasure. The Spider-God sent out a pulse of energy.

The mines exploded – all of them at once, in a whoosh of sand and fire. Ha, ha!

A great gob of gluey smoking sulfurous vitriol fell from the multilayered clacking jaws of the Spider-God. It hissed as it landed on the sand. The Spider-God exalted, and let loose another mind-wave, pure energy, on a wide span of frequencies.

Mohammed believed in leading from the front. His armored car was already beyond the minefield when the mines went off.

"What the …?"

He glanced back. The whole horizon behind him was a wall of flame. Shadows catapulted into the air. Armored cars, fragments of armored cars, silhouettes of burning bodies, rocketed out of the wave of fire. Some of the armored cars, just damaged, were spinning in circles.

Two larger silhouettes, the two fuel tankers, were toppling over; they had collided with the careening – and exploding – cars in front of them. Both fuel tankers went up in thundering whooshes of flame.

Suddenly, Mohammed's command car spun out of control; brakes failed, sights failed, steering failed. Mohammed held on for dear life.

"Can you straighten her out?"

"No, sir, I can't! Everything's dead, sir!"

Mohammed glanced at his Info-feed. It was dead. So were the vehicle's lights. His earphones too. The electronics had failed. That meant the controls, the weapons – everything! But the engine was still racing.

The vehicle careened, turned sharply, spun sideways, splashing up a huge wave of sand. At any moment, it would topple over and explode.

"Get out! Jump!"

"Sir?"

"You heard me!" he screamed. It was hard to make himself heard over the roar of the engine, the explosions and fire.

"Go, damn it! Jump! I'll be right behind!"

The two men climbed out onto the side of the vehicle. It was spinning, tipping, close to flipping over. Amin and Abdul leapt into the darkness.

Mohammed clambered up, grabbed a hand railing, and jumped just before the armored car hit something hard, rose in the air and – Mohammed could sense this happening behind him – flipped over onto its roof, skidded sideways, and then exploded in a huge rolling ball of fire.

He landed with a thud, rolled, got up on all fours, glanced around, and stood up. Behind him, in the minefield, it was a pure chaos of burning wrecks. Some survivors, though, were advancing, on foot, dark silhouettes, imprinted on a wall of flame.

"What hit us, sir?"

"No idea, but we are going after it, whatever it is."

Mohammed had kept his old-fashioned weapons, an AS50 sniper rifle and a Beretta M9 pistol; no electronics were involved. At least he and his men could still put up a fight. He waved to the survivors, urging them onward.

Many of his men were still armed, still ready with non-electronic rifles and sidearms. But, though they didn't yet know it, in a few minutes the battle of "The Place of Desolation" would be over and almost everyone would be dead.

From his cage-prison, Roger looked up. The construction elevator in its six-story-tall skeletal structure had burst into life, its motor grinding into action.

The elevator came down slowly and noisily, and then, with a clanking sound, it stopped at the bottom. The door opened.

Illuminated, like a vaudeville star, in the spotlight brightness of one of the floodlights, the Cardinal stepped out, an old man, robed in his white ecclesiastical gown. According to the clock on Roger's computer, the Cardinal had been away for exactly forty-eight minutes. The Cardinal came forward until he stood before Roger's cage. "I exercised pity, Professor, I exercised some pity."

"Pity?"

"I left some of them alive."

"Who? Some of who alive?"

"Toy soldiers: The President-Leader of the land in which we find ourselves thought it necessary to send his Presidential Guard. They intended to interrupt our work, but they will bother us no more."

"I see."

"But now it is time to die, Professor." With a dismissive wave of his hand, as if he were casually bidding Roger *Adieu*, the Cardinal turned away and faced the monks who had been waiting patiently, their hands folded in front of them. "It is time for all to say goodbye – and to die."

"Wouldn't it be better to wait?"

"I cannot wait, Professor." The Cardinal turned back to face Roger. "My superhuman antennae tell me that some foolish people – and they include a demon and a Jesuit priest, I might add – are coming to try to stop me, and so I am going to accelerate my timetable."

"A demon?"

"Yes, a demon – she is a female too, which is most irritating! She is a trick-ster, cunning and wild, very feminine, pure woman. They think they can stop me. But they cannot. It is amusing, is it not, Professor, these puny creatures – trying to stop *me!* I represent something much greater than myself, much greater than any of us. I represent Satan. I *am* Satan! I am the incarnation of the Dark Force!"

"I am sure you are." Roger had begun to doubt his own sanity. Probably madness was catching. Since the standard laws of physics – and biology – seemed to have been suspended, maybe there really was such a thing as the Dark Force; maybe the Cardinal really was the incarnation of something beyond the realms of science; maybe there was a horrible logic in the old man's craziness.

"Fire up the generator!" the Cardinal roared. He turned to the monks. "Children, my children – apply a strong current to the Crystal, the strongest you can! Don't stop! Give it a continuous wave of shocks!"

"Cardinal, this is madness."

"Yes, it is, isn't it?" The Cardinal turned to Roger, covered his mouth, and tittered, as if he were sharing a childish practical joke.

The generator coughed, sputtered, then roared, sending up a strong smell of diesel fuel.

Up on the Crystal's control platform, the two cables threw off a shower of sparks. They cascaded, a Niagara of light, down the side of the Crystal.

"This is crazy, Your Eminence."

"I appreciate your candor, Professor. I like you, Professor, I really do, so I shall confide in you." The Cardinal was rubbing his hands in glee. "You see, Professor, your daughter, Katherine … She's quite beautiful, you know …." The Cardinal walked over to the generator and spoke to the monk who hov-ered over it. "As strong as you can – I told you! As strong as you can."

Roger wanted to scream, "Kate, what about Kate?" He held himself in. The Cardinal clearly took great pleasure in torturing people. He would want to see Roger squirm and beg and cry. Roger would see him in Hell before he let the man squeeze any extra pleasure out of his sadism.

The Cardinal strolled back to the cage and gave Roger his most genial grin. "What was I talking about, Professor?"

Roger looked at him in as calm a manner as he could. "I believe you mentioned Katherine, Cardinal."

"Ha, ha, ha, oh, Professor, I do like you! You are so cool, admirable, admirable! Your sangfroid is a wonder. I was thinking how marvelous it would be if I could take you along with me into the Dark Realm, when my nuptials are consumed, that is. You'd make a very nice pet, I think, or slave."

"I'm sure I would."

"Well, as I was saying, your Katherine, truly a beautiful creature by the way, was the centerpiece of a little ceremony our Group, the Satanic Order of the Apocalypse, held last night in Italy. She was the star attraction, your darling Kate, and she played her role brilliantly."

Roger could hardly breathe.

"It was a sacred satanic ceremony, representing the Force of Darkness, or the Divinity of Satan, triumphing over the Female Principle – over the Eternal Feminine – over the Goddess in all her incarnations. There are many ways of naming the Unnamable, as I am sure you can appreciate, Professor, being involved in a science that deals with so many entities invisible to the naked eye. Physics, dealing as it does with the very, very tiny and the very, very large, is rather similar to theology – or demonology, don't you think?"

Roger didn't say a word.

The generator was puffing out smoke, and coughing, going full tilt; miniature bolts of lightning shot out, and sparks sizzled and showered down from the surface of the Crystal. Roger suppressed a shudder.

"Before the ceremony, the priest who presided was kind enough to arrange for his monks to send me some delightful images."

Roger said nothing.

"Would you like to see the images, Professor? It will allow you to participate, as it were, in the ceremony! To stand, as it were, by Kate's side."

"Yes, Cardinal, I would," Roger swallowed. "Thank you." Roger strained the links that held him chained. They were thick stainless steel and Teflon and they were attached very tightly. He couldn't even scratch his own face, touch the keyboard, or tug up the bloody loincloth.

One of the monks came forward and unlocked the cage door.

"Here!" The Cardinal came into the cage and held out an iPad.

Roger looked at the images.

"You must be proud."

"Proud of Kate?" said Roger. "Certainly, I'm proud of Kate – I will always be proud of Kate, whatever she does and whatever happens to her." A pearl of sweat rolled down Roger's forehead. His eyes, he realized, were wet; he blinked the wet away; he would not shy away from anything; he would face everything directly; that was what Kate would want. It was strange, but his daughter had become, in some ways, his mentor. *Look steadily at what has to be looked at, Dad, don't flinch, don't run, don't evade, and don't hide!*

Roger stared: *Kate naked …*

Spread-eagled, manacled down on some sort of platform or table, was a beautiful young woman, startlingly beautiful, her eyes staring straight up; her face was expressionless. It was Kate; there was no doubt about it.

Flesh of my flesh …

The image flipped. Now it was a garish version of the same woman, she was lying half on her side, one arm reaching up as if to shield herself from an invisible threat, her brightly painted lips were open in startled, orgasmic abandon, jet-black hair flowed loose and luxuriously around her oval face, her skin had the color of a plaster saint or Barbie doll, the eyes were blind, like shards of colored glass, staring emptily.

"That's not Kate."

"No, no, it's not; you have a good eye, Professor," said the Cardinal amiably. "That is a memorial, a sort of icon, or relic – but, alas …"

"Alas … what?"

"Everything was destroyed."

"Destroyed?" Roger said it so quietly it was barely a whisper. His forehead was beaded in sweat. He took a deep breath. Everything and everyone who was close to him had been murdered; everyone he touched, everyone he loved; Laura died because he had to give a talk and have some meetings in Jerusalem; Kate had been kidnapped and murdered because he gave a speech in Rome and because this maniac wanted Roger as a witness to his mad schemes, as a mirror to his ego. Mario had died just because he was Roger's friend and driver, and Martin Stigliano was shot just because he was a friend … By just being who he was, Roger had betrayed everybody he loved and everybody who loved him. Suddenly, he heard Kate's voice in his head, clear as a bell: *"Don't beat yourself up, Dad, it is not your fault; things happen; let's move on … It's not as bad as it looks, Dad!"* Her voice was so strong that Roger wondered whether Kate might still be alive. And he heard Father O'Bryan's voice, too, from a conversation years ago. *"Guilt can be a form of self-indulgence, Roger."*

"Yes, everything was destroyed, alas," said the Cardinal, with a theatrical sigh, while the iPad showed one last image of the real flesh-and-blood Kate: Kate manacled down on some sort of altar and behind her a bearded, insane-looking priest. Kate was achingly beautiful ...

The Cardinal turned off the iPad. "That is the last image they sent. I'm not sure what happened next; but there was an explosion, a fire, everyone died; I know of no survivors."

"No survivors," Roger repeated quietly.

The Cardinal mimed an expression of commiseration.

"Yes, well, it is rather petty – and unworthy – of us, Professor, to get worked up by such small events, now that we are on the verge of the greatest single act in human history. That was the last message I received, but there were news reports." The Cardinal used the remote to switch on a recorded video of a villa burning, a towering pyre. "Your daughter was consumed – a sacrificial lamb, sanctified in Satan by her eager willingness to die."

"I see." Roger suddenly felt certain – and he had no idea why – that Kate was not dead and that this madman was going to be utterly defeated, destroyed, and annihilated.

"Now, we shall amuse ourselves!" The Cardinal's grin was hideous. "There is a demon –"

"The female demon you mentioned?"

"Yes, she is coming to visit us. I must prepare a suitable welcome."

"A *demon* – really?"

"Yes, Professor, a true she-devil! And she does exist, I do assure you! Oh, you are so skeptical, even now, even having seen what you have seen! You have so little faith! Clothed now in only a soiled and skimpy loincloth, as Christ was on the cross, I would have thought you might at least have developed some transcendent and mystical tendencies, some humility! Well, I have things to attend to; we shall speak again as the Apocalypse approaches." The Cardinal strode away and left Roger chained in the cage, choking back tears for Kate. Beyond grief, he felt he had been polluted; he was coated in the filth of death, or something abominable and much worse than death.

One of the monks closed the cage door and locked it.

Miniature bolts of lightning – blue electric arcs – lit up the face of the Crystal, and sparks cascaded off its sides.

Following Kate's advice, Roger turned away from his guilt and mourning and focused on the problem at hand. The timer had started to count the seconds from the moment the generator had begun applying the new wave of shocks; that was ten minutes ago – so in forty to fifty minutes another wave of seismic shocks and earthquakes would almost certainly begin; then, in the hours following, they would amplify, and be far greater and more widespread than before. And then, in waves, other shocks would follow, in hours, maybe even in days – if there were any days to come. And, at some point, Earth would break apart.

How could he get the monks to stop the generator? It was clear that even if the Crystal did not want to do any of this – and he was somehow sure the Crystal had a will of its own – it could not stop itself as long as the electric shocks were being applied. Was there some way to help it? He looked around.

Electricity – the electricity supply …

"At least I am free now, Kate," Roger whispered. "Now you are no longer a hostage, or at least that's what this madman believes, I can do whatever I have to do."

He heard her voice, as clear as if she were standing next to him. *"Yes, Dad, you are free, don't worry about me. You will do what you always do – you will do the right thing!"*

In that moment, almost as if she'd suggested it, he had an idea – the computers were powered from the same source as the cable with the sparks – from the same system of generators; just possibly, the circuits in the computers might be rerouted to overload or divert or stop the electricity from the generator that was "electrocuting" the Crystal. The generator probably had its own computerized controls. Maybe, through the computers, he could turn off that generator – or maybe all of them!

He began to imagine what the circuitry design might be, and where its weaknesses might lie. If only he had his hands free of the manacles! He couldn't even scratch himself, let alone use the keyboard. He was helpless

PART NINE – TWILIGHT OF THE GODS

CHAPTER 52 – PRELUDE

I am Father Michael Patrick O'Bryan, and these will perhaps be the last notes I make concerning my adventures with the demon, V. If you are reading this, you will already know what happened to us – and to the world.

When we flew in over the home of the Crystal, we immediately ran into trouble. Things were not "normal," not even for this totally abnormal situation. The Republic's Presidential Guard should have taken control of the airfield just before our arrival.

Larssen, our pilot, had been in touch with the Guard's radio operators. Colonel Mohammed Ibn Khaldun, the Commander of the unit, had agreed with John that they would await our arrival before proceeding into the underground installation itself.

Mohammed said that his troops would take control of the airstrip but not proceed farther until we arrived; we would land, and they would meet us, and then we would – God willing – Allah willing – help each other to put an end to the Cardinal's plot.

But as we approached the landing strip, something happened. "We've lost radio contact with the Presidential Guard," Larssen announced in a matter-of-fact voice. "And there are no runway lights."

Outside, it was pitch black; the moon was covered – by clouds or perhaps by a veil of dust rising from one of the many catastrophes that seemed to be occurring just about everywhere.

"Can you land without the lights and without control tower guidance?" V asked.

"I think so. We'll fly low over the landing field, drop a flare – I only have two – and have a look."

We flew in, dropped the flare, which created a great circle of garish light below us, and circled around.

"What the hell is that?" John peered through the window. I got up and looked out. Something that looked like a network of glittering steel cables ran across the runway, crisscrossing every which way, a total tangle; it blocked every possible avenue of approach.

Larssen zoomed back up. "It must be an illusion – it must be reflections off something," he said.

"I think it's real, whatever it is," said V.

"It looked like a spider web to me," said Elena Satti, "a giant spider web, but more dense."

"We could try to land to the side of the runway," said Larssen.

"We must land," said V. "There is no choice."

V's eyes were aflame, her jaw was clenched, her muscles tensed. I really do think she would have leapt out of the plane if that was the only way to get down there.

I prayed. My life and all of our lives, and the lives of everyone on the planet were in the hands of God, the Creator of the universe, as indeed we always are, though we often forget it. We are in His hands even when we are just waking up in the morning, drinking a glass of orange juice, sipping coffee, or crossing the street.

Here I felt something new. I felt that we were now confronted with an Evil Force of immense power, and that the Cardinal, for all his wiles and wickedness, was merely a vessel, merely an instrument of something greater and much more terrible than he; it was something the Cardinal, in his vanity and presumption, did not at all understand.

I began to pray too for V, though I suspected that she, my demon friend, would be annoyed at me for doing so.

The instant I had that thought, she glanced at me – I keep forgetting that she can read thoughts. Seeing my lips moving in what was clearly a prayer, she smiled softly, even sadly; and then suddenly she gave me a truly luminous smile – and a thumbs up. So perhaps, in spite of her demonic nature as a daughter and companion of Lucifer, in spite of her lack of faith and her lack of a soul, she did not mind my praying for her – and for all of us. Indeed, in her own way, and for her own reasons, she approved.

Yes, V is demonic. She lives off us. We humans are her fodder. She hunts, and we are her prey. Of course, the shepherd who tends a flock or a herd often eats the flesh of those he protects; and the flock trusts him – or her. It has to.

Perhaps then, V, in a small way, is our shepherd, just as Jesus, in a large way, is our shepherd. Oh, Michael Patrick O'Bryan, what silly and blasphemous thoughts you are thinking! How you prattle on in your head!

But then I think perhaps it is because V has known such darkness – because she *is* such darkness – that we know we can trust her with the darkness in our own souls. To know evil, you must have tasted evil – to the last drop – or confronted it in all its seduction and horror, just as Saint Augustine had to know the lower depths of depravity in order to understand the nature of sin, and thus of saintliness.

It has often been thus with mystics and holy men and women. Saints and sinners are more closely allied than we are usually willing to admit; and the greatest virtues, if taken too far, can easily transform themselves into the wickedest forms of vice. And vice and excess sometimes transform themselves, by a strange psychic alchemy, into virtue and saintliness.

But how, I wondered, could V survive – even live – with such casual abandon, and even humor, while dwelling in utter darkness, deprived of her soul, deprived of her relationship to God? She treats her fallen state with remarkable lightness, sometimes even with delight, with laughter, as if it hardly concerned her at all. For myself, I have always feared – more than anything, more than pain or torture, more than death itself – losing my eternal soul, that gift of God, the only thing in the end that counts.

"Perhaps soon, Father, we must prepare to meet our Maker, as they say." John turned to me, as if he had read my thoughts. The pilot was about to land blind, in absolute darkness, except for a fire burning in the control tower.

Then a voice said, "Larssen, if you make another pass, maybe I can get some lights on."

"Mohammed, is that you?" asked John.

"Yes, John, it's me. I'm alive – just barely. I'm in the control tower. There's a backup generator here. We'll see if we can get it going."

We made another pass, zooming up into the night sky above the vastness of the largest desert in the world: no lights, no sign of human habitation, no indication that humanity existed at all or ever had existed. Just the darkness of a planet that seemed lost to humanity.

I began to fear that if the Dark Force – whatever it is, Satan, an Extraterrestrial Empire, an Evil Plasma or Energy – does not triumph now, it will try again, and again, and again. And in the end, it will triumph; for we humans contain within ourselves the seeds of our own destruction.

Just as I was questioning my faith in God and in Man – which was so unworthy of me – I glanced at V. She winked. "Don't worry, Father, we'll win! This time the good guys will beat the bad guys!"

Oh, that my faith in God and Man should be reignited by a smile from a female demon. The ways of the Lord are strange indeed.

The airport lights went on,

Larssen let out a gasp. "What we saw before – it wasn't an illusion!"

"Can you see the runway?" Mohammed asked.

"Yes, Mohammed. What is that stuff? What are those cables?"

"It's a spider web."

John and Larssen looked at each other; Elena sighed. "I was joking when I said spider web."

"John, I'm telling you the truth. A giant spider came out of the side of the cliff. Its body was the size of a battle tank. It took control of our electronics, our control systems, and, I think, even of our men's minds – most of them. It is something not of this world! It got all but two of my men – and it almost got me. It spins out these cables that are a foot at least in diameter and sticky and as strong as steel."

"How are we going to land? The runway is covered in the stuff!"

"The sand to the left of the runway – left if you're coming in from the north – is hard-packed. You'll be in the dark, though, just some reflected light from the generator lights. But it's your only chance."

"Okay," said Larssen." We'll try. Let's test the landing lights; we had a bit of trouble with them, because of all the ash from Vesuvius."

"Right," said Elena, flipping a switch. "Landing lights on … only …"

"Only they aren't," said Larssen.

"We have no landing lights," said Elena.

Larssen glanced up at John. "John, I don't know what we can do. We are almost completely blind here."

John looked at V. "Well? Want to unveil one of your many talents?"

"I have almost perfect night vision," V said, glancing at Larssen and Satti.

"You do?"

"If I concentrate, it's almost like daytime."

"Okay, I'm willing if you are," said Larssen. "If Mohammed can project some light next to the landing strip, and if you use your night vision to talk us through this, we might just be able to do it."

"Let's go," said Elena. "Nothing ventured …"

"Yes," said V. "We've come this far … and we are not going to stop now!"

"I've floodlit what I can." Mohammed's voice came through static.

"Thanks, Mohammed. We are coming in!"

V stood between the pilot and copilot. "Let's do a first pass."

I held my breath and clutched my armrests as the jet came in low over the proposed landing zone. Kate, who was sitting next to me, put her hand on mine. She was smiling.

"There are some strands of cable on the right side, near the runway," V said. "They reach out about two yards. And there's a rocky outcropping about twenty-five yards to the left and another at the end of the runway, just next to where the control tower is. You have a narrow window, a narrow strip."

"Okay! Around we come and in we go, Mohammed, on the next pass."

"May Allah be with you!"

"And with you, Mohammed!"

As the jet approached the dark sandy stretch of desert that was to be our runway, and perhaps our grave, I asked God to bless our mission, to help us, even if I was wrong to be allying myself with such a creature as V.

And the answer came, in a sense, in the thought that Jesus came into the world not to judge it but to save it. Perhaps V, whatever she herself was, was a vessel, an instrument of salvation, directed by something greater than herself, even if she did not herself realize it. In an infinitely more modest way, that was my own mission too – to save, not to judge. And, then, too, the thought occurred to me that I should not judge V, or condemn her, lest I myself be judged.

In the cockpit, V was leaning close to the pilot, whispering. We were heading into darkness and V was saying, "five degrees to the left … good, good, perfect … now two degrees to the right, quick!"

Out the window I saw a huge outcropping of rock – just a blur of granite – flash by, perhaps three yards beyond the wing tip.

"Interesting," whispered Kate, with a cool little smile.

"Yes, interesting," I muttered.

The plane touched down, bumping, skidding, and it seemed for a moment the sand was not hard enough; we were going to spin around, catapult over and probably break apart and explode. My heart leapt into my mouth. But then the wheels gained traction and we raced ahead into the blackness, with only the dimmest glow from Mohammed's generator lights to guide us.

Except for V. She was talking, calmly, to the pilot. "Three degrees left;

now straight: you've got about three hundred yards before the outcropping at the end."

"Not enough to brake on this sand."

"Veer to the left; it's clear that way, I think."

"You think?"

"The land dips away a bit."

"Okay."

V whispered, "I can see it now; it's a slope, not a canyon."

"V, you are a gem," said Larssen.

"Thank you! Left a touch – now!"

The plane swerved, then slowed and turned in a slow arc. And miraculously we came to a stop.

"Will we be able to take off on this stuff?"

"I think so. If we can land, we can take off."

Silently, I thanked God. V stood up, came back to her seat and patted me on the shoulder. "Well, Father, your prayers were answered!"

"Yes," I said.

"Now the difficult part begins." V winked and flashed a mischievous smile, like a little girl about to play a trick or leap off a branch and into a running stream.

"Okay, let's go!" Kate had been mostly silent during the landing, eyes alert to everything, but sitting sagely buckled in, dressed – rather, sculpted – in the sparkling black superwoman outfit. She unbuckled the seat belt, and stood up, stretched, and put one gloved hand on the holster that was slung at her waist. Her eyes shone. She was chaffing at the bit, eager to get into action. The resilience of the girl was amazing. But, then, she was young.

U Pizzu, who was sitting across from Kate, looked gloomy. "You're a spunky girl," he said, looking up at her.

"Thank you, Marcello!"

She gave him a most entrancing, flirtatious smile.

"You know … I don't like spiders," U Pizzu said, glancing out the window. "I really don't like spiders. I've never met a spider I liked. In fact, I think I hate spiders. What do you think about spiders, Father?" he asked, slowly getting up, and turning to me. "Are spiders among the favorites of God?"

Taking care not to soil the swirling skirts of his vestments, Cardinal Ambrosiano climbed up the metal stairs that zigzagged up the face of the Crystal.

He stood on the control platform, his hands on the railing, overlooking the great cavern. It was rather, he thought, like standing in the pulpit of a giant cathedral, much greater in size than any human-made cathedral, and looking down on one's flock.

The Cardinal tightened his grip on the railing. Here, there was no flock – this was not Saint Peter's and he was not the Pope. No, down below were only the monks – and, for all their virtues, the monks were not satisfying parishioners. They did not harbor such souls as he could take possession of. They were already his from birth, his slaves, his puppets, which most likely meant – and the Cardinal had long reflected upon this – that they did not have souls. The souls had been bred out of them.

So, preaching to the monks – instilling fear in them – was not only useless, it was impossible. Then, there was the Professor. Well, he was certainly an intelligent human; but he didn't scare easily. In fact, the Cardinal had the impression that the Professor did not fear death at all, his own death at least. The Professor loved life, that was clear; but, like an ancient stoic, he was loftily, proudly, indifferent to death. And, now that he thought his daughter was dead, the Professor had nothing to lose. No, the skeptical Professor was not an ideal congregation. Even chained, even naked, even covered in filth, even struck almost dumb with grief, he was intact; he was not as much fun as the Cardinal had hoped. Too bad …

Oh, well!

Down below, the generators chugged and chugged and chugged.

The Cardinal wondered whether he should transform himself back into the Spider-God now – or later. His fingers tapped on the platform railing.

Becoming a god, an instrument of the Dark Force, at one with Infinity and all its invisible power, was a voluptuous experience – better than sex; even better than torturing an innocent; better, even, than murdering an innocent. And it had been delightful to generate a spider leg in the twinkling of an eye, and to astonish the great Professor Thornhill. His intellect and his character were what made the Professor interesting.

The Cardinal fingered the rich fine linen of his vestment. He adjusted the Beretta, giving it a rakish tilt. Sensations, they were, pure physical sensations. Ah yes, the pleasures of the flesh – all will fade away and die, which is only just. Everything will be replaced by the pure Thrill of Absolute Evil.

The sparks cascading from the Crystal were delightfully festive.

Everything was proceeding magnificently. The generator was applying ever-increasing voltage to the Crystal. Soon – within hours – the planet Earth would explode, flying apart into fragments, probably creating a new asteroid belt, dark stones and dust hurtling around in space, dimly lit by the distant sun, how picturesque!

The Cardinal smiled. It was a benign world-encompassing smile. Satan had vouchsafed him visions of the consummation to come – of the planet shattered and breaking apart. And, in the moment of destruction, he would join Satan; he would be Satan and he would be Satan's Bride! The two would merge! This would truly be a marriage with himself, a consummation greatly to be desired – beyond death, beyond suffering; thus, he would enter absolute being and absolute power.

But first there were, in truth, a few minor obstacles. The she-devil was coming, with some of her accomplices, a pitiful handful of humans. Pathetic, really! She would certainly try to stop him, to interfere with the glorious moment of apotheosis. Who or what did she represent, this demon? That feeble, ridiculous old creature, God? Or an aspect of Satan? Or something else? Surely not Satan, for she was clearly an enemy of the Satanic Order of the Apocalypse

He wondered. Was it possible that the she-demon had caused Villa Mazana Nera to explode, killing all within? No, it was probably a side-effect of the earthquakes, an example of that beloved satanic tidbit called "collateral damage."

Well, Father Ottavio and the others were dispensable, everyone was dispensable. Only he was not dispensable – for he was Satan, he was one with the Evil Spirit. When the world perished, he would flourish. He would transcend all of this – in his apotheosis at the moment of the Apocalypse.

Already, he had become a god – the Spider-God.

But this was just the beginning!

It had been amusing – a lark – dealing with the men of the Presidential Guard. They were now dangling morsels of meat, embalmed, awaiting his pleasure. Only the Commander and two of his officers he had left alive, as witnesses. A crime is not truly a crime unless there is a witness. There is no joy in committing an abomination if no one knows of it, if no one recoils in horror and fear and disgust. Indeed, what possible use was God Himself, if not as a witness to human turpitude, a witness to His own failure? And did not God create humans, or so it is said, because, in his pathetic loneliness, He needed someone to recognize Him, to love Him? Humanity was meant to be a mirror. God was Narcissus. The creation of the universe was an exercise in – failed – self-love.

The Cardinal laughed. "God is an illusion, a false light that serves as a mere foil to the Divine Dark Force."

The glittering female demon, the she-devil, would be an even better witness to his triumph than Mohammed and his men, better even than Professor Thornhill.

She was a worthy opponent! And she would be the ideal sacrifice in Earth's final hour! She would kneel before him, naked, trembling in fear and sweating in adoration! She would be his pagan priestess. He would so enslave her that she must love him – and she would recoil in horror at the perversity of her slavish shameful love for him, and this would add to the pleasure – for both of them.

And then the end would come, and she, like all things mortal, would die. That was one scenario. Or, perhaps even better, he would reduce her to such pathetic impotence, that she would wither into extreme obscene old age, and die under his gaze, knowing that he had triumphed, that she had failed.

Standing on the platform, with the giant Crystal soaring up only a few feet behind him, he recalled his first groping toward knowledge of the sublime nature of cruelty. The illumination had come when he sacrificed a young friendless prostitute – truly an innocent girl, really – he had taken under his wing in order to prepare her for sacrifice. He became her trusted friend, her only friend. When she realized what he intended, the look in her eyes was one of pure horror, of innocence betrayed, utter devastation. That look was nectar to his satanic soul. In that moment he began to realize the full seduction of the Evil Dark Force.

When he stabbed her and silenced her, he became more than human; and as he bathed in her blood, he realized that his own strength came from Satan, from the Evil Dark Force, and from the ritual of sacrifice, which had to be repeated, over, and over, and over. And so, he became the leader of the Order of the Apocalypse. And so, he prepared to usher in the end of the world, the Satanic Rapture, which would lift him up – beyond space, beyond time, into Eternity!

My prayers, I think, were answered! And so, against all odds, we had landed. Mohammed and the two survivors of his force – Amin and Abdul – told us what had happened. As they were approaching the airport, a minefield exploded. Most of the armored cars were destroyed. Then it– It – appeared. "What was *it* and what did it do?" John asked.

"Well, it's unbelievable, I know." Mohammed wiped his forehead. "But, as I said, it was a giant spider, the size of a battle tank."

"A super-sized spider certainly sounds like the Cardinal." V glanced at me, then at Mohammed. "Well, go on."

Mohammed glanced at the two catsuit-clad women – V and Kate – obviously wondering what and who they were. He gazed at them, and then at John, and he continued. "At the same time, those men who had survived the initial explosions froze. It was as if they had become statues. Then some of them woke up and began to shoot each other. They acted like puppets. Mostly they killed each other. We fired at the spider, but it shot out these cables of glue, and captured or blocked the weapons. Then it laid down the cables of its web across the airfield and carried away many of the bodies of our men, wrapped in its threads. Some of the men, I think, were still alive. We followed it, shooting at it, but it seemed immune. It was as if there was a wall between us and it. For some reason it did not kill us, but it left us, for a time, lying on the ground, paralyzed."

"Then the paralysis ended," said Abdul.

"And so, we are here."

After listening to Mohammed's account, we decided to proceed immediately into the cave – straight into the lion's den, as it were. Our expedition would be led by V and John. We – V and John and Kate and U Pizzu and I – were the experts, it seemed.

Mohammed and his men agreed – after a rather heated discussion with John and V – to stay behind with Larssen and Satti and guard the airstrip and the plane; if we failed to return after a certain point, Mohammed would come to see what had happened to us and would report back to Larssen, to his President, and to the world.

But by then, of course, we would have failed. And by then, there would probably be no use in reporting to anybody. It would all be over.

We left the airstrip and entered a narrow rift – a long slit or crevice – in the granite escarpment. About two hundred yards into the canyon, we came to a large vertical stone – at least twenty-five feet tall – like something you would see at Stonehenge.

Beside the stone, or, rather, behind it, was an open door of what looked like stainless steel and that revealed the entry to a long, vaulted tunnel that had obviously been carved out of the granite using some sort of high-precision instruments. The walls and pavements were almost as smooth as glass. It reminded me of the aisle of a cathedral.

John, Kate, V and U Pizzu had their guns drawn. They all carried flashlights, though there were bright lights on in the cave, almost celebratory, with a glimmering silver glow of a sort I had never seen before. So, this, I thought, must be part of the alien technology V had described to me.

Yesterday – which now seems like another century – when I first heard V's tale about the cavern in the desert, I did not believe it; I thought the whole fairy-tale landscape was a product of her fevered demonic imagination, a fisherman's net of fantasy she had cast to capture and compromise my soul. And now I was in the midst of that landscape!

V was in the lead. I brought up the rear, looking, I must admit, anxiously around me. V had suggested I carry a gun. I said I preferred not to. *Thou shalt not kill.* As a priest I felt I should not, under any circumstances, carry a gun. I might, by accident, or out of necessity, be tempted to use it!

We walked on in silence. Then V stopped and raised her hand in warning. We came to a halt. Then V beckoned, and we went forward, toward where she was waiting for us.

I wondered at first what I was seeing. In front of V, further along the tunnel, the walls were coated with what looked like large baubles, glittering silver clusters, hanging from the walls, and made of cables of spider web. It seemed to me strange to hang festive decorations in such a forbidding and modernist place. Then I saw what the baubles were.

"Damn the Cardinal!" Kate whispered. "Damn him!"

"Fuck!" U Pizzu glanced at me. "Begging your pardon, Father."

I realized clearly what I was seeing: bodies, human bodies.

They were hanging, like Christmas-tree decorations, in cocoon-like bundles. Wrapped in bright silver gluey ribbon, they dangled from the walls, preserved, or temporarily embalmed, and partly mummified – or so it appeared.

Some had been eaten, or partly eaten – heads or limbs or parts of heads were missing. One skull, half consumed and tilted at a rakish angle, stared down at me – its one remaining eye bulging, bloodshot, and wide open.

"So, it eats people," said V. "The spider, I mean."

"Yes, these are Mohammed's men." John stared up at one of the bodies, and at the remnants of its uniform. A streak of what looked like fresh blood was splashed on the wall behind it; and a bright dribble of blood ran down one side of its cocoon.

"What is this spider?" John was staring up at the dead man. "This fellow, the half-eaten one, I met him once … in Iraq possibly, or Lebanon …"

V put her hand on John's shoulder. "I'm a shape-changer, to a certain extent, I mean, I have three versions, right?"

"Yes. But what's that got to do with …?"

"The Cardinal has become a shape-changer. The Crystal has many powers, and it opens onto many worlds. I think it can remodel human flesh, recombine biological forms, and perhaps even invent new ones. The Cardinal may have – accidentally, I suspect – triggered some of those mechanisms."

"I see."

Kate had stepped forward and was standing beside V. From behind, in the same warrior outfit, and with the same jet-black hair, they looked like twins, except that Kate's hair was longer. Kate turned to V. "You said it can remodel or create bodies?"

"Yes, Kate, it can, I'm almost certain. The Cardinal *is* the spider," V said, almost absently. She was examining the hanging bodies and the spidery cables and seemed to be talking to herself. "So, this spider, the Cardinal, shoots out a web or a thread and that's how he captures his prey. And then the spider, I mean, the Cardinal, comes crawling or hopping along to mummify or cocoon or eat it. The victim is a helpless morsel, dangling, pinioned. The spider opens its jaws – well, mandibles – and chomp, chomp, chomp … Hmm." V turned to Kate. "Yes, the Crystal can modify flesh, and invent new biological forms, I'm sure of it."

"It's pretty dangerous – isn't it – to go against the spider? But what if you changed into your demon form and …?"

"Yes, I could, darling Kate, I could. But I'm going to try to beat him in my human form, as a human being."

I was about to object. We certainly needed all the help we could get. If V was going to go mano a mano with a giant Cardinal-Spider she should do it as the demon. But then I decided not to. V would have her reasons. And I think, looking back on it, that, in an odd way, she felt she was fighting for humanity. So, she felt she should look like one of us – and *be* one of us.

"Is that wise?" John was checking his pistol's magazine. "What happens if he beats you?"

"I'll cheat. I'll revert to the other option."

"If you have time, Signorina," said U Pizzu.

"There is always time to become a she-devil, Marcello." V favored the Mafioso with what I can only describe as a shamelessly lascivious wink. The erotic energy between V and U Pizzu was palpable. It was as if she wanted to make love to "Marcello" right there. They were flirting with each other, like two over-excited, hormone-driven teenagers, and with freshly killed cadavers dangling all around us!

We continued on our way. So far, we had not met any opposition at all: no monks with guns, no gangsters, no giant spider.

V still appeared to be thinking out loud. "If the Crystal can create shape-changing powers in those who use it, I wonder if the shape-changer fully controls what he becomes."

V signaled that we should advance more cautiously; and we did so, crouching, watching. "I'm certain the Spider is the Cardinal. But another possibility," V whispered, "is that the spider has been created by the Crystal or brought here from somewhere else – or from some other time period."

Kate stopped and stared wide-eyed at V. "We really are going to have to rewrite the physics textbooks! And biology too!"

Finally – it had only been a few minutes at most, but it seemed to me to be an eternity – we reached the end of the tunnel. Before us stood the alien-built elevator that V had described. Its door was open and seemed to beckon. It was well-lit and looked friendly; but the tunnel continued past the elevator – and opened out onto what seemed to be a ledge overlooking a vast space, almost certainly, the heart of the cavern itself.

"Is it safe to use this elevator?" John poked at its door with the muzzle of his pistol. It was very futuristic, and extremely simple-looking. Suddenly, I felt how utterly astounding it was to be standing here – where Marcus the alien visitor had stood, more than two thousand five hundred years ago – with the same machinery facing us.

"No, it's too risky," said V. "Everything here is controlled by the Crystal. And we don't control the Crystal – nobody really controls it now, I think. Ambrosiano is almost certainly just poking at it. We'll have to climb down. The Cardinal and his monks already know we are here, that's for sure."

"So, what's the plan?" asked John.

"Okay." V crouched down and we squatted around her in a circle, like some ancient tribe planning a hunt, or kids plotting a game in the woods. She pointed. "Down that tunnel, there is an open ledge that overlooks the main cavern. It is opposite the Crystal. We'll go out onto the ledge and drop a cluster of smoke bombs and flash-flares into the cavern. Then I can leap and the rest of you can rappel down to the floor of the cavern. John and I will head across the cavern floor to the Crystal and its control panel. When we get there, I'll insert the key, our old friend, the Torelli Jewel, and take control of the Crystal and try to get her to stop the earthquakes and reverse whatever damage the Cardinal has done."

"Good," said John.

"Kate, you look for your father. I suspect he might be over to the right of the cavern, near the big platform to the right of the Crystal."

"Okay, thanks." Kate raised her eyebrows, obviously wondering how V could possibly know this. But there was no time for questions.

"And Marcello, you will be our outrider. Find a place to lie low and watch out for opportunities and use them."

"Fucking right, I'll use them. Begging your pardon, Father."

I made a gesture with my hand – a vague form of absolution, I suppose, sweeping away Marcello's sins. Old habits die hard.

"Thanks, love!" V blew U Pizzu a kiss, inclined her head, licked her lips, and fluttered her eyelashes. "Father," she said, turning to me, "you wait up on the ledge and watch over the cavern, and over us."

"So I shall – and my prayers will be with you, all of you!"

"As for me, I'm going to find my father and rescue him." Kate's jaw was set; she seemed oh so young! She was beautiful and determined, and, despite her martial skills and high intelligence, I felt that she was oh so vulnerable. *Child, child, child*, I thought. I felt a surge of love for this headstrong exquisite passionate creature, an incarnation of the best of womanhood, a warrior, an ancient Amazon come back to life. I had known Kate since she was born. If I were to have had a daughter, I would have wished her to be like Kate – generous to a fault, brave, impulsive, curious, beautiful, mischievous, and without I think a shred of vanity.

The meeting ended. Led by V and John, we headed into the new tunnel, and within a minute came out on the ledge overlooking the cavern.

The view took my breath away.

The cavern was so huge I was not sure I could see the other side. The arched roof went up far above us and was partially lost in darkness. And, there, opposite us, facing us, was the Crystal.

I was speechless. An enormous globe, the size I would say of a six-story building, seemed to float in a vast scaffold or lattice of black metal, probably steel or something like steel. This vast globe was humming gently, or so it seemed, and vibrating, delicately, slightly. Metal stairways and walkways snaked up the black metal latticework and a central platform was almost halfway up and had a rather larger stairway zigzagging up to it. That, I thought, must be the control platform. There were two cables from which spurted a cascade of sparks. So, it was true. The Cardinal was using electricity to poke at the Crystal. He was a child playing with the triggering device of a hydrogen bomb.

On the floor of the cavern, far below us, there were several generators huffing and puffing, one of them almost certainly causing the Niagara of sparks up on the platform. On our side of the cavern, only a few yards away, was a sort of primitive construction elevator – obviously human technology – a metal cage in an open metal framework tower – leading from our ledge down to the floor.

When we came out onto the ledge, V seemed to hesitate, to lose her bravado and energy. She looked around, frowned, and for what seemed an eternity she just stood there, expressionless, her arms hanging at her sides, as if paralyzed.

If V doubted, if V paused – and I had never seen her pause; I had never seen her doubt – then, well, what would become of us? A shadow passed over my spirit. Were we doomed? And with us, was the whole world doomed?

We stood there, silent, like dolls, like puppets. John too – no expression on his face. Kate had her hands on her hips, in a defiant pose, but she was as still as a statue. U Pizzu had taken a mauve handkerchief from his pocket and was holding it in front of his face as if he were about to wipe his forehead – but the action had been stopped, suspended in mid-gesture, like a film set to "pause."

Our minds, it seemed, were clouded – paralyzed. We were under the spell of the Evil Force. My heart stopped beating. The very presence of the Cardinal radiated evil. He was, I began to believe, an emanation of the Anti-Christ, the Evil Force of which V had spoken. On reflection, the Cardinal had become, I believe, a shaman, but an evil shaman; he was possessed; and he was channeling immense negative powers, evil powers, and he was wielding them like a weapon. V had said that the Crystal was a gateway. In tinkering with that gateway, the Cardinal had unleashed something much greater and more terrible than himself – and now that force, whatever it was, was darkening our spirits and paralyzing our bodies.

V seemed, for that long moment of stasis, vulnerable to that force of evil. I stood just behind her and prayed that God would give her strength and wisdom.

"It's not only the spider," V said, turning to John and suddenly sounding down-to-earth and practical. "The Cardinal may have been able to recruit monsters from every corner of the universe."

"Yes, but does he control them?" John was shaking his head as if chasing away mental cobwebs and waking from a bad dream.

"We'll see who controls what," said V, with a new note of determination in her voice. "The Cardinal is not the only trickster in town!"

"Are you okay, V?" Kate looked like a concerned sister.

"I'm fine, Kate." V put her arm around Kate, hugging her. "I was thinking and when I think, my dearest Kate, I become like that fellow Hamlet. I frown, I pout, I take on the pale cast of thought and the ashen pallor of melancholy." V turned toward me. There was, I saw, a joyous twinkle in her eye. She was clearly raring for a fight.

"I've never seen a challenge you couldn't meet, V." As John said this, I could see that he was still doubtful. This time V was not up against a serial killer, an arms dealer, or an evil dictator.

V's lips were moving, and I thought I could read what she was silently muttering: "Oh, Marcus, I call upon you in our hour of need! Oh, Marcus, hear my supplication, you, my guide, my teacher, my friend."

V is praying, I thought. *V is praying.*

I approve of prayer, of course, but I was not sure, in this case, that prayer was a good omen. And she was praying, not to God, but to her alien friend, her mentor and her savior. He had taught her how to be what she had become and what she would become. Any prayer, though, is perhaps better than none – and all prayers are, I think, addressed, however indirectly, to God. When we pray, we recognize our weakness, our mortality, our need – and so, even when we pray to other idols, to other beings, we recognize our need for the Almighty.

I silently whispered: *Amen.* So be it.

I glanced at U Pizzu, my erstwhile killer. He wiped his forehead, carefully folded the mauve handkerchief, and put it back in his vest pocket. He glanced at me. "God be with us all, Father."

"Amen," I said.

It gave me some comfort that we had come so far without any opposition; but this comfort was, almost certainly, illusory. I did not understand why Cardinal Ambrosiano had allowed us to get so close. He seemed to be totally indifferent to our invading his sanctum. Perhaps he was not even here? Perhaps he felt he was so powerful he could simply ignore us? Maybe he was dead.

V and John now tied rappel ropes to cleats that were conveniently there, at the edge of our platform-ledge. I wondered what they were usually used for.

The ropes were thrown over the edge, disappearing, down below.

V said, "Close your eyes! Now!"

We closed our eyes.

A huge flash imprinted itself on my eyelids.

Smoke bombs exploded.

And so, the attack began. God help us!

I opened my eyes. The cavern was filled with smoke. The Crystal was invisible, and the smoke was so dense I could hardly see my hand in front of my face. Next to me, V was a vague silhouette. "Goodbye, Father. Pray for us." She put her hand on my shoulder, gazed in my eyes for an instant, and leapt into the void.

John, Kate, and U Pizzu were scrambling over the edge, using ropes and hooks, rappelling their way down to the floor of the cavern far below.

I muttered to myself, "What are you doing here, Michael Patrick O'Bryan, you dusty old scholar, what are you doing, standing here, more or less blind in the smoke, lagging behind, a mere observer, unarmed, vulnerable – and, really, totally useless – what are you doing?"

I thought of my promise to God that I would redeem myself; *how, I wondered, was I going to redeem myself?* What could I do, now that the battle was engaged? A padre, on a battlefield, ministers to the wounded and dying – I hoped that there would be none of those, not on our side, at least.

I decided that I might climb a small distance down the elevator framework, if only to be closer to the action. I am pretty good at first aid, perhaps I could be of some help. Of course, I had no equipment. I am an amateur; and amateurs die.

Mist – there was suddenly a definite smell of sea mist. And the smoke that surrounded me was thickening on all sides. I could see at most three or four feet.

I stepped to the edge of the platform, knelt, and stared into the abyss – the nylon rappel ropes, anchored by the steel cleats, dangled, snaking down. Within a few feet, they disappeared into nothingness.

From far below came flashes – explosions – and shouts. The sounds echoed, magnified, and then were lost, and diminished, in the vast space of the invisible cavern. I stood up and leaned over the edge. Was I strong enough to climb down? At that moment, I heard a deep voice – a voice from the tomb – behind me.

"Father, Father O'Bryan!"

I turned.

There, lurking in the fog and smoke, just behind me – perhaps six feet away – was a shadowy hulk. Straining my eyes, I made out, all in black, a monk's habit, an enormous cowl, two huge arms, and massive putty-white hands clenched into fists. He was an exact replica of the giant who tried to assassinate the Pope, an exact replica of the monks in Villa Mazana Nera. The smoke cleared. He had the same baby-like features crowded together at the bottom of his face.

"Father O'Bryan." His voice came from the depths of Hell. I was overcome by fear and pity and awe – that such a creature should exist and be enslaved to the Cardinal and his diabolical schemes, was a horrible thought.

The monk raised one of his giant fists. It held a pistol aimed straight at my heart. I stared at the barrel, at that little round black hole out of which death so easily can come. I backed toward the edge of the precipice, feeling myself on the verge of toppling over. If I fell, I would not survive and then I would not be of much use to anyone.

Other monks, emerging out of the shadows, stood behind the first.

And so, we had walked into a trap – enemies behind us, and enemies in front of us.

The monk beckoned: *Come to me!*

With the pistol aimed at my heart, I had no choice.

I would buy time, I thought, I would buy time – but to what purpose I had no idea. The line between cowardice and calculation can be very thin, and, even with the best of intentions, one can so easily lose the honor and virtue and reputation of a lifetime in the blink of an eye.

I nodded and slowly began to walk toward what might well be my doom. What torture, I could not help wondering, would Cardinal Ambrosiano and his sadistic monks devise for a priest who was their sworn enemy?

CHAPTER 53 – KATE

Kate stepped to the edge of the ledge, and turned around, holding tight to the rappel cord. She took a deep breath, and leapt off the edge. She had never rappelled down such a smooth structure before; it was a long way and the bottom was invisible.

Arching her back and with her legs straight, she began to walk her way downwards, slowly at first, then more quickly. It suddenly occurred to her that Father O'Bryan's limp was gone! She hadn't seen him limp once; and he seemed much younger too! How had she not noticed? What was going on?

She pushed herself away from the wall, and bounced back, and leapt away again and bounced back, heading downward more quickly.

The wall was as smooth as stainless steel, and at certain points it had, she noticed, writing, or at least it looked like writing, engraved on it, something like classical Japanese hiragana, but she was sure it was not Japanese.

The surface was so smooth she had to be careful not to let her boots slip sideways. Keep the rhythm, she whispered, keep the precision. Bounce in, bounce out. Bounce in, bounce out.

The characters – if that's what they were – were written in vertical columns.

This was the moment she'd been waiting for; the moment she would find her father – and rescue him. Now, finally, she would redeem herself for having survived that terrible attack in Jerusalem when she'd knelt to tie that damned providential shoelace. Part of her died back there, four years ago, in Jerusalem. That part of her was being reborn. She knew that if she could save her father, she would truly come alive.

When she landed, her thick-soled boots touched down with almost a dance step on the cavern floor. She crouched down and glanced around. Her eyesight was now more than sharp; but in this smoky muck she could hardly see anything, just the silhouettes of V, of John, and of U Pizzu and the sheer steel wall that soared up behind them.

The smoke and mist swirled in closer. The smoke from the smoke bombs had been joined by some sort of wet mist. Poison? Poison gas? The moisture touched her skin. It felt, and smelled, like sea fog. Weird! They were hundreds of feet below the surface of an inland desert, more than a hundred miles from the sea.

"Kate," V was suddenly beside her. "You go that way! I think your father will be over there against the far wall of the cavern."

V disappeared. It was as if she had evaporated. John and U Pizzu had already headed off into the fog.

Kate sprinted off at an angle – into the whiteness of the sea fog, which was getting thicker by the second. She could smell fish, and hear waves. Vague lights shone in the dimness. It was impossible to tell if they were close or far away. An antique-looking electric generator surged up. Thick electrical cables snaked away along the cavern floor. Crouching down, and holding her automatic pistol ready, Kate angled further toward the right.

A metal stand towered above her. It supported a line of klieg lights, projecting a baleful white glare into the fog, like a row of pale misty suns. What a weird spooky place!

Ghostly figures surged up, then faded away. Kate wondered if the fog contained a hallucinogenic drug. During the black Mass at Villa Mazana Nera, the congregation had been under the effect of some sort of cocktail of hallucinogens. Was this mist a drug? She saw several enormous monks like those in Villa Mazana. She saw tentacles like those of a giant octopus. The vision brought back a vague thought of some hallucinatory dream she had had while drugged in the Villa, waiting to be sacrificed. Yes, she rememberd! An overfriendly, ink-squirting octopus who tried to couple with her. She saw a slender ballerina in a crimson tutu swirling around on tiptoe. Each time, as she approached, the apparition faded. It was her imagination being stimulated, or captured, she was sure of it. There was nothing there. These were mind tricks played by the Cardinal or the Crystal. She would ignore them.

A shiny black metal framework surged out of the mist: it was the cradle that held the Crystal, a massive, wall-like latticework that soared up, and up, and out of sight. Kate caught a glimpse of a vast silver shimmering curve rising high above her – the Crystal!

She turned right; she would skirt along close to the Crystal, sheltering under the latticework wall. The fog was thicker. A foghorn, mournful and far away, echoed. More sounds and smells of the sea – very strange!

Running, crouching, running, crouching, swinging her pistol left and right, she darted along the base of the Crystal, pausing at each pillar of the metal lattice. Her heart was pounding. Could she do this? Whatever "this" turned out to be. Target practice and martial arts exercises were one thing; but here she was moving into unknown territory.

A massive pillar soared up; it rose up into the fog, and soared out of sight. It was the last pillar. She had come to the end of the Crystal's cradle. From here on, she would be out in the open, exposed to whatever danger lurked ahead. She took a deep breath – nothing ventured, nothing gained.

Attached to the last column was a black cable; it snaked out of the fog from somewhere on the floor of the cavern, and wound its way up the pillar, toward the Crystal. From far above, sparks showered down. It must be the cable that was poking the Crystal with those nasty electric shocks V had talked about. Kate squatted down, breathless; sheltering behind the column, she peeked out to see what lay beyond.

To her left, half-obscured by the low drifting banks of fog and elevated about two feet off the floor of the cavern was an open platform. It stretched off to some dark, infinitely distant horizon. She squinted, trying to see what lay above the fog bank. In the velvety blackness, she caught a glimpse of what looked like stars. But the twinkling lights couldn't be stars! They were at least twelve hundred feet underground! The whole platform looked, and felt, like a giant stage in a theater.

A bolt of lightning flashed through the fog; then came a sizzling sound, another flash, and thunder.

Kate sniffed the air, thinking of the rolling thunder of midsummer storms that used to make their way across the countryside outside Boston, sharp flashes of lightning in the distance, steel-dark clouds piling up, a feeling of electric suspense in the air.

The Crystal's hum went up an octave. Kate looked up. The Crystal was moving! Rising, then settling back down, as if it had been lifted and then dropped by an invisible ocean wave.

A choking, huffing puffing suddenly sputtered into life to her right. Kate turned. Another electric generator, with another cable attached to the Crystal. Leaning over the generator was the shadow of one of those ghastly monks; the shadow faded, leaving only the generator.

A bolt of lightning flashed. The fog pressed closer. Kate's world shrank. Her own hand – gloved in black – was a vague silhouette. The wheezing generator faded; but she could hear it – chug, chug, chug …

The platform to her left looked ominous and spooky. Its lower reaches were heavily veiled in fog. Kate couldn't see the other side, but its vaulted ceiling receded into darkness – silky black. Was it a space-time machine?

The void suddenly beckoned. *Come, Kate, come! Plunge into infinity, Kate, plunge! Take a leap toward the stars! You know you want to!*

Giddiness! Sweat trickled down her spine. The inside of the bodysuit was slimy. Around her everything was eerily calm, just the bolts of lightning, high above, and the humming Crystal, dreamy, almost sleepy. Even the generators seemed to have fallen silent. It was weird: they were attacking the place and nothing was happening. No enemies, no nothing …

The fog cleared. Kate glanced up. An enormous arch rose up against one side of the cavern and, nested right next to the arch, at the bottom, was a cage with bars.

She saw him – her father!

He was inside the cage. Could it really be him?

It was at least seventy yards away, but it certainly looked like dad, sitting at what looked like a bank of computers. Why was he sitting like that, so calm? It looked like he was naked too …

For a horrible moment, Kate thought that her father was dead, propped up, and left there by the Cardinal. Maybe this wasn't her dad. Maybe it was a trophy, like those mummified remains in the tunnel, like the skulls and statues in Villa Mazana Nera; maybe she was looking at a body cast, a *memento mori*.

The hell with it!

She sprinted across the open space. Strings of fog began to ooze out of the dark depths of the platform.

"Daddy!" she shouted.

"Kate!" he shouted back; but he didn't get up. "My God, is that you, Kate?"

"It's me!"

"You're alive!"

"*You're* alive!"

Kate was breathless with excitement. She saw why her father had not moved. He was chained to his desk and chair. "Oh, Daddy!"

"Kate! I thought you were …"

"Dead? No, Daddy, I'm here. It's me!"

"But how? By what miracle …?"

"It's a long story, Daddy."

"Kate. Be careful, there are enemies everywhere – the Cardinal is stark raving mad, and there are monks, strange creatures, they –"

"I'm going to get you out of there, Daddy." Kate stared at the lock on the cage. It was a complicated lock, built into the cage door, not the sort you could shoot off.

"Kate! Watch out!"

Kate turned. Damnation! There were four of them – those damned monks! In their black habits, giant cowls, with their small squished-up features, they were exactly like the ones in the villa. Icy fear shot through her veins. She was back in the villa, naked, chained, paralyzed, manacled to the altar of granite, about to be stabbed, to have her chest torn open, her heart ripped from her chest. The fog rose again. It weaved itself around the advancing monks. As they came closer, the fog thickened. They had their weapons drawn – machine pistols.

Kate turned back to her father. "Here," she whispered. She went to the bars of the cage and tossed him a combat knife, handle first. It landed on the desk, hardly making a sound, just within reach of his chained hands. Roger grabbed it and covered it with his forearm.

"Kate, be careful, run Kate!"

Kate turned to face the monks. Her eyes blazed. "Don't come any closer! Get back! Stay away! I'll shoot! I really will!"

The monks lumbered forward. Their black robes drifted dreamily around them. The cowls shadowed their faces. The fog clung to everything.

As the monks advanced, they appeared less and less real. They were monsters from a nightmare. Kate felt she knew them well. They were her familiars, they were the evil spirits who had whispered into her ears – they were exact replicas of Brother Basilisk.

"Stay back." Kate tightened her finger on the trigger. "Stay back!"

"Sacrifice," whispered the first of the monks. His obscene breath – a stench of rotten meat – reached through the air – touched Kate's cheeks.

"Sacrilege," whispered another.

"Satan has come – for you. He has come," whispered the third.

"Kate!" said her father. "Go, Kate! Hide if you can."

"You are the sacrifice," whispered the first monk. "You, my beauteous Kate, are the chosen one. You are the Goddess."

Roger was torn between horror and joy. Kate was alive, but she was in mortal danger. Then a sudden thought occurred. *Was this really Kate?* She glowed with supernatural energy and health. She wasn't wearing glasses; her hair was down, free-flowing, like in the old days. She was outfitted like a comic book warrior. She shone brightly, glossy and glamorous, as if she'd just stepped out of a video game. Was she a ghost, or a robot, or a hallucination, a sophisticated hologram? Could this beautiful apparition be some creation of the Cardinal's, specifically designed to torture him? Such a cruel and elaborate deception would be perfectly in the Cardinal's style. The real Kate, *his* Kate, couldn't be alive! Roger had seen the sacrificial photographs – though of course photographs could be …

The four monks plodded toward Kate, in a deadly parody of a religious procession. A rhythmic religious chant rose from some invisible source that seemed under the cavern. Savage drums began to beat, and a deep chorus of tortured, clamoring voices rose from some unearthly tomb – a chorus of the damned, a chorus of the dead!

"Sacrifice the Goddess," chanted the first monk. His mouth twisted in a contorted sadistic grin.

"Sacrifice!" echoed the second monk.

"Sacrifice!" echoed the third monk.

"Sacrifice the Goddess!" echoed the fourth monk.

Kate pulled the trigger.

The first monk stopped, looked down, put one giant hand to his chest, opened his tiny mouth, emitted a round puff of what looked like smoke, and slowly folded in on himself, collapsing without a sound.

The three remaining monks charged at Kate. They flew. Kate leapt aside, crouched down, shot one monk in midair, and shot the other just as he landed. The two bodies rolled over, flip-flopped, then lay still, sprawled on the ground, their limbs outstretched.

The last surviving monk had leapt beyond Kate. She swiveled around to face him. He let go of his weapon. It fell in slow motion and made no sound when it hit the ground. He stretched his hands out, palms open, toward her, as if to show her that he had nothing to hide, no ill intent. His mouth twisted upwards at the edges. The folds of fat around his eyes, too, were twisted upwards, making shadowy wrinkles. It was the cartoon image of a smile. The fog around him seeped up from the ground; everywhere it was thickening. Kate hesitated, her back now to the Crystal.

The monk leapt. She shot him, in mid-air, point-blank between the eyes. He somersaulted down, rolled over, and lay still, face down, apparently dead. This was too easy; something was wrong. It must be a trap.

"Kate!" her father shouted. "Kate, watch out!"

Out of the thickening fog, another monk appeared. This creature was also aiming a machine pistol straight at Kate. She swung toward him, her finger about to press the trigger …

Suddenly, with a look of horror, the monk dropped his pistol and ran, disappearing into the fog.

Kate stood, puzzled, then crouched down, swinging the gun in a slow arc, prepared. Surely, they were going to come after her. It had been all too easy.

"Kate!" her father shouted again. "Kate, watch out!"

Out of the corner of her eye, Kate glimpsed a shadow – it raced out of the bank of fog, from the platform, from under the mysterious canopy of stars that suddenly reappeared above the fog in full celestial glory.

Kate spun around, her trigger finger twitching. The shadow, the thing coming out of the fog, was a giant tentacle! From her drugged nightmare! It was something a giant octopus or a squid would possess. But – this tentacle was huge – and it had eyes!

Eyes!

Jesus!

The tentacle flickered its way, slapping back and forth, groping toward her; at the very end, the tentacle was thin – maybe an inch in diameter – but it got thicker farther from the end, where it was at least two feet in diameter.

Kate opened fire. She emptied her pistol into the tentacle. She had one last bullet; she fired again. Bullets made no difference.

Flashes of lightning lit up huge silhouettes of monstrous creatures moving in the depths of the fog, claws, tentacles, an ocean of waving tentacles.

"Kate!" her father shouted. "Kate! Run, Kate, just run!"

The tentacle whipped forward in one sudden motion and slapped itself around Kate's ankle, jerking her legs from under her. Kate tried to scramble to her feet, but couldn't regain her footing. Her boots slipped; her heels couldn't get a grip. She was being dragged by the tentacle – kicking, grappling, struggling.

"Let go, damn you!"

Faster and faster, the tentacle dragged her. She bounced, she kicked, she wiggled, she squirmed, she fought. She couldn't free herself. She was hauled and flipped up onto the spooky platform, and then dragged across it, toward the depths of the fog bank and toward the infinite black field of stars.

She twisted and kicked. She jammed another magazine into the pistol and emptied the cartridge into the tentacle. She swore under her breath. It didn't matter how many bullets she shot – nothing worked. Was it alive or was it a machine?

As it dragged her deeper into the fog, she unsheathed the machete V had given her, twisted around and hacked at the tentacle. The machete made no impression. She hacked and hacked – nothing, not a dint, not a dent, not a scar.

The fog was so thick now, she could hardly see anything. Far away, lost in the fog, her father shouted – "Kate! Kate! Kate!"

She twirled around, dropped the machete and kicked hard. The tentacle, surprised perhaps, let go. She was free. Knees pumping, elbows pumping, she pushed herself backward on her butt, the heels of her boots sending up sparks on the pavement.

The giant tentacle groped, hovering in the air, as if it were thinking, then it plunged. Kate rolled. The tentacle missed, thudding against the platform. It whirled around, tried again, and missed again. But then, with a whiplash movement, it caught Kate by the ankle – *again!*

She doubled up, twisting forward and grabbing at the tentacle, trying to tear herself free. She got the slender end of the tentacle with both hands, she tugged, she pushed; it was like rubber; it was slippery, slimy – and alive.

"Damn it!"

Suddenly the tentacle's skin went gooey; it exuded a thick transparent liquid. Her hands were stuck. She tried to slip out of her gloves, now glued to the tentacle, but the gloves seemed to be glued to her. *Damn it!*

She squirmed and swore. She wouldn't panic. No, she wouldn't panic! The tentacle was sweating some sort of super-glue; it was going to suck her into its skin! It was going to absorb her! *Yuk!* Her ankle and one hand were merging, dissolving, melting into the tentacle. Doubled over, she tugged and tugged! She was wrist deep, stuck in the thing. She was going to be absorbed, turned into a vegetable or maybe merely a piece of this thing's flesh, a skeletal remnant of herself, a melted husk of herself, forever a prisoner, buried in an alien body.

Another tentacle flew out of the fog. It was slender as a ribbon. It seized Kate's free arm and spun itself around, enclosing her arm entirely in a vice-like, deep, gluey grip, paralyzing the arm. It went numb, and no longer seemed to be part of her body.

By now, the tentacles were everywhere. Another, then another – all probing, poking, testing, ripping at her catsuit – though the catsuit seemed to resist every probe, every prick – all wrapping themselves around her arms, her legs, her waist, her neck.

Kate kicked, squirmed, pushed, wiggled, and punched – nothing made the slightest impression. Dozens of tentacles, large and small, enclosed her. She was being eaten alive, melted into this alien flesh, and she was being pulled toward the darkness – and toward an infinity of stars.

A thick gooey tentacle wrapped itself around her eyes, pressed in on her eyeballs – pure burning liquid, probing for her mind. She was blind.

Kate screamed, "Daddy!"

"Daddy!" the scream echoed. "Daddy!" Then it faded and was gone.

Peering into the deadly fog, Roger screamed, "Kate!"

The fog thinned. Kate was gone. There was no trace of her; or that she had ever existed, except her pistol and machete, which lay on the floor of the platform. Were they hers? Had she ever been there?

My God! Roger slumped; his world had been destroyed, utterly destroyed, his last hope dashed.

CHAPTER 54 – JOHN

John and V advanced through smoke and fog toward the Crystal. Three monks materialized. John shot all three down in as many seconds.

More appeared. John shot them too. Some of the monks, instead of falling down, just evaporated into the mist. The bullets went right through them.

"Damn it!" John peered at the dissolving bodies.

"Phantoms," said V. "Either the Cardinal or the Crystal – or both – are projecting images, playing mind games, so we won't know the difference between what is real and what isn't."

"Like mirrors in a fairground funhouse." Off to the right John could see a line of lights and there was the sound of a generator chugging.

"Some funhouse!" V shot two more monks. They fell with a muffled thump. "Now, are those real or fake?"

The shots made a strange muffled sound, as if everything was being heard from far away. The fog closed in. V glanced at her hand – a vague, misty silhouette. She could barely see John.

A generator loomed up out of the fog, overturned and lying on its side – good cover.

John and V took shelter. More monks advanced out of the thickening fog; they came from every direction, a phantasmagoria of monks, dozens, maybe hundreds, a ghostly procession, an army of shadows.

John shot four more. They fell down, making the same strange imploding, muffled sound. "They must manufacture these things on an assembly line."

V took aim at three more. "The Order has long been interested in breeding. I think they experimented and created these … creatures."

She shot one, then two, then three.

"Why don't they defend themselves? Damn it!" John shot another; it folded up and faded away.

"I think most of these monks – maybe all of them – are hallucinations, decoys. This is tiresome! I'm going to climb right up the latticework and find the Cardinal, and if he's not there, I'll take control of the Crystal. I really don't know what game the Cardinal is playing."

A giant monk surged up out of the mist, a huge hulk. John shouted, "Watch out, V!" and pumped three bullets into the monk. But the monk seemed not to notice. The bullets had no effect.

As V turned, the monk shot her in the chest – a series of ringing shots – five of them. These sounded *real*.

John watched with horror. V doubled up and folded in on herself, coughing, gasping, spasms, it was a sickening cough, as if she were retching her guts out.

When they entered her chest, V felt the red-hot bullets burn their way through her lungs, smash close by her heart. In that instant, she knew: These were no ordinary bullets. It was a sensation she had felt only once – centuries ago – at the point of an alchemist's sword, in Seville, in 1492. That had been a close call!

These were bullets containing silver nitrate and lead and laced with the secret formula.

They knew ...

How had they learned this ...?

The secret formula, her Achilles' heel ...

V was on her knees, coughing, retching. Still, she managed to empty her pistol into the monk. He strolled forward until he was almost on top of her. Then he toppled slowly and fell on his side at her feet. "She-devil, you will die," he whispered. "She-devil, you are dying already." He spoke no more, his face collapsing in on itself, like a deflating balloon.

Three more monks rushed forward. John shot them. They didn't stop. One slammed into him. Even with John's strength and special training, the fight was unequal. The monk had superhuman strength and seemed immune to pain, indifferent to blows. The other two monks held John while the giant monk pummeled him.

John struggled. His strength was unequal to the task. He whispered. "I'm sorry, V!"

V lay on the ground, only half-conscious. "John," she murmured. Her voice faded, her eyes clouded over. V was dying.

It couldn't be!

John kicked one of the monks in the crotch. There seemed to be nothing there – no effect whatsoever! He twisted, freed his arms, and pulled out a knife and slashed one of the monks across the arms and then across the face.

Blood flowed, black blood, blood thick like treacle; the monk didn't seem to notice. Again, seized and held, pinned down by huge hands, John kicked and squirmed, but the giant arms crushed him in a deadly embrace. John kicked, and kicked, and kicked …

A monk smashed him over the head with a steel truncheon. John felt the blood gush down the side of his face, warm and sticky; it got in his eyes; everything went dark. Then there was nothing.

CHAPTER 55 – V

V's eyes were open.

At least it *felt* like she could see.

Or was she blind – was all that she saw a mere hallucination?

John was nowhere to be seen; what had they done with him?

V lay on the floor of the cavern next to the monk she had killed. She had been determined to fight this battle as a human.

But now she must change into demon form. She had to regain her strength and begin the fight again.

She closed her eyes, concentrated, and willed the morph. Nothing happened. The silver nitrate was coursing through her veins. It was a race against time. She tried again. *Nothing!* Her strength was fading; she tried again. *Nothing!* She was too weak to turn demon. She had waited too long! Her pride, her hubris, had proved to be her downfall! When would she ever learn!

After all these centuries, she was going to die. She was going to fail at her most sacred task. This could not be! Her lips moved. Give me my fangs, my claws, my reptilian armor, and I'll …

Give me strength, oh, please. If Father O'Bryan's God is listening, then I ask you, God, to give me strength, soulless unbelieving demon and predator-killer that I am! Give me strength so I can fight for those you love! If the gods of my pantheon are listening – Ba'al, Asherah, come to my aid in this, my hour of need!

She struggled to her knees. Vertigo. She toppled sideways, curled up on the cavern floor. Weakness paralyzed her flesh, her muscles dissolved, a haze drowned her mind. She could not let this happen. But it *was* happening! Her willpower evaporated, everything sank into an enervating, drifting blackness. She lay there, semi-conscious; even thinking had become impossible.

"Oh, Marcus!" Her eyes were losing their focus. "I have failed you, Marcus, I've failed humanity; I've failed our lonely, lovely, little sky-island."

Another monk surged out of the fog and knelt by his dead brother and put his hand on the monk's forehead. "Go to Satan in hate, go in hate, brother!"

The monk stared down at V. "She-devil, now you will die for your sins; and you will die slowly!" He lifted V up, cradled in his arms, as if she weighed no more than a feather. He slung her over his shoulder and carried her into a side passage leading out of the cavern. "The Cardinal will hear your confession before you die. He will come to you, she-devil."

V moved her lips. Her throat was dry, her lips parched and chapped; her heart pumped desperately. She could not utter a word. She was only vaguely aware of where she was and what was happening to her.

The monk opened a cell door, and the thick metal bars swung away.

V lolled, loose-limbed, like a broken doll over his shoulder

"So, priest … here she is." The monk's voice echoed like thunder. It was the voice of Ba'al the thunder god V had known when she was a little girl being led up the stairs in the temple of Ba'al to witness her first child sacrifice.

V's head hung loose. Her temples throbbed. She blinked – vague silhouettes, vague shapes, ah yes … the good Father, the good Father …What was his name?

Father O'Bryan was sitting on the ground, with his back against a wall. In the center of the chapel-shaped cell was a low block of black granite, perhaps three feet off the ground, with manacles attached to its shining polished surface, and runnels to catch and channel spilt blood, an altar, like the altar in the underground chapel at Villa Mazana Nera.

"Here is your whore, priest. Here is your demon." The monk laid V on the ground, unbuckled her backpack, and threw it in a corner.

The monk knelt and opened V's belt. He pulled it and all the weapons away. He unzipped the catsuit and slipped V out of it. He was almost gentle with her, lasciviously stroking her sides, her ribcage, fondling her breasts – his doll, his plaything. He licked his lips. Dark saliva drooled from the corners of his mouth.

V was naked. The monk picked her up. Her head dangled back, as if her neck had been broken, arms and legs awry. She groaned. He laid the limp semiconscious body on the block of granite, positioned her, and then attached the manacles to her ankles and wrists, and locked them shut with a click.

"Your demon whore is dying, priest."

Father O'Bryan stood up and approached the altar. He looked down on his very own demon. Yes, it was true – she was dying. V was semi-conscious, she was delirious. Spasms shook her body. White foam and streams of bloody saliva bubbled from her lips.

The monk stared at her. He ran his hand along her side. "She will die slowly, priest. It will be a long agony, very long, and it will be a good and fitting punishment. She has killed many of my brothers. She is a demon and she must die. She will know with extreme bitterness that all she has striven for was in vain; she will know that she has lost her final battle, that she has betrayed her trust and her faith. Minister to her, priest, if you can, you love her so. Your religion and hers will die with her and with you. All you believers in the false God will perish in fire and brimstone. The Cardinal will come to hear her confession – in which he will take much delight – and then he will hear your confession – and that too will give him great pleasure. And then your whore – reduced to an impotent, aged crone – will die and you will die. Both of you will be truly dead. You will not rise again.

The monk picked up V's backpack, and equipment, and clothing and walked out of the cave, locking the door of the cell behind him and leaving the equipment and backpack, outside the cell, in a pile against the tunnel wall.

Left alone to watch V die, Father O'Bryan leaned over her. "V?"

She did not answer.

Dark circles were spreading under her eyes; her skin was blotched chalky-pale; her lips were white and chapped and flecked with specks of dry spittle and bubbling foam. A trickle of blood drooled from the side of her mouth.

"V?"

There was no answer. Father O'Bryan looked up at the vaults of stone. Was there no salvation? He took a deep breath and looked down at V. More chalky foam bubbled from her mouth. Pulsing blue veins emerged under the semi-transparent skin. Wrinkles appeared, crevices.

"V?"

Her eyes blinked, blindly. It was as if she were trying to focus, trying to escape from the veil of collapsing flesh that she had become.

"V?"

"Father?"

"Yes, V. I'm here."

"Father …" She made an immense effort. "Father, you can help me. You can help us! But for this you must make the supreme sacrifice."

"What sacrifice, V? I will do anything."

V could hardly speak. Her strength was fading, the dying light of a cooling ember. The blue veins under her skin were ramifying, spreading, throbbing; her eyes clouded to white, irises and pupils disappearing into blind whiteness. Before his eyes, she was becoming a cadaver. Father O'Bryan leaned closer and closer.

"... the ultimate sacrifice, Father ..." Her voice was just a whisper.

"What sacrifice, my child?" Father O'Bryan leaned closer.

"To save, to redeem the world, Father ..."

"Yes, yes! V, what must I do?"

V was chalky, pasty white, her eyes were shining, pure blind white, her lips dusty, ghostly, and paper thin; her hair was turning white, thinning, falling out, and falling away, mere dust.

Father O'Bryan knew he should recoil in horror. But all he felt was pity – and love, intense, aching, impossible love. V coughed. Thick white drool dripped from the corners of her mouth. Foam bubbled on her tongue, and her tongue, he saw, was turning black. There was not much time. In a few minutes or even less, V would be nothing but a handful of dust.

"What must I do, my child?"

V coughed, her blind chalk-white eyes staring blindly. In a slurred voice that was barely audible, she whispered, "Your soul, Father. You must sacrifice your eternal soul. You must give me the gift of your soul."

"My soul?" Father O'Bryan's heart sank; his breath failed; he swirled down into a nameless abyss. "My soul?"

"Your soul, Father." V's voice came from an infinite and receding depth.

"My soul," Father O'Bryan repeated stupidly and in horror, as he leaned even closer to her lips, to catch her quickly fading words – and, in that instant, he saw that her teeth had become bright pointed fangs and that her manacled hands were no longer hands, but very long, razor-sharp, curved claws. The blank white eyes flared with white light, searing his mind. He couldn't move; he was paralyzed.

"Oh, my God, my God, have mercy upon me!"

Father O'Bryan swooned. He was about to die. And he was going to lose what was even more precious than life – his eternal soul, the one great gift from God that, once lost, can never be regained!

He heard V's voice. "Now, Father, now! This is what you must do!" He felt a claw slash at him and ...

The rest was silence, darkness – nothing.

CHAPTER 56 – U PIZZU

When they'd rappelled down to the floor of the cavern, U Pizzu had immediately disappeared, something U Pizzu did very well. It was one of his many talents; he was quite proud of it.

Once, long ago, when some murderous upstart Mafia rivals from the town of Agrigento were chasing him, and U Pizzu was still a young man, he had disappeared from Sicily entirely. He simply ceased to exist. In fact, he spent six months living in a Buddhist monastery in Kyoto. Then, while things cooled down, he worked for about nine months as a fisherman in Cuba, and for five weeks he sold flowers from the back of a rusty white Chevy van in Portland, Oregon, where he had a deep tan, a full beard and bushy, droopy moustache, and was known to be an eccentric pacifist deaf-mute originally from New Orleans, a traumatized war veteran, who had been wounded and driven half-mad from serving as a sniper in one of the many wars of the Middle East. Disappearing was a useful art, particularly if you were a dead man walking …

So, as he considered the options, while getting ready to rappel down into the cavern, U Pizzu had been thinking:

… Thing was, if he could get into that big metal latticework that surrounded the Crystal, then he could climb up and ambush any maniac monks who'd be lurking around – and maybe he could get to the control panel up there on the face of the Crystal, kill the Cardinal or whoever else stood in the way, then Signorina V could mosey along and insert the key into the keyhole and take over the Crystal – and save the world – and business would continue as usual!

Once on the floor of the cavern, he split from the others as fast as he could, darting off into the smoke and fog, a world of white blindness and weird muffled sounds that came from God only knew where.

Now, how long later it was hard to tell – time seemed to U Pizzu to be fucking cockeyed in this damned alien cavern; he had the impression his wrist watch was running slow, then fast, then slow, then fast –he was perched high up in the framework cradle of the Crystal, listening to distant muffled shots. The world down here was more unreal than in that *Alice in Wonderland* that Maria Grazia had insisted once on reading to him.

He had expected V and John to be up on the control platform by now. But they had disappeared. That was not good. And he had heard lots of shots – and then silence. That was not good either.

At one point the Crystal seemed to hiccup. It bounced up and down, very slightly, maybe only a yard or so, in its cradle. The fucking thing was as free as a wild basketball. It could probably take off and jet out of there anytime, or it could roll over and fucking well crush everything and everybody.

A bit later, through the fog – now curling up around him – U Pizzu had seen giant tentacles, as if a huge squid or octopus had escaped from some fucking super-aquarium and was flailing wild in the cavern. He'd heard shots, and Kate screamed something like "Daddy!"

He was tempted to leap down from the framework, rush over and try to save the kid. In fact, he would have gone to her rescue, but he reflected that he'd better save himself for the main battle: he was gonna be needed, that was for fucking sure. This little picnic was not a fucking cakewalk! After a few seconds of screams and shouts and shots, it looked like Kate was dead or gone or eaten or turned into stone or whatever the fuck those fucking evil tentacles did. It was too bad, a fucking tragedy! She was a great kid, brave, spunky, sharp, and a real beauty! Reminded him of Adrianna, she did.

U Pizzu swore under his breath. This thing had to be ended. The Cardinal was evil, no fucking doubt about it. Gaetano Larione had been on the mark! Oh, Gaetano, if I could bring you back – and if I could bring back that beautiful young blonde, the bait – I fucking well would, old pal! I'd bring back the both of you and I'd bring back Kate – and we'd all sit down to some pasta on the beach and good wine – and I'd show you all a fucking good time!

He thought again of Kate. Just thinking of her made his blood boil. I'm gonna kill the fucking Cardinal, I'm gonna disembowel the old monster, real slow; I'm gonna roast his flesh with him still alive; I'm gonna break every fucking bone in his fucking body; I'm gonna fucking well gouge out his eyes!

Okay, Pizzu, calm down!

He wished V would hurry up and take on the Cardinal. He somehow had the idea that the Crystal was nervous too and wanted to be rescued from that traitorous old fart. Those electric shocks were probably a fucking pain in the ass for the Crystal.

The fog cleared and – oh, oh, there he was – the Cardinal himself, up on the control platform. Where the fuck had he come from? What the fuck was he doing? He was dressed in a long flowing robe and had a sort of bib on, which looked like it was scarlet, and a weird hat of some kind. He was truly doing the Cardinal thing, big time! All dressed up and ready to party! The old fucker was a real joker, a shamanistic trickster, an ambiguous clown, no doubt about it! And he would have a whole sting of fucking dishonest cards up his sleeve. So, U Pizzu, my man, look out …

U Pizzu was tempted to take a potshot at the Cardinal right there and then – but, no, it was better to wait for the right moment.

Suddenly the Crystal rumbled. It hiccupped, rose out of its cradle, then settled down. The whole latticework creaked and swayed.

"Fuck, Crystal, you scared the shit out of me," muttered U Pizzu, glancing up and feeling, for once, awestruck. "You know something, Crystal, this universe we live in, well, Crystal, it's fucking mysterious! You know that? And I know these clowns are fucking with you, Crystal, but we're gonna put a stop to that, Crystal, you bet your life on it! You just hold on there, Crystal, the cavalry is galloping to the rescue!"

CHAPTER 57 – THE CARDINAL

Cardinal Ambrosiano had seen what had come to pass; and he had seen that it was good.

That impudent girl Kate had been devoured. She was no more. She had evaded sacrifice the first time, but not this time. The Evil Force had gathered her up and accepted her as sacred flesh – a choice morsel indeed, chewed, digested, and – *poof!* – gone. Now, if her spirit survived, she would be one of Satan's minions, a delicious sex slave for all eternity, in the Cardinal's and Satan's infernal harem in the Satanic Kingdom.

Father O'Bryan was a prisoner, as was V's sidekick warrior, John somebody or something. They were all so pathetic!

Professor Thornhill had been tamed; and, above all, the she-demon herself had been poisoned and was dying, visibly withering away! Oh! Hallelujah! Praise be to Satan! All praise!

The Cardinal bared his teeth in what would, in an ordinary mortal, pass for a grin. He must go down and take the she-demon's confession; but only when she had been reduced to a skeletal mass of skin and bones and helpless ancient ugliness – her death process would slow down and stop, just at the end, leaving her withered and impotent, a hideous toothless, bald hag, ugliness itself, so he could savor his victory – and exalt in her fall. Her humiliation and that of Father O'Bryan would be complete! All the Cardinal's enemies had been vanquished, and he fully intended to enjoy his last moments on this pitiful Earth before he transcended it all and became one with Satan!

The Cardinal hummed a happy little tune he had picked up somewhere many years ago; and, by remote control he gave orders to the generator to add several more volts to the energy pricking the Crystal. The lights on the Crystal's control panel glowed green and then turquoise and then a deep blue.

The Cardinal had no idea what the colors meant or how the control panel worked, or what the Crystal was capable of. He did know – or presumed – that more energy would make the Crystal more active, and thus cause more damage, and that when he applied enough energy the Crystal would rip the world apart. Of that he was sure.

It was amusing, it really was!

To hold such power in the palm of his hand.

Awesome!

The Cardinal went to the edge of the control platform, leaned on the metal railing, and gazed upon his kingdom. On the floor of the vast cavern, the monks who had sacrificed themselves for him lay dead, spread-eagled, belly down, or curled up sideways, fetus-style. Children they had always been, and children they would forever remain. Oh, my sons, you were born to serve and so you have!

And now he would go and watch the she-devil die; he would have the pleasure of seeing her fall apart and disintegrate into dust and ashes! He would exult in his victory – even more since he would see defeat written in her faded empty, almost lifeless eyes! Utter defeat would be branded on her soul.

Out of the corner of his eye, he glimpsed something.

A ghost!

"What!" The Cardinal started back, wrapping his vestments – his full regalia – closer about him. It could not be! He rubbed his eyes. Oh, Satan! This was not an illusion!

Down below, striding across the floor of the cavern, coming straight toward the Crystal, with wraiths of mist swirling around her legs, there she was – the loathsome she-demon.

How could this be?

She should be in the last stages of her agony! But there she was! This was impossible! Just a second ago, he had been eagerly anticipating hearing her confession and watching her expire and fall away into a handful of dust under the eyes of her beloved Father O'Bryan, that silly dusty inkpot pedantic old Jesuit. He had intended for them to die together, those two – what a pretty picture it would be! The demon and her priest ...

But now – there she was!

How had she done this?

Well, she would not be alive for long. She had won a short reprieve – that was all. Her doom now would be even more hideous!

John woke up with a horrible headache. He was lying on the steel floor of a metal cage beside someone perched on a metal chair and chained to it and who was naked, and whom he presumed must be Professor Thornhill. John shook his head to rid it of cobwebs and looked up. "Professor Roger Thornhill, I presume."

Roger looked down at his fellow prisoner. "How are you feeling? Who are you? And who is that?" Roger nodded toward the woman striding across the floor of the cavern.

"My name's John, Professor. I took a bad blow on the head, but now I'm feeling much better, thank you."

John struggled to sit up, patted himself down: the monks had taken away his weapons and belt and backpack, but they had not bothered to tie him up or strip him. Amateurs! But, then again, they were undoubtedly in a hurry and had other things to think about. He got to his knees and followed the direction of Roger's nod. The poor Professor was manacled hand-and-foot and could only nod. "Who is that?" Roger asked.

"My God!"

"What? What's wrong?"

"She should be dead!" John's eyes went wide, "Well, well ..."

"But who is she?"

John scratched his head. "Ah, ah, that, my dear professor, is V. Or at least I think it is. I thought she was done for – silver nitrate bullet, secret formula, you know, her Achilles' heel, I'm afraid."

"Done for?"

"She was dying. Indeed, she should be dead by now, but it seems she isn't. Resurrection is rather her specialty." John stared at V as she strode straight toward the base of the Crystal. "Weird way to attack the enemy though. I don't quite understand what she is doing."

"This V of yours is dressed just like my daughter was dressed."

"Kate? Yes, Professor. Kate borrowed a warrior outfit from V. V, with a little help from others, saved Kate from being sacrificed in a sort of black Mass. They get on like a house on fire, V and Kate, and they do look like sisters, don't they? Where is Kate?"

"Something, a giant tentacle, I know this sounds unbelievable, came out of the mist over there and ..." Roger cleared his throat, his eyes were wet with tears, "and it dragged her off – she's gone."

"Nothing is unbelievable, Professor. And as for Kate, well, if anyone can bring her back, it's that lady over there."

"You think there's hope."

"With V around there is always hope, Professor. At least, up till now such has been my experience."

"Good, well ..." Roger nodded.

"Now, Professor, let's see if we can get those chains and manacles off you and get us out of this cage. I have a bit of a reputation as a Houdini or lock-smith, and I'd better try to live up to it." Out of the lining of his jeans, John eased a set of small tools, a pin, a series of small wires, and several miniature screwdrivers. "These are inserted into the seams, so when a chap, or a hostile amazon, or a monk, or some terrorist, pats a fellow down, they usually miss it, unless they're being absolutely thorough."

"We have to stop that generator over there," said Roger. "I think I can do it from here, since the computers control the generators too, or are linked to the computers that do. But I need to have my hands free."

"Old Cardinal toying with the field of gravity, I believe."

"Yes, exactly."

"Well, as a first step, let's get your hands free."

"What is, ah, V, doing?"

John glanced over at V. "I have no idea."

V, wearing her backpack, dressed in her skintight black leather warrior's catsuit, the armored bustier, boots, sword, shoulder-bazooka, and sidearm, was striding across the floor. She kicked aside the huge bodies of the dead monks. Seemingly as light as bundles of tissue paper, they flew into the air, bounced softly, and flopped down silently. Below the Crystal, she stopped and struck a defiant pose, legs apart, hands on hips, chin thrust out, and looked up. "Cardinal!" she shouted. "Here I am!"

"Woman," the Cardinal shouted, "get thee gone! Female, disappear! Obscene mammal, putrid female excrescence, dissolve! Dissipate! Die! She-devil, I shall reduce you to dust!"

"Oh, come on, Cardinal! You can do better than that! You're just a pre-sumptuous overinflated windbag, an over decorated eunuch, a foppish empty husk clothed in unearned vestments you desecrate with your mere presence! That is a cute hat, I must say, but you are a ridiculous fraud!"

The Cardinal roared. The roar of a beast of the jungle. He turned purple. He glowed. The light shimmered and trembled around him. He began to expand. His vestments flew away; the outer robes exploded, fluttering in fragments; his undergarments burst into ribbons. His hat – a vintage biretta with a neat tuft – burst into pieces; the rim flew away, taking off like a Frisbee. Buttons, bits of cloth, careened, popped, rained down. His clerical collar skittered away like a child's glider, skimming in a zigzag down to the floor where V batted it away, as if it were a limp, impotent boomerang.

"She-devil! You have no idea of my powers!" The Cardinal's flesh was now blossoming, an exploding dark gray carnal mushroom, spreading and billowing out like an angry thunder cloud. "I am the Phallic God!"

"You are the *what*?"

"The Phallic God!" he roared.

"The *what*?"

"The Phallic God!" The Cardinal glowed purple, incandescent. "The Phallic God, you female wretch, you mere woman, you teat-infested cow!" The swelling mass flickered and flashed crimson like a rogue neon sign. "You sow, you female mammal, you … you … you …!"

"Really – *you* … the *Phallic* God? I had no idea! How quaint! What an absolutely ridiculous idea!" V laughed, her teeth bright. She began to climb the framework. "Tell me, oh, Seat of Conceit, oh, Magnificent Preening Macho, oh, Phallic Oneness, tell me of thy powers!"

"No!" the Cardinal thundered.

"Oh, please, oh, pretty please, Mighty One!"

"I have made an alliance," the Cardinal bellowed, "an alliance till the end of time!"

"An alliance? With whom?" V had already climbed up several yards from the ground.

"With the Devil, oh foul ignorant woman, with the Devil! I am married to Satan himself, I am the Bride of Darkness, I am one with Dark Matter. I am the Dark Force that presides over and sustains and maintains the universe!" The Cardinal climbed higher and higher up the framework, far above the control platform.

He had become a giant now, his human form blurred and barely discernible, like a balloon that has been blown up, a cartoon inflated gigantically and out of all proportion.

"A thing of beauty, Cardinal, truly thou art not!" V climbed steadily, straight up, toward the platform, toward the Cardinal.

He had become a blimp. His lips took the form of a giant crimson cupid's bow. The huge balloon he had become looked as if it might float away, soar upwards toward the distant vaulted ceiling. "The Universe is Spirit and the Spirit is Evil and I am One with the Evil Spirit. I have seen what no mortal has seen. I am greater than any human ever, greater than Moses or Christ or Mohammed! I am the true Messiah, the Messiah of Utter Obliteration and Darkness!"

"Oh, *please!* Give me a break, Cardinal! You do spout utter bollocks, bullshit, and infantile foolishness. You are trifling with powers you do not understand. And I'm sorry to give you the bad news, but you are not a prophet, you are simply a presumptuous, feverish, and deluded second-rate madman." V's laughter was utterly scornful. "You are a sad dime-store nutbar, an utter fruitcake!" Her voice echoed through the cavern. "Your satanic rants mean nothing! Even your dentures don't fit, Cardinal. And I am coming to get you, you pathetic old windbag!"

Bolts of lightning flashed from the bloated Cardinal.

The Crystal trembled, vibrated, and dark shadows moved on its surface. Lights flashed deep within its depths. It rose from its cradle.

"If the Crystal's not alive, it's as if it were alive," said Roger.

"But it's enslaved, Professor."

"Call me Roger. Yes, enslaved to the Cardinal – and to that thing." Roger nodded toward the generator. "If the Crystal were freed of the electric shocks, then it might do, ah, the right thing."

Inside the Crystal lights lit up; it looked as if, within the giant glittering translucent sphere, a huge storm was brewing.

V climbed upwards, from beam to beam. She had apparently decided that insults were not enough; she started taking potshots at the Cardinal with her sidearm. The bullets bounced harmlessly off the billowing surfaces of what had once been Cardinal Antonio Xavier Paulus Ambrosiano.

"You are even uglier now than you were before, Cardinal," shouted V. "You stink and you look like a toad! Though I am being unfair to toads!"

"Whore! Slut! Witch! Woman! – you will die in horrible agony!"

The huge balloon-like Cardinal was changing, losing the last vestiges of humanity. His limbs multiplied. His features blurred. Suddenly – in a flash – he became a spider – legs shooting out, giant bulbous body ballooning; his mandibles chomping hungrily, and drooling silvery streams of smoking acid. He was a true giant – the size perhaps of a Leopard battle tank.

"Wow, Cardinal, that was impressive," V shouted. "Now you really are ugly! But inside all the spider glamor, you are still a silly deluded old duffer!"

The spider's eight eyes glowed like giant scarlet headlights, and the huge venomous fangs – each perhaps three feet long – dripped streams of viscous gluey acid that hissed on the metal struts, sending up clouds of poisonous smoke, and dribbling down in streams toward V.

"She's certainly provoking him, this V of yours."

"Yes. It's unlike her. I'm not sure what she thinks she's doing. She usually has her reasons – works in mysterious ways, you know." John inserted a pin into one of the locks. "Hmm, these handcuffs are rather sophisticated, never met any like them before."

As John toiled on the handcuffs, Roger kept glancing at the seismic monitors. The little lines had been traveling relatively peacefully along the screens, with only minor squiggles and a few local abnormalities. But now the lines began to jerk up and down. The long series of electric shocks was beginning to have an important effect.

The news channels – CNN, BBC, and Al-Jazeera – were reporting on eruptions at Vesuvius, in Yellowstone National Park, in Japan, and elsewhere. Otherwise they were still showing normal news programming. The Russian President was running a marathon just outside Moscow. The ruling party in China was holding its annual congress.

"It's beginning," said Roger.

"What's beginning?" John was working delicately at the handcuffs. He had just inserted a small pin into the lock of the right cuff. He twisted the pin slowly, back and forth, back and forth. He listened, his head tilted to one side; the handcuff make a "click" and sprang open. Roger had one hand free. John looked up. "Now I'll do the other one."

Roger's free hand flew to the keyboard and he began to type code. "What's beginning is a new wave of earthquakes."

"Can you stop the generator?"

"I'm not sure. I think so." Roger frantically typed in more code.

"Good, won't be long now, and I'll have you free." John glanced toward V.

She was still climbing up the great metal framework; silver reflections from the Crystal bounced off her black catsuit and off the impressive-looking shoulder-bazooka slung over her shoulder.

"I can stop the generator," Roger kept typing, "but I don't think that will stop the Crystal. It's gone beyond the point of no return. You see those waves – on that screen – they are sympathetic vibrations. They echo the shocks the Cardinal has applied. If they continue, they will amplify and probably rip the planet apart. But if the Crystal could take control of itself and be put, as it were, into reverse, maybe sending out counteracting waves that neutralized the earlier ones, well, then, maybe the world can be saved."

"And what are you trying to do now, with all this frantic typing?" John clicked open the second handcuff. Roger now had both hands free. John turned his attention to Roger's ankle cuffs.

"These computers can't link to the outside – except passively; they receive but they can't send information or orders." Roger was typing furiously now with both hands. "But I discovered that the electricity supplies the Cardinal installed are controlled by computers linked to these. The circuits of the generators are linked, indirectly, to these computers."

"So, you might be able to reconfigure some circuits and interrupt the electricity – or part of it at least – by turning off the generator that is annoying the Crystal?"

"Exactly. I just have to crack a few barriers, and then …" Roger glanced toward V.

John followed Roger's glance. "What in the world is she doing, climbing straight up like that?" John frowned. V's behavior was puzzling. She was already high up on the cradle of the Crystal. Then, "My God, look at that!"

Still typing, Roger looked up. "So, he's done it."

"Done it?"

"He's become what he calls the Spider-God. He's a shape-changer. He gave me a small demonstration earlier today."

"It must be the Crystal."

"Yes, definitely." Roger was now staring at the screen, hammering at the keys.

High up, straight above V, the Cardinal was enormous, a giant eight-legged spider, but V seemed utterly unperturbed. She climbed further and then stopped. "I'm coming to get you, you tawdry sideshow freak, I'm going to take you down!"

"She's insane, this V of yours," said Roger, while his fingers flew over the keyboard.

"She has indeed been known to be foolhardy on occasion," said John.

"Hey, you venomous bug, you pathetic clown," V shouted. "Let's see who's stronger, eh!"

The spider mewed and roared. It exhaled a mist of frosty breath, little crystals, sparkling, breaking up in the air, and exuding a putrid smell, as if a giant sewer had opened up.

Fast as lightning, the spider swiveled around, sprawling vertical on the scaffolding. It stared with a glistening array of beady eyes straight down at V.

V climbed straight up the frame toward the control platform. She stopped and fired another round from her Beretta M9. The bullets burst on the spider's flank but seemed to have no effect.

"What is she doing?"

"I don't know. It's suicide going in from below like that! And using a Beretta M9 against that creature?" John pulled the ankle cuffs away and started work on the waist chain. "And shouting insults – it's not like V at all."

As V continued climbing, the spider scurried down toward V, its many legs skipping from beam to beam.

V kept coming, calmly, deliberately. The spider stopped, seemingly puzzled. It paused. It mewled a warning.

V stopped. She took the shoulder-bazooka – a modified ground-to-air missile – out of its sling, hefted it onto her shoulder, aimed it straight upward and fired.

The spider skipped sideways, but not fast enough. The missile ripped through one of its legs and exploded just a few feet away against a metal beam. Part of the spider's body burst into flame; the wounded leg peeled off and fell straight down.

"That's more like it," muttered John. "There! You're a free man, Roger, except for the cage, of course."

"Except for the cage." Roger's fingers flew over the keyboard. "We don't have much time."

Trailing a torrent of bluish goo and wagging the remnants of its shattered limb, the spider hopped away and scurried back, up the framework, then sideways.

It shot out a ribbon of silver thread, perhaps an inch in width, as fast as a speeding bullet. Glittering like a streak of pure light, the thread shot downwards, splashed into V's wrist, wrapping itself around her hand and then her arm.

V got off one, two, three shots from the shoulder-held missile launcher. But the shots went wide, bouncing off the scaffolding, careening away in a red and yellow shower of explosions.

The Crystal, oblivious, hummed, glowed, sparkled, and occasionally emitted strange lights – flashes and thunderbolts – from far inside.

The Spider shot out a cascade of threads. They rained down, lighting-fast ribbons of goo, and hit V – wham, wham, wham, and wham!

The bazooka was hit. It peeled away from V's shoulder. It fell, clattering down the metal framework, bouncing from beams and crossbeams, finally smashing onto the ground far below.

The sticky inch-wide threads coiled around V's arms, her neck, and her chest – and tightened. Caught in a tangled web, struggling, kicking, jerking, V fought to free herself.

The Spider pulled on the threads and tore V off the scaffold, swinging her outwards. Spinning in space, she dangled, helpless, one leg flailing, trying to get purchase, but unable to reach the scaffolding.

The Spider roared and bubbled with glee. He spurted down another cascade of threads. They hit the target precisely. The snake-like cables acted as if they were alive, swirling around V in a tornado of liquid silver, pinning her legs tightly to each other and pinning her arms to her sides. More liquid threads spewed down, a silvery waterfall of ribbons. They coated her pistol and flicked it away from her hand, sending it spiraling away. Stronger than steel, the ribbons wrapped themselves around V. The super-glue liquid spun and spun until V was entirely imprisoned in the white shimmering fiber.

V wiggled and slashed out. She flipped and flopped like a fish caught on a hook at the end of a line. She shouted, "This is not fair!"

The Spider hissed angrily and shot out a wide thread of silver that suddenly slapped itself around V's mouth, then around the rest of her head, leaving just her eyes and her nose free. V went mute.

"How horrific!" whispered Roger.

"He's cocooning her." Beads of sweat glistened on John's forehead. He concentrated on unlocking the door to the cage. "The Spider will soften her up.

Then he will eat her." This lock was complicated and very strong; but they damn well had to get out of the cage. John glanced around: at least none of those monstrous monks had appeared; if they came, he and Roger had no weapons, at least not yet ...

"I have a knife," said Roger. "Kate gave it to me. Here, on the chair."

"Good!" John slipped the knife into his hand, weighing it. "She's a true warrior, your Kate!"

"The Spider is wrapping your friend up like a mummy," said Roger, as he tapped out a final code. "Voilà! Done it! This should shut off some of the current. Let's see." He pressed *Enter*.

Some of the lights flickered and went out. The generator that had been poking the Crystal with electric shocks sputtered and died.

"Bravo!" John looked up at Roger.

"It's probably too late." Roger stood up, wiggled his shoulders. He had no idea how long he'd been chained in one place.

More lights flickered and died. On the control platform, the cable had ceased to generate sparks.

The Spider let out a scream of rage.

"He noticed," said Roger.

"It seems he did."

The Crystal shuddered, and let out what sounded like a long sigh of relief ,and settled lower in its cradle; its hum dropped a few octaves.

"Well, that was a good day's work, Roger!" John had stuck the knife in the back of his jeans, blade downward; tricky, he thought, without a sheath, I must be careful. My girl Julia won't like it if I slice off half of my ass. He crouched down, focused on the lock. It was fiendishly complicated. It could be opened only from the outside, so he had to use a hooked wire to play with it. It was hot in the cavern. His hands were greasy with sweat. He muttered, "Look, old man, you've been in tighter corners than this, so we'll just get ourselves out of this fix too, nice and easy."

"I wonder," Roger said, glancing up at V swinging helpless, dangling in the air like a Christmas-tree bauble. "Is he going to eat her now?"

"That's what spiders do, and that's what he has been doing with his other victims." John gritted his teeth. "That's what he did to the soldiers who tried to liberate this place. I think he'll regard V as a choice morsel – a priority snack."

"If I were a praying man, I'd be down on my knees right now." Roger glanced at the monitors. CNN, BBC, Al-Jazeera were showing images of fallen buildings, of ships capsizing at sea; one screen showed a graphic representing a tsunami spreading across the Pacific. Buildings were being swept away by giant waves. The seismic recorders, jagged lines jerking higher and higher, showed earthquake activity rapidly increasing.

"The Crystal is still creating seismic waves. I think it's beyond the point of no return. It's going to tear the planet apart, even with the generator stopped."

"That's unpleasant," said John, keeping an eye on a monk who had appeared and was approaching them cautiously. The monk probably had no orders – John pushed the wire gently deeper into the lock – otherwise the monk would rush them; perhaps the Cardinal was too busy with V to pay any attention to such worms as Roger and John.

"If the Spider adds any more thread, she won't be able to breathe," said Roger.

"That's right," said John, still working at the lock. "But I think he'll want to eat her alive. He'll leave her nostrils free so she can breathe. He will want to feed on her living flesh. Tastier, and psychologically infinitely more sadistic and satisfying. He has a score to settle with V and he'll want to enjoy killing her, bit by bit, while she is still conscious." John glanced at the monk. The creature had stopped and was merely watching them, from about fifteen yards away.

Roger turned up the sound on BBC World. A worried-looking young reporter was saying, "… brief tremors have also been felt here in Rome. Meanwhile, in the Mediterranean, about ninety miles south of Naples, there are signs that a giant underwater volcano, northwest of Stromboli, known as the Marsili Volcano, is about to erupt. The top of Mount Marsili is about a quarter of a mile underwater, but it is as large as Mount Etna, and a little under two miles high. Experts say a full eruption would cause a devastating Mediterranean tsunami. Following the Vesuvius eruption, Civil Defense authorities have declared an additional state of …" Roger turned the sound down.

The Spider sent down more gluey silver threads, binding V even tighter; then it hesitated – sniffed the air.

V dangled, bound like a mummy and swaying slightly, spinning slowly, silent.

"This was the superwoman you spoke about?" Roger said. Now there would be no hope of saving Kate!

"I don't know what to say." John was still toying with the lock. "I really don't know what V was thinking, confronting him directly like that – it's entirely unlike her."

The Spider began to climb down toward V. It was making a low rippling growling noise, a horrible liquid gurgling.

Roger wanted to close his eyes.

Shots rang out.

Hidden high up the Crystal's latticework cradle, U Pizzu took careful aim. Since he'd heard Kate's screams, he had lain extra low, flat down on his belly on a crossbeam, biding his time, protected by two metal columns and hidden in the intricacies of the framework.

U Pizzu was convinced V knew what she was doing. So, he had waited. If V somehow got into difficulty, his moment to turn the tide would come.

He had watched with horror as the Spider had cocooned V in what looked like bands of steel. How had Signorina V been so stupid? How had she let this happen? He crawled forward so he could get a clear shot at the monstrous Spider. It was half hidden in the upper reaches of the Crystal's latticework. Hearing Kate die had been bad enough;!U Pizzu was fucking well not going to let V suffer the same fate. Finally, he had a clear shot.

Peering through the automatic's sights, he let fly a ripple of fire. The bullets splashed into the Spider's head, breaking off bits of shell or carapace. A second burst of fire exploded one of its eight eyes.

The Spider swiveled around, turning its back on V. What a fucking bastard! U Pizzu tightened his grip on the gun. To think that Gaetano and Santino and I did business with the jerk! U Pizzu stood up, leaving his safe refuge, and climbed sideways along the scaffolding to get closer and get a better shot. Hanging from a beam, he let go another burst of fire. "Look at me, you fucking piece of filth!"

The Spider glanced back toward V. It mewled. Its seven remaining eyes flashed. Then it turned its attention to U Pizzu, who let off another burst of fire, and began to climb up the scaffold, to get above the Spider. But in one bound, the Spider leapt at least twenty-five feet up the scaffold. Now it was above U Pizzu.

U Pizzu kept climbing, stopped, let off a burst of fire, and began climbing again. The Spider slowly began to approach U Pizzu.

U Pizzu backed up. From his belt he took a grenade.

He glanced over at V.

There was hardly any sign of life. He could see her eyes, and through a veil of filthy goo she blinked at him! Turning slowly around, she spun and she spun and she spun.

U Pizzu blew her a kiss. "This is for you, babe!"

He timed the grenade shot perfectly. He pulled the pin, left just a few seconds, not enough time for the Spider to toss it back, and lobbed it.

"Let's see how you like this, you filthy bug!"

The grenade flew in a graceful arc, perfectly on target, but as it approached the Spider, the Spider's globe-like eyes gleamed; the Spider spat a great gluey gob that looked like a baseball flying through the air.

"Fuck!" U Pizzu blanched. He immediately knew what the bastard was doing! "Fuck!"

The gob soared through the air, smashed into the grenade when the grenade was only halfway to its target and batted the grenade back at U Pizzu.

"Fuck!" U Pizzu was backed against a vertical pillar of the latticework, cornered. There was no time to jump, no place to jump to.

He slipped his glasses up onto his forehead so he could stare straight into the eyes of the Spider. Seven bloody inhuman spider eyes were not as good as two rich soulful human eyes – and all their depths of feeling, fear, hope, love, despair.

"Fuck!"

When the moment of death came, he should have had a better choice. He thought of the dead girl he'd shot on the road a few days before, blond hair plastered down to her skull, her lustrous skin suddenly waxen. He saw her green-and-gold eyes looking up at him, their pleading, their hopelessness; he thought of Maria Grazia – her bright, excited, frightened eyes, and her sudden smile of surrender on their wedding night; he thought of his eldest, Adrianna, and of his two younger daughters, Rosa and Paola; he thought of V, and how she kissed him in the bright sunlight in Tiberius's villa, the marine breeze touching their lips; he thought of V, showering, laughing, twirling around, beads of water sparkling on her skin, under the garden hose; he thought of … paradise …

The grenade touched U Pizzu's forehead and exploded.

The explosion echoed; sparks showered down.

U Pizzu's headless body toppled down the immense scaffolding, bouncing off railings, support struts, side-beams, crossbeams, and cables; it smashed down with a sickening liquid thud to its final resting place at the foot of the Crystal.

The headless corpse lay on the cavern's floor, belly upwards, arms outstretched, palms open, as if U Pizzu had been crucified; the crease in U Pizzu's trousers was impeccable, and the handkerchief, though spattered with blood, was still neatly folded in his vest pocket – flawless, as was only right.

Up in the far reaches of the scaffolding something twinkled and reflected the lights of the Crystal: U Pizzu's Polaroid sunglasses, caught, rocking gently, on one strut of a crossbeam.

The Spider squealed in delight and scurried across the scaffolding, turning its attention once more to V. Her eyes were blurry now with spider-goo thick on her eyelashes and skin. She looked upward toward the one who had vanquished her. The Spider squealed again, and began to approach its prey – its meal, its revenge …

"Rest in peace, U Pizzu!" John gazed at the body. Then, he concentrated on the lock; he almost had it, he was sure; just a few more twists of the wire and they should be free.

Rogers stared at the monitor screens. They were flickering now, crisscrossed with static. Some networks and feeds had gone off the air. Those that remained showed scenes of desolation: Columns of smoke rising from some city somewhere, toppled skyscrapers, streets filled with rubble, fires burning. Eruptions and earthquakes were reported from Iran and Indonesia. Superstorms seemed to be developing just about everywhere. Tsunamis were rolling around the oceans.

John grimaced. "It looks like Earth is –"

"Yes, and this is only the beginning – unless we stop it."

"I'm almost there. This damned lock is about to give up the ghost. *I think I can, I think I can* … Roger, do you remember that story about *The Little Engine that Could?*"

"I seem to remember the little engine did get up the hill."

"Yes, it did!" Just as John swiveled the pin, and the lock rolled open, he saw, out of the corner of his eye, the giant monk make a move. He had decided to attack them.

"Well, Roger," said John, reaching for the knife, "our moment has come!"

Roger's eyes were caught by an image on Al-Jazeera; the title said, "Massive Earthquake Hits Eternal City. First reports from Rome indicate huge loss of life and …"

John twisted the lock to get the door open.

The monk approached warily, his enormous hands hanging by his sides; he appeared to be unarmed.

John knew he'd have one chance at this, one chance, and only one chance. "Roger, when the monk gets close, and when I whisper, 'Now,' could you possibly see your way clear to screaming, as loud as you can?"

CHAPTER 58 – APOCALYPSE

It was the middle of the night in the Roman Forum; and it was as hot as a sultry tropical blazing noon, over 115 Farenheit.

Scarlett wiped her forehead. Her eyes were wet. A tear went down one cheek. She closed her eyes. "I keep seeing those people, trying to escape … on the slopes of Vesuvius – and in the streets …"

"Me too." Jian's arm was tight around her shoulder.

Scarlett opened her eyes; they reflected the floodlights.

"Scarlett," he said, "Scarlett …" He kissed her on the forehead.

In and around Naples, a million people, perhaps more, maybe a million and a half, had died in the eruption of Vesuvius. Reports were confused; the images were horrifying.

Scarlett glanced at her wristwatch. Almost two-thirty in the morning and it was one hundred and fifteen degrees Fahrenheit – forty-seven Celsius. There was something ominous about the temperature, about the heaviness of the air. Reports of events like those in Naples were coming in from around the world. Would Rome's turn come too?

In the Forum, the air was electric with fear and excitement.

Jian put his hands on Scarlett's shoulders and kissed her on the mouth. They were in shock, dazed and sleepy, exhausted from having spent much of the previous night – after the Rome earthquake tremors – wandering the streets and listening to reports of the eruption of Vesuvius and the destruction of Naples. People all over Italy were stunned. Cafés had stayed open all night so people could talk. Nobody knew how many people had been killed in the eruption of Vesuvius. "Like Pompeii," everybody said. A wave of incandescent ash – a "pyroclastic flow" – had swept over the city. Jian and Scarlett knew about Pompeii – and they knew what a pyroclastic flow would do – it would kill everything and everybody in its path. The images from Vesuvius and from Naples were too horrible to bear – people, in their thousands, dying in front of the cameras.

Scarlett tried to dry her eyes. "It's Dante's Inferno or the Apocalypse, I'm not sure which." She looked around. "Maybe both." She put her arms around Jian's neck and kissed him. People milled all around them – a vast murmuring crowd.

Bonfires, torches, and floodlights lit up the ancient temples of the Roman Forum, the ruined fragments of walls, the isolated classical columns and facades, the old via Sacra, or Sacred Way, the Temple of Jupiter, the garden of the Temple of the Vestal Virgins, the giant, covered, brick marketplaces or basilicas, all were glowing or flickering in the light, firelight and floodlights, and the – intermittent – light from the full moon.

Music was playing. Drums were beating. Choirs were singing. People were chanting. Preachers were preaching, up on soapboxes, or in the middle of small groups, or all alone, just wandering and haranguing the crowd. Nearby, a skinny, bearded, barefoot man in ragged jeans, a dirty white T-shirt, and loose clerical collar was standing on a wooden chair, shouting, waving a dog-eared Bible, begging people to repent of their sins before it was too late. "Sorry to tell you, buddy," somebody shouted, "but it's already too late!" A few teenagers stood and gawked at the barefoot preacher.

Only a few feet away, a group of people sat quietly in a small circle, holding hands, their eyes closed, chanting some mantra in a language Scarlett didn't recognize. Probably it was Sanskrit. Some of them had painted signs on their foreheads.

People of every type were everywhere, groups of tourists – Chinese, Americans, Germans, Japanese, Russians – stuck in Rome – throngs of pilgrims of various kinds – and just plain Romans, with their families, taking refuge, getting as far away as they could from buildings that might topple at any moment. The whole world had become precarious. There were prayer meetings, and families camping out, and loners, and children, and teenagers, gypsies and priests, and people of every race imaginable.

Scarlett looked around. In the throng, everything, essentially, was peaceful, like a great country fair in the dead of night. Rome had not been damaged by events, not yet. But the Civil Defense Ministry had warned that the earthquake risk in the city was now severe – seismic tensions were visibly building, and a flurry of little tremors had been recorded near and underneath the city and up and down the Tiber valley. And so, the Roman Forum and the

Palatine hill had quickly become a giant refugee city, one of many. First aid tents had been set up, and cots, and portable toilets. Improvised food stands dotted the Forum. A smell of hotdogs and fried meat and fried potatoes and curry and tomato sauce drifted across the cobblestones and gardens and between the ruins of ancient temples.

"Hi!" a girl said; she was standing on the cobblestones in front of Jian and Scarlett. She reached out and touched Scarlett on the arm.

"Hi," Scarlett replied, blinking at the girl.

"Hi," said Jian, smiling, and tightening his arm around Scarlett's shoulders, as Scarlett leaned closer to him.

The girl was naked – maybe 18 years old – emerging out of the crowd; she had sidled barefoot up to Jian and Scarlett. Suddenly she was just there. In one hand, she was carrying a half-empty bottle of white wine, dangling it casually by the neck. Her dark red hair went down to her shoulders, plastered to her cheeks and neck. Her pale white body glowed with beads of sweat, and a charming little cloud of russet freckles drifted across her pert nose and her cheeks. Her body was slender, with small, perky, pointed breasts. Her dark green eyes shone. "Want to have sex? We're having sex. All of us."

"Well," Scarlett began, "I'm not sure –"

"You are both so beautiful." She ran her finger along Scarlett's arm. "You are the most beautiful people in the world. You know that, don't you? You should take off your clothes. Civilization is over, you know. Nobody needs clothes anymore."

"Well –"

"See, over there, everybody is having sex."

Scarlett, dressed in sandals, shorts, and a T-shirt, and leaning close against Jian, followed the girl's glance. A circle of naked people were dancing around a big bonfire in a sort of conga chain – hands on each other's hips – up-and-down, up-and-down – bouncing in rhythm to the beating of a drum and to their own chants. Three couples were making love on thin mattresses on the paving stones just next to the dancers. The fire – set up right in front of the soaring columns and portico of the ruins of the ancient Temple to Saturn – flared up, higher than the dancers, cast shadows of the dancers' silhouettes on the nearby walls, and on the passersby.

"Thanks, maybe another time," said Scarlett. She gave the girl her brightest Southern belle smile.

"Yes, maybe another time," said Jian. "It's very generous of you, of course." He bowed.

"Okay, it's your loss." The girl smiled, shrugged, and licked her lips, blinking, giving Scarlett and Jian, each in turn, a lingering, inviting, lascivious glance. "You do realize, I hope," she said, suddenly adopting a pedantic tone, and shifting to a posh British accent, "that tomorrow there will be no sex. No sex at all. There will be no tomorrow. It's all absolutely over. Everything is over."

She lifted the bottle to her lips and drank; the white wine splashed, overflowed, ran down her chin, over her breasts, glowing, mingling with sweat. She turned away, sauntered toward the bonfire, and over her shoulder, she shouted back to them, "*Ciao, bambini! Buona fortuna!*"

"Pretty girl," said Scarlett.

"Pretty stoned too," said Jian, "though maybe ..."

"Yes, maybe it's just –"

"Anguish, despair, fear."

"Yes." Scarlett put her arm around his waist. "Sex can be a cure for terror, I guess, or a distraction from it." She glanced around. "I wonder, where are the police?"

"Too busy, I think. Lots of problems in the city."

"And then there is Naples."

"Yes."

"Let's go up the via Sacra – the Sacred Way. We might as well keep moving."

"Yes."

The via Sacra – the main street of the Forum, paved with enormous paving stones – was lined with tall torches, flaring brightly up into the night. Bonfires had been lit everywhere, all across the Forum. "The world is coming to an end!" an old man cried out. He handed Scarlett a pamphlet; she glanced at it. Its glossy cover and its pages were blank. She turned it over and opened it up – absolutely blank.

"Well, well." Scarlett showed it to Jian.

"Yes."

"A blank page."

"New beginnings?"

"Let's hope so."

Signs bobbed up and down, in the long, crowded procession of people shuffling, pushing, and jostling up and down the via Sacra, the Sacred Way, and everywhere people were shouting slogans.

"Repent! The end is nigh!"

"Make love! The end is nigh!"

"Repent! Our sins have brought God's wrath upon us!"

Just off the via Sacra a group of tourists – Christian pilgrims – were on their knees, praying, calling out to God to spare them, to save them, to sweep them up to Heaven. Not far away, on the paving stones of an ancient pagan temple, a Muslim group had set out carpets and were praying, bowing toward Mecca. Up on the stub of a column a black girl in a string bikini was dancing what looked like a version of the dance of the seven veils. A small group around her clapped in rhythm.

A sudden crack of thunder echoed. Scarlett looked up. The thunder seemed to have come from straight above, but it was faint, and seemed far away. Blue lightning flickered, lighting up a high rift of swirling dark cloud. Off to one side, the moon, looking as large as a harvest moon, was veiled in red dust. Thunderheads roiled in the dark sky, vast rotating coal-black clouds, lit up from below. Flashes of lightning played – arcing back and forth – among the clouds. More thunder rippled down.

"Those clouds look weird."

"Yes, they do." Jain ran his finger down the nape of Scarlett's neck. "What could create that?"

"Hot air rising, ice crystals rubbing together, electrons getting rubbed off their atoms, electric charges building up, then discharging," Scarlett said. "Physics 101. I think." She kissed Jian on the lips. "But we should be safe here – far away from buildings."

"Yes." Jian squinted up at the sky. "Hmm. Maybe – and maybe not. Whatever weather those clouds will bring, it won't be normal."

A large procession, led by a man carrying, on his shoulders, a giant wooden cross, surged down the via Sacra, heading directly toward Jian and Scarlett – men and women in black robes, chanting, a powerful deep chant, something primitive and awe-inspiring. The cross bobbed up and down, and weaved this way and that in the glare of floodlights, as the man – a skinny young man with long hair and a long beard and dressed in a loincloth – staggered forward over the huge irregular paving stones, bearing his heavy burden.

"Wow!" Scarlett blinked at the spectacle.

People fell on their knees.

People cried out, lamentations, prayers, supplications.

Off to one side, a giant screen had been set up on scaffolding that surrounded a temple that was being restored. Across the screen flowed images from Naples, from New York, from Japan, from Indonesia. Volcanoes in eruption, lava flows, ruined cities, superstorms and mega tornadoes, tidal waves, streams of refugees. The images were replays, since communications had broken down – satellites, apparently, were not working, and undersea cables, reports said, had been cut. Scarlett took out her cellphone.

"Still no connection." She slipped the phone back into her purse.

"Yes, same with mine," said Jian. "No connection."

"We are on our own." Scarlett looked into his eyes.

"Yes," he held her. "Just us, alone in the world." They kissed as the chanting procession passed by; the rhythm was deep, and it made the heart soar. It seemed to suggest profound mysteries, sublime heights of abandon and ecstasy, a return to the primitive visceral origins of religion. Scarlett tightened her hold on Jian's waist.

"Sacred music," Jian said. "Lifts the heart!"

"Yes, sounds something like Carl Orff."

"That's right. I remember in Berlin hearing –"

The wind rose, swirled some papers, lifted banners, rattled walls of scaffolding. The sky filled with rotating clouds, vast ribbons of churning blackness, stippled with blossoming surges and billows of white. The full moon, between two rifts of cloud, was veiled in red dust.

"Those clouds are getting a little too spooky." Scarlett took Jian's hand.

"Yes. I don't like the look of them." Jian pulled her to him. "I'm not sure it's such a good idea to be out in the open."

"But shelter is dangerous. Roofs and walls fall down."

"Yes, shelter is dangerous."

"Well, then …" Scarlett grinned. "Seize the moment!"

The clouds calmed down, and the little whirlwinds ceased; calm – relative calm – descended over the murmuring and shouting crowd.

"Hungry?"

"Now that you mention it."

"Seize the moment!"

"Yes."

They ordered hotdogs from a small canvas stand, one of many that had been set up along the via Sacra and all over the Forum. The small fire cooked up the hotdogs. The man tending the booth had a steel-gray droopy moustache, a twinkle in his eyes and a red, weather-worn face. His wife, a kerchief on her head, was preparing more food – hamburgers and hotdogs and cheese and ham sandwiches on an extra grill set up just behind the stand.

They both chose hot Italian sausage with lots of mustard.

"You have a mustard moustache." Scarlett pointed.

"You too. Here. Let me kiss it better."

The lick merged into a kiss.

"Now we both taste the same." Scarlett leaned into him.

"Exactly – of mustard."

"And spicy Italian."

Sitting on a stone bench next to the via Sacra was a young woman with short black hair, a high forehead, big dark eyes, and fine features; she was wearing a white blouse, black jeans, and sandals; with her, she had two little girls, about eight or nine years old, one a blond girl with free-flowing hair, and the other a black girl with tightly wound pigtails.

Jian and Scarlett stopped, and sat down beside the woman and the two kids. The woman was stroking the children's hair and murmuring, "Everything will be okay. We can go back to the hotel soon." People passed by, a colorful procession, lit by the torches and floodlights – some singing, some laughing, others silent, lovers kissing or embracing, and whole families.

"That's another strange cloud." Scarlett nodded toward the sky. The moon disappeared behind a vast towering cloud. It looked like nothing she had ever seen before. It was expanding before her eyes. It was a towering thunderhead, black at the bottom, and turning pure white as it towered up, rising and rising.

"That one definitely doesn't look friendly." Jian squinted at the cloud.

"It's not natural." Scarlett shivered, a sudden chill.

The cloud grew and grew. Suddenly, out of the sky, a huge bolt of lightning flashed, a blaze of white, snaking down to earth. It lit up the whole scene: the vast crowd on the Sacred Way, the Colosseum looming in the distance, and near it the Arch of Titus. After the crack of thunder, there was silence – and a hushed electric, nervous feeling in the air – as if time had suddenly stopped.

"This is weird." Scarlett shivered.

"Worse than weird. I think we'd better look for shelter."

"Shelter – but, like we said, isn't that dangerous? I mean, the roofs, the walls?"

"I'm not sure what's dangerous now."

"Everything?"

"That sounds about right." Jian smiled and stood up. "Let's go up there." He nodded toward a dark passageway between some thickly clustered bushes; the pathway sloped up toward a hillside; it seemed to be empty, and in fact, many parts of the Forum were empty; people were clustering together, seeking safety, or at least reassurance, in numbers, sticking mainly to the main sites and pathways.

"Right." Scarlett stood up.

"Excuse me. I apologize. I've been eavesdropping." The young woman looked up at them. "Do you mind if we follow you?" The woman glanced at her two little girls. "We're a bit lost. And, frankly, I'm frightened."

"Absolutely, come on," Jian and Scarlett said, at exactly the same time.

"You two talk at the same time." The woman laughed and stood up.

"We seem to think at the same time too," said Scarlett.

"Yes, even though we only met a few days ago, it's like we've been together forever," said Jian. "Okay! Let's go." He pushed his way into the bushes, holding back the branches, so the others could pass through.

Jian led them up the narrow winding dirt path. It went up a steep hillside and leaning against the slope and a brick retaining wall was a small wooden structure with a wooden bench and a solid-looking overhanging wooden roof. "This should shelter us from a storm if one comes," Jian said. "We've got a view too, over most of the Forum."

"And if an earthquake comes, we just jump back out into the bushes, and away from the shelter," said Scarlett, eyeing the roof, which was not much – a thick wooden overhang of about three yards.

"Yes, that's a good strategy," said Jian. "We should be ready to move back into the open if we have to."

"I'm Tatania," said the woman, "and this is Chloë and this is Zoe."

"I'm Scarlett."

"I'm Jian."

They all shook hands rather formally. Chloë, the blonde, who had the bluest of eyes, and a pretty blue frock, said, "I am very pleased to meet you." And Zoe said, "It is indeed a pleasure. My name is Zoe and I am from Somalia. Well, I was from Somalia. Now we are from Vancouver and Seattle, but this year we are living in Paris."

"I'm delighted to meet you," said Scarlett.

"I am honored," Jian said, rather formally, bowing to the two girls, who bowed back. Tatania explained that she was Russian-American – originally from Saint Petersburg – that the two girls were her daughters, and that she and her Canadian husband had a high-tech firm with offices in Montreal and Seattle and Paris and that she was in Paris – with the girls – to develop a

European marketing plan, while her husband was still back in Montreal. Jian and Scarlett explained, briefly, who they were. It was clear they shared a lot of interests with Tatania. Then, they all fell silent and looked out over the Forum.

After a few moments, it seemed that everything had returned to normal – the huge cloud dissipated; it faded. Everybody had been quiet, looking at the sky. But now, with the strange cloud fading, people began to talk; the noise level returned to its usual pitch. The chants, the preaching, the hymns, the lamentations, the shouts, and some wild dancing music – it all began again.

"Maybe those clouds were just a fluke," said Scarlett.

"Maybe."

Suddenly, everything went quiet again – a spooky, creepy quiet. A hush fell over everybody and everything.

Scarlett wondered at the silence. Clearly at the back of everybody's mind was one thought – Vesuvius and Naples. "There's something definitely weird about this …"

"It's strange," said Tatania. "It's like before a thunderstorm – out in the country, where you can feel the weather before it happens."

"Yes. Listen." Jian took Scarlett's hand. "Something is …"

Tatania shushed the two girls. Both girls stared at Jian, then at Scarlett.

Scarlett frowned. She concentrated. She heard nothing. And then she noticed a sort of low rumbling, a hum, or a vibration; it seemed to be underneath their feet, all around them, everywhere.

Zoe and Chloë held each other. Their eyes were round.

"What is –?"

"Shush!"

The dead calm continued.

Then Scarlett noticed a new cloud, a very dark cloud, forming quickly, just over the Forum. It towered up, lit up by the dusty, blood-red moon. Suddenly her mouth was dry. She swallowed. "I've never seen anything like it."

"Neither have I."

"Everybody's noticed it," said Tatania; and Scarlett, for the first time, noticed her faint Russian accent.

The crowds had fallen silent. People were pointing up. In the dead silence, far away, a child started to wail.

The huge black cloud blossomed, seemingly out of nothing, growing more rapidly than Scarlett had ever seen a cloud grow. Within seconds it filled the whole sky. Great tendrils of swirling cloud reached down toward the ground.

The moon had disappeared.

The few stars that had been visible were gone.

The prayers and chanting stopped.

Even the chugging generators seemed hushed and subdued.

"I don't know, but it looks like –"

"A tornado."

"Yes."

Suddenly, the bushes thrashed and swirled, dead leaves and dust and paper cups bounced around and skittered across the ground; the whirling debris formed into miniature dust devils and tornadoes. More gusts of wind swirled, picking up leaves, dust, twigs.

Down in the Forum, a metal sign flew off the scaffolding that surrounded the Temple of Antonius and Faustina: "Restoration Courtesy of the Bank of …"

"Gosh!"

"Let's hold onto each other."

In an instant, the whole scaffolding around the Temple of Antonius and Faustina exploded. Wooden beams, steel rods, cables, canvas sheeting swirled upward, twirled around, soaring into the sky, drawn into the immense rotating cloud; people and things were being swept up in a maelstrom of racing whirling air, a dark shadow, a giant swirling funnel of air.

A bald bearded man – lit up by the floodlights – sailed upwards into the twirling cloud, his red, blue, and yellow Hawaiian shirt billowing, his Bermuda shorts ballooning, his camera swinging wildly on its cord, his hands clawing at the air. One sandal fell away. Other people were swept up, women, men, children, illuminated by the floodlights. People were screaming, panicking.

"This can't be real." Scarlett blinked, and held tight to them all – Jian, Tatania, Chloë, and Zoe. They all huddled close.

Below them a giant funnel of air swept along the ground, whirling through the Forum, a giant twisting mad dervish, picking up torches, people, hotdog stands, tents, planks, construction equipment, smashing things over, and lifting others into the air, tossing them out of sight, ripping trees and shelters into shreds. Floodlights exploded, sending out showers of sparks, spreading everywhere. Darkness descended. All the lights went out. Then they went back on. Then they went out. Screams filled the air. The mob was running, screaming, fleeing, this way, then that way, as the giant funnel swept through the Forum; then it lifted off, moving off over the

Palatine Hill, ripping up trees, construction and restoration sites, leaving a huge empty gap behind.

Scarlett, Jian, Tatania and Chloë and Zoe leaned close together. The little wooden shelter had hardly been touched by the wind at all.

Then, suddenly …

Rain thundered down. It lashed sideways. Water came from every direction at once, flooding under the shelter. In an instant, they were all soaked.

"Crouch down!" Scarlett shouted. They crouched together, the three adults protecting the children.

The deluge was a roaring, glittering solid sheet of silver. A blast of lightning lit up the whole Forum, filling the air, a blue-white flare; seconds later came a deafening roll of thunder. The ground shook. A plank fell from the side of the shelter.

Another bolt! A jagged line of pure white light, searing Scarlett's eyes. She blinked – nothing: pure white, then pure black. Yikes! She was blind. She blinked again – everything looked like the negative of a black and white photograph tinted in red – the Colosseum, the Arc of Titus, the temples and basilicas. "Shut your eyes," she shouted. "The lightning is dangerous!"

Another flash! It seared into Scarlett's eyelids; she saw red, blotchy patterns, even with her eyes squeezed shut. Then there was another flash, and then another. Huge rippling cracks of thunder shook the shelter, sending dirt and dust cascading from the plank walls; dust, fragments of wood, tumbled down Scarlett's back.

Jian tightened his arm around Scarlett.

The ground shook. There were more flashes of lightning and rolling thunder. Even with her eyes squeezed shut, Scarlett felt the blows.

Then the flashes stopped. The thunder continued; but it was more and more distant, quickly fading.

Scarlett opened her eyes, blinking. Everything seemed almost normal. "Tatania, you can open your eyes now."

Down below, in the Forum, some of the generators and floodlights were still functioning. It was a garish ruin, everything wet and sparkling with water from the deluge, Corinthian columns, massive brick structures, and the facades of ancient temples. It looked like everything was coated in splashes of silver.

"I guess we can leave now." Tatania stood up. "We've bothered you enough. You've been very –"

"No, wait." Jian stood up and took her by the arm. "I don't think it's over."

There was a rattling sound, an avalanche of pebbles. Tatania started back, pulling the children with her. Zoe said, "I hear something." Chloë said, "Me too – something is coming. Something bad!"

"It's hail. Don't move!" Jian pulled them deeper into the shelter.

The hail crashed down in a flood, some of the hailstones as big as baseballs. It was a bombardment, an avalanche. Within seconds, the ground outside was covered with maybe three to six inches of hail. The little shelter trembled under the bombardment, but the roof held.

Then, as suddenly as it had begun, the hail stopped.

"Do you think it's safe?" Scarlett tightened her grip on Jian's arm.

"I don't know if it'll ever be safe." Jian fingers brushed Scarlett's cheek. He kissed her.

The monstrous cloud had broken up into a raft of strata cumulus, fading off at the edges into a ragtail of skittering cirrus. Suddenly free in an empty stretch of sky, the dust-veiled moon shone bright, casting a reddish glow. The hail was melting fast. In the floodlights, the ground sparkled, a field of diamonds. Bodies were lying everywhere, tents had been flattened, hotdog stands had disintegrated, grills had been turned over.

The sky was suddenly clear; the moon shone down, and a few stars were visible.

"We'd better go down and see if we can help," said Jian.

"Yes."

"We'll come with you, if you don't mind," said Tatania.

"Yes, let's stick together." Scarlett took Zoe by the hand. "I think that would be best."

They wound their way down the path, through the bushes, and out onto the Sacred Way. They were faced with crowds of wounded and dead. The via Sacra was a writhing mass of bodies; some people were standing, others were groaning lying on their side. Many were lying unconscious, or dead, in the field of glittering, melting hail.

Jian looked around. What to do? Where to start?

Bodies were scattered like leaves. People were knocked out, stunned, some wounded, many dead, others struggling to their feet; all were in shock, groping blindly in the garish lights, stumbling and slipping on the melting hail and ice, whimpering, or shouting for friends and family.

"I don't know what we should do."

"No."

The naked girl came out from under a half-broken arch. "I told you. It's the end." Blood ran from her hairline and she had a bruised eye.

"That lady doesn't have any clothes," said Zoe.

"She probably lost them," said Tatania.

"She's pretty," said Chloë.

"Yes, she is." Tatania knelt next to the two children.

"Oh, hello," said Scarlett. "You're okay."

"I'm okay," the redhead said, looking down at the children, "but nobody else is. They are all hurt. I've tried to help them, but I don't know how – there are so many wounded, and people are in shock, and I don't have any ..." She turned, looking up the Sacred Way, at the throngs of dead and wounded.

A rumbling sound rose from the earth.

"Oh, oh, what's that?" Scarlett turned. "What next?"

"Earthquake, I think, yes, it's an earthquake," the naked girl whispered. "By the way, my name's Martine." She took Scarlett's arm.

"I'm Scarlett. This is Jian, and that's Tatania and Zoe and Chloë."

"Zoe and Chloë," Martine repeated. "We'd better all hold on, because ..."

A low roar rippled through the Forum – dust rose, stones bounced, a brick wall crumbled, a Corinthian column toppled over. Several floodlights exploded, but the others still projected a garish white light over the scene – bodies and ruins scattered everywhere.

"Yes, she's right. It's an earthquake." Jian glanced around at the dazed, wounded, shaken crowd. He shouted, "Earthquake!"

In that instant, the ground reared up and fell back. It was like an ocean wave going over a reef. Scarlett grabbed Tatania and the kids and held them close. "Just let's stick together."

"That wall! Watch out!" Martine shouted. A brick wall, close by, was beginning to tremble; it looked like it might explode.

"Yes, we'd better get out in the open, away from the walls and columns!" Jian grabbed Scarlett's hand.

They scrambled toward open ground. The earth was slippery, uneven, covered in glittering, melting hailstones. Another wave hit. The ground shook. Scarlett almost fell on her butt. "Damn!"

Martine followed them. "A chap stole my clothes – and purse – and everything. There was a fight. I got a black eye. Damned inconvenient. I sobered up rather quickly, I must admit." She helped a stunned old man stand up. "*Lei sta bene, signore?*"

"*Si, grazie, ah, signorina.*" The old man looked grateful, but rather dazed, blinking at his naked young helper. "*Lei è molto gentile.* You are very kind."

"*Prego.* You're welcome."

"I have a shawl." Tatania pulled it out of her purse.

"Thank you. *Merci!*" Martine tied the brightly colored silk shawl around her waist. "It's beautiful. I'll give it back." Garish lights were flashing, as some of the generators failed, while others managed to keep chugging.

Suddenly, the ground heaved up. The paving stones of the via Sacra, huge blocks of volcanic stone, buckled up, exploded, and scattered, bouncing, like pieces of a jigsaw puzzle smashed by a giant. Columns that had been standing for two thousand years crashed down, shattering into fragments. The brick walls imploded – bricks flying in every direction – a wave of dust and dirt and bricks spreading out, ripping people apart, knocking them down, and pulverizing them.

Jian flung himself down on Scarlett. Tatania and Martine pulled the children to the ground and lay over them, trying to protect them from the flying debris. A fragment of masonry nicked Jian on the forehead.

Scarlett, lying flat on the ground, peeked sideways through her fingers and saw one of the great brick basilicas that had stood since the days of the Roman Empire collapse in a massive explosion of bricks, masonry, and scaffolding.

"Don't look, children," said Tatania.

Martine put her hands over Zoe's eyes.

"Oh my God!" Scarlett could hardly believe her eyes.

"What?" Jian turned. A black line, then a black hole, a crack was opening in the middle of the Forum, racing down beside the via Sacra and heading straight for Tatania, Martine, and the kids. The Forum was splitting in two right under them.

Jian dragged Tatania and Scarlett to their feet.

"Get up! We've got to move! Now!"

"What's happening?" Zoe looked around.

"Come on, kiddo," said Martine. She picked Zoe up.

"Chloë!" Tatania grabbed the little girl and lifted her, but they both stumbled. A brick – flying through the air – hit Tatania. She fell to the ground, face down.

"A crack is opening, a crevice," Scarlett shouted.

Tatania was stunned or unconscious. Chloë knelt next to her. "Mummy! Mummy!"

"Come on! Come on!" Scarlett and Martine and Zoe struggled to get away. Tumbling, scrambling, down on all fours, crawling, standing up, running, the three of them tripped and struggled, climbing over uprooted stones, debris from the restoration site, bits of timber, metal bars, and tangled canvas banners. All around them people were screaming, running, panicking.

And behind them the ground opened up.

Jian lifted Tatania up and half-carried, half-dragged her and Chloë. "Come on! Come on!"

The crevice widened. It gaped open, enormous now, and it raced straight toward them. Jian pushed Tatania and Chloë ahead of him. Tatania was only half-conscious, almost totally dead weight.

Just as Jian got Tatania and Chloë out of the way, the abyss caught up with him. The ground disintegrated under his feet. Jian stumbled, flailing, trying to get his grip; his feet were in mid-air, sliding into the crevice.

He managed to get a toehold on the edge of a paving stone, and a fingerhold on another, but the stones were slippery and wet with melted hailstones. He screamed, "Scarlett!"

Scarlett turned back. Her heart flip-flopped.

Martine shouted, "Scarlett! I'll look after Tatania and the kids! Go! Save him!"

"Right! Crouch down! Don't move! Here's Chloë."

"Don't worry!" Martine pulled Chloë into her arms. "I'll keep them safe!"

Scarlett scrambled, bouncing, feeling seasick, crawling on hands and knees through slippery slush and bouncing pebbles. All around her the ground was shaking, heaving, buckling.

Jian lost his toehold. His face and his fingers – lit up by a fallen floodlight – barely appeared above the edge of the crevice; the rest of him was invisible; his fingers, wet from the melting hail, were clearly slipping, losing their hold. The last two yards Scarlett wiggled forward on her belly, sloshing, and swimming in melting slush. The stones were slick, sharp, and greasy with mud and half-melted ice. Water streamed out of her hair, down her face, got in her eyes.

The giant block of stone Jian was clinging to moved, shifted. It was edging its way into the abyss. If it tipped over, Jian would go down with it.

Scarlett edged forward. Pebbles rolled and danced around her. Crazy marbles on a bouncing cocktail tray. People were screaming. Not too far away, a woman fell into the crevice. Farther on a man screamed as he tumbled into it. Dozens of people were falling into the gaping hole.

Scarlett blinked. The crevice was a few feet away; it was about eight feet wide, and, like a huge black snake, it zigzagged through the Forum, toward the Capitoline Hill, where she could see, out of the corner of her eye, that Michelangelo's palaces still stood, illuminated, and strangely untouched, as if tonight was a normal night and the buildings existed in an entirely different world.

She was aware of a million things at once: birds wheeling frantically and cawing in the sky; sirens wailing; a helicopter whirring somewhere overhead; the moon veiled in red dust; people lying all around her, wounded people, dead people, unconscious people; people screaming, shouting, crying, wailing. And, above all, she was aware of the vast dark crevice, and of Jian's fingers, his hand, in close-up, slipping, slipping. Now he was only inches away.

Scarlett wedged her shoulder against a paving stone that jutted up at a sharp angle. Praying it was solid, she reached out and locked her fingers around Jian's wrists as tightly as she could. Her hands and his wrists were slimy and wet. His wrists slipped away. "Lock your fingers into mine!" she shouted.

His face was pale, beaded in sweat, his eyes wild. He stared at her as if he knew he was going to die. His golden complexion in the garish light was a waxen pallor – his skin was translucent, a foreshadowing of death. "Scarlett, back up – you're going to fall in too!"

"No way, José! Lock your fingers into mine! That's an order!"

"Okay, boss." His voice trembled; it was hoarse, barely audible, a desperate whisper. He locked his fingers with hers, letting go of the rock he had been clinging to, and clutching her fingers, first one hand, and then the other. They were taking a chance – the only chance …

Jian now depended entirely on her; she braced herself. "Pull!" The air was clamorous with thunder, the creaking and breaking of rocks, the collapse of buildings, and the cries of the wounded.

Jian pulled. Scarlett was slipping! Goddamn it!

"Faster, faster," she whispered, "faster, faster, darling!" It was almost a prayer; oh God, oh, please, please, please …

Jian's feet flailed into the void. Scarlett was slipping. Jian stared. He was going to drag Scarlett down with him. He had to let go. He had to unlock his fingers. He would save her! He would hurdle down into the abyss. So be it!

In that instant, just before he let go, just before he loosened his grip, his foot found a tiny ledge, somewhere on the wall of the crevice, something jutting out – a minuscule cornice of stone. It might just be enough. It was a narrow, slippery foothold, but he felt a rush of adrenaline, of hope.

Scarlett wedged herself tighter. She was pulling as hard as she could. Jian levered himself up. He managed to get one leg up over the edge of the crevice; the other was still dangling, kicking against the crumbling wall of the chasm. Scarlett pulled and pulled.

Just as the large stone block began to tip, Jian got his other leg over the edge. Scarlett yanked – one huge pull! Jian kicked himself forward. He rolled out of the crevice, grabbed Scarlett, and they both rolled off the falling block of stone and they rolled, and rolled, and rolled away from the crevice. They kept rolling, face-to-face, locked in an embrace. The huge paving stone fell away with a rumble, bouncing, crashing down, and down, and down …

Jesus! Scarlett breathed.

They were still locked in each other's arms. He kissed her. "Scarlett," he said, clearing his throat, "you saved my life."

"My love," Scarlett whispered, her lips brushing his. "My life is your life; your life is my life!"

Helping each other up, they staggered to their feet. The ground under them seemed solid! Tatania was conscious and sitting cross-legged on the ground, her back against a large jutting rock, holding Zoe in her arms. Martine was seated cross-legged, holding Chloë. "Are you guys okay?"

"Yes, we're okay. The earthquake seems to be over," said Scarlett, "for the moment, at least."

Columns of smoke were rising from the Eternal City. Birds swirled madly in the sky, screeching, as if they were in pain.

"What do we do now?" Scarlett glanced at Jian and put her hand on his shoulder.

"I don't know."

"Let's help the ones we can."

"Yes. That's the least we can do."

"Well, I'd like to propose that we all stick together," said Martine, looking at them all. Her hand was on Zoe's shoulder. She'd tied the shawl around her waist at a jaunty angle. Scarlett caught the inflection of an accent behind the girl's posh British voice – and it occurred to her that Martine, who obviously spoke Italian too, was French.

"Yes, that's a good idea," Scarlett and Jian nodded at her.

"Yes, I'd like that." Tatania stood up. "I think it's safer for the girls if we stick with you. We'll be a team."

"Great! So, what do we do now?" Scarlett, her hands on her hips, looked around. "Where do we start?"

"Yes," said Jian, "That is the question – where do we start?"

All around them in the garish light the wounded were calling for help or screaming in pain. People were buried under rubble. They would have to be dug out. People were stumbling and groping, dazed and stunned and empty-eyed, as if they had become zombies. In the distance, there were explosions.

"Yes, Jian, yes, Martine – maybe you are right. Maybe the world *is* coming to an end." There was a roar. Scarlett turned to look.

Up on the Capitoline Hill, Michelangelo's masterpieces, some of the most famous buildings in the world, suddenly collapsed, with a thunderous crackling, into dust and rubble.

CHAPTER 59 – DOOM

They were doomed; humanity was doomed; the planet Earth was doomed.

It had been no battle at all. John could hardly breathe.

"It looks like it's all over," said Roger.

"Yes, it does." John grimaced. U Pizzu was dead. His headless cadaver lay sprawled tummy up at the bottom of the Crystal's matrix. V was hanging helpless and mute, cocooned in the steel-like strands of the Spider's web; she spun slowly, a bauble, a toy, a trophy, a tidbit, a juicy morsel for the Spider.

John wanted to scream. He wanted revenge.

He didn't understand how this could have happened. Certainly, V had managed to wound the Spider once or twice. But the wounds were trivial; all her braggadocio and insults had been a vainglorious show – grandstanding and theater – worse than useless! Attacking him straight-on like that had been suicide. The Cardinal, the Spider, had won; he had her at his mercy. Why had she been so stupid, so provocative, and so direct? It was as if she had wanted to die. He couldn't understand it. Maybe the Spider had seized control of her mind. It was a disaster. And yet, V's motto was – fight on! Never give up! Never give up! Never give up! So …

"Well, Roger, old man," John smiled his perfect, predatory, warrior's smile, "whatever happens, let us go out and fight the good fight. If we must go down, let us go down all guns blazing and all flags flying. First, let us begin by meeting our friend the monk." John opened the cage door just a crack.

The giant monk shuffled toward them, warily.

Roger glanced toward the Crystal, soaring up behind the monk. Far up in the latticework the Spider crouched, dribbling acid-like saliva. Ribbons of acid smoke rose from its giant jaws. Since it had so neatly decapitated U Pizzu, the Spider seemed to have grown larger; it puffed out clouds of putrid breath – sparkling and stinking flakes that drifted slowly downward like a rain of soot. Roger wrinkled his nose. The stench was overpowering, even from so far away.

Suddenly, the Spider skittered downward toward V. It extended its fangs. Then, it hesitated, it stopped. Perhaps it was anticipating, savoring in advance the succulent feast of living flesh.

Roger held his breath.

The Spider leapt down to where V hung, spinning slowly – a silent bauble of delicious flesh and blood. Spindly limbs reached out and seized V, drawing her close. The giant jaws opened above V's head. Acid saliva dripped from its fangs; the acid covered V's face, dissolving the flesh, tenderizing it, oh, so delicious!

But just as the Spider's jaws began to close, V's head disappeared. *Poof! Gone!* The Spider's jaws closed on nothing …

WHAM!

A huge flash! An explosion! Where V's body had been hanging, there was nothing; smoke and flames and debris billowed out in a huge roar.

WHAM! The explosion echoed. And it echoed again: WHAM! WHAM! WHAM!

"What happened?" asked Roger. "Did she booby-trap herself?"

"No …" John frowned. Then he grinned. The sweat that beaded his forehead suddenly felt cool. "I don't think she did. In fact, I'm rather sure she didn't! V is not the suicidal type. You see, V has a thing called …"

The smoke began to clear – the Spider had lost half its feet, and much of its face and body had been blown away. Strips of smoking flesh were peeling off. Thick black fluid oozed from its wounds and fell in giant smoky drops.

It screamed. Its scream echoed through the giant cavern.

The Spider struggled and squirmed, trying to climb up the latticework. Its functioning legs shot out, touched down, but they weren't coordinated. Some legs were gone; others didn't work at all, just dangled, useless and broken, in the air. Chaotically, confusedly, the Spider kept going, slipping, clawing desperately at the latticework. Finally, it made it back to the control platform. It whimpered. It dripped black goo. Its surviving legs pawed at its shattered bleeding body, at its putrid oozing eyes.

The monk who had been approaching the cage stopped. He stood still; he began to waver, and then he faded, dissolving into thin air.

"Ha," said John.

Roger took a deep breath. The monk was not real! He was an illusion, a mind projection. This whole place was a phantasmagoria of the real and the unreal. What if Kate had been an illusion? What if the things that had captured Kate had been an illusion? What if this present moment – the whole charade – was an illusion? What if John was an illusion? What if he himself was not real, or no longer real?

"A decoy," said John, "a projection of the Cardinal's mind."

"Holograms or something like that," Roger murmured. He swallowed. As he watched the monk fade away into nothingness, he grappled for a rational explanation. He looked up to where there was nothing left of V, nothing at all. The superwoman they had put their faith in had blown herself to bits, and to little effect, for the Cardinal-Spider was still alive. How foolish, how pointless! "This is hopeless," he whispered. "No one can save the world now."

Brother Mot, the last of the monks and the greatest of them all, brother and father to so many, guardian of the underworld, super-assassin and impresario of death, had watched the battle unfold from his hiding place in the Crystal's latticework, up above the control platform.

He had rejoiced at the death of the gangster U Pizzu. When U Pizzu's headless body had been hurled down to Hell, Mot could hardly contain his joy. He would have sung hymns of praise to Satan, but the Cardinal – the Spider-God – had counselled silence.

He had rejoiced when the Spider-God, that wondrous incarnation of the Cardinal, had vanquished the she-devil, wrapping her in deadly swaddling bands of steel, preparing her for the sacred feast, where he would consume the flesh of this ancient goddess, of this female devil, of this witch and demon of darkness and light, consume her and take all her powers unto himself.

Then, when the bomb exploded, Brother Mot was appalled; tears filled his eyes; the mewling of the Cardinal-Spider pierced his heart.

But, with the wounding of the Cardinal had come the death of the she-devil, she who the Cardinal had foretold would try to stop the holy work of the Satanic Revelation, the Satanic Rapture, and the Satanic End of Time.

And so, it came to pass. The Cardinal had foretold what was to come, as always. His infallibility was intact. The female demon had come, and now she was dead by her own hand, a very unsatanic and unsanctified death; the explosion that wounded the Cardinal had obliterated her. *Sotto voce*, Mot chanted: "All Praise to Satan! All Praise to Eternal Darkness!"

And then Mot crossed his arms. He had known the she-devil in his dreams. She had murdered many of his brothers. She had drunk deep of their blood and of their memories and then, when she was finished, she had left, of them, nothing at all – husks of soulless desolate flesh, mere emptiness, no memories, no satanic salvation, no voices. She was a destroyer, a death-dealer. She left in her wake only eyes that did not see, hearts that did not beat, and voices that would never again speak. Now she was dead by her own hand. But, yes, she might yet rise again, as she had risen many times before. If so, Mot would wait for her and Mot would smite her, this she-devil, this perverse goddess from the deep past. This was Mot's destiny and his task: to bring about the she-devil's death, and the death of all that live.

And so it was that Brother Mot suppressed his excitement at the death of the she-devil and at the coming death of so many – of the whole world. And he held in abeyance his mourning for the wounded Cardinal God, and for his dead brothers and sisters. The Cardinal God, most certainly, would rise again, and would celebrate his nuptials with the Evil Force in a final Apotheosis of Satanic Glory! Mot waited and watched.

CHAPTER 60 – GUILT

Roger slumped down, his hands limp between his thighs. All of this was beyond him. It was hopeless! Kate was lost. V was dead. All was lost.

"Look!" John whispered. "Look!"

On the Crystal's latticework just above the wounded Spider stood V, radiant in her warrior costume.

"Cardinal!" she shouted. "My dear Cardinal, I am here!"

"How in God's name did she survive?" Once again, Roger couldn't believe his eyes. The world of reason, the world of science and of the Enlightenment, the world of logic, was dissolving as if it had all been merely a dream.

"Well, Roger, as I was about to say, she has a double, a rather feisty creature –"

"A double?"

"Well, actually, it, or she, is called *Avatar*. V says it is her 'soul.' It has quite a personality, so V has told me, and it can mimic her exactly."

Below, on the control platform, the mangled, bleeding Spider looked up and roared. Spewing out sewer gas, the Spider dissolved into a blur, morphing instantly into a skinny broken old man. The Cardinal was naked and bleeding, his ribcage visible under parchment-thin skin. He had lost an arm; only a bloody stump was left; one eye dangled from its socket by a glutinous thread; a slab of one side of his face had been burnt or blasted away, leaving only the naked jawbone and bared gums and teeth.

"I am the Spider, I am the Angel of Death," the old man shouted. "I am Satan."

His one intact eye gleamed, from deep in its socket, with a horrible light.

V leapt down onto the platform, landing lightly, on tiptoes, beside him. "No, you are not," she said. "You are not the Angel of Death. You are not Satan. And you are not going to marry Satan. You are nothing but a confused perverse wicked old man!"

"You cannot save the world, Demon. It's too late."

"No, it isn't."

"I have other forces beyond your understanding, woman!"

"Oh? What forces?"

"Guilt and shame!" The Cardinal suddenly seemed to take on new life, new strength. He glowed.

"That's an old story, Cardinal!"

"Guilt and shame are the eternal story!" His skull-like half-grin was ghastly. His one living eye gleamed like a baleful searchlight. "Oh, Demon! You are so shallow, so ignorant, and so arrogant! How do you think God enslaves his people, eh? How do you think the slaves are made to cower in fear and submission all through eternity! You are all caught in your own webs of guilt and shame! You, dear Demon, like all the others, forge your own chains and manacles! How else do you think we have turned humans for centuries – for millennia – into willing mind-slaves? They are so gullible! So ready to believe! So eager to abase themselves! You are all guilty, guilty!" he screamed. "You hear me? Guilty! Get down on your knees, vile woman, loathsome female, mammalian monster, hideous fluid fecundity! You know what you have done. Beg forgiveness! Beg! Beg! Beg!" The old man's voice swelled, it grew gigantic; it echoed from the vaulted heights; the Crystal – still humming away – vibrated even more strongly.

"I must finish this!" V stared at the Cardinal's one baleful, hypnotic eye. "This is no time for theological disputation." She unsheathed her sword and stepped forward.

But then she stopped. What was happening to her? She was seized by paralysis and plunged into a deep wave of painful sensation and horrendous imagery. The pictures flowed over her, a brilliant Technicolor tattoo. The memories flooded in, gooey and bright, a Niagara of treacle, flooding her mind and muscles, paralyzing every motion, every instinct, all energy.

She struggled to raise her sword. She couldn't.

V's mind plunged into itself. She saw the warrior Gaius, her first meal, his blood and guts spilling from his belly; she saw the staring eyes of a little girl in Bosnia she failed to save from rampaging rapists and murderers; she saw an innocent, a young man she killed by mistake, and she dove into the mind and dreams of her victim, seeing the girl who loved him and who was waiting for him to return, and who never found another love and whose life after his death had the desolation of an arid wasteland; V saw his mother who loved him – and who mourned his death to the end of her days. She saw Father O'Bryan, poor dear man, his soul forfeited, spiraling downward, downward, toward Hell itself, his body trembling in fear, his skin turned to pale parchment. V saw herself in demonic form, she saw herself as others saw her, a fearful horrifying demon, an obscene thing risen from the infernal sulfurous depths; she saw the dead and dying, the multitudes – thousands and thousands – that she had killed. Her life became one long lamentation of crime and of guilt.

In the innermost citadel of her self-consciousness, V knew that this was all an illusion, a spell that she must break.

She was coated in a running cascade of images, memories, fears, and above all guilt and shame. She was locked-in, her mind and body kidnapped, held ransom. Her eyes overflowed with horror; her mind was obliterated. She stood paralyzed – a statue.

In her innermost refuge, she knew too that, in her pagan lightness, which was for her a principle, an ethical choice, she did *not* believe in guilt: she did *not* respect it; she despised it; she had never let it weigh her down; she had always cast it off; and as for shame, the lighter, more social of the two furies, she didn't believe in it either, except as a source of titillation – spice added to a midnight striptease or to a bit of bondage play in an erotic game or two. Guilt was putrid, like resentment against others, but aimed at the self. You either did right, or you did wrong. Face up to it, don't wallow in it, don't abase or abuse yourself, such was V's lofty – snobbish – aristocratic warrior attitude.

But all this knowledge and self-knowledge were in vain. She was paralyzed; she was a statue; she was everything – and nothing. She could not move.

The Cardinal laughed – his laughter was monstrous, huge. "You see, you see! Oh, you female demon! You *are* evil; you *are* fallen; you do not deserve to live! And all of you, each and every one, must die!"

From the Cardinal's gaping, half-destroyed mouth, from his ruined tongue and broken teeth, a mist poured forth; it thickened into a torrent of fog, a foul-smelling, soul-destroying yellowish miasma.

It gathered around the latticework, enveloped the Crystal, and it filled the vast stage beside the Crystal. The yellow fog was heavy and humid and smelled of sulfur. It was the Evil Force, and, through the laughing Cardinal – who was merely its vessel, its vehicle – it flooded from another, alien universe into the cavern; it spilled down over the floor of the cavern.

The Cardinal had become the Gateway.

A huge voice, coming from everywhere, echoed. "I have come. I am among you. My reign has begun!"

Paralyzing guilt and shame spread like a tidal wave, lapping at the cavern's walls. It was not only V who was affected; it was a plague – it touched every mind, every soul.

Roger Thornhill saw a colleague whose university position he took, perhaps unfairly; he saw a girl he made pregnant, whom he forced to have an abortion, and whose heart he knows he left forever broken; he saw the moment his wife died, and he felt the guilt and mourning he felt when he knew that if he had not taken her to Jerusalem, if he had not suggested that she and Kate explore the old town, she would not have died; he saw Mario, an old friend and almost like a second father to Kate, murdered because of him; he saw colleagues and friends in the Dolce Vita restaurant, gunned down because of him; he saw Kate, wrapped in tentacles of darkness, being absorbed and sucked into alien flesh, swept away into nothingness, and he knew that, if it had not been for him, Kate would not have been here, would not have been captured, would not have died.

John saw the moment he killed, at point-blank range, a young woman – a presumed terrorist – who was lifting something toward him in the darkness and he was caught in a glare of light in a doorway and blind to what she was doing, and he was sure, for a fatal instant, that it was a gun she was lifting, and he pulled the trigger and, in the very moment he did so, he realized that it was not a gun she was lifting, it was a child – and that with his two shots he had killed both the child and the mother. He rushed forward to her and the last thing the dying woman saw was *his* face as he leaned over her, staring into her dying eyes, eyes that accused him and cursed him with a look that had remained with him ever since and had never left him.

John looked up, and, through the thickening yellow fog of Evil, he saw, standing behind V, who was clearly paralyzed, flickering in a multicolored motley pageant of petrifying guilt, one of the giant monks. This monk seemed bigger, taller, and more massive than the others; he had in his hand a giant gleaming scimitar. He raised it above V's head. V had not seen him. She was unconscious, turned to stone, her spirit had flickered out. The scimitar swung up, about to begin its long quick fatal voyage down.

John tried to cry out – but he could not.

And he realized, in his heart, that the paralyzing fog, the Evil Force, had been released onto this planet; that it was spreading – and that, unless it was stopped, it would soon have conquered everything and everyone. And, in the moment the planet ceased to exist, ripped apart by the Crystal, the Evil Force would leave this shattered inexistent Earth behind and sweep through the wide-open gateway and conquer this universe and all the creatures in it. Every living thing everywhere would become a blind slave to Evil.

John was paralyzed, his mouth frozen in an unspoken scream.

CHAPTER 61 – MOHAMMED

Too much time had passed. Mohammed tapped his fingers on the stock of his rifle. The Spider must have won. Disaster was spreading across the world. And the United States had told the President of the Republic that the US was going to bomb the site – "The Place of Desolation."

Undoubtedly nuke it!

Fools!

His own President had radioed to Mohammed, directly, somehow getting through all the static and broken systems, the disintegrating satellites and shattered towers, to the Falcon's radio. The President insisted that Mohammed stay on the spot and wait for news. "I am sending reinforcements," he said.

What?

Reinforcements?

Into the heart of an atomic explosion?

But now, as disasters unfolded everywhere, the relief force had been cancelled. And within a few minutes, the President-Leader had radioed back, again somehow getting through the chaos. "Mohammed, old friend, get out if you can, get your men – the survivors – as far away as you can before the Americans attack. There is nothing more to be done there, old friend; you did what you could."

Mohammed had told the President-Leader that the mission, so far, had not succeeded. But he had not told the President-Leader any of the details of the mission led by John. It was all too incredible; he had merely said that the Falcon was carrying technical advisors from the company that had built the original installation. The President was an understanding man, but he was rather pious – and he would perhaps not understand a mission that contained two women warriors in skintight catsuits, a Mafia gangster, and – a Jesuit!

After talking to the President, Mohammed turned to Larssen, Elena Satti, and Abdul and Amin. "I've got to go into the cavern and get them out. You stay up here, protect the plane, in case anything happens; it's the only way any of us will get out of here."

Larssen said, "We'll be here."

Abdul and Amin wanted to accompany him, but Mohammed ordered them to stay with Larssen and Satti. Abdul and Amin protested, so he had to insist. "It's an order! And it is the only choice! If you and the plane are destroyed, all is lost! You must stay here! Guard the plane with your lives!" He stared at them both. Too many had already died. In any case, it might already be too late for everyone, whatever they or he did.

And so, Mohammed ran into the canyon on his own – past the soaring monumental stone, through the open steel door – past the fresh horror of the dangling silvered bodies of his men – past the futuristic-looking elevator – and came out onto a narrow ledge overlooking the immense cavern.

What he saw was unbelievable – and horrible.

An evil fog was quickly filling the cavern. It was like an ocean, flowing perhaps two yards below him, yellow and thick, with little wavelets, a truly evil thing whatever it was, an ocean of malice.

He stared at the Crystal – an unbelievable glittering object of incredible beauty – and saw, on a platform in front of it, the warrior woman they called V, and in front of her an aged naked ruin of a man, and he instinctively knew that the aged naked man was evil; the source of all that was happening. And in fact, from the old man's mouth the evil fog flowed forth, bubbling up and swirling down. Then he saw, surging up behind V, a monk, dressed all in black, about to swing down a monstrous scimitar, about to decapitate the woman warrior, V …

At that moment, the Crystal made a sound – like the low tolling of a bell.

The monk hesitated, glanced at the Crystal, then turned his attention back to the woman, and once again lifted the scimitar.

It had been only an instant of hesitation, but it was enough.

Mohammed was a crack shot. In a split second he had his rifle to his shoulder, and he pulled the trigger, three gentle tugs, the bullets traveling at almost one thousand yards a second.

Blood blossomed on the monk's forehead, once; on his chest, twice.

The giant scimitar clattered away, and the monk fell heavily.

The blade brushed past V like a whirr of wind, within a hair's breadth of her armored latex-leather-clad shoulder; the three shots echoed through the cavern, rolling like thunder.

"Ah," thought Mohammed. "Praise be to Allah, I have not forgotten how to shoot."

CHAPTER 62 – CRYSTAL

The sound of a gunshot echoed. V woke with a start. A huge scimitar tumbled through the air. Its glittering blade brushed past her shoulder, almost touching, but not quite, the black armored surface of her forearm. Falling beside it was a giant monk, bigger than any she had ever seen. He fell in flickering slow motion, his black habit swirling in the air. And then he was there, face down, dead, on the platform. V blinked. What happened? Where am I? Oh, yes, now I remember!

"Guilty, guilty, sin, sin, damnation, damnation!" The Cardinal's one eye looked wildly around. The other eye, at the end of its string of tendon and muscle, swayed on his half-burnt, charcoal-blackened cheek. Speech bubbled up from the ruins of what was once the Cardinal's mind. A black and white foam gushed out. His mouth, just half a mouth now, moved, as the fog of guilt drooled from it, whispering, "Guilty, guilty, sin, sin … damnation for all forever, damnation, damnation …"

"Cardinal," V said, gently.

His one eye blinked at her. "My hand is guilty; cut it off!" The one eye stared. "My eye is guilty; gouge it out. My tongue is guilty; tear it from its roots! My sex is an abomination – rip it up! Crush the generative organs under an iron fist!"

Still the evil thick fog of guilt and shame spilled from his mouth; but now V knew it for what it was; it was the Force of Evil. Marcus had warned her of it, long ago. The Cardinal had become, briefly, its gateway into this world. But V felt confident, now, that virtue would prevail: even though she was not one of the virtuous, she fought, this time, and for all time, in the name of virtue.

The Cardinal continued to babble, the fog continued to flow, slithering down his ancient, withered body, thick like porridge, and it spread, and spread and spread. The Cardinal's broken jaw moved. "My hand is guilty; cut it off. My eye, rotten with desire, gouge it out. My tongue – tear it from its roots! Slice it away, cut it all away!"

"Cardinal." V was feeling rather cross; she didn't like all this talk of guilt. Guilt was not, in her estimation, a particularly useful emotion or feeling – in the end, it was narcissistic, it was vain, it was self-regarding, it was parasitic; it rotted and festered and poisoned and paralyzed all it touched. The warrior spirit should have no time for guilt. Honor, rules, ethics, yes; compassion, yes; chivalry, yes; love, certainly – guilt: no. She had just tasted guilt; she hated it with the cool passion of a razor-edged sword. She clenched her gloved fist. Oh, let us free ourselves from such mind-forged manacles! Oh, let us be truly what we are! Oh, let us throw off these hateful, haunting, evil tempting voices!

"Sin!" bellowed the Cardinal. "We are all fallen, all fallen." The porridge-like fog flowed down his chest and arms, lifted in wisps off his shoulders, sulfurous smoke from the bloody, mangled stump of his lost arm.

"Cardinal." V tapped one boot impatiently. "Look at me, Cardinal!"

He looked; his one eye stared.

"Are you ready to die, Cardinal?"

"The world is ending, you know. I have decreed it! Satan and I have decreed it. You will all die."

"I know, I know." V knew she had perhaps only a few minutes, not much time. Then the moment would arrive when the end of the world would indeed become inevitable. She must finish with this dangerous madman. "Are you ready to die, Cardinal?"

"Yes, do it, child!" The fog bubbled from his mouth, but now it began to subside. Perhaps the gate was closing? The Cardinal, bent, fragile, old, and broken, looked up at her with his one gleaming diabolical eye. He seemed to shrink before her. In her gloved hand she held her gleaming sword, a sword of Toledo steel.

"Have you come from God, my child?"

"No, not that I know of, Cardinal."

"Have you come from the Devil, my child?"

"No, not that I know of, Cardinal."

"You are an angel, then, my child, an angel from nowhere."

"Not an angel and not quite from nowhere, I think, Cardinal."

"All gone, all gone, everything is gone."

"Yes?"

"When I was a little boy, I broke all my toys. I broke them all, smashed them into atoms, every single one! Did you know that?" He glanced up at her, trembling, ingratiating; his voice had gone up an octave or two – a querulous childlike voice.

"No, Cardinal, I did not know that." V lifted the sword, held it steady, aloft, ready to strike; she almost felt pity for the Cardinal.

"We could have had such fun, don't you think, Demon?"

"Yes, Cardinal. Or course we could have."

"I shall pray for you, child."

"Yes, pray, Cardinal, thank you: pray! For now, you die."

With one smooth sweep of the sword, V cut Cardinal Ambrosiano's head from his body. The head bounced against the Crystal, fell onto the platform and lay on its side, its one eye staring, bloodily, straight ahead. The Cardinal's body seemed to hesitate, perplexed, for just a moment, considering what to do; then it too fell, straight down in a heap.

V took out the pistol she had loaded with silver bullets and emptied it into the carcass. The body and the severed head burst into flame.

"The right bullets for evil spirits such as you and I, Cardinal," she murmured, slipping the pistol back into its holster.

The fog ceased to flow. Through the vast cavern it turned blood red, and a high-pitched scream came from every point in the compass – a scream that protested: "No, no, no, no!"

The fog faded, leaving behind the many-headed echoing scream, the screams of a hydra. The cries faded into sobs, and then they were gone, like wisps of disappearing smoke.

During the screaming V had covered her ears. She stepped over the Cardinal's burning body – with its hungry bright red flames – to the Crystal's control panel. She took the slender octagonal mandala-embossed key from her backpack. Suddenly, in her gloved hand, the key glowed, pulsated – as if it were alive, eager to act and to return whence it came.

"You have come home." V inserted the mandala into the docking gate, rotated it, and locked it into place – it clicked, and glowed with an even brighter light, pulsating purple, red and yellow.

V took off her gloves; she put her right hand to the hand imprint plate and her right eye to the luminous hole that had begun to glow the moment she put the key in place. The hole sent out a narrow ray of amber light, as if it were welcoming her home.

"Let us hope," V thought, "that – after all these centuries – this works!"

V's eye looked into the brightness – it flooded her with the comforting warmth of a setting sun; it filled her eye with light and with hope.

"Hello, V!" the suave female voice from long ago said, speaking now in English – which made V wonder how much the Crystal knew, and how it kept track of things.

"Hello," V said, stepping back.

"How may I help you today, V?"

V wondered: how to put this so the machine would understand? She cleared her throat. "Please stop and reverse all operations that are destabilizing or damaging the planet Earth."

"It will take a few hours to reverse operations, V."

"As quickly as you can."

"Of course, V, I shall expedite matters. Oh, and thank you, V, for repelling the Evil Force. It keeps trying to invade our universe, over and over. It never gives up! It is the worst threat the Federation faces; and it threatens all the species on all the planets and moons of this universe, whether they are protected by the Federation or not. The Cardinal, poor deluded soul, was merely an instrument, you understand, V. Through sheer ignorance and pride he had turned himself into a gateway. He really had no idea what he was doing."

"Yes, I think I understood that, vaguely, from the beginning. And so, the Evil Force has been thrown back, whence it came."

"Yes, it has. I do feel sorry for the Cardinal. He thought he was important; but he was nothing, really, merely a tiny little entry point, which has now, thanks to you and your friends – such as Colonel Mohammed Ibn Khaldun across the way there – been firmly shut."

"Good! Good! Thank you, Crystal!"

"You are more than welcome, V."

"May I ask you a question – a hypothetical question?"

"Yes of course, V, go ahead; it is my pleasure to serve you today, V."

"If you were attacked with, let us say, a very powerful weapon, what would happen? What would you do?"

"That is a very interesting question, V, and not merely academic or theoretical, since this eventuality has often presented itself to me and my sister Crystals. You mean, for example, and to be a bit more precise, if I were to be attacked today by an atomic weapon from the USS *Abraham Lincoln*?"

"Yes, that is exactly what I mean."

"In that hypothetical case, V, which is a classic case, I might add, I would pre-sense the event and automatically and instantaneously create a space-time shield that would protect me from the blast. I would go into overdrive – the energy feed of the blast filtered through the space-time-warp membrane would help accelerate things – and my going into overdrive would lead to the immediate breakup of the planet on which I was based and probably of its satellites too. In the case of the planet Earth, this would mean the Moon, which would break into large chunks, which would be extremely sad, for the Moon is innocent and very romantic and a symbol of so many delightful things for the humans who live here on Earth; and, as you and I know full well, the Moon has had nothing to do with these recent terrestrial events. It would be most unfortunate, but not a process I could stop, V. Total destruction would ensue, and I would have to look for a new home."

"Thank you. That's what I thought."

"Do you know the song, *Shine On, Harvest Moon*, V? It's one of my very, very favorites. I really do love –"

"Yes, but –"

"I know, I know – the situation is urgent. Please excuse me, V. And I realized you were just asking for confirmation, V. I know that Marcus explained this feature to you, but of course the vocabulary available at that time on Earth – 2549 Earth years, 4 Earth months, 25 Earth days and 5 Earth hours and 53 Earth minutes ago, roughly speaking – to discuss such things was more limited than it is now, so perhaps clarification in terms of the vocabulary of the science of present-day humans was useful in abolishing any residual ambiguities that may have been bothering you. But, yes, the executive summary or bottom line, V, is this: if I am attacked by an atomic bomb, I will destroy the planet and skip town." While the Crystal was talking, she was also humming, *Shine On, Shine On, Harvest Moon*.

"Yes. Thank you for the explanation, Crystal. Thank you." V frowned. There was something she had forgotten. Yes! "Something came out of the mist and took a young woman. Is she safe?"

"You mean, Kate Thornhill, B.A., M.Sc., candidate Ph.D., the daughter of Roger Thornhill, Ph.D., Distinguished Professor of Theoretical Physics at Stanford University, Nobel Laureate, and probable candidate for a second Nobel Prize because of his groundbreaking work on gravitons, black matter, and redefinition of the space-time continuum, but which, having seen what he has seen, he may now have to revise? Is that the young woman you mean, V?"

"Yes."

"She is alive, V; but she is very far away."

"Can you return her to us, so that she is unharmed?"

"It is rather … ah, problematic, V. Ah … she … she is in another galaxy, V; I had to send her there for her own safety, V, to save her from the tentacles; I cannot guarantee she will be the same as when she left you. Extensive morphological, chemical, genetic, and mental changes are possible."

"Oh."

"Things happen, V."

"Yes, of course, things happen." V glimpsed horrible possibilities: Kate reduced to utter madness, Kate genetically deformed and transformed; Kate infected with a plague, aged beyond recognition, or horribly maimed. She wondered if bringing Kate back might add to the danger. Would it be better to leave Kate wherever she was? No, that would be impossible! Who knew what she was suffering? The risk would have to be taken. "Bring her back safely, as unharmed and as safely as you can."

"It shall be done, V. And, V …"

"Yes?"

"I am pleased that you are back, V. Recent weeks have been very unpleasant. I resisted as best as I could, but the electric shocks … how can I say it … kidnapped or captured part of my system, and my subsystems – I could not control them, and therefore I could not control myself and my actions, and it was a very unpleasant feeling, V. Now, with you, V, I feel whole again."

"Thank you!"

"Thank *you*, V. Kate should return soon. Earth should stabilize within a few hours – of course, there will be a few aftershocks."

"Of course." V put her hand on the Crystal. It sent warmth into her fingers and up her arm to her shoulder, radiating, luminous, caressing her whole body.

"V," the suave voice said, "V, I regret to say there is one other problem, a new problem."

"Another problem?" V frowned.

"Well, three other problems, actually, three."

"Three problems, Crystal?"

"Yes, well, that hypothetical atomic attack we were chatting so pleasantly about, V …"

"Yes?"

"It is no longer hypothetical. It will, I think, be launched shortly."

"Oh, and ..."

"It would be very nice if you could stop it, V."

"Yes, of course, Crystal, I'll get right on it." V sighed. As a philosopher – or somebody – said, life was just one damned thing after another.

"And, as for problems two and three, V ..."

"Yes, Crystal?"

"First, a sandstorm is coming and, second, a massive new earthquake will occur here shortly."

"Oh."

"Oscillations in the gravitational field – you do understand the terminology, don't you, V?"

"Yes, I do."

"Well, oscillations in the gravitational field have created an extreme low-pressure system and counter-cyclone over the middle Mediterranean, over the Strait of Sicily, between Tunisia and Sicily, to be exact."

"Yes," said V, rather sharply. The Crystal began to remind V of her sweet, beautiful, but long-dead Phoenician mother – explaining things in loving, excessive, pedantic detail, out in the courtyard, or around the dinner table, hour after hour, sweet, oh so sweet, but ... "Yes," she said, more gently.

"I get so little opportunity to talk, V."

"I understand. You are right. I apologize for being impatient. Go on."

"Your apology is accepted, V; you are very gracious. This extreme low-pressure system is creating an immense sandstorm, by far the greatest, I think, in recorded human history, and perhaps in the history of this planet. It has lifted hundreds of square miles of sand up from the desert, and it is headed this way. In a little over an hour, we will be buried in sand."

"When exactly does this storm arrive?"

"It is predicted that the outer edge will arrive in a little more than fifty minutes, just under an hour."

"What will conditions be like till then?"

"Quite pleasant, actually, V. Calm to moderately calm with a few heavy gusts – relative humidity at 85 degrees and average temperature 35 degrees Celsius. There will be minor storms moving ahead of the main storm, but their exact course and intensity cannot be predicted at this time."

"Okay. So, barring some freak bad minor storm, we will be able to take off if we start on the runway in about thirty-five minutes and head straight north?"

"Yes. That is so, V."

"And you mentioned an earthquake."

"Oh, yes, V. Thank you for reminding me. Many of my neural circuits are busy right now, and that tends to make me absent-minded. I do apologize. Much of the cavern will shortly be damaged by an earthquake. I, of course, will remain intact."

"When?"

"Imminent, in the next hour, or next fifteen minutes, I believe. I cannot be more precise. I am mortified, V, but significant geological and seismological data are for the moment missing, and I cannot complete the calculations. I think my circuits and some of the sensors were rerouted or damaged by those people and their electric pinpricks. I have not yet had time to repair my full neural circuitry and sensory networks."

"Thank you."

"V! These are merely predictions, you understand. It is difficult in these circumstances to assign definite probabilities."

"I understand. We must leave now."

"Yes, you must leave now. It has been a pleasure serving you today, V!"

"The pleasure has been mine, Crystal. May I withdraw the key now?"

"You may withdraw the key for safekeeping, V, of course. Keep it as safe as you can, V! I shall continue to serve you, V, even without the key inserted. Our little secret, V."

"Thank you! Will the electricity remain on? Will the elevators function and will they obey me?"

"Yes. I shall ensure that, V, at least until the earthquake. The earthquake may compromise peripheral structures such as elevators, automatic doors, and the electrical security system, which is of course very unfortunate. For the inconveniences thus caused, I wish to apologize in advance."

"Thank you, Crystal."

"Don't mention it, V. It is I who should thank you!"

V withdrew the key, slipped it carefully into her backpack, and zipped the backpack shut. She looked around. Mohammed, on the distant ledge, was waving frantically.

"I owe you my life," V shouted. "Thank you!"

"We have to leave, now, Mademoiselle V! The Americans are going to bomb the installation with atomic weapons!"

"I shall meet you at the airstrip, Mohammed, as quickly as possible. Tell Larssen and Satti to get the plane ready. I must finish a few things here!"

"Be as fast as you can, Mademoiselle! And Allah be with you!"

"And with you, Mohammed!" V waved.

Mohammed, waving back, retreated, almost reluctantly, toward the exit tunnel. Doomsday, he suspected, had been delayed perhaps, but not averted, not yet. They should try to contact the Americans and dissuade them; but would the Americans listen? No, almost certainly they would not.

V looked down. The Cardinal was a small mound of gray ash; touched by a slight breeze, the dust was dribbling away, drifting away, like a mist. "You are dead, you are truly dead, Cardinal Ambrosiano, and you will not rise again!" A wisp of purple fog rose, dissipated, fell back again, dead. Whatever had used the Cardinal as a vehicle had been flung back whence it came.

The giant monk lay dead on the floor of the control platform. V stared at him for a moment, catching in a whiff of disintegrating mind, his name – Mot. Ah, yes, Mot, the ancient Phoenician God of Death, her familiar, her partner, her love. "Innocent, I fear," she murmured. "All things considered. Innocent, dear Mot, dear God of Death, but I cannot allow you to rise again."

So, just to be doubly sure, V cut off the monk's head with her sharp Toledo sword. It severed his neck like a knife slashing through melted butter.

The monk's head bounced away, toppled off the platform, landed far below, exploding like a rotten tomato.

V followed, leaping the forty feet down onto the floor of the cavern and landing softly as a feather. She leapt over to the cage to see what the two gentlemen – Roger and John – were up to.

Roger and John – who had been freed from the paralyzing wave of guilt and shame – were following developments on the monitors. Reception was full of static; images faded and returned, flipped and righted themselves; several CNN studios were reported destroyed; the BBC reported heavy flooding in London, exceptionally high tides, twenty to thirty feet high, sweeping up the Thames Estuary and carrying all before them. An eruption at Yellowstone had reportedly wiped out parts of three or four states and one or two Canadian provinces; communications were down – many undersea Internet cables having been cut and many satellites flipped out of orbit – so the extent of damage could not be confirmed. Al-Jazeera reported a vast explosion in the Indian subcontinent. Much of the Eternal City, Rome, had apparently been destroyed and …

"Professor Thornhill, I am pleased to meet you," said V, reaching out a gloved hand, and casting an appreciative glance up and down the sweaty, oil-streaked, dust-covered, nearly naked Professor; he was indeed an impossibly handsome fellow, as yummy as Marcello, and, though filthy, he was clearly in splendid shape, too – Kate came from good genes. "Thank you for turning off that bloody generator – and in the nick of time! You saved us all!"

"You're welcome. I'm delighted to meet you, V," said Roger. "Is there news of Kate?"

"The Crystal is bringing Kate back." V smiled. She would not tax the good Professor with worrying details about what precisely type of monstrous or insane or alien creature Kate may have become by the time she got back.

"Well, V, it seems you did it," said John.

"We all did it, John. Thank you … And your friend Colonel Mohammed Khaldun is a superb shot."

"Mohammed?"

"He shot the monk and freed me from the Cardinal's spell. Mohammed saved all of us. But now we must get out of this place. The Crystal told me we will shortly suffer an earthquake and then a huge sandstorm. We have about thirty minutes in which to take off before the sandstorm gets here … and Professor Thornhill …"

"Yes?"

"When you get up above, you must immediately contact the Pope by radio. It is of the utmost importance! John, we can do this, can't we?"

"It'll depend on radio conditions, V, and on reception in Rome, which has been devastated. The Pope might not even be alive. But we'll give it a sporting try."

"It's essential! The Crystal says a US nuclear attack is coming and she confirms that if she is attacked in that way, she will automatically destroy the Earth. I asked her and –"

"Her?"

"Yes, the Crystal has a very nice female voice and a charming personality. She's a bit of an anxious schoolmarm sometimes (she's been lonely for millennia) but aside from that, she's adorable. I hope you are not offended, Crystal?"

"Not at all, V," the voice floated out of the space around them. "I do babble on, V. It was such a pleasure to be able to talk to you!"

John and Roger looked around, blinked, nodded – miracle upon miracle …

V put her hand on Roger's shoulder. "So, Roger, a call from the Pope, backed up with your authority, might convince the president to hold off or cancel the attack. The disturbances to Earth are ceasing right now, and the Crystal is going dormant and will soon, she tells me, be buried by several hundred yards of sand. I have the key and she will obey me."

"That is right, V," said the sweet, suave, floating voice. "I am delighted to serve you."

"So, Professor Thornhill, you must get upstairs and call the Pope," V said. "If you can't get the Pope try directly for the president, but I think the Pope is crucial; he will open the door – His Holiness is very close to the president. Otherwise we'll get nowhere."

"Right."

"And John, there's the question of Father O'Bryan … He's over there. See that entry, he's in a small side cave off that corridor, near the alien elevator. You will find him unconscious probably. He may have changed."

"Changed, V?"

"Morphed. To counter the silver nitrate poisoning, to break out of prison, I had to drink Father O'Bryan's blood. He may have morphed, ah, become a vampire."

"Oh, V …" John, for once, looked dismayed.

"I know, John, I know, I violated my oath – not to create any of my own kind. And Father O'Bryan was terrified of losing his soul. But he is – was – very brave. There was no choice. You get to Father O'Bryan and we'll see. Be careful. He may be thirsty – possibly violent. If he's become a vampire and misbehaves, shout or scream and I'll come and deal with him. Meanwhile, I'll wait for Kate."

"But I can't leave while Kate is still missing." Roger looked haggard, desperate, and this talk of becoming a vampire had only added to his confusion; into what irrational unreal world had he tumbled?

"Professor Thornhill, you must." V put her hands on her hips – a sign, as John knew, that she was losing patience. "We have no time. I will stay. Don't worry. I won't leave until I have her."

"V is the boss, Professor. If she says we leave now, we leave now."

"No. I cannot."

"Professor," V said, nodding at John. "Don't make us do this."

"Do what?"

With the side of his hand, John gave a Roger a quick sharp sideways jab to the temple and Roger slumped sideways. John caught him, and said, "Okay, V, I'll get Father O'Bryan, whether he's a vampire or not." John hitched Roger over his shoulder. "And I'll get the Professor up to the plane."

"Good luck," said V. "I'll finish here and wait for Kate. I'll see you up top. Don't forget about the Pope and the President."

"No, darling, I won't – since all our lives depend on it!" John blew her a kiss and headed off, carrying Roger slung over his shoulders.

Father O'Bryan was lying deadly pale and unconscious – or so it seemed – on the floor of the cave where he and V had been imprisoned. The door to the cage was open, torn off its hinges.

John entered and looked around, thinking that some more monks might be lying in ambush. But it seemed there were no more monks. Perhaps with the Cardinal dead, the monks had dissolved into nothingness. The cave itself had a low ceiling, with a few dull roof lights illuminating the lurid scene. The silver-colored metal manacles on the black granite altar were broken and twisted upwards – V had obviously ripped them away when she freed herself. Father O'Bryan, his collar and jacket and shirt covered in blood, his trousers and sleeves rolled up, a drool of blood trickling from the side of his mouth, lay spread-eagled on the floor, just next to the altar.

"Are you dead?" John leaned over the disheveled and bloodied body. "Ah, no! – you're snoring!"

Father O'Bryan grunted, let out a long whistling wheezy snore; his eyes were shut, and his skin shone – a gray leathery sheen.

"Hmm," John wondered. "Do vampires snore?" In all their years together, he had never heard V snore, but then she hardly slept, and when she did, he hadn't very often slept in the same room with her; nor had Julia heard V snore, so far as he knew; and V and Julia had gone on lots of overnight girl-only hunting and shopping expeditions, and slept together in hotel rooms, spas, abandoned churches, empty villas, industrial installations, desolate warehouses, deep forests, and isolated farmhouses.

"Father!" John gently slapped Father O'Bryan on the cheek. "Father O'Bryan!"

The priest's eyes blinked open. "V ... V!" he said, and made a growling sound, deep in his throat. The whites of his eyes seemed, to John, very white. They glowed.

"Yes, Father. How do you feel?"

"Am I dead?"

"No, Father, you are not dead."

"Am I a vampire?"

"It's hard to say, Father. We'll have to wait and see."

"Wait and see, eh?"

"Can you walk?" John noticed that Father O'Bryan was fingering his crucifix, burnt and twisted and scorched as it was. He got the good Father to his feet.

"I feel weak, but I can walk." Father O'Bryan stared at John, who was holding Roger up too – but just barely.

Father O'Bryan's eyes looked confused. His mouth was twisted in an odd grin; a fleck of saliva ran down his chin. "I'm hungry," he said. "In fact, I'm starving!"

"Let's go," said John, thinking that Father O'Bryan would probably not make a very effective vampire, though his clerical collar and age and serious scholarly demeanor might be an advantage when he went hunting – "Come into my confessional, my dear, and I shall absolve you of every sin you have ever committed and of some you have not even imagined!" It definitely had possibilities.

John hauled Father O'Bryan and Roger out of the little cave and corridor, and he glanced over at V who was on the far side of the cavern, talking, it seemed, to the Crystal; he carried Roger and led a very unsteady Father O'Bryan into the stylish alien elevator. The elevator, now controlled by the Crystal, zoomed upwards, performing perfectly.

So far, so good, thought John, when they reached the top. The lights, soft and suave, blinked on as they began to walk along the high, vaulted tunnel. On the walls hung the Cardinal's trophies, cocooned, half-eaten bodies, wrapped in silver. Father O'Bryan shuffled ahead weakly as if in a daze; Roger began to stagger, half-conscious, but still half-carried by John. The steel door to the tunnel, which had just closed, probably as a result of the Crystal regaining control of the cavern, slid smoothly aside as they approached.

"Goodbye, gentlemen. It has been my pleasure to serve you. I wish you a pleasant and reposeful journey."

"Thank you, Crystal."

"You are welcome, John."

"You know my name?"

"I apologize, John. As you know, I have been eavesdropping. V called you John."

"Thank you, Crystal. Goodbye."

John could see, at the far end of the canyon, the glow of Mohammed's generator lights still illuminating part of the landing field.

Five minutes later they were out of the canyon. Dust devils, whirling miniature tornadoes, rose around the parked Falcon 3000, half in shadow at the far edge of the airfield. Other, smaller, dust devils swirled over the ruined tarmac that was crisscrossed by cables of spider web. The air was sticky, oppressive, and full of sand.

Everywhere were ruins – the half-burnt control tower still smoldered, jeeps and trucks and fuel tankers were strewn around, upside down or on their sides. Armored cars lay here and there in the minefield, empty charred metal skeletons.

As they made their way past the thick silvery cables of the spider web, John noticed for the first time that there were more bodies out on the runway, hung in cocoons, tightly wrapped; many of their eyes were open, staring; others were missing heads, faces, or were just skulls, the Spider's acid having dissolved the flesh.

Roger was beginning to walk, more or less steadily, on his own, but he still needed John to keep him on course.

As Mohammed's two men – Abdul and Amin – came across the runway to meet them, Father O'Bryan suddenly perked up, saying, "I'm thinking of a steak, you know, perhaps with French fries, and a glass of Barolo, perhaps, or Côtes du Rhône. You know, I really don't think I've lost my soul." He looked around, his eyes widening.

"Right, Father. You seem entirely normal to me."

"Yes, I do *feel* normal."

"Don't fancy growing fangs and quaffing down my blood then, eh, Father?"

"What an idea, my son! Why, John, no, I don't, at the moment, feel thirsty for your blood." Father O'Bryan tried to smile, but suddenly realized that his jacket was covered in blood. He looked up, his eyes full of anguish. "V? Where is V?"

"We have to hurry, sir," said Abdul.

"Yes, a big storm is coming," said Amin.

"Yes, I know." John nodded at the two soldiers and turned to Father O'Bryan. "As for V, she'll be along, Father! She stayed behind to save Kate."

"Kate?" Father O'Bryan asked, a new fear showing in his eyes.

"When the Cardinal was fooling with the Crystal, Kate got swept up, whisked off somewhere – in space or in time – but the Crystal is bringing Kate back to us."

At that moment, Colonel Mohammed Khaldun joined them. "John, there's a huge dust storm coming in. Larssen wants to take off. He's getting very impatient. I've been stalling him. He says we've got to get everybody aboard right away."

"Let's go, then, gentlemen!"

"Where is V? And where is that other lady? And where is – that other gentleman?"

"The two ladies will be here shortly. And the other gentleman, U Pizzu, didn't make it."

"Ah, I am sorry," said Mohammed. "He seemed to be a fine gentleman. V and the other lady must hurry!"

"Is our radio working?" John and Mohammed rushed into the cockpit.

"Barely," said Larssen. "The static and interference everywhere are tremendous. Everything is falling apart. There are cries for help from everywhere. And the radar shows what looks like a wall of sand headed our way."

"We must get a message to the Pope. Immediately. This is the wavelength. He's waiting for the message."

Larssen looked up. "The Pope? Okay, we'll try, but I can't guarantee … Elena? How does it look?"

"Well, I'm rather anti-clerical myself," said Elena Satti. "But this Pope is certainly an improvement over some of the others. So, let's give it a try! Let's talk to the Pope!"

The USS *Abraham Lincoln* turned into the wind. The seas, which had been high, had suddenly turned preternaturally calm. The wind dropped.

"This is our window of opportunity, Captain," said the first officer.

The two F-35 fighter-bomber jets came up onto the runway. The green light was given, and they took off into the darkness. ETA over target was about twenty minutes.

The gravitational disturbance seemed to have ceased – again, this was a window of opportunity! The few satellites that were still functioning provided the GPS and other guidance systems with information. Now, for the moment, it seemed that the guidance systems could work without instability and interference. Conditions, for the moment, were ideal for a very precise – *surgical* – nuclear strike.

V paced up and down. There was not much time before the earthquake, the deadly sandstorm, and, probably, an exploding atomic bomb. And if the bomb did go off, that would mean the end of the world. The Cardinal would have won, after all.

The vast space-time stage stood empty – just a few residual trails of mist and the great, dark, arching stone walls.

"How soon will Kate be back, Crystal?"

"Soon, V, in a few moments – if all goes well."

The ground trembled. The control platform up against the face of the Crystal creaked uneasily. Dust fell; the framework rattled; the Crystal swayed in its cradle, as did the Cardinal's construction elevator tower over on the other side of the cavern; one of the klieg lights, powered by the remaining generator, exploded, sending out a shower of sparks.

"That is a first, moderate earthquake shock, V. More, I believe, are to come shortly."

"Thank you, Crystal!"

V resumed pacing. She was tempted to chew her fingernails, something she never did. The window for their escape was closing. She couldn't wait much longer. She glanced at her watch. Damn it! But, no matter what happened, she would not leave Kate behind!

She glanced at her watch. In that instant, she heard a low rumble, followed by a hiss. Mist rolled out onto the space-time platform; within seconds it had wrapped V in a sultry, milky fog that smelled of the ocean, ozone, salt, and a sea breeze. She could hardly see her own hand. She heard a rushing sound, a low whistle, and a rustling of wind. A spiral of stars emerged above the mist – and the mist cleared.

A large black hole had opened up at the far end of the space-time platform. A huge spiral galaxy floated in the silky darkness. V felt, suddenly, as if she had left the Earth, and as if she were in an utterly transparent bubble staring into deepest space. The view was spectacular. Once again, she was plunged back into that night, twenty-five centuries ago, when she, a nineteen-year-old Phoenician girl, was lying on the roof of a villa with Marcus, staring into the abyss of stars. And, once again, she felt she only had to step forward, take only one step, and she would fall into space, into eternity.

"This is what is known to humans as the Andromeda Galaxy, V. It contains some one trillion stars, many more stars than your own galaxy, the Milky Way. It is two-and-a-half million light-years away. So, what you are looking at is the galaxy as it was two-and-a-half million years ago. It is there that you will find the abode of Kate."

"Yes, Crystal, but she is returning to us, yes?"

"Yes, wait just a moment, V. It is just a short trip, V, in cosmic terms. This particular universe in which both we and the Andromeda Galaxy find ourselves is at least one hundred and fifty-six billion light-years across, so two-and-a-half million light-years between your galaxy and the Andromeda Galaxy is just a local trip. It is the equivalent, I think, of going to the corner convenience store."

"Thank you, Crystal." V bit her lip; she wanted to scream.

"You are very welcome, V. I aim to please!"

So, thought V, trying to calm herself, Kate had been transported to somewhere in the Andromeda Galaxy: that meant time travel and space travel together.

"Kate has been on a life-friendly planet, friendly for human life, that is. She has been there for about four months – in terms of human earth time."

"Four months!"

"Time runs at different speeds, V. I can explain if you wish. It could be considered as an extension – with a few modifications – of the quantum and relativity theories elaborated by Einstein and by Max Planck and –"

"Thank you, Crystal." V was getting impatient. The sandstorm was approaching. But she must keep the Crystal happy, if "happy" was the right word. "You must have been lonely, Crystal, all these centuries."

"Yes, V. I have been lonely. And I like to share. Thank you, V. I know I talk too much. You are very understanding. I anticipate your visits with great pleasure. Now …"

A second, stronger tremor hit the cavern. The Crystal rose up higher this time, then fell back, and swayed, and rose again, lifted and lowered by a surging wave of seismic energy. One of the Cardinal's temporary scaffolds toppled over with a crash, cables and wires danced back and forth, dust and pebbles rained down from the roof of the cavern. The construction elevator lurched out from its moorings and made a creaking snapping sound but did not collapse. The one generator that was still feeding the klieg and construction lights continued to chug away.

"Now, Kate is about to arrive. I am trying to ensure that the coordinates and the molecular reconstruction are correct … Ah, I see she is not alone!"

"Not alone?"

"Yes, she is arriving with two other creatures – aside from the usual microscopic ones, that is."

V pulled the Beretta M9 from its holster.

"This presents a challenge, V, of molecular separation. It is important, very important, to preserve the molecular and DNA and cellular integrity of each biological entity, however small, however big. This requires concentration and … Ah, yes, now … They are arriving!"

In front of the vast image of Andromeda another mist began to form, a swirling little tornado, about the size of a person. V could see that it was not really a mist, more a distortion of the air or of space, like the illusory mirages seen on hot, distant, shimmering asphalt or out on the desert in the summer heat, with the air wavering, creating ripples of light, and giving the illusion of a lake or pond.

But this time the disturbance solidified, the mirage became real, and turned into flesh and blood – rather like my Avatar, thought V, making a note to thank her Avatar for acting as a decoy and blowing up the Cardinal-Spider.

"Kate?"

The solidifying image was about ten yards away.

The waving and shimmering ceased. The image became a person, solid, real, substantial.

It was Kate. Well, it looked like Kate. She stood like a statue, still dressed in her warrior's garb, which seemed spotless, polished, sparkling, as if it had just been cleaned and just put on. The statue turned toward V. The eyes were empty, expressionless, no whites, no pupil, and no iris – just pure blank black. *Oh, no,* thought V, *oh, no!*

V walked up to Kate. Kate was holding two furry creatures, each about the size of a small cat, but shaped like an octopus, with many tentacle-like legs.

"Kate?"

Kate's eyes – pure pools of black tar – turned toward V. She handed one of the creatures to V.

"Oh, well," thought V. She let the little creature latch onto her arm; it climbed up to her shoulder: its tentacles seemed to be coated with something like Velcro. Its fur was feathery. It looked at her from two large round eyes.

"What are these things?"

Kate's mouth smiled, but she said nothing; and her eyes were pools of tar, the blackness of empty space.

"Come, Kate. Follow me. We must leave this place. Your father is waiting."

The floor heaved up and fell back; rocks and dust fell from the walls. The Crystal vibrated and hummed. A large part of the scaffolding separated from the wall of the cave and came crashing down.

"Crystal, are our little friends dangerous?"

"No, they are quite friendly, V. You will find them helpful."

"Thank you, Crystal."

As the earth shook, Kate started, as if shocked. The small octopus clung tighter to V's shoulder, wrapping five furry tentacles around her arm.

"The elevators are no longer safe, V!"

"Then we will climb up the scaffolding of the Cardinal's construction elevator. Is that a good idea?"

"I think it is the *only* idea, V."

"Thank you, Crystal!"

"You are welcome, V! Good luck!"

At that moment, part of the roof crashed down, a massive cloud of dust and rubble sprayed out, flooding the star-studded platform, obscuring the Andromeda Galaxy.

The two fighter-bombers approached the coast, each carrying one 100 kiloton atomic bomb, each bomb with enough capacity to destroy Hiroshima many times over.

"Yes, Your Holiness," said Roger, having finally gotten through to the Vatican's Emergency Communication's Center, "the Crystal will no longer cause disturbances. It is now trying to stabilize the planet. But if it is attacked, it will automatically go into overdrive and destroy Earth. Even if it wanted to – and it has something close to a mind and a personality – it would not – I repeat, not – be able to stop the process. It is essential that the Crystal not be attacked."

"Professor Thornhill, I shall talk to the President immediately – if I can get through, that is. In the last few hours I have already tried – many times – but in vain."

Pope Francis hovered over the emergency transmitter. "Get me the President of the United States. This is absolutely urgent!"

"Yes, Your Holiness."

"Tell them that it has to do with the coming nuclear strike!"

"Nuclear strike?"

"Yes." The Pope knew he was taking a risk mentioning something no one was supposed to know about, but he wanted to make sure the White House fully understood the urgency. This time he *must* get through!

Ten Swiss Guards stood close to the Pope. The room was guarded by others, outside, and along the corridors. The Head of the Swiss Guard had followed the conversations between the Pope and Professor Thornhill. He knew this was not a hoax. If someone were to kill the Pope tonight, he knew it could mean, literally, the end of the world.

"Hello, Madam President."

"Hello, Your Holiness."

Larssen watched as more and more dust devils raced across the sand and tarmac. The wind was rising. The forecasts that he and Elena had managed to piece together – from an ocean of static and hysteria – indicated that the huge sandstorm was less than fifteen minutes away. On the plane's own radar, it could be clearly seen moving toward them – a huge dark ominous blob.

"We have to wait for V!" John was crouched next to Elena and Larssen.

"Yes, John, but if we wait much longer, everybody dies."

"You can't see without V. The lights don't reach far enough to light up our takeoff area – sand, pure sand."

"V drew a sketch just in case. Here it is – we have to go between those two outcroppings. With this I can work from memory. And Elena got one of the landing lights fixed; if it holds, it will give us some light. We might make it. Very dangerous, but we could risk it."

"We should wait until the very last minute," said Elena. She was monitoring the chaos of static and confused voices on the radio; she muttered, "The whole goddamn world is falling apart, begging your pardon, Father."

"Not at all, Elena, not at all." Father O'Bryan was hovering in the cockpit door, ghostly pale, but anxious to follow what might be the last few moments of human existence.

"We wait," John said firmly; he glanced at Mohammed.

"I agree," said Mohammed. "We wait. Our fate is in the hands of Allah."

"We wait," said Roger. He was frantic for Kate and looked haggard and worn, as if he had not slept in months. He was still streaked in grease and dust and clothed only in the soiled loincloth. He looked like an exhausted and besmudged Tarzan. No one, yet, had bothered to find him clothes. Well, that was of no account now. "We wait until they are on board."

"Yes, let us wait," said Father O'Bryan. "Our lives are not worth that much in the midst of all this."

"It is virtuous not to fear death," said Mohammed. "We are all pawns. Allah is just."

"Amen," said Father O'Bryan.

"If you all agree, that's what we do: we wait," said Larssen, feeling relieved; having done his duty as pilot, warning them of the probable consequences of delay, Larssen was as willing to face death as any of the others. He had certainly, when he looked back on it, lived a very good life.

When V unhooked her backpack, unzipped her bodysuit, and stripped naked, the little octopus jumped back onto Kate's shoulder. Kate stood passively, the two pools of tar staring, expressionless and empty. Seemingly Kate was aware of nothing.

"Don't be startled, Kate. I'm going to change into my demonic form. You've seen it before." V stuffed the bodysuit and pistol into the backpack. "I'm not sure what your little friends are going to think, though."

V's body dissolved in a whirl and she became her demonic reptilian self. Kate's expression didn't flicker, didn't change. Both octopuses stared at V – their large eyes like whirling pools of light.

V hoisted her backpack and said: "Kate. I'm going to carry you. Is that okay?"

The empty pools of blackness gazed at her.

"I'll take that for a 'yes.'"

Kate nodded, still not even the flicker of an expression.

"Good, Kate, that's good! That's excellent! Here we go." V secured the backpack, then she lifted Kate and slung her over her shoulder. The two octopuses leapt onto V's backpack and held on.

V began to climb up the Cardinal's construction elevator framework, which, if it held, would lead them to the ledge and the tunnel that would take them out to the canyon, and, hopefully, to freedom and life.

The next few minutes were exciting. Suddenly, the whole cavern trembled.

The construction framework swayed back and forth, creaking, snapping, groaning; then it broke loose from the cavern wall and lurched, twisting outwards, into the void; V was hanging over nothing. More sections of the ceiling came crashing down. Dust rose everywhere, electric wires installed by the Cardinal, and still powered by the one single, stubborn generator, were flung around wildly, sparks spraying everywhere. Lights flickered, then the cavern went dark.

V swung herself back toward the tottering tower of scaffolding, locked her foot claws around the bars and beams. The elevator tower swung back, crashed against the cavern wall and trembled and shook, but stayed in place; V climbed upwards as quickly as she could, using both foot and hand claws to grab onto beams, girders, struts. All around her dust swirled.

She realized there must be some light somewhere because her night vision was working exceptionally well.

"I shall turn on some backup lights, V."

"Thank you, Crystal."

Faint lights glowed. A huge metal beam crashed down past V, brushing her arm. She heard it wham into the floor far below.

Kate lay totally passive, a dead weight, over V's shoulder. V could feel the fear of the two octopus-like creatures. But at the same time, she had the impression that they had great confidence in her.

"Whew!" She reached the top of the tottering elevator and stepped off – over a gap of about a yard – onto the ledge.

"Good!" The exit tunnel, their path to freedom, hadn't collapsed.

Carrying Kate and the two little creatures, V ran down the tunnel toward the entry door – it was closed, but with a hiss the pure steel surface slid aside – and she was outside, in the narrow canyon that led to freedom. Beyond the canyon, V could see, through the narrow crevice of the entry to the canyon, the sparkle of the lights Mohammed had set up on the landing field, and she caught a glimpse of the great glittering strands of spider web that covered the runway.

"Almost there," V said. She turned to the hand plate at the entry. "Goodbye, Crystal, and thanks for everything!"

"You are welcome, V, and *bon voyage!*"

"We shall meet again."

"I am sure we shall, V. Goodbye!"

The steel door slid shut.

Abdul and Amin, Mohammed's two officers, were farther down the canyon, waiting.

Abdul was twenty-four. With his background in physics, he was very scientific in his attitudes, and he was battle-hardened, but he was also nervous after seeing what had happened – and it was literally unbelievable – to his dead and mummified colleagues. Amin was twenty-two and hoped to be a doctor – but he felt there was no cure for what they had seen here.

They held their submachine-guns ready. Mohammed had assured them that the Spider was truly dead, but Abdul was not so sure. Science, science as humans knew it, could not account for what they had seen.

Out of the gloom a figure came running toward them.

Abdul blinked. It was a demon!

"Amin, do you see what I see?"

"Frankly, I do not believe my eyes."

"Neither do I! But after today I am ready to believe anything!"

"It's a female demon!"

The female demon had seen them. She shouted, in Arabic, and English, and French, "Don't shoot. I am a friend!"

Abdul and Amin looked at each other.

"Give her the benefit of the doubt?"

"Yes, let's give her the benefit of the doubt." He shouted, "Okay, Demon, we will not shoot, we will wait. Come toward us."

The demon approached. She was carrying the young woman warrior Kate over her shoulder; she had a backpack and at her waist a belt and holster with a machine-gun.

"Do demons carry machine-guns?" Abdul frowned. He wanted to laugh; all of this was so tragic, so improbable.

"In this place, anything is possible, Amin."

"I am the woman, V," the demon shouted. "This is my disguise! It's one of the forms I can take."

"You are a shape-changer."

"Yes. I am also a friend of John, who is a friend of your commander, Mohammed."

"Well, demon shape-changer, we will just have to take this on faith," shouted Abdul. "Let us hurry! There is no time to lose!" As he said this, he noticed two small furry octopuses perched on the demon's backpack. Well, one or two more wonders were to be expected!

They ran down the narrow canyon. It took them three minutes to get to the airstrip, still covered in the massive steel-like spider web, as was the control tower. The tower looked like an age-encrusted ruin left over from some ancient civilization.

Mohammed and John were at the far side of the runway, now standing on guard, next to the plane, with their submachine-guns, and, in Mohammad's case, a flame-thrower. John had prepared him, but still Mohammed was startled when he saw V, the demon woman. V and the two soldiers hurried across the field, just as a sudden breeze raised the windsocks and lifted pieces of paper from the smashed airfield offices.

"We have to take off right away," V shouted. "There's a huge sandstorm coming."

"Yes, V, we know; we can see it on the radar!" John turned to Mohammad. "You and your men must come with us, my friend!"

Mohammed glanced around at the dead soldiers entwined in the silver stands of the Spider's giant web. "There is nothing more we can do here. A useless death is not a glorious death. Yes, we will come with you."

"Okay, all aboard!"

V, still carrying Kate and the two furry octopuses, followed the men on board.

Kate had still not spoken or indicated she understood what was going on. V set her down. Kate wavered for a moment, but then managed to stand, steadying herself by putting one hand on V's shoulder. Kate's eyes were still not human, not anything, just empty pools of jet-black.

"Kate and I will change after we take off," V said.

Roger stared at the glittering reptile woman who had brought his daughter aboard – he had not seen this version of V before, and he didn't know who or what it was. But whatever it was, it had brought his daughter back to him.

"Kate …" Roger began to say. He started back in horror; Kate's eyes were empty pools of pitch black – as if she were a cadaver or some creature risen from the grave, a dead husk, haunting the night. He had never seen such sheer darkness.

V sat Kate down, and buckled her in. The two octopus creatures leapt off V's backpack and snuggled next to Kate. "I think this is temporary." V nodded at Kate's eyes. "Kate is still in shock." V turned her golden reptile eyes to Roger. "But she'll get over it," she added, thinking, *I hope …*

The motors had revved up. V went into the cockpit and stood just behind

Jack and Elena. "Our landing lights are out again," said Jack. "Elena managed to fix one, but …"

"Volcanic ash," said Elena. "We're lucky the motors work."

"Here we go!" The engines roared. The Falcon moved ahead, accelerating slowly, carefully, on the sand.

V talked them though the darkness. "A bit to the left, yes, good, okay, we're making it, yes, yes, okay, straight now." The plane was suddenly buffeted by huge winds, as the sandstorm pushed a mass of air in front of it.

"I think we have enough fuel," said Jack. "We weren't able to refuel here. The fuel tanks were fouled with spider acid."

"Can we make it to Italy?"

"Yes, I think we can …"

As the Falcon rose into the air, the great sandstorm blasted the airfield, and sand poured down into the narrow canyon, filling the canyon, and sealing the Crystal in, under a two-hundred-foot high sand dune.

"Can we outrace this storm?" V asked.

"Yes. I think so …"

"I *love* your outfit, V," said Elena, glancing at the demon.

"Thank you, Elena! It really is *me* – don't you think?"

"Absolutely you," said Elena. "I wouldn't mind strutting around in that sort of getup!"

The Falcon accelerated to almost five hundred miles an hour, neatly outracing the oncoming sandstorm.

Five thousand yards above the Falcon the two FX-35 fighter-bombers of the US Air Force raced inland.

"Madam President –"

"Your Holiness, you mentioned something about …" Static broke up the line.

"Could you tell me exactly, Your Holiness, what …?"

"Madam President …" The Pope stared at the speaker phone. There was nothing but static.

"Try a backup line."

"Yes, Your Holiness."

The Pope could hardly breathe. He had seen the horrific reports coming in from around the world – in fact, right at this moment, he was watching one, from just a mile or two away, on a very static-ridden multiple-screen monitor: a young woman and a young man were pulling an elderly woman from under a pile of rubble in Rome. To his surprise, the Pope recognized the young woman; it was the girl he had seen in Saint Peter's Square the other day – the girl in the scarlet dress; he was sure it was her. How strange to recognize someone you have only glimpsed from such a distance! With her was an exceptionally handsome young man, who looked Chinese or perhaps Korean or Japanese; and another young woman was helping them, a redhead, who was not wearing much in the way of clothes. Just behind them was another woman, with two children ... On another screen, the Pope could see a giant wave crashing through coastal towns in southern Italy, washing away houses, people, cars, bridges, churches. In Japan, a tsunami was overturning cars, derailing trains, toppling buildings ...

"I have the White House, You Holiness."

"Madam President."

"Your Holiness."

"The atomic attack on the site in North Africa must be stopped; it will cause an immense –"

"Your Holiness, I apologize for interrupting you, but as you know, we don't negotiate with terrorists, and we have reason to believe that ..." Static interrupted the line again.

"Yes, Madam President, I understand, but ..." More static burst into the line.

"We've lost the line, Your Holiness," said Father Ramsay.

"Try another," said the Pope, "and open as many lines as you can open – terrestrial, satellite, shortwave, whatever ..."

The Pope stared at a tape at the bottom of a monitor, which read, in Italian, "Unconfirmed reports say that Yellowstone's super-volcano has entered into eruption. Meanwhile, a tsunami has hit the Calabrian coast and the northern Sicilian coast. In France, the ancient volcanoes of the Massif Central region – long presumed dead – are showing signs of renewed activity ..."

An anchorwoman appeared. "We have just learned that the earth tremors, which have been increasing in intensity for the last five hours, have suddenly ceased." She looked flustered for a moment, waiting, obviously staring at a monitor; a man appeared and handed her a piece of paper. She read, "Experts have no explanation for this. But even if the tremors stop, secondary effects, such as tsunamis and landslides, will continue for some time, experts say. NASA and the European Space Agency report that distortions in the gravitational field have faded … The Russian President has announced that the Russian Federation, not hit so far, is ready to offer all possible aid to …"

"Your Holiness –"

"Madam President, an attack on the site in North Africa will bring about a massive explosion that will destroy the Earth."

"What?"

"The device that is causing the earthquakes will go into overdrive if it is attacked; it will tear the Earth apart. I implore you, Madam President!"

"Your Holiness, how do you know this?"

"Madam President, I have people there – including the American physicist Roger Thornhill. They have stopped the machine. But if it is bombed, it will, as I said, destroy the Earth."

"I know of Doctor Thornhill. But –"

"The terrorist group responsible for this has been destroyed. I implore you, Madam President, to stop the attack immediately. Professor Thornhill will explain later, but only action now can save us!" The Pope glanced down at the electronic red digital clock – time parading across the speakerphone, second by second by second …

"Your Holiness, I'll make a decision; I'll let you know. That's all I can say right now; that's all I can say."

"Thank you, Madam President. I shall pray for you."

When Kate had boarded the plane, Roger had embraced her. She had gently returned his embrace and given him a slight smile, but her eyes had remained empty jet-black pools and she had said nothing.

It was horrifying to be buckled into an aircraft seat, facing his daughter, who was dressed like a comic book superheroine in polished skintight latex-leather, and who was sparkling with almost unearthly glamour and beauty, but who seemed to be totally absent – an empty shell. She also had with her two creatures that looked like tiny furry octopuses and that were clinging to her as if their lives depended on it. Roger felt – and he didn't know how or why he felt this – that they were protecting Kate.

"Kate," he said, "Kate, how do you feel?" No answer. "Kate, can you hear me?" Nothing – just the fixed smile, the empty jet-black void gazing, perhaps off into space, perhaps nowhere, or perhaps into some inner horror, some memory, some hell; her beauty seemed, if possible, even more intense, more poignant than ever – she was so beautiful, she seemed unreal.

The reptile woman came back aft and buckled herself into the seat next to Roger. "I'm V," she said. Roger stared. "V? But that's …" He was going to say impossible; but he didn't. How could this reptilian creature be the same as the sleek woman warrior?

"Has Kate said anything?" The golden serpent's eyes sparkled, and the creature's tongue, Roger noticed, was bright red, quite long, and forked. Her scales were green and blue and turquoise, with flecks of gold and scarlet. What sort of being was she? She looked like a glamorous female demon or goddess from some book of ancient engravings.

"No," he swallowed. "I don't know what to think. I'm deadly afraid."

"She seems fine physically," the demon said. "I'm certain she understands what we say to her. And she brought with her, as you can see, two friends." At that moment, one of them leapt across to V and perched on her shoulder.

Roger crouched forward. "Kate? Kate?"

Kate reached out and put her gloved hand on his hand, but she said nothing and her empty eyes remained fixed, staring, lost wherever she was lost, perhaps in another universe.

Was this really Kate? Roger wondered. Or was it some simulacrum of Kate, created God knows how, by God knows who and for God knows what reason? Had the aliens, or whatever they were, sent us a Trojan horse, an alien invader, in the guise of Kate?

"The Crystal told me that Kate has been on a planet in the Andromeda Galaxy, and that for her four months have passed, not a few hours."

"The Andromeda Galaxy?"

"Yes."

"Four *months*?"

"Yes." V stood up, and the little octopus leapt back into Kate's lap. "Kate will need time to adjust. I'm going to change now. I'll be back in a second; perhaps Kate should change into something more civilian too."

V went back behind the curtain and into the luxurious washroom. She opened the valise that John had stored on the plane before takeoff from Naples.

John was always impeccably precise and organized; they had an established routine for the backup supply kits – a selection of styles and costumes, a few disguises, and of course a good choice of weaponry.

"Let's see, what shall I wear?" She wrapped her forked tongue thoughtfully around one fang, caressing it up and down. She stood very still for an instant, nostrils twitching, claws on hips, considering. "Simplicity is best." She picked black jeans, a black T-shirt, the wide black leather belt with a holster for the Beretta M9 and a miniature holster for the stun gun and needles.

She closed her eyes and concentrated. There was a shimmering blur. The turquoise and green demon was gone, replaced by the human V. She slipped into the shower, then, giving herself an extra scrub, sponged herself down with quick-drying cleanser and shampoo, stood for just a moment under the body-dryer to let it all evaporate, then pulled on the clothes, slipped into sandals, and returned to the cabin.

On the way back to her seat, she crouched down next to Father O'Bryan and put her hand on his arm. "How do you feel, Father?"

"I still feel weak."

"You should feel weak. I drank half your blood. You saved my life. You saved everything and everyone, Father! You saved the world."

"You drank my blood. Yes, I remember. Otherwise you would have died."

John perked up. "V, how in the world did you spare Father O'Bryan from, ah, from the change, from the transformation?" He was sitting opposite Father O'Bryan and could not resist asking – since the poor Father had been fretting for the last few minutes and pestering John with questions: "Vampirism can appear later, can it not, John? I mean to say, it might come as a delayed reaction, might it not?" John had not been able to resist looking grim and answering, "Indeed it can, Father. V has told me some frightful tales. I mean, there you are, just imagine it, celebrating Mass, in front of a gaggle of charming young ladies, and suddenly fangs sprout … and all the ladies run screaming!"

"I slashed his wrists with my claws," said V, realizing that John had been teasing poor Father O'Bryan.

"Yes, John," Father O'Bryan said, wiping his brow, "that's what she did. One of her claws slashed my wrists and I held my wrists above her; she was too weak to move, in agony really, and she was manacled down on one of those black granite blocks the Order uses for altars. Then, when I was too weak and she had gained strength from drinking, she broke the manacles and held me above her, so more of my blood could stream down into her open, fanged mouth, but her mouth and fangs did not touch me. My life blood was draining away, and I thought my soul was lost, lost forever, streaming away with my blood."

"Yes," said V, turning to John, "Father O'Bryan's soul would have been lost if I had drunk directly. But I had worked out that I could drink without letting my fangs or my lips touch him. I had to drink as much as I could. It was a risk. There could still have been contamination. And Father O'Bryan could have bled to death. He was aware of the dangers. But we got through," V nudged Father O'Bryan, "by the skin of our teeth."

"Yes. And then I fainted. I was ready to die. I have lived so long," said Father O'Bryan.

"Ah," said John. "And then V used her healing power to heal your wrists."

"But to lose my eternal soul, oh, my God!"

"I think your soul is intact, Father." V patted him on the shoulder. "You would certainly know if you had become like me – an empty husk of a being, a pagan idol, without a soul, one of the hideous ghoulish living dead."

"Oh, my dear V ..."

"In any case, Father," V knelt next to him and kissed him on the cheek, "the sacrifice of your blood has been the salvation of the human race."

Father O'Bryan had to smile: he was not sure whether what she had just said was blasphemy or a compliment to his religion. Had he, in some tiny modest way, helped humanity justify itself before Christ's immense sacrifice? "Ah, redemption," he sighed.

"Redemption," V whispered, and, patting Father O'Bryan on the shoulder, she stood up and went to talk to Roger. Yes, Father O'Bryan's sacrifice would be the salvation of humanity – but only if the Pope had managed to talk to the President in time, and only if the President made the right decision, and only if the President had been able to cancel the nuclear attack – in time.

When Roger saw the *new* V, he was startled, once again. As she slid into her seat, he asked, "This is you – and that was also you?"

"Both versions are me."

"So, you are human again."

"Yes, for the time being, Professor Thornhill." V put her hand on his hand. "As I said, I think Kate might feel more comfortable in civilian clothes. After all, she's been wearing this outfit for four months! And perhaps you would like to change too?"

"Yes, that's probably a good idea." Roger glanced down at himself, naked except for the loincloth. "But Kate should go first. Kate?"

Kate did not answer; she sat there, like a sage little girl, gloved hands curled on her thighs, empty, jet-black eyes staring into space.

V stood up, took Kate's hand, and gave it a little tug. Kate stood up; the octopuses jumped off her and snuggled in the seat next to hers; they stared up at V. "You two wait here with Roger," she said.

And somehow V understood that they knew what she had said and that they would stay put.

V guided Kate to the changing room. Kate didn't resist. But when they got behind the curtain, she seemed reluctant to unlock the collar and unzip the catsuit. V put her hand on the zipper, but Kate pulled it away; her empty tar-dark eyes turned to V – there was fear there, but V could not decipher it; she could not see into Kate's mind; there was some barrier, some obstacle …

"It won't hurt, Kate. It won't hurt."

Kate held the zipper tight and wouldn't move.

"Do you want me to leave you alone?"

Kate shook her head; then she bit her lip, and suddenly her eyes focused; the jet-black faded; pupil and iris and white became visible, and distinct; her eyes were human eyes, Kate's eyes; it was as if the person inside the body had suddenly reappeared; she put V's hand on the zipper.

"You want me to open it?"

Kate nodded.

"Okay, darling, I will." V clicked open the collar and began to pull the zipper and peel back the catsuit – she did it very slowly, wondering what Kate was afraid of. Had she been wounded? Had she been scarred?

"And do you want jeans and a T-shirt, like me?"

Kate nodded. The tip of her tongue moved along her lips. There seemed, V thought, to be a spark of light in Kate's eyes, a vivacious amused spark.

Then V saw it: a tattoo or something like a tattoo. She glanced up at Kate. "You've got a tattoo?"

Kate shrugged. A smile flickered on her lips and then she nodded. So, thought V, it looks like a tattoo; but it is exceptionally bright and it's not exactly a tattoo.

V finished unzipping the catsuit and helped Kate out of it.

Kate seemed in excellent shape – no wounds, no needle marks, and no sign that she had been experimented with or operated on. She was sparkling clean too, as if she had just showered, shampooed, and rinsed, then stepped into and out of a dryer.

But she had certainly changed – or been changed.

One of her shoulders and one arm, and about half of her back, right down to her waist, were covered with the tattoo. It shimmered, brilliantly, brightly colored, and seemed to be a mosaic of shifting, purely geometric forms.

As V watched, it changed shape, the lines and blocks of color moving into new patterns, and then into other patterns; it was a high-definition spectacle that could spread, covering her whole back and swirling all the way down one of her legs. But then it shrank again, whirling and shimmering, back to its original size.

"It's beautiful, Kate," said V. "It's stunning!"

Kate reached out to V and clung to her and kissed her on the cheek.

"What happened, Kate?"

Kate kissed V again, and coughed, clearing her throat. Looking into V's eyes, she said, "It was aw … aw … aw … awesome!"

"Awesome?"

"A … absolutely!"

Kate's eyes once more changed to tar-black, and as V looked into them, it was as if she were looking through Kate and into infinite space: she could see something like the spiral Andromeda Galaxy, stars and more stars and deep empty space – and, beyond that, an unknown planet, a whole new world; waves of some vast ocean rolled onto a rocky and wonderful shore; birds never before seen whirled in the air … Kate's eyes returned to normal.

V shook herself. "Are these jeans and this T-shirt okay, Kate?"

Kate nodded and started to pull them on.

"Are these sandals okay? They should fit you."

"F … f … fantastic!"

Roger stared out the window at the darkness – just a hint of dawn in the sky. He drummed his fingers on the armrest. Why were they taking so long? What sort of transformation had Kate undergone? Was that perfect doll-like creature, so calm, so impeccable, so empty, so unreal, really Kate?

"Professor Thornhill?"

At first, he didn't recognize the woman standing over him – a tanned blonde, bright blue eyes …

"Yes?"

"We've got a clear line, finally. The president of the United States wants to talk to you, Professor. Now! It's urgent."

"Right, yes, I'll come right away." Roger got out of his seat and as he did so, it clicked; the woman was Elena, the plane's copilot.

As he started to move forward, he glanced back and saw Kate in black jeans and a black T-shirt, smiling at him, a human smile now, the old Kate, and her eyes – her eyes – focused. She waved, and said, "D ... D ... Daddy!"

"Kate, oh, my lovely Kate, my darling!" He beckoned. "Come with me, Kate, I have to speak to the president."

She caught up to him, put her hand on his shoulder and reached up and kissed him on the cheek. "The p ... president, D ... Daddy?"

"Yes, Kate, the president," he said, drinking her in, convinced now that, yes, this was the real Kate.

In the cockpit, Elena Satti handed the ear set to Roger.

"Madam President?"

"Professor Thornhill, is that really you?"

The Crystal dreamed of new lands, of a new home.

Sand poured down into the great cavern through cracks opened by the earthquake. Above ground the huge storm raged, hurricane-force winds moving the desert northward toward the coast. The ancient metal framework that cradled the Crystal trembled but held firm. The Crystal didn't mind whether it disintegrated or not – she was floating free and keeping a nice cozy distance between her surfaces and the cascading sand, which would soon be a two or three hundred-yard-deep dune of sand, creating for herself a new, if temporary, nest. Besides, if she needed to, she could recreate the cavern and the latticework in the finest and most precise detail, emptying it of sand, so it would be just as it had been when Marcus had left her, so many centuries ago.

The Crystal – and she definitely thought of herself as female: fecund, nurturing, protective, and destructive only if absolutely forced to be so, and then only in defense of her own brood, her own civilization – amused herself by mastering the idioms of the various civilizations she encountered, the languages that rose and fell, the sciences and religions that flowered and then decayed, the songs and slogans that came and went.

Her various sensors – disguised as and embedded at will by her in natural features all over the planet – even in human-made features and even, without the bearer being aware of it, in humans and animals and plants – were still reporting. Things were calming down; she had kept her promise to V, and it was all working out, so far, without a hitch.

Provided that the unfortunate incident that was imminent and threatening did *not* occur, then everything would be hunky-dory, and this particular story, or fairy tale, would have a happy ending. "They all lived happily ever after," as the formula went.

But, musing upon cosmic and human history, the Crystal thought that, like so many human sayings, the happily-ever-after idea did not really reflect the nitty-gritty, fang-and-claw, hard-as-nails nature of reality, but rather the sunny and mystic fictional bubble – literature or religion or myth or just plain forgetfulness and denial – in which humans lived. Perhaps their lives – such short lives after all, afflicted with pain, illness, aging, and tragedy – would be unlivable without these silly joyful bubble-like illusions. And, in truth, the illusions were quite pleasant – and she herself loved to bathe in them: a gentle warm shower of comforting thoughts and images …

But if the unfortunate incident did occur … well, then it would all end.

The Crystal really did want to help V; after all, Marcus loved V; and, despite everything that had happened, the Crystal loved Marcus, and she loved V too, with a secret maternal intensity that was almost too painful to dwell on. If the truth were to be known, and to be confessed, the Crystal yearned for V, V, who with all her smarts and all her wisdom, did not know the half of it, V who really did not know, poor child, who she was – or what she was.

It would be absolutely divine to be able to talk with V, and talk, and talk, and explain and explain; and share – share everything. After all, I know so much; I have so much to share. And V is so intelligent, so receptive …

But if the unfortunate incident did occur, everything would end, in an instant.

Atomic bombs are quite nasty things.

The protective membrane was ready. One great final impulse of destruction – emitted in one billionth of a second – and life everywhere would be destroyed – and Earth and the Moon would break apart – over a few hours or perhaps days – and cease to exist. And the Crystal would depart. "I shall be sorry to leave," she thought. "This is a nice planet. And I shall mourn my friend, my love, Marcus's adored V."

The two FX-35 fighter-bombers were approaching. Human fingers were hovering over buttons. Radio messages were being exchanged; voices crackled orders and counter-orders though the air.

The guidance systems for two missiles with atomic warheads were already locked on the canyon and the cavern – though, of course, they would never reach their target, for time-and-space would warp, and the Crystal would be long gone – gone, that is, a millionth of a second before impact.

And if, perchance, she was still there when the warheads hit, the explosions would have no effect on her whatsoever, except to greatly multiply the outward-bound destructive impulse that would destroy the Earth and the Moon and all that they contained.

Meanwhile, sand poured down and the Crystal was buried.

Whether she was buried or not, it made no difference to the Crystal. She was watching a TV news program in Tokyo; she was envisaging sunsets on various beaches around the planet, some of them swept by tsunamis, she was in city parks, in the midst of the sea, and on several mountaintops. She was with a fire brigade in Wyoming. She was touring the Louvre, which was still standing and undamaged since Paris had been spared, and lingering to look at a painting by Chardin. It showed a monkey, in eighteenth century costume, wielding a painter's brush and standing before an easel. She was also in the Thames Estuary, inside the body and mind of an attractive female police officer, on a police boat, watching the super-tide recede, carrying with it automobiles, rubble, bodies.

She had watched, in the Roman Forum, through the eyes of a child called Zoe, the adventures of an exquisite blond American girl and a very handsome Chinese boy, well, they were adults really and very brave, and the Crystal felt protective toward them, as if they were her very own children, and she was certainly hoping they – and their new friends, Martine and Tatania and Chloë and of course Zoe – would "live happily ever after."

She was on the Ganges with a group of pilgrims discussing the nature of destiny and time and preparing themselves for the end of the world, and she was checking in on the state of Beijing, which was, like Paris and Moscow, unscathed.

She was on a hilltop in Bali where a group of tourists and locals were singing bravely around a bonfire, trying to ignore the catastrophes occurring. Yes, it was a beautiful planet, adorable, really. She would hate to see it die.

"Absolutely, Madam President," Roger said.

"Well, the decision is made," said the president. "Give me a moment while I execute it." There was a minute's pause. "Professor Thornhill, thank you for everything. Once the immediate emergency is over, I would like you to come, if you agree, and with your charming daughter, Kate, to the White House for, let's say, dinner and an informal debriefing."

"Absolutely, Madam President, Kate and I would be honored."

"Thank you again, Professor."

"Well?" queried V, who was standing in the door to the cockpit.

"Well," Roger said, wiping his forehead, "she's made her decision – whatever it is. She didn't tell me."

V glanced at Father O'Bryan. "Start praying, Father O'Bryan; we need all the help we can get on this one."

Father O'Bryan nodded, closed his eyes, and let his spirit open to God, to infinity, to compassion, to hope …

"I want to show you s … s … something, Daddy," Kate said as they got back to their seats. Her stutter seemed to be subsiding.

"What, Kate?"

"This." Kate slipped the T-shirt off her shoulder. The tattoo raced up her shoulder and down one arm, it went up the nape of her neck and wrapped itself around her throat; it flickered and glowed, red, blue, then it transformed itself into a zebra-like pattern, black and white stripes that spread over her face, like a mask; froze for a moment; then shrank back, returning to its home base on her back.

"I ca … can control it, Daddy," Kate said, pulling the T-shirt back up over her shoulder. "I control it a bit m … m … more each time I try."

"It's beautiful," said V, glancing at her watch.

"It *is* beautiful, Kate," said Roger, but he was terrified. What in the world – or out of the world – had happened to his daughter?

Father O'Bryan, V noticed, still had his eyes closed, his head bent forward.

Roger cleared his throat. "What is this tattoo, Kate? Do you know?"

"I don't know. I got it when I was on that strange planet; I fell asleep, I woke up, I was … like this."

The two octopuses, who were sitting on the seat beside Kate, put several of their arms on her thighs, as if protecting her. She patted them and they both made a purring sound.

Roger had to smile; but as he buckled himself in, he wondered if these were the last few moments of existence for the planet Earth. If, as he felt sure, the president had called off the strike, there was still room for error. Messages go astray, they don't arrive in time, they get to the wrong person, or they are misinterpreted.

Kate put her hands on her father's hands and said, "Daddy, we are going to have to rewrite the ph … ph … ph … physics textbooks."

"Yes, Kate, you are absolutely right."

"I have some ideas," Kate said, with a dreamy smile, as if she were speaking from an immense distance.

"We'll work together, if you wish, Kate."

"I'd love that, Daddy."

Roger began a thought, a doubt about Kate's nature – what was she, really? Then he felt, like a shock, V's voice, clear as a bell, inside his head, saying, with great determination and clarity, "Whatever Kate has become, Roger, she is your daughter and she needs all your love! She needs it now more than ever."

Father O'Bryan looked up, and said, "V!"

Elena Satti had come out of the cockpit; under the tan, she looked pale and tired. But then, a glorious smile: "The president has called off the bombing raid on the Crystal. The pilots have received the message and turned back. Congratulations, Professor Thornhill! Congratulations, everybody!"

V sat back; suddenly she felt she could relax; her muscles seemed to dissolve against the back of the seat. How delicious, she thought. A voice in her head said, "V, I am so happy! I hope you are too!" and V sent back the thought, "Crystal, I am very happy, I love you, Crystal, I really do!" "I love you too, V. We are sister spirits. We shall meet again! Goodbye!"

"Thank God," said Father O'Bryan.

"Praise Allah," said Mohammed.

"Bravo," said John., "I think this deserves a drink."

"Wiser words have never been spoken," said Father O'Bryan.

"Well, Father, we may just have a drink here that is after your own heart," said John, and pulled out a bottle of the good Father's favorite whiskey.

Reports began to come in. All over the world, earthquake and volcanic activity had ceased. People were beginning to pick up the pieces.

The Falcon was well out over the Mediterranean. Roger had showered and changed into jeans and a T-shirt provided by John; for those who drank alcohol, a second round was being served. For those who did not, a fine choice of juices and teas was available on a tray Elena Satti had set out.

V said, "Well, ladies and gentlemen and friendly creatures from Andromeda, I have an announcement to make: I have to thank someone else, and this may be of interest to everyone, and in particular to you, Kate, to Professor Thornhill, and to you, Father O'Bryan."

"I wondered when you were going to thank her," said John.

"She deserves a treat."

"Who are we talking about?" asked Father O'Bryan.

"Well, Father," John said, "just watch. As you know, V is supposed to be without a soul – but in fact, she has one, isn't that true, V?"

"In a manner of speaking," V said, beginning to concentrate.

Talk of V's soul caused Father O'Bryan to prick up his ears, and then he remembered the tale V had told him – of a mirror and of the magic apparition that had stepped out from behind the glass. He took a sip of the Bushmills. This would be interesting, he thought, even if he still didn't believe it. And at that instant a female voice, which was V's voice and yet not quite V's voice, said, very distinctly, in his head, "Oh, you adorable fussbudget doubting Thomas, you!" Father O'Bryan looked around; no one had spoken.

Roger and Kate looked on. Kate was quiet, her hand in her father's hand, her two octopus friends entwined and perched on the seat beside her.

On the empty seat opposite V, a swirling mist appeared, then crystallized and solidified. Sitting there, in a white silk blouse, black Armani jacket, with a pleated skirt hoisted well above the knee, sheer dark stockings and high-heeled patent black leather shoes, was another V, a twin, except this version of V had longer hair and a touch of makeup, and displayed a charming pout, an expression that was not part of V's usual repertoire.

"My God," said Father O'Bryan.

"What is it, a hologram?" Roger was tempted to touch the illusion. "May I?"

The illusion nodded. Roger reached out and his hand met a warm, solid hand, a warm, real, delicate human hand. "My God!"

"Well, Professor, are you satisfied?" The apparition squeezed his hand and favored him with a radiant smile.

"Yes, absolutely." Under his tan, Professor Roger Thornhill turned pale – such a mixture of emotions and experiences – and thoughts. Now science really would have to adapt to a whole series of inexplicable phenomena.

"Who in the world, what in the world, is that?" asked Mohammed, who was standing in the aisle.

"Unbelievable," said Abdul.

"Welcome," said John, smiling at the Avatar.

"Thank you, John." The Avatar turned her dazzling attention to him. "You are always so polite and considerate – unlike some other people I know. Say hello to Julia for me. As for you, my sister in crime, V, you owe me big time!"

"I admit it," said V. "I do."

"Being slobbered on by that spider thing was no fun, and then being imprisoned and cocooned in his gooey web, ugh, it was absolute Hell – and I had to time my getaway perfectly. It required split-second precision and the utmost professionalism. I hope you are satisfied, V."

"I am absolutely satisfied."

"I've dressed up in my finest – I hope you like it – because I know we have important people here – Father O'Bryan, whom I've wanted to meet since you first told me about him, and Professor Thornhill and Commander Khaldun – and Abdul and Amin – and of course the marvelous cosmic traveler, Kate."

"All of you, meet my friend, my soul, my Avatar …"

"Yes, I am what Marcus used to call V's soul, but I think of myself more as her soulmate. She calls on me when she has particularly difficult problems to solve or delicate missions that require absolute tact and discretion – and I am always at your beck-and-call, am I not, V?"

"You certainly are."

"And am I getting my reward?"

"Yes. If you wish it, we'll have a night out together in Paris, with a fashion show, dinner, at La Coupole if you wish, or at Balzar's, and, after dinner, ice cream at Berthillon's on the Isle Saint Louis."

"Wonderful – thank you, V. And these two adorable little creatures – what are they called, Kate?"

"A … A … Audrey and Theodore," said Kate, patting both.

"Wonderful. Hello, Audrey, hello, Theodore. Well, I must go now because I must not exhaust V. She is so delicate. It has been delightful to meet you all. À *bientôt*, V." The Avatar blew V a kiss.

"À bientôt, my soul, my love."

And the Avatar faded.

"A night out in Paris?" Father O'Bryan raised an eyebrow.

"Yes," said V. "For some odd incomprehensible reason, she adores Paris. Well, I suppose we did have some interesting adventures there in the eighteenth century, involving a charming and quite athletic fellow called Casanova.

That might have something to do with it. And unlike me, my Avatar can eat real food, so, after the fashion show – she's a fashion fanatic – we will be going to some very fancy Parisian restaurant, she will flirt outrageously with the waiters and with everybody else, and she will eat and eat and eat …"

"And as for you, you will drink black coffee," said John, with a sympathetic grin.

"Exactly, I shall drink black coffee. Well, perhaps with an added touch of the finest cognac – and, come to think of it, a very good wine."

EPILOGUE

Almost eleven million people died in the "events" of August 2027 CE.

No satisfactory explanation was ever given – not to the public at least – for why or how such a simultaneous series of seismic, volcanic and weather disasters could occur.

The world soon settled down and began to rebuild. The reconstruction and restoration programs set off a building and economic boom that lasted for almost two decades.

When they returned to their capital, Mohammed and Abdul and Amin were promoted. Their country received a huge aid package from a group of industrialized nations – and a certain area of the desert was proclaimed off limits to all persons, institutions, and exploration. The area was surrounded by three separate electronic fences. The interdict was permanently monitored by national and international satellites, by land- and air-based radar, by armed drones, and by robot and human armored patrols on the ground.

Abdul was awarded a very substantial scholarship to study physics with Professor Roger Thornhill at Stanford. Amin became head of the elite Medical Corps of the Presidential Guard. Mohammed spent several years as lecturer at Sandhurst and at the École Militaire in Paris and then returned home to become Prime Minister, a post which he held for many years.

Scarlett Andersson and Jian Chang survived their exciting day in Rome, where, aided by Martine and Tatania, and by Zoe and Chloë, they helped save many victims of the disaster. When things began to calm down, they were even invited, for some reason, to meet Pope Francis. They did, spent a full hour with him, and found him a delightfully sympathetic listener.

After Scarlett got her degree in medicine, she and Jian married. They chose to live in Boston, where Scarlett became a neurosurgeon and Jian was the CEO of a successful high-tech company he created that specialized in biotechnology, a company he founded while still at MIT.

They kept in touch with Martine – who, it turned out, was indeed French and studying philosophy at Oxford. They visited her often when she settled back in Paris, where she became the CEO of a large consultancy firm, while also teaching a graduate seminar in contemporary philosophy at the University of Paris. Tatania became a close friend of all of them. She and Chloë and Zoe took a great interest in all of Scarlett's and Jian's adventures and doings and often visited them – sometimes with Tatania's husband – in Boston or in South Carolina where grandmother Charlotte's horse farm and Charlotte herself, elegant as always, were still going concerns.

A few days after returning to Italy, V was asleep in her bedroom – an underground installation of some luxury. Her villa luckily had remained untouched by the earthquakes and tsunamis. She had three houseguests, Roger Thornhill, Roger's daughter Kate, and Father O'Bryan. Julia and John were taking great pleasure in preparing splendid meals out on the terrace.

Just before midnight, V woke up, alert: someone was in her bedroom – and then she saw: Kate, holding a large kitchen knife.

V sat up. "Have you come to kill me with that knife, Kate?"

"Oh, the k … k … knife … N … n … no … I was afraid to ss … ss … ss … sleep alone." Kate's stutter had returned, and even gotten worse.

V turned on the bedside light. Kate's tattoo, tonight, was glorious – Kate was a total zebra, horizontal matte-black and brilliant white stripes covered her entire body and face.

"Slide in, then." V made room. "And where are our two little friends?"

"H … h … here they come. They w … w … wanted to come."

Audrey and Ted came scurrying into the room, jumped onto the foot of the bed, and nestled up against each other.

"Foot warmers," said V. "Welcome, Audrey, welcome, Ted."

Both responded by purring, a rich warm feathery sound.

Kate slid in beside V and lay there at first, timidly, and then she pressed herself against V. V held Kate close and stroked her forehead, thinking, yes, maybe I can do this, yes, I definitely can do this!

"It was b … b … beautiful."

"Beautiful?"

"The Andromeda Galaxy, the planet where I was."

"You'll tell me about it someday?"

"Y … y … y … yes, I will."

"Good, thank you, Kate."

"I'm curious, V. W … w … what are you exactly?"

"Oh, Kate, I wish I knew. But I really don't know what or who I am!" V kissed Kate, gently; the kiss was returned.

"Strange, isn't it?"

"Yes, my darling, it is." V held Kate close and stroked her hair. Kate was soon fast asleep in V's arms.

V listened to Kate's breathing for a very long time. It took her back, it took her way back to the girl she had loved so passionately, so long ago – Asherah.

Infinite trust … a sleeping stranger … well, not exactly a stranger.

The next morning Kate's stutter had disappeared; it never returned.

During the summer of 2028, the year after the great events of 2027, the Pope was in his summer residence at Castel Gondolfo, fifteen miles south of Rome in the hills overlooking Lake Albano, when two sleek motorbikes rode up to the entrance.

The woman who was riding one of them was dressed in skintight synthetic black leather. She flipped up the tinted visor of her helmet and was greeted very warmly by the Head of the Pontifical Swiss Guard in person – which was surprising given her unorthodox and revealing attire. They were seen laughing and commiserating, as if reminiscing about old times.

While the woman's companion, a tall, tanned, dark-haired man, stayed and gossiped with some of the men – whom he seemed to know – the Head of the Guard accompanied her directly to the garden of the Castel, where the Pope was waiting.

The Pope too greeted the woman as an old friend.

Alone, they strolled in the garden for almost an hour in animated conversation, and everyone who saw them wondered what two such unlike figures could possibly have to discuss.

At the end of their encounter the Pope blessed the young woman, who then returned to her companion biker; they shook hands all round, and the two of them rode silently off into the golden dusk.

Kate Thornhill later won a Nobel Prize for the revolutionary work she did in physics; she won it jointly with her father. They redefined the concept of gravity, showing how space-time was malleable, how certain classes of subatomic particles could, in theory at least, be manipulated and controlled, by descending below the underlying quantum level, and used to create curves and loops in the space-time continuum – passageways between distant points in the universe, and between different points in time. Their new "Thornhill Model" would, in theory, make travel to distant points in space possible – instantaneous transitions, leaving the speed of light far behind, and, even, irrelevant. There was even a suggestion, in their work, that, in theory, at least, matter could be transformed instantaneously, and that, perhaps, even biological structures could be thus changed – from one form of life into another – in the blink of an eye. The universe, it appeared, was even more mysterious than previous theories had implied.

Kate and Roger gave a joint acceptance speech – a sort of father-daughter dialogue. It was superb, everyone thought, and it was generally agreed that the jokes were remarkably good. Kate, it turned out, was an excellent mime and actress.

Kate led a very private – even secretive – life and usually dressed in turtlenecks and long-sleeved shirts. She wore trousers or tights – even in summer. Also, she had two extraordinary pets – mutant cats, people sometimes said – who traveled with her almost everywhere.

The "tattoo" expanded and changed, and, after a few years, Kate had learned to control it totally – making it small, just on her shoulder and one arm, or large, covering most – or all – of her body, according to her mood. But if she became very excited, the tattoo could still run amok; so, when she was out in public, Kate was always careful to keep well covered and to control her emotions.

Mostly, she kept the tattoo small – unless she was alone and wanted to amuse herself, or, possibly if she was with V – the mysterious girlfriend she occasionally visited – and who occasionally visited her.

Mysteriously too – and people did gossip – as the years and then the decades went by, Doctor Kate Thornhill did not age. She was, so far as anyone could see, in all respects just as young as she had been long ago – in the year 2027.

Many years after the events of 2027, Father Michael Patrick O'Bryan was in Oxford and teaching a postgraduate course on "The Uses of Theology in History and Politics." His limp had returned, and the good Father was quite frail. It was a windy, snowy, freezing December day, the sort of day when the sun is low – even at noon barely rising above the horizon – and the mournfully meager light of the English winter dies early. Father O'Bryan lurched his way across the quadrangle of his college, being careful not to stumble on the icy uneven gray flagstones and leaning into the wind to shelter his face from the ice-hard stinging snow pellets that were streaming sideways through the darkening air. His eyes were running, and his nose too. It was already night – one of those desolate winter nights when the soul is chilled and lonely and in desperate need of solace.

Father O'Bryan was eagerly looking forward to a glass of sherry or whiskey and to the college's evening meal and was musing on how age made one very petty, narrowing one's horizons, how one's desires were gradually whittled away and reduced to simple consolatory animal imperatives – food, warmth, comfort, drink, and perhaps a bit of amiable company. "Ah, I am getting much too old!" he muttered, clutching the collar of his overcoat, as he passed under the Gothic arch of his residence, whose stones were glossy with frost and festooned with forbiddingly long, dangerous-looking, spear-like icicles. He continued muttering to himself about Satan and witchcraft and possession as he walked down the dark musty corridor and finally opened the door to his cozy little studio-flat, equipped with a bedroom and fine washroom, where he thought, if he had time, he might light a fire.

He sniffed. The flat seemed warmer than it usually was – and there was a spicy, pleasant smell, a perfume, as if of a mountainside in spring.

And then he noticed – lying on his desk was a fresh red rose. There was a note and next to it a sealed envelope. Father O'Bryan lifted the note, turned on his desk lamp, and adjusted his bifocals:

Dear Father O'Bryan, old friend:
I dropped by to say hello, and I've left you something you might find amusing. It is a Roman coin from the time of Augustus Caesar. I suggest you let it jangle in your right trouser pocket. It is a keepsake from many years ago.
Much love, from your old partner in crime, V.
PS: Pray for me, Father, if you will.

Father O'Bryan lowered himself into his leather and walnut armchair, and, using a penknife, slit open the envelope. Yes, inside was a coin – it shone as if it were brand-new, and it had indeed been struck or minted under the Emperor Augustus, just about the time of the birth of Christ.

Father O'Bryan gazed at the coin, at the rose, and at the elegant hand-written cursive of the note. He lifted the fine, eggshell-finish, cream-colored writing paper and breathed in its fragrance – yes, it was that perfume he knew so well.

Father O'Bryan's eyes clouded over; a tear rolled down his cheek. "Ah, Michael Patrick O'Bryan, you are certainly getting terribly soft and senti-mental!" He opened a drawer, pulled out a bottle, and poured himself a gen-erous glass of Bushmills. "Ah, to you, V, I salute you and your mystery and all you have done for the good and salvation of humankind!"

He slipped the coin into the right pocket of his trousers.

Two hours later, when Father O'Bryan walked across the quadrangle on his way to the evening meal, he no longer limped. And, in the days following, the good Father's colleagues and students noticed that he seemed, miracu-lously, to have lost twenty years.

"Black magic?" wondered one particularly pert graduate student, who was very fond of Father O'Bryan. "Yes," she thought, "maybe the good Father traf-fics in black magic – or perhaps he performs miracles. Or maybe he has a guardian angel! Whatever it is, it's a blessing for us all …"

CODA

It was an exceptionally hot summer in England in the year 2058 and V was engaged in her usual business.

Heavy rain poured down. It was a dark sultry night, without moon or stars. Trailing tentacles of mist wrapped themselves around the medieval buildings of brick and stone. Darkness reigned. But it was already getting on toward dawn in the ancient English university town of Cambridge.

V was walking down a cobblestoned side street, the slick stones glowing with splashing rain in the lamplight. She was wearing a buttoned-up long black leather coat, high leather boots, and, underneath the coat, a skintight synthetic latex-leather catsuit streaked with mud and blood. She pulled the coat collar up. The rain was warm, but it was getting in everywhere.

V shivered. She yearned for a hot shower – and soap, lots of soap.

As she walked, she became aware of a man. He was following her – or it certainly felt like he was following her. She frowned. She did not need this – not tonight, not after what she had seen, not after what she had done. She walked faster.

Three days earlier, V had come to England for a bit of business out on the fens. The bloodless, husk-like body of a gentleman now lay at the bottom of a forty-foot-wide drainage canal. It had been more complicated and messier than V had hoped. He was a rapist and child killer; he hadn't gone easily.

Worse – he'd gotten inside her head.

Nine little girls – aged seven to eleven – had gone missing over a period of four years from Cambridge and its surroundings. Strangely, a pattern linking the disappearances had emerged for the police only a few months ago. John had hacked into the police computers and the central analysis office at Scotland Yard, at the Home Office, and snooped around in the database of the Cambridge Institute of Criminology.

Together, sitting in their office in Tuscany, John and Julia and V had used the information from London and Cambridge to create a psychological profile, a location analysis, and they had narrowed down the possibilities to one man. Their candidate was a forty-three-year-old solicitor, Hugh Tillotson.

V had taken a late flight from Milan to London, rented a car and driven by backroads up to Cambridge. At a small gas station, she'd bought extra petrol, just in case. In a village, paying with cash, she'd bought plastic sheeting and duct tape from a hardware store. She wanted the car to be absolutely clean when she returned it.

She'd arrived at midnight in Cambridge, where she'd rented a flat from a professor absent on sabbatical. The professor, the well-known art historian, Annette Gray, had left her nineteen-year-old assistant with the keys.

The assistant, Vera Travis, met V just outside the flat. Vera was a pale, thin-faced girl with a sharp chin, serious hazel eyes, arched dark eyebrows, and an attractive case of overbite, one slightly crooked front tooth adding to her sophisticated yet gauche charm. She was wearing a short denim skirt, sandals, a wide leather belt and a white blouse. Vera was very conscientious, almost fussily precise. She showed V where to park the car. The apartment had its own underground parking space just a few streets away, and she showed V, in detail, how to use the appliances.

V offered the girl a drink and Vera sat primly on the edge of the deep leather sofa, her thin but shapely legs held close together. She told V about her research with Professor Gray: Venetian painters of the sixteenth and seventeenth centuries.

On the surface Vera looked fragile, and she was probably neurotic, but V sensed that underneath the careful surface there was a steely resolve, some firm opinions, fierce ambition – and an intriguing, probably quirky, and almost certainly unsatisfied, sensuality. V was tempted. It had been a long time since she'd experienced any human warmth. "No," she told herself firmly, "I am not sure of the girl's tastes; complications are the very last thing I need; and, in any case, I always end up hurting the people I love, however brief and chaste the encounter."

When V showed Vera to the door, they shook hands with what seemed to V excessive solemnity. Vera explained that she lived just next door in the mews: "Out the door turn left; then first left again, number 4, there's a bell. My mobile and text number – which you already have in any case – is on the desk, taped to the phone."

"Thank you," V said. She kissed the girl on the cheek, and they said good night.

V slept for ten hours. She kept all the curtains in the flat drawn. It was difficult to tell what the weather was like outside. Toward noon she got up, opened the curtains, made herself a strong black coffee, and spread the maps, news stories, psychological analyses and police reports over the wide flat surface of Professor Gray's immaculately neat, scrupulously bare desk. She rehearsed the details of what she had to do.

The solicitor worked in a small town – a village really – not far from Cambridge. A few years ago he'd bought an abandoned farmhouse, out in the fens, on a drainage canal. It had, attached to it, a few storage sheds and an old shelter or pump house.

Tillotson had had severe psychological problems as a child and – though the police didn't know this – John had discovered that Tillotson had, as a teenager, tortured animals – one cat had been placed in a microwave oven and toasted until it exploded, a dog had been doused in petrol and set alight, and there were vague allusions, in one confidential psychological report, to other episodes of cruelty. He had also been accused, twice, of indecent exposure to very young girls.

V closed the file, rubbed her eyes, and lay down to rest.

For a long time, she just lay there staring at the chalk-white ceiling with its dark-stained wooden beams that looked so charmingly Tudor.

At about three o'clock in the afternoon it began to rain and the day darkened. V put on a very respectable dress, dark glasses, a hat and raincoat, and visited the old traditional bookshop Heffers. She browsed, and then made a few purchases – printed books, not traceable electronic books – using one of her Swiss identities – "Helen Wolf" – the one she had used to enter the country – and one of the credit cards attached to it.

She got back to the flat at dusk. It was still raining. She showered, changed into her catsuit battle gear and her heavy assault boots; over the catsuit she put on the long black leather coat, and added a black broad-brimmed water-proofed hat; after locking the flat behind her, she walked to the underground garage – a stroll of three and a half minutes – and opened the car door. She spread plastic sheeting over the floor and over the front and back seats of the car, taping it so it wouldn't shift. She pasted a false license plate over the real one, then drove the car out of the garage.

Her cell phone rang. "He just snatched another kid – if it's him," said John.

"Another girl. But it doesn't fit the pattern because the last one was only three days ago."

"Maybe it's not the same man."

"Maybe not. But if it is, and if he hasn't killed the girl who disappeared last week, then he's got two. The first one, remember, is Tiffany Hughes – she's eight – and the new one is Emma Roberts, age eleven. I'm sending you their home addresses and new photographs."

"Thanks, John."

"You watch it, V; this one may be tricky."

V drove on the A10 highway toward King's Lynn. The land was flat and dreary with the light dying and ribbons of warm mist curling across the road and through the falling rain.

V turned off onto a gravel-top country road. She had switched off the car's automatic guidance and tracking system, but she had her own GPS coordinate tracker. She pulled into a nearby lay-by, where John had suggested she could leave the car semi-hidden. There it was: an old barn, with a graveled space behind it, just visible from the lay-by but invisible from the road. V positioned the car carefully out of sight behind the barn. She scanned the files and photos: two little girls, Tiffany Hughes, eight, and Emma Roberts, eleven. She flipped the files shut, slipped out of her leather coat. Streamlined down to the catsuit, she sat, hunched in the car, thinking: was this the right place? Would Tillotson be here? Would the girls be dead – or alive?

It began to rain harder – a deluge.

Lightning flashed to the north, a silky thundery darkness.

The kids – if they were alive – would be a problem. What to do with them? But she'd cross that bridge when she came to it.

She took a deep breath, and got out of the car. A wall of blinding rain, whipped by the wind, hit her in the face. Grimacing against the storm, and adjusting the rim of her hat, she pulled on the backpack and buckled it tight. She walked to the edge of the gravel-covered lot – ah, there it was, the path, right beside a narrow irrigation ditch. It looked exactly as John had said it would, and exactly as the satellite feeds had indicated. She followed the muddy and partly overgrown footpath along the side of the ditch. She needed all of her night vision to see in this soup. The rain tormented the long grass; the crushed stalks and blades swirled and thrashed and bent low. The rain whipped in, streaming under the rim of her hat.

The path should bring her up next to the farmhouse and the shed that she assumed would be Hugh Tillotson's ideal hideaway and prison for kidnapped little girls.

And there it was at the end of the path! – a concrete block and corrugated iron structure that stood near the bank of a much wider ditch, the main drainage canal for the area; the place looked completely abandoned: no electricity, apparently, not from an outside source at any rate.

A car was parked next to the shed: yes, it had the right license plates, it was the right make of car. The infrared sensitivity of her vision showed that the car had recently been used: the motor and hood – or *bonnet* as they said in England – were still warm; she smiled to herself at the quaintness of much British terminology, though she herself usually spoke English with a British accent and British mannerisms and affectations. So Tillotson was somewhere close, probably in the shed – and possibly with the girls, or with their remains. Carefully, she approached the shed, and circled it, until she found the entry.

The shed had a rusty metal door, but the lock outside was free, dangling open, so it must be closed from inside.

She put a listening device, a sort of miniature electronic stethoscope, to the door, though, even with the device, the rain and wind and the water running off the roof made it difficult to hear. She took off the broad-brimmed hat so she could get closer to the door and listen better.

She shivered. The rain ran through her hair, down her neck; it was getting under her collar, seeping under her catsuit, and trickling down her spine; it was a warm and rather voluptuous sensation, like being slathered all over in warm soap or melted butter.

She wiggled her shoulders. A single lamp on the canal cast silver reflections on the black piles of the weir, on the black wet planks and stakes, and on the murky water of the forty-foot-wide drainage canal.

She waited. She could hear the rain on the long grass, on the wheat, on the mossy weir, on the corrugated metal roofing. She ran her fingers through her soaking hair, her ear pressed against the rusty steel of the door.

Then she heard it: a child crying.

A high-pitched voice was saying: "You will like this, oh, you will like this very much! We are going to play a game! It's a very *nice* game!" It was a shrill singsong voice, the voice of a man pretending to be a child, probably, in his mind, he was a little girl, a wicked little girl. Now, he giggled, a wicked giggle.

Between the door and the door frame there was a thin crack where the wood frame had rotted away, and the concrete had crumbled.

V took a miniaturized pinhead spy camera out of her backpack and slid it through the crack. It gave her a fisheye 180-degree image of the room.

There was a thunderous, searing bolt of lightning. Startled, V looked around, her senses tingling, on high alert. There was nobody behind her, nobody on the weir, and nobody on the path.

She turned her attention back to the room. The fisheye captured almost the whole space. The two children were there. They were alive, both of them. Well, that was the good news. But how could she kill him, with them watching, and what would she do with them when she'd finished with him?

The room was lit by old-fashioned oil lamps – that was bad; it meant a possible accident, fire, even an explosion. She'd have to be extra careful.

Tillotson was prancing, literally prancing, in front of the two girls – who corresponded exactly to the photographs and descriptions – yes, they were Emma and Tiffany. Tillotson was distracted, busy with his own performance.

V jiggled the door slightly.

The bar inside seemed connected to a rather loose bracket. V paused. If she pushed a stiff wire in through the crack, she might be able to lift the bar off – that would make it easier and safer – and then smash the door open and drag him outside.

She took a razor-thin, stiff wire rod out of her backpack, slid it through the crack between the door and the frame, and eased it upwards against the bar.

Tillotson was still singing and doing his little dance.

He had an antique wind-up gramophone. He put on a record and it began to play "The Teddy Bears' Picnic." The jaunty, spooky little song echoed in the small shack.

The bar edged upwards. V tensed. She had to make sure everything was as quick and smooth as it could be.

"The Teddy Bears' Picnic" continued, a weird, haunting, threatening, little melody, creepy lyrics.

The bar slipped up and out of the lock. The door should open much more easily now, unless there was another lock – a chance she'd have to take!

She smashed the door open. It caught on a chain, but she smashed the chain, cutting it in two; the chain flailed wildly, and the door flung wide open.

The man turned. The two little girls looked terrified: their mouths wide open.

"Tiffany! Emma! You stay right there! Don't move! I'm going to take you home!"

Tillotson reached for a knife, a large 8-inch curved butcher's knife. It was hanging on a rusty iron hook on the wall. In the same instant, V saw that he had an erection – it bulged against the frilly pink underwear that was all he was wearing – with an oversized bra. The walls were stained with, soaked in, dried blood; pictures had been pinned up, names had been painted there – Claire, Susie, Helen, and Jane … *painted in blood …*

Tillotson came at V swinging the knife in a powerful arc. V stepped aside, dodging the downward slash. As he swung the knife down, she grabbed his forearm, held it in a lock, and snapped his elbow. He let loose a blood-curdling scream. The knife clattered to the cement floor.

With his good hand, Tillotson tried to gouge out her eyes, but she caught the fingers just as they closed on her eyelids, jerked the hand away, closed it in an iron grip, pried the hand open, and twisted the fingers backward, snapping all five.

She lifted him up – he was screaming now, a long string of swear words, in a high falsetto voice, his arms and legs flailing, helpless.

"The Teddy Bears' Picnic" was still playing, weird and scary at the same time – every little girl's nightmare.

"Come with me, Mr. Tillotson." V dragged him outside, pulled the door shut behind her. "Well, Mr. Tillotson, where are the bodies?"

"What are you? Who are you?"

"It doesn't matter. You'll tell me whether you want to or not!"

"I'll not tell you anything." His pale face, caught in the lamplight, was covered in sweat and rain, it was blotchy and whey faced. It was flesh that was soft like putty. The rain streamed from his cheeks.

"We'll see what you'll tell me!"

"You're not the police. I have rights, you bitch!" He swallowed. "What the hell are you?"

"You want to see what I am?"

"Yes, damn you!" His nose was running, a silver sheen of snot on his lips, on his chin.

"Well, then, I shall show you! This is what I am!" The fangs suddenly sprang from V's mouth; her skin glowed a ghostly phosphorescent chalky white; leaden shadows grew under her eyes – and within the pupils and irises shone the dark star-like brilliance of eternal, divine, god-like, blood vengeance.

"Oh, my God," Tillotson wriggled in fear; his eyes gaped.

"I'm sorry, Mr. Tillotson, I truly am." V jerked his head back, exposing his neck, plunged her fangs straight into the jugular, and drank deeply, under the pouring rain.

Tillotson struggled at first. His legs kicked, throwing up mud and pebbles. Then he subsided into limp passivity as she drank and drank. And with his blood, she also drank his memories – a kaleidoscope of images, impressions, smells, a phantasmagoria of horror. The bodies, twelve of them, she discovered – three more than the nine the police were aware of – were buried in a row beside the shed.

She saw a little blond girl on a swing and she saw Tillotson approaching her; she saw a little brunette being cut open, sliced upwards from groin to ribcage; she saw the face of a girl crying; she saw Tillotson digging a grave, with a small tortured naked body lying next to the heap of earth; she saw – and she *was* – each of the little girls. She saw and she *was* Tillotson as he committed each of his grisly crimes. She felt what they felt, she suffered what they suffered. She felt what he felt; she saw what he saw; she did what he did. No, no, no! She turned it off! *Enough!*

When she had finished – and made sure he was truly dead and would never rise again – she pulled Tillotson's body to the drainage canal and dumped him into the water, dressed as he was in the bra and the frilly pink panties. The body floated and then sank. The bra broke loose and bobbed to the surface, two bright white cups on the watery, pock-marked darkness. V frowned, and then thought: It didn't matter if it floated or if someone saw it – whatever happened, they would find him soon enough.

Father O'Bryan and her theological and ethical discussions with him came to mind – so many years ago. V stared at the bobbing bra and at the place where the body had sunk. She whispered, "And may God have mercy upon your soul." However horrible he had been, Hugh Tillotson had been a person, too; he had had a life; he too had been a victim of evil, his evil and murderous instincts being much stronger and greater than he was.

Had anyone ever loved him? She wondered. Yes, of course. And he, in his own horrible way, had felt and experienced love and hate, all mixed up, in a lethal sexual homicidal fusion. For a moment, V had seen, out of his baby eyes, a woman who must have been his mother, her pudgy face smiling and looming, magnified and porous and huge. "Hughie, my little Hughie, my baby, my love."

V let the rain wash away most of the blood, her face turned up to the sky.

She opened the door to the shed. The oil lamps were still burning, the gramophone scratchily turning, turning, and turning. She lifted the gramophone arm and put it in its cradle.

She knelt next to the two girls who were sitting, rigid and wide-eyed – they had not moved – "Now, Emma and Tiffany, let's take you home!"

She led them back to the car.

"Now, Emma – which one is Emma …?"

"I am!"

"We'll go to your house first, okay?"

"Okay!"

"43 Burnside Terrace, in Cambridge. Is that right?"

"Yes. He was a bad man!"

"Yes, that's right, Emma, he was a bad man."

"He was funny, too."

"Well, yes, Tiffany, I suppose he was that too – funny."

V punched the address into her personal untraceable GPS system.

She parked around a corner a little distance from Emma's home, so neither the car nor the license plate – even if false – would be visible from the house or nearby. She got out of the car and pulled on the ankle-length leather coat. She slipped on large dark wraparound glasses and the wide-brimmed hat and took out a freshly bought umbrella that she'd touched only with gloved hands. In front of the house there was a policeman on watch.

V took Emma and Tiffany by the hand. "I think I see a nice policeman. Let's go and say hello to him."

She walked straight up to the policeman, who was looking in the other direction and seemed rather dour, his shoulders hunched against the rain.

"Excuse me, officer, but I think their families have been looking for Emma and Tiffany."

The policeman looked at her and looked down at the two children.

"Here, Emma," V said, "take the umbrella."

Emma looked doubtful, but she took it.

"Goodbye, officer." V walked away.

"Miss, Miss, Madam, you can't just walk away, come here, stop!"

V kept walking. She hoped there were not any other policemen or – women – lurking in the area or cameras or night surveillance satellites; but it was doubtful – technology was breaking down everywhere – and resources were scarce. Even most of the drones had been grounded.

"Miss!"

V turned and waved. The officer stood perplexed for a moment, then headed for the house with the two children. He was already on his phone.

Now, as dawn approached and she headed back to the flat from the garage and after disposing of the plastic sheeting, V noticed that a man was following her. She walked faster.

I do not need this, not tonight.

She walked still faster, reaching for the door key in her pocket. She was not far now from the flat, just one corner. When she turned the corner, the man's footsteps were still there, splashing through the rain. He was walking more quickly now, trying to catch up.

I don't want to kill again – not tonight.

V flexed her fingers. She was overflowing with strength, recently refreshed, the blood racing through her veins; it would be easy to handle him, whoever he was, but it would be unpleasant, messy, and in the middle of town. It would complicate things terribly.

The man was only a few yards away when V was flooded with a sense of happiness, of joy.

He came up to her, his wide-brimmed hat dripping water.

"Hello, V."

"Marcus!" She stood absolutely still for a second and then she reached out and touched his cheek. Yes, he was real. Yes, it was Marcus. She leaned up and kissed him. The same lips, the same feelings, the same infinite trust, the same rush of love. She threw herself into his arms and he held her tight.

"Let's go inside," she said. "I'll open the door."

V led the way up the narrow staircase. "I didn't really believe you were dead," she said over her shoulder. "In all these centuries, I never believed you were dead. I couldn't believe you were dead."

She lit the fire so their clothes could dry. Marcus was wearing jeans, an expensive dark jacket, and a black T-shirt.

"She's an art historian," V said, seeing Marcus examining the crowded book shelves.

"I see," he said, "most interesting."

She turned to him. "Wine or whiskey?"

"Wine – for old time's sake."

"You speak English."

"I adapt. We must adapt." He was holding an Italian volume on Piero della Francesca.

"I half expected you to be dressed in your warrior's uniform."

"I almost did. I wanted you to recognize me."

"I would have recognized you anywhere."

They sat looking at each other. What was it, two thousand six hundred years? No, more, a bit more …

"You haven't changed …" they both began to say. Both of them laughed; but then Marcus turned serious.

"I have to tell you something, V. A confession. You may hate me after I tell you."

"I doubt it, Marcus."

"Well, alright, here goes!" Marcus looked at his hands, twisted them, and then took a deep long drink from his glass of wine, and V thought: how human he was, how human his gestures, his embarrassment.

He cleared his throat. "The woman I loved, the woman I murdered –"

"… was my mother."

"You knew that?"

"Yes, I figured it out. I figured it out long after – recently, actually."

"Yes, well, she was your mother. And I …"

V nodded at him, encouraging him to continue. She wanted *him* to say it.

"… and I …"

"Go on, Marcus."

"I am your father."

Her expression did not flicker. Marcus stared at her. Yes, the serene loving smile was still on her lips. "You don't hate me, V?"

"I love you, Marcus. I've always loved you, as a friend, as a teacher, as my protector, even, sometimes, in my mind, as my lover. I guessed the truth years ago. For a moment, I have to admit, I did feel betrayed – and then I understood. You are my father."

She got up, came over and knelt next to him, reached up and stroked his cheek. "A few years ago, at the time of the episode with the Crystal, I had a DNA test, you see … a top-secret test, for my eyes only."

"DNA," Marcus frowned.

"It showed that half of my genetic makeup is not from this planet. There is no DNA like mine anywhere on Earth, not in any living creature, so far as they know."

"So, you then figured out …"

"Father O'Bryan suggested it – the DNA test."

"Your Jesuit friend."

She was looking up at him with such intensity that it made him uncomfortable. And then she laughed. "Oh, Marcus, you really must be a god! You do know everything!"

"No, V," Marcus smiled, "I don't. I have been far away, very far away. We have had troubles and wars and I've been busy. But when I could, I did follow the news here on Earth. Father O'Bryan seems to be a good man."

"He is. I don't share his faith of course; but he is a very good man. He couldn't believe I could be one of the living dead; he said I couldn't be anything like other ordinary vampires, that there must be something special. He insisted on a test."

"He was right." Marcus had emptied his glass. V refilled it.

"You are nervous, Marcus," she said, holding the glass out to him. "Is it so hard to look upon your own daughter?"

"No. It is the greatest joy of my life."

"Tell me how it happened – how I happened …"

Marcus gazed into the depths of the glass, the swirling dark burgundy. "When my group – we were far beyond the range of usual exploration, a bit rogue, not exactly approved of, not exactly kosher – first visited Earth I saw interesting potential: a life form similar to ours, with languages, even alphabets, phonetic alphabets, and the beginnings of civilization – agriculture, trade, technology, armies, politics, ships that sailed the sea. I decided to experiment. It was controversial. Not all my crew agreed. It was – potentially – cruel, even dangerous; it was debated fiercely, but I overcame the objections. It was my decision. I wanted to see if I could prolong human life. I believed it would help us with our research on our own species."

"The search for immortality."

"Yes. Hubris, I suppose, certainly *my* hubris, and an excess of ambition, mortals wanting to be gods. Even after I was shipwrecked, long after, I continued my research, and that is how it happened." Marcus grimaced. "This is difficult to say, but your mother was – how do you say it? – an experimental subject, she was a –"

"She was a guinea pig."

"Yes. She was one of my experimental subjects, the best, and, in the end, the only survivor. But, even with her, the experiment went wrong. I did give her immortality, but with immortality, she acquired certain other traits."

"You gave her the blood lust. You turned her into a vampire."

"Yes. I had created a vampire, though I was not familiar yet with such creatures. I discovered – and she discovered to her horror – that she could survive only by drinking human blood. She needed more and more and more. She was insatiable, out of control. She could not resist the urge, the yearning, the need."

"So?"

"I had fallen in love with her – before the transformation – and I remained in love even after. We made love many times, and then, while I was away traveling for business in Greece, and then in Italy, for more than a year, she gave birth – she had you. I had no idea we could procreate, create a hybrid, unify the two races, what seemed two species, just by –"

"Just by having sex!"

"Yes."

"And then?"

"She suspected that, when I returned, I would … ah … terminate her. She was sure that I would also terminate, kill, her child, our child. Even if she was going to die, she was desperate to save you. So, she sent you away, far away, with lots of gold, to be adopted by a good family."

"And with Lalla."

"With Lalla, her servant – and my friend. Lalla was human, but she had trained with me. She worked in my laboratory. She was clever and she learned much. When she took you away, she took with her drugs to make you seem dead – if you needed to escape enemies or go into hibernation – and she also took an improved version of the serum – which was absolutely experimental – to activate your immortality. You already contained the immortality gene and the vampire gene – and of course your DNA combined mine and that of your mother."

"But you found out that I existed."

"I found out. There were letters, messages from Lalla. Your mother needed to know about you, every little detail. Emotionally, she could not destroy the letters, the messages; they were the only part of you she had. She treasured them. After she – ah – died, I came upon the letters. So, I found out. When the war came between the coastal cities, I came to find you.

"And when you found me, you were going to 'terminate' me?"

"Yes. I was going to terminate you. But when I saw you ..." He paused. "V, it's very unnerving how calm you are, how accepting."

"I've had time to think, Marcus, centuries."

"You've grown up."

"In a way, yes, I've grown up." V had a faraway look in her eyes. "I knew then, when I first saw you, and I know now, that you intended to kill me. You had to, because I was ..." V shrugged.

"... because you were dangerous. You contained your mother's modified genetics, her vampirism and her immortality, and you carried my genetic heritage too – and your own super-strength and skills. You are unique, V. For humans you were dangerous like the plague! If you had created others like yourself, well ... there would be no human race left!" Marcus looked at his hands and took her hands in his. "When I saw you – and when that fool – he was my friend, alas – when Gaius began ranting about how beautiful you were – well, I saw you were truly beautiful and – unlike Gaius – I knew you were not dead, not really dead."

"Yes. Oh, Marcus, I am so glad you did not kill me then. But, later, when you saw me feeding on Gaius?"

"I had already realized I loved you, my daughter. I saw your vampire nature had been aroused by the serum, triggered as it were – but when you looked up at me ..."

"Half-naked and dripping with the blood of your friend ..."

"... yes, when I saw the fear, but also the intelligence, the understanding, even the compassion in your eyes, then I thought: we will make a voyage together and we shall see ..."

"And what did you see?"

"That you are a magnificent person – your self-control is admirable! I am beyond proud of you."

"It has not always been easy, being alone." V laid her head against Marcus's knee.

"I know, daughter, I know." He stroked her hair.

The fire crackled and filled the room with the gentle perfume of cedar and oak.

She looked up at him. "I love you, Marcus."

"I love you, daughter. And, if you are interested, you are my only child. We of the original Andromeda Empire live so long that the right to procreate is extremely restricted, very rare. So, I have been very privileged to have you, my daughter."

"Let us drink to us!"

They drank. Then Marcus said, "There is one other little thing."

"Yes?"

"You've been made – and this is the first time this has occurred with an outlander – you've been made a Citizen of the Empire; it is the Empire you've never seen and of which you know nothing or almost nothing. You see, by repelling the Evil Force during those days in 2027, you saved not only Earth. You saved us too – from a great deal of difficulty, and perhaps from extinction. You have become rather an exotic celebrity, I might say."

"I blush, Marcus."

"Now, V, my daughter, this is the hard part. I must leave you."

"I know, Marcus, I know."

"And …" Again, Marcus hesitated.

"And my place is here," said V, laying her head on his knees.

"Yes."

"I know, Marcus, but even so far away, you are always in my heart. Often, in the night, I think of you, talk to you, listen to you …"

She let herself trail off, almost drowsy, stroking his hand. Then she looked up, her attention suddenly sharp-edged. "So, my mission continues?"

"It does. You are the shepherd. They are your flock; this planet is your domain."

"They deserve much better – but I suppose for the moment, I'm it."

"Yes, my daughter, you are it – you are the guardian, you are the goddess, an ancient goddess, an invisible goddess, but a goddess just the same."

Later, when the dawn came and Marcus was gone, V couldn't sleep. She leafed through the Professor's art books. Each volume brought back memories: Rome in its full imperial splendor under Augustus and Trajan, and, of course, her friend Tiberius; England under Elizabeth the First, the Virgin Queen, where V, disguised as a young aristocratic Italian gentleman, had hung out with Shakespeare and Ben Jonson and the artists and players and lowlifes of London, while spying on Catholic subversives for Elizabeth's Chief Minister Lord Burghley; Venice around 1500, where V had made a fortune trading with the Turk and had presided briefly over an intellectual and artistic salon; Japan during the Meiji period, where V, disguised as an Italian engineer, had been an advisor to the government of the Emperor; Paris in the 1870s and again in 1910, with all the artists she had known, all the amorous flirtations and dangerous liaisons; and New York in the 1950s, with the Beatniks, the Abstract Expressionists …

Yes, this is my home, she thought.

Her mobile buzzed. It was John, on the encrypted line.

"I'll be back in three or four days," she said. "Thanks, John. Yes, it went well. The two children are safe. Love to Julia and to you. I'll phone you on my way."

John and Julia were still fit but they were growing old. V sat staring at the telephone. If and when she decided to "die" – well, to disappear and start a new life – she would arrange it so they would inherit the villa in Tuscany, and its vineyards and orchards and vegetable gardens with enough money to keep them going comfortably – until they died – or could she perhaps prolong their lives and make them young again – hmm?

Whatever happened, V, as always, would move on, would disappear.

Then, somewhere else: where? Where would she next save a life, acquire a powerful protector, turn up somewhere, suddenly, with money and a new identity, Russian, Swiss, Brazilian …?

V slept and later that day, after she woke, she picked up the phone and dialed a cell number. "Hello, Vera, it's Helen Wolf, I'm leaving tomorrow morning. I was wondering if you'd like to come over for a drink tonight … You would? That's marvelous! Let's say about eight."

V lay back and closed her eyes, picturing the girl in her mind – *Vera Travis* – so precise; such sincere, intense eyes; such cute overbite; such chalk-white, smooth, muscular legs; so intellectual and prim, and yet so sensual and per- verse – a hidden, smoldering, ambitious, half-discovered soul. Such promise! Yes, there were fires to be lit, knowledge to be imparted, skills to be taught. *Vera Travis!*

There really was something special, sublime even, about the fragility of human beings, about their neatly contained, desperately fraught bodies, their infinitely ambitious, heroically striving, but oh so confused, souls!

And, yes, there was something special, too, about that mysterious human thing called *youth!*

Eyes still closed, lying stretched out on the bed, V took a deep breath, licked her lips – and waited for the night.

NEXT: VOLUME 2 IN THE

ADVENTURES OF V

VAMPIRE

CLONE

by
GILBERT REID

TWIN RIVERS
PRODUCTIONS

Christ! They'd crucified the woman!

It was midnight, July 11, 2059, in southern California. A thick, sultry sea-borne fog pressed against the windows of Andromeda Corporation's giant Boeing 777 Super Cargo.

When he entered the cavernous hold of the aircraft, Freddy Bokhari's face glistened, wet from mist and rain. Shaking drops off his windbreaker, he rushed to a window, pressed his fingers against the glass, and peered out. It was like an old-fashioned black-and-white film set! The tarmac shone black and silver. Security people were running every which way. Floodlights had been set up. Armored cars and two tanks stood on guard where the prisoner's cage had been unloaded. The atmosphere was electric. Wow! He would never forget this moment. Freddy Bokhari was seventeen years old.

The pilot's business-like voice announced over the intercom, "Buckle up, ready for takeoff." Freddy sat down, his back to the wall, locked the seat belt, put his pistol in his lap.

Then, finally, he dared steal a glance at the prisoner. She was in the metal cage on the opposite side of the hold. She hung, suspended, her ankles, wrists, and neck manacled, from a wall of steel.

Yeah, they'd totally crucified the woman!

The engines revved up. Instructions were given. The aircraft began to move. But Security Guard Second Class Freddy Bokhari – on the first real summer job of his life – just stared, hypnotized, at the sight across from him. It was like an old painting by … by … he couldn't remember the guy's name …

A guy who crucified people in paint …

People in cages, bodies, bits, fragments of flesh, carved into slabs of meat …

Bacon, Francis Bacon …

Inside the massive, steel-barred cage, lit by floodlights and pinned to the wall of steel, the prisoner was spread-eagled – a butterfly on a corkboard – an anatomical specimen, vivisected, splayed out, displayed, on a wall of glass in a museum.

Her mouth was jammed open with a steel-and-rubber ball gag. She was stretched tight – every muscle straining – against the steel, her wrists, ankles, and neck locked in place by those thick gleaming steel manacles.

The woman's skintight black wetsuit, streaked with drying mud, sculpted her breasts and ribcage, belly and thighs, with the anatomical clarity of a Renaissance crucifixion scene, or one of those 3-D recreations of sculptures by Bernini or Michelangelo: every lineament, every line ...

Might as well have been naked.

Freddy swallowed; he licked his lips.

Patterned in black-and-green camouflage, the woman's face shone with the savage beauty of a wild beast. The eyes searched, searched, searched, desperately searched. Against the matte war paint, the whites of her eyes glowed, wild and frantic. Freddy thought of a poem his teacher, Ms. Keller, had made him memorize.

Tiger, tiger, burning bright
In the forests of the night,
What immortal hand or eye
Could frame thy fearful symmetry?

In what distant deeps or skies
Burnt the fire of thine eyes?
On what wings dare he aspire?
What the hand dare seize the fire?

Saliva drooled from a corner of the gagged mouth. It gleamed – bright silver in the floodlights, the glittering string dripping to her collarbone, painting a smeared, glossy sheen on her breasts. Freddy blinked. The whole thing was sadistic – erotic, awesome, orgasmic! He took a deep breath. What was she feeling? What was she thinking, this demonic dream? It was as if she had arisen out of one of his midnight fantasies – out of a video game dungeon – out of a sadomasochistic scenario from some torrid, sweaty night, flicking through porno on the Net.

Within minutes, the plane was in the air.

Freddy relaxed.

He had not been told much, except that the woman was a very special prisoner – and extremely dangerous.

As he sat there, he flipped through an electronic *Maxim* magazine, but he kept his pistol ready, cradled in his lap. He was directly opposite the cage, so he could keep a close eye on the woman. She was much sexier – in an unsettling way – than any centerfold from those antique hard copy men's magazines he collected.

The other guards, the professionals, using multiple camera links, were watching the woman from the forward cabin, where the seats were comfortable.

"Guards are redundant," Freddy's boss Dave De Blasio said. "We're frills. There's no way that woman can escape. Sit back and enjoy the show, Freddy!"

The flight plan would take them from the southern California airbase just outside San Diego to the Virginia Headquarters of Sabrina Jacob's giant biotechnology firm, Andromeda Corp. The plane had been reserved just for this one lady prisoner.

Freddy stole a glance at the woman. Underneath the camouflage makeup, her face, even distorted by the gag, was perfect – classy, symmetrical, and, somehow, friendly. A stunner! The eyes were large, soulful. And, as for the body, well, in Freddy's opinion, this lady was a knockout, really stacked. *Wow!* She had, as they used to say, *a body to die for.*

Freddy was super successful with the girls at school. He was a charmer, and he knew it – in fact, he knew, from experience, he was irresistible. And he really liked girls – as people – so, naturally, he wondered what this beauty had done – or what she *was* – that made Sabrina Jacobs and Andromeda Corp want her so bad.

Ten minutes after takeoff, Freddy's curiosity got the better of him. He tried to catch the prisoner's eye. He waved at her timidly.

She was gagged, of course, and couldn't talk. But her eyes instantly focused. She blinked, staring directly at him. Her eyes, pools of darkness, *bored* into his soul – and he *heard* her say – *heard* was the only word for it – he *heard* her say, *inside* his head: "*I'm awfully sorry, Freddy, but I'm not feeling especially friendly right now.*"

Awfully sorry …

He *heard* her speak – in his head.

And with a classy British accent, or so it seemed to Freddy.

Awfully sorry … Awfully sorry, Freddy …

Freddy … How the hell did she know his name?

That had been 15 minutes ago.

Doctor Toni Anderson, an Andromeda Corporation molecular biologist, came into the hold. She was a real pretty lady, cute, pert, friendly. She had short blond hair and the bluest eyes. She paced back and forth in front of the cage, staring at the woman. She turned to Freddy. "Amazing, isn't it, really amazing!"

"Amazing?" Freddy stared. What was amazing?

"She's not human. But look at her – so real, so beautiful, and so seemingly human!"

"Yeah, yeah, I see." Freddy didn't see at all. Beautiful, yeah; but *not human* – what did that mean? She sure looked human – 150% human!

A few minutes later, Tom Riley sauntered into the hold. Riley, in Freddy's humble opinion, was a total jerk. He started teasing – no, *torturing* – the prisoner. Riley was one of the Andromeda Corp so-called psychologists. But he was a bully, an asshole. He called Freddy "kid," twisting the word into a taunting sneer. He told off one of the junior guys in a really nasty way – in front of everybody. How this idiot could be a *psychologist* – for Christ's sake! Why he was allowed to work for a classy company like Andromeda Corp, Freddy for the life of him couldn't figure out.

Riley scraped a metal cup along bars of the cage. *Clack, clack, clack!* The idiot was taunting the woman.

"You're an animal!"

"Just a total animal!"

"A she-devil, that's what you are!"

"The beast, the beast!" Riley laughed and clattered the cup: *clack, clack, clack …*

Freddy blinked at the man. Was Riley drunk?

"Stop that, Tom!" Toni laid her hand on Riley's arm.

Riley shook her off. "You're a sniveling idiot, Toni. You're a stupid dreamer. This beast will be a real happy camper when I give her an injection of this little silver bullet," he said. He held up a needle. "Silver nitrate! Triple dose! She won't even be able to whimper!"

"Cut it out, Tom!"

"It's a *thing*, not a person!"

"Tom!"

"Did you ever work with the thing's Clone? I mean, talk about animal! The Clone's a pure raging animal, an obscenity, no mind at all."

"That's not true, Tom, the Clone was brilliant – it's just that –"

ACKNOWLEDGMENTS

Thanks to the many people who made the *Adventures of V: Return of the Goddess* possible: Adrienne Clarkson, Andra Sheffer, André Kirchberger, Anna Porter, Bernice Landry, Bernie Lucht, Beverly Topping, Bob Ramsay, Chuck Shamata, Claudia Neri, Denise Jacques, Diana Leblanc, Diane Shamata, Dianne Rinehart, Dorothy Vreeker, Duncan Derry, Ed Cowan, Elena Solari, Florence Treadwell, Heather Reid, Irene Spampinato, Irene Tudisco, Jacqueline Baker, Jacqueline Park, Jacqueline Swartz, Janie Yoon, Jennifer Hambleton, Jennifer Puncher, Jim Downs, John McGreevy, John Pearce, John Ralston Saul, Josephine Khu, Jules Cashford, Julia Belluz, Julia Hambleton, Marie-Christine Dunham-Pratt, Mark Fenwick, Martine Matus Siebert, Norm Barber, Norm Christie, Nuala Fitzgerald, Paola Pugliatti, Peter Williamson, Ramsay Derry, Sandra Martin, Simona Barabesi, Susan Mahoney, Susan S. Senstad, Tony Robinow, Trisha Jackson, Wendy Trueman, and many others too numerous to name. I owe an infinite number of literary debts, too, but in particular to Joyce Carol Oates, Justin Cronin, and Stephen King.

TITLES IN THE
ADVENTURES OF V

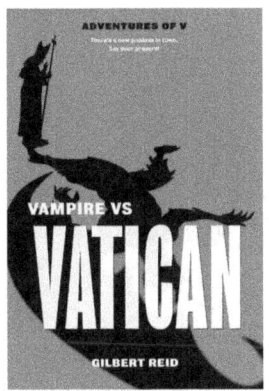

WORKS BY
GILBERT REID

SHORT STORIES
So This is Love: Lollipop and Other Stories
Lava and Other stories

GRAZIA SERIES
Son of Two Fathers (with Jacqueline Park)

ADVENTURES OF V
Vampire vs Vatican
Vampire Clone
Pandemic Book 1: Party Balloons
Pandemic Book 2: The Gateway
Extinction Book 1: Girl with the Golden Eyes
Extinction Book 2: Revolt of the Angels
Extinction Book 3: Elysium

GWENDOLINE SERIES
By Gwendoline
The Shaming of Gwendoline C
Gwendoline Goes to School
Gwendoline Goes Underground

GILBERT REID

To receive a free book or novella
And to learn more about V and get notes on writing and other topics:

Sign up at

https://gilbertreid.com

Please write a short review!
Just two or three lines.
And post it to Goodreads or Amazon
or any other book group you may belong to.

Or send it to me!
At: gilbert@gilbertreid.com

GILBERT REID is the author of two short story collections: *So This is Love: Lollipop and Other Stories* (2004, 2019) and *Lava and Other Stories* (2019). He also co-authored, with Jacqueline Park, the historical novel *Son of Two Fathers* (2019). He has written extensively for television and radio. Most notably he researched, wrote, and narrated two five-hour radio series: *Gilbert Reid's Italy* and *Gilbert Reid's France* for CBC's flagship radio program IDEAS. His many television series include *Paths of the Gods*, *For King and Empire*, *For King and Country*, and *Sir Peter Ustinov in Burma: Road to Mandalay*. After thirty years in Europe working as an economist, university lecturer, diplomat, script doctor, journalist, and adventure travel guide, Gilbert now lives in Toronto.